THE ULTIMATE HITCHHIKER'S GUIDE TO THE GALAXY

DOUGLAS ADAMS

THE ULTIMATE HITCHHIKER'S GUIDE TO THE GALAXY

DEL REY • NEW YORK

A Del Rey ® Book
Published by The Random House Publishing Group

Published in the United States by Del Rey, an imprint of Random House, a division of
Penguin Random House LLC, New York. This edition was previously published by
Random House Value Publishing as *The Ultimate Hitchhiker's Guide* and also in
separate volumes.

randomhousebooks.com

ISBN 978-0-345-45374-7

Manufactured in the United States of America

First Ballantine Books Edition: May 2002

42   41   40   39   38   37

Contents

Foreword:
What Was He Like, Douglas Adams?

He was tall, very tall. He had an air of cheerful diffidence. He combined a razor-sharp intellect and understanding of what he was doing with the puzzled look of someone who had backed into a profession that surprised him in a world that perplexed him. And he gave the impression that, all in all, he was rather enjoying it.

He was a genius, of course. It's a word that gets tossed around a lot these days, and it's used to mean pretty much anything. But Douglas *was* a genius, because he saw the world differently, and more importantly, he could communicate the world he saw. Also, once you'd seen it his way you could never go back.

Douglas Noel Adams was born in 1952 in Cambridge, England (shortly before the announcement of an even more influential DNA, deoxyribonucleic acid). He was a self-described "strange child" who did not learn to speak until he was four. He wanted to be a nuclear physicist ("I never made it because my arithmetic was so bad"), then went to Cambridge to study English, with ambitions that involved becoming part of the tradition of British writer/performers (of which the members of Monty Python's Flying Circus are the best-known example).

When he was eighteen, drunk in a field in Innsbruck, hitchhiking across Europe, he looked up at the sky filled with stars and thought, "Somebody ought to write the Hitchhiker's Guide to the Galaxy." Then he went to sleep and almost, but not quite, forgot all about it.

He left Cambridge in 1975 and went to London where his many writing and performing projects tended, in the main, not to happen. He worked with former Python Graham Chapman writing scripts and sketches for abortive projects (among them a show for Ringo Starr which contained the germ of *Starship Titanic*) and with writer-producer John Lloyd (they pitched a series called *Snow Seven and the White Dwarfs*, a comedy about two astronomers in an observatory on Mt. Everest—"The idea for that was minimum casting, minimum set, and we'd just try to sell the series on cheapness").

He liked science fiction, although he was never a fan. He supported himself through this period with a variety of odd jobs: he was, for example, a hired bodyguard for an oil-rich Arabian family, a job that entailed wearing a suit and sitting in hotel corridors through the night listening to the ding of passing elevators.

In 1977 BBC radio producer (and well-known mystery author) Simon Brett commissioned him to write a science fiction comedy for BBC Radio Four. Douglas originally imagined a series of six half-hour comedies called *The Ends of the Earth*—funny stories which at the end of each, the world would end. In the first episode, for example, the Earth would be destroyed to make way for a cosmic freeway.

But, Douglas soon realized, if you are going to destroy the Earth, you need someone to whom it matters. Someone like a reporter for, yes, the *Hitchhiker's Guide to the Galaxy*. And someone else . . . a man who was called Alaric B in Douglas's original proposal. At the last moment Douglas crossed out Alaric B and wrote above it Arthur Dent. A normal name for a normal man.

For those people listening to BBC Radio 4 in 1978 the show came as a revelation. It was funny—genuinely witty, surreal, and smart. The series was produced by Geoffrey Perkins, and the last two episodes of the first series were co-written with John Lloyd.

(I was a kid who discovered the series—accidentally, as most listeners did—with the second episode. I sat in the car in the driveway, getting cold, listening to Vogon poetry, and then the ideal radio line "Ford, you're turning into an infinite number of penguins," and I was happy; perfectly, unutterably happy.)

By now, Douglas had a real job. He was the script editor for the long-running BBC SF series Doctor Who, in the Tom Baker days.

Pan Books approached him about doing a book based on the radio series, and Douglas got the manuscript for *The Hitchhiker's Guide to the Galaxy* in to his editors at Pan slightly late (according to legend they telephoned him and asked, rather desperately, where he was in the book, and how much more he had to go. He told them. "Well," said his editor, making the best of a bad job, "just finish the page you're on and we'll send a motorbike around to pick it up in half an hour"). The book, a paperback original, became a surprise bestseller, as did, less surprisingly, its four sequels. It spawned a bestselling text-based computer game.

The Hitchhiker's Guide to the Galaxy sequence used the tropes of science fiction to talk about the things that concerned Douglas, the world he observed, his thoughts on Life, the Universe, and Everything. As we moved into a world where people really did think that digital watches

were a pretty neat thing, the landscape had become science fiction and
Douglas, with a relentless curiosity about matters scientific, an instinct
for explanation, and a laser-sharp sense of where the joke was, was in
a perfect position to comment upon, to explain, and to describe that
landscape.

I read a lengthy newspaper article recently demonstrating that *Hitchhiker's* was in fact a lengthy tribute to Lewis Carroll (something that
would have come as a surprise to Douglas, who had disliked the little of
Alice in Wonderland he read). Actually, the literary tradition that Douglas
was part of was, at least initially, the tradition of English Humor Writing
that gave us P. G. Wodehouse (whom Douglas often cited as an influence,
although most people tended to miss it because Wodehouse didn't write
about spaceships).

Douglas Adams did not enjoy writing, and he enjoyed it less as time
went on. He was a bestselling, acclaimed, and much-loved novelist who
had not set out to be a novelist, and who took little joy in the process of
crafting novels. He loved talking to audiences. He liked writing screenplays. He liked being at the cutting edge of technology and inventing and
explaining with an enthusiasm that was uniquely his own. Douglas's
ability to miss deadlines became legendary. ("I love deadlines," he said
once. "I love the whooshing sound they make as they go by.")

He died in May 2001—too young. His death surprised us all, and left a
huge, Douglas Adams–sized hole in the world. We had lost both the man
(tall, affable, smiling gently at a world that baffled and delighted him)
and the mind.

He left behind a number of novels, as often-imitated as they are, ulti-
mately, inimitable. He left behind characters as delightful as Marvin the
Paranoid Android, Zaphod Beeblebrox and Slartibartfast. He left sen-
tences that will make you laugh with delight as they rewire the back of
your head.

And he made it look so easy.

—*Neil Gaiman,*
January 2002

(Long before Neil Gaiman was the bestselling author of novels like *American Gods* and
Neverwhere, or graphic novels like *The Sandman* sequence, he wrote a book called *Don't
Panic*, a history of Douglas Adams and the *Hitchhiker's Guide to the Galaxy*.)

Introduction:
A GUIDE TO THE GUIDE

Some unhelpful remarks from the author

The history of *The Hitchhiker's Guide to the Galaxy* is now so complicated that every time I tell it I contradict myself, and whenever I do get it right I'm misquoted. So the publication of this omnibus edition seemed like a good opportunity to set the record straight—or at least firmly crooked. Anything that is put down wrong here is, as far as I'm concerned, wrong for good.

The idea for the title first cropped up while I was lying drunk in a field in Innsbruck, Austria, in 1971. Not particularly drunk, just the sort of drunk you get when you have a couple of stiff Gössers after not having eaten for two days straight, on account of being a penniless hitchhiker. We are talking of a mild inability to stand up.

I was traveling with a copy of the *Hitch Hiker's Guide to Europe* by Ken Walsh, a very battered copy that I had borrowed from someone. In fact, since this was 1971 and I still have the book, it must count as stolen by now. I didn't have a copy of *Europe on Five Dollars a Day* (as it then was) because I wasn't in that financial league.

Night was beginning to fall on my field as it spun lazily underneath me. I was wondering where I could go that was cheaper than Innsbruck, revolved less and didn't do the sort of things to me that Innsbruck had done to me that afternoon. What had happened was this. I had been walking through the town trying to find a particular address, and being thoroughly lost I stopped to ask for directions from a man in the street. I knew this mightn't be easy because I don't speak German, but I was still surprised to discover just how much difficulty I was having communicating with this particular man. Gradually the truth dawned on me as we struggled in vain to understand each other that of all the people in Innsbruck I could have stopped to ask, the one I had picked did not speak English, did not speak French and was also deaf and dumb. With a series of sincerely apologetic hand movements, I disentangled myself, and a few minutes later, on another street, I stopped and asked another man who also turned out to be deaf and dumb, which was when I bought the beers.

I ventured back onto the street. I tried again.

When the third man I spoke to turned out to be deaf and dumb and also blind I began to feel a terrible weight settling on my shoulders; wherever I looked the trees and buildings took on dark and menacing aspects. I pulled my coat tightly around me and hurried lurching down the street, whipped by a sudden gusting wind. I bumped into someone and stammered an apology, but he was deaf and dumb and unable to understand me. The sky loured. The pavement seemed to tip and spin. If I hadn't happened then to duck down a side street and pass a hotel where a convention for the deaf was being held, there is every chance that my mind would have cracked completely and I would have spent the rest of my life writing the sort of books for which Kafka became famous and dribbling.

As it is I went to lie in a field, along with my *Hitch Hiker's Guide to Europe*, and when the stars came out it occurred to me that if only someone would write a *Hitchhiker's Guide to the Galaxy* as well, then I for one would be off like a shot. Having had this thought I promptly fell asleep and forgot about it for six years.

I went to Cambridge University. I took a number of baths—and a degree in English. I worried a lot about girls and what had happened to my bike. Later I became a writer and worked on a lot of things that were almost incredibly successful but in fact just failed to see the light of day. Other writers will know what I mean.

My pet project was to write something that would combine comedy and science fiction, and it was this obsession that drove me into deep debt and despair. No one was interested, except finally one man: a BBC radio producer named Simon Brett who had had the same idea, comedy and science fiction. Although Simon only produced the first episode before leaving the BBC to concentrate on his own writing (he is best known in the United States for his excellent Charles Paris detective novels), I owe him an immense debt of gratitude for simply getting the thing to happen in the first place. He was succeeded by the legendary Geoffrey Perkins.

In its original form the show was going to be rather different. I was feeling a little disgruntled with the world at the time and had put together about six different plots, each of which ended with the destruction of the world in a different way, and for a different reason. It was to be called "The Ends of the Earth."

While I was filling in the details of the first plot—in which the Earth was demolished to make way for a new hyperspace express route—I realized that I needed to have someone from another planet around to tell the reader what was going on, to give the story the context it needed. So I had to work out who he was and what he was doing on the Earth.

I decided to call him Ford Prefect. (This was a joke that missed American audiences entirely, of course, since they had never heard of the rather oddly named little car, and many thought it was a typing error for Perfect.) I explained in the text that the minimal research my alien character had done before arriving on this planet had led him to think that this name would be "nicely inconspicuous." He had simply mistaken the dominant life form.

So how would such a mistake arise? I remembered when I used to hitchhike through Europe and would often find that the information or advice that came my way was out of date or misleading in some way. Most of it, of course, just came from stories of other people's travel experiences.

At that point the title *The Hitchhiker's Guide to the Galaxy* suddenly popped back into my mind from wherever it had been hiding all this time. Ford, I decided, would be a researcher who collected data for the *Guide*. As soon as I started to develop this particular notion, it moved inexorably to the center of the story, and the rest, as the creator of the original Ford Prefect would say, is bunk.

The story grew in the most convoluted way, as many people will be surprised to learn. Writing episodically meant that when I finished one episode I had no idea about what the next one would contain. When, in the twists and turns of the plot, some event suddenly seemed to illuminate things that had gone before, I was as surprised as anyone else.

I think that the BBC's attitude toward the show while it was in production was very similar to that which Macbeth had toward murdering people—initial doubts, followed by cautious enthusiasm and then greater and greater alarm at the sheer scale of the undertaking and still no end in sight. Reports that Geoffrey and I and the sound engineers were buried in a subterranean studio for weeks on end, taking as long to produce a single sound effect as other people took to produce an entire series (and stealing everybody else's studio time in which to do so), were all vigorously denied but absolutely true.

The budget of the series escalated to the point that it could have practically paid for a few seconds of *Dallas*. If the show hadn't worked...

The first episode went out on BBC Radio 4 at 10:30 P.M. on Wednesday, March 8, 1978, in a huge blaze of no publicity at all. Bats heard it. The odd dog barked.

After a couple of weeks a letter or two trickled in. So—someone out there had listened. People I talked to seemed to like Marvin the Paranoid Android, whom I had written in as a one-scene joke and had only developed further at Geoffrey's insistence.

Then some publishers became interested, and I was commissioned by Pan Books in England to write up the series in book form. After a lot of procrastination and hiding and inventing excuses and having baths, I managed to get about two-thirds of it done. At this point they said, very pleasantly and politely, that I had already passed ten deadlines, so would I please just finish the page I was on and let them have the damn thing.

Meanwhile, I was busy trying to write another series and was also writing and script editing the TV series "Dr. Who," because while it was all very pleasant to have your own radio series, especially one that somebody had written in to say they had heard, it didn't exactly buy you lunch.

So that was more or less the situation when the book *The Hitchhiker's Guide to the Galaxy* was published in England in September 1979 and appeared on the *Sunday Times* mass market best-seller list at number one and just stayed there. Clearly, somebody had been listening.

This is where things start getting complicated, and this is what I was asked, in writing this Introduction, to explain. The *Guide* has appeared in so many forms—books, radio, a television series, records and soon to be a major motion picture—each time with a different story line that even its most acute followers have become baffled at times.

Here then is a breakdown of the different versions—not including the various stage versions, which haven't been seen in the States and only complicate the matter further.

The radio series began in England in March 1978. The first series consisted of six programs, or "fits" as they were called. Fits 1 thru 6. Easy. Later that year, one more episode was recorded and broadcast, commonly known as the Christmas episode. It contained no reference of any kind to Christmas. It was called the Christmas episode because it was first broadcast on December 24, which is not Christmas Day. After this, things began to get increasingly complicated.

In the fall of 1979, the first *Hitchhiker* book was published in England, called *The Hitchhiker's Guide to the Galaxy*. It was a substantially expanded version of the first four episodes of the radio series, in which some of the characters behaved in entirely different ways and others behaved in exactly the same ways but for entirely different reasons, which amounts to the same thing but saves rewriting the dialogue.

At roughly the same time a double record album was released, which was, by contrast, a slightly contracted version of the first four episodes of the radio series. These were not the recordings that were originally broadcast but wholly new recordings of substantially the same scripts. This was done because we had used music off gramophone records as incidental music for the series, which is fine on radio, but makes commercial release impossible.

In January 1980, five new episodes of "The Hitchhiker's Guide to the Galaxy" were broadcast on BBC Radio, all in one week, bringing the total number to twelve episodes.

In the fall of 1980, the second *Hitchhiker* book was published in England, around the same time that Harmony Books published the first book in the United States. It was a very substantially reworked, reedited and contracted version of episodes 7, 8, 9, 10, 11, 12, 5 and 6 (in that order) of the radio series "The Hitchhiker's Guide to the Galaxy." In case that seemed too straightforward, the book was called *The Restaurant at the End of the Universe*, because it included the material from radio episode 5 of "The Hitchhiker's Guide to the Galaxy," which was set in a restaurant called Milliways, otherwise known as the Restaurant at the End of the Universe.

At roughly the same time, a second record album was made featuring a heavily rewritten and expanded version of episodes 5 and 6 of the radio series. This record album was also called The Restaurant at the End of the Universe.

Meanwhile, a series of six television episodes of "The Hitchhiker's Guide to the Galaxy" was made by the BBC and broadcast in January 1981. This was based, more or less, on the first six episodes of the radio series. In other words, it incorporated most of the book *The Hitchhiker's Guide to the Galaxy* and the second half of the book *The Restaurant at the End of the Universe*. Therefore, though it followed the basic structure of the radio series, it incorporated revisions from the books, which didn't.

In January 1982 Harmony Books published *The Restaurant at the End of the Universe* in the United States.

In the summer of 1982, a third *Hitchhiker* book was published simultaneously in England and the United States, called *Life, the Universe and Everything*. This was not based on anything that had already been heard or seen on radio or television. In fact it flatly contradicted episodes 7, 8, 9, 10, 11 and 12 of the radio series. These episodes of "The Hitchhiker's Guide to the Galaxy," you will remember, had already been incorporated in revised form in the book called *The Restaurant at the End of the Universe.*

At this point I went to America to write a film screenplay which was completely inconsistent with most of what has gone on so far, and since that film was then delayed in the making (a rumor currently has it that filming will start shortly before the Last Trump), I wrote a fourth and last book in the trilogy, *So Long, and Thanks for All the Fish.* This was published in Britain and the USA in the fall of 1984 and it effectively contradicted everything to date, up to and including itself.

As if this all were not enough I wrote a computer game for Infocom called *The Hitchhiker's Guide to the Galaxy,* which bore only fleeting resemblances to anything that had previously gone under that title, and in collaboration with Geoffrey Perkins assembled *The Hitchhiker's Guide to the Galaxy: The Original Radio Scripts* (published in England and the USA in 1985). Now this was an interesting venture. The book is, as the title suggests, a collection of all the radio scripts, as broadcast, and it is therefore the only example of one Hitchhiker publication accurately and consistently reflecting another. I feel a little uncomfortable with this—which is why the introduction to that book was written *after* the final and definitive one you are now reading and, of course, flatly contradicts it.

People often ask me how they can leave the planet, so I have prepared some brief notes.

How to Leave the Planet

1. Phone NASA. Their phone number is (713) 483-3111. Explain that it's very important that you get away as soon as possible.

2. If they do not cooperate, phone any friend you may have in the White House—(202) 456-1414—to have a word on your behalf with the guys at NASA.

3. If you don't have any friends in the White House, phone the Kremlin (ask the overseas operator for 0107-095-295-9051). They don't have any friends there either (at least, none to speak of), but they do seem to have a little influence, so you may as well try.

4. If that also fails, phone the Pope for guidance. His telephone number is 011-39-6-6982, and I gather his switchboard is infallible.

5. If all these attempts fail, flag down a passing flying saucer and explain that it's vitally important you get away before your phone bill arrives.

Douglas Adams

Los Angeles 1983 and
London 1985/1986

The Hitchhiker's Guide to the Galaxy

For Jonny Brock and Clare Gorst
and all other Arlingtonians
for tea, sympathy and a sofa

Far out in the uncharted backwaters of the unfashionable end of the Western Spiral arm of the Galaxy lies a small unregarded yellow sun.

Orbiting this at a distance of roughly ninety-eight million miles is an utterly insignificant little blue-green planet whose ape-descended life forms are so amazingly primitive that they still think digital watches are a pretty neat idea.

This planet has—or rather had—a problem, which was this: most of the people living on it were unhappy for pretty much of the time. Many solutions were suggested for this problem, but most of these were largely concerned with the movements of small green pieces of paper, which is odd because on the whole it wasn't the small green pieces of paper that were unhappy.

And so the problem remained; lots of the people were mean, and most of them were miserable, even the ones with digital watches.

Many were increasingly of the opinion that they'd all made a big mistake in coming down from the trees in the first place. And some said that even the trees had been a bad move, and that no one should ever have left the oceans.

And then, one Thursday, nearly two thousand years after one man had been nailed to a tree for saying how great it would be to be nice to people for a change, a girl sitting on her own in a small café in Rickmansworth suddenly realized what it was that had been going wrong all this time, and she finally knew how the world could be made a good and happy place. This time it was right, it would work, and no one would have to get nailed to anything.

Sadly, however, before she could get to a phone to tell anyone about it, a terrible, stupid catastrophe occurred, and the idea was lost for ever.

This is not her story.

But it is the story of that terrible, stupid catastrophe and some of its consequences.

It is also the story of a book, a book called The Hitchhiker's Guide to the Galaxy—not an Earth book, never published on Earth, and until the terrible catastrophe occurred, never seen or even heard of by any Earthman.

Nevertheless, a wholly remarkable book.

In fact, it was probably the most remarkable book ever to come out of the great publishing corporations of Ursa Minor—of which no Earthman had ever heard either.

Not only is it a wholly remarkable book, it is also a highly successful one—more popular than the Celestial Home Care Omnibus, *better selling than* Fifty-three More Things to Do in Zero Gravity, *and more controversial than Oolon Coluphid's trilogy of philosophical blockbusters,* Where God Went Wrong, Some More of God's Greatest Mistakes *and* Who Is This God Person Anyway?

In many of the more relaxed civilizations on the Outer Eastern Rim of the Galaxy, the Hitchhiker's Guide *has already supplanted the great* Encyclopedia Galactica *as the standard repository of all knowledge and wisdom, for though it has many omissions and contains much that is apocryphal, or at least wildly inaccurate, it scores over the older, more pedestrian work in two important respects.*

First, it is slightly cheaper; and second, it has the words DON'T PANIC *inscribed in large friendly letters on its cover.*

But the story of this terrible, stupid Thursday, the story of its extraordinary consequences, and the story of how these consequences are inextricably intertwined with this remarkable book begins very simply.

It begins with a house.

Chapter 1

The house stood on a slight rise just on the edge of the village. It stood on its own and looked out over a broad spread of West Country farmland. Not a remarkable house by any means—it was about thirty years old, squattish, squarish, made of brick, and had four windows set in the front of a size and proportion which more or less exactly failed to please the eye.

The only person for whom the house was in any way special was Arthur Dent, and that was only because it happened to be the one he lived in. He had lived in it for about three years, ever since he had moved out of London because it made him nervous and irritable. He was about thirty as well, tell, dark-haired and never quite at ease with himself. The thing that used to worry him most was the fact that people always used to ask him what he was looking so worried about. He worked in local radio which he always used to tell his friends was a lot more interesting than they probably thought. It was, too—most of his friends worked in advertising.

On Wednesday night it had rained very heavily, the lane was wet and muddy, but the Thursday morning sun was bright and clear as it shone on Arthur Dent's house for what was to be the last time.

It hadn't properly registered yet with Arthur that the council wanted to knock it down and build a bypass instead.

At eight o'clock on Thursday morning Arthur didn't feel very good. He woke up blearily, got up, wandered blearily round his room, opened a window, saw a bulldozer, found his slippers, and stomped off to the bathroom to wash.

Toothpaste on the brush—so. Scrub.

Shaving mirror—pointing at the ceiling. He adjusted it. For a moment it reflected a second bulldozer through the bathroom window. Properly adjusted, it reflected Arthur Dent's bristles. He shaved them off, washed, dried and stomped off to the kitchen to find something pleasant to put in his mouth.

Kettle, plug, fridge, milk, coffee. Yawn.

The word *bulldozer* wandered through his mind for a moment in search of something to connect with.

The bulldozer outside the kitchen window was quite a big one.

He stared at it.

"Yellow," he thought, and stomped off back to his bedroom to get dressed.

Passing the bathroom he stopped to drink a large glass of water, and another. He began to suspect that he was hung over. Why was he hung over? Had he been drinking the night before? He supposed that he must have been. He caught a glint in the shaving mirror. "Yellow," he thought, and stomped on to the bedroom.

He stood and thought. The pub, he thought. Oh dear, the pub. He vaguely remembered being angry, angry about something that seemed important. He'd been telling people about it, telling people about it at great length, he rather suspected: his clearest visual recollection was of glazed looks on other people's faces. Something about a new bypass he'd just found out about. It had been in the pipeline for months only no one seemed to have known about it. Ridiculous. He took a swig of water. It would sort itself out, he'd decided, no one wanted a bypass, the council didn't have a leg to stand on. It would sort itself out.

God, what a terrible hangover it had earned him though. He looked at himself in the wardrobe mirror. He stuck out his tongue. "Yellow," he thought. The word *yellow* wandered through his mind in search of something to connect with.

Fifteen seconds later he was out of the house and lying in front of a big yellow bulldozer that was advancing up his garden path.

Mr. L. Prosser was, as they say, only human. In other words he was a carbon-based bipedal life form descended from an ape. More specifically he was forty, fat and shabby and worked for the local council. Curiously enough, though he didn't know it, he was also a direct male-line descendant of Genghis Khan, though intervening generations and racial mixing had so juggled his genes that he had no discernible Mongoloid characteristics, and the only vestiges left in Mr. L. Prosser of his mighty ancestry were a pronounced stoutness about the tum and a predilection for little fur hats.

He was by no means a great warrior; in fact he was a nervous, worried man. Today he was particularly nervous and worried because something had gone seriously wrong with his job, which was to see that Arthur Dent's house got cleared out of the way before the day was out.

"Come off it, Mr. Dent," he said, "you can't win, you know. You can't lie in front of the bulldozer indefinitely." He tried to make his eyes blaze fiercely but they just wouldn't do it.

Arthur lay in the mud and squelched at him.

"I'm game," he said, "we'll see who rusts first."

"I'm afraid you're going to have to accept it," said Mr. Prosser, gripping his fur hat and rolling it round the top of his head; "this bypass has got to be built and it's going to be built!"

"First I've heard of it," said Arthur, "why's it got to be built?"

Mr. Prosser shook his finger at him for a bit, then stopped and put it away again.

"What do you mean, why's it got to be built?" he said. "It's a bypass. You've got to build bypasses."

Bypasses are devices that allow some people to dash from point A to point B very fast while other people dash from point B to point A very fast. People living at point C, being a point directly in between, are often given to wonder what's so great about point A that so many people from point B are so keen to get there, and what's so great about point B that so many people from point A are so keen to get there. They often wish that people would just once and for all work out where the hell they wanted to be.

Mr. Prosser wanted to be at point D. Point D wasn't anywhere in particular, it was just any convenient point a very long way from points A, B and C. He would have a nice little cottage at point D, with axes over the door, and spend a pleasant amount of time at point E, which would be the nearest pub to point D. His wife of course wanted climbing roses, but he wanted axes. He didn't know why—he just liked axes. He flushed hotly under the derisive grins of the bulldozer drivers.

He shifted his weight from foot to foot, but it was equally uncomfortable on each. Obviously somebody had been appallingly incompetent and he hoped to God it wasn't him.

Mr. Prosser said, "You were quite entitled to make any suggestions or protests at the appropriate time, you know."

"Appropriate time?" hooted Arthur. "Appropriate time? The first I knew about it was when a workman arrived at my home yesterday. I asked him if he'd come to clean to windows and he said no, he'd come to demolish the house. He didn't tell me straight away of course. Oh no. First he wiped a couple of windows and charged me a fiver. Then he told me."

"But Mr. Dent, the plans have been available in the local planning office for the last nine months."

"Oh yes, well, as soon as I heard I went straight round to see them, yesterday afternoon. You hadn't exactly gone out of your way to call attention to them, had you? I mean, like actually telling anybody or anything."

"But the plans were on display..."

"On display? I eventually had to go down to the cellar to find them."

"That's the display department."

"With a flashlight."

"Ah, well, the lights had probably gone."

"So had the stairs."

"But look, you found the notice, didn't you?"

"Yes," said Arthur, "yes I did. It was on display in the bottom of a locked filing cabinet stuck in a disused lavatory with a sign on the door saying 'Beware of the Leopard.' "

A cloud passed overhead. It cast a shadow over Arthur Dent as he lay propped up on his elbow in the cold mud. It cast a shadow over Arthur Dent's house. Mr. Prosser frowned at it.

"It's not as if it's a particularly nice house," he said.

"I'm sorry, but I happen to like it."

"You'll like the bypass."

"Oh, shut up," said Arthur Dent. "Shut up and go away, and take your bloody bypass with you. You haven't got a leg to stand on and you know it."

Mr. Prosser's mouth opened and closed a couple of times while his mind was for a moment filled with inexplicable but terribly attractive visions of Arthur Dent's house being consumed with fire and Arthur himself running screaming from the blazing ruin with at least three hefty spears protruding from his back. Mr. Prosser was often bothered with visions like these and they made him feel very nervous. He stuttered for a moment and then pulled himself together.

"Mr. Dent," he said.

"Hello? Yes?" said Arthur.

"Some factual information for you. Have you any idea how much damage that bulldozer would suffer if I just let it roll straight over you?"

"How much?" said Arthur.

"None at all," said Mr. Prosser, and stormed nervously off wondering why his brain was filled with a thousand hairy horsemen all shouting at him.

By a curious coincidence, "None at all" is exactly how much suspicion the ape-descendant Arthur Dent had that one of his closest friends was not descended from an ape, but was in fact from a small planet somewhere in the vicinity of Betelgeuse and not from Guildford as he usually claimed.

Arthur Dent had never, ever suspected this.

This friend of his had first arrived on the planet Earth some fifteen Earth years previously, and he had worked hard to blend himself into Earth society—with, it must be said, some success. For instance, he had spent those fifteen years pretending to be an out-of-work actor, which was plausible enough.

He had made one careless blunder though, because he had skimped a bit on his preparatory research. The information he had gathered had led him to choose the name "Ford Prefect" as being nicely inconspicuous.

He was not conspicuously tall, his features were striking but not conspicuously handsome. His hair was wiry and gingerish and brushed backward from the temples. His skin seemed to be pulled backward from the nose. There was something very slightly odd about him, but it was difficult to say what it was. Perhaps it was that his eyes didn't seem to blink often enough and when you talked to him for any length of time your eyes began involuntarily to water on his behalf. Perhaps it was that he smiled slightly too broadly and gave people the unnerving impression that he was about to go for their neck.

He struck most of the friends he had made on Earth as an eccentric, but a harmless one—an unruly boozer with some oddish habits. For instance, he would often gate-crash university parties, get badly drunk and start making fun of any astrophysicists he could find till he got thrown out.

Sometimes he would get seized with oddly distracted moods and stare into the sky as if hypnotized until someone asked him what he was doing. Then he would start guiltily for a moment, relax and grin.

"Oh, just looking for flying saucers," he would joke, and everyone would laugh and ask him what sort of flying saucers he was looking for.

"Green ones!" he would reply with a wicked grin, laugh wildly for a moment and then suddenly lunge for the nearest bar and buy an enormous round of drinks.

Evenings like this usually ended badly. Ford would get out of his skull on whisky, huddle in a corner with some girl and explain to her in slurred phrases that honestly the color of the flying saucers didn't matter that much really.

Thereafter, staggering semiparalytic down the night streets, he would often ask passing policemen if they knew the way to Betelgeuse. The policemen would usually say something like, "Don't you think it's about time you went off home, sir?"

"I'm trying to, baby, I'm trying to," is what Ford invariably replied on these occasions.

In fact what he was really looking for when he stared distractedly into the sky was any kind of flying saucer at all. The reason he said green was that green was the traditional space livery of the Betelgeuse trading scouts.

Ford Prefect was desperate that any flying saucer at all would arrive soon because fifteen years was a long time to get stranded anywhere, particularly somewhere as mind-bogglingly dull as the Earth.

Ford wished that a flying saucer would arrive soon because he knew how to flag flying saucers down and get lifts from them. He knew how to see the Marvels of the Universe for less than thirty Altairian dollars a day.

In fact, Ford Prefect was a roving researcher for that wholly remarkable book, *The Hitchhiker's Guide to the Galaxy*.

Human beings are great adapters, and by lunchtime life in the environs of Arthur's house had settled into a steady routine. It was Arthur's accepted role to lie squelching in the mud making occasional demands to see his lawyer, his mother or a good book; it was Mr. Prosser's accepted role to tackle Arthur with the occasional new ploy such as the For the Public Good talk, or the March of Progress talk, the They Knocked My House Down Once You Know, Never Looked Back talk and various other cajoleries and threats; and it was the bulldozer drivers' accepted role to sit around drinking coffee and experimenting with union regulations to see how they could turn the situation to their financial advantage.

The Earth moved slowly in its diurnal course.

The sun was beginning to dry out the mud that Arthur lay in.

A shadow moved across him again.

"Hello, Arthur," said the shadow.

Arthur looked up and squinting into the sun was startled to see Ford Prefect standing above him.

"Ford! Hello, how are you?"

"Fine," said Ford, "look, are you busy?"

"Am I *busy?*" exclaimed Arthur. "Well, I've just got all these bulldozers and things to lie in front of because they'll knock my house down if I don't, but other than that ... well, no, not especially, why?"

They don't have sarcasm on Betelgeuse, and Ford Prefect often failed to notice it unless he was concentrating. He said, "Good, is there anywhere we can talk?"

"What?" said Arthur Dent.

For a few seconds Ford seemed to ignore him, and stared fixedly into the sky like a rabbit trying to get run over by a car. Then suddenly he squatted down beside Arthur.

"We've got to talk," he said urgently.

"Fine," said Arthur, "talk."

"And drink," said Ford. "It's vitally important that we talk and drink. Now. We'll go to the pub in the village."

He looked into the sky again, nervous, expectant.

"Look, don't you understand?" shouted Arthur. He pointed at Prosser. "That man wants to knock my house down!"

Ford glanced at him, puzzled.

"Well, he can do it while you're away, can't he?" he asked.

"But I don't want him to!"

"Ah."

"Look, what's the matter with you, Ford?" said Arthur.

"Nothing. Nothing's the matter. Listen to me—I've got to tell you the most important thing you've ever heard. I've got to tell you now, and I've got to tell you in the saloon bar of the Horse and Groom."

"But why?"

"Because you're going to need a very stiff drink."

Ford stared at Arthur, and Arthur was astonished to find his will beginning to weaken. He didn't realize that this was because of an old drinking game that Ford learned to play in the hyperspace ports that served the madranite mining belts in the star system of Orion Beta.

The game was not unlike the Earth game called Indian wrestling, and was played like this:

Two contestants would sit either side of a table, with a glass in front of each of them.

Between them would be placed a bottle of Janx Spirit (as immortalized in that ancient Orion mining song, "Oh, don't give me none more of that Old Janx Spirit/No, don't you give me none more of that Old Janx Spirit/For my head will fly, my tongue will lie, my eyes will fry and I may die/Won't you pour me one more of that sinful Old Janx Spirit").

Each of the two contestants would then concentrate their will on the bottle and attempt to tip it and pour spirit into the glass of his opponent, who would then have to drink it.

The bottle would then be refilled. The game would be played again. And again.

Once you started to lose you would probably keep losing, because one of the effects of Janx Spirit is to depress telepsychic power.

As soon as a predetermined quantity had been consumed, the final loser would have to perform a forfeit, which was usually obscenely biological.

Ford Prefect usually played to lose.

Ford stared at Arthur, who began to think that perhaps he did want to go to the Horse and Groom after all.

"But what about my house...?" he asked plaintively.

Ford looked across to Mr. Prosser, and suddenly a wicked thought struck him.

"He wants to knock your house down?"

"Yes, he wants to build..."

"And he can't because you're lying in front of his bulldozer?"

"Yes, and..."

"I'm sure we can come to some arrangement," said Ford. "Excuse me!" he shouted.

Mr. Prosser (who was arguing with a spokesman for the bulldozer drivers about whether or not Arthur Dent constituted a mental health hazard, and how much they should get paid if he did) looked around. He was surprised and slightly alarmed to see that Arthur had company.

"Yes? Hello?" he called. "Has Mr. Dent come to his senses yet?"

"Can we for the moment," called Ford, "assume that he hasn't?"

"Well?" sighed Mr. Prosser.

"And can we also assume," said Ford, "that he's going to be staying here all day?"

"So?"

"So all your men are going to be standing around all day doing nothing?"

"Could be, could be..."

"Well, if you're resigned to doing that anyway, you don't acually need him to lie here all the time do you?"

"What?"

"You don't," said Ford patiently, "actually need him here."

Mr. Prosser thought about this.

"Well, no, not as such..." he said, "not exactly *need*..."

Prosser was worried. He thought that one of them wasn't making a lot of sense.

Ford said, "So if you would just like to take it as read that he's actually here, then he and I could slip off down to the pub for half an hour. How does that sound?"

Mr. Prosser thought it sounded perfectly potty.

"That sounds perfectly reasonable..." he said in a reassuring tone of voice, wondering who he was trying to reassure.

"And if you want to pop off for a quick one yourself later on," said Ford, "we can always cover for you in return."

"Thank you very much," said Mr. Prosser, who no longer knew how to play this at all, "thank you very much, yes, that's very kind..." He frowned, then smiled, then tried to do both at once, failed, grasped hold of his fur hat and rolled it fitfully round the top of his head. He could only assume that he had just won.

"So," continued Ford Prefect, "if you would just like to come over here and lie down..."

"What?" said Mr. Prosser.

"Ah, I'm sorry," said Ford, "perhaps I hadn't made myself fully clear. Somebody's got to lie in front of the bulldozers, haven't they? Or there won't be anything to stop them driving into Mr. Dent's house, will there?"

"What?" said Mr. Prosser again.

"It's very simple," said Ford, "my client, Mr. Dent, says that he will stop lying here in the mud on the sole condition that you come and take over from him."

"What are you talking about?" said Arthur, but Ford nudged him with his shoe to be quiet.

"You want me," said Prosser, spelling out this new thought to himself, "to come and lie there..."

"Yes."

"In front of the bulldozer?"

"Yes."

"Instead of Mr. Dent."

"Yes."

"In the mud."

"In, as you say, the mud."

As soon as Mr. Prosser realized that he was substantially the loser after all, it was as if a weight lifted itself off his shoulders: this was more like the world as he knew it. He sighed.

"In return for which you will take Mr. Dent with you down to the pub?"

"That's it," said Ford, "that's it exactly."

Mr. Prosser took a few nervous steps forward and stopped.

"Promise?" he said.

"Promise," said Ford. He turned to Arthur.

"Come on," he said to him, "get up and let the man lie down."

Arthur stood up, feeling as if he was in a dream.

Ford beckoned to Prosser, who sadly, awkwardly, sat down in the mud. He felt that his whole life was some kind of dream and he sometimes wondered whose it was and whether they were enjoying it. The mud folded itself round his bottom and his arms and oozed into his shoes.

Ford looked at him severely.

"And no sneaky knocking Mr. Dent's house down while he's away, all right?" he said.

"The mere thought," growled Mr. Prosser, "hadn't even begun to speculate," he continued, settling himself back, "about the merest possibility of crossing my mind."

He saw the bulldozer drivers' union representative approaching and let his head sink back and closed his eyes. He was trying to marshal his arguments for proving that he did not now constitute a mental health hazard himself. He was far from certain about this—his mind seemed to be full of noises, horses, smoke and the stench of blood. This always happened when he felt miserable or put upon, and he had never been able to explain it to himself. In a high dimension of which we know nothing, the mighty Khan bellowed with rage, but Mr. Prosser only trembled slightly and whimpered. He began to feel little pricks of water behind his eyelids. Bureaucratic cock-ups, angry men lying in mud, indecipherable strangers handing out inexplicable humiliation and an unidentified army of horsemen laughing at him in his head—what a day.

What a day. Ford Prefect knew that it didn't matter a pair of dingo's kidneys whether Arthur's house got knocked down or not now.

Arthur remained very worried.

"But can we trust him?" he said.

"Myself I'd trust him to the end of the Earth," said Ford.

"Oh yes," said Arthur, "and how far's that?"

"About twelve minutes away," said Ford, "come on, I need a drink."

Chapter 2

Here's what the Encyclopedia Galactica *has to say about alcohol. It says that alcohol is a colorless volatile liquid formed by the fermentation of sugars and also notes its intoxicating effect on certain carbon-based life forms.*

The Hitchhiker's Guide to the Galaxy *also mentions alcohol. It says that the best drink in existence is the Pan Galactic Gargle Blaster.*

It says that the effect of drinking a Pan Galactic Gargle Blaster is like having your brains smashed out by a slice of lemon wrapped round a large gold brick.

The Guide *also tells you on which planets the best Pan Galactic Gargle Blasters are mixed, how much you can expect to pay for one and what voluntary organizations exist to help you rehabilitate afterward.*

The Guide *even tells you how you can mix one yourself.*

Take the juice from one bottle of the Ol' Janx Spirit, it says.

Pour into it one measure of water from the seas of Santraginus V—Oh, that Santraginean seawater, it says. Oh, those Santraginean fish!

Allow three cubes of Arcturan Mega-gin to melt into the mixture (it must be properly iced or the benzine is lost).

Allow four liters of Fallian marsh gas to bubble through it, in memory of all those happy hikers who have died of pleasure in the Marshes of Fallia.

Over the back of a silver spoon float a measure of Qualactin Hypermint extract, redolent of all the heady odors of the dark Qualactin Zones, subtle, sweet and mystic.

Drop in the tooth of an Algolian Suntiger. Watch it dissolve, spreading the fires of the Algolian Suns deep into the heart of the drink.

Sprinkle Zamphuor.

Add an olive.

Drink . . . but . . . very carefully . . .

The Hitchhiker's Guide to the Galaxy *sells rather better than the* Encyclopedia Galactica.

"Six pints of bitter," said Ford Prefect to the barman of the Horse and Groom. "And quickly please, the world's about to end."

The barman of the Horse and Groom didn't deserve this sort of treatment; he was a dignified old man. He pushed his glasses up his nose and blinked at Ford Prefect. Ford ignored him and stared out the window, so the barman looked instead at Arthur, who shrugged helplessly and said nothing.

So the barman said, "Oh yes, sir? Nice weather for it," and started pulling pints.

He tried again. "Going to watch the match this afternoon then?"

Ford glanced round at him.

"No, no point," he said, and looked back out the window.

"What's that, foregone conclusion then, you reckon, sir?" said the barman. "Arsenal without a chance?"

"No no," said Ford, "it's just that the world's about to end."

"Oh yes, sir, so you said," said the barman, looking over his glasses this time at Arthur. "Lucky escape for Arsenal if it did."

Ford looked back at him, genuinely surprised.

"No, not really," he said. He frowned.

The barman breathed in heavily. "There you are, sir, six pints," he said.

Arthur smiled at him wanly and shrugged again. He turned and smiled wanly at the rest of the pub just in case any of them had heard what was going on.

None of them had, and none of them could understand what he was smiling at them for.

A man sitting next to Ford at the bar looked at the two men, looked at the six pints, did a swift burst of mental arithmetic, arrived at an answer he liked and grinned a stupid hopeful grin at them.

"Get off," said Ford, "they're ours," giving him a look that would have made an Algolian Suntiger get on with what it was doing.

Ford slapped a five-pound note on the bar. He said, "Keep the change."

"What, from a fiver? Thank you, sir."

"You've got ten minutes left to spend it."

The barman decided simply to walk away for a bit.

"Ford," said Arthur, "would you please tell me what the hell is going on?"

"Drink up," said Ford, "you've got three pints to get through."

"Three pints?" said Arthur. "At lunchtime?"

The man next to Ford grinned and nodded happily. Ford ignored him. He said, "Time is an illusion. Lunchtime doubly so."

"Very deep," said Arthur, "you should send that in to the *Reader's Digest.* They've got a page for people like you."

"Drink up."

"Why three pints all of a sudden?"

"Muscle relaxant, you'll need it."

"Muscle relaxant?"

"Muscle relaxant."

Arthur stared into his beer.

"Did I do anything wrong today," he said, "or has the world always been like this and I've been too wrapped up in myself to notice?"

"All right," said Ford, "I'll try to explain. How long have we known each other?"

"How long?" Arthur thought. "Er, about five years, maybe six," he said. "Most of it seemed to make some kind of sense at the time."

"All right," said Ford. "How would you react if I said that I'm not from Guildford after all, but from a small planet somewhere in the vicinity of Betelgeuse?"

Arthur shrugged in a so-so sort of way.

"I don't know," he said, taking a pull of beer. "Why, do you think it's the sort of thing you're likely to say?"

Ford gave up. It really wasn't worth bothering at the moment, what with the world being about to end. He just said, "Drink up."

He added, perfectly factually, "The world's about to end."

Arthur gave the rest of the pub another wan smile. The rest of the pub frowned at him. A man waved at him to stop smiling at them and mind his own business.

"This must be Thursday," said Arthur to himself, sinking low over his beer. "I never could get the hang of Thursdays."

Chapter 3

On this particular Thursday, something was moving quietly through the ionosphere many miles above the surface of the planet; several somethings in fact, several dozen huge yellow chunky slablike somethings, huge as office blocks, silent as birds. They soared with ease, basking in electromagnetic rays from the star Sol, biding their time, grouping, preparing.

The planet beneath them was almost perfectly oblivious of their presence, which was just how they wanted it for the moment. The huge yellow something went unnoticed at Goonhilly, they passed over Cape Canaveral without a blip, Woomera and Jodrell Bank looked straight through them, which was a pity because it was exactly the sort of thing they'd been looking for all these years.

The only place they registered at all was on a small black device called a Sub-Etha Sens-O-Matic which winked away quietly to itself. It nestled in the darkness inside a leather satchel which Ford Prefect habitually wore slung around his neck. The contents of Ford Prefect's satchel were quite interesting in fact and would have made any Earth physicist's eyes pop out of his head, which is why he always concealed them by keeping a couple of dogeared scripts for plays he pretended he was auditioning for stuffed in the top. Besides the Sub-Etha Sens-O-Matic and the scripts he had an Electronic Thumb—a short squat black rod, smooth and matt with a couple of flat switches and dials at one end; he also had a device that looked rather like a largish electronic calculator. This had about a hundred tiny flat press buttons and a screen about four inches square on which any one of a million "pages" could be summoned at a moment's notice. It looked insanely complicated, and this was one of the reasons why the snug plastic cover it fitted into had the words DON'T PANIC printed on it in large friendly letters. The other reason was that this device was in fact that most remarkable of all books ever to come out of the great publishing corporations of Ursa Minor—*The Hitchhiker's Guide to the Galaxy*. The reason why it was published in the form of a micro sub meson electronic component is that if it were printed in normal book form, an interstellar hitchhiker would require several inconveniently large buildings to carry it around in.

Beneath that in Ford Prefect's satchel were a few ballpoints, a notepad and a largish bath towel from Marks and Spencer.

The Hitchhiker's Guide to the Galaxy *has a few things to say on the subject of towels.*

A towel, it says, is about the most massively useful thing an interstellar hitchhiker can have. Partly it has great practical value. You can wrap it around you for warmth as you bound across the cold moons of Jaglan Beta; you can lie on it on the brilliant marble-sanded beaches of Santraginus V, inhaling the heady sea vapors; you can sleep under it beneath the stars which shine so redly on the desert world of Kakrafoon; use it to sail a miniraft down the slow heavy River Moth; wet it for use in hand-to-hand combat; wrap it round your head to ward off noxious fumes or avoid the gaze of the Ravenous Bugblatter Beast of Traal (a mind-bogglingly stupid animal, it assumes that if you can't see it, it can't see you—daft as a brush, but very very ravenous); you can wave your towel in emergencies as a distress signal, and of course dry yourself off with it if it still seems to be clean enough.

More importantly, a towel has immense psychological value. For some reason, if a strag (strag: nonhitchhiker) discovers that a hitchhiker has his towel with him, he will automatically assume that he is also in possession of a toothbrush, washcloth, soap, tin of biscuits, flask, compass, map, ball of string, gnat spray, wet-weather gear, space suit etc., etc. Furthermore, the strag will then happily lend the hitchhiker any of these or a dozen other items that the hitchhiker might accidentally have "lost." What the strag will think is that any man who can hitch the length and breadth of the Galaxy, rough it, slum it, struggle against terrible odds, win through and still know where his towel is, is clearly a man to be reckoned with.

Hence a phrase that has passed into hitchhiking slang, as in "Hey, you sass that hoopy Ford Prefect? There's a frood who really knows where his towel is." *(Sass: know, be aware of, meet, have sex with; hoopy: really together guy; frood: really amazingly together guy.)*

Nestling quietly on top of the towel in Ford Prefect's satchel, the Sub-Etha Sens-O-Matic began to wink more quickly. Miles above the surface of the planet the huge yellow somethings began to fan out. At Jodrell Bank, someone decided it was time for a nice relaxing cup of tea.

"You got a towel with you?" said Ford suddenly to Arthur.

Arthur, struggling through his third pint, looked round at him.

"Why? What, no . . . should I have?" He had given up being surprised, there didn't seem to be any point any longer.

Ford clicked his tongue in irritation.

"Drink up," he urged.

At that moment the dull sound of a rumbling crash from outside filtered through the low murmur of the pub, through the sound of the jukebox, through the sound of the man next to Ford hiccupping over the whisky Ford had eventually bought him.

Arthur choked on his beer, leaped to his feet.

"What's that?" he yelped.

"Don't worry," said Ford, "they haven't started yet."

"Thank God for that," said Arthur, and relaxed.

"It's probably just your house being knocked down," said Ford, downing his last pint.

"What?" shouted Arthur. Suddenly Ford's spell was broken. Arthur looked wildly around him and ran to the window.

"My God, they are! They're knocking my house down. What the hell am I doing in the pub, Ford?"

"It hardly makes any difference at this stage," said Ford, "let them have their fun."

"Fun?" yelped Arthur. "Fun!" He quickly checked out the window again that they were talking about the same thing.

"Damn their fun!" he hooted, and ran out of the pub furiously waving a nearly empty beer glass. He made no friends at all in the pub that lunchtime.

"Stop, you vandals! You home wreckers!" bawled Arthur. "You half-crazed Visigoths, stop, will you!"

Ford would have to go after him. Turning quickly to the barman he asked for four packets of peanuts.

"There you are, sir," said the barman, slapping the packets on the bar, "twenty-eight pence if you'd be so kind."

Ford was very kind—he gave the barman another five-pound note and told him to keep the change. The barman looked at it and then looked at Ford. He suddenly shivered: he experienced a momentary sensation that he didn't understand because no one on Earth had ever experienced it before. In moments of great stress, every life form that exists gives out a tiny subliminal signal. This signal simply communicates an exact and almost pathetic sense of how far that being is from the place of his birth. On Earth it is never possible to be farther than sixteen thousand miles from your birthplace, which really isn't very far, so such signals are too minute to be noticed. Ford Prefect was at this moment under great stress, and he was born six hundred light-years away in the near vicinity of Betelgeuse.

The barman reeled for a moment, hit by a shocking, incomprehensible sense of distance. He didn't know what it meant, but he looked at Ford Prefect with a new sense of respect, almost awe.

"Are you serious, sir?" he said in a small whisper which had the effect of silencing the pub. "You think the world's going to end?"

"Yes," said Ford.

"But, this afternoon."

Ford had recovered himself. He was at his flippest.

"Yes," he said gaily, "in less than two minutes I would estimate."

The barman couldn't believe this conversation he was having, but he couldn't believe the sensation he had just had either.

"Isn't there anything we can do about it then?" he said.

"No, nothing," said Ford, stuffing the peanuts into his pocket.

Someone in the hushed bar suddenly laughed raucously at how stupid everyone had become.

The man sitting next to Ford was a bit sozzled by now. His eyes weaved their way up to Ford.

"I thought," he said, "that if the world was going to end we were meant to lie down or put a paper bag over our head or something."

"If you like, yes," said Ford.

"That's what they told us in the army," said the man, and his eyes began the long trek back toward his whisky.

"Will that help?" asked the barman.

"No," said Ford, and gave him a friendly smile. "Excuse me," he said, "I've got to go." With a wave, he left.

The pub was silent for a moment longer and then, embarrassingly enough, the man with the raucous laugh did it again. The girl he had dragged along to the pub with him had grown to loathe him dearly over the last hour, and it would probably have been a great satisfaction to her to know that in a minute and a half or so he would suddenly evaporate into a whiff of hydrogen, ozone and carbon monoxide. However,. when the moment came she would be too busy evaporating herself to notice it.

The barman cleared his throat. He heard himself say, "Last orders, please."

The huge yellow machines began to sink downward and to move faster.

Ford knew they were there. This wasn't the way he had wanted it.

Running up the lane, Arthur had nearly reached his house. He didn't notice how cold it had suddenly become, he didn't notice the wind, he didn't notice the sudden irrational squall of rain. He didn't notice anything but the caterpillar bulldozers crawling over the rubble that had been his home.

"You barbarians!" he yelled. "I'll sue the council for every penny it's got! I'll have you hung, drawn and quartered! And whipped! And boiled ... until ... until ... until you've had enough."

Ford was running after him very fast. Very very fast.

"And then I will do it again!" yelled Arthur. "And when I've finished I will take all the little bits, and I will *jump* on them!"

Arthur didn't notice that the men were running from the bulldozers; he didn't notice that Mr. Prosser was staring hectically into the sky. What Mr. Prosser had noticed was that huge yellow somethings were screaming through the clouds. Impossibly huge yellow somethings.

"And I will carry on jumping on them," yelled Arthur, still running, "until I get blisters, or I can think of anything even more unpleasant to do, and then ..."

Arthur tripped, and fell headlong, rolled and landed flat on his back. At last he noticed that something was going on. His finger shot upward.

"What the hell's that?" he shrieked.

Whatever it was raced across the sky in its monstrous yellowness, tore the sky apart with mind-boggling noise and leaped off into the distance leaving the gaping air to shut behind it with a *bang* that drove your ears six feet into your skull.

Another one followed and did exactly the same thing only louder.

It's difficult to say exactly what the people on the surface of the planet were doing now, because they didn't really know what they were doing themselves. None of it made a lot of sense—running into houses, running out of houses, howling noiselessly at the noise. All around the world city streets exploded with people, cars skidded into each other as the noise fell on them and then rolled off like a tidal wave over hills and valleys, deserts and oceans, seeming to flatten everything it hit.

Only one man stood and watched the sky, stood with terrible sadness in his eyes and rubber bungs in his ears. He knew exactly what was happening and had known ever since his Sub-Etha Sens-O-Matic had started winking in the dead of night beside his pillow and wakened him with a start. It was what he had waited for all these years, but when he had deciphered the signal pattern sitting alone in his small dark room, a coldness had gripped him and squeezed his heart. Of all the races in all of the Galaxy who could have come and said a big hello to planet Earth, he thought, didn't it just have to be the Vogons.

Still, he knew what he had to do. As the Vogon craft screamed through the air high above him he opened his satchel. He threw away a copy of *Joseph and the Amazing Technicolor Dreamcoat*, he threw away a copy of *Godspell*: he wouldn't need them where he was going. Everything was ready, everything was prepared.

He knew where his towel was.

A sudden silence hit the Earth. If anything it was worse than the noise. For a while nothing happened.

The great ships hung motionless in the sky, over every nation on Earth. Motionless they hung, huge, heavy, steady in the sky, a blasphemy against nature. Many people went straight into shock as their minds tried to encompass what they were looking at. The ships hung in the sky in much the same way that bricks don't.

And still nothing happened.

Then there was a slight whisper, a sudden spacious whisper of open ambient sound. Every hi-fi set in the world, every radio, every television, every cassette recorder, every woofer, every tweeter, every mid-range driver in the world quietly turned itself on.

Every tin can, every dustbin, every window, every car, every wineglass, every sheet of rusty metal became activated as an acoustically perfect sounding board.

Before the Earth passed away it was going to be treated to the very ultimate in sound reproduction, the greatest public address system ever built. But there was no concert, no music, no fanfare, just a simple message.

"*People of Earth, your attention, please,*" a voice said, and it was wonderful. Wonderful perfect quadrophonic sound with distortion levels so low as to make a brave man weep.

"*This is Prostetnic Vogon Jeltz of the Galactic Hyperspace Planning Council,*" the voice continued. "*As you will no doubt be aware, the plans for development of the outlying regions of the Galaxy require the building of a hyperspatial express route through your star system, and regrettably your planet is one of those scheduled for demolition. The process will take slightly less than two of your Earth minutes. Thank you."*

The PA died away.

Uncomprehending terror settled on the watching people of Earth. The terror moved slowly through the gathered crowds as if they were iron filings on a sheet of board and a magnet was moving beneath them. Panic sprouted again, desperate fleeing panic, but there was nowhere to flee to.

Observing this, the Vogons turned on their PA again. It said:

"There's no point in acting all surprised about it. All the planning charts and demolition orders have been on display in your local planning department in Alpha Centauri for fifty of your Earth years, so you've had plenty of time to lodge any formal complaint and it's far too late to start making a fuss about it now."

The PA fell silent again and its echo drifted across the land. The huge ships turned slowly in the sky with easy power. On the underside of each a hatchway opened, an empty black square.

By this time somebody somewhere must have manned a radio transmitter, located a wavelength and broadcast a message back to the Vogon ships, to plead on behalf of the planet. Nobody ever heard what they said, they only heard the reply. The PA slammed back into life again. The voice was annoyed. It said:

"What do you mean, you've never been to Alpha Centauri? For heaven's sake, mankind, it's only four light-years away, you know. I'm sorry, but if you can't be bothered to take an interest in local affairs that's your own lookout.

"Energize the demolition beams."

Light poured out of the hatchways.

"I don't know," said the voice on the PA, *"apathetic bloody planet, I've no sympathy at all."* It cut off.

There was a terrible ghastly silence.

There was a terrible ghastly noise.

There was a terrible ghastly silence.

The Vogon Constructor Fleet coasted away into the inky starry void.

Chapter 4

Far away on the opposite spiral arm of the Galaxy, five hundred thousand light-years from the star Sol, Zaphod Beeblebrox, President of the Imperial Galactic Government, sped across the seas of Damogran, his ion drive delta boat winking and flashing in the Damogran sun.

Damogran the hot; Damogran the remote; Damogran the almost totally unheard of.

Damogran, secret home of the Heart of Gold.

The boat sped on across the water. It would be some time before it reached its destination because Damogran is such an inconveniently arranged planet. It consists of nothing but middling to large desert islands separated by very pretty but annoyingly wide stretches of ocean.

The boat·sped on.

Because of this topographical awkwardness Damogran has always remained a deserted planet. This is why the Imperial Galactic Government chose Damogran for the Heart of Gold project, because it was so deserted and the Heart of Gold project was so secret.

The boat zipped and skipped across the sea, the sea that lay between the main islands of the only archipelago of any useful size on the whole planet. Zaphod Beeblebrox was on his way from the tiny spaceport on Easter Island (the name was an entirely meaningless coincidence—in Galactic-speke, *easter* means small, flat and light-brown) to the Heart of Gold Island, which by another meaningless coincidence was called France.

One of the side effects of work on the Heart of Gold was a whole string of pretty meaningless coincidences.

But it was not in any way a coincidence that today, the day of culmination of the project, the great day of unveiling, the day that the Heart of Gold was finally to be introduced to a marveling Galaxy, was also a great day of culmination for Zaphod Beeblebrox. It was for the sake of this day that he had first decided to run for the presidency, a decision that had sent shock waves of astonishment throughout the Imperial Galaxy. Zaphod Beeblebrox? *President?* Not *the* Zaphod Beeblebrox? Not *the* President? Many had seen it as clinching proof that the whole of known creation had finally gone bananas.

Zaphod grinned and gave the boat an extra kick of speed.

Zaphod Beeblebrox, adventurer, ex-hippie, good-timer (crook? quite possibly), manic self-publicist, terribly bad at personal relationships, often thought to be completely out to lunch.

President?

No one had gone bananas, not in that way at least.

Only six people in the entire Galaxy understood the principle on which the Galaxy was governed, and they knew that once Zaphod Beeblebrox had announced his intention to run as President it was more or less a fait accompli: he was ideal presidency fodder.*

What they completely failed to understand was why Zaphod was doing it.

He banked sharply, shooting a wild wall of water at the sun.

Today was the day; today was the day when they would realize what Zaphod had been up to. Today was what Zaphod Beeblebrox's presidency was all about. Today was also his two-hundredth birthday, but that was just another meaningless coincidence.

As he skipped his boat across the seas of Damogran he smiled quietly to himself about what a wonderful, exciting day it was going to be. He relaxed and spread his two arms lazily along the seat back. He steered with an extra arm he'd recently had fitted just beneath his right one to help improve his ski-boxing.

---

*President: full title President of the Imperial Galactic Government.

The term *Imperial* is kept though it is now an anachronism. The hereditary Emperor is nearly dead and has been for many centuries. In the last moments of his dying coma he was locked in a stasis field which keeps him in a state of perpetual unchangingness. All his heirs are now long dead, and this means that without any drastic political upheaval, power has simply and effectively moved a rung or two down the ladder, and is now seen to be vested in a body that used to act simply as advisers to the Emperor—an elected governmental assembly headed by a President elected by that assembly. In fact it vests in no such place.

The President in particular is very much a figurehead—he wields no real power whatsoever. He is apparently chosen by the government, but the qualities he is required to display are not those of leadership but those of finely judged outrage. For this reason the President is always a controversial choice, always an infuriating but fascinating character. His job is not to wield power but to draw attention away from it. On those criteria Zaphod Beeblebrox is one of the most successful Presidents the Galaxy has ever had—he has already spent two of his ten presidential years in prison for fraud. Very very few people realize that the President and the Government have virtually no power at all, and of these few people only six know whence ultimate political power is wielded. Most of the others secretly believe that the ultimate decision-making process is handled by a computer. They couldn't be more wrong.

"Hey," he cooed to himself, "you're a real cool boy, you." But his nerves sang a song shriller than a dog whistle.

The island of France was about twenty miles long, five miles across the middle, sandy and crescent-shaped. In fact, it seemed to exist not so much as an island in its own right as simply a means of defining the sweep and curve of a huge bay. This impression was heightened by the fact that the inner coastline of the crescent consisted almost entirely of steep cliffs. From the top of the cliff the land sloped slowly down five miles to the opposite shore.

On top of the cliffs stood a reception committee.

It consisted in large part of the engineers and researchers who had built the Heart of Gold—mostly humanoid, but here and there were a few reptiloid atomineers, two or three green sylphlike maximegalaticians, an octopodic physuculturalist or two and a Hooloovoo (a Hooloovoo is a superintelligent shade of the color blue). All except the Hooloovoo were resplendent in their multicolored ceremonial lab coats; the Hooloovoo had been temporarily refracted into a free-standing prism for the occasion.

There was a mood of immense excitement thrilling through all of them. Together and between them they had gone to and beyond the furthest limits of physical laws, restructured the fundamental fabric of matter, strained, twisted and broken the laws of possibility and impossibility, but still the greatest excitement of all seemed to be to meet a man with an orange sash round his neck. (An orange sash was what the President of the Galaxy traditionally wore.) It might not even have made much difference to them if they'd known exactly how much power the President of the Galaxy actually wielded: none at all. Only six people in the Galaxy knew that the job of the Galactic President was not to wield power but to attract attention away from it.

Zaphod Beeblebrox was amazingly good at his job.

The crowd gasped, dazzled by sun and seamanship, as the presidential speedboat zipped round the headland into the bay. It flashed and shone as it came skating over the sea in wide skidding turns.

In fact, it didn't need to touch the water at all, because it was supported on a hazy cushion of ionized atoms, but just for effect it was fitted with thin finblades which could be lowered into the water. They slashed sheets of water hissing into the air, carved deep gashes in the sea which swayed crazily and sank back foaming in the boat's wake as it careered across the bay.

Zaphod loved effect: it was what he was best at.

He twisted the wheel sharply, the boat skidded round in a wild scything skid beneath the cliff face and dropped to rest lightly on the rocking waves.

Within seconds he ran out onto the deck and waved and grinned at over three billion people. The three billion people weren't actually there, but they watched his every gesture through the eyes of a small robot tri-D camera which hovered obsequiously in the air nearby. The antics of the President always made amazingly popular tri-D: that's what they were for.

He grinned again. Three billion and six people didn't know it, but today would be a bigger antic than anyone had bargained for.

The robot camera homed in for a close-up on the more popular of his two heads and he waved again. He was roughly humanoid in appearance except for the extra head and third arm. His fair tousled hair stuck out in random directions, his blue eyes glinted with something completely unidentifiable, and his chins were almost always unshaven.

A twenty-foot-high transparent globe floated next to his boat, rolling and bobbing, glistening in the brilliant sun. Inside it floated a wide semicircular sofa upholstered in glorious red leather: the more the globe bobbed and rolled, the more the sofa stayed perfectly still, steady as an upholstered rock. Again, all done for effect as much as anything.

Zaphod stepped through the wall of the globe and relaxed on the sofa. He spread his two arms along the back and with the third brushed some dust off his knee. His heads looked about, smiling; he put his feet up. At any moment, he thought, he might scream.

Water boiled up beneath the bubble, it seethed and spouted. The bubble surged into the air, bobbing and rolling on the water spout. Up, up it climbed, throwing stilts of light at the cliff. Up it surged on the jet, the water falling from beneath it, crashing back into the sea hundreds of feet below.

Zaphod smiled, picturing himself.

A thoroughly ridiculous form of transport, but a thoroughly beautiful one.

At the top of the cliff the globe wavered for a moment, tipped onto a railed ramp, rolled down it to a small concave platform and riddled to a halt.

To tremendous applause Zaphod Beeblebrox stepped out of the bubble, his orange slash blazing in the light.

The President of the Galaxy had arrived.

He waited for the applause to die down, then raised his hand in greeting. "Hi," he said.

A government spider sidled up to him and attempted to press a copy of his prepared speech into his hands. Pages three to seven of the original version were at the moment floating soggily on the Damogran Sea some five miles out from the bay. Pages one and two had been salvaged by a Damogran Frond Crested Eagle and had already become incorporated into an extraordinary new form of nest which the eagle had invented. It was constructed largely of papier-mâché and it was virtually impossible for a newly hatched baby eagle to break out of it. The Damogran Frond Crested Eagle had heard of the notion of survival of the species but wanted no truck with it.

Zaphod Beeblebrox would not be needing his set speech and he gently deflected the one being offered him by the spider.

"Hi," he said again.

Everyone beamed at him, or at least, nearly everyone. He singled out Trillian from the crowd. Trillian was a girl that Zaphod had picked up recently while visiting a planet, just for fun, incognito. She was slim, darkish, humanoid, with long waves of black hair, a full mouth, an odd little knob of a nose and ridiculously brown eyes. With her red head scarf knotted in that particular way and her long flowing silky brown dress, she looked vaguely Arabic. Not that anyone there had ever heard of an Arab of course. The Arabs had very recently ceased to exist, and even when they had existed they were five hundred thousand light-years from Damogran. Trillian wasn't anybody in particular, or so Zaphod claimed. She just went around with him rather a lot and told him what she thought of him.

"Hi, honey," he said to her.

She flashed him a quick tight smile and looked away. Then she looked back for a moment and smiled more warmly—but by this time he was looking at something else.

"Hi," he said to a small knot of creatures from the press who were standing nearby wishing that he would stop saying *Hi* and get on with the quotes. He grinned at them particularly because he knew that in a few moments he would be giving them one hell of a quote.

The next thing he said though was not a lot of use to them. One of the officials of the party had irritably decided that the President was clearly not in a mood to read the deliciously turned speech that had been written for him, and had flipped the switch on the remote-control device in his pocket. Away in front of them a huge white dome that bulged against the sky cracked down the middle, split and slowly folded itself down into the ground. Everyone gasped although they had known perfectly well it was going to do that because they'd built it that way.

Beneath it lay uncovered a huge starship, one hundred and fifty meters long, shaped like a sleek running shoe, perfectly white and mind-bogglingly beautiful. At the heart of it, unseen, lay a small gold box which carried within it the most brain-wrenching device ever conceived, a device that made this starship unique in the history of the Galaxy, a device after which the ship had been named—the Heart of Gold.

"Wow," said Zaphod Beeblebrox to the Heart of Gold. There wasn't much else he could say.

He said it again because he knew it would annoy the press. "Wow."

The crowd turned their faces back toward him expectantly. He winked at Trillian, who raised her eyebrows and widened her eyes at him. She knew what he was about to say and thought him a terrible show-off.

"That is really amazing," he said. "That really is truly amazing. That is so amazingly amazing I think I'd like to steal it."

A marvelous presidential quote, absolutely true to form. The crowd laughed appreciatively, the newsmen gleefully punched buttons on their Sub-Etha News-Matics and the President grinned.

As he grinned his heart screamed unbearably and he fingered the small Paralyso-Matic bomb that nestled quietly in his pocket.

Finally he could bear it no more. He lifted his heads up to the sky, let out a wild whoop in major thirds, threw the bomb to the ground and ran forward through the sea of suddenly frozen beaming smiles.

Prostetnic Vogon Jeltz was not a pleasant sight, even for other Vogons. His highly domed nose rose high above a small piggy forehead. His dark green rubbery skin was thick enough for him to play the game of Vogon Civil Service politics, and play it well, and waterproof enough for him to survive indefinitely at sea depths of down to a thousand feet with no ill effects.

Not that he ever went swimming of course. His busy schedule would not allow it. He was the way he was because billions of years ago when the Vogons had first crawled out of the sluggish primeval seas of Vogsphere, and had lain panting and heaving on the planet's virgin shores . . . when the first rays of the bright young Vogsol sun had shone across them that morning, it was as if the forces of evolution had simply given up on them there and then, had turned aside in disgust and written them off as an ugly and unfortunate mistake. They never evolved again: they should never have survived.

The fact that they did is some kind of tribute to the thick-willed slug-brained stubbornness of these creatures. *Evolution?* they said to themselves, *Who needs it?*, and what nature refused to do for them they simply did without until such time as they were able to rectify the gross anatomical inconveniences with surgery.

Meanwhile, the natural forces on the planet Vogsphere had been working overtime to make up for their earlier blunder. They brought forth scintillating jeweled scuttling crabs, which the Vogons ate, smashing their shells with iron mallets; tall aspiring trees of breathtaking slenderness and color which the Vogons cut down and burned the crabmeat with; elegant gazellelike creatures with silken coats and dewy eyes which the Vogons would catch and sit on. They were no use as transport because their backs would snap instantly, but the Vogons sat on them anyway.

Thus the planet Vogsphere whiled away the unhappy millennia until the Vogons suddenly discovered the principles of interstellar travel. Within a few short Vog years every last Vogon had migrated to the Megabrantis cluster, the political hub of the Galaxy, and now formed the immensely powerful backbone of the Galactic Civil Service. They have attempted to acquire learning, they have attempted to acquire style and social graces, but in most respects the modern Vogon is little different from his primitive forebears. Every year they import twenty-seven thousand scintillating jeweled scuttling crabs from their native planet and while away a happy drunken night smashing them to bits with iron mallets.

Prostetnic Vogon Jeltz was a fairly typical Vogon in that he was thoroughly vile. Also, he did not like hitchhikers.

Somewhere in a small dark cabin buried deep in the intestines of Prostetnic Vogon Jeltz's flagship, a small match flared nervously. The owner of the match was not a Vogon, but he knew all about them and was right to be nervous. His name was Ford Prefect.*

He looked about the cabin but could see very little; strange monstrous shadows loomed and leaped with the tiny flickering flame, but all was quiet. He breathed a silent thank you to the Dentrassis. The Dentrassis are an unruly tribe of gourmands, a wild but pleasant bunch whom the Vogons had recently taken to employing as catering staff on their long-haul fleets, on the strict understanding that they keep themselves very much to themselves.

This suited the Dentrassis fine, because they loved Vogon money, which is one of the hardest currencies in space, but loathed the Vogons themselves. The only sort of Vogon a Dentrassi liked to see was an annoyed Vogon.

It was because of this tiny piece of information that Ford Prefect was not now a whiff of hydrogen, ozone and carbon monoxide.

He heard a slight groan. By the light of the match he saw a heavy shape

*Ford Prefect's original name is only pronounceable in an obscure Betelgeusian dialect, now virtually extinct since the Great Collapsing Hrung Disaster of Gal./Sid./Year 03758 which wiped out all the old Praxibetel communities on Betelgeuse Seven. Ford's father was the only man on the entire planet to survive the Great Collapsing Hrung Disaster, by an extraordinary coincidence that he was never able satisfactorily to explain. The whole episode is shrouded in deep mystery: in fact no one ever knew what a Hrung was nor why it had chosen to collapse on Betelgeuse Seven particularly. Ford's father, magnanimously waving aside the clouds of suspicion that had inevitably settled around him, came to live on Betelgeuse Five, where he both fathered and uncled Ford; in memory of his now dead race he christened him in the ancient Praxibetel tongue.

Because Ford never learned to say his original name, his father eventually died of shame, which is still a terminal disease in some parts of the Galaxy. The other kids at school nicknamed him Ix, which in the language of Betelgeuse Five translates as "boy who is not able satisfactorily to explain what a Hrung is, nor why it should choose to collapse on Betelgeuse Seven."

moving slightly on the floor. Quickly he shook the match out, reached in his pocket, found what he was looking for and took it out. He ripped it open and shook it. He crouched on the floor. The shape moved again.

Ford Prefect said, "I bought some peanuts."

Arthur Dent moved, and groaned again, muttering incoherently.

"Here, have some," urged Ford, shaking the packet again, "if you've never been through a matter transference beam before you've probably lost some salt and protein. The beer you had should have cushioned your system a bit."

"Whhhrrr..." said Arthur Dent. He opened his eyes. "It's dark," he said.

"Yes," said Ford Prefect, "it's dark."

"No light," said Arthur Dent. "Dark, no light."

One of the things Ford Prefect had always found hardest to understand about humans was their habit of continually stating and repeating the very very obvious, as in *It's a nice day*, or *You're very tall*, or *Oh dear you seem to have fallen down a thirty-foot well, are you all right?* At first Ford had formed a theory to account for this strange behavior. If human beings don't keep exercising their lips, he thought, their mouths probably seize up. After a few months' consideration and observation he abandoned this theory in favor of a new one. If they don't keep on exercising their lips, he thought, their brains start working. After a while he abandoned this one as well as being obstructively cynical and decided he quite liked human beings after all, but he always remained desperately worried about the terrible number of things they didn't know about.

"Yes," he agreed with Arthur, "no light." He helped Arthur to some peanuts. "How do you feel?" he asked him.

"Like a military academy," said Arthur, "bits of me keep on passing out."

Ford stared at him blankly in the darkness.

"If I asked you where the hell we were," said Arthur weakly, "would I regret it?"

Ford stood up. "We're safe," he said.

"Oh good," said Arthur.

"We're in a small galley cabin," said Ford, "in one of the spaceships of the Vogon Constructor Fleet."

"Ah," said Arthur, "this is obviously some strange usage of the word *safe* that I wasn't previously aware of."

Ford struck another match to help him search for a light switch.

Monstrous shadows leaped and loomed again. Arthur struggled to his feet and hugged himself apprehensively. Hideous alien shapes seemed to throng about him, the air was thick with musty smells which sidled into his lungs without identifying themselves, and a low irritating hum kept his brain from focusing.

"How did we get here?" he asked, shivering slightly.

"We hitched a lift," said Ford.

"Excuse me?" said Arthur. "Are you trying to tell me that we just stuck out our thumbs and some green bug-eyed monster stuck his head out and said, 'Hi fellas, hop right in, I can take you as far as the Basingstoke roundabout'?"

"Well," said Ford, "the Thumb's an electronic sub-etha signaling device, the roundabout's at Barnard's Star six light-years away, but otherwise, that's more or less right."

"And the bug-eyed monster?"

"Is green, yes."

"Fine," said Arthur, "when can I go home?"

"You can't," said Ford Prefect, and found the light switch.

"Shade your eyes . . ." he said, and turned it on.

Even Ford was surprised.

"Good grief," said Arthur, "is this really the interior of a flying saucer?"

Prostetnic Vogon Jeltz heaved his unpleasant green body round the control bridge. He always felt vaguely irritable after demolishing populated planets. He wished that someone would come and tell him that it was all wrong so that he could shout at them and feel better. He flopped as heavily as he could onto his control seat in the hope that it would break and give him something to be genuinely angry about, but it only gave a complaining sort of creak.

"Go away!" he shouted at a young Vogon guard who entered the bridge at that moment. The guard vanished immediately, feeling rather relieved. He was glad it wouldn't now be him who delivered the report they'd just received. The report was an official release which said that a wonderful new form of spaceship drive was at this moment being unveiled at a Government research base on Damogran which would henceforth make all hyperspatial express routes unnecessary.

Another door slid open, but this time the Vogon captain didn't shout because it was the door from the galley quarters where the Dentrassis prepared his meals. A meal would be most welcome.

A huge furry creature bounded through the door with his lunch tray. It was grinning like a maniac.

Prostetnic Vogon Jeltz was delighted. He knew that when a Dentrassi looked that pleased with itself there was something going on somewhere on the ship that he could get very angry indeed about.

Ford and Arthur stared around them.

"Well, what do you think?" said Ford.

"It's a bit squalid, isn't it?"

Ford frowned at the grubby mattresses, unwashed cups and unidentifiable bits of smelly alien underwear that lay around the cramped cabin.

"Well, this is a working ship, you see," said Ford. "These are the Dentrassis' sleeping quarters."

"I thought you said they were called Vogons or something."

"Yes," said Ford, "the Vogons run the ship, the Dentrassis are the cooks; they let us on board."

"I'm confused," said Arthur.

"Here, have a look at this," said Ford. He sat down on one of the mattresses and rummaged about in his satchel. Arthur prodded the mattress nervously and then sat on it himself: in fact he had very little to be nervous about, because all mattresses grown in the swamps of Sqornshellous Zeta are very thoroughly killed and dried before being put to service. Very few have ever come to life again.

Ford handed the book to Arthur.

"What is it?" asked Arthur.

The Hitchhiker's Guide to the Galaxy. It's a sort of electronic book. It tells you everything you need to know about anything. That's its job."

Arthur turned it over nervously in his hands.

"I like the cover," he said. " 'Don't Panic.' It's the first helpful or intelligible thing anybody's said to me all day."

"I'll show you how it works," said Ford. He snatched it from Arthur, who was still holding it as if it were a two-week-dead lark, and pulled it out of its cover.

"You press this button here, you see, and the screen lights up, giving you the index."

A screen, about three inches by four, lit up and characters began to flicker across the surface.

"You want to know about Vogons, so I entered that name so." His fingers tapped some more keys. "And there we are."

The words *Vogon Constructor Fleets* flared in green across the screen.

Ford pressed a large red button at the bottom of the screen and words began to undulate across it. At the same time, the book began to speak the entry as well in a still, quiet, measured voice. This is what the book said:

"Vogon Constructor Fleets. Here is what to do if you want to get a lift from a Vogon: forget it. They are one of the most unpleasant races in the Galaxy—not actually evil, but bad-tempered, bureaucratic, officious and callous. They wouldn't even lift a finger to save their own grandmothers from the Ravenous Bugblatter Beast of Traal without orders signed in triplicate, sent in, sent back, queried, lost, found, subjected to public inquiry, lost again, and finally buried in soft peat for three months and recycled as firelighters.

"The best way to get a drink out of a Vogon is to stick your finger down his throat, and the best way to irritate him is to feed his grandmother to the Ravenous Bugblatter Beast of Traal.

"On no account allow a Vogon to read poetry at you."

Arthur blinked at it.

"What a strange book. How did we get a lift then?"

"That's the point, it's out of date now," said Ford, sliding the book back into its cover. "I'm doing the field research for the new revised edition, and one of the things I'll have to do is include a bit about how the Vogons now employ Dentrassi cooks, which gives us a rather useful little loophole."

A pained expression crossed Arthur's face. "But who are the Dentrassis?" he said.

"Great guys," said Ford. "They're *the* best cooks and the best drink mixers and they don't give a wet slap about anything else. And they'll always help hitchhikers aboard, partly because they like the company, but mostly because it annoys the Vogons. Which is exactly the sort of thing you need to know if you're an impoverished hitchhiker trying to see the marvels of the Universe for less than thirty Altairian dollars a day. And that's my job. Fun, isn't it?"

Arthur looked lost.

"It's amazing," he said, and frowned at one of the other mattresses.

"Unfortunately I got stuck on the Earth for rather longer than I intended," said Ford. "I came for a week and got stuck for fifteen years."

"But how did you get there in the first place then?"

"Easy, I got a lift with a teaser."

"A teaser?"

"Yeah."

"Er, what is..."

"A teaser? Teasers are usually rich kids with nothing to do. They cruise around looking for planets that haven't made interstellar contact yet and buzz them."

"Buzz them?" Arthur began to feel that Ford was enjoying making life difficult for him.

"Yeah," said Ford, "they buzz them. They find some isolated spot with very few people around, then land right by some poor unsuspecting soul whom no one's ever going to believe and then strut up and down in front of him wearing silly antennas on their head and making *beep beep* noises. Rather childish really." Ford leaned back on the mattress with his hands behind his head and looked infuriatingly pleased with himself.

"Ford," insisted Arthur, "I don't know if this sounds like a silly question, but what am I doing here?"

"Well, you know that," said Ford, "I rescued you from the Earth."

"And what's happened to the Earth?"

"Ah. It's been demolished."

"Has it," said Arthur levelly.

"Yes. It just boiled away into space."

"Look," said Arthur, "I'm a bit upset about that."

Ford frowned to himself and seemed to roll the thought around his mind.

"Yes, I can understand that," he said at last.

"Understand that!" shouted Arthur. "Understand that!

Ford sprang up.

"Keep looking at the book!" he hissed urgently.

"What?"

"Don't Panic."

"I'm not panicking!"

"Yes, you are."

"All right, so I'm panicking, what else is there to do?"

"You just come along with me and have a good time. The Galaxy's a fun place. You'll need to have this fish in your ear."

"I beg your pardon?" asked Arthur, rather politely he thought.

Ford was holding up a small glass jar which quite clearly had a small yellow fish wriggling around in it. Arthur blinked at him. He wished there was something simple and recognizable he could grasp hold of. He would have felt safe if alongside the Dentrassis' underwear, the piles of Sqornshellous mattresses and the man from Betelgeuse holding up a small yellow fish and offering to put it in his ear he had been able to see just a small packet of cornflakes. But he couldn't, and he didn't feel safe.

Suddenly a violent noise leaped at them from no source that he could identify. He gasped in terror at what sounded like a man trying to gargle while fighting off a pack of wolves.

"Shush!" said Ford. "Listen, it might be important."

"Im . . . important?"

"It's the Vogon captain making an announcement on the tannoy."

"You mean that's how the Vogons talk?"

"Listen!"

"But I can't speak Vogon!"

"You don't need to. Just put this fish in your ear."

Ford, with a lightning movement, clapped his hand to Arthur's ear, and he had the sudden sickening sensation of the fish slithering deep into his aural tract. Gasping with horror he scrabbled at his ear for a second or so, but then slowly turned goggle-eyed with wonder. He was experiencing the aural equivalent of looking at a picture of two black silhouetted faces and suddenly seeing it as a picture of a white candlestick. Or of looking at a lot of colored dots on a piece of paper which suddenly resolve themselves into the figure six and mean that your optician is going to charge you a lot of money for a new pair of glasses.

He was still listening to the howling gargles, he knew that, only now it had somehow taken on the semblance of perfectly straightforward English.

This is what he heard . . .

Chapter 6

*H*owl howl gargle howl gargle howl howl howl gargle howl gargle howl howl gargle gargle howl gargle gargle gargle howl slurrp uuuurgh should have a good time. Message repeats. This is your captain speaking, so stop whatever you're doing and pay attention. First of all I see from our instruments that we have a couple of hitchhikers aboard. Hello, wherever you are. I just want to make it totally clear that you are not at all welcome. I worked hard to get where I am today, and I didn't become captain of a Vogon constructor ship simply so I could turn it into a taxi service for a load of degenerate freeloaders. I have sent out a search party, and as soon as they find you I will put you off the ship. If you're very lucky I might read you some of my poetry first.

"Secondly, we are about to jump into hyperspace for the journey to Barnard's Star. On arrival we will stay in dock for a seventy-two-hour refit, and no one's to leave the ship during that time. I repeat, all planet leave is canceled. I've just had an unhappy love affair, so I don't see why anybody else should have a good time. Message ends."

The noise stopped.

Arthur discovered to his embarrassment that he was lying curled up in a small ball on the floor with his arms wrapped round his head. He smiled weakly.

"Charming man," he said. "I wish I had a daughter so I could forbid her to marry one..."

"You wouldn't need to," said Ford. "They've got as much sex appeal as a road accident. No, don't move," he added as Arthur began to uncurl himself, "you'd better be prepared for the jump into hyperspace. It's unpleasantly like being drunk."

"What's so unpleasant about being drunk?"

"You ask a glass of water."

Arthur thought about this.

"Ford," he said.

"Yeah?"

"What's this fish doing in my ear?"

"It's translating for you. It's a Babel fish. Look it up in the book if you like."

He tossed over *The Hitchhiker's Guide to the Galaxy* and then curled himself up into a fetal ball to prepare himself for the jump.

At that moment the bottom fell out of Arthur's mind.

His eyes turned inside out. His feet began to leak out of the top of his head.

The room folded flat around him, spun around, shifted out of existence and left him sliding into his own navel.

They were passing through hyperspace.

"The Babel fish," said *The Hitchhiker's Guide to the Galaxy* quietly, *"is small, yellow and leechlike, and probably the oddest thing in the Universe. It feeds on brainwave energy received not from its own carrier but from those around it. It absorbs all unconscious mental frequencies from this brainwave energy to nourish itself with. It then excretes into the mind of its carrier a telepathic matrix formed by combining the conscious thought frequencies with nerve signals picked up from the speech centers of the brain which has supplied them. The practical upshot of all this is that if you stick a Babel fish in your ear you can instantly understand anything said to you in any form of language. The speech patterns you actually hear decode the brainwave matrix which has been fed into your mind by your Babel fish.*

"Now it is such a bizarrely improbable coincidence that anything so mind-bogglingly useful could have evolved purely by chance that some thinkers have chosen to see it as a final and clinching proof of the nonexistence of God.

"The argument goes something like this: 'I refuse to prove that I exist,' says God, 'for proof denies faith, and without faith I am nothing.'

" 'But,' says Man, 'the Babel fish is a dead giveaway, isn't it? It could not have evolved by chance. It proves you exist, and so therefore, by your own arguments, you don't. QED.'

" 'Oh dear,' says God, 'I hadn't thought of that,' and promptly vanishes in a puff of logic.

" 'Oh, that was easy,' says Man, and for an encore goes on to prove that black is white and gets himself killed on the next zebra crossing.

"Most leading theologians claim that this argument is a load of dingo's kidneys, but that didn't stop Oolon Colluphid making a small fortune when he used it as the central theme of his best-selling book, Well That about Wraps It Up for God.

"Meanwhile, the poor Babel fish, by effectively removing all barriers to communication between different races and cultures, has caused more and bloodier wars than anything else in the history of creation."

Arthur let out a low groan. He was horrified to discover that the kick through hyperspace hadn't killed him. He was now six light-years from the place that the Earth would have been if it still existed.

The Earth.

Visions of it swam sickeningly through his nauseated mind. There was no way his imagination could feel the impact of the whole Earth having gone, it was too big. He prodded his feelings by thinking that his parents and his sister had gone. No reaction. He thought of all the people he had been close to. No reaction. Then he thought of a complete stranger he had been standing behind in the queue at the supermarket two days before and felt a sudden stab—the supermarket was gone, everyone in it was gone. Nelson's Column had gone! Nelson's Column had gone and there would be no outcry, because there was no one left to make an outcry. From now on Nelson's Column only existed in his mind. England only existed in his mind—his mind, stuck here in this dank smelly steel-lined spaceship. A wave of claustrophobia closed in on him.

England no longer existed. He'd got that—somehow he's got it. He tried again. America, he thought, has gone. He couldn't grasp it. He decided to start smaller again. New York has gone. No reaction. He'd never seriously believed it existed anyway. The dollar, he thought, has sunk for ever. Slight tremor there. Every Bogart movie has been wiped, he said to himself, and that gave him a nasty knock. McDonald's, he thought. There is no longer any such thing as a McDonald's hamburger.

He passed out. When he came round a second later he found he was sobbing for his mother.

He jerked himself violently to his feet.

"Ford!"

Ford looked up from where he was sitting in a corner humming to himself. He always found the actual traveling-through-space part of space travel rather trying.

"Yeah?" he said.

"If you're a researcher on this book thing and you were on Earth, you must have been gathering material on it."

"Well,, I was able to extend the original entry a bit, yes."

"Let me see what is says in this edition then, I've got to see it."

"Yeah, okay." He passed it over again.

Arthur grabbed hold of it and tried to stop his hands shaking. He pressed the entry for the relevant page. The screen flashed and swirled and resolved into a page of print. Arthur stared at it.

"It doesn't have an entry!" he burst out.

Ford looked over his shoulder.

"Yes, it does," he said, "down there, see at the bottom of the screen, just above Eccentrica Gallumbits, the triple-breasted whore of Eroticon 6."

Arthur followed Ford's finger, and saw where it was pointing. For a moment it still didn't register, then his mind nearly blew up.

"What? *Harmless?* Is that all it's got to say? *Harmless!* One word!"

Ford shrugged.

"Well, there are a hundred billion stars in the Galaxy, and only a limited amount of space in the book's microprocessors," he said, "and no one knew much about the Earth, of course."

"Well, for God's sake, I hope you managed to rectify that a bit."

"Oh yes, well, I managed to transmit a new entry off to the editor. He had to trim it a bit, but it's still an improvement."

"And what does it say now?" asked Arthur.

"Mostly harmless," admitted Ford with a slightly embarrassed cough.

"Mostly harmless!" shouted Arthur.

"What was that noise?" hissed Ford.

"It was me shouting," shouted Arthur.

"No! Shut up!" said Ford. "I think we're in trouble."

"You think we're in trouble!"

Outside the door were the clear sounds of marching footsteps.

"The Dentrassis?" whispered Arthur.

"No, those are steel-tipped boots," said Ford.

There was a sharp ringing rap on the door.

"Then who is it?" said Arthur.

"Well," said Ford, "if we're lucky it's just the Vogons come to throw us into space."

"And if we're unlucky?"

"If we're unlucky," said Ford grimly, "the captain might be serious in his threat that he's going to read us some of his poetry first...."

Chapter 7

Vogon poetry is of course the third worst in the Universe. The second worst is that of the Azgoths of Kria. During a recitation by their Poet Master Grunthos the Flatulent of his poem "Ode to a Small Lump of Green Putty I Found in My Armpit One Midsummer Morning" four of his audience died of internal hemorrhaging, and the President of the Mid-Galactic Arts Nobbling Council survived by gnawing one of his own legs off. Grunthos is reported to have been "disappointed" by the poem's reception, and was about to embark on a reading of his twelve-book epic entitled *My Favorite Bathtime Gurgles* when his own major intestine, in a desperate attempt to save life and civilization, leaped straight up through his neck and throttled his brain.

The very worst poetry of all perished along with its creator, Paula Nancy Millstone Jennings of Greenbridge, Essex, England, in the destruction of the planet Earth.

Prostetnic Vogon Jeltz smiled very slowly. This was done not so much for effect as because he was trying to remember the sequence of muscle movements. He had had a terribly therapeutic yell at his prisoners and was now feeling quite relaxed and ready for a little callousness.

The prisoners sat in Poetry Appreciation chairs—strapped in. Vogons suffered no illusions as to the regard their works were generally held in. Their early attempts at composition had been part of a bludgeoning insistence that they be accepted as a properly evolved and cultured race, but now the only thing that kept them going was sheer bloody-mindedness.

The sweat stood out cold on Ford Prefect's brow, and slid round the electrodes strapped to his temples. These were attached to a battery of electronic equipment—imagery intensifiers, rhythmic modulators, alliterative residulators and simile dumpers—all designed to heighten the experience of the poem and make sure that not a single nuance of the poet's thought was lost.

Arthur Dent sat and quivered. He had no idea what he was in for, but he knew that he hadn't liked anything that had happened so far and didn't think things were likely to change.

The Vogon began to read—a fetid little passage of his own devising.

"*Oh freddled gruntbuggly . . .*" he began. Spasms wracked Ford's body—this was worse than even he'd been prepared for.

"*? . . . thy micturations are to me/ As plurdled gabbleblotchits on a lurgid bee.*"

"Aaaaaaargggggghhhhhh!" went Ford Prefect, wrenching his head back as lumps of pain thumped through it. He could dimly see beside him Arthur lolling and rolling in his seat. He clenched his teeth.

"*Groop I implore thee,*" continued the merciless Vogon, "*my foonting turlingdromes.*"

His voice was rising to a horrible pitch of impassioned stridency. "*And hooptiously drangle me with crinkly bindlewurdles,/ Or I will rend thee in the gobberwarts with my blurglecruncheon, see if I don't!*"

"Nnnnnnnnnnnyyyyyyyyuuuuuuurrrrrrrggggggghhhhh!" cried Ford Prefect and threw one final spasm as the electronic enhancement of the last line caught him full blast across the temples. He went limp.

Arthur lolled.

"Now, Earthlings . . ." whirred the Vogon (he didn't know that Ford Prefect was in fact from a small planet somewhere in the vicinity of Betelgeuse, and wouldn't have cared if he had), "I present you with a simple choice! Either die in the vacuum of space, or . . ." he paused for melodramatic effect, "tell me how good you thought my poem was!"

He threw himself backward into a huge leathery bat-shaped seat and watched them. He did the smile again.

Ford was rasping for breath. He rolled his dusty tongue round his parched mouth and moaned.

Arthur said brightly, "Actually I quite liked it."

Ford turned and gaped. Here was an approach that had quite simply not occurred to him.

The Vogon raised a surprised eyebrow that effectively obscured his nose and was therefore no bad thing.

"Oh good . . ." he whirred, in considerable astonishment.

"Oh yes," said Arthur, "I thought that some of the metaphysical imagery was really particularly effective."

Ford continued to stare at him, slowly organizing his thoughts around this totally new concept. Were they really going to be able to bareface their way out of this?

"Yes, do continue . . ." invited the Vogon.

"Oh . . . and, er . . . interesting rhythmic devices too," continued Arthur, "which seemed to counterpoint the . . . er . . . er . . ." he floundered.

Ford leaped to his rescue, hazarding " . . . counterpoint the surrealism of the underlying metaphor of the . . . er . . ." He floundered too, but Arthur was ready again.

" . . . humanity of the . . ."

"*Vogonity,*" Ford hissed at him.

"Ah yes, Vogonity—sorry—of the poet's compassionate soul"—Arthur felt he was on a homestretch now—"which contrives through the medium of the verse structure to sublimate this, transcend that, and come to terms with the fundamental dichotomies of the other"—he was reaching a triumphant crescendo—"and one is left with a profound and vivid insight into . . . into . . . er . . ." (which suddenly gave out on him). Ford leaped in with the coup de grace:

"Into whatever it was the poem was about!" he yelled. Out of the corner of his mouth: "Well done, Arthur, that was very good."

The Vogon perused them. For a moment his embittered racial soul had been touched, but he thought no—too little too late. His voice took on the quality of a cat snagging brushed nylon.

"So what you're saying is that I write poetry because underneath my mean callous heartless exterior I really just want to be loved," he said. He paused, "Is that right?"

Ford laughed a nervous laugh. "Well, I mean, yes," he said, "don't we all, deep down, you know . . . er . . ."

The Vogon stood up.

"No, well, you're completely wrong," he said, "I just write poetry to throw my mean callous heartless exterior into sharp relief. I'm going to throw you off the ship anyway. Guard! Take the prisoners to number three airlock and throw them out!"

"What?" shouted Ford.

A huge young Vogon guard stepped forward and yanked them out of their straps with his huge blubbery arms.

"You can't throw us into space," yelled Ford, "we're trying to write a book."

"Resistance is useless!" shouted the Vogon guard back at him. It was the first phrase he'd learned when he joined the Vogon Guard Corps.

The captain watched with detached amusement and then turned away.

Arthur stared round him wildly.

"I don't want to die now!" he yelled. "I've still got a headache! I don't want to go to heaven with a headache, I'd be all cross and wouldn't enjoy it!"

The guard grasped them both firmly round the neck, and bowing deferentially toward his captain's back, hoicked them both protesting out of the bridge. A steel door closed and the captain was on his own again. He hummed quietly and mused to himself, lightly fingering his notebook of verses.

"Hmmm," he said, *"counterpoint the surrealism of the underlying metaphor...."* He considered this for a moment, and then closed the book with a grim smile.

"Death's too good for them," he said.

The long steel-lined corridor echoed to the feeble struggles of the two humanoids clamped firmly under rubbery Vogon armpits.

"This is great," spluttered Arthur, "this is really terrific. Let go of me, you brute!"

The Vogon guard dragged them on.

"Don't you worry," said Ford, "I'll think of something." He didn't sound hopeful.

"Resistance is useless!" bellowed the guard.

"Just don't say things like that," stammered Ford. "How can anyone maintain a positive mental attitude if you're saying things like that?"

"My God," complained Arthur, "you're talking about a positive mental attitude and you haven't even had your planet demolished today. I woke up this morning and thought I'd have a nice relaxed day, do a bit of reading, brush the dog.... It's now just after four in the afternoon and I'm already being thrown out of an alien spaceship six light-years from the smoking remains of the Earth!" He spluttered and gurgled as the Vogon tightened his grip.

"All right," said Ford, "just stop panicking!"

"Who said anything about panicking?" snapped Arthur. "This is still just the culture shock. You wait till I've settled down into the situation and found my bearings. *Then* I'll start panicking!"

"Arthur, you're getting hysterical. Shut up!" Ford tried desperately to think, but was interrupted by the guard shouting again.

"Resistance is useless!"

"And you can shut up as well!" snapped Ford.

"Resistance is useless!"

"Oh, give it a rest," said Ford. He twisted his head till he was looking straight up into his captor's face. A thought struck him.

"Do you really enjoy this sort of thing?" he asked suddenly.

The Vogon stopped dead and a look of immense stupidity seeped slowly over his face.

"Enjoy?" he boomed. "What do you mean?"

"What I mean," said Ford, "is does it give you a full, satisfying life? Stomping around, shouting, pushing people out of spaceships..."

The Vogon stared up at the low steel ceiling and his eyebrows almost rolled over each other. His mouth slacked. Finally he said, "Well, the hours are good...."

"They'd have to be," agreed Ford.

Arthur twisted his head round to look at Ford.

"Ford, what are you doing?" he asked in an amazed whisper.

"Oh, just trying to take an interest in the world around me, okay?" he said. "So the hours are pretty good then?" he resumed.

The Vogon stared down at him as sluggish thoughts moiled around in the murky depths.

"Yeah," he said, "but now you come to mention it, most of the actual minutes are pretty lousy. Except..." he thought again, which required looking at the ceiling, "except some of the shouting I quite like." He filled his lungs and bellowed, "Resistance is..."

"Sure, yes," interrupted Ford hurriedly, "you're good at that, I can tell. But if it's mostly lousy," he said, slowly giving the words time to reach their mark, "then why do you do it? What is it? The girls? The leather? The machismo? Or do you just find that coming to terms with the mindless tedium of it all presents an interesting challenge?"

Arthur looked backward and forward between them in bafflement.

"Er..." said the guard, "er... er... I dunno. I think I just sort of... do it really. My aunt said that spaceship guard was a good career for a young Vogon—you know, the uniform, the low-slung stun ray holster, the mindless tedium..."

"There you are, Arthur," said Ford with the air of someone reaching the conclusion of his argument, "you think you've got problems."

Arthur rather thought he had. Apart from the unpleasant business with his home planet the Vogon guard had half-throttled him already and he didn't like the sound of being thrown into space very much.

"Try and understand *his* problem," insisted Ford. "Here he is, poor lad, his entire life's work is stamping around, throwing people off spaceships..."

"And shouting," added the guard.

"And shouting, sure," said Ford, patting the blubbery arm clamped round his neck in friendly condescension, "and he doesn't even know why he's doing it!"

Arthur agreed this was very sad. He did this with a small feeble gesture, because he was too asphyxiated to speak.

Deep rumblings of bemusement came from the guard.

"Well. Now you put it like that I suppose..."

"Good lad!" encouraged Ford.

"But all right," went on the rumblings, "so what's the alternative?"

"Well," said Ford, brightly but slowly, "stop doing it, of course! Tell them," he went on, "you're not going to do it any more." He felt he ought to add something to that, but for the moment the guard seemed to have his mind occupied pondering that much.

"Eerrrrrmmmmmmmmmmmmmmmmmmmmmmmmmmmm..." said the guard, "erm, well, that doesn't sound that great to me."

Ford suddenly felt the moment slipping away.

"Now wait a minute," he said, "that's just the start, you see, there's more to it than that, you see...."

But at that moment the guard renewed his grip and continued his original purpose of lugging his prisoners to the airlock. He was obviously quite touched.

"No, I think if it's all the same to you," he said, "I'd better get you both shoved into this airlock and then go and get on with some other bits of shouting I've got to do."

It wasn't all the same to Ford Prefect at all.

"Come on now... but look!" he said, less slowly, less brightly.

"Huhhhhgggggggnnnnnnn..." said Arthur without any clear inflection.

"But hang on," pursued Ford, "there's music and art and things to tell you about yet! Arrggghhh!"

"Resistance is useless," bellowed the guard, and then added, "You see, if I keep it up I can eventually get promoted to Senior Shouting Officer, and there aren't usually many vacancies for nonshouting and nonpushing-people-about officers, so I think I'd better stick to what I know."

They had now reached the airlock—a large circular steel hatchway of massive strength and weight let into the inner skin of the craft. The guard operated a control and the hatchway swung smoothly open.

"But thanks for taking an interest," said the Vogon guard. "Bye now." He flung Ford and Arthur through the hatchway into the small chamber within. Arthur lay panting for breath. Ford scrambled round and flung his shoulder uselessly against the reclosing hatchway.

"But listen," he shouted to the guard, "there's a whole world you don't know anything about . . . here, how about this?" Desperately he grabbed for the only bit of culture he knew offhand—he hummed the first bar of Beethoven's "Fifth."

"*Da da da dum!* Doesn't that stir anything in you?"

"No," said the guard, "not really. But I'll mention it to my aunt."

If he said anything further after that it was lost. The hatchway sealed itself tight, and all sound was lost except the faint distant hum of the ship's engines.

They were in a brightly polished cylindrical chamber about six feet in diameter and ten feet long.

Ford looked round it, panting.

"Potentially bright lad I thought," he said, and slumped against the curved wall.

Arthur was still lying in the curve of the floor where he had fallen. He didn't look up. He just lay panting.

"We're trapped now, aren't we?"

"Yes," said Ford, "we're trapped."

"Well, didn't you think of anything? I thought you said you were going to think of something. Perhaps you thought of something and I didn't notice."

"Oh yes, I thought of something," panted Ford.

Arthur looked up expectantly.

"But unfortunately," continued Ford, "it rather involved being on the other side of this airtight hatchway." He kicked the hatch they'd just been thrown through.

"But it was a good idea, was it?"

"Oh yes, very neat."

"What was it?"

"Well, I hadn't worked out the details yet. Not much point now, is there?"

"So . . . er, what happens next?" asked Arthur.

"Oh, er, well, the hatchway in front of us will open automatically in a few moments and we will shoot out into deep space I expect and asphyxiate. If you take a lungful of air with you you can last for up to thirty seconds, of course . . ." said Ford. He stuck his hands behind his back, raised his eyebrows and started to hum an old Betelgeusian battle hymn. To Arthur's eyes he suddenly looked very alien.

"So this is it," said Arthur, "we are going to die."

"Yes," said Ford, "except . . . no! Wait a minute!" He suddenly lunged across the chamber at something behind Arthur's line of vision. "What's this switch?" he cried.

"What? Where?" cried Arthur, twisting round.

"No, I was only fooling," said Ford, "we are going to die after all."

He slumped against the wall again and carried on the tune from where he left off.

"You know," said Arthur, "it's at times like this, when I'm trapped in a Vogon airlock with a man from Betelgeuse, and about to die of asphyxiation in deep space, that I really wish I'd listened to what my mother told me when I was young."

"Why, what did she tell you?"

"I don't know, I didn't listen."

"Oh." Ford carried on humming.

"This is terrific," Arthur thought to himself, "Nelson's Column has gone, McDonald's has gone, all that's left is me and the words *Mostly harmless*. Any second now all that will be left is *Mostly harmless*. And yesterday the planet seemed to be going so well."

A motor whirred.

A slight hiss built into a deafening roar of rushing air as the outer hatchway opened onto an empty blackness studded with tiny, impossibly bright points of light. Ford and Arthur popped into outer space like corks from a toy gun.

The Hitchhiker's Guide to the Galaxy *is a wholly remarkable book. It has been compiled and recompiled many times over many years and under many different editorships. It contains contributions from countless numbers of travelers and researchers.*

The introduction begins like this:

"Space," *it says,* "is big. Really big. You just won't believe how vastly hugely mind-bogglingly big it is. I mean, you may think it's a long way down the road to the chemist, but that's just peanuts to space. Listen . . ." *and so on.*

(After a while the style settles down a bit and it begins to tell you things you really need to know, like the fact that the fabulously beautiful planet Bethselamin is now so worried about the cumulative erosion by ten billion visiting tourists a year that any net imbalance between the amount you eat and the amount you excrete while on the planet is surgically removed from your body weight when you leave: so every time you go to the lavatory there it is vitally important to get a receipt.)

To be fair though, when confronted by the sheer enormity of the distances between the stars, better minds than the one responsible for the Guide's introduction have faltered. Some invite you to consider for a moment a peanut in Reading and a small walnut in Johannesburg, and other such dizzying concepts.

The simple truth is that interstellar distances will not fit into the human imagination.

Even light, which travels so fast that it takes most races thousands of years to realize that it travels at all, takes time to journey between the stars. It takes eight minutes to journey from the star Sol to the place where the Earth used to be, and four years more to arrive at Sol's nearest stellar neighbor, Alpha Proxima.

For light to reach the other side of the Galaxy, for it to reach Damogran, for instance, takes rather longer: five hundred thousand years.

The record for hitchhiking this distance is just under five years, but you don't get to see much on the way.

The Hitchhiker's Guide to the Galaxy *says that if you hold a lungful of air you can survive in the total vacuum of space for about thirty seconds. However, it does go on to say that what with space being the mind-boggling size it is the chances of getting picked up by another ship within those thirty seconds are two to the power of two hundred and seventy-six thousand, seven hundred and nine to one against.*

By a totally staggering coincidence, that is also the telephone number of an Islington flat where Arthur once went to a very good party and met a very nice girl whom he totally failed to get off with—she went off with a gate-crasher.

Though the planet Earth, the Islington flat and the telephone have all now been demolished, it is comforting to reflect that they are all in some small way commemorated by the fact that twenty-nine seconds later Ford and Arthur were rescued.

Chapter 9

A computer chattered to itself in alarm as it noticed an airlock open and close itself for no apparent reason.

This was because reason was in fact out to lunch.

A hole had just appeared in the Galaxy. It was exactly a nothingth of a second long, a nothingth of an inch wide, and quite a lot of millions of light-years from end to end.

As it closed up, lots of paper hats and party balloons fell out of it and drifted off through the Universe. A team of seven three-foot-high market analysts fell out of it and died, partly of asphyxiation, partly of surprise.

Two hundred and thirty-nine thousand lightly fried eggs fell out of it too, materializing in a large wobbly heap on the famine-struck land of Poghril in the Pansel system.

The whole Poghril tribe had died out from famine except for one last man who died of cholesterol poisoning some weeks later.

The nothingth of a second for which the hole existed reverberated backward and forward through time in a most improbable fashion. Somewhere in the deeply remote past it seriously traumatized a small random group of atoms drifting through the empty sterility of space and made them cling together in the most extraordinarily unlikely patterns. These patterns quickly learned to copy themselves (this was part of what was so extraordinary about the patterns) and went on to cause massive trouble on every planet they drifted on to. That was how life began in the Universe.

Five wild Event Maelstroms swirled in vicious storms of unreason and spewed up a pavement.

On the pavement lay Ford Prefect and Arthur Dent gulping like half-spent fish.

"There you are," gasped Ford, scrabbling for a finger hold on the pavement as it raced through the Third Reach of the Unknown, "I told you I'd think of something."

"Oh sure," said Arthur, "sure."

"Bright idea of mine," said Ford, "to find a passing spaceship and get rescued by it."

The real Universe arched sickeningly away beneath them. Various pretend ones flitted silently by, like mountain goats. Primal light exploded, splattering space-time as with gobbets of Jell-O. Time blossomed, matter shrank away. The highest prime number coalesced quietly in a corner and hid itself away for ever.

"Oh, come off it," said Arthur, "the chances against it were astronomical."

"Don't knock it, it worked," said Ford.

"What sort of ship are we in?" asked Arthur as the pit of eternity yawned beneath them.

"I don't know," said Ford, "I haven't opened my eyes yet."

"No, nor have I," said Arthur.

The Universe jumped, froze, quivered and splayed out in several unexpected directions.

Arthur and Ford opened their eyes and looked about in considerable surprise.

"Good God," said Arthur, "it looks just like the sea front at Southend."

"Hell, I'm relieved to hear you say that," said Ford.

"Why?"

"Because I thought I must be going mad."

"Perhaps you are. Perhaps you only thought I said it."

Ford thought about this.

"Well, did you say it or didn't you?" he asked.

"I think so," said Arthur.

"Well, perhaps we're both going mad."

"Yes," said Arthur, "we'd be mad, all things considered, to think this was Southend."

"Well, do you think this is Southend?"

"Oh yes."

"So do I."

"Therefore we must be mad."

"Nice day for it."

"Yes," said a passing maniac.

"Who was that?" asked Arthur.

"Who—the man with the five heads and the elderberry bush full of kippers?"

"Yes."

"I don't know. Just someone."

"Ah."

They both sat on the pavement and watched with a certain unease as huge children bounced heavily along the sand and wild horses thundered through the sky taking fresh supplies of reinforced railings to the Uncertain Areas.

"You know," said Arthur with a slight cough, "if this is Southend, there's something very odd about it. . . ."

"You mean the way the sea stays steady as a rock and the buildings keep washing up and down?" said Ford. "Yes, I thought that was odd too. In fact," he continued as with a huge bang Southend split itself into six equal segments which danced and spun giddily round each other in lewd and licentious formations, "there is something altogether very strange going on."

Wild yowling noises of pipes and strings seared through the wind, hot doughnuts popped out of the road for ten pence each, horrid fish stormed out of the sky and Arthur and Ford decided to make a run for it.

They plunged through heavy walls of sound, mountains of archaic thought, valleys of mood music, bad shoe sessions and footling bats and suddenly heard a girl's voice.

It sounded quite a sensible voice, but it just said, "Two to the power of one hundred thousand to one against and falling," and that was all.

Ford skidded down a beam of light and spun round trying to find a source for the voice but could see nothing he could seriously believe in.

"What was that voice?" shouted Arthur.

"I don't know," yelled Ford, "I don't know. It sounded like a measurement of probability."

"Probability? What do you mean?"

"Probability. You know, like two to one, three to one, five to four against. It said two to the power of one hundred thousand to one against. That's pretty improbable, you know."

A million-gallon vat of custard upended itself over them without warning.

"But what does it mean?" cried Arthur.

"What, the custard?"

"No, the measurement of improbability!"

"I don't know. I don't know at all. I think we're on some kind of spaceship."

"I can only assume," said Arthur, "that this is not the first-class compartment."

Bulges appeared in the fabric of space-time. Great ugly bulges.

"Haaaauuurrgghhh . . ." said Arthur, as he felt his body softening and bending in unusual directions. "Southend seems to be melting away . . . the stars are swirling . . . a dustbowl . . . my legs are drifting off into the sunset . . . my left arm's come off too." A frightening thought struck him. "Hell," he said, "how am I going to operate my digital watch now?" He wound his eyes desperately around in Ford's direction.

"Ford," he said, "you're turning into a penguin. Stop it."

Again came the voice.

"Two to the power of seventy-five thousand to one against and falling."

Ford waddled around his pond in a furious circle.

"Hey, who are you?" he quacked. "Where are you? What's going on and is there any way of stopping it?"

"Please relax," said the voice pleasantly, like a stewardess in an airliner with only one wing and two engines, one of which is on fire, "you are perfectly safe."

"But that's not the point!" raged Ford. "The point is that I am now a perfectly safe penguin, and my colleague here is rapidly running out of limbs!"

"It's all right, I've got them back now," said Arthur.

"Two to the power of fifty thousand to one against and falling," said the voice.

"Admittedly," said Arthur, "they're longer than I usually like them, but . . ."

"Isn't there anything," squawked Ford in avian fury, "you feel you ought to be telling us?"

The voice cleared its throat. A giant petit four lolloped off into the distance.

"Welcome," the voice said, "to the Starship Heart of Gold."

The voice continued.

"Please do not be alarmed," it said, "by anything you see or hear around you. You are bound to feel some initial ill effects as you have been rescued from certain death at an improbability level of two to the power of two hundred and seventy-six thousand to one against—possibly much higher. We are now cruising at a level of two to the power of twenty-five thousand to one against and falling, and we will be restoring normality just as soon as we are sure what is normal anyway. Thank you. Two to the power of twenty thousand to one against and falling."

The voice cut out.

Ford and Arthur were in a small luminous pink cubicle.

Ford was wildly excited.

"Arthur!" he said, "this is fantastic! We've been picked up by a ship powered by the Infinite Improbability Drive! This is incredible! I heard rumors about it before! They were all officially denied, but they must have done it! They've built the Improbability Drive! Arthur, this is . . . Arthur? What's happening?"

Arthur had jammed himself against the door to the cubicle, trying to hold it closed, but it was ill fitting. Tiny furry little hands were squeezing themselves through the cracks, their fingers were ink-stained; tiny voices chattered insanely.

Arthur looked up.

"Ford!" he said, "there's an infinite number of monkeys outside who want to talk to us about this script for *Hamlet* they've worked out."

Chapter 10

The Infinite Improbability Drive is a wonderful new method of crossing vast interstellar distances in a mere nothingth of a second, without all that tedious mucking about in hyperspace. It was discovered by a lucky chance, and then developed into a governable form of propulsion by the Galactic Government's research team on Damogran.

This, briefly, is the story of its discovery.

The principle of generating small amounts of *finite* improbability by simply hooking the logic circuits of a Bambleweeny 57 Sub-Meson Brain to an atomic vector plotter suspended in a strong Brownian Motion producer (say a nice hot cup of tea) were of course well understood—and such generators were often used to break the ice at parties by making all the molecules in the hostess's undergarments leap simultaneously one foot to the left, in accordance with the Theory of Indeterminacy.

Many respectable physicists said that they weren't going to stand for this, partly because it was a debasement of science, but mostly because they didn't get invited to those sorts of parties.

Another thing they couldn't stand was the perpetual failure they encountered in trying to construct a machine which could generate the *infinite* improbability field needed to flip a spaceship across the mind-paralyzing-distances between the farthest stars, and in the end they grumpily announced that such a machine was virtually impossible.

Then, one day, a student who had been left to sweep up the lab after a particularly unsuccessful party found himself reasoning this way:

If, he thought to himself, such a machine is a *virtual* impossibility, then it must logically be a *finite* improbability. So all I have to do in order to make one is to work out exactly how improbable it is, feed that figure into the finite improbability generator, give it a fresh cup of really hot tea . . . and turn it on!

He did this, and was rather startled to discover that he had managed to create the long-sought-after golden Infinite Improbability generator out of thin air.

It startled him even more when just after he was awarded the Galactic Institute's Prize for Extreme Cleverness he got lynched by a rampaging mob of respectable physicists who had finally realized that the one thing they really couldn't stand was a smart-ass.

The improbability-proof control cabin of the Heart of Gold looked like a perfectly conventional spaceship except that it was perfectly clean because it was so new. Some of the control seats hadn't had the plastic wrapping taken off yet. The cabin was mostly white, oblong, and about the size of a smallish restaurant. In fact it wasn't perfectly oblong: the two long walls were raked round in a slight parallel curve, and all the angles and corners of the cabin were contoured in excitingly chunky shapes. The truth of the matter is that it would have been a great deal simpler and more practical to build the cabin as an ordinary three-dimensional oblong room, but then the designers would have got miserable. As it was the cabin looked excitingly purposeful, with large video screens ranged over the control and guidance system panels on the concave wall, and long banks of computers set into the convex wall. In one corner a robot sat humped, its gleaming brushed steel head hanging loosely between its gleaming brushed steel knees. It too was fairly new, but though it was beautifully constructed and polished it somehow looked as if the various parts of its more or less humanoid body didn't quite fit properly. In fact they fitted perfectly well, but something in its bearing suggested that they might have fitted better.

Zaphod Beeblebrox paced nervously up and down the cabin, brushing his hands over pieces of gleaming equipment and giggling with excitement.

Trillian sat hunched over a clump of instruments reading off figures. Her voice was carried round the tannoy system of the whole ship.

"Five to one against and falling . . ." she said, *"four to one against and falling . . . three to one . . . two . . . one . . . probability factor of one to one . . . we have normality, I repeat we have normality."* She turned her microphone off—then turned it back on—with a slight smile and continued: *"Anything you still can't cope with is therefore your own problem. Please relax. You will be sent for soon."*

Zaphod burst out in annoyance, "Who are they, Trillian?"

Trillian spun her seat round to face him and shrugged.

"Just a couple of guys we seem to have picked up in open space," she said. "Section ZZ, Plural Z Alpha."

"Yeah, well, that's a very sweet thought, Trillian," complained Zaphod, "but do you really think it's wise under the circumstances? I mean, here we are on the run and everything, we must have the police of half the Galaxy after us by now, and we stop to pick up hitchhikers. Okay, so ten out of ten for style, but minus several million for good thinking, yeah?"

He tapped irritably at a control panel. Trillian quietly moved his hand before he tapped anything important. Whatever Zaphod's qualities of mind might include—dash, bravado, conceit—he was mechanically inept and could easily blow the ship up with an extravagant gesture. Trilllian had come to suspect that the main reason he had had such a wild and successful life was that he never really understood the significance of anything he did.

"Zaphod," she said patiently, "they were floating unprotected in open space . . . you wouldn't want them to have died, would you?"

"Well, you know . . . no. Not as such, but . . ."

"Not as such? Not die as such? But?" Trillian cocked her head on one side.

"Well, maybe someone else might have picked them up later."

"A second later and they would have been dead."

"Yeah, so if you'd taken the trouble to think about the problem a bit longer it would have gone away."

"You'd have been happy to let them die?"

"Well, you know, not happy as such, but . . ."

"Anyway," said Trillian, turning back to the controls, "I didn't pick them up."

"What do you mean? Who picked them up then?"

"The ship did."

"Huh?"

"The ship did. All by itself."

"Huh?"

"While we were in Improbability Drive."

"But that's incredible."

"No, Zaphod. Just very very improbable."

"Er, yeah."

"Look, Zaphod," she said, patting his arm, "don't worry about the aliens. They're just a couple of guys, I expect. I'll send the robot down to get them and bring them up here. Hey, Marvin!"

In the corner, the robot's head swung up sharply, but then wobbled about imperceptibly. It pulled itself up to its feet as if it was about five pounds heavier than it actually was, and made what an outside observer would have thought was a heroic effort to cross the room. It stopped in front of Trillian and seemed to stare through her left shoulder.

"I think you ought to know I'm feeling very depressed," it said. Its voice was low and hopeless.

"Oh God," muttered Zaphod, and slumped into a seat.

"Well," said Trillian in a bright compassionate tone, "here's something to occupy you and keep your mind off things."

"It won't work," droned Marvin, "I have an exceptionally large mind."

"Marvin!" warned Trillian.

"All right," said Marvin, "what do you want me to do?"

"Go down to number two entry bay and bring the two aliens up here under surveillance."

With a microsecond pause, and a finely calculated micromodulation of pitch and timbre—nothing you could actually take offense at—Marvin managed to convey his utter contempt and horror of all things human.

"Just that?" he said.

"Yes," said Trillian firmly.

"I won't enjoy it," said Marvin.

Zaphod leaped out of his seat.

"She's not asking you to enjoy it," he shouted, "just do it, will you?"

"All right," said Marvin, like the tolling of a great cracked bell, "I'll do it."

"Good . . ." snapped Zaphod, "great . . . thank you . . ."

Marvin turned and lifted his flat-topped triangular red eyes up toward him.

"I'm not getting you down at all, am I?" he said pathetically.

"No no, Marvin," lilted Trillian, "that's just fine, really. . . ."

"I wouldn't like to think I was getting you down."

"No, don't worry about that," the lilt continued, "you just act as comes naturally and everything will be just fine."

"You're sure you don't mind?" probed Marvin.

"No, no, Marvin," lilted Trillian, "that's just fine, really . . . just part of life."

Marvin flashed her an electronic look.

"Life," said Marvin, "don't talk to me about life."

He turned hopelessly on his heel and lugged himself out of the cabin. With a satisfied hum and a click the door closed behind him.

"I don't think I can stand that robot much longer, Zaphod," growled Trillian.

The Encyclopedia Galactica *defines a robot as a mechanical apparatus designed to do the work of a man. The marketing division of the Sirius Cybernetics*

Corporation defines a robot as "Your Plastic Pal Who's Fun to Be With."

The Hitchhiker's Guide to the Galaxy *defines the marketing division of the Sirius Cybernetics Corporation as "a bunch of mindless jerks who'll be the first against the wall when the revolution comes," with a footnote to the effect that the editors would welcome applications from anyone interested in taking over the post of robotics correspondent.*

Curiously enough, an edition of the Encyclopedia Galactica *that had the good fortune to fall through a time warp from a thousand years in the future defined the marketing division of the Sirius Cybernetics Corporation as "a bunch of mindless jerks who were the first against the wall when the revolution came."*

The pink cubicle had winked out of existence, the monkeys had sunk away to a better dimension. Ford and Arthur found themselves in the embarkation area of the ship. It was rather smart.

"I think this ship's brand new," said Ford.

"How can you tell?" asked Arthur. "Have you got some exotic device for measuring the age of metal?"

"No, I just found this sales brochure lying on the floor. It's a lot of 'the Universe can be yours' stuff. Ah! Look, I was right."

Ford jabbed at one of the pages and showed it to Arthur.

"It says: *'Sensational new breakthrough in Improbability Physics. As soon as the ship's drive reaches Infinite Improbability it passes through every point in the Universe. Be the envy of other major governments.'* Wow, this is big league stuff."

Ford hunted excitedly through the technical specs of the ship, occasionally gasping with astonishment at what he read—clearly Galactic astrotechnology had moved ahead during the years of his exile.

Arthur listened for a short while, but being unable to understand the vast majority of what Ford was saying, he began to let his mind wander, trailing his fingers along the edge of an incomprehensible computer bank. He reached out and pressed an invitingly large red button on a nearby panel. The panel lit up with the words *Please do not press this button again*. He shook himself.

"Listen," said Ford, who was still engrossed in the sales brochure, "they make a big thing of the ship's cybernetics. *'A new generation of Sirius Cybernetics Corporation robots and computers, with the new GPP feature.'* "

"GPP feature?" said Arthur. "What's that?"

"Oh, it says *Genuine People Personalities*."

"Oh," said Arthur, "sounds ghastly."

A voice behind them said, "It is." The voice was low and hopeless and accompanied by a slight clanking sound. They spun round and saw an abject steel man standing hunched in the doorway.

"What?" they said.

"Ghastly," continued Marvin, "it all is. Absolutely ghastly. Just don't even talk about it. Look at this door," he said, stepping through it. The irony circuits cut in to his voice modulator as he mimicked the style of the sales brochure. " *'All the doors in this spaceship have a cheerful and sunny disposition. It is their pleasure to open for you, and their satisfaction to close again with the knowledge of a job well done.'* "

As the door closed behind them it became apparent that it did indeed have a satisfied sighlike quality to it. *"Hummmmmmmyummmmmmmm ah!"* it said.

Marvin regarded it with cold loathing while his logic circuits chattered with disgust and tinkered with the concept of directing physical violence against it. Further circuits cut in saying, *Why bother? What's the point? Nothing is worth getting involved in.* Further circuits amused themselves by analyzing the molecular components of the door, and of the humanoids' brain cells. For a quick encore they measured the level of hydrogen emissions in the surrounding cubic parsec of space and then shut down again in boredom. A spasm of despair shook the robot's body as he turned.

"Come on," he droned, "I've been ordered to take you down to the bridge. Here I am, brain the size of a planet and they ask me to take you down to the bridge. Call that *job satisfaction?* 'Cos I don't."

He turned and walked back to the hated door.

"Er, excuse me," said Ford following after him, "which government owns this ship?"

Marvin ignored him.

"You watch this door," he muttered, "it's about to open again. I can tell by the intolerable air of smugness it suddenly generates."

With an ingratiating little whine the door slid open again and Marvin stomped through.

"Come on," he said.

The others followed quickly and the door slid back into place with pleased little clicks and whirrs.

"Thank you the marketing division of the Sirius Cybernetics Corporation," said Marvin, and trudged desolately up the gleaming curved corridor that stretched out before them. *"Let's build robots with Genuine People Personalities,"* they said. So they tried it out with me. I'm a personality prototype. You can tell, can't you?"

Ford and Arthur muttered embarrassed little disclaimers.

"I hate that door," continued Marvin. "I'm not getting you down at all, am I?"

"Which government . . ." started Ford again.

"No government owns it," snapped the robot, "it's been stolen."

"Stolen?"

"Stolen?" mimicked Marvin.

"Who by?" asked Ford.

"Zaphod Beeblebrox."

Something extraordinary happened to Ford's face. At least five entirely separate and distinct expressions of shock and amazement piled up on it in a jumbled mess. His left leg, which was in midstride, seemed to have difficulty in finding the floor again. He stared at the robot and tried to disentangle some dartoid muscles.

"Zaphod Beeblebrox . . . ?" he said weakly.

"Sorry, did I say something wrong?" said Marvin, dragging himself on regardless. "Pardon me for breathing, which I never do anyway so I don't know why I bother to say it, oh God, I'm so depressed. Here's another of those self-satisfied doors. *Life!* Don't talk to me about life."

"No one even mentioned it," muttered Arthur irritably. "Ford, are you all right?"

Ford stared at him. "Did that robot say Zaphod Beeblebrox?" he said.

A loud clatter of gunk music flooded through the Heart of Gold cabin as Zaphod searched the sub-etha radio wave bands for news of himself. The machine was rather difficult to operate. For years radios had been operated by means of pressing buttons and turning dials; then as the technology became more sophisticated the controls were made touch-sensitive—you merely had to brush the panels with your fingers; now all you had to do was wave your hand in the general direction of the components and hope. It saved a lot of muscular expenditure, of course, but meant that you had to sit infuriatingly still if you wanted to keep listening to the same program.

Zaphod waved a hand and the channel switched again. More gunk music, but this time it was a background to a news announcement. The news was always heavily edited to fit the rhythms of the music.

"... *and news reports brought to you here on the sub-etha wave band, broadcasting around the Galaxy around the clock,*" squawked a voice, "*and we'll be saying a big hello to all intelligent life forms everywhere... and to everyone else out there, the secret is to bang the rocks together, guys. And of course, the big news story tonight is the sensational theft of the new Improbability Drive prototype ship by none other than Galactic President Zaphod Beeblebrox. And the question everyone's asking is... has the Big Z finally flipped? Beeblebrox, the man who invented the Pan Galactic Gargle Blaster, ex-confidence trickster, once described by Eccentrica Gallumbits as the Best Bang since the Big One, and recently voted the Worst Dressed Sentient Being in the Known Universe for the seventh time... has he got an answer this time? We asked his private brain care specialist Gag Halfrunt...*"

The music swirled and dived for a moment. Another voice broke in, presumably Halfrunt. He said "*Vell, Zaphod's just zis guy, you know?*" but got no further because an electric pencil flew across the cabin and through the radio's on/off-sensitive airspace. Zaphod turned and glared at Trillian— she had thrown the pencil.

"Hey," he said, "what you do that for?"

Trillian was tapping her finger on a screenful of figures.

"I've just thought of something," she said.

"Yeah? Worth interrupting a news bulletin about me for?"

"You hear enough about yourself as it is."

"I'm very insecure. We know that."

"Can we drop your ego for a moment? This is important."

"If there's anything more important than my ego around, I want it caught and shot now." Zaphod glared at her again, then laughed.

"Listen," she said, "we picked up those couple of guys..."

"What couple of guys?"

"The couple of guys we picked up."

"Oh yeah," said Zaphod, "those couple of guys."

"We picked them up in sector ZZ, Plural Z Alpha."

"Yeah?" said Zaphod, and blinked.

Trillian said quietly, "Does that mean anything to you?"

"Mmmm," said Zaphod, "ZZ, Plural Z Alpha. ZZ, Plural Z Alpha?"

"Well?" said Trillian.

"Er... what does the Z mean?" said Zaphod.

"Which one?"

"Any one."

One of the major difficulties Trillian experienced in her relationship with Zaphod was learning to distinguish between him pretending to be stupid just to get people off their guard, pretending to be stupid because he couldn't be bothered to think and wanted someone else to do it for him, pretending to be outrageously stupid to hide the fact that he actually didn't understand what was going on, and really being genuinely stupid. He was renowned for being amazingly clever and quite clearly was so—but not all the time, which obviously worried him, hence the act. He preferred people to be puzzled rather than contemptuous. This above all appeared to Trillian to be genuinely stupid, but she could no longer be bothered to argue about it.

She sighed and punched up a star map on the visiscreen so she could make it simple for him, whatever his reasons for wanting it to be that way.

"There," she pointed, "right there."

"Hey... yeah!" said Zaphod.

"Well?" she said.

"Well what?"

Parts of the inside of her head screamed at other parts of the inside of her head. She said, very calmly, "It's the same sector you originally picked me up in."

He looked at her and then looked back at the screen.

"Hey, yeah," he said, "now that is wild. We should have zapped straight into the middle of the Horsehead Nebula. How did we come to be there? I mean, that's nowhere."

She ignored this.

"Improbability Drive," she said patiently. "You explained it to me yourself. We pass through every point in the Universe, you know that."

"Yeah, but that's one wild coincidence, isn't it?"

"Yes."

"Picking someone up at that point? Out of the whole of the Universe to choose from? That's just too . . . I want to work this out. Computer!"

The Sirius Cybernetics Shipboard Computer, which controlled and permeated every particle of the ship, switched into communication mode.

"Hi there!" it said brightly and simultaneously spewed out a tiny ribbon of ticker tape just for the record. The ticker tape said, *Hi there!*

"Oh God," said Zaphod. He hadn't worked with this computer for long but had already learned to loathe it.

The computer continued, brash and cheery as if it were selling detergent.

"I want you to know that whatever your problem, I am here to help you solve it."

"Yeah, yeah," said Zaphod. "Look, I think I'll just use a piece of paper."

"Sure thing," said the computer, spilling out its message into a waste bin at the same time, "I understand. If you ever want . . ."

"Shut up!" said Zaphod, and snatching up a pencil sat down next to Trillian at the console.

"Okay, okay," said the computer in a hurt tone of voice and closed down its speech channel again.

Zaphod and Trillian pored over the figures that the Improbability flight-path scanner flashed silently up in front of them.

"Can we work out," said Zaphod, "from their point of view what the Improbability of their rescue was?"

"Yes, that's a constant," said Trillian, "two to the power of two hundred and seventy-six thousand, seven hundred and nine to one against."

"That's high. They're two lucky lucky guys."

"Yes."

"But relative to what we were doing when the ship picked them up . . ."

Trillian punched up the figures. They showed two-to-the-power-of-Infinity-minus-one to one against (an irrational number that only has a conventional meaning in Improbability Physics).

"It's pretty low," continued Zaphod with a slight whistle.

"Yes," agreed Trillian, and looked at him quizzically.

"That's one big whack of Improbability to be accounted for. Something pretty improbable has got to show up on the balance sheet if it's all going to add up into a pretty sum."

Zaphod scribbled a few sums, crossed them out and threw the pencil away.

"Bat's dos, I can't work it out."

"Well?"

Zaphod knocked his two heads together in irritation and gritted his teeth.

"Okay," he said. "Computer!"

The voice circuits sprang to life again.

"Why, hello there!" they said (ticker tape, ticker tape). "All I want to do is make your day nicer and nicer and nicer . . ."

"Yeah, well, shut up and work something out for me."

"Sure thing," chattered the computer, "you want a probability forecast based on . . ."

"Improbability data, yeah."

"Okay," the computer continued. "Here's an interesting little notion. Did you realize that most people's lives are governed by telephone numbers?"

A pained look crawled across one of Zaphod's faces and on to the other one.

"Have you flipped?" he said.

"No, but you will when I tell you that . . ."

Trillian gasped. She scrabbled at the buttons on the Improbability flight-path screen.

"Telephone number?" she said. "Did that thing say *telephone number?*"

Numbers flashed up on the screen.

The computer had paused politely, but now it continued.

"What I was about to say was that . . ."

"Don't bother, please," said Trillian.

"Look, what is this?" said Zaphod.

"I don't know," said Trillian, "but those aliens—they're on the way up to the bridge with that wretched robot. Can we pick them up on any monitor cameras?"

Chapter 13

Marvin trudged on down the corridor, still moaning.

"And then of course I've got this terrible pain in all the diodes down my left-hand side . . ."

"No?" said Arthur grimly as he walked along beside him. "Really?"

"Oh yes," said Marvin, "I mean I've asked for them to be replaced but no one ever listens."

"I can imagine."

Vague whistling and humming noises were coming from Ford. "Well well well," he kept saying to himself, "Zaphod Beeblebrox . . ."

Suddenly Marvin stopped, and held up a hand.

"You know what's happened now, of course?"

"No, what?" said Arthur, who didn't want to know.

"We've arrived at another of those doors."

There was a sliding door let into the side of the corridor. Marvin eyed it suspiciously.

"Well?" said Ford impatiently. "Do we go through?"

"Do we go through?" mimicked Marvin. "Yes. This is the entrance to the bridge. I was told to take you to the bridge. Probably the highest demand that will be made on my intellectual capacities today, I shouldn't wonder."

Slowly, with great loathing, he stepped toward the door, like a hunter stalking his prey. Suddenly it slid open.

"Thank you," it said, *"for making a simple door very happy."*

Deep in Marvin's thorax gears ground.

"Funny," he intoned funereally, "how just when you think life can't possibly get any worse it suddenly does."

He heaved himself through the door and left Ford and Arthur staring at each other and shrugging their shoulders. From inside they heard Marvin's voice again.

"I suppose you'll want to see the aliens now," he said. "Do you want me to sit in a corner and rust, or just fall apart where I'm standing?"

"Yeah, just show them in, would you, Marvin?" came another voice.

Arthur looked at Ford and was astonished to see him laughing.

"What's . . ."

"Shhh," said Ford, "come on in."

He stepped through into the bridge.

Arthur followed him in nervously and was astonished to see a man lolling back in a chair with his feet on a control console picking the teeth in his right-hand head with his left hand. The right-han head seemed to be thoroughly preoccupied with this task, but the left-hand one was grinning a broad, relaxed, nonchalant grin. The number of things that Arthur couldn't believe he was seeing was fairly large. His jaw flopped about at a loose end for a while.

The peculiar man waved a lazy wave at Ford and with an appalling affectation of nonchalance said, "Ford, hi, how are you? Glad you could drop in."

Ford was not going to be outcooled.

"Zaphod," he drawled, "great to see you, you're looking well, the extra arm suits you. Nice ship you've stolen."

Arthur goggled at him.

"You mean you know this guy?" he said, waving a wild finger at Zaphod.

"Know him!" exclaimed Ford, "he's . . ." he paused, and decided to do the introductions the other way round.

"On, Zaphod, this is a friend of mine, Arthur Dent," he said. "I saved him when his planet blew up."

"Oh sure," said Zaphod, "hi, Arthur, glad you could make it." His right-hand head looked round casually, said "hi" and went back to having its teeth picked.

Ford carried on. "And Arthur," he said, "this is my semicousin Zaphod Beeb . . ."

"We've met," said Arthur sharply.

When you're cruising down the road in the fast lane and you lazily sail past a few hard-driving cars and are feeling pretty pleased with yourself and then accidentally change down from fourth to first instead of third thus making your engine leap out of your hood in a rather ugly mess, it tends to throw you off your stride in much the same way that this remark threw Ford Prefect off his.

"Er . . . what?" he said.

"I said we've met."

Zaphod gave an awkward start of surprise and jabbed a gum sharply.

"Hey . . . er, have we? Hey . . . er . . . "

Ford rounded on Arthur with an angry flash in his eyes. Now he felt he was back on home ground he suddenly began to resent having lumbered himself with this ignorant primitive who knew as much about the affairs of the Galaxy as an Ilford-based gnat knew about life in Peking.

"What do you mean you've met?" he demanded. "This is Zaphod Beeblebrox from Betelgeuse Five, you know, not bloody Martin Smith from Croydon."

"I don't care," said Arthur coldly. "We've met, haven't we, Zaphod Beeblebrox—or should I say . . . Phil?"

"What?" shouted Ford.

"You'll have to remind me," said Zaphod. "I've a terrible memory for species."

"It was at a party," pursued Arthur.

"Yeah, well, I doubt that," said Zaphod.

"Cool it, will you, Arthur!" demanded Ford.

Arthur would not be deterred. "A party six months ago. On Earth . . . England . . ."

Zaphod shook his head with a tight-lipped smile.

"London," insisted Arthur, "Islington."

"Oh," said Zaphod with a guilty start, *"that* party."

This wasn't fair on Ford at all. He looked backward and forward between Arthur and Zaphod. "What?" he said to Zaphod. "You don't mean to say you've been on that miserable little planet as well, do you?"

"No, of course not," said Zaphod breezily. "Well, I may have just dropped in briefly, you know, on my way somewhere . . ."

"But I was stuck there for fifteen years!"

"Well, I didn't know that, did I?"

"But what were you doing there?"

"Looking about, you know."

"He gate-crashed a party," said Arthur, trembling with anger, "a fancy dress party . . ."

"It would have to be, wouldn't it?" said Ford.

"At this party," persisted Arthur, "was a girl . . . oh, well, look, it doesn't matter now. The whole place has gone up in smoke anyway . . ."

"I wish you'd stop sulking about that bloody planet," said Ford. "Who was the lady?"

"Oh, just somebody. Well all right, I wasn't doing very well with her. I'd been trying all evening. Hell, she was something though. Beautiful, charming, devastatingly intelligent, at last I'd got her to myself for a bit and was plying her with a bit of talk when this friend of yours barges up and says 'Hey, doll, is this guy boring you? Why don't you talk to me instead? I'm from a different planet.' I never saw her again."

"Zaphod?" exclaimed Ford.

"Yes," said Arthur, glaring at him and trying not to feel foolish. "He only had the two arms and the one head and he called himself Phil, but..."

"But you must admit he did turn out to be from another planet," said Trillian, wandering into sight at the other end of the bridge. She gave Arthur a pleasant smile which settled on him like a ton of bricks and then turned her attention to the ship's controls again.

There was silence for a few seconds, and then out of the scrambled mess of Arthur's brain crawled some words.

"Tricia McMillan?" he said. "What are you doing here?"

"Same as you," she said, "I hitched a lift. After all, with a degree in math and another in astrophysics what else was there to do? It was either that or the dole queue again on Monday."

"Infinity minus one," chattered the computer. "Improbability sum now complete."

Zaphod looked about him, at Ford, at Arthur, and then at Trillian.

"Trillian," he said, "is this sort of thing going to happen every time we use the Improbability Drive?"

"Very probably, I'm afraid," she said.

Chapter 14

The Heart of Gold fled on silently through the night of space, now on conventional photon drive. Its crew of four were ill at ease knowing that they had been brought together not of their own volition or by simple coincidence, but by some curious perversion of physics—as if relationships between people were susceptible to the same laws that governed the relationships between atoms and molecules.

As the ship's artificial night closed in they were each grateful to retire to separate cabins and try to rationalize their thoughts.

Trillian couldn't sleep. She sat on a couch and stared at a small cage which contained her last and only links with Earth—two white mice that she had insisted Zaphod let her bring. She had expected never to see the planet again, but she was disturbed by her negative reaction to the news of the planet's destruction. It seemed remote and unreal and she could find no thoughts to think about it. She watched the mice scurrying round the cage and running furiously in their little plastic treadwheels till they occupied her whole attention. Suddenly she shook herself and went back on to the bridge to watch over the tiny flashing lights and figures that charted the ship's progress through the void. She wished she knew what it was she was trying not to think about.

Zaphod couldn't sleep. He also wished he knew what it was that he wouldn't let himself think about. For as long as he could remember he'd suffered from a vague nagging feeling of being not all there. Most of the time he was able to put this thought aside and not worry about it, but it had been reawakened by the sudden, inexplicable arrival of Ford Prefect and Arthur Dent. Somehow it seemed to conform to a pattern that he couldn't see.

Ford couldn't sleep. He was too excited about being back on the road again. Fifteen years of virtual imprisonment were over, just as he was finally beginning to give up hope. Knocking about with Zaphod for a bit promised to be a lot of fun, though there seemed to be something faintly odd about his semicousin that he couldn't put his finger on. The fact that he had become President of the Galaxy was frankly astonishing, as was the manner of his leaving the post. Was there a reason behind it? There would be no point in asking Zaphod, he never appeared to have a reason for anything he did at all: he had turned unfathomability into an art form. He attacked everything in life with a mixture of extraordinary genius and naive incompetence and it was often difficult to tell which was which.

Arthur slept: he was terribly tired.

There was a tap at Zaphod's door. It slid open.

"Zaphod . . . ?"

"Yeah?"

Trillian stood outlined in the oval of light.

"I think we just found what you came to look for."

"Hey, yeah?"

Ford gave up the attempt to sleep. In the corner of his cabin was a small computer screen and keyboard. He sat at it for a while and tried to compose a new entry for the *Guide* on the subject of Vogons but couldn't think of anything vitriolic enough so he gave that up too, wrapped a robe round himself and went for a walk to the bridge.

As he entered he was surprised to see two figures hunched excitedly over the instruments.

"See? The ship's about to move into orbit," Trillian was saying. "There's a planet out there. It's at the exact coordinates you predicted."

Zaphod heard a noise and looked up.

"Ford!" he hissed. "Hey, come and take a look at this."

Ford went and had a look at it. It was a series of figures flickering over a screen.

"You recognize those Galactic coordinates?" said Zaphod.

"No."

"I'll give you a clue. Computer!"

"Hi, gang!" enthused the computer. "This is getting real sociable, isn't it?"

"Shut up," said Zaphod, "and show up the screens."

Light on the bridge sank. Pinpoints of light played across the consoles and reflected in four pairs of eyes that stared up at the external monitor screens.

There was absolutely nothing on them.

"Recognize that?" whispered Zaphod.

Ford frowned.

"Er, no," he said.

"What do you see?"

"Nothing."

"Recognize it?"

"What are you talking about?"

"We're in the Horsehead Nebula. One whole vast dark cloud."

"And I was meant to recognize that from a blank screen?"

"Inside a dark nebula is the only place in the Galaxy you'd see a dark screen."

"Very good."

Zaphod laughed. He was clearly very excited about something, almost childishly so.

"Hey, this is really terrific, this is just far too much!"

"What's so great about being stuck in a dust cloud?" said Ford.

"What would you reckon to find here?" urged Zaphod.

"Nothing."

"No stars? No planets?"

"No."

"Computer!" shouted Zaphod, "rotate angle of vision through one-eighty degrees and don't talk about it!"

For a moment it seemed that nothing was happening, then a brightness glowed at the edge of the huge screen. A red star the size of a small plate crept across it followed quickly by another one—a binary system. Then a vast crescent sliced into the corner of the picture—a red glare shading away into deep black, the night side of the planet.

"I've found it!" cried Zaphod, thumping the console. "I've found it!"

Ford stared at it in astonishment.

"What is it?" he said.

"That..." said Zaphod, "is the most improbable planet that ever existed."

Chapter 15

(Excerpt from *The Hitchhiker's Guide to the Galaxy*, page 634784, section 5a. Entry: *Magrathea*)

Far back in the mists of ancient time, in the great and glorious days of the former Galactic Empire, life was wild, rich and largely tax free. Mighty starships plied their way between exotic suns, seeking adventure and reward among the farthest reaches of Galactic space. In those days spirits were brave, the stakes were high, men were real men, women were real women and small furry creatures from Alpha Centauri were real small furry creatures from Alpha Centauri. And all dared to brave unknown terrors, to do mighty deeds, to boldly split infinitives that no man had split before—and thus was the Empire forged.

Many men of course became extremely rich, but this was perfectly natural and nothing to be ashamed of because no one was really poor—at least no one worth speaking of. And for all the richest and most successful merchants life inevitably became rather dull and niggly, and they began to imagine that this was therefore the fault of the worlds they'd settled on. None of them was entirely satisfactory: either the climate wasn't quite right in the later part of the afternoon, or the day was half an hour too long, or the sea was exactly the wrong shade of pink.

And thus were created the conditions for a staggering new form of specialist industry: custom-made luxury planet building. The home of this industry was the planet Magrathea, where hyperspatial engineers sucked matter through white holes in space to form it into dream planets—gold planets, platinum planets, soft rubber planets with lots of earthquakes—all lovingly made to meet the exacting standards that the Galaxy's richest men naturally came to expect.

But so successful was this venture that Magrathea itself soon became the richest planet of all time and the rest of the Galaxy was reduced to abject poverty. And so the system broke down, the Empire collapsed, and a long sullen silence settled over a billion hungry worlds, disturbed only by the pen scratchings of scholars as they labored into the night over smug little treatises on the value of a planned political economy.

Magrathea itself disappeared and its memory soon passed into the obscurity of legend.

In these enlightened days, of course, no one believes a word of it.

Chapter 16

Arthur awoke to the sound of argument and went to the bridge. Ford was waving his arms about.

"You're crazy, Zaphod," he was saying, "Magrathea is a myth, a fairy story, it's what parents tell their kids about at night if they want them to grow up to become economists, it's..."

"And that's what we are currently in orbit about," insisted Zaphod.

"Look, I can't help what you may personally be in orbit around," said Ford, "but this ship..."

"Computer!" shouted Zaphod.

"Oh no..."

"Hi there! This is Eddie, your shipboard computer, and I'm feeling just great, guys, and I know I'm just going to get a bundle of kicks out of any program you care to run through me."

Arthur looked inquiringly at Trillian. She motioned him to come on in but keep quiet.

"Computer," said Zaphod, "tell us what our present trajectory is."

"A real pleasure, feller," it burbled; "we are currently in orbit at an altitude of three hundred miles around the legendary planet of Magrathea."

"Proving nothing," said Ford. "I wouldn't trust that computer to speak my weight."

"I can do that for you, sure," enthused the computer, punching out more ticker tape. "I can even work out your personality problems to ten decimal places if it will help."

Trillian interrupted.

"Zaphod," she said, "any minute now we will be swinging round to the daylight side of this planet," adding, "whatever it turns out to be."

"Hey, what do you mean by that? The planet's where I predicted it would be, isn't it?"

"Yes, I know there's a planet there. I'm not arguing with anyone, it's just that I wouldn't know Magrathea from any other lump of cold rock. Dawn's coming up if you want it."

"Okay, okay," muttered Zaphod, "let's at least give our eyes a good time. Computer!"

"Hi there! What can I . . ."

"Just shut up and give us a view of the planet again."

A dark featureless mass once more filled the screens—the planet rolling away beneath them.

They watched for a moment in silence, but Zaphod was fidgety with excitement.

"We are now traversing the night side . . ." he said in a hushed voice. The planet rolled on.

"The surface of the planet is now three hundred miles beneath us . . ." he continued. He was trying to restore a sense of occasion to what he felt should have been a great moment. Magrathea! He was piqued by Ford's skeptical reaction. Magrathea!

"In a few seconds," he continued, "we should see . . . there!"

The moment carried itself. Even the most seasoned star tramp can't help but shiver at the spectacular drama of a sunrise seen from space, but a binary sunrise is one of the marvels of the Galaxy.

Out of the utter blackness stabbed a sudden point of blinding light. It crept up by slight degrees and spread sideways in a thin crescent blade, and within seconds two suns were visible, furnaces of light, searing the black edge of the horizon with white fire. Fierce shafts of color streaked through the thin atmosphere beneath them.

"The fires of dawn . . . !" breathed Zaphod. "The twin suns of Soulianis and Rahm . . . !"

"Or whatever," said Ford quietly.

"Soulianis and Rahm!" insisted Zaphod.

The suns blazed into the pitch of space and a low ghostly music floated through the bridge: Marvin was humming ironically because he hated humans so much.

As Ford gazed at the spectacle of light before them excitement burned inside him, but only the excitement of seeing a strange new planet; it was enough for him to see it as it was. It faintly irritated him that Zaphod had to impose some ludicrous fantasy onto the scene to make it work for him. All this Magrathea nonsense seemed juvenile. Isn't it enough to see that a garden is beautiful without having to believe that there are fairies at the bottom of it too?

All this Magrathea business seemed totally incomprehensible to Arthur. He edged up to Trillian and asked her what was going on.

"I only know what Zaphod's told me," she whispered. "Apparently Magrathea is some kind of legend from way back which no one seriously believes in. Bit like Atlantis on Earth, except that the legends say the Magratheans used to manufacture planets."

Arthur blinked at the screens and felt he was missing something important. Suddenly he realized what it was.

"Is there any tea on this spaceship?" he asked.

More of the planet was unfolding beneath them as the Heart of Gold streaked along its orbital path. The suns now stood high in the black sky, the pyrotechnics of dawn were over, and the surface of the planet appeared bleak and forbidding in the common light of day—gray, dusty and only dimly contoured. It looked dead and cold as a crypt. From time to time promising features would appear on the distant horizon—ravines, maybe mountains, maybe even cities—but as they approached the lines would soften and blur into anonymity and nothing would transpire. The planet's surface was blurred by time, by the slow movement of the thin stagnant air that had crept across it for century upon century.

Clearly, it was very very old.

A moment of doubt came to Ford as he watched the gray landscape move beneath them. The immensity of time worried him, he could feel it as a presence. He cleared his throat.

"Well, even supposing it is . . . "

"It is," said Zaphod.

"Which it isn't," continued Ford. "What do you want with it anyway? There's nothing there."

"Not on the surface," said Zaphod.

"All right, just supposing there's something, I take it you're not here for the sheer industrial archeology of it all. What are you after?"

One of Zaphod's heads looked away. The other one looked round to see what the first was looking at, but it wasn't looking at anything very much.

"Well," said Zaphod airily, "it's partly the curiosity, partly a sense of adventure, but mostly I think it's the fame and the money. . . . "

Ford glanced at him sharply. He got a very strong impression that Zaphod hadn't the faintest idea why he was there at all.

"You know, I don't like the look of that planet at all," said Trillian, shivering.

"Ah, take no notice," said Zaphod; "with half the wealth of the former Galactic Empire stored on it somewhere it can afford to look frumpy."

Bullshit, thought Ford. Even supposing this was the home of some ancient civilization now gone to dust, even supposing a number of exceedingly unlikely things, there was no way that vast treasures of wealth were going to be stored there in any form that would still have meaning now. He shrugged.

"I think it's just a dead planet," he said.

"The suspense is killing me," said Arthur testily.

Stress and nervous tension are now serious social problems in all parts of the Galaxy, and it is in order that this situation should not be in any way exacerbated that the following facts will now be revealed in advance.

The planet in question *is* in fact the legendary Magrathea.

The deadly missile attack shortly to be launched by an ancient automatic defense system will result merely in the breakage of three coffee cups and a mouse cage, the bruising of somebody's upper arm, and the untimely creation and sudden demise of a bowl of petunias and an innocent sperm whale.

In order that some sense of mystery should still be preserved, no revelation will yet be made concerning whose upper arm sustains the bruise. This fact may safely be made the subject of suspense since it is of no significance whatsoever.

Chapter 17

After a fairly shaky start to the day, Arthur's mind was beginning
to reassemble itself from the shell-shocked fragments the previous day had left him with. He had found a Nutri-Matic
machine which had provided him with a plastic cup filled
with a liquid that was almost, but not quite, entirely unlike tea. The way it
functioned was very interesting. When the *Drink* button was pressed it
made an instant but highly detailed examination of the subject's taste buds,
a spectroscopic analysis of the subject's metabolism and then sent tiny
experimental signals down the neural pathways to the taste centers of the
subject's brain to see what was likely to go down well. However, no one
knew quite why it did this because it invariably delivered a cupful of liquid
that was almost, but not quite, entirely unlike tea. The Nutri-Matic was
designed and manufactured by the Sirius Cybernetics Corporation whose
complaints department now covers all the major landmasses of the first
three planets in the Sirius Tau Star system.

Arthur drank the liquid and found it reviving. He glanced up at the
screens again and watched a few more hundred miles of barren grayness
slide past. It suddenly occurred to him to ask a question that had been
bothering him.

"Is it safe?" he said.

"Magrathea's been dead for five million years," said Zaphod; "of course
it's safe. Even the ghosts will have settled down and raised families by
now."

At which point a strange and inexplicable sound thrilled suddenly
through the bridge—a noise as of a distant fanfare; a hollow, reedy,
insubstantial sound. It preceded a voice that was equally hollow, reedy and
insubstantial. The voice said, *"Greetings to you . . . "*

Someone from the dead planet was talking to them.

"Computer!" shouted Zaphod.

"Hi there!"

"What the photon is it?"

"Oh, just some five-million-year-old tape that's being broadcast at us."

"A what? A recording?"

"Shush!" said Ford. "It's carrying on."

The voice was old, courteous, almost charming, but was underscored with quite unmistakable menace.

"*This is a recorded announcement,*" it said, "*as I'm afraid we're all out at the moment. The commercial council of Magrathea thanks you for your esteemed visit . . .*"

("A voice from ancient Magrathea!" shouted Zaphod. "Okay, okay," said Ford.)

"*. . . but regrets,*" continued the voice, "*that the entire planet is temporarily closed for business. Thank you. If you would care to leave your name and the address of a planet where you can be contacted, kindly speak when you hear the tone.*"

A short buzz followed, then silence.

"They want to get rid of us," said Trillian nervously. "What do we do?"

"It's just a recording," said Zaphod. "We keep going. Got that, computer?"

"I got it," said the computer and gave the ship an extra kick of speed. They waited.

After a second or so came the fanfare once again, and then the voice.

"*We would like to assure you that as soon as our business is resumed announcements will be made in all fashionable magazines and color supplements, when our clients will once again be able to select from all that's best in contemporary geography.*" The menace in the voice took on a sharper edge. "*Meanwhile, we thank our clients for their kind interest and would ask them to leave. Now.*"

Arthur looked round the nervous faces of his companions.

"Well, I suppose we'd better be going then, hadn't we?" he suggested.

"Shhh!" said Zaphod. "There's absolutely nothing to be worried about."

"Then why's everyone so tense?"

"They're just interested!" shouted Zaphod. "Computer, start descent into the atmosphere and prepare for landing."

This time the fanfare was quite perfunctory, the voice now distinctly cold.

"*It is most gratifying,*" it said, "*that your enthusiasm for our planet continues unabated, and so we would like to assure you that the guided missiles currently converging with your ship are part of a special service we extend to all of our most enthusiastic clients, and the fully armed nuclear warheads are of course merely a courtesy detail. We look forward to your custom in future lives. . . . Thank you.*"

The voice snapped off.

"Oh," said Trillian.

"Er..." said Arthur.

"Well?" said Ford.

"Look," said Zaphod, "will you get it into your heads? That's just a recorded message. It's millions of years old. It doesn't apply to us, get it?"

"What," said Trillian quietly, "about the missiles?"

"Missiles? Don't make me laugh."

Ford tapped Zaphod on the shoulder and pointed at the rear screen. Clear in the distance behind them two silver darts were climbing through the atmosphere toward the ship. A quick change of magnification brought them into close focus—two massively real rockets thundering through the sky. The suddenness of it was shocking.

"I think they're going to have a very good try at applying to us," said Ford.

Zaphod stared at them in astonishment.

"Hey, this is terrific!" he said. "Someone down there is trying to kill us!"

"Terrific," said Arthur.

"But don't you see what this means?"

"Yes. We're going to die."

"Yes, but apart from that."

"*Apart* from that?"

"It means we must be on to something!"

"How soon can we get off it?"

Second by second the image of the missiles on the screen grew larger. They had swung round now on to a direct homing course so that all that could be seen of them now was the warheads, head-on.

"As a matter of interest," said Trillian, "what are we going to do?"

"Just keep cool," said Zaphod.

"Is that all?" shouted Arthur.

"No, we're also going to... er... take evasive action!" said Zaphod with a sudden access of panic. "Computer, what evasive action can we take?"

"Er, none, I'm afraid, guys," said the computer.

"Or something," said Zaphod, "... er..." he said.

"There seems to be something jamming my guidance systems," explained the computer brightly, "impact minus forty-five seconds. Please call me Eddie if it will help you to relax."

Zaphod tried to run in several equally decisive directions simultaneously.

"Right!" he said. "Er . . . we've got to get manual control of this ship."

"Can you fly her?" asked Ford pleasantly.

"No, can you?"

"No."

"Trillian, can you?"

"No."

"Fine," said Zaphod, relaxing. "We'll do it together."

"I can't either," said Arthur, who felt it was time he began to assert himself.

"I'd guessed that," said Zaphod. "Okay, computer, I want full manual control now."

"You got it," said the computer.

Several large desk panels slid open and banks of control consoles sprang up out of them, showering the crew with bits of expanded polystyrene packaging and balls of rolled-up cellophane: these controls had never been used before.

Zaphod stared at them wildly.

"Okay, Ford," he said, "full retro thrust and ten degrees starboard. Or something . . ."

"Good luck, guys," chirped the computer, "impact minus thirty seconds. . . ."

Ford leaped to the controls—only a few of them made any immediate sense to him so he pulled those. The ship shook and screamed as its guidance rocket jets tried to push it every which way simultaneously. He released half of them and the ship spun around in a tight arc and headed back the way it had come, straight toward the oncoming missiles.

Air cushions ballooned out of the walls in an instant as everyone was thrown against them. For a few seconds the inertial forces held them flattened and squirming for breath, unable to move. Zaphod struggled and pushed in manic desperation and finally managed a savage kick at a small lever that formed part of the guidance system.

The lever snapped off. The ship twisted sharply and rocketed upward. The crew were hurled violently back across the cabin. Ford's copy of *The Hitchhiker's Guide to the Galaxy* smashed into another section of the control console with the combined result that the *Guide* started to explain to anyone who cared to listen about the best ways of smuggling Antarean parakeet glands out of Antares (an Antarean parakeet gland stuck on a small stick is a revolting but much-sought-after cocktail delicacy and very large sums of money are often paid for them by very rich idiots who want to impress other very rich idiots), and the ship suddenly dropped out of the sky like a stone.

It was of course more or less at this moment that one of the crew sustained a nasty bruise to the upper arm. This should be emphasized because, as has already been revealed, they escape otherwise completely unharmed and the deadly nuclear missiles do not eventually hit the ship. The safety of the crew is absolutely assured.

"Impact minus twenty seconds, guys..." said the computer.

"Then turn the bloody engines back on!" bawled Zaphod.

"Oh, sure thing, guys," said the computer. With a subtle roar the engines cut back in, the ship smoothly flattened out of its dive and headed back toward the missiles again.

The computer started to sing.

" *'When you walk through the storm...'* " it whined nasally, " *'hold your head up high...'* "

Zaphod screamed at it to shut up, but his voice was lost in the din of what they quite naturally assumed was approaching destruction.

" *'And don't... be afraid... of the dark!'* " Eddie wailed.

The ship, in flattening out, had in fact flattened out upside down and lying on the ceiling as they were it was now totally impossible for any of the crew to reach the guidance systems.

" *'At the end of the storm...'* " crooned Eddie.

The two missiles loomed massively on the screens as they thundered toward the ship.

" *'is a golden sky...'* "

But by an extraordinarily lucky chance they had not yet fully corrected their flight paths to that of the erratically weaving ship, and they passed right under it.

" *'And the sweet silver song of the lark'....* Revised impact time fifteen seconds, fellas.... *'Walk on through the wind...'* "

The missiles banked round in a screeching arc and plunged back in pursuit.

"This is it," said Arthur watching them. "We are now quite definitely going to die, aren't we?"

"I wish you'd stop saying that," shouted Ford.

"Well, we are, aren't we?"

"Yes."

" *'Walk on through the rain...'* " sang Eddie.

A thought struck Arthur. He struggled to his feet.

"Why doesn't anyone turn on this Improbability Drive thing?" he said. "We could probably reach that."

"What are you, crazy?" said Zaphod. "Without proper programming anything could happen."

"Does that matter at this stage?" shouted Arthur.

" '*Though your dreams be tossed and blown . . .* ' " sang Eddie.

Arthur scrambled up on to one of the excitingly chunky pieces of molded contouring where the curve of the wall met the ceiling.

" '*Walk on, walk on, with hope in your heart . . .* ' "

"Does anyone know why Arthur can't turn on the Improbability Drive?" shouted Trillian.

" '*And you'll never walk alone.*' . . . Impact minus five seconds, it's been great knowing you guys, God bless. . . . '*You'll ne . . . ver . . . walk . . . alone!*' "

"I said," yelled Trillian, "does anyone know . . ."

The next thing that happened was a mind-mangling explosion of noise and light.

nd the next thing that happened after that was that the Heart of
Gold continued on its way perfectly normally with a rather
fetchingly redesigned interior. It was somewhat larger, and
done out in delicate pastel shades of green and blue. In the
center a spiral staircase, leading nowhere in particular, stood in a spray of
ferns and yellow flowers and next to it a stone sundial pedestal housed the
main computer terminal. Cunningly deployed lighting and mirrors created
the illusion of standing in a conservatory overlooking a wide stretch of
exquisitely manicured garden. Around the periphery of the conservatory
area stood marble-topped tables on intricately beautiful wrought-iron legs.
As you gazed into the polished surface of the marble the vague forms of
instruments became visible, and as you touched them the instruments
materialized instantly under your hands. Looked at from the correct angles
the mirrors appeared to reflect all the required data read-outs, though it
was far from clear where they were reflected from. It was in fact
sensationally beautiful.

Relaxing in a wickerwork sun chair, Zaphod Beeblebrox said, "What the
hell happened?"

"Well, I was just saying," said Arthur lounging by a small fish pool,
"there's this Improbability Drive switch over here . . ." he waved at where
it had been. There was a potted plant there now.

"But where are we?" said Ford, who was sitting on the spiral staircase, a
nicely chilled Pan Galactic Gargle Blaster in his hand.

"Exactly where we were, I think . . ." said Trillian, as all about them the
mirrors suddenly showed them an image of the blighted landscape of
Magrathea, which still scooted along beneath them.

Zaphod leaped out of his seat.

"Then what's happened to the missiles?" he said.

A new and astounding image appeared in the mirrors.

"They would appear," said Ford doubtfully, "to have turned into a bowl
of petunias and a very surprised-looking whale . . ."

"At an Improbability factor," cut in Eddie, who hadn't changed a bit, "of eight million, seven hundred and sixty-seven thousand, one hundred and twenty-eight to one against."

Zaphod stared at Arthur.

"Did you think of that, Earthman?" he demanded.

"Well," said Arthur, "all I did was . . ."

"That's very good thinking, you know. Turn on the Improbability Drive for a second without first activating the proofing screens. Hey, kid, you just saved our lives, you know that?"

"Oh," said Arthur, "well, it was nothing really. . . ."

"Was it?" said Zaphod. "Oh well, forget it then. Okay, computer, take us in to land."

"But . . ."

"I said forget it."

Another thing that got forgotten was the fact that against all probability a sperm whale had suddenly been called into existence several miles above the surface of an alien planet.

And since this is not a naturally tenable position for a whale, this poor innocent creature had very little time to come to terms with its identity as a whale before it then had to come to terms with not being a whale any more.

This is a complete record of its thought from the moment it began its life till the moment it ended it.

Ah . . . ! What's happening? it thought.

Er, excuse me, who am I?

Hello?

Why am I here? What's my purpose in life?

What do I mean by who am I?

Calm down, get a grip now . . . oh! this is an interesting sensation, what is it? It's a sort of . . . yawning, tingling sensation in my . . . my . . . well, I suppose I'd better start finding names for things if I want to make any headway in what for the sake of what I shall call an argument I shall call the world, so let's call it my stomach.

Good. Ooooh, it's getting quite strong. And hey, what about this whistling roaring sound going past what I'm suddenly going to call my head? Perhaps I can call that . . . wind! Is that a good name? It'll do . . . perhaps I can find a better name for it later when I've found out what it's for. It must be something very important because there certainly seems to be a hell of a lot of it. Hey! What's this thing? This . . . let's call it a tail—yeah, tail. Hey! I can really thrash it about pretty good, can't I? Wow! Wow! That feels great! Doesn't seem to achieve very much but I'll probably find out what it's for later on. Now, have I built up any coherent picture of things yet?

No.

Never mind, hey, this is really exciting, so much to find out about, so much to look forward to, I'm quite dizzy with anticipation . . .

Or is it the wind?

There really is a lot of that now, isn't there?

And wow! Hey! What's this thing suddenly coming toward me very fast? Very, very fast. So big and flat and round, it needs a big wide-sounding name like . . . ow . . . ound . . . round . . . ground! That's it! That's a good name—ground!

I wonder if it will be friends with me?

And the rest, after a sudden wet thud, was silence.

Curiously enough, the only thing that went through the mind of the bowl of petunias as it fell was Oh no, not again. Many people have speculated that if we knew exactly why the bowl of petunias had thought that we would know a lot more about the nature of the Universe than we do now.

Chapter 19

Are we taking this robot with us?" said Ford, looking with distaste at Marvin, who was standing in an awkward hunched posture in the corner under a small palm tree.

Zaphod glanced away from the mirror screens which presented a panoramic view of the blighted landscape on which the Heart of Gold had now landed.

"Oh, the Paranoid Android," he said. "Yeah, we'll take him."

"But what are you supposed to do with a manically depressed robot?"

"You think you've got problems," said Marvin, as if he was addressing a newly occupied coffin, "what are you supposed to do if you *are* a manically depressed robot? No, don't bother to answer that, I'm fifty thousand times more intelligent than you and even I don't know the answer. It gives me a headache just trying to think down to your level."

Trillian burst in through the door from her cabin.

"My white mice have escaped!" she said.

An expression of deep worry and concern failed to cross either of Zaphod's faces.

"Nuts to your white mice," he said.

Trillian glared an upset glare at him, and disappeared again.

It is possible that her remark would have commanded greater attention had it been generally realized that human beings were only the third most intelligent life form present on the planet Earth, instead of (as was generally thought by most independent observers) the second.

"Good afternoon, boys."

The voice was oddly familiar, but oddly different. It had a matriarchal twang. It announced itself to the crew as they arrived at the airlock hatchway that would let them out on the planet surface.

They looked at each other in puzzlement.

"It's the computer," explained Zaphod. "I discovered it had an emergency back-up personality that I thought might work out better."

"Now this is going to be your first day out on a strange new planet," continued Eddie's new voice, "so I want you all wrapped up snug and warm, and no playing with any naughty bug-eyed monsters."

Zaphod tapped impatiently on the hatch.

"I'm sorry," he said, "I think we might be better off with a slide rule."

"Right!" snapped the computer. "Who said that?"

"Will you open up the exit hatch, please, computer?" said Zaphod, trying not to get angry.

"Not until whoever said that owns up," urged the computer, stamping a few synapses closed.

"Oh God," muttered Ford, slumped against a bulkhead. He started to count to ten. He was desperately worried that one day sentient life forms would forget how to do this. Only by counting could humans demonstrate their independence of computers.

"Come on," said Eddie sternly.

"Computer..." began Zaphod.

"I'm waiting," interrupted Eddie. "I can wait all day if necessary...."

"Computer..." said Zaphod again, who had been trying to think of some subtle piece of reasoning to put the computer down with, and had decided not to bother competing with it on its own ground, "if you don't open that exit hatch this moment I shall zap straight off to your major data banks and reprogram you with a very large ax, got that?"

Eddie, shocked, paused and considered this.

Ford carried on counting quietly. This is about the most aggressive thing you can do to a computer, the equivalent of going up to a human being and saying *Blood... blood... blood... blood...*

Finally Eddie said quietly, "I can see this relationship is something we're all going to have to work at," and the hatchway opened.

An icy wind ripped into them, they hugged themselves warmly and stepped down the ramp on to the barren dust of Magrathea.

"It'll all end in tears, I know it," shouted Eddie after them, and closed the hatchway again.

A few minutes later he opened and closed the hatchway again in response to a command that caught him entirely by surprise.

ive figures wandered slowly over the blighted land. Bits of it were dullish gray, bits of it dullish brown, the rest of it rather less interesting to look at. It was like a dried-out marsh, now barren of all vegetation and covered with a layer of dust about an inch thick. It was very cold.

Zaphod was clearly rather depressed about it. He stalked off by himself and was soon lost to sight behind a slight rise in the ground.

The wind stung Arthur's eyes and ears, and the stale thin air clasped his throat. However, the thing that was stung most was his mind.

"It's fantastic . . ." he said, and his own voice rattled his ears. Sound carried badly in this thin atmosphere.

"Desolate hole, if you ask me," said Ford. "I could have more fun in a cat litter." He felt a mounting irritation. Of all the planets in all the star systems of all the Galaxy—many wild and exotic, seething with life—didn't he just have to turn up at a dump like this after fifteen years of being a castaway? Not even a hot-dog stand in evidence. He stooped down and picked up a cold clod of earth, but there was nothing underneath it worth crossing thousands of light-years to look at.

"No," insisted Arthur, "don't you understand, this is the first time I've actually stood on the surface of another planet . . . a whole alien world . . . ! Pity it's such a dump though."

Trillian hugged herself, shivered and frowned. She could have sworn she saw a slight and unexpected movement out of the corner of her eye, but when she glanced in that direction all she could see was the ship, still and silent, a hundred yards or so behind them.

She was relieved when a second or so later they caught sight of Zaphod standing on top of the ridge of ground and waving to them to come and join him.

He seemed to be excited, but they couldn't clearly hear what he was saying because of the thinnish atmosphere and the wind.

As they approached the ridge of higher ground they became aware that it seemed to be circular—a crater about a hundred and fifty yards wide. Round the outside of the crater the sloping ground was spattered with black and red lumps. They stopped and looked at a piece. It was wet. It was rubbery.

With horror they suddenly realized that it was fresh whalemeat.

At the top of the crater's lip they met Zaphod.

"Look," he said, pointing into the crater.

In the center lay the exploded carcass of a lonely sperm whale that hadn't lived long enough to be disappointed with its lot. The silence was only disturbed by the slight involuntary spasms of Trillian's throat.

"I suppose there's no point in trying to bury it?" murmured Arthur, and then wished he hadn't.

"Come," said Zaphod, and started back down into the crater.

"What, down there?" said Trillian with severe distaste.

"Yeah," said Zaphod, "come on, I've got something to show you."

"We can see it," said Trillian.

"Not that," said Zaphod, "something else. Come on."

They all hesitated.

"Come on," insisted Zaphod, "I've found a way in."

"*In?*" said Arthur in horror.

"Into the interior of the planet! An underground passage. The force of the whale's impact cracked it open, and that's where we have to go. Where no man has trod these five million years, into the very depths of time itself. . . ."

Marvin started his ironical humming again.

Zaphod hit him and he shut up.

With little shudders of disgust they all followed Zaphod down the incline into the crater, trying very hard to avoid looking at its unfortunate creator.

"Life," said Marvin dolefully, "loathe it or ignore it, you can't like it."

The ground had caved in where the whale had hit it, revealing a network of galleries and passages, now largely obstructed by collapsed rubble and entrails. Zaphod had made a start clearing a way into one of them, but Marvin was able to do it rather faster. Dank air wafted out of its dark recesses, and as Zaphod shone a flashlight into it, little was visible in the dusty gloom.

"According to the legends," he said, "the Magratheans lived most of their lives underground."

"Why's that?" said Arthur. "Did the surface become too polluted or overpopulated?"

"No, I don't think so," said Zaphod. "I think they just didn't like it very much."

"Are you sure you know what you're doing?" said Trillian, peering nervously into the darkness. "We've been attacked once already, you know."

"Look, kid, I promise you the live population of this planet is nil plus the four of us, so come on, let's get on in there. Er, hey, Earthman . . ."

"Arthur," said Arthur.

"Yeah, could you just sort of keep this robot with you and guard this end of the passageway. Okay?"

"Guard?" said Arthur. "What from? You just said there's no one here."

"Yeah, well, just for safety, okay?" said Zaphod.

"Whose? Yours or mine?"

"Good lad. Okay, here we go."

Zaphod scrambled down into the passage, followed by Trillian and Ford.

"Well, I hope you all have a really miserable time," complained Arthur.

"Don't worry," Marvin assured him, "they will."

In a few seconds they had disappeared from view.

Arthur stamped around in a huff, and then decided that a whale's graveyard is not on the whole a good place to stamp around in.

Marvin eyed him balefully for a moment, and then turned himself off.

Zaphod marched quickly down the passageway, nervous as hell, but trying to hide it by striding purposefully. He flung the beam around. The walls were covered in dark tiles and were cold to the touch, the air thick with decay.

"There, what did I tell you?" he said. "An inhabited planet. Magrathea," and he strode on through the dirt and debris that littered the tile floors.

Trillian was reminded unavoidably of the London Underground, though it was less thoroughly squalid.

At intervals along the walls the tiles gave way to large mosaics—simple angular patterns in bright colors. Trillian stopped and studied one of them but could not interpret any sense in them. She called to Zaphod.

"Hey, have you any idea what these strange symbols are?"

"I think they're just strange symbols of some kind," said Zaphod, hardly glancing back.

Trillian shrugged and hurried after him.

From time to time a doorway led either to the left or right into smallish chambers which Ford discovered to be full of derelict computer equipment. He dragged Zaphod into one to have a look. Trillian followed.

"Look," said Ford, "you reckon this is Magrathea . . ."

"Yeah," said Zaphod, "and we heard the voice, right?"

"Okay, so I've bought the fact that it's Magrathea—for the moment. What you have so far said nothing about is how in the Galaxy you found it. You didn't just look it up in a star atlas, that's for sure."

"Research. Government archives. Detective work. Few lucky guesses. Easy."

"And then you stole the Heart of Gold to come and look for it with?"

"I stole it to look for a lot of things."

"A lot of things?" said Ford in surprise. "Like what?"

"I don't know."

"What?"

"I don't know what I'm looking for."

"Why not?"

"Because . . . because . . . I think it might be because if I knew I wouldn't be able to look for them."

"What, are you crazy?"

"It's a possibility I haven't ruled out yet," said Zaphod quietly. "I only know as much about myself as my mind can work out under its current conditions. And its current conditions are not good."

For a long time nobody said anything as Ford gazed at Zaphod with a mind suddenly full of worry.

"Listen, old friend, if you want to . . ." started Ford eventually.

"No, wait . . . I'll tell you something," said Zaphod. "I freewheel a lot. I get an idea to do something, and, hey, why not, I do it. I reckon I'll become President of the Galaxy, and it just happens, it's easy. I decide to steal this ship. I decide to look for Magrathea, and it all just happens. Yeah, I work out how it can best be done, right, but it always works out. It's like having a Galacticredit card which keeps on working though you never send off the checks. And then whenever I stop and think—why did I want to do something?—how did I work out how to do it?—I get a very strong desire just to stop thinking about it. Like I have now. It's a big effort to talk about it."

Zaphod paused for a while. For a while there was silence. Then he frowned and said, "Last night I was worrying about this again. About the fact that part of my mind just didn't seem to work properly. Then it occurred to me that the way it seemed was that someone else was using my mind to have good ideas with, without telling me about it. I put the two ideas together and decided that maybe that somebody had locked off part of my mind for that purpose, which was why I couldn't use it. I wondered if there was a way I could check.

"I went to the ship's medical bay and plugged myself into the encephalographic screen. I went through every major screening test on both my heads—all the tests I had to go through under Government medical officers before my nomination for presidency could be properly ratified. They showed up nothing. Nothing unexpected at least. They showed that I was clever, imaginative, irresponsible, untrustworthy, extrovert, nothing you couldn't have guessed. And no other anomalies. So I started inventing further tests, completely at random. Nothing. Then I tried superimposing the results from one head on top of the results from the other head. Still nothing. Finally I got silly, because I'd given it all up as nothing more than an attack of paranoia. Last thing I did before I packed it in was take the superimposed picture and look at it through a green filter. You remember I was always superstitious about the color green when I was a kid? I always wanted to be a pilot on one of the trading scouts?"

Ford nodded.

"And there it was," said Zaphod, "clear as day. A whole section in the middle of both brains that related only to each other and not to anything else around them. Some bastard had cauterized all the synapses and electronically traumatized those two lumps of cerebellum."

Ford stared at him, aghast. Trillian had turned white.

"Somebody *did* that to you?" whispered Ford.

"Yeah."

"But have you any idea who? Or why?"

"Why? I can only guess. But I do know who the bastard was."

"You know? How do you know?"

"Because they left their initials burned into the cauterized synapses. They left them there for me to see."

Ford stared at him in horror and felt his skin begin to crawl.

"Initials? Burned into your brain?"

"Yeah."

"Well, what were they, for God's sake?"

Zaphod looked at him in silence again for a moment. Then he looked away.

"Z.B.," he said quietly.

At that moment a steel shutter slammed down behind them and gas started to pour into the chamber.

"I'll tell you about it later," choked Zaphod as all three passed out.

On the surface of Magrathea Arthur wandered about moodily. Ford had thoughtfully left him his copy of *The Hitchhiker's Guide to the Galaxy* to while away the time with. He pushed a few buttons at random.

The Hitchhiker's Guide to the Galaxy *is a very unevenly edited book and contains many passages that simply seemed to its editors like a good idea at the time.*

One of these (the one Arthur now came across) supposedly relates the experiences of one Veet Voojagig, a quiet young student at the University of Maximegalon, who pursued a brilliant academic career studying ancient philology, transformational ethics and the wave harmonic theory of historical perception, and then, after a night of drinking Pan Galactic Gargle Blasters with Zaphod Beeblebrox, became increasingly obsessed with the problem of what had happened to all the ballpoints he'd bought over the past few years.

There followed a long period of painstaking research during which he visited all the major centers of ballpoint loss throughout the Galaxy and eventually came up with a quaint little theory which quite caught the public imagination at the time. Somewhere in the cosmos, he said, along with all the planets inhabited by humanoids, reptiloids, fishoids, walking treeoids and superintelligent shades of the color blue, there was also a planet entirely given over to ballpoint life forms. And it was to this planet that unattended ballpoints would make their way, slipping away quietly through wormholes in space to a world where they knew they could enjoy a uniquely ballpointoid life-style, responding to highly ballpoint-oriented stimuli, and generally leading the ballpoint equivalent of the good life.

And as theories go this was all very fine and pleasant until Veet Voojagig suddenly claimed to have found this planet, and to have worked there for a while driving a limousine for a family of cheap green retractables, whereupon he was taken away, locked up, wrote a book and was finally sent into tax exile, which is the usual fate reserved for those who are determined to make fools of themselves in public.

When one day an expedition was sent to the spatial coordinates that Voojagig had claimed for this planet they discovered only a small asteroid inhabited by a solitary old man who claimed repeatedly that nothing was true, though he was later discovered to be lying.

There did, however, remain the question of both the mysterious sixty thousand Altairian dollars paid yearly into his Brantisvogan bank account, and of course Zaphod Beeblebrox's highly profitable secondhand ballpoint business.

Arthur read this, and put the book down.

The robot still sat there, completely inert.

Arthur got up and walked to the top of the crater. He walked around the crater. He watched two suns set magnificently over Magrathea.

He went back down into the crater. He woke the robot up because even a manically depressed robot is better to talk to than nobody.

"Night's falling," he said. "Look, robot, the stars are coming out."

From the heart of a dark nebula it is possible to see very few stars, and only very faintly, but they were there to be seen.

The robot obediently looked at them, then looked back.

"I know," he said. "Wretched, isn't it?"

"But that sunset! I've never seen anything like it in my wildest dreams . . . the two suns! It was like mountains of fire boiling into space."

"I've seen it," said Marvin. "It's rubbish."

"We only ever had the one sun at home," persevered Arthur. "I came from a planet called Earth, you know."

"I know," said Marvin, "you keep going on about it. It sounds awful."

"Ah no, it was a beautiful place."

"Did it have oceans?"

"Oh yes," said Arthur with a sigh, "great wide rolling blue oceans . . ."

"Can't bear oceans," said Marvin.

"Tell me," inquired Arthur, "do you get on well with other robots?"

"Hate them," said Marvin. "Where are you going?"

Arthur couldn't bear any more. He had got up again.

"I think I'll just take another walk," he said.

"Don't blame you," said Marvin and counted five hundred and ninety-seven billion sheep before falling asleep again a second later.

Arthur slapped his arms about himself to try and get his circulation a little more enthusiastic about its job. He trudged back up the wall of the crater.

Because the atmosphere was so thin and because there was no moon, nightfall was very rapid and it was by now very dark. Because of this, Arthur practically walked into the old man before he noticed him.

He was standing with his back to Arthur watching the very last glimmers of light sink into blackness behind the horizon. He was tallish, elderly and dressed in a single long gray robe. When he turned, his face was thin and distinguished, careworn but not unkind, the sort of face you would happily bank with. But he didn't turn yet, not even to react to Arthur's yelp of surprise.

Eventually the last rays of the sun vanished completely, and he turned. His face was still illuminated from somewhere, and when Arthur looked for the source of the light he saw that a few yards away stood a small craft of some kind—a small Hovercraft, Arthur guessed. It shed a dim pool of light around it.

The man looked at Arthur, sadly it seemed.

"You choose a cold night to visit our dead planet," he said.

"Who . . . who are you?" stammered Arthur.

The man looked away. Again a look of sadness seemed to cross his face.

"My name is not important," he said.

He seemed to have something on his mind. Conversation was clearly something he felt he didn't have to rush at. Arthur felt awkward.

"I . . . er . . . you startled me . . ." he said, lamely.

The man looked round to him again and slightly raised his eyebrows.

"Hmmm?" he said.

"I said you startled me."

"Do not be alarmed, I will not harm you."

Arthur frowned at him. "But you shot at us! There were missiles . . ." he said.

The man gazed into the pit of the crater. The slight glow from Marvin's eyes cast very faint red shadows on the huge carcass of the whale.

The man chuckled slightly.

"An automatic system," he said and gave a small sigh. "Ancient computers ranged in the bowels of the planet tick away the dark millennia, and the ages hang heavy on their dusty data banks. I think they take the occasional potshot to relieve the monotony."

He looked gravely at Arthur and said, "I'm a great fan of science, you know."

"Oh... er, really?" said Arthur, who was beginning to find the man's curious, kindly manner disconcerting.

"Oh yes," said the old man and simply stopped talking again.

"Ah," said Arthur, "er..." He had an odd feeling of being like a man in the act of adultery who is surprised when the woman's husband wanders into the room, changes his trousers, passes a few idle remarks about the weather and leaves again.

"You seem ill at ease," said the old man with polite concern.

"Er, no... well, yes. Actually, you see, we weren't really expecting to find anybody about in fact. I sort of gathered that you were all dead or something..."

"Dead?" said the old man. "Good gracious me, no, we have but slept."

"Slept?" said Arthur incredulously.

"Yes, through the economic recession, you see," said the old man, apparently unconcerned about whether Arthur understood a word he was talking about or not.

Arthur had to prompt him again.

"Er, economic recession?"

"Well, you see, five million years ago the Galactic economy collapsed, and seeing that custom-built planets are something of a luxury commodity, you see..."

He paused and looked at Arthur.

"You know we built planets, do you?" he asked solemnly.

"Well, yes," said Arthur, "I'd sort of gathered..."

"Fascinating trade," said the old man, and a wistful look came into his eyes, "doing the coastlines was always my favorite. Used to have endless fun doing the little bits in fjords... so anyway," he said, trying to find his thread again, "the recession came and we decided it would save a lot of bother if we just slept through it. So we programmed the computers to revive us when it was all over."

The man stifled a very slight yawn and continued.

"The computers were index-linked to the Galactic stock-market prices, you see, so that we'd all be revived when everybody else had rebuilt the economy enough to afford our rather expensive services."

Arthur, a regular *Guardian* reader, was deeply shocked at this.

"That's a pretty unpleasant way to behave, isn't it?"

"Is it?" asked the old man mildly. "I'm sorry, I'm a bit out of touch."

He pointed down into the crater.

"Is that robot yours?" he said.

"No," came a thin metallic voice from the crater, "I'm mine."

"If you'd call it a robot," muttered Arthur. "It's more a sort of electronic sulking machine."

"Bring it," said the old man. Arthur was quite surprised to hear a note of decision suddenly present in the old man's voice. He called to Marvin, who crawled up the slope making a big show of being lame, which he wasn't.

"On second thoughts," said the old man, "leave it here. You must come with me. Great things are afoot." He turned toward his craft which, though no apparent signal had been given, now drifted quietly toward them through the dark.

Arthur looked down at Marvin, who now made an equally big show of turning round laboriously and trudging off down into the crater again muttering sour nothings to himself.

"Come," called the old man, "come now or you will be late."

"Late?" said Arthur. "What for?"

"What is your name, human?"

"Dent. Arthur Dent," said Arthur.

"Late, as in the late Dentarthurdent," said the old man, sternly. "It's a sort of threat, you see." Another wistful look came into his tired old eyes. "I've never been very good at them myself, but I'm told they can be very effective."

Arthur blinked at him.

"What an extraordinary person," he muttered to himself.

"I beg your pardon?" said the old man.

"Oh, nothing, I'm sorry," said Arthur in embarrassment. "All right, where do we go?"

"In my aircar," said the old man, motioning Arthur to get into the craft which had settled silently next to them. "We are going deep into the bowels of the planet where even now our race is being revived from its five-million-year slumber. Magrathea awakes."

Arthur shivered involuntarily as he seated himself next to the old man. The strangeness of it, the silent bobbing movement of the craft as it soared into the night sky, quite unsettled him.

He looked at the old man, his face illuminated by the dull glow of tiny lights on the instrument panel.

"Excuse me," he said to him, "what is your name, by the way?"

"My name?" said the old man, and the same distant sadness came into his face again. He paused. "My name," he said, "is Slartibartfast."

Arthur practically choked.

"I beg your pardon?" he spluttered.

"Slartibartfast," repeated the old man quietly.

"Slartibartfast?"

The old man looked at him gravely.

"I said it wasn't important," he said.

The aircar sailed through the night.

Chapter 23

It is an important and popular fact that things are not always what they seem. For instance, on the planet Earth, man had always assumed that he was more intelligent than dolphins because he had achieved so much—the wheel, New York, wars and so on—while all the dolphins had ever done was muck about in the water having a good time. But conversely, the dolphins had always believed that they were far more intelligent than man—for precisely the same reasons.

Curiously enough, the dolphins had long known of the impending destruction of the planet Earth and had made many attempts to alert mankind to the danger; but most of their communications were misinterpreted as amusing attempts to punch footballs or whistle for tidbits, so they eventually gave up and left the Earth by their own means shortly before the Vogons arrived.

The last ever dolphin message was misinterpreted as a surprisingly sophisticated attempt to do a double-backward somersault through a hoop while whistling the "Star-Spangled Banner," but in fact the message was this: *So long and thanks for all the fish.*

In fact there was only one species on the planet more intelligent than dolphins, and they spent a lot of their time in behavioral research laboratories running round inside wheels and conducting frighteningly elegant and subtle experiments on man. The fact that once again man completely misinterpreted this relationship was entirely according to these creatures' plans.

Silently the aircar coasted through the cold darkness, a single soft glow of light that was utterly alone in the deep Magrathean night. It sped swiftly. Arthur's companion seemed sunk in his own thoughts, and when Arthur tried on a couple of occasions to engage him in conversation again he would simply reply by asking if he was comfortable enough, and then left it at that.

Arthur tried to gauge the speed at which they were traveling, but the blackness outside was absolute and he was denied any reference points. The sense of motion was so soft and slight he could almost believe they were hardly moving at all.

Then a tiny glow of light appeared in the far distance and within seconds had grown so much in size that Arthur realized it was traveling toward them at a colossal speed, and he tried to make out what sort of craft it might be. He peered at it, but was unable to discern any clear shape, and suddenly gasped in alarm as the aircar dipped sharply and headed downward in what seemed certain to be a collision course. Their relative velocity seemed unbelievable, and Arthur had hardly time to draw breath before it was all over. The next thing he was aware of was an insane silver blur that seemed to surround him. He twisted his head sharply round and saw a small black point dwindling rapidly in the distance behind them, and it took him several seconds to realize what had happened.

They had plunged into a tunnel in the ground. The colossal speed had been their own, relative to the glow of light which was a stationary hole in the ground, the mouth of the tunnel. The insane blur of silver was the circular wall of the tunnel down which they were shooting, apparently at several hundred miles an hour.

He closed his eyes in terror.

After a length of time which he made no attempt to judge, he sensed a slight subsidence in their speed and some while later became aware that they were gradually gliding to a gentle halt.

He opened his eyes again. They were still in the silver tunnel, threading and weaving their way through what appeared to be a crisscross warren of converging tunnels. When they finally stopped it was in a small chamber of curved steel. Several tunnels also had their termini here, and at the farther end of the chamber Arthur could see a large circle of dim irritating light. It was irritating because it played tricks with the eyes, it was impossible to focus on it properly or tell how near or far it was. Arthur guessed (quite wrongly) that it might be ultraviolet.

Slartibartfast turned and regarded Arthur with his solemn old eyes.

"Earthman," he said, "we are now deep in the heart of Magrathea."

"How did you know I was an Earthman?" demanded Arthur.

"These things will become clear to you," said the old man gently, "at least," he added with slight doubt in his voice, "clearer than they are at the moment."

He continued: "I should warn you that the chamber we are about to pass into does not literally exist within our planet. It is a little too . . . large. We are about to pass through a gateway into a vast tract of hyperspace. It may disturb you."

Arthur made nervous noises.

Slartibartfast touched a button and added, not entirely reassuringly, "It scares the willies out of me. Hold tight."

The car shot forward straight into the circle of light, and suddenly Arthur had a fairly clear idea of what infinity looked like.

It wasn't infinity in fact. Infinity itself looks flat and uninteresting. Looking up into the night sky is looking into infinity—distance is incomprehensible and therefore meaningless. The chamber into which the aircar emerged was anything but infinite, it was just very very very big, so big that it gave the impression of infinity far better than infinity itself.

Arthur's senses bobbed and spun as, traveling at the immense speed he knew the aircar attained, they climbed slowly through the open air, leaving the gateway through which they had passed an invisible pinprick in the shimmering wall behind them.

The wall.

The wall defied the imagination—seduced it and defeated it. The wall was so paralyzingly vast and sheer that its top, bottom and sides passed away beyond the reach of sight. The mere shock of vertigo could kill a man.

The wall appeared perfectly flat. It would take the finest laser-measuring equipment to detect that as it climbed, apparently to infinity, as it dropped dizzily away, as it planed out to either side, it also curved. It met itself again thirteen light seconds away. In other words the wall formed the inside of a hollow sphere, a sphere over three million miles across and flooded with unimaginable light.

"Welcome," said Slartibartfast as the tiny speck that was the aircar, traveling now at three times the speed of sound, crept imperceptibly forward into the mind-boggling space, "welcome," he said, "to our factory floor."

Arthur stared about him in a kind of wonderful horror. Ranged away before them, at distances he could neither judge nor even guess at, were a series of curious suspensions, delicate traceries of metal and light hung about shadowy spherical shapes that hung in the space.

"This," said Slartibartfast, "is where we make most of our planets, you see."

"You mean," said Arthur, trying to form the words, "you mean you're starting it all up again now?"

"No no, good heavens, no," exclaimed the old man, "no, the Galaxy isn't nearly rich enough to support us yet. No, we've been awakened to perform just one extraordinary commission for very . . . special clients from another dimension. It may interest you . . . there in the distance in front of us."

Arthur followed the old man's finger till he was able to pick out the floating structure he was pointing out. It was indeed the only one of the many structures that betrayed any sign of activity about it, though this was more a subliminal impression than anything one could put one's finger on.

At that moment, however, a flash of light arced through the structure and revealed in stark relief the patterns that were formed on the dark sphere within. Patterns that Arthur knew, rough blobby shapes that were as familiar to him as the shapes of words, part of the furniture of his mind. For a few seconds he sat in stunned silence as the images rushed around his mind and tried to find somewhere to settle down and make sense.

Part of his brain told him that he knew perfectly well what he was looking at and what the shapes represented while another quite sensibly refused to countenance the idea and abdicated responsibility for any further thinking in that direction.

The flash came again, and this time there could be no doubt.

"The Earth . . ." whispered Arthur.

"Well, the Earth Mark Two in fact," said Slartibartfast cheerfully. "We're making a copy from our original blueprints."

There was a pause.

"Are you trying to tell me," said Arthur, slowly and with control, "that you originally . . . *made* the Earth?"

"Oh yes," said Slartibartfast. "Did you ever go to a place . . . I think it was called Norway?"

"No," said Arthur, "no, I didn't."

"Pity," said Slartibartfast, "that was one of mine. Won an award, you know. Lovely crinkly edges. I was most upset to hear of its destruction."

"*You* were upset!"

"Yes. Five minutes later and it wouldn't have mattered so much. It was a quite shocking cock-up."

"Huh?" said Arthur.

"The mice were furious."

"The *mice* were furious?"

"Oh yes," said the old man mildly.

"Yes, well, so I expect were the dogs and cats and duckbilled platypuses, but . . ."

"Ah, but they hadn't paid for it, you see, had they?"

"Look," said Arthur, "would it save you a lot of time if I just gave up and went mad now?"

For a while the aircar flew on in awkward silence. Then the old man tried patiently to explain.

"Earthman, the planet you lived on was commissioned, paid for, and run by mice. It was destroyed five minutes before the completion of the purpose for which it was built, and we've got to build another one."

Only one word was registering with Arthur.

"*Mice?*" he said.

"Indeed, Earthman."

"Look, sorry, are we talking about the little white furry things with the cheese fixation and women standing on tables screaming in early sixties sitcoms?"

Slartibartfast coughed politely.

"Earthman," he said, "it is sometimes hard to follow your mode of speech. Remember I have been asleep inside this planet of Magrathea for five million years and know little of these early sixties sitcoms of which you speak. These creatures you call mice, you see, they are not quite as they appear. They are merely the protrusion into our dimension of vastly hyperintelligent pandimensional beings. The whole business with the cheese and the squeaking is just a front."

The old man paused, and with a sympathetic frown continued. "They've been experimenting on you, I'm afraid."

Arthur thought about this for a second, and then his face cleared.

"Ah no," he said, "I see the source of the misunderstanding now. No, look, you see what happened was that we used to do experiments on *them*. They were often used in behavioral research, Pavlov and all that sort of stuff. So what happened was that the mice would be set all sorts of tests, learning to ring bells, run round mazes and things so that the whole nature of the learning process could be examined. From our observations of their behavior we were able to learn all sorts of things about our own. . . ."

Arthur's voice trailed off.

"Such subtlety . . ." said Slartibartfast, "one has to admire it."

"What?" said Arthur.

"How better to disguise their real natures, and how better to guide your thinking. Suddenly running down a maze the wrong way, eating the wrong bit of cheese, unexpectedly dropping dead of myxomatosis. If it's finely calculated the cumulative effect is enormous."

He paused for effect.

"You see, Earthman, they really are particularly clever hyperintelligent pandimensional beings. Your planet and people have formed the matrix of an organic computer running a ten-million-year research program. . . . Let me tell you the whole story. It'll take a little time."

"Time," said Arthur weakly, "is not currently one of my problems."

There are of course many problems connected with life, of which some of the most popular are *Why are people born? Why do they die? Why do they want to spend so much of the intervening time wearing digital watches?*

Many many millions of years ago a race of hyperintelligent pandimensional beings (whose physical manifestation in their own pandimensional universe is not dissimilar to our own) got so fed up with the constant bickering about the meaning of life which used to interrupt their favorite pastime of Brockian Ultra Cricket (a curious game which involved suddenly hitting people for no readily apparent reason and then running away) that they decided to sit down and solve their problems once and for all.

And to this end they built themselves a stupendous super computer which was so amazingly intelligent that even before its data banks had been connected up it had started from *I think therefore I am* and got as far as deducing the existence of rice pudding and income tax before anyone managed to turn it off.

It was the size of a small city.

Its main console was installed in a specially designed executive office, mounted on an enormous executive desk of finest ultramahogany topped with rich ultrared leather. The dark carpeting was discreetly sumptuous, exotic pot plants and tastefully engraved prints of the principal computer programmers and their families were deployed liberally about the room, and stately windows looked out upon a tree-lined public square.

On the day of the Great On-Turning two soberly dressed programmers with briefcases arrived and were shown discreetly into the office. They were aware that this day they would represent their entire race in its greatest moment, but they conducted themselves calmly and quietly as they seated themselves deferentially before the desk, opened their briefcases and took out their leather-bound notebooks.

Their names were Lunkwill and Fook.

For a few moments they sat in respectful silence, then, after exchanging a quiet glance with Fook, Lunkwill leaned forward and touched a small black panel.

The subtlest of hums indicated that the massive computer was now in total active mode. After a pause it spoke to them in a voice rich, resonant and deep.

It said: "What is this great task for which I, Deep Thought, the second greatest computer in the Universe of Time and Space, have been called into existence?"

Lunkwill and Fook glanced at each other in surprise.

"Your task, O computer..." began Fook.

"No, wait a minute, this isn't right," said Lunkwill, worried. "We distinctly designed this computer to be the greatest one ever and we're not making do with second best. Deep Thought," he addressed the computer, "are you not as we designed you to be, the greatest, most powerful computer in all time?"

"I described myself as the second greatest," intoned Deep Thought, "and such I am."

Another worried look passed between the two programmers. Lunkwill cleared his throat.

"There must be some mistake," he said, "are you not a greater computer than the Milliard Gargantubrain at Maximegalon which can count all the atoms in a star in a millisecond?"

"The Milliard Gargantubrain?" said Deep Thought with unconcealed contempt. "A mere abacus—mention it not."

"And are you not," said Fook leaning anxiously forward, "a greater analyst than the Googleplex Star Thinker in the Seventh Galaxy of Light and Ingenuity which can calculate the trajectory of every single dust particle throughout a five-week Dangrabad Beta sand blizzard?"

"A five-week sand blizzard?" said Deep Thought haughtily. "You ask this of me who have contemplated the very vectors of the atoms in the Big Bang itself? Molest me not with this pocket calculator stuff."

The two programmers sat in uncomfortable silence for a moment. Then Lunkwill leaned forward again.

"But are you not," he said, "a more fiendish disputant than the Great Hyperlobic Omni-Cognate Neutron Wrangler of Ciceronicus Twelve, the Magic and Indefatigable?"

"The Great Hyperlobic Omni-Cognate Neutron Wrangler," said Deep Thought, thoroughly rolling the r's, "could talk all four legs off an Arcturan Mega-Donkey—but only I could persuade it to go for a walk afterward."

"Then what," asked Fook, "is the problem?"

"There is no problem," said Deep Thought with magnificent ringing tones. "I am simply the second greatest computer in the Universe of Space and Time."

"But the *second?*" insisted Lunkwill. "Why do you keep saying the second? You're surely not thinking of the Multicorticoid Perspicutron Titan Muller, are you? Or the Pondermatic? Or the . . ."

Contemptuous lights flashed across the computer's console.

"I spare not a single unit of thought on these cybernetic simpletons!" he boomed. "I speak of none but the computer that is to come after me!"

Fook was losing patience. He pushed his notebook aside and muttered, "I think this is getting needlessly messianic."

"You know nothing of future time," pronounced Deep Thought, "and yet in my teeming circuitry I can navigate the infinite delta streams of future probability and see that there must one day come a computer whose merest operational parameters I am not worthy to calculate, but which it will be my fate eventually to design."

Fook sighed heavily and glanced across to Lunkwill.

"Can we get on and ask the question?" he said.

Lunkwill motioned him to wait.

"What computer is this of which you speak?" he asked.

"I will speak of it no further in this present time," said Deep Thought. "Now. Ask what else of me you will that I may function. Speak."

They shrugged at each other. Fook composed himself.

"O Deep Thought computer," he said, "the task we have designed you to perform is this. We want you to tell us . . ." he paused, "the Answer!"

"The Answer?" said Deep Thought. "The Answer to what?"

"Life!" urged Fook.

"The Universe!" said Lunkwill.

"Everything!" they said in chorus.

Deep Thought paused for a moment's reflection.

"Tricky," he said finally.

"But can you do it?"

Again, a significant pause.

"Yes," said Deep Thought, "I can do it."

"There is an answer?" said Fook with breathless excitement.

"A simple answer?" added Lunkwill.

"Yes," said Deep Thought. "Life, the Universe, and Everything. There is an answer. But," he added, "I'll have to think about it."

A sudden commotion destroyed the moment: the door flew open and two angry men wearing the coarse faded-blue robes and belts of the Cruxwan University burst into the room, thrusting aside the ineffectual flunkie who tried to bar their way.

"We demand admission!" shouted the younger of the two men elbowing a pretty young secretary in the throat.

"Come on," shouted the older one, "you can't keep us out!" He pushed a junior programmer back through the door.

"We demand that you can't keep us out!" bawled the younger one, though he was now firmly inside the room and no further attempts were being made to stop him.

"Who are you?" said Lunkwill, rising angrily from his seat. "What do you want?"

"I am Majikthise!" announced the older one.

"And I demand that I am Vroomfondel!" shouted the younger one.

Majikthise turned on Vroomfondel. "It's all right," he explained angrily, "you don't need to demand that."

"All right!" bawled Vroomfondel, banging on a nearby desk. "I am Vroomfondel, and that is *not* a demand, that is a solid *fact*! What we demand is solid *facts!*"

"No, we don't!" exclaimed Majikthise in irritation. "That is precisely what we don't demand!"

Scarcely pausing for breath, Vroomfondel shouted, "We *don't* demand solid facts! What we demand is a total *absence* of solid facts. I demand that I may or may not be Vroomfondel!"

"But who the devil are you?" exclaimed an outraged Fook.

"We," said Majikthise, "are Philosophers."

"Though we may not be," said Vroomfondel, waving a warning finger at the programmers.

"Yes, we *are*," insisted Majikthise. "We are quite definitely here as representatives of the Amalgamated Union of Philosophers, Sages, Luminaries and Other Thinking Persons, and we want this machine off, and we want it off *now!*"

"What's the problem?" said Lunkwill.

"I'll tell you what the problem is, mate," said Majikthise, "demarcation, that's the problem!"

"We demand," yelled Vroomfondel, "that demarcation may or may not be the problem!"

"You just let the machines get on with the adding up," warned Majikthise, "and we'll take care of the eternal verities, thank you very much. You want to check your legal position, you do, mate. Under law the Quest for Ultimate Truth is quite clearly the inalienable prerogative of your working thinkers. Any bloody machine goes and actually *finds* it and we're straight out of a job, aren't we? I mean, what's the use of our sitting up half the night arguing that there may or may not be a God if this machine only goes and gives you his bleeding phone number the next morning?"

"That's right," shouted Vroomfondel, "we demand rigidly defined areas of doubt and uncertainty!"

Suddenly a stentorian voice boomed across the room.

"Might *I* make an observation at this point?" inquired Deep Thought.

"We'll go on strike!" yelled Vroomfondel.

"That's right!" agreed Majikthise. "You'll have a national Philosophers' strike on your hands!"

The hum level in the room suddenly increased as several ancillary bass driver units, mounted in sedately carved and varnished cabinet speakers around the room, cut in to give Deep Thought's voice a little more power.

"All I wanted to say," bellowed the computer, "is that my circuits are now irrevocably committed to calculating the answer to the Ultimate Question of Life, the Universe, and Everything." He paused and satisfied himself that he now had everyone's attention, before continuing more quietly. "But the program will take me a little while to run."

Fook glanced impatiently at his watch.

"How long?" he said.

"Seven and half million years," said Deep Thought.

Lunkwill and Fook blinked at each other.

"Seven and a half million years!" they cried in chorus.

"Yes," declaimed Deep Thought, "I said I'd have to think about it, didn't I? And it occurs to me that running a program like this is bound to create an enormous amount of popular publicity for the whole area of philosophy in general. Everyone's going to have their own theories about what answer I'm eventually going to come up with, and who better to capitalize on that media market than you yourselves? So long as you can keep disagreeing with each other violently enough and maligning each other in the popular press, and so long as you have clever agents, you can keep yourselves on the gravy train for life. How does that sound?"

The two philosophers gaped at him.

"Bloody hell," said Majikthise, "now that is what I call thinking. Here, Vroomfondel, why do we never think of things like that?"

"Dunno," said Vroomfondel in an awed whisper; "think our brains must be too highly trained, Majikthise."

So saying, they turned on their heels and walked out of the door and into a life-style beyond their wildest dreams.

Yes, very salutary," said Arthur, after Slartibartfast had related the salient points of this story to him, "but I don't understand what all this has got to do with the Earth and mice and things."

"That is but the first half of the story, Earthman," said the old man. "If you would care to discover what happened seven and a half million years later, on the great day of the Answer, allow me to invite you to my study where you can experience the events yourself on our Sens-O-Tape records. That is, unless you would care to take a quick stroll on the surface of New Earth. It's only half completed, I'm afraid—we haven't even finished burying the artificial dinosaur skeletons in the crust yet, then we have the Tertiary and Quaternary Periods of the Cenozoic Era to lay down, and..."

"No, thank you," said Arthur, "it wouldn't be quite the same."

"No," said Slartibartfast, "it won't be," and he turned the aircar round and headed back toward the mind-numbing wall.

Slartibartfast's study was a total mess, like the results of an explosion in a public library. The old man frowned as they stepped in.

"Terribly unfortunate," he said, "a diode blew in one of the life-support computers. When we tried to revive our cleaning staff we discovered they'd been dead for nearly thirty thousand years. Who's going to clear away the bodies, that's what I want to know. Look, why don't you sit yourself down over there and let me plug you in?"

He gestured Arthur toward a chair which looked as if it had been made out of the rib cage of a stegosaurus.

"It was made out of the rib cage of a stegosaurus," explained the old man as he pottered about fishing bits of wire out from under tottering piles of paper and drawing instruments. "Here," he said, "hold these," and passed a couple of stripped wire ends to Arthur.

The instant he took hold of them a bird flew straight through him.

He was suspended in midair and totally invisible to himself. Beneath him was a pretty tree-lined city square, and all around it as far as the eye could see were white concrete buildings of airy spacious design but somewhat the worse for wear—many were cracked and stained with rain. Today, however, the sun was shining, a fresh breeze danced lightly through the trees, and the odd sensation that all the buildings were quietly humming was probably caused by the fact that the square and all the streets around it were thronged with cheerful excited people. Somewhere a band was playing, brightly colored flags were fluttering in the breeze and the spirit of carnival was in the air.

Arthur felt extraordinarily lonely stuck up in the air above it all without so much as a body to his name, but before he had time to reflect on this a voice rang out across the square and called for everyone's attention.

A man standing on a brightly dressed dais before the building which clearly dominated the square was addressing the crowd over a tannoy.

"O people who wait in the shadow of Deep Thought!" he cried out. "Honored Descendants of Vroomfondel and Majikthise, the Greatest and

Most Truly Interesting Pundits the Universe has ever known, the Time of Waiting is over!"

Wild cheers broke out among the crowd. Flags, streamers and wolf whistles sailed through the air. The narrower streets looked rather like centipedes rolled over on their backs and frantically waving their legs in the air.

"Seven and a half million years our race has waited for this Great and Hopefully Enlightening Day!" cried the cheerleader. "The Day of the Answer!"

Hurrahs burst from the ecstatic crowd.

"Never again," cried the man, "never again will we wake up in the morning and think *Who am I? What is my purpose in life? Does it really, cosmically speaking, matter if I don't get up and go to work?* For today we will finally learn once and for all the plain and simple answer to all these nagging little problems of Life, the Universe and Everything!"

As the crowd erupted once again, Arthur found himself gliding through the air and down toward one of the large stately windows on the first floor of the building behind the dais from which the speaker was addressing the crowd.

He experienced a moment's panic as he sailed straight toward the window, which passed when a second or so later he found he had gone right through the solid glass without apparently touching it.

No one in the room remarked on his peculiar arrival, which is hardly surprising as he wasn't there. He began to realize that the whole experience was merely a recorded projection which knocked six-track seventy-millimeter into a cocked hat.

The room was much as Slartibartfast had described it. In seven and a half million years it had been well looked after and cleaned regularly every century or so. The ultramahogany desk was worn at the edges, the carpet a little faded now, but the large computer terminal sat in sparkling glory on the desk's leather top, as bright as if it had been constructed yesterday.

Two severely dressed men sat respectfully before the terminal and waited.

"The time is nearly upon us," said one, and Arthur was surprised to see a word suddenly materialize in thin air just by the man's neck. The word was LOONQUAWL, and it flashed a couple of times and then disappeared again. Before Arthur was able to assimilate this the other man spoke and the word PHOUCHG appeared by his neck.

"Seventy-five thousand generations ago, our ancestors set this program in motion," the second man said, "and in all that time we will be the first to hear the computer speak."

"An awesome prospect, Phouchg," agreed the first man, and Arthur suddenly realized he was watching a recording with subtitles.

"We are the ones who will hear," said Phouchg, "the answer to the great question of Life . . . !"

"The Universe . . . !" said Loonquawl.

"And Everything . . . !"

"Shhh," said Loonquawl with a slight gesture, "I think Deep Thought is preparing to speak!"

There was a moment's expectant pause while panels slowly came to life on the front of the console. Lights flashed on and off experimentally and settled down into a businesslike pattern. A soft low hum came from the communication channel.

"Good morning," said Deep Thought at last.

"Er . . . good morning, O Deep Thought," said Loonquawl nervously, "do you have . . . er, that is . . ."

"An answer for you?" interrupted Deep Thought majestically. "Yes. I have."

The two men shivered with expectancy. Their waiting had not been in vain.

"There really is one?" breathed Phouchg.

"There really is one," confirmed Deep Thought.

"To Everything? To the great Question of Life, the Universe and Everything?"

"Yes."

Both of the men had been trained for this moment, their lives had been a preparation for it, they had been selected at birth as those who would witness the answer, but even so they found themselves gasping and squirming like excited children.

"And you're ready to give it to us?" urged Loonquawl.

"I am."

"Now?"

"Now," said Deep Thought.

They both licked their dry lips.

"Though I don't think," added Deep Thought, "that you're going to like it."

"Doesn't matter!" said Phouchg. "We must know it! Now!"

"Now?" inquired Deep Thought.

"Yes! Now..."

"All right," said the computer, and settled into silence again. The two men fidgeted. The tension was unbearable.

"You're really not going to like it," observed Deep Thought.

"Tell us!"

"All right," said Deep Thought. "The Answer to the Great Question..."

"Yes...!"

"Of Life, the Universe and Everything..." said Deep Thought.

"Yes...!"

"Is..." said Deep Thought, and paused.

"Yes...!"

"Is..."

"Yes...!!!...?"

"Forty-two," said Deep Thought, with infinite majesty and calm.

t was a long time before anyone spoke.

Out of the corner of his eye Phouchg could see the sea of tense expectant faces down in the square outside.

"We're going to get lynched, aren't we?" he whispered.

"It was a tough assignment," said Deep Thought mildly.

"Forty-two!" yelled Loonquawl. "Is that all you've got to show for seven and a half million years' work?"

"I checked it very thoroughly," said the computer, "and that quite definitely is the answer. I think the problem, to be quite honest with you, is that you've never actually known what the question is."

"But it was the Great Question! The Ultimate Question of Life, the Universe and Everything," howled Loonquawl.

"Yes," said Deep Thought with the air of one who suffers fools gladly, "but what actually *is* it?"

A slow stupefied silence crept over the men as they stared at the computer and then at each other.

"Well, you know, it's just Everything...everything..." offered Phouchg weakly.

"Exactly!" said Deep Thought. "So once you do know what the question actually is, you'll know what the answer means."

"Oh, terrific," muttered Phouchg, flinging aside his notebook and wiping away a tiny tear.

"Look, all right, all right," said Loonquawl, "can you just please *tell* us the question?"

"The Ultimate Question?"

"Yes!"

"Of Life, the Universe and Everything?"

"Yes!"

Deep Thought pondered for a moment.

"Tricky," he said.

"But can you do it?" cried Loonquawl.

Deep Thought pondered this for another long moment.

Finally: "No," he said firmly.

Both men collapsed onto their chairs in despair.

"But I'll tell you who can," said Deep Thought.

They both looked up sharply.

"Who? Tell us!"

Suddenly Arthur began to feel his apparently nonexistent scalp begin to crawl as he found himself moving slowly but inexorably forward toward the console, but it was only a dramatic zoom on the part of whoever had made the recording, he assumed.

"I speak of none but the computer that is to come after me," intoned Deep Thought, his voice regaining its accustomed declamatory tones. "A computer whose merest operational parameters I am not worthy to calculate—and yet I will design it for you. A computer that can calculate the Question to the Ultimate Answer, a computer of such infinite and subtle complexity that organic life itself shall form part of its operational matrix. And you yourselves shall take on new forms and go down into the computer to navigate its ten-million-year program! Yes! I shall design this computer for you. And I shall name it also unto you. And it shall be called . . . the Earth."

Phouchg gaped at Deep Thought.

"What a dull name," he said, and great incisions appeared down the length of his body. Loonquawl too suddenly sustained horrific gashes from nowhere. The Computer console blotched and cracked, the walls flickered and crumbled and the room crashed upward into its own ceiling. . . .

Slartibartfast was standing in front of Arthur holding the two wires.

"End of the tape," he explained.

Chapter 29

"Zaphod! Wake up!"

"Mmmmmwwwwwerrrr?"

"Hey, come on, wake up."

"Just let me stick to what I'm good at, yeah?" muttered Zaphod, and rolled away from the voice back to sleep.

"Do you want me to kick you?" said Ford.

"Would it give you a lot of pleasure?" said Zaphod, blearily.

"No."

"Nor me. So what's the point? Stop bugging me." Zaphod curled himself up.

"He got a double dose of the gas," said Trillian, looking down at him, "two windpipes."

"And stop talking," said Zaphod, "it's hard enough trying to sleep anyway. What's the matter with the ground? It's all cold and hard."

"It's gold," said Ford.

With an amazingly balletic movement Zaphod was standing and scanning the horizon, because that was how far the gold ground stretched in every direction, perfectly smooth and solid. It gleamed like ... it's impossible to say what it gleamed like because nothing in the Universe gleams in quite the same way that a planet made of solid gold does.

"Who put all that there?" yelped Zaphod, goggle-eyed.

"Don't get excited," said Ford, "it's only a catalog."

"A who?"

"A catalog," said Trillian, "an illusion."

"How can you say that?" cried Zaphod, falling to his hands and knees and staring at the ground. He poked it and prodded it. It was very heavy and very slightly soft—he could mark it with his fingernail. It was very yellow and very shiny, and when he breathed on it his breath evaporated off it in that very peculiar and special way that breath evaporates off solid gold.

"Trillian and I came round a while ago," said Ford. "We shouted and yelled till somebody came and then carried on shouting and yelling till they got fed up and put us in their planet catalog to keep us busy till they were ready to deal with us. This is all Sens-O-Tape."

Zaphod stared at him bitterly.

"Ah, shit," he said, "you wake me up from my own perfectly good dream to show me somebody else's." He sat down in a huff.

"What's that series of valleys over there?" he said.

"Hallmark," said Ford. "We had a look."

"We didn't wake you earlier," said Trillian. "The last planet was knee-deep in fish."

"Fish?"

"Some people like the oddest things."

"And before that," said Ford, "we had platinum. Bit dull. We thought you'd like to see this one though."

Seas of light glared at them in one solid blaze wherever they looked.

"Very pretty," said Zaphod petulantly.

In the sky a huge green catalog number appeared. It flickered and changed, and when they looked around again so had the land.

As with one voice they all went, "Yuch."

The sea was purple. The beach they were on was composed of tiny yellow and green pebbles, presumably terribly precious stones. The mountains in the distance seemed soft and undulating and red peaks. Nearby stood a solid silver beach table with a frilly mauve parasol and silver tassles.

In the sky a huge sign appeared, replacing the catalog number. It said, *Whatever your tastes, Magrathea can cater for you. We are not proud.*

And five hundred entirely naked women dropped out of the sky on parachutes.

In a moment the scene vanished and left them in a springtime meadow full of cows.

"Ow!" said Zaphod. "My brains!"

"You want to talk about it?" said Ford.

"Yeah, okay," said Zaphod, and all three sat down and ignored the scenes that came and went around them.

"I figure this," said Zaphod. "Whatever happened to my mind, I did it. And I did it in such a way that it wouldn't be detected by the Government screening tests. And I wasn't to know anything about it myself. Pretty crazy, right?"

The other two nodded in agreement.

"So I reckon, what's so secret that I can't let anybody know I know it, not the Galactic Government, not even myself? And the answer is I don't know. Obviously. But I put a few things together and I can begin to guess. When did I decide to run for President? Shortly after the death of President Yooden Vranx. You remember Yooden, Ford?"

"Yeah," said Ford, "he was that guy we met when we were kids, the Arcturan captain. He was a gas. He gave us conkers when you bust your way into his megafreighter. Said you were the most amazing kid he'd ever met."

"What's all this?" said Trillian.

"Ancient history," said Ford, "when we were kids together on Betelgeuse. The Arcturan megafreighters used to carry most of the bulky trade between the Galactic Center and the outlying regions. The Betelgeuse trading scouts used to find the markets and the Arcturans would supply them. There was a lot of trouble with space pirates before they were wiped out in the Dordellis wars, and the megafreighters had to be equipped with the most fantastic defense shields known to Galactic science. They were real brutes of ships, and huge. In orbit round a planet they would eclipse the sun.

"One day, young Zaphod here decides to raid one. On a trijet scooter designed for stratosphere work, a mere kid. I mean forget it, it was crazier than a mad monkey. I went along for the ride because I'd got some very safe money on him not doing it, and didn't want him coming back with fake evidence. So what happens? We get in his trijet which he had souped up into something totally other, crossed three parsecs in a matter of weeks, bust our way into a megafreighter I still don't know how, marched on to the bridge waving toy pistols and demanded conkers. A wilder thing I have not known. Lost me a year's pocket money. For what? Conkers."

"The captain was this really amazing guy, Yooden Vranx," said Zaphod. "He gave us food, booze—stuff from really weird parts of the Galaxy—lots of conkers, of course, and we had just the most incredible time. Then he teleported us back. Into the maximum security wing of the Betelgeuse state prison. He was a cool guy. Went on to become President of the Galaxy."

Zaphod paused.

The scene around them was currently plunged into gloom. Dark mists swirled round them and elephantine shapes lurked indistinctly in the shadows. The air was occasionally rent with the sounds of illusory beings murdering other illusory beings. Presumably enough people must have liked this sort of thing to make it a paying proposition.

"Ford," said Zaphod quietly.

"Yeah?"

"Just before Yooden died he came to see me."

"What? You never told me."

"No."

"What did he say? What did he come to see you about?"

"He told me about the Heart of Gold. It was his idea that I should steal it."

"*His* idea?"

"Yeah," said Zaphod, "and the only possible way of stealing it was to be at the launching ceremony."

Ford gaped at him in astonishment for a moment, and then roared with laughter.

"Are you telling me," he said, "that you set yourself up to become President of the Galaxy just to steal that ship?"

"That's it," said Zaphod with the sort of grin that would get most people locked away in a room with soft walls.

"But why?" said Ford. "What's so important about having it?"

"Dunno," said Zaphod. "I think if I'd consciously known what was so important about it and what I would need it for it would have showed up on the brain screening tests and I would never have passed. I think Yooden told me a lot of things that are still locked away."

"So you think you went and mucked about inside your own brain as a result of Yooden talking to you?"

"He was a hell of a talker."

"Yeah, but Zaphod, old mate, you want to look after yourself, you know."

Zaphod shrugged.

"I mean, don't you have any inkling of the reasons for all this?" asked Ford.

Zaphod thought hard about this and doubts seemed to cross his mind.

"No," he said at last, "I don't seem to be letting myself into any of my secrets. Still," he added on further reflection, "I can understand that. I wouldn't trust myself further than I could spit a rat."

A moment later, the last planet in the catalog vanished from beneath them and the solid world resolved itself again.

They were sitting in a plush waiting room full of glasstop tables and design awards.

A tall Magrathean man was standing in front of them.

"The mice will see you now," he said.

So there you have it," said Slartibartfast, making a feeble and perfunctory attempt to clear away some of the appalling mess of his study. He picked up a piece of paper from the top of a pile, but then couldn't think of anywhere else to put it, so he put it back on top of the original pile which promptly fell over. "Deep Thought designed the Earth, we built it and you lived on it."

"And the Vogons came and destroyed it five minutes before the program was completed," added Arthur, not unbitterly. "Yes," said the old man, pausing to gaze hopelessly round the room. "Ten million years of planning and work gone just like that. Ten million years, Earthman, can you conceive of that kind of time span? A galactic civilization could grow from a single worm five times over in that time. Gone." He paused. "Well, that's bureaucracy for you," he added.

"You know," said Arthur thoughtfully, "all this explains a lot of things. All through my life I've had this strange unaccountable feeling that something was going on in the world, something big, even sinister, and no one would tell me what it was."

"No," said the old man, "that's just perfectly normal paranoia. Everyone in the Universe has that."

"Everyone?" said Arthur. "Well, if everyone has that perhaps it means something! Perhaps somewhere outside the Universe we know . . ."

"Maybe. Who cares?" said Slartibartfast before Arthur got too excited. "Perhaps I'm old and tired," he continued, "but I always think that the chances of finding out what really is going on are so absurdly remote that the only thing to do is to say hang the sense of it and just keep yourself occupied. Look at me: I design coastlines. I got an award for Norway."

He rummaged around in a pile of debris and pulled out a large Plexiglas block with his name on it and a model of Norway molded into it.

"Where's the sense in that?" he said. "None that I've been able to make out. I've been doing fjords all my life. For a fleeting moment they become fashionable and I get a major award."

He turned it over in his hands with a shrug and tossed it aside carelessly, but not so carelessly that it didn't land on something soft.

"In this replacement Earth we're building they've given me Africa to do and of course I'm doing it with all fjords again because I happen to like them, and I'm old-fashioned enough to think that they give a lovely baroque feel to a continent. And they tell me it's not equatorial enough. Equatorial!" He gave a hollow laugh. "What does it matter? Science has achieved some wonderful things, of course, but I'd far rather be happy than right any day."

"And are you?"

"No. That's where it all falls down, of course."

"Pity," said Arthur with sympathy. "It sounded like quite a good life-style otherwise."

Somewhere on the wall a small white light flashed.

"Come," said Slartibartfast, "you are to meet the mice. Your arrival on the planet has caused considerable excitement. It has already been hailed, so I gather, as the third most improbable event in the history of the Universe."

"What were the first two?"

"Oh, probably just coincidences," said Slartibartfast carelessly. He opened the door and stood waiting for Arthur to follow.

Arthur glanced around him once more, and then down at himself, at the sweaty disheveled clothes he had been lying in the mud in on Thursday morning.

"I seem to be having tremendous difficulty with my life-style," he muttered to himself.

"I beg your pardon?" asked the old man mildly.

"Oh, nothing," said Arthur, "only joking."

Chapter 31

It is of course well known that careless talk costs lives, but the full scale of the problem is not always appreciated.

For instance, at the very moment that Arthur said, "I seem to be having tremendous difficulty with my life-style," a freak wormhole opened up in the fabric of the space-time continuum and carried his words far far back in time across almost infinite reaches of space to a distant Galaxy where strange and warlike beings were poised on the brink of frightful interstellar battle.

The two opposing leaders were meeting for the last time.

A dreadful silence fell across the conference table as the commander of the Vl'hurgs, resplendent in his black jeweled battle shorts, gazed levelly at the G'Gugvuntt leader squatting opposite him in a cloud of green sweet-smelling steam, and, with a million sleek and horribly beweaponed star cruisers poised to unleash electric death at his single word of command, challenged the vile creature to take back what it had said about his mother.

The creature stirred in his sickly broiling vapor, and at that very moment the words *I seem to be having tremendous difficulty with my life-style* drifted across the conference table.

Unfortunately, in the Vl'hurg tongue this was the most dreadful insult imaginable, and there was nothing for it but to wage terrible war for centuries.

Eventually, of course, after their Galaxy had been decimated over a few thousand years, it was realized that the whole thing had been a ghastly mistake, and so the two opposing battle fleets settled their few remaining differences in order to launch a joint attack on our own Galaxy—now positively identified as the source of the offending remark.

For thousands more years, the mighty ships tore across the empty wastes of space and finally dived screaming on to the first planet they came across—which happened to be the Earth—where due to a terrible miscalculation of scale the entire battle fleet was accidentally swallowed by a small dog.

Those who study the complex interplay of cause and effect in the history of the Universe say that this sort of thing is going on all the time, but that we are powerless to prevent it.

"It's just life," they say.

A short aircar trip brought Arthur and the old Magrathean to a doorway. They left the car and went through the door into a waiting room full of glass-topped tables and Plexiglas awards. Almost immediately a light flashed above the door at the other side of the room and they entered.

"Arthur! You're safe!" a voice cried.

"Am I?" said Arthur, rather startled. "Oh, good."

The lighting was rather subdued and it took him a moment or so to see Ford, Trillian and Zaphod sitting round a large table beautifully decked out with exotic dishes, strange sweetmeats and bizarre fruits. They were stuffing their faces.

"What happened to you?" demanded Arthur.

"Well," said Zaphod, attacking a boneful of grilled muscle, "our guests here have been gassing us and zapping our minds and being generally weird and have now given us a rather nice meal to make it up to us. Here," he said, hoicking out a lump of evil-smelling meat from a bowl, "have some Vegan Rhino's cutlet. It's delicious if you happen to like that sort of thing."

"Hosts?" said Arthur. "What hosts? I don't see any..."

A small voice said, "Welcome to lunch, Earth creature."

Arthur glanced around and suddenly yelped.

"Ugh!" he said. "There are mice on the table!"

There was an awkward silence as everyone looked pointedly at Arthur.

He was busy staring at two white mice sitting in what looked like whisky glasses on the table. He heard the silence and glanced around at everyone.

"Oh!" he said, with sudden realization. "Oh, I'm sorry, I wasn't quite prepared for..."

"Let me introduce you," said Trillian. "Arthur, this is Benjy mouse."

"Hi," said one of the mice. His whiskers stroked what must have been a touch sensitive panel on the inside of the whisky glasslike affair, and it moved forward slightly.

"And this is Frankie mouse."

The other mouse said, "Pleased to meet you," and did likewise.

Arthur gaped.

"But aren't they..."

"Yes," said Trillian, "they are the mice I brought with me from the Earth."

She looked him in the eye and Arthur thought he detected the tiniest resigned shrug.

"Could you pass me that bowl of grated Arcturan Mega-Donkey?" she said.

Slartibartfast coughed politely.

"Er, excuse me," he said.

"Yes, thank you, Slartibartfast," said Benjy mouse sharply, "you may go."

"What? Oh . . . er, very well," said the old man, slightly taken aback, "I'll just go and get on with some of my fjords then."

"Ah, well, in fact that won't be necessary," said Frankie mouse. "It looks very much as if we won't be needing the new Earth any longer." He swiveled his pink little eyes. "Not now that we have found a native of the planet who was there seconds before it was destroyed."

"What?" cried Slartibartfast, aghast. "You can't mean that! I've got a thousand glaciers poised and ready to roll over Africa!"

"Well, perhaps you can take a quick skiing holiday before you dismantle them," said Frankie acidly.

"Skiing holiday!" cried the old man. "Those glaciers are works of art! Elegantly sculpted contours, soaring pinnacles of ice, deep majestic ravines! It would be sacrilege to go skiing on high art!"

"Thank you, Slartibartfast," said Benjy firmly. "That will be all."

"Yes, sir," said the old man coldly, "thank you very much. Well, goodbye, Earthman," he said to Arthur, "hope the life-style comes together."

With a brief nod to the rest of the company he turned and walked sadly out of the room.

Arthur stared after him, not knowing what to say.

"Now," said Benjy mouse, "to business."

Ford and Zaphod clinked their glasses together.

"To business!" they said.

"I beg your pardon?" said Benjy.

Ford looked round.

"Sorry, I thought you were proposing a toast," he said.

The two mice scuttled impatiently around in their glass transports. Finally they composed themselves, and Benjy moved forward to address Arthur.

"Now, Earth creature," he said, "the situation we have in effect is this. We have, as you know, been more or less running your planet for the last ten million years in order to find this wretched thing called the Question to the Ultimate Answer."

"Why?" said Arthur sharply.

"No—we already thought of that one," said Frankie interrupting, "but it doesn't fit the answer. *Why? Forty-two* . . . you see, it doesn't work."

"No," said Arthur, "I mean, why have you been doing it?"

"Oh, I see," said Frankie. "Well, eventually just habit I think, to be brutally honest. And this is more or less the point—we're sick to the teeth with the whole thing, and the prospect of doing it all over again on account of those whinnet-ridden Vogons quite frankly gives me the screaming heebie-jeebies, you know what I mean? It was by the merest lucky chance that Benjy and I finished our particular job and left the planet early for a quick holiday, and have since manipulated our way back to Magrathea by the good offices of your friends."

"Magrathea is a gateway back to our own dimension," put in Benjy.

"Since then," continued his murine colleague, "we have had an offer of a quite enormously fat contract to do the 5D chat show and lecture circuit back in our own dimensional neck of the woods, and we're very much inclined to take it."

"I would, wouldn't you, Ford?" said Zaphod promptingly.

"Oh yes," said Ford, "jump at it, like a shot."

Arthur glanced at them, wondering what all this was leading up to.

"But we've got to have *product*, you see," said Frankie. "I mean, ideally we still need the Question to the Ultimate Answer in some form or other."

Zaphod leaned forward to Arthur.

"You see," he said, "if they're just sitting there in the studio looking very relaxed and, you know, just mentioning that they happen to know the Answer to Life, the Universe and Everything, and then eventually have to admit that in fact it's Forty-two, then the show's probably quite short. No follow-up, you see."

"We have to have something that *sounds* good," said Benjy.

"Something that *sounds* good?" exclaimed Arthur. "A Question to the Ultimate Answer that *sounds* good? From a couple of mice?"

The mice bristled.

"Well, I mean, *yes* idealism, *yes* the dignity of pure research, *yes* the pursuit of truth in all its forms, but there comes a point I'm afraid where you begin to suspect that if there's any *real* truth, it's that the entire multidimensional infinity of the Universe is almost certainly being run by a bunch of maniacs. And if it comes to a choice between spending yet another ten million years finding that out, and on the other hand just taking the money and running, then I for one could do with the exercise," said Frankie.

"But . . ." started Arthur, hopelessly.

"Hey, will you get this, Earthman," interrupted Zaphod. "You are a last generation product of that computer matrix, right, and you were there right up to the moment your planet got the finger, yeah?"

"Er . . ."

"So your brain was an organic part of the penultimate configuration of the computer program," said Ford, rather lucidly he thought.

"Right?" said Zaphod.

"Well," said Arthur doubtfully. He wasn't aware of ever having felt an organic part of anything. He had always seen this as one of his problems.

"In other words," said Benjy, steering his curious little vehicle right over to Arthur, "there's a good chance that the structure of the question is encoded in the structure of your brain—so we want to buy it off you."

"What, the question?" said Arthur.

"Yes," said Ford and Trillian.

"For lots of money," said Zaphod.

"No, no," said Frankie, "it's the brain we want to buy."

"What!"

"Well, who would miss it?" inquired Benjy.

"I thought you said you could just read his brain electronically," protested Ford.

"Oh yes," said Frankie, "but we'd have to get it out first. It's got to be prepared."

"Treated," said Benjy.

"Diced."

"Thank you," shouted Arthur, tipping up his chair and backing away from the table in horror.

"It could always be replaced," said Benjy reasonably, "if you think it's important."

"Yes, an electronic brain," said Frankie, "a simple one would suffice."

"A simple one!" wailed Arthur.

"Yeah," said Zaphod with a sudden evil grin, "you'd just have to program it to say *What?* and *I don't understand* and *Where's the tea?* Who'd know the difference?"

"What?" cried Arthur, backing away still farther.

"See what I mean?" said Zaphod, and howled with pain because of something that Trillian did at that moment.

"*I'd* notice the difference," said Arthur.

"No, you wouldn't," said Frankie mouse, "you'd be programmed not to."

Ford made for the door.

"Look, I'm sorry, mice, old lads," he said. "I don't think we've got a deal."

"I rather think we have to have a deal," said the mice in chorus, all the charm vanishing from their piping little voices in an instant. With a tiny whining shriek their two glass transports lifted themselves off the table, and swung through the air toward Arthur, who stumbled farther backward into a blind corner, utterly unable to cope or think of anything.

Trillian grabbed him desperately by the arm and tried to drag him toward the door, which Ford and Zaphod were struggling to open, but Arthur was deadweight—he seemed hypnotized by the airborne rodents swooping toward him.

She screamed at him, but he just gaped.

With one more yank, Ford and Zaphod got the door open. On the other side of it was a small pack of rather ugly men who they could only assume were the heavy mob of Magrathea. Not only were they ugly themselves, but the medical equipment they carried with them was also far from pretty. They charged.

So—Arthur was about to have his head cut open, Trillian was unable to help him and Ford and Zaphod were about to be set upon by several thugs a great deal heavier and more sharply armed than they were.

All in all it was extremely fortunate that at that moment every alarm on the planet burst into an ear-splitting din.

E*mergency! Emergency!"* blared the klaxons throughout Magrathea. *"Hostile ship has landed on planet. Armed intruders in section 8A. Defense stations, defense stations!"*

The two mice sniffed irritably round the fragments of their glass transports where they lay shattered on the floor. "Damnation," muttered Frankie mouse, "all that fuss over two pounds of Earthling brain." He scuttled round and about, his pink eyes flashing, his fine white coat bristling with static. "The only thing we can do now," said Benjy, crouching and stroking his whiskers in thought, "is to try and fake a question, invent one that will sound plausible."

"Difficult," said Frankie. He thought. "How about *What's yellow and dangerous?*"

Benjy considered this for a moment.

"No, no good," he said. "Doesn't fit the answer."

They sank into silence for a few seconds.

"All right," said Benjy. *"What do you get if you multiply six by seven?"*

"No, no, too literal, too factual," said Frankie, "wouldn't sustain the punters' interest."

Again they thought.

Then Frankie said, "Here's a thought. *How many roads must a man walk down?*"

"Ah!" said Benjy. "Aha, now that does sound promising!" He rolled the phrase around a little. "Yes," he said, "that's excellent! Sounds very significant without actually tying you down to meaning anything at all. *How many roads must a man walk down? Forty-two.* Excellent, excellent, that'll fox 'em. Frankie, baby, we are made!"

They performed a scampering dance in their excitement.

Near them on the floor lay several rather ugly men who had been hit about the head with some heavy design awards.

Half a mile away, four figures pounded up a corridor looking for a way out. They emerged into a wide open-plan computer bay. They glanced about wildly.

"Which way you reckon, Zaphod?" said Ford.

"At a wild guess, I'd say down here," said Zaphod, running off down to the right between a computer bank and the wall. As the others started after him he was brought up short by a Kill-O-Zap energy bolt that cracked through the air inches in front of him and fried a small section of adjacent wall.

A voice on a bullhorn said, "Okay, Beeblebrox, hold it right there. We've got you covered."

"Cops!" hissed Zaphod, and spun around in a crouch. "You want to try a guess at all, Ford?"

"Okay, this way," said Ford, and the four of them ran down a gangway between two computer banks.

At the end of the gangway appeared a heavily armored and space-suited figure waving a vicious Kill-O-Zap gun.

"We don't want to shoot you, Beeblebrox!" shouted the figure.

"Suits me fine!" shouted Zaphod back, and dived down a wide gap between two data process units.

The others swerved in behind him.

"There are two of them," said Trillian. "We're cornered."

They squeezed themselves down in an angle between a large computer data bank and the wall.

They held their breath and waited.

Suddenly the air exploded with energy bolts as both the cops opened fire on them simultaneously.

"Hey, they're shooting at us," said Arthur, crouching in a tight ball. "I thought they said they didn't want to do that."

"Yeah, I thought they said that," agreed Ford.

Zaphod stuck a head up for a dangerous moment.

"Hey," he said, "I thought you said you didn't want to shoot us!" and ducked again.

They waited.

After a moment a voice replied, "It isn't easy being a cop!"

"What did he say?" whispered Ford in astonishment.

"He said it isn't easy being a cop."

"Well, surely that's his problem, isn't it?"

"I'd have thought so."

Ford shouted out, "Hey, listen! I think we've got enough problems of our own having you shooting at us, so if you could avoid laying *your* problems on us as well, I think we'd all find it easier to cope!"

Another pause, and then the bullhorn again.

"Now see here, guy," said the voice, "you're not dealing with any dumb two-bit trigger-pumping morons with low hairlines, little piggy eyes and no conversation, we're a couple of intelligent caring guys that you'd probably quite like if you met us socially! I don't go around gratuitously shooting people and then bragging about it afterward in seedy space-rangers bars, like some cops I could mention! I go around shooting people gratuitously and then I agonize about it afterward for hours to my girlfriend!"

"And I write novels!" chimed in the other cop. "Though I haven't had any of them published yet, so I better warn you, I'm in a *meeeean* mood!"

Ford's eyes popped halfway out of their sockets. "Who are these guys?" he said.

"Dunno," said Zaphod, "I think I preferred it when they were shooting."

"So are you going to come quietly," shouted one of the cops again, "or are you going to let us blast you out?"

"Which would you prefer?" shouted Ford.

A millisecond later the air about them started to fry again, as bolt after bolt of Kill-O-Zap hurled itself into the computer bank in front of them.

The fusillade continued for several seconds at unbearable intensity.

When it stopped, there were a few seconds of near-quietness as the echoes died away.

"You still there?" called one of the cops.

"Yes," they called back.

"We didn't enjoy doing that at all," shouted the other cop.

"We could tell," shouted Ford.

"Now, listen to this, Beeblebrox, and you better listen good!"

"Why?" shouted back Zaphod.

"Because," shouted the cop, "it's going to be very intelligent, and quite interesting and humane! Now—either you all give yourselves up now and let us beat you up a bit, though not very much of course because we are firmly opposed to needless violence, or we blow up this entire planet and possibly one or two others we noticed on our way out here!"

"But that's crazy!" cried Trillian. "You wouldn't do that!"

"Oh yes, we would," shouted the cop, "wouldn't we?" he asked the other one.

"Oh yes, we'd have to, no question," the other one called back.

"But why?" demanded Trillian.

"Because there are some things you have to do even if you are an enlightened liberal cop who knows all about sensitivity and everything!"

"I just don't believe these guys," muttered Ford, shaking his head.

One cop shouted to the other, "Shall we shoot them again for a bit?"

"Yeah, why not?"

They let fly another electric barrage.

The heat and noise was quite fantastic. Slowly, the computer bank was beginning to disintegrate. The front had almost all melted away, and thick rivulets of molten metal were winding their way back toward where they were squatting. They huddled farther back and waited for the end.

Chapter 33

But the end never came, at least not then.

Quite suddenly the barrage stopped, and the sudden silence afterward was punctuated by a couple of strangled gurgles and thuds.

The four stared at each other.

"What happened?" said Arthur.

"They stopped," said Zaphod with a shrug.

"Why?"

"Dunno, do you want to go and ask them?"

"No."

They waited.

"Hello?" called out Ford.

No answer.

"That's odd."

"Perhaps it's a trap."

"They haven't the wit."

"What were those thuds?"

"Dunno."

They waited for a few more seconds.

"Right," said Ford, "I'm going to have a look."

He glanced round at the others.

"Is no one going to say, *No, you can't possibly, let me go instead?*"

They all shook their heads.

"Oh well," he said, and stood up.

For a moment, nothing happened.

Then, after a second or so, nothing continued to happen. Ford peered through the thick smoke that was billowing out of the burning computer.

Cautiously he stepped out into the open.

Still nothing happened.

Twenty yards away he could dimly see through the smoke the space-suited figure of one of the cops. He was lying in a crumpled heap on the ground. Twenty yards in the other direction lay the second man. No one else was anywhere to be seen.

This struck Ford as being extremely odd.

Slowly, nervously, he walked toward the first one. The body lay reassuringly still as he approached it, and continued to lie reassuringly still as he reached it and put his foot down on the Kill-O-Zap gun that still dangled from its limp fingers.

He reached down and picked it up, meeting no resistance.

The cop was quite clearly dead.

A quick examination revealed him to be from Blagulon Kappa—he was a methane-breathing life form, dependent on his space suit for survival in the thin oxygen atmosphere of Magrathea.

The tiny life-support system computer on his backpack appeared unexpectedly to have blown up.

Ford poked around in it in considerable astonishment. These miniature suit computers usually had the full back-up of the main computer back on the ship, with which they were directly linked through the sub-etha. Such a system was fail-safe in all circumstances other than total feedback malfunction, which was unheard of.

He hurried over to the prone figure, and discovered that exactly the same impossible thing had happened to him, presumably simultaneously.

He called the others over to look. They came, shared his astonishment, but not his curiosity.

"Let's get shot of this hole," said Zaphod. "If whatever I'm supposed to be looking for is here, I don't want it." He grabbed the second Kill-O-Zap gun, blasted a perfectly harmless accounting computer and rushed out into the corridor, followed by the others. He very nearly blasted hell out of an aircar that stood waiting for them a few yards away. The aircar was empty, but Arthur recognized it as belonging to Slartibartfast.

It had a note from him pinned to part of its sparse instrument panel. The note had an arrow drawn on it, pointing at one of the controls.

It said, *This is probably the best button to press.*

Chapter 34

The aircar rocketed them at speeds in excess of R17 through the steel tunnels that led out on to the appalling surface of the planet which was now in the grip of yet another drear morning twilight. Ghastly gray light congealed on the land.

R is a velocity measure, defined as a reasonable speed of travel that is consistent with health, mental well-being and not being more than, say, five minutes late. It is therefore clearly an almost infinitely variable figure according to circumstances, since the first two factors vary not only with speed taken as an absolute, but also with awareness of the third factor. Unless handled with tranquility this equation can result in considerable stress, ulcers and even death.

R17 is not a fixed velocity, but it is clearly far too fast.

The aircar flung itself through the air at R17 and above, deposited them next to the Heart of Gold which stood starkly on the frozen ground like a bleached bone, and then precipitately hurled itself back in the direction whence they had come, presumably on important business of its own.

Shivering, the four of them stood and looked at the ship.

Beside it stood another one.

It was the Blagulon Kappa policecraft, a bulbous sharklike affair, slate-green in color and smothered with black stenciled letters of varying degrees of size and unfriendliness. The letters informed anyone who cared to read them as to where the ship was from, what section of the police it was assigned to, and where the power feeds should be connected.

It seemed somehow unnaturally dark and silent, even for a ship whose two-man crew was at that moment lying asphyxiated in a smoke-filled chamber several miles beneath the ground. It is one of those curious things that is impossible to explain or define, but one can sense when a ship is completely dead.

Ford could sense it and found it most mysterious—a ship and two policemen seemed to have gone spontaneously dead. In his experience the Universe simply didn't work like that.

The other three could sense it too, but they could sense the bitter cold even more and hurried back into the Heart of Gold suffering from an acute attack of no curiosity.

Ford stayed, and went to examine the Blagulon ship. As he walked, he nearly tripped over an inert steel figure lying face down in the cold dust.

"Marvin!" he exclaimed. "What are you doing?"

"Don't feel you have to take any notice of me, please," came a muffled drone.

"But how are you, metalman?" said Ford.

"Very depressed."

"What's up?"

"I don't know," said Marvin, "I've never been there."

"Why," said Ford squatting down beside him and shivering, "are you lying face down in the dust?"

"It's a very effective way of being wretched," said Marvin. "Don't pretend you want to talk to me, I know you hate me."

"No, I don't."

"Yes, you do, everybody does. It's part of the shape of the Universe. I only have to talk to somebody and they begin to hate me. Even robots hate me. If you just ignore me I expect I shall probably go away."

He jacked himself up to his feet and stood resolutely facing the opposite direction.

"That ship hated me," he said dejectedly, indicating the policecraft.

"That ship?" said Ford in sudden excitement. "What happened to it? Do you know?"

"It hated me because I talked to it."

"You *talked* to it?" exclaimed Ford. "What do you mean you talked to it?"

"Simple. I got very bored and depressed, so I went and plugged myself in to its external computer feed. I talked to the computer at great length and explained my view of the Universe to it," said Marvin.

"And what happened?" pressed Ford.

"It committed suicide," said Marvin, and stalked off back to the Heart of Gold.

Chapter 35

That night, as the Heart of Gold was busy putting a few light-years between itself and the Horsehead Nebula, Zaphod lounged under the small palm tree on the bridge trying to bang his brain into shape with massive Pan Galactic Gargle Blasters; Ford and Trillian sat in a corner discussing life and matters arising from it; and Arthur took to his bed to flip through Ford's copy of *The Hitchhiker's Guide to the Galaxy*. Since he was going to have to live in the place, he reasoned, he'd better start finding out something about it.

He came across this entry.

It said: *"The History of every major Galactic Civilization tends to pass through three distinct and recognizable phases, those of Survival, Inquiry and Sophistication, otherwise known as the How, Why and Where phases.*

"For instance, the first phase is characterized by the question How can we eat? *the second by the question* Why do we eat? *and the third by the question* Where shall we have lunch?"

He got no further before the ship's intercom buzzed into life.

"Hey, Earthman? You hungry, kid?" said Zaphod's voice.

"Er, well, yes, a little peckish, I suppose," said Arthur.

"Okay, baby, hold tight," said Zaphod. "We'll take in a quick bite at the Restaurant at the End of the Universe."

The Restaurant at the End of the Universe

To Jane and James

with many thanks
    to Geoffrey Perkins for achieving the Improbable
    to Paddy Kingsland, Lisa Braun and Alick Hale Munro for helping him
    to John Lloyd for his help with the original Milliways script
    to Simon Brett for starting the whole thing off

to the Paul Simon album *One Trick Pony* which I played incessantly while writing this book. Five years is far too long

And with very special thanks to Jacqui Graham for infinite patience, kindness and food in adversity

There is a theory which states that if ever anyone discovers exactly what the Universe is for and why it is here, it will instantly disappear and be replaced by something even more bizarre and inexplicable.

There is another which states that this has already happened.

Chapter 1

The story so far:

In the beginning the Universe was created.

This has made a lot of people very angry and been widely regarded as a bad move.

Many races believe that it was created by some sort of god, though the Jatravartid people of Viltvodle VI believe that the entire Universe was in fact sneezed out of the nose of a being called the Great Green Arkleseizure.

The Jatravartids, who live in perpetual fear of the time they call The Coming of the Great White Handkerchief, are small blue creatures with more than fifty arms each, who are therefore unique in being the only race in history to have invented the aerosol deodorant before the wheel.

However, the Great Green Arkleseizure Theory is not widely accepted outside Viltvodle VI and so, the Universe being the puzzling place it is, other explanations are constantly being sought.

For instance, a race of hyperintelligent pan-dimensional beings once built themselves a gigantic supercomputer called Deep Thought to calculate once and for all the Question to the Ultimate Answer of Life, the Universe and Everything.

For seven and a half million years, Deep Thought computed and calculated, and in the end announced that the answer was in fact Forty-two—and so another, even bigger, computer had to be built to find out what the actual question was.

And this computer, which was called the Earth, was so large that it was frequently mistaken for a planet—especially by the strange apelike beings who roamed its surface, totally unaware that they were simply part of a gigantic computer program.

And this is very odd, because without that fairly simple and obvious piece of knowledge, nothing that ever happened on the Earth could possibly make the slightest bit of sense.

Sadly, however, just before the critical moment of read-out, the Earth was unexpectedly demolished by the Vogons to make way—so they claimed—for a new hyperspace bypass, and so all hope of discovering a meaning for life was lost for ever.

Or so it would seem.

Two of these strange, apelike creatures survived.

Arthur Dent escaped at the very last moment because an old friend of his, Ford Prefect, suddenly turned out to be from a small planet somewhere in the vicinity of Betelgeuse and not from Guildford as he had hitherto claimed; and, more to the point, he knew how to hitch rides on flying saucers.

Tricia McMillan—or Trillian—had skipped the planet six months earlier with Zaphod Beeblebrox, the then President of the Galaxy.

Two survivors.

They are all that remains of the greatest experiment ever conducted—to find the Ultimate Question and the Ultimate Answer of Life, the Universe and Everything.

And, less than half a million miles from where their starship is drifting lazily through the inky blackness of space, a Vogon ship is moving slowly toward them.

Like all Vogon ships it looked as if it had been not so much designed as congealed. The unpleasant yellow lumps and edifices which protruded from it at unsightly angles would have disfigured the looks of most ships, but in this case that was sadly impossible. Uglier things have been spotted in the skies, but not by reliable witnesses.

In fact to see anything much uglier than a Vogon ship you would have to go inside it and look at a Vogon. If you are wise, however, this is precisely what you will avoid doing because the average Vogon will not think twice before doing something so pointlessly hideous to you that you will wish you had never been born—or (if you are a clearer minded thinker) that the Vogon had never been born.

In fact, the average Vogon probably wouldn't even think once. They are simple-minded, thick-willed, slug-brained creatures, and thinking is not really something they are cut out for. Anatomical analysis of the Vogon reveals that its brain was originally a badly deformed, misplaced and dyspeptic liver. The fairest thing you can say about them, then, is that they know what they like, and what they like generally involves hurting people and, wherever possible, getting very angry.

One thing they don't like is leaving a job unfinished—particularly this Vogon, and particularly—for various reasons—this job.

This Vogon was Captain Prostetnic Vogon Jeltz of the Galactic Hyperspace Planning Council, and he it was who had had the job of demolishing the so-called "planet" Earth.

He heaved his monumentally vile body round in his ill-fitting, slimy seat and stared at the monitor screen on which the starship *Heart of Gold* was being systematically scanned.

It mattered little to him that the *Heart of Gold*, with its Infinite Improbability Drive, was the most beautiful and revolutionary ship ever built. Aesthetics and technology were closed books to him and, had he had his way, burned and buried books as well.

It mattered even less to him that Zaphod Beeblebrox was aboard. Zaphod Beeblebrox was now the ex-President of the Galaxy, and though every police force in the Galaxy was currently pursuing both him and this ship he had stolen, the Vogon was not interested.

He had other fish to fry.

It has been said that Vogons are not above a little bribery and corruption in the same way that the sea is not above the clouds, and this was certainly true in his case. When he heard the words *integrity* or *moral rectitude* he reached for his dictionary, and when he heard the chink of ready money in large quantities he reached for the rule book and threw it away.

In seeking so implacably the destruction of the Earth and all that therein lay he was moving somewhat above and beyond the call of his professional duty. There was even some doubt as to whether the said bypass was actually going to be built, but the matter had been glossed over.

He grunted a repellent grunt of satisfaction.

"Computer," he croaked, "get me my brain care specialist on the line."

Within a few seconds the face of Gag Halfrunt appeared on the screen, smiling the smile of a man who knew he was ten light-years away from the Vogon face he was looking at. Mixed up somewhere in the smile was a glint of irony too. Though the Vogon persistently referred to him as "my private brain care specialist" there was not a lot of brain to take care of, and it was in fact Halfrunt who was employing the Vogon. He was paying him an awful lot of money to do some very dirty work. As one of the Galaxy's most prominent and successful psychiatrists, he and a consortium of his colleagues were quite prepared to spend an awful lot of money when it seemed that the entire future of psychiatry might be at stake.

"Well," he said, "hello my Captain of Vogons Prostetnic, and how are we feeling today?"

The Vogon Captain told him that in the last few hours he had wiped out nearly half his crew in a disciplinary exercise.

Halfrunt's smile did not flicker for an instant.

"Well," he said, "I think this is perfectly normal behavior for a Vogon, you know? The natural and healthy channeling of the aggressive instincts into acts of senseless violence."

"That," rumbled the Vogon, "is what you always say."

"Well again," said Halfrunt, "I think that this is perfectly normal behavior for a psychiatrist. Good. We are clearly both very well adjusted in our mental attitudes today. Now tell me, what news of the mission?"

"We have located the ship."

"Wonderful," said Halfrunt, "wonderful! And the occupants?"

"The Earthman is there."

"Excellent! And . . . ?"

"A female from the same planet. They are the last."

"Good, good," beamed Halfrunt. "Who else?"

"The man Prefect."

"Yes?"

"And Zaphod Beeblebrox."

For an instant Halfrunt's smile flickered.

"Ah, yes," he said, "I had been expecting this. It is most regrettable."

"A personal friend?" inquired the Vogon, who had heard the expression somewhere once and decided to try it out.

"Ah, no," said Halfrunt, "in my profession you know, we do not make personal friends."

"Ah," grunted the Vogon, "professional detachment."

"No," said Halfrunt cheerfully, "we just don't have the knack."

He paused. His mouth continued to smile, but his eyes frowned slightly.

"But Beeblebrox, you know," he said, "he is one of my most profitable clients. He has personality problems beyond the dreams of analysts."

He toyed with this thought a little before reluctantly dismissing it.

"Still," he said, "you are ready for your task?"

"Yes."

"Good. Destroy the ship immediately."

"What about Beeblebrox?"

"Well," said Halfrunt brightly, "Zaphod's just this guy, you know?"

He vanished from the screen.

The Vogon Captain pressed a communicator button which connected him with the remains of his crew.

"Attack," he said.

At that precise moment Zaphod Beeblebrox was in his cabin swearing very loudly. Two hours ago, he had said that they would go for a quick bite at the Restaurant at the End of the Universe, whereupon he had had a blazing row with the ship's computer and stormed off to his cabin shouting that he would work out the Improbability factors with a pencil.

The *Heart of Gold*'s Improbability Drive made it the most powerful and unpredictable ship in existence. There was nothing it couldn't do, provided you knew exactly how improbable it was that the thing you wanted it to do would even happen.

He had stolen it when, as President, he was meant to be launching it. He didn't know exactly why he had stolen it, except that he liked it.

He didn't know why he had become President of the Galaxy, except that it seemed a fun thing to be.

He did know that there were better reasons than these, but that they were buried in a dark, locked off section of his two brains. He wished the dark, locked off section of his two brains would go away because they occasionally surfaced momentarily and put strange thoughts into the light, fun sections of his mind and tried to deflect him from what he saw as being the basic business of his life, which was to have a wonderfully good time.

At the moment he was not having a wonderfully good time. He had run out of patience and pencils and was feeling very hungry.

"Starpox!" he shouted.

At that same precise moment, Ford Prefect was in midair. This was not because of anything wrong with the ship's artificial gravity field, but because he was leaping down the stairwell which led to the ship's personal cabins. It was a very high jump to do in one bound and he landed awkwardly, stumbled, recovered, raced down the corridor sending a couple of miniature service robots flying, skidded around the corner, burst into Zaphod's door and explained what was on his mind.

"Vogons," he said.

A short while before this, Arthur Dent had set out from his cabin in search of a cup of tea. It was not a quest he embarked upon with a great deal of optimism, because he knew that the only source of hot drinks on the entire ship was a benighted piece of equipment produced by the Sirius Cybernetics Corporation. It was called a Nutri-Matic Drinks Synthesizer, and he had encountered it before.

It claimed to produce the widest possible range of drinks personally matched to the tastes and metabolism of whoever cared to use it. When put to the test, however, it invariably produced a plastic cup filled with a liquid which was almost, but not quite, entirely unlike tea.

He attempted to reason with the thing.

"Tea," he said.

"Share and Enjoy," the machine replied and provided him with yet another cup of the sickly liquid.

He threw it away.

"Share and Enjoy," the machine repeated and produced another one.

"Share and Enjoy" is the company motto of the hugely successful Sirius Cybernetics Corporation Complaints Division, which now covers the major land masses of three medium-sized planets and is the only part of the Corporation to have shown a consistent profit in recent years.

The motto stands—or rather stood—in three mile high illuminated letters near the Complaints Department spaceport on Eadrax. Unfortunately its weight was such that shortly after it was erected, the ground beneath the letters caved in and they dropped for nearly half their length through the offices of many talented young Complaints executives—now deceased.

The protruding upper halves of the letters now appear, in the local language, to read "Go stick your head in a pig," and are no longer illuminated, except at times of special celebration.

Arthur threw away a sixth cup of the liquid.

"Listen, you machine," he said, "you claim you can synthesize any drink in existence, so why do you keep giving me the same undrinkable stuff?"

"Nutrition and pleasurable sense data," burbled the machine. "Share and Enjoy."

"It tastes filthy!"

"If you have enjoyed the experience of this drink," continued the machine, "why not share it with your friends?"

"Because," said Arthur tartly, "I want to keep them. Will you try to comprehend what I'm telling you? That drink..."

"That drink," said the machine sweetly, "was individually tailored to meet your personal requirements for nutrition and pleasure."

"Ah," said Arthur, "so I'm a masochist on a diet am I?"

"Share and Enjoy."

"Oh, shut up."

"Will that be all?"

Arthur decided to give up.

"Yes," he said.

Then he decided he'd be damned if he'd give up.

"No," he said, "look, it's very, very simple... all I want... is a cup of tea. You are going to make one for me. Keep quiet and listen."

And he sat. He told the Nutri-Matic about India, he told it about China, he told it about Ceylon. He told it about broad leaves drying in the sun. He told it about silver teapots. He told it about summer afternoons on the lawn. He told it about putting in the milk before the tea so it wouldn't get scalded. He even told it (briefly) about the history of the East India Company.

"So that's it, is it?" said the Nutri-Matic when he had finished.

"Yes," said Arthur, "that is what I want."

"You want the taste of dried leaves boiled in water?"

"Er, yes. With milk."

"Squirted out of a cow?"

"Well, in a manner of speaking I suppose..."

"I'm going to need some help with this one," said the machine tersely. All the cheerful burbling had dropped out of its voice and it now meant business.

"Well, anything I can do," said Arthur.

"You've done quite enough," the Nutri-Matic informed him.

It summoned up the ship's computer.

"Hi there!" said the ship's computer.

The Nutri-Matic explained about tea to the ship's computer. The computer boggled, linked logic circuits with the Nutri-Matic and together they lapsed into a grim silence.

Arthur watched and waited for a while, but nothing further happened.

He thumped it, but still nothing happened.

Eventually he gave up and wandered up to the bridge.

In the empty wastes of space, the *Heart of Gold* hung still. Around it blazed the billion pinpricks of the Galaxy. Towards it crept the ugly yellow lump of the Vogon ship.

Does anyone have a kettle?" Arthur asked as he walked on to the bridge, and instantly began to wonder why Trillian was yelling at the computer to talk to her, Ford was thumping it and Zaphod was kicking it, and also why there was a nasty yellow lump on the vision screen.

He put down the empty cup he was carrying and walked over to them. "Hello?" he said.

At that moment Zaphod flung himself over to the polished marble surfaces that contained the instruments that controlled the conventional photon drive. They materialized beneath his hands and he flipped over to manual control. He pushed, he pulled, he pressed and he swore. The photon drive gave a sickly shudder and cut out again.

"Something up?" said Arthur.

"Hey, didja hear that?" muttered Zaphod as he leaped now for the manual controls on the Infinite Improbability Drive, "the monkey spoke!"

The Improbability Drive gave two small whines and then also cut out.

"Pure history, man," said Zaphod, kicking the Improbability Drive, "a talking monkey!"

"If you're upset about something..." said Arthur.

"Vogons!" snapped Ford. "We're under attack!"

Arthur gibbered.

"Well, what are you doing? Let's get out of here!"

"Can't. Computer's jammed."

"Jammed?"

"It says all its circuits are occupied. There's no power anywhere in the ship."

Ford moved away from the computer terminal, wiped a sleeve across his forehead and slumped back against the wall.

"Nothing we can do," he said. He glared at nothing and bit his lip.

When Arthur had been a boy at school, long before the Earth had been demolished, he had used to play football. He had not been at all good at it, and his particular speciality had been scoring own goals in important matches. Whenever this happened he used to experience a peculiar tingling round the back of his neck that would slowly creep up across his cheeks and heat his brow. The image of mud and grass and lots of little jeering boys flinging it at him suddenly came vividly to his mind at this moment.

A peculiar tingling sensation at the back of his neck was creeping up across his cheeks and heating his brow.

He started to speak, and stopped.

He started to speak again and stopped again.

Finally he managed to speak.

"Er," he said. He cleared his throat.

"Tell me," he continued, and said it so nervously that the others all turned to stare at him. He glanced at the approaching yellow blob on the vision screen.

"Tell me," he said again, "did the computer say what was occupying it? I just ask out of interest...."

Their eyes were riveted on him.

"And, er...well, that's it really, just asking."

Zaphod put out a hand and held Arthur by the scruff of the neck.

"What have you done to it, Monkeyman?" he breathed.

"Well," said Arthur, "nothing in fact. It's just that I think a short while ago it was trying to work out how to..."

"Yes?"

"Make some tea."

"That's right, guys," the computer sang out suddenly, "just coping with that problem right now, and wow, it's a biggy. Be with you in a while." It lapsed back into a silence that was only matched for sheer intensity by the silence of the three people staring at Arthur Dent.

As if to relieve the tension, the Vogons chose that moment to start firing.

The ship shook, the ship thundered. Outside, the inch thick force shield around it blistered, crackled and spat under the barrage of a dozen 30-Megahurt Definit-Kil Photrazon Cannon, and looked as if it wouldn't be around for long. Four minutes is how long Ford Prefect gave it.

"Three minutes and fifty seconds," he said a short while later.

"Forty-five seconds," he added at the appropriate time. He flicked idly at some useless switches, then gave Arthur an unfriendly look.

"Dying for a cup of tea, eh?" he said. "Three minutes and forty seconds."

"Will you stop counting!" snarled Zaphod.

"Yes," said Ford Prefect, "in three minutes and thirty-five seconds."

Aboard the Vogon ship, Prostetnic Vogon Jeltz was puzzled. He had expected a chase, he had expected an exciting grapple with tractor beams, he had expected to have to use the specially installed Sub-Cyclic Normality Assert-i-Tron to counter the *Heart of Gold*'s Infinite Improbability Drive; but the Sub-Cyclic Normality Assert-i-Tron lay idle as the *Heart of Gold* just sat there and took it.

A dozen 30-Megahurt Definit-Kil Photrazon Cannon continued to blaze away at the *Heart of Gold*, and still it just sat there and took it.

He tested every sensor at his disposal to see if there was any subtle trickery afoot, but no subtle trickery was to be found.

He didn't know about the tea of course.

Nor did he know exactly how the occupants of the *Heart of Gold* were spending the last three minutes and thirty seconds of life they had left to spend.

Quite how Zaphod Beeblebrox arrived at the idea of holding a seance at this point is something he was never quite clear on.

Obviously the subject of death was in the air, but more as something to be avoided than harped upon.

Possibly the horror that Zaphod experienced at the prospect of being reunited with his deceased relatives led on to the thought that they might just feel the same way about him and, what's more, be able to do something about helping to postpone this reunion.

Or again it might just have been one of the strange promptings that occasionally surfaced from that dark area of his mind that he had inexplicably locked off prior to becoming President of the Galaxy.

"You want to talk to your great-grandfather?" boggled Ford.

"Yeah."

"Does it have to be *now*?"

The ship continued to shake and thunder. The temperature was rising. The light was getting dimmer—all the energy the computer didn't require for thinking about tea was being pumped into the rapidly fading force field.

"Yeah!" insisted Zaphod. "Listen, Ford, I think he may be able to help us."

"Are you sure you mean *think*? Pick your words with care."

"Suggest something else we can do."

"Er, well..."

"Okay, round the central console. Now. Come on! Trillian, Monkey-man, move."

They clustered round the central console in confusion, sat down and, feeling exceptionally foolish, held hands. With his third hand Zaphod turned off the lights.

Darkness gripped the ship.

Outside, the thunderous roar of the Definit-Kil Cannon continued to rip at the force field.

"Concentrate," hissed Zaphod, "on his name."

"What is it?" asked Arthur.

"Zaphod Beeblebrox the Fourth."

"What?"

"Zaphod Beeblebrox the Fourth. Concentrate!"

"The Fourth?"

"Yeah. Listen, I'm Zaphod Beeblebrox, my father was Zaphod Beeblebrox the Second, my grandfather Zaphod Beeblebrox the Third..."

"What?"

"There was an accident with a contraceptive and a time machine. Now concentrate!"

"Three minutes," said Ford Prefect.

"Why," said Arthur Dent, "are we doing this?"

"Shut up," suggested Zaphod Beeblebrox.

Trillian said nothing. What, she thought, was there to say?

The only light on the bridge came from two dim red triangles in a far corner where Marvin the Paranoid Android sat slumped, ignoring all and ignored by all, in a private and rather unpleasant world of his own.

Round the central console four figures hunched in tight concentration trying to blot from their minds the terrifying shuddering of the ship and the fearful roar that echoed through it.

They concentrated.

Still they concentrated.

And still they concentrated.

The seconds ticked by.

On Zaphod's brows stood beads of sweat, first of concentration, then of frustration and finally of embarrassment.

At last he let out a cry of anger, snatched back his hands from Trillian and Ford and stabbed at the light switch.

"Ah, I was beginning to think you'd never turn the lights on," said a voice. "No, not too bright please, my eyes aren't what they once were."

Four figures jolted upright in their seats. Slowly they turned their heads to look, though their scalps showed a distinct propensity to try and stay in the same place.

"Now. Who disturbs me at this time?" said the small, bent, gaunt figure standing by the sprays of fern at the far end of the bridge. His two small wispy-haired heads looked so ancient that it seemed they might hold dim memories of the birth of the galaxies themselves. One lolled in sleep, the other squinted sharply at them. If his eyes weren't what they once were, they must once have been diamond cutters.

Zaphod stuttered nervously for a moment. He gave the intricate little double nod which is the traditional Betelgeusian gesture of familial respect.

"Oh . . . er, hi Great-granddad . . ." he breathed.

The little old figure moved closer toward them. He peered through the dim light. He thrust out a bony finger at his great grandson.

"Ah," he snapped, "Zaphod Beeblebrox. The last of our great line. Zaphod Beeblebrox the Nothingth."

"The First."

"The Nothingth," spat the figure. Zaphod hated his voice. It always seemed to him to screech like fingernails across the blackboard of what he liked to think of as his soul.

He shifted awkwardly in his seat.

"Er, yeah," he muttered. "Er, look, I'm really sorry about the flowers, I meant to send them along, but you know, the shop was fresh out of wreaths and . . ."

"You forgot!" snapped Zaphod Beeblebrox the Fourth.

"Well . . ."

"Too busy. Never think of other people. The living are all the same."

"Two minutes, Zaphod," whispered Ford in an awed whisper.

Zaphod fidgeted nervously.

"Yeah, but I did mean to send them," he said. "And I'll write to my great-grandmother as well, just as soon as we get out of this. . . ."

"Your great-grandmother," mused the gaunt little figure to himself.

"Yeah," said Zaphod, "er, how is she? Tell you what, I'll go and see her. But first we've just got to . . ."

"Your *late* great-grandmother and I are very well," rasped Zaphod Beeblebrox the Fourth.

"Ah. Oh."

"But very disappointed in you, young Zaphod. . . ."

"Yeah, well . . ." Zaphod felt strangely powerless to take charge of this conversation, and Ford's heavy breathing at his side told him that the seconds were ticking away fast. The noise and the shaking had reached terrifying proportions. He saw Trillian's and Arthur's faces white and unblinking in the gloom.

"Er, Great-grandfather..."

"We've been following your progress with considerable despondency..."

"Yeah, look, just at the moment you see..."

"Not to say contempt!"

"Could you sort of listen for a moment...?"

"I mean what exactly are you doing with your life?"

"I'm being attacked by a Vogon fleet!" cried Zaphod. It was an exaggeration, but it was his only opportunity so far of getting the basic point of the exercise across.

"Doesn't surprise me in the least," said the little old figure with a shrug.

"Only it's happening right now, you see," insisted Zaphod feverishly.

The spectral ancestor nodded, picked up the cup Arthur Dent had brought in and looked at it with interest.

"Er...Great-granddad—"

"Did you know," interrupted the ghostly figure, fixing Zaphod with a stern look, "the Betelgeuse Five has now developed a very slight eccentricity in its orbit?"

Zaphod didn't and found the information hard to concentrate on what with all the noise and the imminence of death and so on.

"Er, no...look," he said.

"Me spinning in my grave!" barked the ancestor. He slammed the cup down and pointed a quivering, sticklike see-through finger at Zaphod.

"Your fault!" he screeched.

"One minute thirty," muttered Ford, his head in his hands.

"Yeah, look Great-granddad, can you actually help because..."

"Help?" exclaimed the old man as if he'd been asked for a weasel.

"Yeah, help, and like, now, because otherwise..."

"Help!" repeated the old man as if he'd been asked for a lightly grilled weasel in a bun with French fries. He stood amazed.

"You go swanning your way round the Galaxy with your"—the ancestor waved a contemptuous hand—"with your disreputable friends, too busy to put flowers on my grave, plastic ones would have done, would have been quite appropriate from you, but no. Too busy. Too modern.

Too skeptical—till you suddenly find yourself in a bit of a fix and come over suddenly all astrally minded!"

He shook his head—carefully, so as not to disturb the slumber of the other one, which was already becoming restive.

"Well, I don't know, young Zaphod," he continued, "I think I'll have to think about this one."

"One minute ten," said Ford hollowly.

Zaphod Beeblebrox the Fourth peered at him curiously.

"Why does that man keep talking in numbers?" he said.

"Those numbers," said Zaphod tersely, "are the time we've got left to live."

"Oh," said his great-grandfather. He grunted to himself. "Doesn't apply to me, of course," he said and moved off to a dimmer recess of the bridge in search of something else to poke around at.

Zaphod felt he was teetering on the edge of madness and wondered if he shouldn't just jump over and have done with it.

"Great-grandfather," he said, "it applies to us! We are still alive, and we are about to lose our lives."

"Good job too.'

"What?"

"What use is your life to anyone? When I think of what you've made of it the phrase 'pig's ear' comes irresistibly to mind."

"But I was President of the Galaxy, man!"

"Huh," muttered his ancestor. "And what kind of a job is that for a Beeblebrox?"

"Hey, what? Only President you know! Of the whole Galaxy!"

"Conceited little megapuppy."

Zaphod blinked in bewilderment.

"Hey—er, what are you at, man? I mean Great-grandfather."

The hunched up little figure stalked up to his great-grandson and tapped him sternly on the knee. This had the effect of reminding Zaphod that he was talking to a ghost because he didn't feel a thing.

"You know and I know what being President means, young Zaphod. You know because you've been it, and I know because I'm dead and it gives one such a wonderfully uncluttered perspective. We have a saying up here. 'Life is wasted on the living.' "

"Yeah," said Zaphod bitterly, "very good. Very deep. Right now I need aphorisms like I need holes in my heads."

"Fifty seconds," grunted Ford Prefect.

"Where was I?" said Zaphod Beeblebrox the Fourth.

"Pontificating," said Zaphod Beeblebrox.

"Oh yes."

"Can this guy," muttered Ford quietly to Zaphod, "actually in fact help us?"

"Nobody else can," whispered Zaphod.

Ford nodded despondently.

"Zaphod!" the ghost was saying, "you became President of the Galaxy for a reason. Have you forgotten?"

"Could we go into this later?"

"Have you forgotten?" insisted the ghost.

"Yeah! Of course I forgot! I had to forget. They screen your brain when you get the job, you know. If they'd found my head full of tricksy ideas I'd have been right out on the streets again with nothing but a fat pension, secretarial staff, a fleet of ships and a couple of slit throats."

"Ah," nodded the ghost in satisfaction, "then you do remember!"

He paused for a moment.

"Good," he said and the noise stopped.

"Forty-eight seconds," said Ford. He looked again at his watch and tapped it. He looked up.

"Hey, the noise has stopped," he said.

A mischievous twinkle gleamed in the ghost's hard little eyes.

"I've slowed down time for a moment," he said, "just for a moment you understand. I would hate you to miss all I have to say."

"No, you listen to me, you see-through old bat," said Zaphod leaping out of his chair, "A—Thanks for stopping time and all that, great, terrific, wonderful, but B—no thanks for the homily, right? I don't know what this great thing I'm meant to be doing is, and it looks to me as if I was supposed not to know. And I resent that, right?

"The old me knew. The old me cared. Fine, so far so good. Except that the old me cared so much that he actually got inside his own brain—my own brain—and locked off the bits that knew and cared, because if I knew and cared I wouldn't be able to do it. I wouldn't be able to go and be President, and I wouldn't be able to steal this ship, which must be the important thing.

"But this former self of mine killed himself off, didn't he, by changing my brain? Okay, that was his choice. This new me has its own choices to make, and by a strange coincidence those choices involve not knowing and not caring about this big number, whatever it is. That's what he wanted, that's what he got.

"Except this old self of mine tried to leave himself in control, leaving orders for me in the bit of my brain he locked off. Well, I don't want to know, and I don't want to hear them. That's my choice. I'm not going to be anybody's puppet, particularly not my own."

Zaphod banged on the console in fury, oblivious of the dumbfounded looks he was attracting.

"The old me is dead!" he raved. "Killed himself! The dead shouldn't hang about trying to interfere with the living!"

"And yet you summon me up to help you out of a scrape," said the ghost.

"Ah," said Zaphod, sitting down again, "well that's different, isn't it?"

He grinned at Trillian weakly.

"Zaphod," rasped the apparition, "I think the only reason I waste my breath on you is that being dead I don't have any other use for it."

"Okay," said Zaphod, "why don't you tell me what the big secret is. Try me."

"Zaphod, you knew when you were President of the Galaxy, as did Yooden Vranx before you, that the President is nothing. A cipher. Somewhere in the shadows behind is another man, being, something, with ultimate power. That man, or being, or something, you must find—the man who controls this Galaxy, and—we suspect—others. Possibly the entire Universe."

"Why?"

"Why?" exclaimed an astonished ghost. "Why? Look around you, lad, does it look to you as if it's in very good hands?"

"It's all right."

The old ghost glowered at him.

"I will not argue with you. You will simply take this ship, this Improbability Drive ship, to where it is needed. You will do it. Don't think you can escape your purpose. The Improbability Field controls you, you are in its grip. What's this?"

He was standing tapping at one of the terminals of Eddie the Shipboard Computer. Zaphod told him.

"What's it doing?"

"It is trying," said Zaphod with wonderful restraint, "to make tea."

"Good," said his great-grandfather, "I approve of that. Now Zaphod," he said, turning and wagging a finger at him, "I don't know if you are really capable of succeeding in your job. I think you will not be able to avoid it. However, I am too long dead and too tired to care as much as I did. The principal reason I am helping you now is that I couldn't bear the thought of you and your modern friends slouching about up here. Understood?"

"Yeah, thanks a bundle."

"Oh, and Zaphod?"

"Er, yeah?"

"If you ever find you need help again, you know, if you're in trouble, need a hand out of a tight corner..."

"Yeah?"

"Please don't hesitate to get lost."

Within the space of one second, a bolt of light flashed from the wizened old ghost's hands to the computer, the ghost vanished, the bridge filled with billowing smoke and the *Heart of Gold* leaped an unknown distance through the dimensions of time and space.

T en light-years away, Gag Halfrunt jacked up his smile by several notches. As he watched the picture on his vision screen, relayed across the sub-ether from the bridge of the Vogon ship, he saw the final shreds of the *Heart of Gold*'s force shield ripped away, and the ship itself vanish in a puff of smoke.

Good, he thought.

The end of the last stray survivors of the demolition he had ordered on the planet Earth, he thought.

The final end of this dangerous (to the psychiatric profession) and subversive (also to the psychiatric profession) experiment to find the Question to the Ultimate Answer of Life, the Universe and Everything, he thought.

There would be some celebration with his fellows tonight, and in the morning they would meet again their unhappy, bewildered and highly profitable patients, secure in the knowledge that the Meaning of Life would not now be, once and for all, well and truly sorted out, he thought.

"Family's always embarrassing, isn't it?" said Ford to Zaphod as the smoke began to clear.

He paused, he looked about.

"Where's Zaphod?" he said.

Arthur and Trillian looked about blankly. They were pale and shaken and didn't know where Zaphod was.

"Marvin?" said Ford, "where's Zaphod?"

A moment later he said:

"Where's Marvin?"

The robot's corner was empty.

The ship was utterly silent. It lay in thick black space. Occasionally it rocked and swayed. Every instrument was dead, every vision screen was dead. They consulted the computer. It said:

"I regret I have been temporarily closed to all communication. Meanwhile, here is some light music."

They turned off the light music.

They searched every corner of the ship in increasing bewilderment and alarm. Everywhere was dead and silent. Nowhere was there any trace of Zaphod or of Marvin.

One of the last areas they checked was the small bay in which the Nutri-Matic machine was located.

On the delivery plate of the Nutri-Matic Drink Synthesizer was a small tray, on which sat three bone china cups and saucers, a bone china jug of milk, a silver teapot full of the best tea Arthur had ever tasted and a small printed note saying "Wait."

Chapter 5

Ursa Minor Beta is, some say, one of the most appalling places in the known Universe.

Although it is excruciatingly rich, horrifyingly sunny and more full of wonderfully exciting people than a pomegranate is of pips, it can hardly be insignificant that when a recent edition of *Playbeing* magazine headlined an article with the words "When you are tired of Ursa Minor Beta you are tired of life," the suicide rate there quadrupled overnight.

Not that there are any nights on Ursa Minor Beta.

It is a West zone planet which by an inexplicable and somewhat suspicious freak of topography consists almost entirely of subtropical coastline. By an equally suspicious freak of temporal relastatics, it is nearly always Saturday afternoon just before the beach bars close.

No adequate explanation for this has been forthcoming from the dominant life forms on Ursa Minor Beta, who spend most of their time attempting to achieve spiritual enlightenment by running round swimming pools, and inviting Investigation Officials from the Galactic Geo-Temporal Control Board to "have a nice diurnal anomaly."

There is only one city on Ursa Minor Beta, and that is only called a city because the swimming pools are slightly thicker on the ground there than elsewhere.

If you approach Light City by air—and there is no other way of approaching it, no roads, no port facilities—if you don't fly they don't want to see you in Light City—you will see why it has this name. Here the sun shines brightest of all, glittering on the swimming pools, shimmering on the white, palm-lined boulevards, glistening on the healthy bronzed specks moving up and down them, gleaming off the villas, the hazy airpads, the beach bars and so on.

Most particularly it shines on a building, a tall, beautiful building consisting of two thirty-story white towers connected by a bridge halfway up their length.

The building is the home of a book, and was built here on the proceeds of an extraordinary copyright lawsuit fought between the book's editors and a breakfast cereal company.

The book is a guide book, a travel book.

It is one of the most remarkable, certainly the most successful, books ever to come out of the great publishing corporations of Ursa Minor—more popular than *Life Begins at Five Hundred and Fifty*, better selling than *The Big Bang Theory—A Personal View* by Eccentrica Gallumbits (the tripled-breasted whore of Eroticon Six) and more controversial then Oolon Colluphid's latest blockbusting title *Everything You Never Wanted to Know About Sex but Have Been Forced to Find Out.*

(And in many of the more relaxed civilizations on the Outer Eastern Rim of the Galaxy, it has long supplanted the great *Encyclopedia Galactica* as the standard repository of all knowledge and wisdom, for though it has many omissions and contains much that is apocryphal, or at least wildly inaccurate, it scores over the older more pedestrian work in two important respects. First, it is slightly cheaper, and secondly it has the words DON'T PANIC printed in large friendly letters on its cover.)

It is of course that invaluable companion for all those who want to see the marvels of the known Universe for less than thirty Altairian dollars a day—*The Hitchhiker's Guide to the Galaxy.*

If you stood with your back to the main entrance lobby of the *Guide* offices (assuming you had landed by now and freshened up with a quick dip and shower) and then walked east, you would pass along the leafy shade of Life Boulevard, be amazed by the pale golden color of the beaches stretching away to your left, astounded by the mind-surfers floating carelessly along two feet above the waves as if this was nothing special, surprised and eventually slightly irritated by the giant palm trees that hum tuneless nothings throughout the daylight hours, in other words continuously.

If you then walked to the end of Life Boulevard you would enter the Lalamatine district of shops, bolonut trees and pavement cafés where the UM-Betans come to relax after a hard afternoon's relaxation on the beach. The Lalamatine district is one of those very few areas which doesn't enjoy a perpetual Saturday afternoon—it enjoys instead the cool of a perpetual early Saturday evening. Behind it lie the nightclubs.

If, on this particular day, afternoon, stretch of eveningtime—call it what you will—you had approached the second pavement café on the right, you would have seen the usual crowd of UM-Betans chatting, drinking, looking very relaxed and casually glancing at each other's watches to see how expensive they were.

You would also have seen a couple of rather disheveled-looking hitchhikers from Algol who had recently arrived on an Arcturan Megafreighter aboard which they had been roughing it for a few days. They were angry and bewildered to discover that here, within sight of the *Hitchhiker's Guide* building itself, a simple glass of fruit juice cost the equivalent of over sixty Altairian dollars.

"Sell out," one of them said, bitterly.

If at that moment you had then looked at the next table you would have seen Zaphod Beeblebrox sitting and looking very startled and confused.

The reason for his confusion was that five seconds earlier he had been sitting on the bridge of the starship *Heart of Gold.*

"Absolute sell out," said the voice again.

Zaphod looked nervously out of the corners of his eyes at the two disheveled hitchhikers at the next table. Where the hell was he? How had he got there? Where was his ship? His hand felt the arm of the chair on which he was sitting, and then the table in front of him. They seemed solid enough. He sat very still.

"How can they sit and write a guide for hitchhikers in a place like this?" continued the voice. "I mean look at it. Look at it!"

Zaphod was looking at it. Nice place, he thought. But where? And why?

He fished in his pocket for his two pairs of sunglasses. In the same pocket he felt a hard, smooth, unidentified lump of very heavy metal. He pulled it out and looked at it. He blinked at it in surprise. Where had he got that? He returned it to his pocket and put on the sunglasses, annoyed to discover that the metal object had scratched one of the lenses. Nevertheless, he felt much more comfortable with them on. They were a double pair of Joo Janta 200 Super-Chromatic Peril Sensitive Sunglasses, which had been specially designed to help people develop a relaxed attitude to danger. At the first hint of trouble they turn totally black and thus prevent you from seeing anything that might alarm you.

Apart from the scratch the lenses were clear. He relaxed, but only a little bit.

The angry hitchhiker continued to glare at his monstrously expensive fruit juice.

"Worst thing that ever happened to the *Guide*, moving to Ursa Minor Beta," he grumbled; "they've all gone soft. You know, I've even heard that they've created a whole electronically synthesized Universe in one of their offices so they can go and research stories during the day and still go to parties in the evening. Not that day and evening mean much in this place."

Ursa Minor Beta, thought Zaphod. At least he knew where he was now.

He assumed that this must be his great-grandfather's doing, but why?

Much to his annoyance, a thought popped into his mind. It was very clear and very distinct, and he had now come to recognize these thoughts for what they were. His instinct was to resist them. They were the preordained promptings from the dark and locked off parts of his mind.

He sat still and ignored the thought furiously. It nagged at him. He ignored it. It nagged at him. He ignored it. It nagged at him. He gave in to it.

What the hell, he thought, go with the flow. He was too tired, confused and hungry to resist. He didn't even know what the thought meant.

Hello? Yes? Megadodo Publications, home of the *Hitchhiker's Guide to the Galaxy*, the most totally remarkable book in the whole of the known Universe, can I help you?" said the large pink-winged insect into one of the seventy phones lined up along the vast chrome expanse of the reception desk in the foyer of the *Hitchhiker's Guide to the Galaxy* offices. It fluttered its wings and rolled its eyes. It glared at all the grubby people cluttering up the foyer, soiling the carpets and leaving dirty handmarks on the upholstery. It adored working for the *Hitchhiker's Guide to the Galaxy*, it just wished there was some way of keeping all the hitchhikers away. Weren't they meant to be hanging around dirty spaceports or something? It was certain that it had read something somewhere in the book about the importance of hanging around dirty spaceports. Unfortunately most of them seemed to come and hang around in this nice clean shiny foyer immediately after hanging around in extremely dirty spaceports. And all they ever did was complain. It shivered its wings.

"What?" it said into the phone. "Yes, I passed on your message to Mr. Zarniwoop, but I'm afraid he's too cool to see you right now. He's on an intergalactic cruise."

It waved a petulant tentacle at one of the grubby people who was angrily trying to engage its attention. The petulant tentacle directed the angry person to look at the notice on the wall to its left and not to interrupt an important phone call.

"Yes," said the insect, "he is in his office, but he's on an intergalactic cruise. Thank you so much for calling." It slammed down the phone.

"Read the notice," it said to the angry man who was trying to complain about one of the more ludicrous and dangerous pieces of misinformation contained in the book.

The Hitchhiker's Guide to the Galaxy is an indispensable companion to all those who are keen to make sense of life in an infinitely complex and confusing Universe, for though it cannot hope to be useful or informative on all matters, it does at least make the reassuring claim, that where it is inaccurate it is at least *definitively* inaccurate. In cases of major discrepancy it's always reality that's got it wrong.

This was the gist of the notice. It said "The *Guide* is definitive. Reality is frequently inaccurate."

This has led to some interesting consequences. For instance, when the Editors of the *Guide* were sued by the families of those who had died as a result of taking the entry on the planet Traal literally (it said "Ravenous Bugblatter Beasts often make a very good meal for visiting tourists" instead of "Ravenous Bugblatter Beasts often make a very good meal *of* visiting tourists"), they claimed that the first version of the sentence was the more aesthetically pleasing, summoned a qualified poet to testify under oath that beauty was truth, truth beauty and hoped thereby to prove that the guilty party in this case was Life itself for failing to be either beautiful or true. The judges concurred, and in a moving speech held that Life itself was in contempt of court, and duly confiscated it from all those there present before going off to enjoy a pleasant evening's ultragolf.

Zaphod Beeblebrox entered the foyer. He strode up to the insect receptionist.

"Okay," he said, "where's Zarniwoop? Get me Zarniwoop."

"Excuse me, sir?" said the insect icily. It did not care to be addressed in this manner.

"Zarniwoop. Get him, right? Get him now."

"Well, sir," snapped the fragile little creature, "if you could be a little cool about it. . . ."

"Look," said Zaphod, "I'm up to here with cool, okay? I am so amazingly cool you could keep a side of meat in me for a month. I am so hip I have difficulty seeing over my pelvis. Now will you move before I blow it?"

"Well, if you'd let me explain, *sir*," said the insect, tapping the most petulant of all the tentacles at its disposal, "I'm afraid that isn't possible right now as Mr. Zarniwoop is on an intergalactic cruise."

Hell, thought Zaphod.

"When's he going to be back?" he said.

"Back, sir? He's in his office."

Zaphod paused while he tried to sort this particular thought out in his mind. He didn't succeed.

"This cat's on an intergalactic cruise . . . in his *office?*" He leaned forward and gripped the tapping tentacle.

"Listen, three eyes," he said, "don't you try to outweird me, I get stranger things than you free with my breakfast cereal."

"Well, just who do you think you are, honey?" flounced the insect, quivering its wings in rage. "Zaphod Beeblebrox or something?"

"Count the heads," said Zaphod in a low rasp.

The insect blinked at him. It blinked at him again.

"You *are* Zaphod Beeblebrox?" it squeaked.

"Yeah," said Zaphod, "but don't shout it out or they'll all want one."

"*The* Zaphod Beeblebrox?"

"No, just *a* Zaphod Beeblebrox; didn't you hear I come in six packs?"

The insect rattled its tentacles together in agitation.

"But, sir," it squealed, "I just heard on the sub-ether radio report. It said you were dead...."

"Yeah, that's right," said Zaphod, "I just haven't stopped moving yet. Now. Where do I find Zarniwoop?"

"Well, sir, his office is on the fifteenth floor, but—"

"But he's on an intergalactic cruise, yeah, yeah, how do I get to him?"

"The newly installed Sirius Cybernetics Corporation Happy Vertical People Transporters are in the far corner, sir. But, sir..."

Zaphod was turning to go. He turned back.

"Yeah?" he said.

"Can I ask you why you want to see Mr. Zarniwoop?"

"Yeah," said Zaphod, who was unclear on this point himself, "I told myself I had to."

"Come again, sir?"

Zaphod leaned forward, conspiratorially.

"I just materialized out of thin air in one of your cafés," he said, "as a result of an argument with the ghost of my great-grandfather. No sooner had I got there than my former self, the one that operated on my brain, popped into my head and said 'Go see Zarniwoop.' I have never heard of the cat. That is all I know. That and the fact that I've got to find the man who rules the Universe."

He winked.

"Mr. Beeblebrox, sir," said the insect in awed wonder, "you're so weird you should be in movies."

"Yeah," said Zaphod patting the thing on a glittering pink wing, "and you, baby, should be in real life."

The insect paused for a moment to recover from its agitation and then reached out a tentacle to answer a ringing phone.

A metal hand restrained it.

"Excuse me," said the owner of the metal hand in a voice that would have made an insect of a more sentimental disposition collapse in tears.

This was not such an insect, and it couldn't stand robots.

"Yes, *sir*," it snapped, "can I help you?"

"I doubt it," said Marvin.

"Well, in that case, if you'll just excuse me. . . ." Six of the phones were now ringing. A million things awaited the insect's attention.

"No one can help me," intoned Marvin.

"Yes, sir, well . . ."

"Not that anyone's tried of course." The restraining metal hand fell limply by Marvin's side. His head hung forward very slightly.

"Is that so," the insect said tartly.

"Hardly worth anyone's while to help a menial robot, is it?"

"I'm sorry, sir, if . . ."

"I mean, where's the percentage in being kind or helpful to a robot if it doesn't have any gratitude circuits?"

"And you don't have any?" said the insect, who didn't seem to be able to drag itself out of this conversation.

"I've never had occasion to find out," Marvin informed it.

"Listen, you miserable heap of maladjusted metal . . ."

"Aren't you going to ask me what I want?"

The insect paused. Its long thin tongue darted out and licked its eyes and darted back again.

"Is it *worth* it?" it asked.

"Is anything?" said Marvin immediately.

"*What . . . do . . . you . . . want?*"

"I'm looking for someone."

"Who?" hissed the insect.

"Zaphod Beeblebrox," said Marvin, "he's over there."

The insect shook with rage. It could hardly speak.

"Then why did you ask *me*?" it screamed.

"I just wanted something to talk to," said Marvin.

"What!"

"Pathetic, isn't it?"

With a grinding of gears Marvin turned and trundled off. He caught up with Zaphod approaching the elevators. Zaphod spun around in astonishment.

"Hey . . . Marvin?" he said. "Marvin! How did you get here?"

Marvin was forced to say something which came very hard to him.

"I don't know," he said.

"But—"

"One moment I was sitting in your ship feeling very depressed, and the next moment I was standing here feeling utterly miserable. An Improbability Field I expect."

"Yeah," said Zaphod, "I expect my great-grandfather sent you along to keep me company."

"Thanks a bundle, Granddad," he added to himself under his breath.

"So, how are you?" he said aloud.

"Oh, fine," said Marvin, "if you happen to like being me, which personally I don't."

"Yeah, yeah," said Zaphod as the elevator doors opened.

"Hello," said the elevator sweetly, "I am to be your elevator for this trip to the floor of your choice. I have been designed by the Sirius Cybernetics Corporation to take you, the visitor to the *Hitchhiker's Guide to the Galaxy*, into these their offices. If you enjoy your ride, which will be swift and pleasurable, then you may care to experience some of the other elevators which have recently been installed in the offices of the Galactic tax department, Boobiloo Baby Foods and the Sirian State Mental Hospital, where many ex-Sirius Cybernetics Corporation executives will be delighted to welcome your visits, sympathy and happy tales of the outside world."

"Yeah," said Zaphod, stepping into it, "what else do you do besides talk?"

"I go up," said the elevator, "or down."

"Good," said Zaphod, "we're going up."

"Or down," the elevator reminded him.

"Yeah, okay, up please."

There was a moment of silence.

"Down's very nice," suggested the elevator hopefully.

"Oh yeah?"

"Super."

"Good," said Zaphod, "now will you take us up?"

"May I ask you," inquired the elevator in its sweetest, most reasonable voice, "if you've considered all the possibilities that down might offer you?"

Zaphod knocked one of his heads against the inside wall. He didn't need this, he thought to himself, this of all things he had no need of. He hadn't asked to be here. If he was asked at this moment where he would like to be he would probably have said ne would like to be lying on the beach with at least fifty beautiful women and a small team of experts working out new ways they could be nice to him, which was his usual reply. To this he would probably have added something passionate on the subject of food.

One thing he didn't want to be doing was chasing after the man who ruled the Universe, who was only doing a job which he might as well keep at, because if it wasn't him it would only be someone else. Most of all he didn't want to be standing in an office block arguing with an elevator.

"Like what other possibilities?" he said wearily.

"Well," the voice trickled on like honey on biscuits, "there's the basement, the microfiles, the heating system . . . er . . ."

It paused.

"Nothing particularly exciting," it admitted, "but they are alternatives."

"Holy Zarquon," muttered Zaphod, "did I *ask* for an existential elevator?" He beat his fists against the wall.

"What's the matter with the thing?" he spat.

"It doesn't want to go up," said Marvin simply. "I think it's afraid."

"Afraid?" cried Zaphod. "Of what? Heights? An elevator that's afraid of heights?"

"No," said the elevator miserably, "of the future. . . ."

"The *future*?" exclaimed Zaphod. "What does the wretched thing want, a pension plan?"

At that moment a commotion broke out in the reception hall behind them. From the walls around them came the sound of suddenly active machinery.

"We can all see into the future," whispered the elevator in what sounded like terror, "it's part of our programming."

Zaphod looked out of the elevator—an agitated crowd had gathered round the elevator area, pointing and shouting.

Every elevator in the building was coming down, very fast.

He ducked back in.

"Marvin," he said, "just get this elevator to go up, will you? We've got to get to Zarniwoop."

"Why?" asked Marvin dolefully.

"I don't know," said Zaphod, "but when I find him, he'd better have a very good reason for me wanting to see him."

Modern elevators are strange and complex entities. The ancient electric winch and "maximum-capacity-eight-persons" jobs bear as much relation to a Sirius Cybernetics Corporation Happy Vertical People Transporter as a packet of mixed nuts does to the entire west wing of the Sirian State Mental Hospital.

This is because they operate on the curious principle of "defocused temporal perception." In other words they have the capacity to see dimly into the immediate future, which enables the elevator to be on the right floor to pick you up even before you knew you wanted it, thus eliminating all the tedious chatting, relaxing and making friends that people were previously forced to do while waiting for elevators.

Not unnaturally, many elevators imbued with intelligence and precognition became terribly frustrated with the mindless business of going up and down, up and down, experimented briefly with the notion of going sideways, as a sort of existential protest, demanded participation in the decision-making process and finally took to squatting in basements sulking.

An impoverished hitchhiker visiting any planets in the Sirius star system these days can pick up easy money working as a counselor for neurotic elevators.

At the fifteenth floor the elevator doors snapped open quickly.

"Fifteenth," said the elevator, "and remember, I'm only doing this because I like your robot."

Zaphod and Marvin bundled out of the elevator which instantly snapped its doors shut and dropped as fast as its mechanism would take it.

Zaphod looked around warily. The corridor was deserted and silent and gave no clue as to where Zarniwoop might be found. All the doors that let off the corridor were closed and unmarked.

They were standing close to the bridge which led across from one tower of the building to the other. Through a large window the brilliant sun of Ursa Minor Beta threw blocks of light in which danced small specks of dust. A shadow flitted past momentarily.

"Left in the lurch by a lift," muttered Zaphod, who was feeling at his least jaunty.

They both stood and looked in both directions.

"You know something?" said Zaphod to Marvin.

"More than you can possibly imagine."

"I'm dead certain this building shouldn't be shaking," Zaphod said.

It was just a light tremor through the soles of his feet—and another one. In the sunbeams the flecks of dust danced more vigorously. Another shadow flitted past.

Zaphod looked at the floor.

"Either," he said, not very confidently, "they've got some vibro system for toning up your muscles while you work, or . . ."

He walked across to the window and suddenly stumbled because at that moment his Joo Janta 200 Super-Chromatic Peril Sensitive Sunglasses had turned utterly black. A large shadow flitted past the window with a sharp buzz.

Zaphod ripped off his sunglasses, and as he did so the building shook with a thunderous roar. He leaped to the window.

"Or," he said, "this building's being bombed!"

Another roar cracked through the building.

"Who in the Galaxy would want to bomb a publishing company?" asked Zaphod, but never heard Marvin's reply because at that moment the building shook with another bomb attack. He tried to stagger back to the elevator—a pointless maneuver he realized, but the only one he could think of.

Suddenly, at the end of a corridor leading at right angles from this one, he caught sight of a figure as it lunged into view, a man. The man saw him.

"Beeblebrox, over here!" he shouted.

Zaphod eyed him with distrust as another bomb blast rocked the building.

"No," called Zaphod. "Beeblebrox over here! Who are you?"

"A friend!" shouted back the man. He ran toward Zaphod.

"Oh yeah?" said Zaphod. "Anyone's friend in particular, or just generally well-disposed to people?"

The man raced along the corridor, the floor bucking beneath his feet like an excited blanket. He was short, stocky and weatherbeaten and his clothes looked as if they'd been twice around the Galaxy and back with him in them.

"Do you know," Zaphod shouted in his ear when he arrived, "your building's being bombed?"

The man indicated his awareness.

It suddenly stopped being light. Glancing round at the window to see why, Zaphod gaped as a huge sluglike, gunmetal-green spacecraft crept through the air past the building. Two more followed it.

"The government you deserted is out to get you, Zaphod," hissed the man. "They've sent a squadron of Frogstar Fighters."

"Frogstar Fighters!" muttered Zaphod. "Zarquon!"

"You get the picture?"

"What are Frogstar Fighters?" Zaphod was sure he'd heard someone talk about them when he was President, but he never paid much attention to official matters.

The man was pulling him back through a door. He went with him.

With a searing whine a small black spiderlike object shot through the air and disappeared down the corridor.

"What was that?" hissed Zaphod.

"Frogstar Scout robot class A out looking for you," said the man.

"Hey, yeah?"

"Get down!"

From the opposite direction came a larger black spiderlike object. It zapped past them.

"And that was . . . ?"

"A Frogstar Scout robot class B out looking for you."

"And that?" said Zaphod, as a third one seared through the air.

"A Frogstar Scout robot class C out looking for you."

"Hey," chuckled Zaphod to himself, "pretty stupid robots, eh?"

From over the bridge came a massive rumbling hum. A gigantic black shape was moving over it from the opposite tower, the size and shape of a tank.

"Holy photon, what's that?" breathed Zaphod.

"A tank," said the man. "Frogstar Scout robot class D come to get you."

"Should we leave?"

"I think we should."

"Marvin!" called Zaphod.

"What do you want?"

Marvin rose from a pile of rubble farther down the corridor and looked at them.

"You see that robot coming toward us?"

Marvin looked at the gigantic black shape edging forward toward them over the bridge. He looked down at his own small metal body. He looked back up at the tank.

"I suppose you want me to stop it," he said.

"Yeah."

"While you save your skins."

"Yeah," said Zaphod, "get in there!"

"Just so long," said Marvin, "as I know where I stand."

The man tugged at Zaphod's arm, and Zaphod followed him off down the corridor.

A point occurred to him about this.

"Where are we going?" he said.

"Zarniwoop's office."

"Is this any time to keep an appointment?"

"Come on."

Chapter 7

Marvin stood at the end of the bridge corridor. He was not in fact a particularly small robot. His silver body gleamed in the dusty sunbeams and shook with the continual barrage which the building was still undergoing.

He did, however, look pitifully small as the gigantic black tank rolled to a halt in front of him. The tank examined him with a probe. The probe withdrew.

Marvin stood there.

"Out of my way little robot," growled the tank.

"I'm afraid," said Marvin, "that I've been left here to stop you."

The probe extended again for a quick recheck. It withdrew again.

"You? Stop me?" roared the tank. "Go on!"

"No, really I have," said Marvin simply.

"What are you armed with?" roared the tank in disbelief.

"Guess," said Marvin.

The tank's engines rumbled, its gears ground. Molecule-size electronic relays deep in its microbrain flipped backward and forward in consternation.

"Guess?" said the tank.

Zaphod and the as yet unnamed man lurched up one corridor, down a second and along a third. The building continued to rock and shudder and this puzzled Zaphod. If they wanted to blow the bulding up, why was it taking so long?

With difficulty they reached one of a number of totally anonymous unmarked doors and heaved at it. With a sudden jolt it opened and they fell inside.

All this way, thought Zaphod, all this trouble, all this not-lying-on-the-beach-having-a-wonderful-time, and for what? A single chair, a single desk and a single dirty ashtray in an undecorated office. The desk, apart from a bit of dancing dust and single, revolutionary new form of paper clip, was empty.

"Where," said Zaphod, "is Zarniwoop?" feeling that his already tenuous grasp of the point of this whole exercise was beginning to slip.

"He's on an intergalactic cruise," said the man.

Zaphod tried to size the man up. Earnest type, he thought, not a barrel of laughs. He probably apportioned a fair whack of his time to running up and down heaving corridors, breaking down doors and making cryptic remarks in empty offices.

"Let me introduce myself," the man said. "My name is Roosta, and this is my towel."

"Hello Roosta," said Zaphod.

"Hello, towel," he added as Roosta held out to him a rather nasty old flowery towel. Not knowing what to do with it, he shook it by the corner.

Outside the window, one of the huge sluglike, gunmetal-green spaceships growled past.

"Yes, go on," said Marvin to the huge battle machine, "you'll never guess."

"Errrmmm . . ." said the machine, vibrating with unaccustomed thought, "laser beams?"

Marvin shook his head solemnly.

"No," muttered the machine in its deep guttural rumble. "Too obvious. Antimatter ray?" it hazarded.

"Far too obvious," admonished Marvin.

"Yes," grumbled the machine, somewhat abashed. "Er . . . how about an electron ram?"

This was new to Marvin.

"What's that?" he said.

"One of these," said the machine with enthusiasm.

From its turret emerged a sharp prong which spat a single lethal blaze of light. Behind Marvin a wall roared and collapsed as a heap of dust. The dust billowed briefly, then settled.

"No," said Marvin, "not one of those."

"Good though, isn't it?"

"Very good," agreed Marvin.

"I know," said the Frogstar battle machine, after another moment's consideration, "you must have one of those new Xanthic Restructron Destabilized Zenon Emitters!"

"Nice, aren't they?" said Marvin.

"That's what you've got?" said the machine in considerable awe.

"No," said Marvin.

"Oh," said the machine, disappointed, "then it must be . . ."

"You're thinking along the wrong lines," said Marvin. "You're failing to take into account something fairly basic in the relationship between men and robots."

"Er, I know," said the battle machine, "is it ...?" It trailed off into thought again.

"Just think," urged Marvin, "they left me, an ordinary, menial robot, to stop you, a gigantic heavy-duty battle machine, while they ran off to save themselves. What do you think they would leave me with?"

"Oooh, er," muttered the machine in alarm, "something pretty damn devastating I should expect."

"Expect!" said Marvin. "Oh yes, expect. I'll tell you what they gave me to protect myself with, shall I?"

"Yes, all right," said the battle machine, bracing itself.

"Nothing," said Marvin.

There was a dangerous pause.

"*Nothing*?" roared the battle machine.

"Nothing at all," intoned Marvin dismally, "not an electronic sausage."

The machine heaved about with fury.

"Well, doesn't that just take the biscuit!" it roared. "Nothing, eh? Just don't think, do they?"

"And me," said Marvin in a soft low voice, "with this terrible pain in all the diodes down my left side."

"Makes you spit, doesn't it?"

"Yes," agreed Marvin with feeling.

"Hell, that makes me angry," bellowed the machine. "Think I'll smash that wall down!"

The electron ram stabbed out another searing blaze of light and took out the wall next to the machine.

"How do you think I feel?" said Marvin bitterly.

"Just ran off and left you, did they?" the machine thundered.

"Yes," said Marvin.

"I think I'll shoot down their bloody ceiling as well!" raged the tank.

It took out the ceiling of the bridge.

"That's very impressive," murmured Marvin.

"You ain't seen nothing yet," promised the machine. "I can take out this floor too, no trouble!"

It took out the floor too.

"Hell's bells!" the machine roared as it plummeted fifteen stories and smashed itself to bits on the ground below.

"What a depressingly stupid machine," said Marvin and trudged away.

o, do we just sit here, or what?" said Zaphod angrily; "what do these guys out here want?"

"You, Beeblebrox," said Roosta. "They're going to take you to the Frogstar—the most totally evil world in the Galaxy."

"Oh yeah?" said Zaphod. "They'll have to come and get me first."

"They have come and got you," said Roosta. "Look out the window."

Zaphod looked, and gaped.

"The ground's going away!" he gasped. "Where are they taking the ground?"

"They're taking the building," said Roosta. "We're airborne."

Clouds streaked past the office window.

Out in the open air again Zaphod could see the ring of dark green Frogstar Fighters around the uprooted tower of the building. A network of force beams radiated in from them and held the tower in a firm grip.

Zaphod shook his head in perplexity.

"What have I done to deserve this?" he said. "I walk into a building, they take it away."

"It's not what you've done they're worried about," said Roosta, "it's what you're going to do."

"Well don't I get a say in that?"

"You did, years ago. You'd better hold on, we're in for a fast and bumpy journey."

"If I ever meet myself," said Zaphod, "I'll hit myself so hard I won't know what's hit me."

Marvin trudged in through the door, looked at Zaphod accusingly, slumped in a corner and switched himself off.

On the bridge of the *Heart of Gold*, all was silent. Arthur stared at the rack in front of him and thought. He caught Trillian's eyes as she looked at him inquiringly. He looked back at the rack.

Finally he saw it.

He picked up five small plastic squares and laid them on the board that lay just in front of the rack.

The five squares had on them the five letters *E, X, Q, U,* and *I.* He laid them next to the letters *S, I, T, E.*

"Exquisite," he said, "on a triple word score. Scores rather a lot I'm afraid."

The ship bumped and scattered some of the letters for the nth time.

Trillian sighed and started to sort them out again.

Up and down the silent corridors echoed Ford Prefect's feet as he stalked the ship thumping dead instruments.

Why did the ship keep shaking? he thought.

Why did it rock and sway?

Why could he not find out where they were?

Where, basically, were they?

The left-hand tower of the *Hitchhiker's Guide to the Galaxy* offices streaked through interstellar space at a speed never equaled either before or since by any other office block in the Universe.

In a room halfway up it, Zaphod Beeblebrox strode angrily.

Roosta sat on the edge of the desk doing some routine towel maintenance.

"Hey, where did you say this building was flying to?" demanded Zaphod.

"The Frogstar," said Roosta, "the most totally evil place in the Universe."

"Do they have food there?" said Zaphod.

"Food? You're going to the Frogstar and you're worried about whether they've got food?"

"Without food I may not make it to the Frogstar."

Out of the window, they could see nothing but the flickering light of the force beams, and vague green streaks which were presumably the distorted shapes of the Frogstar Fighters. At this speed, space itself was invisible, and indeed unreal.

"Here, suck this," said Roosta, offering Zaphod his towel.

Zaphod stared at him as if he expected a cuckoo to leap out of his forehead on a small spring.

"It's soaked in nutrients," explained Roosta.

"What are you, a messy eater or something?" said Zaphod.

"The yellow stripes are high in protein, the green ones have vitamin B and C complexes, the little pink flowers contain wheatgerm extract."

Zaphod took and looked at it in amazement.

"What are the brown stains?" he asked.

"Bar-B-Q sauce," said Roosta, "for when I get sick of wheatgerm."

Zaphod sniffed it doubtfully.

Even more doubtfully, he sucked a corner. He spat it out again.

"Ugh," he stated.

"Yes," said Roosta, "when I've had to suck that end I usually need to suck the other end a bit too."

"Why," asked Zaphod suspiciously, "what's in that?"

"Antidepressants," said Roosta.

"I've gone right off this towel, you know," said Zaphod handing it back.

Roosta took it back from him, swung himself off the desk, walked around it, sat in the chair and put his feet up.

"Beeblebrox," he said, sticking his hands behind his head, "have you any idea what's going to happen to you on the Frogstar?"

"They're going to feed me?" hazarded Zaphod hopefully.

"They're going to feed you," said Roosta, "into the Total Perspective Vortex!"

Zaphod had never heard of this. He believed that he had heard of all the fun things in the Galaxy, so he assumed that the Total Perspective Vortex was not fun. He asked Roosta what it was.

"Only," said Roosta, "the most savage psychic torture a sentient being can undergo."

Zaphod nodded a resigned nod.

"So," he said, "no food, huh?"

"Listen!" said Roosta urgently. "You can kill a man, destroy his body, break his spirit, but only the Total Perspective Vortex can annihilate a man's soul! The treatment lasts seconds, but the effects last the rest of your life!"

"You ever had a Pan Galactic Gargle Blaster?" asked Zaphod sharply.

"This is worse."

"Phreeow!" admitted Zaphod, much impressed.

"Any idea why these guys might want to do this to me?" he added a moment later.

"They believe it will be the best way of destroying you forever. They know what you're after."

"Could they drop me a note and let me know as well?"

"You know," said Roosta, "you know, Beeblebrox. You want to meet the man who rules the Universe."

"Can he cook?" said Zaphod. On reflection he added:

"I doubt if he can. If he could cook a good meal he wouldn't worry about the rest of the Universe. I want to meet a cook."

Roosta sighed heavily.

"What are you doing here anyway?" demanded Zaphod, "what's all this got to do with you?"

"I'm just one of those who planned this thing, along with Zarniwoop, along with Yooden Vranx, along with your great-grandfather, along with you, Beeblebrox."

"Me?"

"Yes, you. I was told you had changed, I didn't realize how much."

"But . . ."

"I am here to do one job. I will do it before I leave you."

"What job, man? What are you talking about?"

"I will do it before I leave you."

Roosta lapsed into an impenetrable silence.

Zaphod was terribly glad.

Chapter 9

The air around the second planet of the Frogstar system was stale and unwholesome.

The dank winds that swept continually over its surface swept over salt flats, dried up marshland, tangled and rotting vegetation and the crumbling remains of ruined cities. No life moved across its surface. The ground, like that of many planets in this part of the Galaxy, had long been deserted.

The howl of the wind was desolate enough as it gusted through the old decaying houses of the cities; it was more desolate as it whipped about the bottoms of the tall black towers that swayed uneasily here and there about the surface of this world. At the top of these towers lived colonies of large, scraggy, evil-smelling birds, the sole survivors of the civilization that once lived here.

The howl of the wind was at its most desolate, however, when it passed over a pimple of a place set in the middle of a wide gray plain on the outskirts of the largest of the abandoned cities.

This pimple of a place was the thing that had earned this world the reputation of being the most totally evil place in the Galaxy. From without it was simply a steel dome about thirty feet across. From within it was something more monstrous than the mind can comprehend.

About a hundred yards or so away, and separated from it by a pockmarked and blasted stretch of the most barren land imaginable was what would probably have to be described as a landing pad of sorts. That is to say that scattered over a largish area were the ungainly hulks of two or three dozen crash-landed buildings.

Flitting over and around these buildings was a mind, a mind that was waiting for something.

The mind directed its attention into the air, and before very long a distant speck appeared, surrounded by a ring of smaller specks.

The larger speck was the left-hand tower of the *Hitchhiker's Guide to the Galaxy* office building, descending through the stratosphere of Frogstar World B.

As it descended, Roosta suddenly broke the long uncomfortable silence that had grown up between the two men.

He stood up and gathered his towel into a bag. He said:

"Beeblebrox, I will now do the job I was sent here to do."

Zaphod looked up at him from where he was sitting in a corner sharing unspoken thoughts with Marvin.

"Yeah?" he said.

"The building will shortly be landing. When you leave the building, do not go out of the door," said Roosta, "go out of the window."

"Good luck," he added, and walked out of the door, disappearing from Zaphod's life as mysteriously as he had entered it.

Zaphod leaped up and tried the door, but Roosta had already locked it. He shrugged and returned to the corner.

Two minutes later, the building crash-landed amongst the other wreckage. Its escort of Frogstar Fighters deactivated their force beams and soared off into the air again, bound for Frogstar World A, an altogether more congenial spot. They never landed on Frogstar World B. No one did. No one ever walked on its surface other than the intended victims of the Total Perspective Vortex.

Zaphod was badly shaken by the crash. He lay for a while in the silent dusty rubble to which most of the room had been reduced. He felt that he was at the lowest ebb he had ever reached in his life. He felt bewildered, he felt lonely, he felt unloved. Eventually he felt he ought to get whatever it was over with.

He looked around the cracked and broken room. The wall had split round the door frame, and the door hung open. The window, by some miracle, was closed and unbroken. For a while he hesitated, then he thought that if his strange and recent companion had been through all that he had been through just to tell him what he had told him, then there must be a good reason for it. With Marvin's help he got the window open. Outside it, the cloud of dust aroused by the crash, and the hulks of the other buildings with which this one was surrounded, effectively prevented Zaphod from seeing anything of the world outside.

Not that this concerned him unduly. His main concern was what he saw when he looked down. Zarniwoop's office was on the fifteenth floor. The building had landed at a tilt of about forty-five degrees, but still the descent looked heart-stopping.

Eventually, stung by the continuous series of contemptuous looks that Marvin appeared to be giving him, he took a deep breath and clambered out on to the steeply inclined side of the building. Marvin followed him, and together they began to crawl slowly and painfully down the fifteen floors that separated them from the ground.

As he crawled, the dank air and dust choked his lungs, his eyes smarted and the terrific distance down made his heads spin.

The occasional remark from Marvin of the order of "This is the sort of thing you life forms enjoy, is it? I ask merely for information," did little to improve his state of mind.

About halfway down the side of the shattered building they stopped to rest. It seemed to Zaphod as he lay there panting with fear and exhaustion that Marvin seemed a mite more cheerful than usual. Eventually he realized this wasn't so. The robot just seemed cheerful in comparison with his own mood.

A large, scraggy black bird came flapping through the slowly settling clouds of dust and, stretching down its scrawny legs, landed on an inclined window ledge a couple of yards from Zaphod. It folded its ungainly wings and teetered awkwardly on its perch.

Its wingspan must have been something like six feet, and its head and neck seemed curiously large for a bird. Its face was flat, the beak underdeveloped, and halfway along the underside of its wings the vestiges of something handlike could be clearly seen.

In fact, it looked almost human.

It turned its heavy eyes on Zaphod and clicked its beak in a desultory fashion.

"Go away," said Zaphod.

"Okay," muttered the bird morosely and flapped off into the dust again.

Zaphod watched its departure in bewilderment.

"Did that bird just talk to me?" he asked Marvin nervously. He was quite prepared to believe the alternative explanation, that he was in fact hallucinating.

"Yes," confirmed Marvin.

"Poor souls," said a deep, ethereal voice in Zaphod's ear.

Twisting around violently to find the source of the voice nearly caused Zaphod to fall off the building. He grabbed savagely at a protruding window fitting and cut his hand on it. He hung on, breathing heavily.

The voice had no visible source whatsoever—there was no one there. Nevertheless, it spoke again.

"A tragic history behind them, you know. A terrible blight."

Zaphod looked wildly about. The voice was deep and quiet. In other circumstances it would even be described as soothing. There is, however, nothing soothing about being addressed by a disembodied voice out of nowhere, particularly when you are, like Zaphod Beeblebrox, not at your best and hanging from a ledge eight stories up a crashed building.

"Hey, er . . ." he stammered.

"Shall I tell you their story?" inquired the voice quietly.

"Hey, who are you?" panted Zaphod. "Where are you?"

"Later then, perhaps," murmured the voice. "I am Gargravarr. I am the Custodian of the Total Perspective Vortex."

"Why can't I see . . . ?"

"You will find your progress down the building greatly facilitated," the voice lifted, "if you move about two yards to your left. Why don't you try it?"

Zaphod looked and saw a series of short horizontal grooves leading all the way down the side of the building. Gratefully he shifted himself across to them.

"Why don't I see you again at the bottom?" said the voice in his ear, and as it spoke it faded.

"Hey," called out Zaphod, "where are you . . . ?"

"It'll only take you a couple of minutes . . ." said the voice very faintly.

"Marvin," said Zaphod earnestly to the robot squatting dejectedly next to him, "did a . . . did a voice just . . . ?"

"Yes," Marvin replied tersely.

Zaphod nodded. He took out his Peril Sensitive Sunglasses again. They were completely black, and by now quite badly scratched by the unexpected metal object in his pocket. He put them on. He would find his way down the building more comfortably if he didn't actually have to look at what he was doing.

Minutes later he clambered over the ripped and mangled foundations of the building and, once more removing his sunglasses, he dropped to the ground.

Marvin joined him a moment or so later and lay face down in the dust and rubble, from which position he seemed disinclined to move.

"Ah, there you are," said the voice suddenly in Zaphod's ear. "Excuse me leaving you like that; it's just that I have a terrible head for heights. At least," it added wistfully, "I did have a terrible head for heights."

Zaphod looked around slowly and carefully, just to see if he had missed something which might be the source of the voice. All he saw, however, was the dust, the rubble and the towering hulks of the encircling buildings.

"Hey, er, why can't I see you?" he said. "Why aren't you here?"

"*I* am here," said the voice slowly. "My body wanted to come but it's a bit busy at the moment. Things to do, people to see." After what seemed like a sort of ethereal sigh it added, "You know how it is with bodies."

Zaphod wasn't sure about this.

"I thought I did," he said.

"I only hope it's gone in for a rest cure," continued the voice; "the way it's been living recently it must be on its last elbows."

"Elbows?" said Zaphod. "Don't you mean last legs?"

The voice said nothing for a while. Zaphod looked around uneasily. He didn't know if it had gone or was still there or what it was doing. Then the voice spoke again.

"So, you are to be put into the Vortex, yes?"

"Er, well," said Zaphod with a very poor attempt at nonchalance, "this cat's in no hurry, you know. I can just slouch about and take in a look at the local scenery, you know?"

"Have you seen the local scenery?" asked the voice of Gargravarr.

"Er, no."

Zaphod clambered over the rubble, and rounded the corner of one of the wrecked buildings that was obscuring his view.

He looked out at the landscape of Frogstar World B.

"Ah, okay," he said. "I'll just sort of slouch about then."

"No," said Gargravarr, "the Vortex is ready for you now. You must come. Follow me."

"Er, yeah?" said Zaphod. "And how am I meant to do that?"

"I'll hum for you," said Gargravarr. "Follow the humming."

A soft keening sound drifted through the air, a pale, sad sound that seemed to be without any kind of focus. It was only be listening very carefully that Zaphod was able to detect the direction from which it was coming. Slowly, dazedly, he stumbled off in its wake. What else was there to do?

Chapter 10

The Universe, as has been observed before, is an unsettlingly big place, a fact which for the sake of a quiet life most people tend to ignore.

Many would happily move to somewhere rather smaller of their own devising, and this is what most beings in fact do.

For instance, in one corner of the Eastern Galactic Arm lies the large forest planet Oglaroon, the entire "intelligent" population of which lives permanently in one fairly small and crowded nut tree. In which tree they are born, live, fall in love, carve tiny speculative articles in the bark on the meaning of life, the futility of death and the importance of birth control, fight a few extremely minor wars and eventually die strapped to the underside of some of the less accessible outer branches.

In fact the only Oglaroonians who ever leave their tree are those who are hurled out of it for the heinous crime of wondering whether any of the other trees might be capable of supporting life at all, or indeed whether the other trees are anything other than illusions brought on by eating too many Oglanuts.

Exotic though this behavior may seem, there is no life form in the galaxy which is not in some way guilty of the same thing, which is why the Total Perspective Vortex is as horrific as it is.

For when you are put into the Vortex you are given just one momentary glimpse of the entire unimaginable infinity of creation, and somewhere in it a tiny little marker, a microscopic dot on a microscopic dot, which says "You are here."

The gray plain stretched before Zaphod, a ruined, shattered plain. The wind whipped wildly over it.

Visible in the middle was the steel pimple of the dome. This, gathered Zaphod, was where he was going. This was the Total Perspective Vortex.

As he stood and gazed bleakly at it, a sudden inhuman wail of terror emanated from it as of a man having his soul burned from his body. It screamed above the wind and died away.

Zaphod started with fear and his blood seemed to turn to liquid helium.

"Hey, what was that?" he muttered voicelessly.

"A recording," said Gargravarr, "of the last man who was put in the Vortex. It is always played to the next victim. A sort of prelude."

"Hey, it really sounds bad..." stammered Zaphod. "Couldn't we maybe slope off to a party or something for a while, think it over?"

"For all I know," said Gargravarr's ethereal voice, "I'm probably at one. My body that is. It goes to a lot of parties without me. Says I only get in the way. Hey ho."

"What is all this with your body?" said Zaphod, anxious to delay whatever it was that was going to happen to him.

"Well, it's... it's busy you know," said Gargravarr hesitantly.

"You mean it's got a mind of its own?" said Zaphod.

There was a long and slightly chilly pause before Gargravarr spoke again.

"I have to say," he replied eventually, "that I find that remark in rather poor taste."

Zaphod muttered a bewildered and embarrassed apology.

"No matter," said Gargravarr, "you weren't to know."

The voice fluttered unhappily.

"The truth is," it continued in tones which suggested he was trying very hard to keep it under control, "the truth is that we are currently undergoing a period of legal trial separation. I suspect it will end in divorce."

The voice was still again, leaving Zaphod with no idea of what to say. He mumbled uncertainly.

"I think we were probably not very well-suited," said Gargravarr again at length; "we never seemed to be happy doing the same things. We always had the greatest arguments over sex and fishing. Eventually we tried to combine the two, but that only led to disaster, as you can probably imagine. And now my body refuses to let me in. It won't even see me...."

He paused again, tragically. The wind whipped across the plain.

"It says I only inhibit it. I pointed out that in fact I was meant to inhabit it, and it said that that was exactly the sort of smart alec remark that got right up a body's left nostril, and so we left it. It will probably get custody of my forename."

"Oh...?" said Zaphod faintly. "And what's that?"

"Pizpot," said the voice. "My name is Pizpot Gargravarr. Says it all really, doesn't it?"

"Errr..." said Zaphod sympathetically.

"And that is why I, as a disembodied mind, have this job, Custodian of the Total Perspective Vortex. No one will ever walk on the ground of this planet. Except the victims of the Vortex—they don't really count I'm afraid."

"Ah ..."

"I'll tell you the story. Would you like to hear it?"

"Er ..."

"Many years ago this was a thriving, happy planet—people, cities, shops, a normal world. Except that on the high streets of these cities there were slightly more shoe shops than one might have thought necessary. And slowly, insidiously, the numbers of these shoe shops were increasing. It's a well-known economic phenomenon but tragic to see it in operation, for the more shoe shops there were, the more shoes they had to make and the worse and more unwearable they became. And the worse they were to wear, the more people had to buy to keep themselves shod, and the more the shops proliferated, until the whole economy of the place passed what I believe is termed the Shoe Event Horizon, and it became no longer economically possible to build anything other than shoe shops. Result—collapse, ruin and famine. Most of the population died out. Those few who had the right kind of genetic instability mutated into birds—you've seen one of them—who cursed their feet, cursed the ground and vowed that none should walk on it again. Unhappy lot. Come, I must take you to the Vortex."

Zaphod shook his head in bemusement and stumbled forward across the plain.

"And you," he said, "you come from this hellhole pit, do you?"

"No no," said Gargravarr, taken aback, "I come from the Frogstar World C. Beautiful place. Wonderful fishing. I flit back there in the evenings. Though all I can do now is watch. The Total Perspective Vortex is the only thing on this planet with any function. It was built here because no one else wanted it on their doorstep."

At that moment another dismal scream rent the air and Zaphod shuddered.

"What can do that to a guy?" he breathed.

"The Universe," said Gargravarr simply, "the whole infinite Universe. The infinite suns, the infinite distances between them and yourself an invisible dot on an invisible dot, infinitely small."

"Hey, I'm Zaphod Beeblebrox, man, you know," muttered Zaphod trying to flap the last remnants of his ego.

Gargravarr made no reply, but merely resumed his mournful humming till they reached the tarnished steel dome in the middle of the plain.

As they reached it, a door hummed open in the side, revealing a small darkened chamber within.

"Enter," said Gargravarr.

Zaphod started with fear.

"Hey, what, now?" he said.

"Now."

Zaphod peered nervously inside. The chamber was very small. It was steel-lined and there was hardly space in it for more than one man.

"It . . . er . . . it doesn't look like any kind of Vortex to me," said Zaphod.

"It isn't," said Gargravarr, "it's just the elevator. Enter."

With infinite trepidation Zaphod stepped into it. He was aware of Gargravarr being in the elevator with him, though the disembodied man was not for the moment speaking.

The elevator began its descent.

"I must get myself into the right frame of mind for this," muttered Zaphod.

"There is no right frame of mind," said Gargravarr sternly.

"You really know how to make a guy feel inadequate."

"I don't. The Vortex does."

At the bottom of the shaft, the rear of the elevator opened up and Zaphod stumbled out into a smallish, functional, steel-lined chamber.

At the far side of it stood a single upright steel box, just large enough for a man to stand in.

It was that simple.

It connected to a small pile of components and instruments via a single thick wire.

"Is that it?" said Zaphod in surprise.

"That is it."

Didn't look too bad, thought Zaphod.

"And I get in there, do I?" said Zaphod.

"You get in there," said Gargravarr, "and I'm afraid you must do it now."

"Okay, okay," said Zaphod.

He opened the door of the box and stepped in.

Inside the box he waited.

After five seconds there was a click, and the entire Universe was there in the box with him.

Chapter 11

The Total Perspective Vortex derives its picture of the whole Universe on the principle of extrapolated matter analyses.

To explain—since every piece of matter in the Universe is in some way affected by every other piece of matter in the Universe, it is in theory possible to extrapolate the whole of creation—every sun, every planet, their orbits, their composition and their economic and social history from, say, one small piece of fairy cake.

The man who invented the Total Perspective Vortex did so basically in order to annoy his wife.

Trin Tragula—for that was his name—was a dreamer, a thinker, a speculative philosopher or, as his wife would have it, an idiot.

And she would nag him incessantly about the utterly inordinate amount of time he spent staring out into space, or mulling over the mechanics of safety pins, or doing spectrographic analyses of pieces of fairy cake.

"Have some sense of proportion!" she would say, sometimes as often as thirty-eight times in a single day.

And so he built the Total Perspective Vortex—just to show her.

And into one end he plugged the whole of reality as extrapolated from a piece of fairy cake, and into the other end he plugged his wife: so that when he turned it on she saw in one instant the whole infinity of creation and herself in relation to it.

To Trin Tragula's horror, the shock completely annihilated her brain; but to his satisfaction he realized that he had proved conclusively that if life is going to exist in a Universe of this size, then the one thing it cannot afford to have is a sense of proportion.

The door of the Vortex swung open.

From his disembodied mind Gargravarr watched dejectedly. He had rather liked Zaphod Beeblebrox in a strange sort of way. He was clearly a man of many qualities, even if they were mostly bad ones.

He waited for him to flop forward out of the box, as they all did.

Instead, he stepped out.

"Hi!" he said.

"Beeblebrox..." gasped Gargravarr's mind in amazement.

"Could I have a drink please?" said Zaphod.

"You...you...have been in the Vortex?" stammered Gargravarr.

"You saw me, kid."

"And it was working?"

"Sure was."

"And you saw the whole infinity of creation?"

"Sure. Really neat place, you know that?"

Gargravarr's mind was reeling in astonishment. Had his body been with him it would have sat down heavily with its mouth hanging open.

"And you saw yourself," said Gargravarr, "in relation to it all?"

"Oh, yeah yeah."

"But...what did you experience?"

Zaphod shrugged smugly.

"It just told me what I knew all the time. I'm a really terrific and great guy. Didn't I tell you, baby, I'm Zaphod Beeblebrox!"

His gaze passed over the machinery which powered the Vortex and suddenly stopped, startled.

He breathed heavily.

"Hey," he said, "is that really a piece of fairy cake?"

He ripped the small piece of confectionery from the sensors with which it was surrounded.

"If I told you how much I needed this," he said ravenously, "I wouldn't have time to eat it."

He ate it.

short while later he was running across the plain in the direction of the ruined city.

The dank air wheezed heavily in his lungs and he frequently stumbled with the exhaustion he was still feeling. Night was beginning to fall too, and the rough ground was treacherous.

The elation of his recent experience was still with him though. The whole Universe. He had seen the whole Universe stretching to infinity around him—everything. And with it had come the clear and extraordinary knowledge that he was the most important thing in it. Having a conceited ego is one thing. Actually being told by a machine is another.

He didn't have time to reflect on this matter.

Gargravarr had told him that he would have to alert his masters as to what had happened, but that he was prepared to leave a decent interval before doing so. Enough time for Zaphod to make a break and find somewhere to hide.

What he was going to do he didn't know, but feeling that he was the most important person in the Universe gave him the confidence to believe that something would turn up.

Nothing else on this blighted planet could give him much grounds for optimism.

He ran on, and soon reached the outskirts of the abandoned city.

He walked along cracked and gaping roads riddled with scrawny weeds, the holes filled with rotting shoes. The buildings he passed were so crumbled and decrepit he thought it unsafe to enter any of them. Where could he hide? He hurried on.

After a while the remains of a wide sweeping road led off from the one down which he was walking, and at its end lay a vast low building, surrounded with sundry smaller ones, the whole surrounded by the remains of a perimeter barrier. The large main building still seemed reasonably solid, and Zaphod turned off to see if it might provide him with . . . well with anything.

He approached the building. Along one side of it—the front it would seem since it faced a wide concreted apron area—were three gigantic doors, maybe sixty feet high. The far one of these was open, and toward this, Zaphod ran.

Inside, all was gloom, dust and confusion. Giant cobwebs lay over everything. Part of the infrastructure of the building had collapsed, part of the rear wall had caved in and a thick choking dust lay inches over the floor.

Through the heavy gloom huge shapes loomed, covered with debris.

The shapes were sometimes cylindrical, sometimes bulbous, sometimes like eggs, or rather cracked eggs. Most of them were split open or falling apart, some were mere skeletons.

They were all spacecraft, all derelict.

Zaphod wandered in frustration among the hulks. There was nothing here that remotely approached the serviceable. Even the mere vibration of his footsteps caused one precarious wreck to collapse further into itself.

Toward the rear of the building lay one old ship, slightly larger than the others, and buried beneath even deeper piles of dust and cobwebs. Its outline, however, seemed unbroken. Zaphod approached it with interest, and as he did so, he tripped over an old feedline.

He tried to toss the feedline aside, and to his surprise discovered that it was still connected to the ship.

To his utter astonishment he realized that the feedline was also humming slightly.

He stared at the ship in disbelief, and then back down at the feedline in his hands.

He tore off his jacket and threw it aside. Crawling along on his hands and knees he followed the feedline to the point where it connected with the ship. The connection was sound, and the slight humming vibration was more distinct.

His heart was beating fast. He wiped away some grime and laid an ear against the ship's side. He could hear only a faint, indeterminate noise.

He rummaged feverishly among the debris lying on the floor all about him and found a short length of tubing and a nonbiodegradable plastic cup. Out of this he fashioned a crude stethoscope and placed it against the side of the ship.

What he heard made his brains turn somersaults.

The voice said:

"Transtellar Cruise Lines would like to apologize to passengers for the continuing delay to this flight. We are currently awaiting the loading of our complement of small lemon-soaked paper napkins for your comfort, refreshment and hygiene during the journey. Meanwhile we thank you for your patience. The cabin crew will shortly be serving coffee and biscuits again."

Zaphod staggered backward, staring wildly at the ship.

He walked around for a few moments in a daze. In so doing he suddenly caught sight of a giant departure board still hanging, but by only one support, from the ceiling above him. It was covered with grime, but some of the figures were still discernible.

Zaphod's eyes searched among the figures, then made some brief calculations. His eyes widened.

"Nine hundred years . . ." he breathed to himself. That was how late the ship was.

Two minutes later he was on board.

As he stepped out of the airlock, the air that greeted him was cool and fresh—the air conditioning was still working.

The lights were still on.

He moved out of the small entrance chamber into a short narrow corridor and stepped nervously down it.

Suddenly a door opened and a figure stepped out in front of him.

"Please return to your seat, sir," said the android stewardess and, turning her back on him, she walked on down the corridor in front of him.

When his heart had started beating again he followed her. She opened the door at the end of the corridor and walked through.

He followed her through the door.

They were now in the passenger compartment and Zaphod's heart stopped still again for a moment.

In every seat sat a passenger, strapped into his or her seat.

The passengers' hair was long and unkempt, their fingernails were long, the men wore beards.

All of them were quite clearly alive—but sleeping.

Zaphod had the creeping horrors.

He walked slowly down the aisle as in a dream. By the time he was halfway down the aisle, the stewardess had reached the other end. She turned and spoke.

"Good afternoon ladies and gentlemen," she said sweetly. "Thank you for bearing with us during this slight delay. We will be taking off as soon as we possibly can. If you would like to wake up now I will serve you coffee and biscuits."

There was a slight hum.

At that moment, all the passengers awoke.

They awoke screaming and clawing at the straps and life support systems that held them tightly in their seats. They screamed and bawled and hollered till Zaphod thought his ears would shatter.

They struggled and writhed as the stewardess patiently moved up the aisle placing a small cup of coffee and a packet of biscuits in front of each one of them.

Then one of them rose from his seat.

He turned and looked at Zaphod.

Zaphod's skin was crawling all over his body as if it was trying to get off. He turned and ran from the bedlam.

He plunged through the door and back into the corridor.

The man pursued him.

He raced in a frenzy to the end of the corridor, through the entrance chamber and beyond. He arrived on the flight deck, slammed and bolted the door behind him. He leaned back against the door breathing hard.

Within seconds, a hand started beating on the door.

From somewhere on the flight deck a metallic voice addressed him.

"Passengers are not allowed on the flight deck. Please return to your seat, and wait for the ship to take off. Coffee and biscuits are being served. This is your autopilot speaking. Please return to your seat."

Zaphod said nothing. He breathed hard; behind him the hand continued to knock on the door.

"Please return to your seat," repeated the autopilot. "Passengers are not allowed on the flight deck."

"I'm not a passenger," panted Zaphod.

"Please return to your seat."

"I am not a passenger!" shouted Zaphod again.

"Please return to your seat."

"I am not a . . . hello, can you hear me?"

"Please return to your seat."

"You're the autopilot?" said Zaphod

"Yes," said the voice from the flight console.

"You're in charge of this ship?"

"Yes," said the voice again, "there has been a delay. Passengers are to be kept temporarily in suspended animation, for their comfort and convenience. Coffee and biscuits are served every year, after which passengers are returned to suspended animation for their continued comfort and convenience. Departure will take place when the flight stores are complete. We apologize for the delay."

Zaphod moved away from the door, on which the pounding now ceased. He approached the flight console.

"Delay?" he cried. "Have you seen the world outside this ship? It's a wasteland, a desert. Civilization's been and gone, man. There are no lemon-soaked paper napkins on the way from anywhere!"

"The statistical likelihood," continued the autopilot primly, "is that other civilizations will arise. There will one day be lemon-soaked paper napkins. Till then there will be a short delay. Please return to your seat."

"But . . ."

But at that moment the door opened. Zaphod spun around to see the man who had pursued him standing there. He carried a large briefcase. He was smartly dressed, and his hair was short. He had no beard and no long fingernails.

"Zaphod Beeblebrox," he said, "my name is Zarniwoop. I believe you wanted to see me."

Zaphod Beeblebrox withered. His mouths said foolish things. He dropped into a chair.

"Oh man, oh man, where did you spring from?" he said.

"I have been waiting here for you," he said in a businesslike tone.

He put the briefcase down and sat in another chair.

"I am glad you followed instructions," he said. "I was a bit nervous that you might have left my office by the door rather than the window. Then you would have been in trouble."

Zaphod shook his heads at him and burbled.

"When you entered the door of my office, you entered my electronically synthesized Universe," he explained. "If you had left by the door you would have been back in the real one. The artificial one works from here."

He patted his briefcase smugly.

Zaphod glared at him with resentment and loathing.

"What's the difference?" he muttered.

"Nothing," said Zarniwoop, "they are identical. Oh—except that I think the Frogstar Fighters are gray in the real Universe."

"What's going on?" spat Zaphod.

"Simple," said Zarniwoop. His self-assurance and smugness made Zaphod seethe.

"Very simple," repeated Zarniwoop. "I discovered the coordinates at which this man could be found—the man who rules the Universe, and discovered that his world was protected by an Unprobability Field. To protect my secret—and myself—I retreated to the safety of this totally artificial Universe and hid myself away in a forgotten cruise liner. I was secure. Meanwhile, you and I..."

"You and *I?*" said Zaphod angrily. "You mean I knew you?"

"Yes," said Zarniwoop, "we knew each other well."

"I had no taste," said Zaphod and resumed a sullen silence.

"Meanwhile, you and I arranged that you would steal the Improbability Drive ship—the only one which could reach the ruler's world—and bring it to me here. This you have now done I trust, and I congratulate you." He smiled a tight little smile which Zaphod wanted to hit with a brick.

"Oh, and in case you were wondering," added Zarniwoop, "this Universe was created specifically for you to come to. You are therefore the most important person in this Universe. You would never," he said with an even more brickable smile, "have survived the Total Perspective Vortex in the real one. Shall we go?"

"Where?" said Zaphod sullenly. He felt collapsed.

"To your ship. The *Heart of Gold.* You did bring it, I trust?"

"No."

"Where is your jacket?"

Zaphod looked at him in mystification.

"My jacket? I took it off. It's outside."

"Good, we will go and find it."

Zarniwoop stood up and gestured to Zaphod to follow him.

Out in the entrance chamber again, they could hear the screams of the passengers being fed coffee and biscuits.

"It has not been a pleasant experience waiting for you," said Zarniwoop.

"Not pleasant for *you!*" bawled Zaphod. "How do you think...?"

Zarniwoop held up a silencing finger as the hatchway swung open. A few feet away from them they could see Zaphod's jacket lying in the debris.

"A very remarkable and very powerful ship," said Zarniwoop. "Watch."

As they watched, the pocket on the jacket suddenly bulged. It split, it ripped. The small metal model of the *Heart of Gold* that Zaphod had been bewildered to discover in his pocket was growing.

It grew, it continued to grow. It reached, after two minutes, its full size.

"At an Improbability Level," said Zarniwoop, "of...oh I don't know, but something very large."

Zaphod swayed.

"You mean I had it with me all the time?"

Zarniwoop smiled. He lifted up his briefcase and opened it.

He twisted a single switch inside it.

"Goodbye artificial Universe," he said; "hello real one!"

The scene before them shimmered briefly—and reappeared exactly as before.

"You see?" said Zarniwoop. "Exactly the same."

"You mean," repeated Zaphod tautly, "that I had it with me all the time?"

"Oh yes," said Zarniwoop, "of course. That was the whole point."

"That's it," said Zaphod. "You can count me out, from here on in you can count me out. I've had all I want of this. You play your own games."

"I'm afraid you cannot leave," said Zarniwoop, "you are entwined in the Improbability Field. You cannot escape."

He smiled the smile that Zaphod had wanted to hit and this time Zaphod hit it.

Chapter 13

Ford Prefect bounded up to the bridge of the *Heart of Gold.*
"Trillian! Arthur!" he shouted. "It's working! The ship's reactivated!"

Trillian and Arthur were asleep on the floor.

"Come on, you guys, we're going, we're off," he said kicking them awake.

"Hi there, guys!" twittered the computer. "It's really great to be back with you again, I can tell you, and I just want to say that . . . "

"Shut up," said Ford. "Tell us where the hell we are."

"Frogstar World B, and man it's a dump," said Zaphod running onto the bridge. "Hi, guys, you must be so amazingly glad to see me you can't even find words to tell me what a cool frood I am."

"What a what?" said Arthur blearily, picking himself up from the floor and not taking any of this in.

"I know how you feel," said Zaphod. "I'm so great even I get tongue-tied talking to myself. Hey it's good to see you Trillian, Ford, Monkey-man. Hey, er, computer . . . "

"Hi there, Mr. Beeblebrox, sir, sure is a great honor to . . . "

"Shut up and get us out of here, fast fast fast."

"Sure thing, fella, where do you want to go?"

"Anywhere, doesn't matter," shouted Zaphod. "Yes it does!" he said again. "We want to go to the nearest place to eat!"

"Sure thing," said the computer happily and a massive explosion rocked the bridge.

When Zarniwoop entered a minute or so later with a black eye, he regarded the four wisps of smoke with interest.

Chapter 14

Four inert bodies sank through spinning blackness. Consciousness had died, cold oblivion pulled the bodies down and down into the pit of unbeing. The roar of silence echoed dismally around them and they sank at last into a dark and bitter sea of heaving red that slowly engulfed them, seemingly forever.

After what seemed an eternity the sea receded and left them lying on a cold hard shore, the flotsam and jetsam of the stream of Life, the Universe and Everything.

Cold spasms shook them, lights danced sickeningly around them. The cold hard shore tipped and spun and then stood still. It shone darkly—it was a very highly polished cold hard shore.

A green blur watched them disapprovingly.

It coughed.

"Good evening, madam, gentlemen," it said. "Do you have a reservation?"

Ford Prefect's consciousness snapped back like elastic, making his brain smart. He looked up woozily at the green blur.

"Reservation?" he said weakly.

"Yes, sir," said the green blur.

"Do you need a reservation for the afterlife?"

In so far as it is possible for a green blur to arch its eyebrows disdainfully, this is what the green blur now did.

"Afterlife, sir?" it said.

Arthur Dent was grappling with his consciousness the way one grapples with a lost bar of soap in the bath.

"Is this the afterlife?" he stammered.

"Well, I assume so," said Ford Prefect trying to work out which way was up. He tested the theory that it must lie in the opposite direction from the cold hard shore on which he was lying, and staggered to what he hoped were his feet.

"I mean, he said, swaying gently, "there's no way we could have survived that blast, is there?"

"No," muttered Arthur. He had raised himself on to his elbows but it didn't seem to improve things. He slumped down again.

"No," said Trillian, standing up, "no way at all."

A dull hoarse gurgling sound came from the floor. It was Zaphod Beeblebrox attempting to speak.

"I certainly didn't survive," he gurgled. "I was a total goner. Wham bang and that was it."

"Yeah, thanks to you," said Ford, "we didn't stand a chance. We must have been blown to bits. Arms, legs everywhere."

"Yeah," said Zaphod struggling noisily to his feet.

"If the lady and gentlemen would care to order drinks..." said the green blur, hovering impatiently beside them.

"Kerpow, splat," continued Zaphod, "instantaneously zonked into our component molecules. Hey, Ford," he said, identifying one of the slowly solidifying blurs around him, "did you get that thing of your whole life flashing before you?"

"You got that too?" said Ford. "Your whole life?"

"Yeah," said Zaphod, "at least I assume it was mine. I spend a lot of time out of my skulls you know."

He looked around him at the various shapes that were at last becoming proper shapes instead of vague and wobbling shapeless shapes.

"So..." he said.

"So what?" said Ford.

"So here we are," said Zaphod hesitantly, "lying dead..."

"Standing," Trillian corrected him.

"Er, standing dead," continued Zaphod, "in this desolate..."

"Restaurant," said Arthur Dent who had got to his feet and could now, much to his surprise, see clearly. That is to say, the thing that surprised him was not that he could see, but what he could see.

"Here we are," continued Zaphod doggedly, "standing dead in this desolate..."

"Five star," said Trillian.

"Restaurant," concluded Zaphod.

"Odd, isn't it?" said Ford.

"Er, yeah."

"Nice chandeliers though," said Trillian.

They looked about themselves in bemusement.

"It's not so much an afterlife," said Arthur, "more a sort of *après vie*."

The chandeliers were in fact a little on the flashy side and the low vaulted ceiling from which they hung would not, in an ideal Universe, have been painted in that particular shade of deep turquoise, and even if it had been it wouldn't have been highlighted by concealed moodlighting. This is not, however, an ideal Universe, as was further evidenced by the eye-crossing patterns of the inlaid marble floor, and the way in which the fronting for the eighty-yard-long marble-topped bar had been made. The fronting for the eighty-yard-long marble-topped bar had been made by stitching together nearly twenty thousand Antarean Mosaic Lizard skins, despite the fact that the twenty thousand lizards concerned had needed them to keep their insides in.

A few smartly dressed creatures were lounging casually at the bar or relaxing in the richly colored body-hugging seats that were deployed here and there about the bar area. A young Vl'Hurg officer and his green steaming young lady passed through the large smoked glass doors at the far end of the bar into the dazzling light of the main body of the Restaurant beyond.

Behind Arthur was a large curtained bay window. He pulled aside the corner of the curtain and looked out at a bleak and dreary landscape, gray, pockmarked and dismal, a landscape which under normal circumstances would have given Arthur the creeping horrors. These were not, however, normal circumstances, for the thing that froze his blood and made his skin try to crawl up his back and off the top of his head was the sky. The sky was ...

An attendant flunky politely drew the curtain back into place.

"All in good time, sir," he said.

Zaphod's eyes flashed.

"Hey, wait a minute, you dead guys," he said. "I think we're missing some ultraimportant thing here, you know. Something somebody said and we missed it."

Arthur was profoundly relieved to turn his attention from what he had just seen.

He said, "I said it was a sort of *après* ..."

"Yeah, and don't you wish you hadn't?" said Zaphod. "Ford?"

"I said it was odd."

"Yeah, shrewd but dull, perhaps it was—"

"Perhaps," interrupted the green blur who had by this time resolved into the shape of a small wizened dark-suited green waiter, "perhaps you would care to discuss the matter over drinks. ..."

"Drinks!" cried Zaphod. "That was it! See what you miss if you don't stay alert."

"Indeed, sir," said the waiter patiently. "If the lady and gentlemen would care to take drinks before dinner..."

"Dinner!" Zaphod exclaimed with passion. "Listen, little green person, my stomach could take you home and cuddle you all night for the mere idea."

"...and the Universe," continued the waiter, determined not to be deflected on his home stretch, "will explode later for your pleasure."

Ford's head swiveled slowly toward him. He spoke with feeling.

"Wow," he said, "what sort of drinks do you serve in this place?"

The waiter laughed a polite little waiter's laugh.

"Ah," he said, "I think sir has perhaps misunderstood me."

"Oh, I hope not," breathed Ford.

The waiter coughed a polite little waiter's cough.

"It is not unusual for our customers to be a little disorientated by the time journey," he said, "so if I might suggest—"

"Time journey?" said Zaphod.

"Time journey?" said Ford.

"Time journey?" said Trillian.

"You mean this isn't the afterlife?" said Arthur.

The waiter smiled a polite little waiter's smile. He had almost exhausted his polite little waiter repertoire and would soon be slipping into his role of a rather tight-lipped and sarcastic little waiter.

"Afterlife, sir?" he said. "No, sir."

"And we're not dead?" said Arthur.

The waiter tightened his lips.

"Aha, ha," he said. "Sir is most evidently alive, otherwise I would not attempt to serve sir."

In an extraordinary gesture which it is pointless attempting to describe, Zaphod Beeblebrox slapped both his foreheads with two of his arms and one of his thighs with the other.

"Hey, guys," he said, "this is crazy. We did it. We finally got to where we were going. This is Milliways!"

"Milliways!" said Ford.

"Yes, sir," said the waiter, laying on the patience with a trowel, "this is Milliways—the Restaurant at the End of the Universe."

"End of what?" said Arthur.

"The Universe," repeated the waiter, very clearly and unnecessarily distinctly.

"When did that end?" said Arthur.

"In just a few minutes, sir," said the waiter. He took a deep breath. He didn't need to do this since his body was supplied with the peculiar assortment of gases it required for survival from a small intravenous device strapped to his leg. There are times, however, when whatever your metabolism you have to take a deep breath.

"Now, if you would care to order your drinks at last," he said, "I will then show you to your table."

Zaphod grinned two manic grins, sauntered over to the bar and bought most of it.

Chapter 15

The Restaurant at the End of the Universe is one of the most extraordinary ventures in the entire history of catering. It has been built on the fragmented remains of... it *will* be built on the fragmented... that is to say it will have been built by this time, and indeed has been—

One of the major problems encountered in time travel is not that of accidentally becoming your own father or mother. There is no problem involved in becoming your own father or mother that a broad-minded and well-adjusted family can't cope with. There is no problem about changing the course of history—the course of history does not change because it all fits together like a jigsaw. All the important changes have happened before the things they were supposed to change and it all sorts itself out in the end.

The major problem is quite simply one of grammar, and the main work to consult in this matter is Dr. Dan Streetmentioner's *Time Traveler's Handbook of 1001 Tense Formations*. It will tell you, for instance, how to describe something that was about to happen to you in the past before you avoided it by time-jumping forward two days in order to avoid it. The event will be described differently according to whether you are talking about it from the standpoint of your own natural time, from a time in the further future, or a time in the further past and is further complicated by the possibility of conducting conversations while you are actually traveling from one time to another with the intention of becoming your own mother or father.

Most readers get as far as the Future Semiconditionally Modified Subinverted Plagal Past Subjunctive Intentional before giving up; and in fact in later editions of the book all the pages beyond this point have been left blank to save on printing costs.

The Hitchhiker's Guide to the Galaxy skips lightly over this tangle of academic abstraction, pausing only to note that the term "Future Perfect" has been abandoned since it was discovered not to be.

To resume:

The Restaurant at the End of the Universe is one of the most extraordinary ventures in the entire history of catering.

It is built on the fragmented remains of an eventually ruined planet which is (wioll haven be) enclosed in a vast time bubble and projected forward in time to the precise moment of the End of the Universe.

This is, many would say, impossible.

In it, guests take (willan on-take) their places at table and eat (willan on-eat) sumptuous meals while watching (willing watchen) the whole of creation explode around them.

This, many would say, is equally impossible.

You can arrive (mayan arrivan on-when) for any sitting you like without prior (late fore-when) reservation because you can book retrospectively, as it were, when you return to your own time (you can have on-book haventa forewhen presooning returningwenta retrohome).

This is, many would now insist, absolutely impossible.

At the Restaurant you can meet and dine with (mayan meetan con with dinan on when) a fascinating cross-section of the entire population of space and time.

This, it can be explained patiently, is also impossible.

You can visit it as many times as you like (mayan on-visit re-onvisiting . . . and so on—for further tense correction consult Dr. Street-mentioner's book) and be sure of never meeting yourself, because of the embarrassment this usually causes.

This, even if the rest were true, which it isn't, is patently impossible, say the doubters.

All you have to do is deposit one penny in a savings account in your own era, and when you arrive at the End of Time the operation of compound interest means that the fabulous cost of your meal has been paid for.

This, many claim, is not merely impossible but clearly insane, which is why the advertising executives of the star system of Bastablon came up with this slogan: "If you've done six impossible things this morning, why not round it off with breakfast at Milliways, the Restaurant at the End of the Universe?"

Chapter 16

At the bar, Zaphod was rapidly becoming as tired as a newt. His heads knocked together and his smiles were coming out of sync. He was miserably happy.

"Zaphod," said Ford, "while you're still capable of speech, would you care to tell me what the photon happened? Where have you been? Where have we been? Small matter, but I'd like it cleared up."

Zaphod's left head sobered up, leaving his right to sink further into the obscurity of drink.

"Yeah," he said, "I've been around. They want me to find the man who rules the Universe, but I don't care to meet him. I believe the man can't cook."

His left head watched his right head saying this and then nodded.

"True," it said, "have another drink."

Ford had another Pan Galactic Gargle Blaster, the drink which has been described as the alcoholic equivalent of a mugging—expensive and bad for the head. Whatever had happened, Ford decided, he didn't really care too much.

"Listen, Ford," said Zaphod, "everything's cool and froody."

"You mean everything's under control."

"No," said Zaphod, "I do not mean everything's under control. That would not be cool and froody. If you want to know what happened let's just say I had the whole situation in my pocket. Okay?"

Ford shrugged.

Zaphod giggled into his drink. It frothed up over the side of the glass and started to eat its way into the marble bar top.

A wild-skinned sky-gypsy approached them and played electric violin at them until Zaphod gave him a lot of money and he agreed to go away again.

The gypsy approached Arthur and Trillian sitting in another part of the bar.

"I don't know what this place is," said Arthur, "but I think it gives me the creeps."

"Have another drink," said Trillian. "Enjoy yourself."

"Which?" said Arthur. "The two are mutually exclusive."

"Poor Arthur, you're not really cut out for this life, are you?"

"You call this life?"

"You're beginning to sound like Marvin."

"Marvin's the clearest thinker I know. How do you think we make this violinist go away?"

The waiter approached.

"Your table is ready," he said.

Seen from the outside, which it never is, the Restaurant resembles a giant glittering starfish beached on a forgotten rock. Each of its arms houses the bars, the kitchens, the force-field generators which protect the entire structure and the decayed hunk of planet on which it sits, and the Time Turbines which slowly rock the whole affair backward and forward across the crucial moment.

In the center sits the gigantic golden dome, almost a complete globe, and it was into this area that Zaphod, Ford, Arthur and Trillian now passed.

At least five tons of glitter alone had gone into it before them, and covered every available surface. The other surfaces were not available because they were already encrusted with jewels, precious seashells from Santraginus, gold leaf, mosaic tiles, lizard skins and a million unidentifiable embellishments and decorations. Glass glittered, silver shone, gold gleamed, Arthur Dent goggled.

"Wowee," said Zaphod. "Zappo."

"Incredible!" breathed Arthur. "The people...! The things...!"

"The things," said Ford Prefect quietly, "are also people."

"The people..." resumed Arthur, "the...other people..."

"The lights...!" said Trillian.

"The tables..." said Arthur.

"The clothes...!" said Trillian.

The waiter thought they sounded like a couple of bailiffs.

"The End of the Universe is very popular," said Zaphod threading his way unsteadily through the throng of tables, some made of marble, some of rich ultramahogany, some even of platinum, and at each a party of exotic creatures chatting among themselves and studying menus.

"People like to dress up for it," continued Zaphod. "Gives it a sense of occasion."

The tables were fanned out in a large circle around a central stage area where a small band was playing light music, at least a thousand tables was

Arthur's guess, and interspersed among them were swaying palms, hissing fountains, grotesque statuary, in short, all the paraphernalia common to all restaurants where little expense has been spared to give the impression that no expense has been spared. Arthur glanced round, half expecting to see someone making an American Express commercial.

Zaphod lurched into Ford, who lurched back into Zaphod.

"Wowee," said Zaphod.

"Zappo," said Ford.

"My great-granddaddy must have really screwed up the computer's works, you know," said Zaphod. "I told it to take us to the nearest place to eat and it sends us to the End of the Universe. Remind me to be nice to it one day."

He paused.

"Hey, everybody's here you know. Everybody who was anybody."

"Was?" said Arthur.

"At the End of the Universe you have to use the past tense a lot," said Zaphod, " 'cause everything's been done, you know. Hi, guys," he called out to a nearby party of giant iguana lifeforms. "How did you do?"

"Is that Zaphod Beeblebrox?" asked one iguana of another iguana.

"I think so," replied the second iguana.

"Well, doesn't that just take the biscuit," said the first iguana.

"Funny old thing, life," said the second iguana.

"It's what you make it," said the first and they lapsed back into silence. They were waiting for the greatest show in the Universe.

"Hey, Zaphod," said Ford, grabbing for his arm and, on account of the third Pan Galactic Gargle Blaster, missing. He pointed a swaying finger.

"There's an old mate of mine," he said. "Hotblack Desiato! See the man at the platinum table with the platinum suit on?"

Zaphod tried to follow Ford's finger with his eyes but it made him feel dizzy. Finally he saw.

"Oh yeah," he said, then recognition came a moment later. "Hey," he said, "did that guy ever make it megabig! Wow, bigger than the biggest thing ever. Other than me."

"Who's he supposed to be?" asked Trillian.

"Hotblack Desiato?" said Zaphod in astonishment. "You don't know? You never heard of Disaster Area?"

"No," said Trillian, who hadn't.

"The biggest," said Ford, "loudest . . ."

" . . . rock band in the history of . . ." he searched for the word.

" . . . history itself," said Zaphod.

"No," said Trillian.

"Zowee," said Zaphod, "here we are at the End of the Universe and you haven't even lived yet. Did you miss out."

He led her off to where the waiter had been waiting all this time at the table. Arthur followed them feeling very lost and alone.

Ford waded off through the throng to renew an old acquaintance.

"Hey, er, Hotblack," he called out, "how you doing? Great to see you big boy, how's the noise? You're looking great, really very, very fat and unwell. Amazing." He slapped the man on the back and was mildly surprised that it seemed to elicit no response. The Pan Galactic Gargle Blasters swilling around inside him told him to plunge on regardless.

"Remember the old days?" he said. "We used to hang out, right? The Bistro Illegal, remember? Slim's Throat Emporium? The Evildrome Boozarama, great days, eh?"

Hotblack Desiato offered no opinion as to whether they were great days or not. Ford was not perturbed.

"And when we were hungry we'd pose as public health inspectors, you remember that? And go around confiscating meals and drinks, right? Till we got food poisoning. Oh, and then there were the long nights of talking and drinking in those smelly rooms above the Café Lou in Gretchen Town, New Betel, and you were always in the next room trying to write songs on your ajuitar and we all hated them. And you said you didn't care, and we said we did because we hated them so much." Ford's eyes were beginning to mist over.

"And you said you didn't want to be a star," he continued, wallowing in nostalgia, "because you despised the star system. And we said—Hadra and Sulijoo and me—that we didn't think you had the option. And what do you do now? You *buy* star systems!"

He turned and solicited the attention of those at nearby tables.

"Here," he said, "is a man who *buys* star systems!"

Hotblack Desiato made no attempt either to confirm or deny this fact, and the attention of the temporary audience waned rapidly.

"I think someone's drunk," muttered a purple bushlike being into his wineglass.

Ford staggered slightly, and sat down heavily on the chair facing Hotblack Desiato.

"What's that number you do?" he said, unwisely grabbing at a bottle for support and tipping it over—into a nearby glass as it happened. Not to waste a happy accident, he drained the glass.

"That really huge number," he continued, "how does it go? 'Bwarm! Bwarm! Baderr!!' something, and in the stage act you do it ends up with this ship crashing right into the sun, and you actually *do* it!"

Ford crashed his fist into his other hand to illustrate this feat graphically. He knocked the bottle over again.

"Ship! Sun! Wham bang!" he cried. "I mean forget lasers and stuff, you guys are into solar flares and *real* sunburn! Oh, and terrible songs."

His eyes followed the stream of liquid glugging out of the bottle onto the table. Something ought to be done about it, he thought.

"Hey, you want a drink?" he said. It began to sink into his squelching mind that something was missing from this reunion, and that the missing something was in some way connected with the fact that the fat man sitting opposite him in the platinum suit and the silvery hat had not yet said "Hi, Ford" or "Great to see you after all this time," or in fact anything at all. More to the point he had not yet even moved.

"Hotblack?" said Ford.

A large meaty hand landed on his shoulder from behind and pushed him aside. He slid gracelessly off his seat and peered upward to see if he could spot the owner of this discourteous hand. The owner was not hard to spot, on account of his being something of the order of seven feet tall and not slightly built with it. In fact he was built the way one builds leather sofas, shiny, lumpy and with lots of solid stuffing. The suit into which the man's body had been stuffed looked as if its only purpose in life was to demonstrate how difficult it was to get this sort of body into a suit. The face had the texture of an orange and the color of an apple, but there the resemblance to anything sweet ended.

"Kid . . ." said a voice which emerged from the man's mouth as if it had been having a really rough time down in his chest.

"Er, yeah?" said Ford conversationally. He staggered back to his feet again and was disappointed that the top of his head didn't come further up the man's body.

"Beat it," said the man.

"Oh yeah?" said Ford, wondering how wise he was being. "And who are you?"

The man considered this for a moment. He wasn't used to being asked this sort of question. Nevertheless, after a while he came up with an answer.

"I'm the guy who's telling you to beat it," he said, "before you get it beaten for you."

"Now listen," said Ford nervously—he wished his head would stop spinning, settle down and get to grips with the situation—"Now listen," he continued, "I am one of Hotblack's oldest friends and . . ."

He glanced at Hotblack Desiato, who still hadn't moved so much as an eyelash.

" . . . and . . ." said Ford again, wondering what would be a good word to say after "and."

The large man came up with a whole sentence to go after "and." He said it.

"And I am Mr. Desiato's bodyguard," it went, "and I am responsible for his body, and I am not responsible for yours, so take it away before it gets damaged."

"Now wait a minute," said Ford.

"No minutes!" boomed the bodyguard. "No waiting! Mr. Desiato speaks to no one!"

"Well, perhaps you'd let him say what he thinks about the matter himself," said Ford.

"He speaks to no one!" bellowed the bodyguard.

Ford glanced anxiously at Hotblack again and was forced to admit to himself that the bodyguard seemed to have the facts on his side. There was still not the slightest sign of movement, let alone keen interest in Ford's welfare.

"Why?" said Ford. "What's the matter with him?"

The bodyguard told him.

The *Hitchhiker's Guide to the Galaxy* notes that Disaster Area, a plutonium rock band from the Gagrakacka Mind Zones, are generally held to be not only the loudest rock band in the Galaxy, but in fact the loudest noise of any kind at all. Regular concert goers judge that the best sound balance is usually to be heard from within large concrete bunkers some thirty-seven miles from the stage, while the musicians themselves play their instruments by remote control from within a heavily insulated spaceship which stays in orbit around the planet—or more frequently around a completely different planet.

Their songs are on the whole very simple and mostly follow the familiar theme of boy-being meets girl-being beneath a silvery moon, which then explodes for no adequately explored reason.

Many worlds have now banned their act altogether, sometimes for artistic reasons, but most commonly because the band's public address system contravenes local strategic arms limitations treaties.

This has not, however, stopped their earnings from pushing back the boundaries of pure hypermathematics, and their chief research accountant has recently been appointed Professor of Neomathematics at the University of Maximegalon, in recognition of both his General and his Special Theories of Disaster Area Tax Returns, in which he proves that the whole fabric of the space-time continuum is not merely curved, it is in fact totally bent.

Ford staggered back to the table where Zaphod, Arthur and Trillian were sitting waiting for the fun to begin.

"Gotta have some food," said Ford.

"Hi, Ford," said Zaphod. "You speak to the big noise boy?"

Ford waggled his head noncommittally.

"Hotblack? I sort of spoke to him, yeah."

"What'd he say?"

"Well, not a lot really. He's...er..."

"Yeah?"

"He's spending a year dead for tax reasons. I've got to sit down."

He sat down.

The waiter approached.

"Would you like to see the menu?" he said. "Or would you like to meet the Dish of the Day?"

"Huh?" said Ford.

"Huh?" said Arthur.

"Huh?" said Trillian.

"That's cool," said Zaphod. "We'll meet the meat."

In a small room in one of the arms of the Restaurant complex a tall, thin, gangling figure pulled aside a curtain and oblivion looked him in the face.

It was not a pretty face, perhaps because oblivion had looked him in it so many times. It was too long for a start, the eyes too sunken and hooded, the cheeks too hollow, his lips were too thin and too long, and when they parted his teeth looked too much like a recently polished bay window. The hands that held the curtain were long and thin too: they were also cold. They lay lightly along the folds of the curtain and gave the impression that if he didn't watch them like a hawk they would crawl away of their own accord and do something unspeakable in a corner.

He let the curtain drop and the terrible light that had played on his features went off to play somewhere more healthy. He prowled around his small chamber like a mantis contemplating an evening's preying, finally settling on a rickety chair by a trestle table, where he leafed through a few sheets of jokes.

A bell rang.

He pushed the thin sheaf of papers aside and stood up. His hands brushed limply over some of the one million rainbow-colored sequins with which his jacket was festooned, and he was gone through the door.

In the Restaurant the lights dimmed, the band quickened its pace, a single spotlight stabbed down into the darkness of the stairway that led up to the center of the stage.

Up the stairs bounded a tall brilliantly colored figure. He burst onto the stage, tripped lightly up to the microphone, removed it from its stand with one swoop of his long thin hand and stood for a moment bowing left and right to the audience, acknowledging their applause and displaying to them his bay window. He waved to his particular friends in the audience even though there weren't any there, and waited for the applause to die down.

He held up his hand and smiled a smile that stretched not merely from

ear to ear, but seemed to extend some way beyond the mere confines of his
face.

"Thank you, ladies and gentlemen!" he cried. "Thank you very much.
Thank you so much."

He eyed them with a twinkling eye.

"Ladies and gentlemen," he said, "the Universe as we know it has now
been in existence for over one hundred and seventy thousand million
billion years and will be ending in a little over half an hour. So, welcome
one and all to Milliways, the Restaurant at the End of the Universe!"

With a gesture he deftly conjured another round of spontaneous
applause. With another gesture he cut it.

"I am your host for tonight," he said. "My name is Max Quordlepleen..." (Everybody knew this, his act was famous throughout the
known Galaxy, but he said it for the fresh applause it generated, which he
acknowledged with a disclaiming smile and wave.) "...and I've just come
straight from the very very other End of Time, where I've been hosting a
show at the Big Bang Burger Bar—where I can tell you we had a very
exciting evening, ladies and gentlemen—and I will be with you right
through this historic occasion, the End of History itself!"

Another burst of applause died away quickly as the lights dimmed down
further. On every table candles ignited themselves spontaneously, eliciting a
slight gasp from all the diners and wreathing them in a thousand tiny
flickering lights and a million intimate shadows. A tremor of excitement
thrilled through the darkened Restaurant as the vast golden dome above
them began very very slowly to dim, to darken, to fade.

Max's voice was hushed as he continued.

"So, ladies and gentlemen," he breathed, "the candles are lit, the band
plays softly and as the force-shielded dome above us fades into transpar-
ency, revealing a dark and sullen sky hung heavy with the ancient light of
livid swollen stars, I can see we're all in for a fabulous evening's apocalypse!"

Even the soft tootling of the band faded away as stunned shock
descended on all those who had not seen this sight before.

A monstrous, grisly light poured in on them
—a hideous light
—a boiling, pestilential light
—a light that would have disfigured hell.

The Universe was coming to an end.

For a few interminable seconds the Restaurant spun silently through the raging void. Then Max spoke again.

"For those of you who ever hoped to see the light at the end of the tunnel," he said, "this is it."

The band struck up again.

"Thank you, ladies and gentlemen," cried Max, "I'll be back with you again in just a moment, and meanwhile I leave you in the very capable hands of Mr. Reg Nullify and his Cataclysmic Combo. Big hand please, ladies and gentlemen, for Reg and the boys!"

The baleful turmoil of the skies continued.

Hesitantly the audience began to clap and after a moment or so normal conversation resumed. Max began his round of the tables, swapping jokes, shouting with laughter, earning his living.

A large dairy animal approached Zaphod Beeblebrox's table, a large fat meaty quadruped of the bovine type with large watery eyes, small horns and what might almost have been an ingratiating smile on its lips.

"Good evening," it lowed and sat back heavily on its haunches, "I am the main Dish of the Day. May I interest you in parts of my body?" It harrumphed and gurgled a bit, wriggled its hind quarters into a more comfortable position and gazed peacefully at them.

Its gaze was met by looks of startled bewilderment from Arthur and Trillian, a resigned shrug from Ford Prefect and naked hunger from Zaphod Beeblebrox.

"Something off the shoulder perhaps?" suggested the animal. "Braised in a white wine sauce?"

"Er, *your* shoulder?" said Arthur in a horrified whisper.

"But naturally my shoulder, sir," mooed the animal contentedly, "nobody else's is mine to offer."

Zaphod leapt to his feet and started prodding and feeling the animal's shoulder appreciatively.

"Or the rump is very good," murmured the animal. "I've been exercising it and eating plenty of grain, so there's a lot of good meat there." It gave a mellow grunt, gurgled again and started to chew the cud. It swallowed the cud again.

"Or a casserole of me perhaps?" it added.

"You mean this animal actually wants us to eat it?" whispered Trillian to Ford.

"Me?" said Ford, with a glazed look in his eyes. "I don't mean anything."

"That's absolutely horrible," exclaimed Arthur, "the most revolting thing I've ever heard."

"What's the problem, Earthman?" said Zaphod, now transferring his attention to the animal's enormous rump.

"I just don't want to eat an animal that's standing there inviting me to," said Arthur. "It's heartless."

"Better than eating an animal that doesn't want to be eaten," said Zaphod.

"That's not the point," Arthur protested. Then he thought about it for a moment. "All right," he said, "maybe it is the point. I don't care, I'm not going to think about it now. I'll just...er..."

The Universe raged about him in its death throes.

"I think I'll just have a green salad," he muttered.

"May I urge you to consider my liver?" asked the animal, "it must be very rich and tender by now, I've been force-feeding myself for months."

"A green salad," said Arthur emphatically.

"A green salad?" said the animal, rolling his eyes disapprovingly at Arthur.

"Are you going to tell me," said Arthur, "that I shouldn't have green salad?"

"Well," said the animal, "I know many vegetables that are very clear on that point. Which is why it was eventually decided to cut through the whole tangled problem and breed an animal that actually wanted to be eaten and was capable of saying so clearly and distinctly. And here I am."

It managed a very slight bow.

"Glass of water please," said Arthur.

"Look," said Zaphod, "we want to eat, we don't want to make a meal of the issues. Four rare steaks please, and hurry. We haven't eaten in five hundred and seventy-six thousand million years."

The animal staggered to its feet. It gave a mellow gurgle.

"A very wise choice, sir, if I may say so. Very good," it said. "I'll just nip off and shoot myself."

He turned and gave a friendly wink to Arthur.

"Don't worry, sir," he said, "I'll be very humane."

It waddled unhurriedly off to the kitchen.

A matter of minutes later the waiter arrived with four huge steaming steaks. Zaphod and Ford wolfed straight into them without a second's hesitation. Trillian paused, then shrugged and started into hers.

"Hey, Earthman," said Zaphod with a malicious grin on the face that wasn't stuffing itself, "what's eating you?"

And the band played on.

All around the Restaurant people and things relaxed and chatted. The air was filled with talk of this and that, and with the mingled scents of exotic plants, extravagant foods and insidious wines. For an infinite number of miles in every direction the universal cataclysm was gathering to a stupefying climax. Glancing at his watch, Max returned to the stage with a flourish.

"And now, ladies and gentlemen," he beamed, "is everyone having one last wonderful time?"

"Yes," called out the sort of people who call out "yes" when comedians ask them if they're having a wonderful time.

"That's wonderful," enthused Max, "absolutely wonderful. And as the photon storms gather in swirling crowds around us, preparing to tear apart the last of the red hot suns, I know you're all going to settle back and enjoy with me what I know we will all find an immensely exciting and terminal experience."

He paused. He caught the audience with a glittering eye.

"Believe me, ladies and gentlemen," he said, "there is nothing penultimate about this one."

He paused again. Tonight his timing was immaculate. Time after time he had done this show, night after night. Not that the word *night* had any meaning here at the extremity of time. All there was was the endless repetition of the final moment, as the Restaurant rocked slowly forward over the brink of time's farthest edge—and back again. This "night" was good though, the audience was writhing in the palm of his sickly hand. His voice dropped. They had to strain to hear him.

"This," he said, "really is the absolute end, the final chilling desolation, in which the whole majestic sweep of creation becomes extinct. This, ladies and gentlemen, is the proverbial 'it.' "

He dropped his voice still lower. In the stillness, a fly would not have dared clear its throat.

"After this," he said, "there is nothing. Void. Emptiness. Oblivion. Absolute nothing. . . ."

His eyes glittered again—or did they twinkle?

"Nothing . . . except, of course, for the desserts and a fine selection of Aldebaran liqueurs!"

The band gave him a music sting. He wished they wouldn't, he didn't need it, not an artist of his caliber. He could play the audience like his own musical instrument. They were laughing with relief. He followed on.

"And for once," he cried cheerily, "you don't need to worry about having a hangover in the morning—because there won't *be* any more mornings!"

He beamed at his happy, laughing audience. He glanced up at the sky, going through the same death routine every night, but his glance was only for a fraction of a second. He trusted it to do its job, as one professional trusts another.

"And now," he said, strutting about the stage, "at the risk of putting a damper on the wonderful sense of doom and futility here this evening, I would like to welcome a few parties."

He pulled a card from his pocket.

"Do we have"—he put up a hand to hold back the cheers—"Do we have a party here from the Zansellquasure Flamarion Bridge Club from beyond the Vortvoid of Qvarne? Are they here?"

A rousing cheer came from the back, but he pretended not to hear. He peered around trying to find them.

"Are they here?" he asked again, to elicit a louder cheer.

He got it, as he always did.

"Ah, there they are. Well, last bids, lads—and no cheating, remember this is a very solemn moment."

He lapped up the laughter.

"And do we also have, do we have . . . a party of minor deities from the Halls of Asgard?"

Away to his right came a rumble of thunder. Lightning arced across the stage. A small group of hairy men with helmets sat looking very pleased with themselves, and raised their glasses to him.

Has-beens, he thought to himself.

"Careful with that hammer, sir," he said.

They did their trick with the lightning again. Max gave them a very thin-lipped smile.

"And thirdly," he said, "thirdly a party of Young Conservatives from Sirius B, are they here?"

A party of smartly dressed young dogs stopped throwing rolls at each other and started throwing rolls at the stage. They yapped and barked unintelligibly.

"Yes," said Max, "well, this is all your fault, you realize that?"

"And finally," said Max, quieting the audience down and putting on his solemn face, "finally I believe we have with us here tonight, a party of believers, very devout believers, from the Church of the Second Coming of the Great Prophet Zarquon."

There were about twenty of them, sitting right out on the edge of the floor, ascetically dressed, sipping mineral water nervously and staying apart from the festivities. They blinked resentfully as the spotlight was turned on them.

"There they are," said Max, "sitting there, patiently. He said he'd come again, and he's kept you waiting a long time, so let's hope he's hurrying fellas, because he's only got eight minutes left!"

The party of Zarquon's followers sat rigid, refusing to be buffeted by the waves of uncharitable laughter which swept over them.

Max restrained his audience.

"No, but seriously though, folks, seriously though, no offense meant. No, I know we shouldn't make fun of deeply held beliefs, so I think a big hand please for the Great Prophet Zarquon . . ."

The audience clapped respectfully.

" . . . wherever he's gone to!"

He blew a kiss to the stony-faced party and returned to the center of the stage.

He grabbed a tall stool and sat on it.

"It's marvelous though," he rattled on, "to see so many of you here tonight—no, isn't it though? Yes, absolutely marvelous. Because I know that so many of you come here time and time again, which I think is really wonderful, to come and watch this final end of everything, and then return home to your own eras . . . and raise families, strive for new and better societies, fight terrible wars for what you know to be right. . . . It really gives one hope for the future of all lifekind. Except of course"—he waved at the blitzing turmoil above and around them—"that we know it hasn't got one. . . ."

Arthur turned to Ford—he hadn't quite got this place worked out in his mind.

"Look, surely," he said, "if the Universe is about to end . . . don't we go with it?"

Ford gave him a three-Pan-Galactic-Gargle-Blaster look, in other words a rather unsteady one.

"No," he said, "look," he said, "as soon as you come into this dive you get held in this sort of amazing force-shielded temporal warp thing. I think."

"Oh," said Arthur. He turned his attention back to a bowl of soup he'd managed to get from the waiter to replace his steak.

"Look," said Ford. "I'll show you."

He grabbed at a napkin off the table and fumbled hopelessly with it.

"Look," he said again, "imagine this napkin, right, as the temporal Universe, right? And this spoon as a transductional mode in the matter curve..."

It took him a while to say this last part, and Arthur hated to interrupt him.

"That's the spoon I was eating with," he said.

"All right," said Ford, "imagine *this* spoon"—he found a small wooden spoon on a tray of relishes—"this spoon"—but found it rather tricky to pick up—"no, better still this fork...."

"Hey, would you let go of my fork?" snapped Zaphod.

"All right," said Ford, "all right, all right. Why don't we say...why don't we say that this wineglass is the temporal Universe...."

"What, the one you've just knocked on the floor?"

"Did I do that?"

"Yes."

"All right," said Ford, "forget that. I mean...I mean, look, do you know—do you know how the Universe actually began for a kick off?"

"Probably not," said Arthur, who wished he'd never embarked on any of this.

"All right," said Ford, "imagine this. Right. You get this bath. Right. A large round bath. And it's made of ebony."

"Where from?" said Arthur. "Harrods was destroyed by the Vogons."

"Doesn't matter."

"So you keep saying."

"Listen."

"All right."

"You get this bath, see? Imagine you've got this bath. And it's ebony. And it's conical."

"Conical?" said Arthur. "What sort of..."

"Shhh!" said Ford. "It's conical. So what you do is, you see, you fill it with fine white sand, all right? Or sugar. Fine white sand, and/or sugar. Anything. Doesn't matter. Sugar's fine. And when it's full, you pull the plug out...are you listening?"

"I'm listening."

"You pull the plug out, and it all just twirls away, twirls away you see, out of the plughole."

"I see."

"You don't see. You don't see at all. I haven't got to the clever bit yet. You want to hear the clever bit?"

"Tell me the clever bit."

"I'll tell you the clever bit."

Ford thought for a moment, trying to remember what the clever bit was.

"The clever bit," he said, "is this. You film it happening."

"Clever," agreed Arthur.

"You get a movie camera, and you film it happening."

"Clever."

"That's not the clever bit. This is the clever bit, I remember now that this is the clever bit. The clever bit is that you then thread the film in the projector . . . backward!"

"Backward?"

"Yes. Threading it backward is definitely the clever bit. So then, you just sit and watch it, and everything just appears to spiral upward out of the plughole and fill the bath. See?"

"And that's how the Universe began, is it?" said Arthur.

"No," said Ford, "but it's a marvelous way to relax."

He reached for his wineglass.

"Where's my wineglass?" he said.

"It's on the floor."

"Ah."

Tipping back his chair to look for it, Ford collided with the small green waiter who was approaching the table carrying a portable telephone.

Ford excused himself to the waiter explaining that it was because he was extemely drunk.

The waiter said that that was quite all right and that he perfectly understood.

Ford thanked the waiter for his kind indulgence, attempted to tug his forelock, missed by six inches and slid under the table.

"Mr. Zaphod Beeblebrox?" inquired the waiter.

"Er, yeah?" said Zaphod, glancing up from his third steak.

"There is a phone call for you."

"Hey, what?"

"A phone call, sir."

"For me? Here? Hey, but who knows where I am?"

One of his minds raced. The other dawdled lovingly over the food it was still shoveling in.

"Excuse me if I carry on, won't you?" said his eating head and carried on.

There were now so many people after him he'd lost count. He shouldn't have made such a conspicuous entrance. Hell, why not though, he thought. How do you know you're having fun if there's no one watching you have it?

"Maybe somebody here tipped off the Galactic Police," said Trillian. "Everyone saw you come in."

"You mean they want to arrest me over the phone?" said Zaphod. "Could be. I'm a pretty dangerous dude when I'm cornered."

"Yeah," said the voice from under the table, "you go to pieces so fast people get hit by the shrapnel."

"Hey, what is this, Judgment Day?" snapped Zaphod.

"Do we get to see that as well?" asked Arthur nervously.

"I'm in no hurry," muttered Zaphod. "Okay, so who's the cat on the phone?" He kicked Ford. "Hey, get up there, kid," he said to him. "I may need you."

"I am not," said the waiter, "personally acquainted with the metal gentleman in question, sir. . . ."

"Metal?"

"Yes, sir."

"Did you say metal?"

"Yes, sir. I said that I am not personally acquainted with the metal gentleman in question. . . ."

"Okay, carry on."

"But I am informed that he has been awaiting your return for a considerable number of millennia. It seems you left here somewhat precipitately."

"*Left* here?" said Zaphod. "Are you being strange? We only just arrived here."

"Indeed, sir," persisted the waiter doggedly, "but before you arrived here, sir, I understand that you left here."

Zaphod tried this in one brain, then in the other.

"You're saying," he said, "that before we arrived here, we left here?"

This is going to be a long night, thought the waiter.

"Precisely, sir," he said.

"Put your analyst on danger money, baby," advised Zaphod.

"No, wait a minute," said Ford, emerging above table level again, "where exactly is here?"

"To be absolutely exact, sir, it is Frogstar World B."

"But we just *left* there," protested Zaphod. "We left there and came to the Restaurant at the End of the Universe."

"Yes, sir," said the waiter, feeling that he was now into the home stretch and running well, "the one was constructed on the ruins of the other."

"Oh," said Arthur brightly, "you mean we've traveled in time but not in space."

"Listen, you semievolved simian," cut in Zaphod, "go climb a tree will you?"

Arthur bristled.

"Go bang your heads together, four-eyes," he advised Zaphod.

"No, no," the waiter said to Zaphod, "your monkey has got it right, sir."

Arthur stuttered in fury and said nothing apposite, or indeed coherent.

"You jumped forward...I believe five hundred and seventy-six thousand million years while staying in exactly the same place," explained the waiter. He smiled. He had a wonderful feeling that he had finally won though against what had seemed to be insuperable odds.

"That's it!" said Zaphod. "I got it. I told the computer to send us to the nearest place to eat, that's exactly what it did. Give or take five hundred and seventy-six thousand million years or whatever, we never moved. Neat."

They all agreed this was very neat.

"But who," said Zaphod, "is the cat on the phone?"

"Whatever happened to Marvin?" said Trillian.

Zaphod clapped his hands to his heads.

"The Paranoid Android! I left him moping about on Frogstar World B."

"When was this?"

"Well, er, five hundred and seventy-six thousand million years ago I suppose," said Zaphod. "Hey, er, hand me the raprod, Plate Captain."

The little waiter's eyebrows wandered about his forehead in confusion.

"I beg your pardon, sir?" he said.

"The phone, waiter," said Zaphod, grabbing it off him. "Shee, you guys are so unhip it's a wonder your bums don't fall off."

"Indeed, sir."

"Hey, Marvin, is that you?" said Zaphod into the phone. "How you doing, kid?"

There was a long pause before a thin low voice came up the line.

Zaphod cupped his hand over the phone.

"It's Marvin," he said.

"Hey, Marvin," he said into the phone again, "we're having a great time. Food, wine, a little personal abuse and the Universe going foom. Where can we find you?"

Again the pause.

"You don't have to pretend to be interested in me you know," said Marvin at last. "I know perfectly well I'm only a menial robot."

"Okay, okay," said Zaphod, "but where are you?"

" 'Reverse primary thrust, Marvin,' that's what they say to me, 'open airlock number three, Marvin. Marvin, can you pick up that piece of paper?' Can I pick up that piece of paper! Here I am, brain the size of a planet and they ask me to . . . "

"Yeah, yeah," sympathized Zaphod hardly at all.

"But I'm quite used to being humiliated," droned Marvin, "I can even go and stick my head in a bucket of water if you like. Would you like me to go and stick my head in a bucket of water? I've got one ready. Wait a minute."

"Er, hey, Marvin . . . " interrupted Zaphod, but it was too late. Sad little clunks and gurgles came up the line.

"What's he saying?" asked Trillian.

"Nothing," said Zaphod, "he just phoned up to wash his head at us."

"There," said Marvin, coming back on the line and bubbling a bit, "I hope that gave satisfaction. . . . "

"Yeah, yeah," said Zaphod, "now will you please tell us where you are?"

"I'm in the parking lot," said Marvin.

"The parking lot?" said Zaphod. "What are you doing there?"

"Parking cars, what else does one do in a parking lot?"

"Okay, hang in there, we'll be right down."

In one movement Zaphod leaped to his feet, threw down the phone and wrote "Hotblack Desiato" on the bill.

"Come on, guys," he said, "Marvin's in the parking lot. Let's get on down."

"What's he doing in the parking lot?" asked Arthur.

"Parking cars, what else? Dum dum."

"But what about the End of the Universe? We'll miss the big moment."

"I've seen it. It's rubbish," said Zaphod, "nothing but a gnab gib."

"A what?"

"Opposite of a big bang. Come on, let's get zappy."

Few of the other diners paid them any attention as they weaved their way through the Restaurant to the exit. Their eyes were riveted on the horror of the skies.

"An interesting effect to watch for," Max was telling them, "is in the upper left-hand quadrant of the sky, where if you look very carefully you can see the star system Hastromil boiling away into the ultraviolet. Anyone here from Hastromil?"

There were one or two slightly hesitant cheers from somewhere at the back.

"Well," said Max beaming cheerfully at them, "it's too late to worry about whether you left the gas on now."

The main reception foyer was almost empty but Ford nevertheless weaved his way through it.

Zaphod grasped him firmly by the arm and maneuvered him
into a cubicle standing to one side of the entrance hall.

"What are you doing to him?" asked Arthur.

"Sobering him up," said Zaphod and pushed a coin into a slot. Lights
flashed, gases swirled.

"Hi," said Ford stepping out a moment later, "where are we going?"

"Down to the parking lot, come on."

"What about the personnel Time Teleports?" said Ford. "Get us
straight back to the *Heart of Gold.*"

"Yeah, but I've cooled on that ship. Zarniwoop can have it. I don't want
to play his games. Let's see what we can find."

A Sirius Cybernetics Corporation Happy Vertical People Transporter
took them down deep into the substrata beneath the Restaurant. They
were glad to see it had been vandalized and didn't try to make them happy
as well as take them down.

At the bottom of the shaft the elevator doors opened and a blast of cold
stale air hit them.

The first thing they saw on leaving the elevator was a long concrete wall
with over fifty doors in it offering lavatory facilities for all of fifty major life
forms. Nevertheless, like every parking lot in the Galaxy throughout the
entire history of parking lots, this parking lot smelled predominantly of
impatience.

They turned a corner and found themselves on a moving catwalk that
traversed a vast cavernous space that stretched off into the dim distance.

It was divided off into bays each of which contained a spaceship
belonging to one of the diners upstairs, some smallish and utilitarian mass
production models, others vast shining limoships, the playthings of the
very rich.

Zaphod's eyes sparkled with something that may or may not have been
avarice as he passed over them. In fact it's best to be clear on this point—
avarice is definitely what it was.

"There he is," said Trillian. "Marvin, down there."

They looked where she was pointing. Dimly they could see a small metal figure listlessly rubbing a small rag on one remote corner of a giant silver suncruiser.

At short intervals along the moving catwalk, wide transparent tubes led down to floor level. Zaphod stepped off the catwalk into one of these and floated gently downward. The others followed. Thinking back to this later. Arthur Dent thought it was the single most enjoyable experience of his travels in the Galaxy.

"Hey, Marvin," said Zaphod, striding over toward to him. "Hey, kid, are we pleased to see you."

Marvin turned, and insofar as it is possible for a totally inert metal face to look reproachful, this is what it did.

"No you're not," he said, "no one ever is."

"Suit yourself," said Zaphod and turned away to ogle the ships. Ford went with him.

Only Trillian and Arthur actually went up to Marvin.

"No, really we are," said Trillian and patted him in a way that he disliked intensely, "hanging around waiting for us all this time."

"Five hundred and seventy-six thousand million, three thousand five hundred and seventy-nine years." said Marvin. "I counted them."

"Well, here we are now," said Trillian, feeling—quite correctly in Marvin's view—that it was a slightly foolish thing to say.

"The first ten million years were the worst," said Marvin, "and the second ten million years, they were the worst too. The third ten million I didn't enjoy at all. After that I went into a bit of a decline."

He paused just long enough to make them feel they ought to say something, and then interrupted.

"It's the people you meet in this job that really get you down," he said and paused again.

Trillian cleared her throat.

"Is that . . ."

The best conversation I had was over forty million years ago," continued Marvin.

Again the pause.

"Oh d—"

"And that was with a coffee machine."

He waited.

"That's a—"

"You don't like talking to me do you?" said Marvin in a low desolate tone.

Trillian talked to Arthur instead.

Farther down the chamber Ford Prefect had found something of which he very much liked the look, several such things in fact.

"Zaphod," he said in a quiet voice, "just look at some of these little star trolleys. . . . "

Zaphod looked and liked.

The craft they were looking at was in fact pretty small but extraordinary, and very much a rich kid's toy. It was not much to look at. It resembled nothing so much as a paper dart about twenty feet long made of thin but tough metal foil. At the rear end was a small horizontal two-man cockpit. It had a tiny charm-drive engine, which was not capable of moving it at any great speed. The thing it did have, however, was a heat-sink.

The heat-sink had a mass of some two thousand billion tons and was contained within a black hole mounted in an electromagnetic field situated halfway along the length of the ship, and this heat-sink enabled the craft to be maneuvered to within a few miles of a yellow sun, there to catch and ride the solar flares that burst out from its surface.

Flare riding is one of the most exotic and exhilarating sports in existence, and those who can dare and afford to do it are among the most lionized men in the Galaxy. It is also of course stupefyingly dangerous—those who don't die riding invariably die of sexual exhaustion at one of the Daedalus Club's Après-Flare parties.

Ford and Zaphod looked and passed on.

"And this baby," said Ford, "the tangerine star buggy with the black sunbusters . . . "

Again, the star buggy was a small ship—a totally misnamed one in fact, because the one thing it couldn't manage was interstellar distances. Basically it was a sporty planet hopper dolled up to look like something it wasn't. Nice lines though. They passed on.

The next one was a big one and thirty yards long—a coach-limoship and obviously designed with one aim in mind, that of making the beholder sick with envy. The paintwork and accessory detail clearly said "Not only am I rich enough to afford this ship, I am also rich enough not to take it seriously." It was wonderfully hideous.

"Just look at it," said Zaphod, "multicluster quark drive, perspulex running boards. Got to be a Lazlar Lyricon custom job."

He examined every inch.

"Yes," he said, "look, the infrapink lizard emblem on the neutrino cowling. Lazlar's trademark. The man has no shame."

"I was passed by one of these mothers once, out by the Axel Nebula," said Ford. "I was going flat out and this thing just strolled past me, star drive hardly ticking over. Just incredible."

Zaphod whistled appreciatively.

"Ten seconds later," said Ford, "it smashed straight into the third moon of Jaglan Beta."

"Yeah, right?"

"Amazing-looking ship though. Looks like a fish, moves like a fish, steers like a cow."

Ford looked round the other side.

"Hey, come see," he called out, "there's a big mural painted on this side. A bursting sun—Disaster Area's trademark. This must be Hotblack's ship. Lucky old bugger. They do this terrible song you know which ends with a stuntship crashing into the sun. Meant to be an amazing spectacle. Expensive in stuntships though."

Zaphod's attention however was elsewhere. His attention was riveted on the ship standing next to Hotblack Desiato's limo. His mouths hung open.

"That," he said, "that . . . is really bad for the eyes. . . ."

Ford looked. He too stood astonished.

It was a ship of classic, simple design, like a flattened salmon, twenty yards long, very clean, very sleek. There was just one remarkable thing about it.

"It's so . . . *black*!" said Ford Prefect. "You can hardly make out its shape . . . light just seems to fall into it!"

Zaphod said nothing. He had simply fallen in love.

The blackness of it was so extreme that it was almost impossible to tell how close you were standing to it.

"Your eyes just slide off it . . ." said Ford in wonder. It was an emotional moment. He bit his lip.

Zaphod moved forward to it, slowly, like a man possessed—or more accurately like a man who wanted to possess. His hand reached out to stroke it. His hand stopped. His hand reached out to stroke it again. His hand stopped again.

"Come and feel this surface," he said in a hushed voice.

Ford put his hand out to feel it. His hand stopped.

"You . . . you can't . . ." he said.

"See?" said Zaphod. "It's just totally frictionless. This must be one mother of a mover. . . ."

He turned to look at Ford seriously. At least, one of his heads did—the other stayed gazing in awe at the ship.

"What do you reckon, Ford?" he said.

"You mean . . . er"—Ford looked over his shoulder—"you mean stroll off with it? You think we should?"

"No."

"Nor do I."

"But we're going to, aren't we?"

"How can we not?"

They gazed a little longer, till Zaphod suddenly pulled himself together.

"We better shift soon," he said. "In a moment or so the Universe will have ended and all the Captain Creeps will be pouring down here to find their bourge-mobiles."

"Zaphod," said Ford.

"Yeah?"

"How do we do it?"

"Simple," said Zaphod. He turned. "Marvin!" he called.

Slowly, laboriously and with a million little clanking and creaking noises that he had learned to simulate, Marvin turned round to answer the summons.

"Come on over here," said Zaphod. "We've got a job for you."

Marvin trudged toward them.

"I won't enjoy it," he said.

"Yes, you will," enthused Zaphod, "there's a whole new life stretching out ahead of you."

"Oh, not another one," groaned Marvin.

"Will you shut up and listen!" hissed Zaphod. "This time there's going to be exicitement and adventure and really wild things."

"Sounds awful," Marvin said.

"Marvin! All I'm trying to ask you . . ."

"I suppose you want me to open this spaceship for you?"

"What? Er . . . yes. Yeah, that's right," said Zaphod jumpily. He was keeping at least three eyes on the entrance. Time was short.

"Well, I wish you'd just tell me rather than try to engage my enthusiasm," said Marvin, "because I haven't got one."

He walked on up to the ship, touched it, and a hatchway swung open. Ford and Zaphod stared at the opening.

"Don't mention it," said Marvin. "Oh, you didn't." He trudged away again.

Arthur and Trillian clustered around.

"What's happening?" asked Arthur.

"Look at this," said Ford. "Look at the interior of this ship."

"Weirder and weirder," breathed Zaphod.

"It's black," said Ford. "Everything in it is just totally black. . . ."

In the Restaurant, things were fast approaching the moment after which there wouldn't be any more moments.

All eyes were fixed on the dome, other than those of Hotblack Desiato's bodyguard, which were looking intently at Hotblack Desiato, and those of Hotblack Desiato himself which the bodyguard had closed out of respect.

The bodyguard leaned forward over the table. Had Hotblack Desiato been alive, he probably would have deemed this a good moment to lean back, or even go for a short walk. His bodyguard was not a man who improved with proximity. On account of his unfortunate condition, however, Hotblack Desiato remained totally inert.

"Mr. Desiato, sir?" whispered the bodyguard. Whenever he spoke, it looked as if the muscles on either side of his mouth were clambering over each other to get out of the way.

"Mr. Desiato? Can you hear me?"

Hotblack Desiato, quite naturally, said nothing.

"Hotblack?" hissed the bodyguard.

Again, quite naturally, Hotblack Desiato did not reply. Supernaturally, however, he did.

On the table in front of him a wineglass rattled, and a fork rose an inch or so and tapped against the glass. It settled on the table again.

The bodyguard gave a satisfied grunt.

"It's time we were going, Mr. Desiato," muttered the bodyguard, "don't want to get caught in the rush, not in your condition. You want to get to the next gig nice and relaxed. There was a really big audience for it. One of the best. Kakrafoon. Five hundred and seventy-six thousand and two million years ago. Had you been looking forward to it?"

The fork rose again, paused, waggled in a noncommittal sort of way and dropped again.

"Ah, come on," said the bodyguard, "it's going to have been great. You knocked 'em cold." The bodyguard would have given Dr. Dan Streetmentioner an apoplectic attack.

"The black ship going into the sun always gets 'em, and the new one's a beauty. Be real sorry to see it go. If we get on down there, I'll set the black ship autopilot and we'll cruise off in the limo. Okay?"

The fork tapped once in agreement, and the glass of wine mysteriously emptied itself.

The bodyguard wheeled Hotblack Desiato's chair out of the Restaurant.

"And now," cried Max from the center of the stage, "the moment you've all been waiting for!" He flung his arms into the air. Behind him, the band went into a frenzy of percussion and rolling synthochords. Max had argued with them about this but they had claimed it was in their contract that that's what they would do. His agent would have to sort it out.

"The skies begin to boil!" he cried. "Nature collapses into the screaming void! In twenty seconds' time, the Universe itself will be at an end! See where the light of infinity bursts in upon us!"

The hideous fury of destruction blazed about them—and at that moment a still small trumpet sounded as from an infinite distance. Max's eyes swiveled round to glare at the band. None of them seemed to be playing a trumpet. Suddenly a wisp of smoke was swirling and shimmering on the stage next to him. The trumpet was joined by more trumpets. Over five hundred times Max had done this show, and nothing like this had ever happened before. He drew back in alarm from the swirling smoke, and as he did so, a figure slowly materialized inside, the figure of an ancient man, bearded, robed, and wreathed in light. In his eyes were stars and on his brow a golden crown.

"What's this?" whispered Max, wild-eyed. "What's happening?"

At the back of the Restaurant the stony-faced party from the Church of the Second Coming of the Great Prophet Zarquon leaped ecstatically to their feet chanting and crying.

Max blinked in amazement. He threw up his arms to the audience.

"A big hand please, ladies and gentlemen," he hollered, "for the Great Prophet Zarquon! He has come! Zarquon has come again!"

Thunderous applause broke out as Max strode across the stage and handed his microphone to the Prophet.

Zarquon coughed. He peered round at the assembled gathering. The stars in his eyes twinkled uneasily. He handled the microphone with confusion.

"Er..." he said, "hello. Er, look, I'm sorry I'm a bit late. I've had the most ghastly time, all sorts of things cropping up at the last moment."

He seemed nervous of the expectant awed hush. He cleared his throat.

"Er, how are we for time?" he said. "Have I just got a min—"

And so the Universe ended.

One of the major selling points of that wholly remarkable travel book, *The Hitchhiker's Guide to the Galaxy*, apart from its relative cheapness and the fact that it has the words DON'T PANIC written in large friendly letters on its cover, is its compendious and occasionally accurate glossary. The statistics relating to the geo-social nature of the Universe, for instance, are deftly set out between pages nine hundred and thirty-eight thousand three hundred and twenty-four and nine hundred and thirty-eight thousand three hundred and twenty-six; and the simplistic style in which they are written is partly explained by the fact that the editors, having to meet a publishing deadline, copied the information off the back of a packet of breakfast cereal, hastily embroidering it with a few footnotes in order to avoid prosecution under the incomprehensibly tortuous Galactic Copyright laws.

It is interesting to note that a later and wilier editor sent the book backward in time through a temporal warp, and then successfully sued the breakfast cereal company for infringement of the same laws.

Here is a sample:

The Universe—some information to help you live in it.

1 AREA: Infinite.

The Hitchhiker's Guide to the Galaxy *offers this definition of the word "Infinite."*
Infinite: *Bigger than the biggest thing ever and then some. Much bigger than that in fact, really amazingly immense, a totally stunning size, real "wow, that's big," time. Infinity is just so big that, by comparison, bigness itself looks really titchy. Gigantic multiplied by colossal multiplied by staggeringly huge is the sort of concept we're trying to get across here.*

2 IMPORTS: None.

It is impossible to import things into an infinite area, there being no outside to import things in from.

3 EXPORTS: None.

See Imports.

4 POPULATION: None.

It is known that there are an infinite number of worlds, simply because there is an infinite amount of space for them to be in. However, not every one of them is inhabited. Therefore, there must be a finite number of inhabited worlds. Any finite number divided by infinity is as near to nothing as makes no odds, so the average population of all the planets in the Universe can be said to be zero. From this it follows that the population of the whole Universe is also zero, and that any people you may meet from time to time are merely the products of a deranged imagination.

5 MONETARY UNITS: None.

In fact there are three freely convertible currencies in the Galaxy, but none of them count. The Altairian Dollar has recently collapsed, the Flainian Pobble Bead is only exchangeable for other Flainian Pobble Beads, and the Triganic Pu has its own very special problems. Its exchange rate of eight Ningis to one Pu is simple enough, but since a Ningi is a triangular rubber coin six thousand eight hundred miles along each side, no one has ever collected enough to own one Pu. Ningis are not negotiable currency, because the Galactibanks refuse to deal in fiddling small change. From this basic premise it is very simple to prove that the Galactibanks are also the product of a deranged imagination.

6 ART: None.

The function of art is to hold the mirror up to nature, and there simply isn't a mirror big enough—see point one.

7 SEX: None.

Well, in fact there is an awful lot of this, largely because of the total lack of money, trade, banks, art or anything else that might keep all the nonexistent people of the Universe occupied.

However, it is not worth embarking on a long discussion of it now because it really is terribly complicated. For further information see Guide Chapters seven, nine, ten, eleven, fourteen, sixteen, seventeen, nineteen, twenty-one to eighty-four inclusive, and in fact most of the rest of the Guide.

Chapter 20

The Restaurant continued existing, but everything else had stopped. Temporal relastatics held it and protected it in a nothingness that wasn't merely a vacuum, it was simply nothing—there was nothing in which a vacuum could be said to exist. The force-shielded dome had once again been rendered opaque, the party was over, the diners were leaving, Zarquon had vanished along with the rest of the Universe, the Time Turbines were preparing to pull the Restaurant back across the brink of time in readiness for the lunch sitting, and Max Quordlepleen was back in his small curtained dressing room trying to raise his agent on the tempophone.

In the parking lot stood the black ship, closed and silent.

Into the parking lot came the late Mr. Hotblack Desiato, propelled along the moving catwalk by his bodyguard.

They descended one of the tubes. As they approached the limoship a hatchway swung down from its side, engaged the wheels of the wheelchair and drew it inside. The bodyguard followed, and having seen his boss safely connected up to his death-support system, moved up to the small cockpit. Here he operated the remote control system which activated the autopilot in the black ship lying next to the limo, thus causing great relief to Zaphod Beeblebrox who had been trying to start the thing for over ten minutes.

The black ship glided smoothly forward out of its bay, turned and moved down the central causeway swiftly and quietly. At the end it accelerated rapidly, flung itself into the temporal launch chamber and began the long journey back into the distant past.

The Milliways Lunch Menu quotes, by permission, a passage from *The Hitchhiker's Guide to the Galaxy*. The passage is this:

The History of every major Galactic Civilization tends to pass through three distinct and recognizable phases, those of Survival, Inquiry and Sophistication, otherwise known as the How, Why, and Where phases.

For instance, the first phase is characterized by the question "How can we eat?", the second by the question "Why do we eat?" and the third by the question, "Where shall we have lunch?"

The Menu goes on to suggest that Milliways, the Restaurant at the End of the Universe, would be a very agreeable and sophisticated answer to that third question.

What it doesn't go on to say is that though it will usually take a large civilization many thousands of years to pass through the How, Why and Where phases, small social groupings under stressful conditions can pass through them with extreme rapidity.

"How are we doing?" said Arthur Dent.

"Badly," said Ford Prefect.

"Where are we going?" said Trillian.

"I don't know," said Zaphod Beeblebrox.

"Why not?" demanded Arthur Dent.

"Shut up," suggested Zaphod Beeblebrox and Ford Prefect.

"Basically, what you're trying to say," said Arthur Dent, ignoring this suggestion, "is that we're out of control."

The ship was rocking and swaying sickeningly as Ford and Zaphod tried to wrest control from the autopilot. The engines howled and whined like tired children in a supermarket.

"It's the wild color scheme that freaks me," said Zaphod whose love affair with this ship had lasted almost three minutes into the flight. "Every time you try to operate one of these weird black controls that are labeled in black on a black background, a little black light lights up black to let you know you've done it. What is this? Some kind of galactic hyperhearse?"

The walls of the swaying cabin were also black, the ceiling was black, the seats—which were rudimentary since the only important trip this ship was designed for was supposed to be unmanned—were black, the control panel was black, the instruments were black, the little screws that held them in place were black, the thin tufted nylon floor covering was black, and when they had lifted up a corner of it they had discovered that the foam underlay also was black.

"Perhaps whoever designed it had eyes that responded to different wavelengths," offered Trillian.

"Or didn't have much imagination," muttered Arthur.

"Perhaps," said Marvin, "he was feeling very depressed."

In fact, though they weren't to know it, the decor had been chosen in honor of its owner's sad, lamented, and tax deductible condition.

The ship gave a particularly sickening lurch.

"Take it easy," pleaded Arthur, "you're making me space sick."

"Time sick," said Ford. "We're plummeting backward through time."

"Thank you," said Arthur, "now I think I really am going to be ill."

"Go ahead," said Zaphod, "we could do with a little color about the place."

"This is meant to be polite after-dinner conversation, is it?" snapped Arthur.

Zaphod left the controls to Ford to figure out, and lurched over to Arthur.

"Look, Earthman," he said angrily, "you've got a job to do, right? The Question to the Ultimate Answer, right?"

"What, that thing?" said Arthur. "I thought we'd forgotten about that."

"Not me, baby. Like the mice said, it's worth a lot of money in the right quarters. And it's all locked up in that head thing of yours."

"Yes but—"

"But nothing! Think about it. The Meaning of Life! We get our fingers on that we can hold every shrink in the Galaxy up to ransom, and that's worth a bundle. I owe mine a mint."

Arthur took a deep breath without much enthusiasm.

"All right," he said, "but where do we start? How should I know? They say the Ultimate Answer or whatever is Forty-two, how am I supposed to know what the question is? It could be anything. I mean, what's six times seven?"

Zaphod looked at him hard for a moment. Then his eyes blazed with excitement.

"Forty-two!" he cried.

Arthur wiped his palm across his forehead.

"Yes," he said patiently, "I know that."

Zaphod's faces fell.

"I'm just saying the question could be anything at all," said Arthur, "and I don't see how I'm meant to know."

"Because," hissed Zaphod, "you were there when your planet did the big firework."

"We have a thing on Earth . . ." began Arthur.

"Had," corrected Zaphod.

" . . . called tact. Oh, never mind. Look, I just don't know."

A low voice echoed dully around the cabin.

"I know," said Marvin.

Ford called out from the controls he was still fighting a losing battle with.

"Stay out of this, Marvin," he said. "This is organism talk."

"It's printed in the Earthman's brainwave patterns," continued Marvin, "but I don't suppose you'll be very interested in knowing that."

"You mean," said Arthur, "you mean you can see into my mind?"

"Yes," said Marvin.

Arthur stared in astonishment.

"And...?" he said.

"It amazes me how you can manage to live in anything that small."

"Ah," said Arthur, "abuse."

"Yes," confirmed Marvin.

"Ah, ignore him," said Zaphod, "he's only making it up."

"Making it up?" said Marvin, swiveling his head in a parody of astonishment. "Why should I want to make anything up? Life's bad enough as it is without wanting to invent any more of it."

"Marvin," said Trillian in the gentle, kindly voice that only she was still capable of assuming in talking to this misbegotten creature, "if you knew all along, why then didn't you tell us?"

Marvin's head swiveled back to her.

"You didn't ask," he said simply.

"Well, we're asking you now, metal man," said Ford, turning round to look at him.

At that moment the ship suddenly stopped rocking and swaying, the engine pitch settled down to a gentle hum.

"Hey, Ford," said Zaphod, "that sounds good. Have you worked out the controls on this boat?"

"No," said Ford, "I just stopped fiddling with them. I reckon we just go to wherever this ship is going and get off it fast."

"Yeah, right," said Zaphod.

"I could tell you weren't really interested," murmured Marvin to himself and slumped into a corner and switched himself off.

"Trouble is," said Ford, "that the one instrument in this whole ship that is giving any reading is worrying me. If it is what I think it is, and if it's saying what I think it's saying, then we've already gone too far back into the past. Maybe as much as two million years before our own time."

Zaphod shrugged.

"Time is bunk," he said.

"I wonder who this ship belongs to anyway," said Arthur.

"Me," said Zaphod.

"No. Who it really belongs to."

"Really me," insisted Zaphod. "Look, property is theft, right? Therefore theft is property. Therefore this ship is mine, okay?"

"Tell the ship that," said Arthur.

Zaphod strode over to the console.

"Ship," he said, banging on the panels, "this is your new owner speaking to . . ."

He got no further. Several things happened at once.

The ship dropped out of time travel mode and reemerged into real space.

All the controls on the console, which had been shut down for the time trip, now lit up.

A large vision screen above the console winked into life revealing a wide starscape and a single very large sun dead ahead of them.

None of these things, however, were responsible for the fact that Zaphod was at the same moment hurled bodily backward against the rear of the cabin, as were all the others.

They were hurled back by a single thunderous clap of noise that thudded out of the monitor speakers surrounding the vision screen.

Down on the dry, red world of Kakrafoon, in the middle of the vast Rudlit Desert, the stage technicians were testing the sound system.

That is to say, the sound system was in the desert, not the technicians. They had retreated to the safety of Disaster Area's giant control ship which hung in orbit some four hundred miles above the surface of the planet, and they were testing the sound from there. Anyone within five miles of the speaker silos wouldn't have survived the tuning up.

If Arthur Dent had been within five miles of the speaker silos then his expiring thought would have been that in both size and shape the sound rig closely resembled Manhattan. Risen out of the silos, the neutron phase speaker stacks towered monstrously against the sky, obscuring the banks of plutonium reactors and seismic amps behind them.

Buried deep in concrete bunkers beneath the city of speakers lay the instruments that the musicians would control from their ship, the massive photon-ajuitar, the bass detonator and the Megabang drum complex.

It was going to be a noisy show.

Aboard the giant control ship, all was activity and bustle. Hotblack Desiato's limoship, a mere tadpole beside it, had arrived and docked, and the lamented gentleman was being transported down the high vaulted corridors to meet the medium who was going to interpret his psychic impulses onto the ajuitar keyboard.

A doctor, a logician and a marine biologist had also just arrived, flown in at phenomenal expense from Maximegalon to try to reason with the lead singer who had locked himself in the bathroom with a bottle of pills and was refusing to come out till it could be proved conclusively to him that he wasn't a fish. The bass player was busy machine-gunning his bedroom and the drummer was nowhere on board.

Frantic inquiries led to the discovery that he was standing on a beach on Santraginus V over a hundred light-years away where, he claimed, he had been happy for over half an hour now and had found a small stone that would be his friend.

The band's manager was profoundly relieved. It meant that for the seventeenth time on this tour the drums would be played by a robot and that therefore the timing of the cymbalistics would be right.

The sub-ether was buzzing with the communications of the stage technicians testing the speaker channels, and it was this that was being relayed to the interior of the black ship.

Its dazed occupants lay against the back wall of the cabin, and listened to the voices on the monitor speakers.

"Okay, channel nine on power," said a voice, "testing channel fifteen...."

Another thumping crack of noise walloped through the ship.

"Channel fifteen A-okay," said another voice.

A third voice cut in.

"The black stuntship is now in position," it said, "it's looking good. Gonna be a great sundive. Stage computer on line?"

A computer voice answered.

"On line," it said.

"Take control of the black ship."

"Black ship locked into trajectory program, on standby."

"Testing channel twenty."

Zaphod leaped across the cabin and switched frequencies on the sub-ether receiver before the next mind-pulverizing noise hit them. He stood there quivering.

"What," said Trillian in a small quiet voice, "does sundive mean?"

"It means," said Marvin, "that the ship is going to dive into the sun. Sun.... Dive. It's very simple to understand. What do you expect if you steal Hotblack Desiato's stuntship?"

"How do you know," said Zaphod in a voice that would make a Vegan snow lizard feel chilly, "that this is Hotblack Desiato's stuntship?"

"Simple," said Marvin. "I parked it for him."

"Then why... didn't... you... tell us!"

"You said you wanted excitement and adventure and really wild things."

"This is awful," said Arthur unnecessarily in the pause which followed.

"That's what I said," confirmed Marvin.

On a different frequency, the sub-ether receiver had picked up a public broadcast, which now echoed around the cabin.

" ... fine weather for the concert here this afternoon. I'm standing here in front of the stage," the reporter lied, "in the middle of the Rudlit Desert, and with the aid of hyperbinoptic glasses I can just about make out the huge audience cowering there on the horizon all around me. Behind me the speaker stacks rise like a sheer cliff face, and high above me the sun is shining away and doesn't know what's going to hit it. The environmentalist lobby do know what's going to hit it, and they claim that the concert will cause earthquakes, tidal waves, hurricanes, irreparable damage to the atmosphere and all the usual things that environmentalists usually go on about.

"But I've just had a report that a representative of Disaster Area met with the environmentalists at lunchtime, and had them all shot, so nothing now lies in the way of..."

Zaphod switched it off. He turned to Ford.

"You know what I'm thinking?" he said.

"I think so," said Ford.

"Tell me what you think I'm thinking."

"I think you're thinking it's time we got off this ship."

"I think you're right," said Zaphod.

"I think you're right," said Ford.

"How?" said Arthur.

"Quiet," said Ford and Zaphod, "we're thinking."

"So this is it," said Arthur, "we're going to die."

"I wish you'd stop saying that," said Ford.

It is worth repeating at this point the theories that Ford had come up with, on his first encounter with human beings, to account for their peculiar habit of continually stating and restating the very very obvious, as in "It's a nice day," or "You're very tall," or "So this is it, we're going to die."

His first theory was that if human beings didn't keep exercising their lips, their mouths probably shriveled up.

After a few months of observation he had come up with a second theory, which was this—"If human beings don't keep exercising their lips, their brains start working."

In fact, this second theory is more literally true of the Belcerebon people of Kakrafoon.

The Belcerebon people used to cause great resentment and insecurity among neighboring races by being one of the most enlightened, accomplished and, above all, quiet civilizations in the Galaxy.

As a punishment for this behavior, which was held to be offensively self-righteous and provocative, a Galactic Tribunal inflicted on them that most cruel of all social diseases, telepathy. Consequently, in order to prevent themselves broadcasting every slightest thought that crosses their minds to anyone within a five mile radius, they now have to talk very loudly and continuously about the weather, their little aches and pains, the match this afternoon and what a noisy place Kakrafoon has suddenly become.

Another method of temporarily blotting out their minds is to play host to a Disaster Area concert.

The timing of the concert was critical.

The ship had to begin its dive before the concert began in order to hit the sun six minutes and thirty-seven seconds before the climax of the song to which it related, so that the light of the solar flares had time to travel out to Kakrafoon.

The ship had already been diving for several minutes by the time that Ford Prefect had completed his search of the other compartments of the black ship. He burst back into the cabin.

The sun of Kakrafoon loomed terrifyingly large on the vision screen, its blazing white inferno of fusing hydrogen nuclei growing moment by moment as the ship plunged onward, unheeding the thumping and banging of Zaphod's hands on the control panel. Arthur and Trillian had the fixed expressions of rabbits on a night road who think that the best way of dealing with approaching headlights is to stare them out.

Zaphod spun around, wild-eyed.

"Ford," he said, "how many escape capsules are there?"

"None," said Ford.

Zaphod gibbered.

"Did you *count* them?" he yelled.

"Twice," said Ford. "Did you manage to raise the stage crew on the radio?"

"Yeah," said Zaphod bitterly, "I said there were a whole bunch of people on board, and they said to say 'hi' to everybody."

Ford goggled.

"Didn't you tell them who you were?"

"Oh yeah. They said it was a great honor. That and something about a restaurant bill and my executors."

Ford pushed Arthur aside roughly and leaned forward over the control console.

"Does *none* of this function?" he said savagely.

"All overridden."

"Smash the autopilot."

"Find it first. Nothing connects."

There was a moment's cold silence.

Arthur was stumbling around the back of the cabin. He stopped suddenly.

"Incidentally," he said, "what does teleport mean?"

Another moment passed.

Slowly, the others turned to face him.

"Probably the wrong moment to ask," said Arthur. "It's just I remember hearing you use the word a short while ago and I only bring it up because . . ."

"Where," said Ford Prefect quietly, "does it say teleport?"

"Well, just over here in fact," said Arthur, pointing at a dark control box in the rear of the cabin. "Just under the word *emergency*, above the word *system* and beside the sign saying *out of order.*"

In the pandemonium that instantly followed, the only action to follow was that of Ford Prefect lunging across the cabin to the small black box that Arthur had indicated and stabbing repeatedly at the single small black button set into it.

A six-foot square panel slid open beside it revealing a compartment which resembled a multiple shower unit that had found a new function in life as an electrician's junk store. Half-finished wiring hung from the ceiling, a jumble of abandoned components lay strewn on the floor, and the programming panel lolled out of the cavity in the wall into which it should have been secured.

A junior Disaster Area accountant, visiting the shipyard where this ship was being constructed, had demanded to know of the works foreman why the hell they were fitting an extremely expensive teleport into a ship which only had one important journey to make, and that unmanned. The foreman had explained that the teleport was available at a ten percent discount and the accountant had explained that this was immaterial; the foreman had explained that it was the finest, most powerful and sophisticated teleport that money could buy and the accountant had explained that the money did not wish to buy it; the foreman had explained that people would still need to enter and leave the ship and the accountant had explained that the ship sported a perfectly serviceable door; the foreman had explained that the accountant could go and boil his head and the accountant had explained to the foreman that the thing approaching him rapidly from his left was a knuckle sandwich. After the explanations had been concluded, work was discontinued on the teleport which subsequently passed unnoticed on the invoice as "Sund. explns." at five times the price.

"Hell's donkeys," muttered Zaphod as he and Ford attempted to sort through the tangle of wiring.

After a moment or so Ford told him to stand back. He tossed a coin into the teleport and jiggled a switch on the lolling control panel. With a crackle and spit of light, the coin vanished.

"That much of it works," said Ford, "however, there is no guidance system. A matter transference teleport with no guidance programming could put you . . . well, anywhere."

The sun of Kakrafoon loomed huge on the screen.

"Who cares," said Zaphod; "we go where we go."

"And," said Ford, "there is no autosystem. We couldn't all go. Someone would have to stay and operate it."

A solemn moment shuffled past. The sun loomed larger and larger.

"Hey, Marvin kid," said Zaphod brightly, "how you doing?"

"Very badly I suspect," muttered Marvin.

A shortish while later, the concert on Kakrafoon reached an unexpected climax.

The black ship with its single morose occupant had plunged on schedule into the nuclear furnace of the sun. Massive solar flares licked out from it millions of miles into space, thrilling and in a few cases spilling the dozen or so flare riders who had been coasting close to the surface of the sun in anticipation of the moment.

Moments before the flare light reached Kakrafoon the pounding desert cracked along a deep faultline. A huge and hitherto undetected underground river lying far beneath the surface gushed to the surface to be followed seconds later by the eruption of millions of tons of boiling lava that flowed hundreds of feet into the air, instantaneously vaporizing the river both above and below the surface in an explosion that echoed to the far side of the world and back again.

Those—very few—who witnessed the event and survived swear that the whole hundred thousand square miles of the desert rose into the air like a mile-thick pancake, flipped itself over and fell back down. At that precise moment the solar radiation from the flares filtered through the clouds of vaporized water and struck the ground.

A year later, the hundred thousand square mile desert was thick with flowers. The structure of the atmosphere around the planet was subtly altered. The sun blazed less harshly in the summer, the cold bit less bitterly in the winter, pleasant rain fell more often and slowly the desert world of

Kakrafoon became a paradise. Even the telepathic power with which the people of Kakrafoon had been cursed was permanently dispersed by the force of the explosion.

A spokesman for Disaster Area—the one who had had all the environmentalists shot—was later quoted as saying that it had been "a good gig."

Many people spoke movingly of the healing powers of music. A few skeptical scientists examined the records of the events more closely, and claimed that they had discovered faint vestiges of a vast artificially induced Improbability Field drifting in from a nearby region of space.

Arthur woke up and instantly regretted it. Hangovers he'd had, but never anything on this scale. This was it, this was the big one, this was the ultimate pits. Matter transference beams, he decided, were not as much fun as, say, a good solid kick in the head.

Being for the moment unwilling to move on account of a dull stomping throb he was experiencing, he lay awhile and thought. The trouble with most forms of transport, he thought, is basically that not one of them is worth all the bother. On Earth—when there had been an Earth, before it was demolished to make way for a new hyperspace bypass—the problem had been with cars. The disadvantages involved in pulling lots of black sticky slime from out of the ground where it had been safely hidden out of harm's way, turning it into tar to cover the land with, smoke to fill the air with and pouring the rest into the sea, all seemed to outweigh the advantages of being able to get more quickly from one place to another—particularly when the place you arrived at had probably become, as a result of this, very similar to the place you had left, i.e., covered with tar, full of smoke and short of fish.

And what about matter transference beams? Any form of transport which involved tearing you apart atom by atom, flinging those atoms through the sub-ether, and then jamming them back together again just when they were getting their first taste of freedom for years had to be bad news.

Many people had thought exactly this before Arthur Dent and had even gone to the lengths of writing songs about it. Here is one that used regularly to be chanted by huge crowds outside the Sirius Cybernetics Corporation Teleport Systems factory on Happi-Werld III:

Aldebaran's great, okay,
Algol's pretty neat,
Betelgeuse's pretty girls
Will knock you off your feet.
They'll do anything you like
Real fast and then real slow,

But if you have to take me apart to get me there
Then I don't want to go.

Singing,
Take me apart, take me apart,
What a way to roam
And if you have to take me apart to get me there
I'd rather stay at home.

Sirius is paved with gold
So I've heard it said
By nuts who then go on to say
"See Tau before you're dead."
I'll gladly take the high road
Or even take the low,
But if you have to take me apart to get me there
Then I, for one, won't go.

Singing,
Take me apart, take me apart,
You must be off your head,
And if you try to take me apart to get me there
I'll stay right here in bed.

. . . and so on. Another favorite song was much shorter:

I teleported home one night
With Ron and Sid and Meg.
Ron stole Meggie's heart away
And I got Sidney's leg.

Arthur felt the waves of pain slowly receding, though he was still aware of
a dull stomping throb. Slowly, carefully, he stood up.

"Can you hear a dull stomping throb?" said Ford Prefect.

Arthur spun around and wobbled uncertainly. Ford Prefect was approaching, looking red-eyed and pasty.

"Where are we?" gasped Arthur.

Ford looked around. They were standing in a long curving corridor
which stretched out of sight in both directions. The outer steel wall—
which was painted in that sickly shade of pale green which they use in

schools, hospitals and mental asylums to keep the inmates subdued—curved over the tops of their heads to where it met the inner perpendicular wall which, oddly enough, was covered in dark brown hessian wall weave. The floor was of dark green ribbed rubber.

Ford moved over to a very thick dark transparent panel set in the outer wall. It was several layers deep, yet through it he could see pinpoints of distant stars.

"I think we're in a spaceship of some kind," he said.

Down the corridor came the sound of a dull stomping throb.

"Trillian?" called Arthur nervously. "Zaphod?"

Ford shrugged.

"Nowhere about," he said, "I've looked. They could be anywhere. An unprogrammed teleport can throw you light-years in any direction. Judging by the way I feel I should think we've traveled a very long way indeed."

"How do you feel?"

"Bad."

"Do you think they're . . ."

"Where they are, how they are, there's no way we can know and no way we can do anything about it. Do what I do."

"What?"

"Don't think about it."

Arthur turned this thought over in his mind, reluctantly saw the wisdom of it, tucked it up and put it away. He took a deep breath.

"Footsteps!" exclaimed Ford suddenly.

"Where?"

"That noise. That stomping throb. Pounding feet. Listen!"

Arthur listened. The noise echoed round the corridor at them from an indeterminate distance. It was the muffled sound of pounding footsteps, and it was noticeably louder.

"Let's move," said Ford sharply. They both moved—in opposite directions.

"Not that way," said Ford. "That's where they're coming from."

"No, it's not," said Arthur. "They're coming from that way."

"They're not, they're . . ."

They both stopped. They both turned. They both listened intently. They both agreed with each other. They both set off in opposite directions again.

Fear gripped them.

From both directions the noise was getting louder.

A few yards to their left another corridor ran at right angles to the inner wall. They ran to it and hurried along it. It was dark, immensely long and, as they passed down it, gave them the impression that it was getting colder and colder. Other corridors gave off it to the left and right, each very dark and each subjecting them to sharp blasts of icy air as they passed.

They stopped for a moment in alarm. The further down the corridor they went, the louder became the sound of pounding feet.

They pressed themselves back against the cold wall and listened furiously. The cold, the dark and the drumming of disembodied feet was getting to them badly. Ford shivered, partly with the cold, but partly with the memory of stories his favorite mother used to tell him when he was a mere slip of a Betelgeusian, ankle high to an Arcturan Megagrasshopper: stories of death ships, haunted hulks that roamed restlessly round the obscurer regions of deep space infested with demons or the ghosts of forgotten crews; stories too of incautious travelers who found and entered such ships; stories of— Then Ford remembered the brown hessian wall weave in the first corridor and pulled himself together. However ghosts and demons may choose to decorate their death hulks, he thought to himself, he would lay any money you liked it wasn't with hessian wall weave. He grasped Arthur by the arm.

"Back the way we came," he said firmly and they started to retrace their steps.

A moment later they leaped like startled lizards down the nearest corridor junction as the owners of the drumming feet suddenly hove into view directly in front of them.

Hidden behind the corner they goggled in amazement as about two dozen overweight men and women pounded past them in track suits panting and wheezing in a manner that would make a heart surgeon gibber.

Ford Prefect stared after them.

"Joggers!" he hissed, as the sound of their feet echoed away up and down the network of corridors.

"Joggers?" whispered Arthur Dent.

"Joggers," said Ford Prefect with a shrug.

The corridor they were concealed in was not like the others. It was very short, and ended at a large steel door. Ford examined it, discovered the opening mechanism and pushed it wide.

The first thing that hit their eyes was what appeared to be a coffin.

And the next four thousand nine hundred and ninety-nine things that hit their eyes were also coffins.

The vault was low ceilinged, dimly lit and gigantic. At the far end, about three hundred yards away, an archway let through to what appeared to be a similar chamber, similarly occupied. Ford Prefect let out a low whistle as he stepped down to the floor of the vault.

"Wild," he said.

"What's so great about dead people?" asked Arthur, nervously stepping down after him.

"Dunno," said Ford. "Let's find out, shall we?"

On closer inspection the coffins seemed to be more like sarcophagi. They stood about waist high and were constructed of what appeared to be white marble, which is almost certainly what it was—something that only appeared to be white marble. The tops were semitranslucent, and through them could dimly be perceived the features of their late and presumably lamented occupants. They were humanoid, and had clearly left the troubles of whatever world it was they came from far behind them, but beyond that little else could be discerned.

Rolling slowly round the floor between the sarcophagi was a heavy, oily white gas which Arthur at first thought might be there to give the place a little atmosphere until he discovered that it also froze his ankles. The sarcophagi too were intensely cold to the touch.

Ford suddenly crouched down beside one of them. He pulled a corner of his towel out of his satchel and started to rub furiously at something.

"Look, there's a plaque on this one," he explained to Arthur. "It's frosted over."

He rubbed the frost clear and examined the engraved characters. To Arthur they looked like the footprints of a spider that had had one too many of whatever it is that spiders have on a night out, but Ford instantly recognized an early form of Galactic Eezzeereed.

"It says 'Golgafrincham Ark Fleet, Ship B, Hold Seven, Telephone Sanitizer Second Class'—and a serial number."

"A telephone sanitizer?" said Arthur. "A dead telephone sanitizer?"

"Best kind."

"But what's he doing here?"

Ford peered through the top at the figure within.

"Not a lot," he said, and suddenly flashed one of those grins of his which always made people think he'd been overdoing things recently and should try to get some rest.

He scampered over to another sarcophagus. A moment's brisk towel work and he anounced:

"This one's a dead hairdresser. Hoopy!"

The next sarcophagus revealed itself to be the last resting place of an advertising account executive; the one after that contained a secondhand car salesman, third class.

An inspection hatch let into the floor suddenly caught Ford's attention, and he squatted down to unfasten it, thrashing away at the clouds of freezing gas that threatened to envelope him.

A thought occurred to Arthur.

"If these are just coffins," he said, "why are they kept so cold?"

"Or, indeed, why are they kept anyway," said Ford, tugging the hatchway open. The gas poured down through it. "Why in fact is anyone going to all the trouble and expense of carting five thousand dead bodies through space?"

"Ten thousand," said Arthur, pointing at the archway through which the next chamber was dimly visible.

Ford stuck his head down through the floor hatchway. He looked up again.

"Fifteen thousand," he said. "There's another lot down there."

"Fifteen million," said a voice.

"That's a lot," said Ford. "A lot a lot."

"Turn around slowly," barked the voice, "and put your hands up. Any other move and I blast you into tiny tiny bits."

"Hello?" said Ford, turning round slowly, putting his hands up and not making any other move.

"Why," said Arthur Dent, "isn't anyone ever pleased to see us?"

Standing silhouetted in the doorway through which they had entered the vault was the man who wasn't pleased to see them. His displeasure was communicated partly by the barking hectoring quality of his voice and partly by the viciousness with which he waved a long silver Kill-O-Zap gun at them. The designer of the gun had clearly not been instructed to beat about the bush. "Make it evil," he'd been told. "Make it totally clear that this gun has a right end and a wrong end. Make it totally clear to anyone standing at the wrong end that things are going badly for them. If that means sticking all sort of spikes and prongs and blackened bits all over it then so be it. This is not a gun for hanging over the fireplace or sticking in the umbrella stand, it is a gun for going out and making people miserable with."

Ford and Arthur looked at the gun unhappily.

The man with the gun moved from the door and circled around them. As he came into the light they could see his black and gold uniform on which the buttons were so highly polished that they shone with an intensity that would have made an approaching motorist flash his lights in annoyance.

He gestured at the door.

"Out," he said. People who can supply that amount of firepower don't need to supply verbs as well. Ford and Arthur went out, closely followed by the wrong end of the Kill-O-Zap gun and the buttons.

Turning into the corridor they were jostled by twenty-four oncoming joggers, now showered and changed, who swept on past them into the vault. Arthur turned to watch them in confusion.

"Move!" screamed their captor.

Arthur moved.

Ford shrugged and moved.

In the vault the joggers went to twenty-four empty sarcophagi along the side wall, opened them, climbed in and fell into twenty-four dreamless sleeps.

Chapter 24

Er, Captain..."

"Yes, Number One?"

"Just had a sort of report thingy from Number Two."

"Oh dear."

High up in the bridge of the ship, the Captain stared out into the infinite reaches of space with mild irritation. From where he reclined beneath a wide domed bubble he could see before and above him the vast panorama of stars through which they were moving—a panorama that had thinned out noticeably during the course of the voyage. Turning and looking backward, over the vast two-mile bulk of the ship he could see the far denser mass of stars behind them which seemed to form almost a solid band. This was the view through the Galactic center from which they were traveling, and indeed had been traveling for years, at a speed that he couldn't quite remember at the moment, but he knew it was terribly fast. It was something approaching the speed of something or other, or was it three times the speed of something else? Jolly impressive anyway. He peered into the bright distance behind the ship, looking for something. He did this every few minutes or so, but never found what he was looking for. He didn't let it worry him though. The scientists chaps had been very insistent that everything was going to be perfectly all right providing nobody panicked and everybody got on and did their bit in an orderly fashion.

He wasn't panicking. As far as he was concerned everything was going splendidly. He dabbed at his shoulder with a large frothy sponge. It crept back into his mind that he was feeling mildly irritated about something. Now what was all that about? A slight cough alerted him to the fact that the ship's first officer was still standing nearby.

Nice chap, Number One. Not of the very brightest, had the odd spot of difficulty tying his shoelaces, but jolly good officer material for all that. The Captain wasn't a man to kick a chap when he was bending over trying to do up his shoelaces, however long it took him. Not like that ghastly Number Two, strutting about all over the place, polishing his buttons, issuing reports every hour: "Ship's still moving, Captain." "Still on course,

Captain." "Oxygen levels still being maintained, Captain." "Give it a miss," was the Captain's vote. Ah yes, that was the thing that had been irritating him. He peered down at Number One.

"Yes, Captain, he was shouting something or other about having found some prisoners. . . ."

The Captain thought about this. Seemed pretty unlikely to him, but he wasn't one to stand in his officers' way.

"Well, perhaps that'll keep him happy for a bit," he said. "He's always wanted some."

Ford Prefect and Arthur Dent trudged onward up the ship's apparently endless corridors. Number Two marched behind them barking the occasional order about not making any false moves or trying any funny stuff. They seemed to have passed at least a mile of continuous brown hessian wall weave. Finally they reached a large steel door which slid open when Number Two shouted at it.

They entered.

To the eyes of Ford Prefect and Arthur Dent, the most remarkable thing about the ship's bridge was not the fifty-foot diameter hemispherical dome which covered it, and through which the dazzling display of stars shone down on them: to people who have eaten at the Restaurant at the End of the Universe, such wonders are commonplace. Nor was it the bewildering array of instruments that crowded the long circumferential wall around them. To Arthur this was exactly what spaceships were traditionally supposed to look like, and to Ford it looked thoroughly antiquated: it confirmed his suspicions that Disaster Area's stuntship had taken them back at least a million, if not two million, years before their own time.

No, the thing that really caught them off balance was the bathtub.

The bathtub stood on a six-foot pedestal of rough-hewn blue water crystal and was of a baroque monstrosity not often seen outside the Maximegalon Museum of Diseased Imaginings. An intestinal jumble of plumbing had been picked out in gold leaf rather than decently buried at midnight in an unmarked grave; the taps and shower attachment would have made a gargoyle jump.

As the dominant certerpiece of a starship bridge it was terribly wrong, and it was with the embittered air of a man who knew this that Number Two approached it.

"Captain, sir!" he shouted through clenched teeth—a difficult trick but he'd had years during which to perfect it.

A large genial face and genial foam-covered arm popped up above the rim of the monstrous bath.

"Ah, hello, Number Two," said the Captain, waving a cheery sponge, "having a nice day?"

Number Two snapped even further to attention than he already was.

"I have brought you the prisoners I located in freezer bay seven, sir!" he yapped.

Ford and Arthur coughed in confusion.

"Er... hello," they said.

The Captain beamed at them. So Number Two had really found some prisoners. Well, good for him, thought the Captain, nice to see a chap doing what he's best at.

"Oh, hello there," he said to them. "Excuse me not getting up, just having a quick bath. Well, jynnan tonnyx all round then. Look in the fridge Number One."

"Certainly, sir."

It is a curious fact, and one to which no one knows quite how much importance to attach, that something like 85 percent of all known worlds in the Galaxy, be they primitive or highly advanced, have invented a drink called jynnan tonnyx, or gee-N-N-T'N-ix, or jinond-o-nicks, or any one of a thousand or more variations on the same phonetic theme. The drinks themselves are not the same, and vary between the Sivolvian "chinanto/mnigs" which is ordinary water served at slightly above room temperature, and the Gagrakackan "tzjin-anthony-ks" which kills cows at a hundred paces; and in fact the one common factor between all of them, beyond the fact that the names sound the same, is that they were all invented and named *before* the worlds concerned made contact with any other worlds.

What can be made of this fact? It exists in total isolation. As far as any theory of structural linguistics is concerned it is right off the graph, and yet it persists. Old structural linguists get very angry when young structural linguists go on about it. Young structural linguists get deeply excited about it and stay up late at night convinced that they are very close to something of profound importance, and end up becoming old structural linguists before their time, getting very angry with the young ones. Structural linguistics is a bitterly divided and unhappy discipline, and a large number of its practitioners spend too many nights drowning their problems in Ouisghian Zodahs.

Number Two stood before the Captain's bathtub trembling with frustration.

"Don't you want to interrogate the prisoners, sir?" he squealed.

The Captain peered at him in bemusement.

"Why on Golgafrincham should I want to do that?" he asked.

"To get information out of them, sir! To find out why they came here!"

"Oh no, no, no," said the Captain. "I expect they just dropped in for a quick jynnan tonnyx, don't you?"

"But, sir, they're my prisoners! I must interrogate them!"

The Captain looked at them doubtfully.

"Oh all right," he said, "if you must. Ask them what they want to drink."

A hard cold gleam came into Number Two's eyes. He advanced slowly on Ford Prefect and Arthur Dent.

"All right, you scum," he growled, "you vermin..." He jabbed Ford with the Kill-O-Zap gun.

"Steady on, Number Two," admonished the Captain gently.

"What do you want to drink?!!" Number Two screamed.

"Well the jynnan tonnyx sounds very nice to me," said Ford. "What about you, Arthur?"

Arthur blinked.

"What? Oh, er, yes," he said.

"With ice or without?!" bellowed Number Two.

"Oh, with, please," said Ford.

"Lemon??!!"

"Yes, please," said Ford, "and do you have any of those little biscuits? You know, the cheesey ones?"

"I'm asking the questions!!!!" howled Number Two, his body quaking with apoplectic fury.

"Er, Number Two..." said the Captain softly.

"Sir?!"

"Shove off, would you, there's a good chap. I'm trying to have a relaxing bath."

Number Two's eyes narrowed and became what are known in the Shouting and Killing People trade as cold slits, the idea presumably being to give your opponent the impression that you have lost your glasses or are having difficulty keeping awake. Why this is frightening is an, as yet, unresolved problem.

He advanced on the Captain, his (Number Two's) mouth a thin hard line. Again, tricky to know why this is understood as fighting behavior. If, while wandering through the jungle of Traal, you were suddenly to come upon the fabled Ravenous Bugblatter Beast, you would have reason to be grateful if its mouth was a thin hard line rather than, as it usually is, a gaping mass of slavering fangs.

"May I remind you, sir," hissed Number Two at the Captain, "that you have now been in that bath for over *three years?!*" This final shot delivered, Number Two spun on his heel and stalked off to a corner to practice darting eye movements in the mirror.

The Captain squirmed in his bath. He gave Ford Prefect a lame smile.

"Well, you need to relax a lot in a job like mine," he said.

Ford slowly lowered his hands. It provoked no reaction. Arthur lowered his.

Treading very slowly and carefully, Ford moved over to the bath pedestal. He patted it.

"Nice," he lied.

He wondered if it was safe to grin. Very slowly and carefully, he grinned. It was safe.

"Er..." he said to the Captain.

"Yes?" said the Captain.

"I wonder," said Ford, "could I ask you actually what your job is in fact?"

A hand tapped him on the shoulder. He spun around.

It was the first officer.

"Your drinks," he said.

"Ah, thank you," said Ford. He and Arthur took their jynnan tonnyx. Arthur sipped his, and was surprised to discover it tasted very like a whisky and soda.

"I mean, I couldn't help noticing," said Ford, also taking a sip, "the bodies. In the hold."

"Bodies?" said the Captain in surprise.

Ford paused and thought to himself. Never take anything for granted, he thought. Could it be that the Captain doesn't know he's got fifteen million dead bodies on his ship?

The Captain was nodding cheerfully at him. He also appeared to be playing with a rubber duck.

Ford looked around. Number Two was staring at him in the mirror, but only for an instant: his eyes were constantly on the move. The first officer was just standing there holding the drinks tray and smiling benignly.

"Bodies?" said the Captain again.

Ford licked his lips.

"Yes," he said, "all those dead telephone sanitizers and account executives, you know, down in the hold."

The Captain stared at him. Suddenly he threw back his head and laughed.

"Oh, they're not dead," he said. "Good Lord, no, no, they're frozen. They're going to be revived."

Ford did something he very rarely did. He blinked.

Arthur seemed to come out of a trance.

"You mean you've got a hold full of frozen hairdressers?" he said.

"Oh yes," said the Captain. "Millions of them. Hairdressers, tired TV producers, insurance salesmen, personnel officers, security guards, public relations executives, management consultants, you name it. We're going to colonize another planet."

Ford wobbled very slightly.

"Exciting, isn't it?" said the Captain.

"What, with that lot?" said Arthur.

"Ah, now don't misunderstand me," said the Captain. "We're just one of the ships in the Ark Fleet. We're the 'B' Ark, you see. Sorry, could I just ask you to run a bit more hot water for me?"

Arthur obliged, and a cascade of pink frothy water swirled around the bath. The Captain let out a sigh of pleasure.

"Thank you so much, my dear fellow. Do help yourselves to more drinks of course."

Ford tossed down his drink, took the bottle from the first officer's tray and refilled his glass to the top.

"What," he said, "is a 'B' Ark?"

"This is," said the Captain, and swished the foamy water around joyfully with the duck.

"Yes," said Ford, "but—"

"Well, what happened you see was," said the Captain, "our planet, the world from which we have come, was, so to speak, doomed."

"Doomed?"

"Oh yes. So what everyone thought was, let's pack the whole population into some giant spaceships and go and settle on another planet."

Having told this much of his story, he settled back with a satisfied grunt.

"You mean a less doomed one?" prompted Arthur.

"What did you say dear fellow?"

"A less doomed planet. You were going to settle on."

"Are going to settle on, yes. So it was decided to build three ships, you see, three Arks in Space, and . . . I'm not boring you, am I?"

"No, no," said Ford firmly, "it's fascinating."

"You know it's delightful," reflected the Captain, "to have someone else to talk to for a change."

Number Two's eyes darted feverishly about the room again and then settled back on the mirror, like a pair of flies briefly distracted from their favorite piece of month-old meat.

"Trouble with a long journey like this," continued the Captain, "is that you end up just talking to yourself a lot, which gets terribly boring because half the time you know what you're going to say next."

"Only half the time?" asked Arthur in surprise.

The Captain thought for a moment.

"Yes, about half, I'd say. Anyway—where's the soap?" He fished around and found it.

"Yes, so anyway," he resumed, "the idea was that into the first ship, the 'A' ship, would go all the brilliant leaders, the scientists, the great artists, you know, all the achievers; and then into the third, or 'C' ship, would go all the people who did the actual work, who made things and did things; and then into the 'B' ship—that's us—would go everyone else, the middlemen, you see."

He smiled happily at them.

"And we were sent off first," he concluded, and hummed a little bathing tune.

The little bathing tune, which had been composed for him by one of his world's most exciting and prolific jingle writers (who was currently asleep in hold thirty-six some nine hundred yards behind them) covered what would otherwise have been an awkward moment of silence. Ford and Arthur shuffled their feet and furiously avoided each other's eyes.

"Er . . ." said Arthur after a moment, "what exactly was it that was wrong with your planet then?"

"Oh, it was doomed, as I said," said the Captain. "Apparently it was going to crash into the sun or something. Or maybe it was that the moon was going to crash into us. Something of the kind. Absolutely terrifying prospect whatever it was."

"Oh," said the first officer suddenly, "I thought it was that the planet was going to be invaded by a gigantic swarm of twelve-foot piranha bees. Wasn't that it?"

Number Two spun around, eyes ablaze with a cold hard light that only comes with the amount of practice he was prepared to put in.

"That's not what I was told!" he hissed. "My commanding officer told me that the entire planet was in imminent danger of being eaten by an enormous mutant star goat!"

"Oh really..." said Ford Prefect.

"Yes! A monstrous creature from the pit of hell with scything teeth ten thousand miles long, breath that would boil oceans, claws that could tear continents from their roots, a thousand eyes that burned like the sun, slavering jaws a million miles across, a monster such as you have never...never...ever..."

"And they made sure they sent you lot off first, did they?" inquired Arthur.

"Oh yes," said the Captain, "well, everyone said, very nicely I thought, that it was very important for morale to feel that they would be arriving on a planet where they could be sure of a good haircut and where the phones were clean."

"Oh yes," agreed Ford, "I can see that would be very important. And the other ships, er...they followed on after you, did they?"

For a moment the Captain did not answer. He twisted round in his bath and gazed backward over the huge bulk of the ship toward the bright galactic center. He squinted into the inconceivable distance.

"Ah. Well, it's funny you should say that," he said and allowed himself a slight frown at Ford Prefect, "because curiously enough we haven't heard a peep out of them since we left five years ago....But they must be behind us somewhere."

He peered off into the distance again.

Ford peered with him and gave a thoughtful frown.

"Unless of course," he said softly, "they were eaten by the goat...."

"Ah yes..." said the Captain with a slight hesitancy creeping into his voice, "the goat...." His eyes passed over the solid shapes of the instruments and computers that lined the bridge. They winked away innocently at him. He stared out at the stars, but none of them said a word. He glanced at his first and second officers, but they seemed lost in their own thoughts for a moment. He glanced at Ford Prefect who raised his eyebrows at him.

"It's a funny thing, you know," said the Captain at last, "but now that I actually come to tell the story to someone else...I mean does it strike you as odd, Number One?"

"Errrrrrrrrrrr..." said Number One.

"Well," said Ford, "I can see that you've got a lot of things you're going to want to talk about, so, thanks for the drinks, and if you could sort of drop us off at the nearest convenient planet . . ."

"Ah, well that's a little difficult you see," said the Captain, "because our trajectory thingy was preset before we left Golgafrincham, I think partly because I'm not very good with figures. . . ."

"You mean we're stuck here on this ship?" exclaimed Ford, suddenly losing patience with the whole charade. "When are you meant to be reaching this planet you're meant to be colonizing?"

"Oh, we're nearly there I think," said the Captain, "any second now. It's probably time I was getting out of this bath in fact. Oh, I don't know though, why stop just when I'm enjoying it?"

"So we're actually going to land in a minute?" said Arthur.

"Well, not so much *land*, in fact, not actually land as such, no . . . er—"

"What are you talking about?" asked Ford sharply.

"Well," said the Captain, picking his way through the words carefully, "I think as far as I can remember we were programmed to crash on it."

"Crash?" shouted Ford and Arthur.

"Er, yes," said the Captain, "yes, it's all part of the plan, I think. There was a terribly good reason for it which I can't quite remember at the moment. It was something to do with . . . er . . ."

Ford exploded.

"You're a load of useless bloody loonies!" he shouted.

"Ah yes, that was it," beamed the Captain, "that was the reason."

The *Hitchhiker's Guide to the Galaxy* has this to say about the planet of Golgafrincham: *It is a planet with an ancient and mysterious history, rich in legend, red, and occasionally green with the blood of those who sought in times gone by to conquer her; a land of parched and barren landscapes, of sweet and sultry air heady with the scent of the perfumed springs that trickle over its hot and dusty rocks and nourish the dark and musky lichens beneath; a land of fevered brows and intoxicated imaginings, particularly among those who taste the lichens; a land also of cool and shaded thoughts among those who have learned to forswear the lichens and find a tree to sit beneath; a land also of steel and blood and heroism; a land of the body and of the spirit. This was its history.*

And in all this ancient and mysterious history, the most mysterious figures of all were without doubt those of the Great Circling poets of Arium. These Circling Poets used to live in remote mountain passes where they would lie in wait for small bands of unwary travelers, circle around them, and throw rocks at them.

And when the travelers cried out, saying why didn't they go away and get on with writing some poems instead of pestering people with all this rock-throwing business, they would suddenly stop, and then break into one of the seven hundred and ninety-four great Song Cycles of Vassillian. These songs were all of extraordinary beauty, and even more extraordinary length, and all fell into exactly the same pattern.

The first part of each song would tell how there once went forth from the City of Vassillian a party of five sage princes with four horses. The princes, who are of course brave, noble and wise, travel widely in distant lands, fight giant ogres, pursue exotic philosophies, take tea with weird gods and rescue beautiful monsters from ravening princesses before finally announcing that they have achieved enlightenment and that their wanderings are therefore accomplished.

The second, and much longer, part of each song would then tell of all their bickerings about which one of them is going to have to walk back.

All this lay in the planet's remote past. It was, however, a descendant of one of these eccentric poets who invented the spurious tales of impending doom which enabled the people of Golgafrincham to rid themselves of an entire useless third of their population. The other two-thirds stayed firmly at home and lived full, rich and happy lives until they were all suddenly wiped out by a virulent disease contracted from a dirty telephone.

Chapter 26

That night the ship crash-landed onto an utterly insignificant little blue-green planet which circled a small unregarded yellow sun in the uncharted backwaters of the unfashionable end of the Western spiral arm of the Galaxy.

In the hours preceding the crash Ford Prefect had fought furiously but in vain to unlock the controls of the ship from their preordained flight path. It had quickly become apparent to him that the ship had been programmed to convey its payload safely, if uncomfortably, to its new home but to cripple itself beyond all hope of repair in the process.

Its screaming, blazing descent through the atmosphere had stripped away most of its superstructure and outer shielding, and its final inglorious bellyflop into a murky swamp had left its crew only a few hours of darkness during which to revive and offload its deep-frozen and unwanted cargo, for the ship began to settle almost at once, slowly upending its gigantic bulk in the stagnant slime. Once or twice during the night it was starkly silhouetted against the sky as burning meteors—the detritus of its descent—flashed across the sky.

In the gray predawn light it let out an obscene roaring gurgle and sank forever into the stinking depths.

When the sun came up that morning it shed its thin watery light over a vast area heaving with wailing hairdressers, public relations executives, opinion pollsters and the rest, all clawing their way desperately to dry land.

A less strong-minded sun would probably have gone straight back down again, but it continued to climb its way through the sky and after a while the influence of its warming rays began to have some restoring effect on the feebly struggling creatures.

Countless numbers had, unsurprisingly, been lost to the swamp in the night, and millions more had been sucked down with the ship, but those who survived still numbered hundreds of thousands and as the day wore on they crawled out over the surrounding countryside, each looking for a few square feet of solid ground on which to collapse and recover from their nightmare ordeal.

Two figures moved farther afield.

From a nearby hillside Ford Prefect and Arthur Dent watched the horror of which they could not feel a part.

"Filthy dirty trick to pull," muttered Arthur.

Ford scraped a stick along the ground and shrugged.

"An imaginative solution to a problem I'd have thought," he said.

"Why can't people just learn to live together in peace and harmony?" said Arthur.

Ford gave a loud, very hollow laugh.

"Forty-two!" he said with a malicious grin. "No, doesn't work. Never mind."

Arthur looked at him as if he'd gone mad and, seeing nothing to indicate to the contrary, realized that it would be perfectly reasonable to assume that this had in fact happened.

"What do you think will happen to them all?" he said after a while.

"In an infinite Universe anything can happen," said Ford. "Even survival. Strange but true."

A curious look came into his eyes as they passed over the landscape and then settled again on the scene of misery below them.

"I think they'll manage for a while," he said.

Arthur looked up sharply.

"Why do you say that?" he said

Ford shrugged.

"Just a hunch," he said, and refused to be drawn on any further questions.

"Look," he said suddenly.

Arthur followed his pointing finger. Down among the sprawling masses a figure was moving—or perhaps lurching would be a more accurate description. He appeared to be carrying something on his shoulder. As he lurched from prostrate form to prostrate form he seemed to wave whatever the something was at them in a drunken fashion. After a while he gave up the struggle and collapsed in a heap.

Arthur had no idea what this was meant to mean to him.

"Movie camera," said Ford. "Recording the historic moment."

"Well, I don't know about you," said Ford again after a moment, "but I'm off."

He sat awhile in silence.

After a while this seemed to require comment.

"Er, when you say you're off, what do you mean exactly?" said Arthur.

"Good question," said Ford. "I'm getting total silence."

Looking over his shoulder Arthur saw that he was twiddling with knobs on a small black box. Ford had already introduced this box to Arthur as a Sub-Etha Sens-O-Matic, but Arthur had merely nodded absently and not pursued the matter. In his mind the Universe still divided into two parts—the Earth, and everything else. The Earth having been demolished to make way for a hyperspace bypass meant that this view of things was a little lopsided, but Arthur tended to cling to that lopsidedness as being his last remaining contact with his home. Sub-Etha Sens-O-Matics belonged firmly in the "everything else" category.

"Not a sausage," said Ford, shaking the thing.

Sausage, thought Arthur to himself as he gazed listlessly at the primitive world about him, what I wouldn't give for a good Earth sausage.

"Would you believe," said Ford in exasperation, "that there are no transmissions of any kind within light-years of this benighted tip? Are you listening to me?"

"What?" said Arthur.

"We're in trouble," said Ford.

"Oh," said Arthur. This sounded like month-old news to him.

"Until we pick up anything on this machine," said Ford, "our chances of getting off this planet are zero. It may be some freak standing wave effect in the planet's magnetic field—in which case we just travel round and round till we find a clear reception area. Coming?"

He picked up his gear and strode off.

Arthur looked down the hill. The man with the movie camera had struggled back up to his feet just in time to film one of his colleagues collapsing.

Arthur picked a blade of grass and strode off after Ford.

I trust you had a pleasant meal?" said Zarniwoop to Zaphod and Trillian as they rematerialized on the bridge of the starship *Heart of Gold* and lay panting on the floor.

Zaphod opened some eyes and glowered at him.

"You," he spat. He staggered to his feet and stomped off to find a chair to slump into. He found one and slumped into it.

"I have programmed the computer with the Improbability Coordinates pertinent to our journey," said Zarniwoop. "We will arrive there very shortly. Meanwhile, why don't you relax and prepare yourself for the meeting?"

Zaphod said nothing. He got up again and marched over to a small cabinet from which he pulled a bottle of old Janx Spirit. He took a long pull at it.

"And when this is all done," said Zaphod savagely, "it's done, all right? I'm free to go and do what the hell I like and lie on beaches and stuff?"

"It depends what transpires from the meeting," said Zarniwoop.

"Zaphod, who is this man?" said Trillian shakily, wobbling to her feet. "What's he doing here? Why's he on our ship?"

"He's a very stupid man," said Zaphod, "who wants to meet the man who rules the Universe."

"Ah," said Trillian, taking the bottle from Zaphod and helping herself, "a social climber."

Chapter 28

The major problem—*one* of the major problems, for there are several—one of the many major problems with governing people is that of whom you get to do it; or rather of who manages to get people to let them do it to them.

To summarize: it is a well-known fact that those people who must *want* to rule people are, ipso facto, those least suited to do it. To summarize the summary: anyone who is capable of getting themselves made President should on no account be allowed to do the job. To summarize the summary of the summary: people are a problem.

And so this is the situation we find: a succession of Galactic Presidents who so much enjoy the fun and palaver of being in power that they very rarely notice that they're not.

And somewhere in the shadows behind them—who?

Who can possibly rule if no one who wants to do it can be allowed to?

On a small obscure world somewhere in the middle of nowhere in particular—nowhere, that is, that could ever be found, since it is protected by a vast field of Unprobability to which only six men in this Galaxy have a key—it was raining.

It was bucketing down, and had been for hours. It beat the top of the sea into a mist, it pounded the trees, it churned and slopped a stretch of scrubby land near the sea into a mudbath.

The rain pelted and danced on the corrugated iron roof of the small shack that stood in the middle of this patch of scrubby land. It obliterated the small rough pathway that led from the shack down to the seashore and smashed apart the neat piles of interesting shells which had been placed there.

The noise of the rain on the roof of the shack was deafening within, but went largely unnoticed by its occupant, whose attention was otherwise engaged.

He was a tall shambling man with rough straw-colored hair that was damp from the leaking roof. His clothes were shabby, his back was hunched, and his eyes, though open, seemed closed.

In his shack was an old beaten-up armchair, an old scratched table, an old mattress, some cushions and a stove that was small but warm.

There was also an old and slightly weatherbeaten cat, and this was currently the focus of the man's attention. He bent his shambling form over it.

"Pussy, pussy, pussy," he said, "coochicoochicoochicoo... pussy want his fish? Nice piece of fish... pussy want it?"

The cat seemed undecided on the matter. It pawed rather condescendingly at the piece of fish the man was holding out, and then got distracted by a piece of dust on the floor.

"Pussy not eat his fish, pussy get thin and waste away, I think," said the man. Doubt crept into his voice.

"I imagine this is what will happen," he said, "but how can I tell?"

He proffered the fish again.

"Pussy think," he said, "eat fish or not eat fish. I think it is better if I don't get involved." He sighed.

"I think fish is nice, but then I think that rain is wet, so who am I to judge?"

He left the fish on the floor for the cat, and retired to his seat.

"Ah, I seem to see you eating it," he said at last, as the cat exhausted the entertainment possibilities of the speck of dust and pounced onto the fish.

"I like it when I see you eat fish," said the man, "because in my mind you will waste away if you don't."

He picked up from the table a piece of paper and the stub of a pencil. He held one in one hand and the other in the other, and experimented with the different ways of bringing them together. He tried holding the pencil under the paper, then over the paper, then next to the paper. He tried wrapping the paper round the pencil, he tried rubbing the stubby end of the pencil against the paper and then he tried rubbing the sharp end of the pencil against the paper. It made a mark, and he was delighted with the discovery, as he was every day. He picked up another piece of paper from the table. This had a crossword on it. He studied it briefly and filled in a couple of clues before losing interest.

He tried sitting on one of his hands and was intrigued by the feel of the bones of his hip.

"Fish come from far away," he said, "or so I'm told. Or so I imagine I'm told. When the men come, or when in my mind the men come in their six black shiny ships, do they come in your mind too? What do you see, pussy?"

He looked at the cat, which was more concerned with getting the fish down as rapidly as possible than it was with these speculations.

"And when I hear their questions, do you hear questions? What do their voices mean to you? Perhaps you just think they're singing songs to you." He reflected on this, and saw the flaw in the supposition.

"Perhaps they are singing songs to you," he said, "and I just think they're asking me questions."

He paused again. Sometimes he would pause for days, just to see what it was like.

"Do you think they came today?" he said. "I do. There's mud on the floor, cigarettes and whisky on the table, fish on a plate for you and a memory of them in my mind. Hardly conclusive evidence I know, but then all evidence is circumstantial. And look what else they've left me."

He reached over to the table and pulled some things off it.

"Crosswords, dictionaries and a calculator."

He played with the calculator for an hour, while the cat went to sleep and the rain outside continued to pour. Eventually he put the calculator aside.

"I think I must be right in thinking they ask me questions," he said. "To come all that way and leave all these things just for the privilege of singing songs to you would be very strange behavior. Or so it seems to me. Who can tell, who can tell."

From the table he picked up a cigarette and lit it with a spill from the stove. He inhaled deeply and sat back.

"I think I saw another ship in the sky today," he said at last. "A big white one. I've never seen a big white one, just the six black ones. And the six green ones. And the others who say they come from so far away. Never a big white one. Perhaps six small black ones can look like one big white one at certain times. Perhaps I would like a glass of whisky. Yes, that seems more likely."

He stood up and found a glass that was lying on the floor by his mattress. He poured in a measure from his whisky bottle. He sat again.

"Perhaps some other people are coming to see me," he said.

A hundred yards away, pelted by the torrential rain, lay the *Heart of Gold*.

Its hatchway opened, and three figures emerged, huddling into themselves to keep the rain off their faces.

"In there?" shouted Trillian above the noise of the rain.

"Yes," said Zarniwoop.

"That shack?"

"Yes."

"Weird," said Zaphod.

"But it's in the middle of nowhere," said Trillian. "We must have come to the wrong place. You can't rule the Universe from a shack."

They hurried through the pouring rain, and arrived, wet through, at the door. They knocked. They shivered.

The door opened.

"Hello?" said the man.

"Ah, excuse me," said Zarniwoop, "I have reason to believe . . ."

"Do you rule the Universe?" said Zaphod.

The man smiled at him.

"I try not to," he said. "Are you wet?"

Zaphod looked at him in astonishment.

"Wet?" he cried. "Doesn't it look as if we're wet?"

"That's how it looks to me," said the man, "but how you feel about it might be an altogether different matter. If you find warmth makes you dry, you'd better come in."

They went in.

They looked around the tiny shack, Zarniwoop with slight distaste, Trillian with interest, Zaphod with delight.

"Hey, er..." said Zaphod, "what's your name?"

The man looked at them doubtfully.

"I don't know. Why, do you think I should have one? It seems very odd to give a bundle of vague sensory perceptions a name."

He invited Trillian to sit in the chair. He sat on the edge of the chair, Zarniwoop leaned stiffly against the table and Zaphod lay on the mattress.

"Wowee!" said Zaphod. "The seat of power!" He tickled the cat.

"Listen," said Zarniwoop, "I must ask you some questions."

"All right," said the man kindly, "you can sing to my cat if you like."

"Would he like that?" asked Zaphod.

"You'd better ask him," said the man.

"Does he talk?" said Zaphod.

"I have no memory of him talking," said the man, "but I am very unreliable."

Zarniwoop pulled some notes out of a pocket.

"Now," he said, "you do rule the Universe, do you?"

"How can I tell?" said the man.

Zarniwoop ticked off a note on the paper.

"How long have you been doing this?"

"Ah," said the man, "this is a question about the past, is it?"

Zarniwoop looked at him in puzzlement. This wasn't exactly what he had been expecting.

"Yes," he said.

"How can I tell," said the man, "that the past isn't a fiction designed to account for the discrepancy between my immediate physical sensations and my state of mind?"

Zarniwoop stared at him. The steam began to rise from his sodden clothes.

"So you answer all questions like this?" he said.

The man answered quickly.

"I say what it occurs to me to say when I think I hear people say things. More I cannot say."

Zaphod laughed happily.

"I'll drink to that," he said and pulled out the bottle of Janx Spirit. He leaped and handed the bottle to the ruler of the Universe, who took it with pleasure.

"Good on you, great ruler," he said, "tell it like it is."

"No, listen to me," said Zarniwoop, "people come to you, do they? In ships . . ."

"I think so," said the man. He handed the bottle to Trillian.

"And they ask you," said Zarniwoop, "to make decisions for them? About people's lives, about worlds, about economies, about wars, about everything going on out there in the Universe?"

"Out there?" said the man. "Out where?"

"Out there!" said Zarniwoop, pointing at the door.

"How can you tell there's anything out there?" said the man politely. "The door's closed."

The rain continued to pound the roof. Inside the shack it was warm.

"But you know there's a whole Universe out there!" cried Zarniwoop. "You can't dodge your responsibilities by saying they don't exist!"

The ruler of the Universe thought for a long while while Zarniwoop quivered with anger.

"You're very sure of your facts," he said at last. "I couldn't trust the thinking of a man who takes the Universe—if there is one—for granted."

Zarniwoop still quivered, but was silent.

"I only decide about my Universe," continued the man quietly. "My Universe is my eyes and my ears. Anything else is hearsay."

"But don't you believe in anything?"

The man shrugged and picked up his cat.

"I don't understand what you mean," he said.

"You don't understand that what you decide in this shack of yours affects the lives and fates of millions of people? This is all monstrously wrong!"

"I don't know. I've never met all these people you speak of. And neither, I suspect, have you. They only exist in words we hear. It is folly to say you know what is happening to other people. Only they know, if they exist. They have their own Universes of their eyes and ears."

Trillian said:

"I think I'm just popping outside for a moment."

She left and walked into the rain.

"Do you believe other people exist?" insisted Zarniwoop.

"I have no opinion. How can I say?"

"I'd better see what's up with Trillian," said Zaphod and slipped out. Outside, he said to her:

"I think the Universe is in pretty good hands, yeah?"

"Very good," said Trillian. They walked off into the rain.

Inside, Zarniwoop continued.

"But don't you understand that people live or die on your word?"

The ruler of the Universe waited for as long as he could. When he heard the faint sound of the ship's engines starting, he spoke to cover it.

"It's nothing to do with me," he said. "I am not involved with people. The Lord knows I am not a cruel man."

"Ah!" barked Zarniwoop, "you say 'The Lord.' You believe in something!"

"My cat," said the man benignly, picking it up and stroking it. "I call him The Lord. I am kind to him."

"All right," said Zarniwoop, pressing home his point, "how do you know he exists? How do you know he knows you to be kind, or enjoys what he thinks of as your kindness?"

'I don't," said the man with a smile, "I have no idea. It merely pleases me to behave in a certain way to what appears to be a cat. Do you behave any differently? Please, I think I am tired."

Zarniwoop heaved a thoroughly dissatisfied sigh and looked about.

"Where are the other two?" he said suddenly.

"What other two?" said the ruler of the Universe, settling back into his chair and refilling his whisky glass.

"Beeblebrox and the girl! The two who were here!"

"I remember no one. The past is a fiction to account for..."

"Stuff it," snapped Zarniwoop and ran out into the rain. There was no ship. The rain continued to churn the mud. There was no sign to show where the ship had been. He hollered into the rain. He turned and ran back to the shack and found it locked.

The ruler of the Universe dozed lightly in his chair. After a while he played with the pencil and the paper again and was delighted when he discovered how to make a mark with the one on the other. Various noises continued outside, but he didn't know whether they were real or not. He then talked to his table for a week to see how it would react.

Chapter 30

The stars came out that night, dazzling in their brilliance and clarity. Ford and Arthur had walked more miles than they had any means of judging and finally stopped to rest. The night was cool and balmy, the air pure, the Sub-Etha Sens-O-Matic totally silent.

A wonderful stillness hung over the world, a magical calm which combined with the soft fragrances of the woods, the quiet chatter of insects and the brilliant light of the stars to soothe their jangled spirits. Even Ford Prefect, who had seen more worlds than he could count on a long afternoon, was moved to wonder if this was the most beautiful he had ever seen. All that day they had passed through rolling green hills and valleys, richly covered with grasses, wild scented flowers and tall thickly leaved trees; the sun had warmed them, light breezes had kept them cool, and Ford Prefect had checked his Sub-Etha Sens-O-Matic at less and less frequent intervals, and had exhibited less and less annoyance at its continued silence. He was beginning to think he liked it here.

Cool though the night air was they slept soundly and comfortably in the open and awoke a few hours later with the light dewfall, feeling refreshed but hungry. Ford had stuffed some small rolls into his satchel at Milliways and they breakfasted on these before moving on.

So far they had wandered purely at random, but now they struck out firmly eastward, feeling that if they were going to explore this world they should have some clear idea of where they had come from and where they were going.

Shortly before noon they had their first indication that the world they had landed on was not an uninhabited one: a half-glimpsed face among the trees, watching them. It vanished at the moment they both saw it, but the image they were both left with was of a humanoid creature, curious to see them but not alarmed. Half an hour later they glimpsed another such face, and ten minutes after that another.

A minute later they stumbled into a wide clearing and stopped short.

Before them in the middle of the clearing stood a group of about two dozen men and women. They stood still and quiet facing Ford and Arthur.

Around some of the women huddled some small children and behind the group was a ramshackle array of small dwellings made of mud and branches.

Ford and Arthur held their breath.

The tallest of the men stood little over five feet high, they all stooped forward slightly, had longish arms and lowish foreheads, and clear bright eyes with which they stared intently at the strangers.

Seeing that they carried no weapons and made no move toward them, Ford and Arthur relaxed slightly.

For a while the two groups simply stared at each other, neither side making any move. The natives seemed puzzled by the intruders, and while they showed no sign of aggression they were quite clearly not issuing any invitations.

Nothing happened.

For a full two minutes nothing continued to happen.

After two minutes Ford decided it was time something happened.

"Hello," he said.

The women drew their children slightly closer to them.

The men made hardly any discernible move and yet their whole disposition made it clear that the greeting was not welcome—it was not resented in any great degree, it was just not welcome.

One of the men, who had been standing slightly forward of the rest of the group and who might therefore have been their leader, stepped forward. His face was quiet and calm, almost serene.

"Ugghhhuuggghhhrrrr uh uh ruh uurgh," he said quietly.

This caught Arthur by surprise. He had grown so used to receiving an instantaneous and unconscious translation of everything he heard via the Babel fish lodged in his ear that he had ceased to be aware of it, and he was only reminded of its presence now by the fact that it didn't seem to be working. Vague shadows of meaning had flickered at the back of his mind, but there was nothing he could get any firm grasp on. He guessed, correctly as it happens, that these people had as yet evolved no more than the barest rudiments of language, and that the Babel fish was therefore powerless to help. He glanced at Ford, who was infinitely more experienced in these matters.

"I think," said Ford out of the corner of his mouth, "he's asking us if we'd mind walking on around the edge of the village."

A moment later, a gesture from the man-creature seemed to confirm this.

"Ruurgggghhhh urrgggh; urgh urgh (uh ruh) rruurruuh ug," continued the man-creature.

"The general gist," said Ford, "as far as I can make out, is that we are welcome to continue our journey in any way we like, but if we would walk around his village rather than through it it would make them all very happy."

"So what do we do?"

"I think we make them happy," said Ford.

Slowly and watchfully they walked around the perimeter of the clearing. This seemed to go down very well with the natives who bowed to them very slightly and then went about their business.

Ford and Arthur continued their journey through the wood. A few hundred yards past the clearing they suddenly came upon a small pile of fruit lying in their path—berries that looked remarkably like raspberries and strawberries, and pulpy, green-skinned fruit that looked remarkably like pears.

So far they had steered clear of the fruit and berries they had seen, though the trees and bushes were laden with them.

"Look at it this way," Ford Prefect had said, "fruit and berries on strange planets either make you live or make you die. Therefore the point at which to start toying with them is when you're going to die if you don't. That way you stay ahead. The secret of healthy hitchhiking is to eat junk food."

They looked at the pile that lay in their path with suspicion. It looked so good it made them almost dizzy with hunger.

"Look at it this way," said Ford, "er..."

"Yes?" said Arthur.

"I'm trying to think of a way of looking at it which means we get to eat it," said Ford.

The leaf-dappled sun gleamed on the plump skins of the things which looked like pears. The things which looked like raspberries and strawberries were fatter and riper than any Arthur had ever seen, even in ice cream commercials.

"Why don't we eat them and think about it afterward?" he said.

"Maybe that's what they want us to do."

"All right, look at it this way...."

"Sounds good so far."

"It's there for us to eat. Either it's good or it's bad, either they want to feed us or to poison us. If it's poisonous and we don't eat it they'll just attack us some other way. If we don't eat, we lose out either way."

"I like the way you're thinking," said Ford. "Now eat one."

Hesitantly, Arthur picked up one of the things that looked like pears.

"I always thought that about the Garden of Eden story," said Ford.

"Eh?"

"Garden of Eden. Tree. Apple. That bit, remember?"

"Yes, of course I do."

"Your God person puts an apple tree in the middle of a garden and says, do what you like guys, oh, but don't eat the apple. Surprise surprise, they eat it and he leaps out from behind a bush shouting 'Gotcha.' It wouldn't have made any difference if they hadn't eaten it."

"Why not?"

"Because if you're dealing with somebody who has the sort of mentality which likes leaving hats on the pavement with bricks under them you know perfectly well they won't give up. They'll get you in the end."

"What are you talking about?"

"Never mind, eat the fruit."

"You know, this place almost looks like the Garden of Eden."

"Eat the fruit."

"Sounds quite like it too."

Arthur took a bite from the thing which looked like a pear.

"It's a pear," he said.

A few moments later, when they had eaten the lot, Ford Prefect turned round and called out.

"Thank you. Thank you very much," he called, "you're very kind."

They went on their way.

For the next fifty miles of their journey eastward they kept on finding the occasional gift of fruit lying in their path, and though they once or twice had a quick glimpse of a native man-creature among the trees, they never again made direct contact. They decided they rather liked a race of people who made it clear that they were grateful simply to be left alone.

The fruit and berries stopped after fifty miles, because that was where the sea started.

Having no pressing calls on their time they built a raft and crossed the sea. It was relatively calm, only about sixty miles wide and they had a reasonably pleasant crossing, landing in a country that was at least as beautiful as the one they had left.

Life was, in short, ridiculously easy and for a while at least they were able to cope with the problems of aimlessness and isolation by deciding to ignore them. When the craving for company became too great they would know where to find it, but for the moment they were happy to feel that the Golgafrinchans were hundreds of miles behind them.

Nevertheless, Ford Prefect began to use his Sub-Etha Sens-O-Matic more often again. Only once did he pick up a signal, but that was so faint and from such enormous distance that it depressed him more than the silence that had otherwise continued unbroken.

On a whim they turned northward. After weeks of traveling they came to another sea, built another raft and crossed it. This time it was harder going, the climate was getting colder. Arthur suspected a streak of masochism in Ford Prefect—the increasing difficulty of the journey seemed to give him a sense of purpose that was otherwise lacking. He strode onward relentlessly.

Their journey northward brought them into steep mountainous terrain of breathtaking sweep and beauty. The vast, jagged, snow-covered peaks ravished their senses. The cold began to bite into their bones.

They wrapped themselves in animal skins and furs which Ford Prefect acquired by a technique he once learned from a couple of ex-Pralite monks running a mind-surfing resort in the Hills of Hunian.

The Galaxy is littered with ex-Pralite monks, all on the make, because the mental control techniques the Order have evolved as a form of devotional discipline are, frankly, sensational—and extraordinary numbers of monks leave the Order just after they have finished their devotional training and just before they take their final vows to stay locked in small metal boxes for the rest of their lives.

Ford's technique seemed to consist mainly of standing still for a while and smiling.

After a while an animal—a deer perhaps—would appear from out of the trees and watch him cautiously. Ford would continue to smile at it, his eyes would soften and shine, and he would seem to radiate a deep and universal love, a love which reached out to embrace all of creation. A wonderful quietness would descend on the surrounding countryside, peaceful and serene, emanating from this transfigured man. Slowly the deer would approach, step by step, until it was almost nuzzling him, whereupon Ford Prefect would reach out to it and break its neck.

"Pheromone control," he said it was. "You just have to know how to generate the right smell."

A few days after landing in this mountainous land they hit a coastline which swept diagonally before them from the southwest to the northeast, a coastline of monumental grandeur: deep majestic ravines, soaring pinnacles of ice—fjords.

For two further days they scrambled and climbed over the rocks and glaciers, awestruck with beauty.

"Arthur!" yelled Ford suddenly.

It was the afternoon of the second day. Arthur was sitting on a high rock watching the thundering sea smashing itself against the craggy promontories.

"Arthur!" yelled Ford again.

Arthur looked to where Ford's voice had come from, carried faintly in the wind.

Ford had gone to examine a glacier, and Arthur found him there crouching by the solid wall of the blue ice. He was tense with excitement—his eyes darted up to meet Arthur's.

"Look," he said, "look!"

Arthur looked. He saw the solid wall of blue ice.

"Yes," he said, "it's a glacier. I've already seen it."

"No," said Ford, "you've looked at it, you haven't seen it. Look."

Ford was pointing deep into the heart of the ice.

Arthur peered—he saw nothing but vague shadows.

"Move back from it," insisted Ford, "look again."

Arthur moved back and looked again.

"No," he said, and shrugged. "What am I supposed to be looking for?"

And suddenly he saw it.

"You see it?"

He saw it.

His mouth started to speak, but his brain decided it hadn't got anything to say yet and shut it again. His brain then started to contend with the problem of what his eyes told it they were looking at, but in doing so relinquished control of the mouth which promptly fell open again. Once more gathering up the jaw, his brain lost control of his left hand which then wandered around in an aimless fashion. For a second or so the brain tried to catch the left hand without letting go of the mouth and simultaneously tried to think about what was buried in the ice, which is probably why the legs went and Arthur dropped restfully to the ground.

The thing that had been causing all this neural upset was a network of shadows in the ice, about eighteen inches beneath the surface. Looked at from the right angle they resolved into the solid shapes of letters from an alien alphabet, each about three feet high; and for those, like Arthur, who couldn't read Magrathean there was above the letters the outline of a face hanging in the ice.

It was an old face, thin and distinguished, careworn but not unkind.

It was the face of the man who had won an award for designing the coastline they now knew themselves to be standing on.

A thin whine filled the air. It whirled and howled through the trees, upsetting the squirrels. A few birds flew off in disgust. The noise danced and skittered round the clearing. It whooped, it rasped, it generally offended.

The Captain, however, regarded the lone bagpiper with an indulgent eye. Little could disturb his equanimity; indeed, once he had got over the loss of his gorgeous bath during that unpleasantness in the swamp all those months ago he had begun to find his new life remarkably congenial. A hollow had been scooped out of a large rock which stood in the middle of the clearing, and in this he would bask daily while attendants sloshed water over him. Not particularly warm water, it must be said, as they hadn't yet worked out a way of heating it. Never mind, that would come, and in the meantime search parties were scouring the countryside far and wide for a hot spring, preferably one in a nice leafy glade, and if it was near a soap mine—perfection. To those who said that they had a feeling soap wasn't found in mines, the Captain had ventured to suggest that perhaps that was because no one had looked hard enough, and this possibility had been reluctantly acknowledged.

No, life was very pleasant, and the great thing about it was that when the hot spring was found, complete with leafy glade *en suite,* and when in the fullness of time the cry came reverberating across the hills that the soap mine had been located and was producing five hundred cakes a day it would be more pleasant still. It was very important to have things to look forward to.

Wail, wail, screech, wail, howl, honk, squeak went the bagpipes, increasing the Captain's already considerable pleasure at the thought that any moment now they might stop. That was something he looked forward to as well.

What else was pleasant? he asked himself. Well, so many things; the red and gold of the trees, now that autumn was approaching; the peaceful chatter of scissors a few feet from his bath where a couple of hairdressers were exercising their skills on a dozing art director and his assistant; the sunlight gleaming off the six shiny telephones lined up along the edge of his rock-hewn bath. The only thing nicer than a phone that didn't ring all the time (or indeed at all) was six phones that didn't ring all the time (or indeed at all).

Nicest of all was the happy murmur of all the hundreds of people slowly assembling in the clearing around him to watch the afternoon committee meeting.

The Captain punched his rubber duck playfully on the beak. The afternoon committee meetings were his favorite.

Other eyes watched the assembling crowds. High in a tree on the edge of the clearing squatted Ford Prefect, lately returned from foreign climes. After his six-month journey he was lean and healthy, his eyes gleamed, he wore a reindeer-skin coat; his beard was as thick and his face as bronzed as a country-rock singer's.

He and Arthur Dent had been watching the Golgafrinchans for almost a week now, and Ford had decided it was time to stir things up a bit.

The clearing was now full. Hundreds of men and women lounged around, chatting, eating fruit, playing cards and generally having a fairly relaxed time of it. Their track suits were now all dirty and even torn, but they all had immaculately styled hair. Ford was puzzled to see that many of them had stuffed their track suits full of leaves and wondered if this was meant to be some form of insulation against the coming winter. Ford's eyes narrowed. They couldn't be interested in botany all of a sudden could they?

In the middle of these speculations the Captain's voice rose above the hubbub.

"All right," he said, "I'd like to call this meeting to some sort of order, if that's at all possible. Is that all right with everybody?" He smiled genially. "In a minute. When you're all ready."

The talking gradually died away and the clearing fell silent, except for the bagpiper who seemed to be in some wild and uninhabitable musical world of his own. A few of those in his immediate vicinity threw some leaves to him. If there was any reason for this then it escaped Ford Prefect for the moment.

A small group of people had clustered round the Captain and one of them was clearly preparing to speak. He did this by standing up, clearing his throat and then gazing off into the distance as if to signify to the crowd that he would be with them in a minute.

The crowd of course were riveted and all turned their eyes on him.

A moment of silence followed, which Ford judged to be the right dramatic moment to make his entry. The man turned to speak.

Ford dropped down out of the tree.

"Hi there," he said.

The crowd swiveled round.

"Ah, my dear fellow," called out the Captain, "got any matches on you? Or a lighter? Anything like that?"

"No," said Ford, sounding a little deflated. It wasn't what he'd prepared. He decided he'd better be a little stronger on the subject.

"No, I haven't," he continued. "No matches. Instead I bring you news ..."

"Pity," said the Captain. "We've all run out you see. Haven't had a hot bath in weeks."

Ford refused to be headed off.

"I bring you news," he said, "of a discovery that might interest you."

"Is it on the agenda?" snapped the man whom Ford had interrupted.

Ford smiled a broad country-rock singer smile.

"Now, come on," he said.

"Well, I'm sorry," said the man huffily, "but speaking as a management consultant of many years' standing, I must insist on the importance of observing the committee structure."

Ford looked around the crowd.

"He's mad, you know," he said, "this is a prehistoric planet."

"Address the chair!" snapped the management consultant.

"There isn't a chair," explained Ford, "there's only a rock."

The management consultant decided that testiness was what the situation now called for.

"Well, call it a chair," he said testily.

"Why not call it a rock?" asked Ford.

"You obviously have no conception," said the management consultant, now abandoning testiness in favor of good old-fashioned hauteur, "of modern business methods."

"And you have no conception of where you are," said Ford.

A girl with a strident voice leaped to her feet and used it.

"Shut up, you two," she said, "I want to table a motion."

"You mean boulder a motion," tittered a hairdresser.

"Order, order!" yapped the management consultant.

"All right," said Ford, "let's see how you're doing." He plunked himself down on the ground to see how long he could keep his temper.

The Captain made a sort of conciliatory harrumphing noise.

"I would like to call to order," he said pleasantly, "the five hundred and seventy-third meeting of the colonization committee of Fintlewoodle-wix...."

Ten seconds, thought Ford, as he leaped to his feet again.

"This is futile," he exclaimed. "Five hundred and seventy-three committee meetings and you haven't even discovered fire yet!"

"If you would care," said the girl with the strident voice, "to examine the agenda sheet—"

"Agenda rock," trilled the hairdresser happily.

"Thank you, I've made that point," muttered Ford.

"...you...will...see..." continued the girl firmly, "that we are having a report from the hairdressers' Fire Development Subcommittee today."

"Oh...ah—" said the hairdresser with a sheepish look, which is recognized the whole Galaxy over as meaning "Er, will next Tuesday do?"

"All right," said Ford, rounding on him. "What have you done? What are you going to do? What are your thoughts on fire development?"

"Well, I don't know," said the hairdresser. "All they gave me was a couple of sticks...."

"So what have you done with them?"

Nervously, the hairdresser fished in his track suit top and handed over the fruits of his labor to Ford.

Ford held them up for all to see.

"Curling tongs," he said.

The crowd applauded.

"Never mind," said Ford. "Rome wasn't burned in a day."

The crowd hadn't the faintest idea what he was talking about, but they loved it nevertheless. They applauded.

"Well, you're obviously being totally naive of course," said the girl. "When you've been in marketing as long as I have you'll know that before any new product can be developed it has to be properly researched. We've got to find out what people want from fire, how they relate to it, what sort of image it has for them."

The crowd were tense. They were expecting something wonderful from Ford.

"Stick it up your nose," he said.

"Which is precisely the sort of thing we need to know," insisted the girl. "Do people want fire that can be fitted nasally?"

"Do you?" Ford asked the crowd.

"Yes!" shouted some.

"No!" shouted others happily.

They didn't know, they just thought it was great.

"And the wheel," said the Captain, "what about this wheel thingy? It sounds a terribly interesting project."

"Ah," said the marketing girl, "well, we're having a little difficulty there."

"Difficulty?" exclaimed Ford. "Difficulty? What do you mean, difficulty? It's the single simplest machine in the entire Universe!"

The marketing girl soured him with a look.

"All right, Mr. Wiseguy," she said, "you're so clever, you tell us what color it should be."

The crowd went wild. One up to the home team, they thought. Ford shrugged his shoulders and sat down again.

"Almighty Zarquon," he said, "have none of you done anything?"

As if in answer to his question there was a sudden clamor of noise from the entrance to the clearing. The crowd couldn't believe the amount of entertainment they were getting this afternoon: in marched a squad of about a dozen men dressed in the remnants of their Golgafrinchan 3rd Regiment dress uniforms. About half of them still carried Kill-O-Zap guns, the rest now carried spears which they struck together as they marched. They looked bronzed, healthy and utterly exhausted and bedraggled. They clattered to a halt and banged to attention. One of them fell over and never moved again.

"Captain, sir!" cried Number Two—for he was their leader—"Permission to report, sir!"

"Yes, Number Two, welcome back and all that. Find any hot springs?" said the Captain despondently.

"No, sir!"

"Thought you wouldn't."

Number Two strode through the crowd and presented arms before the bath.

"We have discovered another continent!"

"When was this?"

"It lies across the sea..." said Number Two, narrowing his eyes significantly, "to the east!"

"Ah."

Number Two turned to face the crowd. He raised his gun above his head. This is going to be great, thought the crowd.

"We have declared war on it!"

Wild abandoned cheering broke out in all corners of the clearing—this was beyond all expectation.

"Wait a minute," shouted Ford Prefect. "Wait a minute!"

He leaped to his feet and demanded silence. After a while he got it, or at least the best silence he could hope for under the circumstances: the circumstances were that the bagpiper was spontaneously composing a national anthem.

"Do we have to have the piper?" demanded Ford.

"Oh yes," said the Captain, "we've given him a grant."

Ford considered opening this idea up for debate but quickly decided that that way madness lay. Instead he slung a well judged rock at the piper and turned to face Number Two.

"War?" he said.

"Yes!" Number Two gazed contemptuously at Ford Prefect.

"On the next continent?"

"Yes! Total warfare! The war to end all wars!"

"But there's no one even living there yet!"

Ah, interesting, thought the crowd, nice point.

Number Two's gaze hovered undisturbed. In this respect his eyes were like a couple of mosquitos that hover purposefully three inches from your nose and refuse to be deflected by arm thrashes, fly swats or rolled newspapers.

"I know that," he said, "but there will be one day! So we have left an open-ended ultimatum."

"What?"

"And blown up a few military installations."

The Captain leaned forward out of his bath.

"Military installations, Number Two?" he said.

For a moment the eyes wavered.

"Yes, sir, well potential military installations. All right ... trees."

The moment of uncertainty passed—his eyes flicked like whips over his audience.

"And," he roared, "we interrogated a gazelle!"

He flipped his Kill-O-Zap smartly under his arm and marched off through the pandemonium that had now erupted throughout the ecstatic crowd. A few steps was all he managed before he was caught up and carried shoulder high for a lap of honor around the clearing.

Ford sat and idly tapped a couple of stones together.

"So what else have you done?" he inquired after the celebrations had died down.

"We have started a culture," said the marketing girl.

"Oh yes?" said Ford.

"Yes. One of our film producers is already making a fascinating documentary about the indigenous cavemen of the area."

"They're not cavemen."

"They look like cavemen."

"Do they live in caves?"

"Well . . ."

"They live in huts."

"Perhaps they're having their caves redecorated," called out a wag from the crowd.

Ford rounded on him angrily.

"Very funny," he said, "but have you noticed that they're dying out?"

On their journey back, Ford and Arthur had come across two derelict villages and the bodies of many natives in the woods, where they had crept away to die. Those that still lived seemed stricken and listless, as if they were suffering from some disease of the spirit rather than the body. They moved sluggishly and with an infinite sadness. Their future had been taken away from them.

"Dying out!" repeated Ford. "Do you know what that means?"

"Er . . . we shouldn't sell them any life insurance?" called out the wag again.

Ford ignored him, and appealed to the whole crowd.

"Can you try and understand," he said, "that it's just since we've arrived here that they've started dying out!"

"In fact that comes over terribly well in this film," said the marketing girl, "and just gives it that poignant twist which is the hallmark of the really great documentary. The producer's very committed."

"He should be," muttered Ford.

"I gather," said the girl, turning to address the Captain who was beginning to nod off, "that he wants to make one about you next, Captain."

"Oh really?" he said, coming to with a start. "That's awfully nice."

"He's got a very strong angle on it, you know, the burden of responsibility, the loneliness of command. . . ."

The Captain hummed and hahed about this for a moment.

"Well, I wouldn't overstress that angle, you know," he said finally. "One's never alone with a rubber duck."

He held the duck aloft and it got an appreciative round from the crowd.

All this while, the management consultant had been sitting in stony silence, his fingertips pressed to his temples to indicate that he was waiting and would wait all day if it was necessary.

At this point he decided he would not wait all day after all, he would merely pretend that the last half hour hadn't happened.

He rose to his feet.

"If," he said tersely, "we could for a moment move on to the subject of fiscal policy..."

"Fiscal policy!" whooped Ford Prefect. "Fiscal policy!"

The management consultant gave him a look that only a lungfish could have copied.

"Fiscal policy..." he repeated, "that is what I said."

"How can you have money," demanded Ford, "if none of you actually produces anything? It doesn't grow on trees you know."

"If you would allow me to continue..."

Ford nodded dejectedly.

"Thank you. Since we decided a few weeks ago to adopt the leaf as legal tender, we have, of course, all become immensely rich."

Ford stared in disbelief at the crowd who were murmuring appreciatively at this and greedily fingering the wads of leaves with which their track suits were stuffed.

"But we have also," continued the management consultant, "run into a small inflation problem on account of the high level of leaf availability, which means that, I gather, the current going rate has something like three deciduous forests buying one ship's peanut."

Murmurs of alarm came from the crowd. The management consultant waved them down.

"So in order to obviate this problem," he continued, "and effectively revalue the leaf, we are about to embark on a massive defoliation campaign, and... er, burn down all the forests. I think you'll all agree that's a sensible move under the circumstances."

The crowd seemed a little uncertain about this for a second or two until someone pointed out how much this would increase the value of the leaves in their pockets whereupon they let out whoops of delight and gave the management consultant a standing ovation. The accountants among them looked forward to a profitable autumn.

"You're all mad," explained Ford Prefect.

"You're absolutely barmy," he suggested.

"You're a bunch of raving nutters," he opined.

The tide of opinion was beginning to turn against him. What had started out as excellent entertainment had now, in the crowd's view, deteriorated into mere abuse, and since this abuse was in the main directed at them they wearied of it.

Sensing this shift in the wind, the marketing girl turned on him.

"Is it perhaps in order," she demanded, "to inquire what you've been doing all these months then? You and that other interloper have been missing since the day we arrived."

"We've been on a journey," said Ford. "We went to try and find out something about this planet."

"Oh," said the girl archly, "doesn't sound very productive to me."

"No? Well, have I got news for you, my love. We have discovered this planet's future."

Ford waited for this statement to have its effect. It didn't have any. They didn't know what he was talking about.

He continued.

"It doesn't matter a pair of fetid dingo's kidneys what you all choose to do from now on. Burn down the forests, anything, it won't make a scrap of difference. Your future history has already happened. Two million years you've got and that's it. At the end of that time your race will be dead, gone and good riddance to you. Remember that, two million years!"

The crowd muttered to itself in annoyance. People as rich as they had suddenly become shouldn't be obliged to listen to this sort of gibberish. Perhaps they could tip the fellow a leaf or two and he would go away.

They didn't need to bother. Ford was already stalking out of the clearing, pausing only to shake his head at Number Two who was already firing his Kill-O-Zap into some neighboring trees.

He turned back once.

"Two million years!" he said and laughed.

"Well," said the Captain with a soothing smile, "still time for a few more baths. Could someone pass me the sponge? I just dropped it over the side."

A mile or so away through the wood, Arthur Dent was too busily engrossed with what he was doing to hear Ford Prefect approach.

What he was doing was rather curious, and this is what it was: on a wide flat piece of rock he had scratched out the shape of a large square, subdivided into one hundred and sixty-nine smaller squares, thirteen to a side.

Furthermore he had collected together a pile of smallish flattish stones and scratched the shape of a letter on to each. Sitting morosely around the rock were a couple of the surviving local native men to whom Arthur Dent was trying to introduce the curious concept embodied in these stones.

So far they had not done well. They had attempted to eat some of them, bury others and throw the rest of them away. Arthur had finally encouraged one of them to lay a couple of stones on the board he had scratched out, which was not even as far as he'd managed to get the day before. Along with the rapid deterioration in the morale of these creatures, there seemed to be a corresponding deterioration in their actual intelligence.

In an attempt to egg them along, Arthur set out a number of letters on the board himself, and then tried to encourage the natives to add some more themselves.

It was not going well.

Ford watched quietly from beside a nearby tree.

"No," said Arthur to one of the natives who had just shuffled some of the letters round in a fit of abysmal dejection, "Q scores ten you see, and it's on a triple word score, so...look, I've explained the rules to you...no, no, look please, put down that jawbone...All right, we'll start again. And try to concentrate this time."

Ford leaned his elbow against the tree and his hand against his head.

"What are you doing, Arthur?" he asked quietly.

Arthur looked up with a start. He suddenly had a feeling that all this might look slightly foolish. All he knew was that it had worked like a dream on him when he was a child. But things were different then, or rather would be.

"I'm trying to teach the cavemen to play Scrabble," he said.

"They're not cavemen," said Ford.

"They look like cavemen."

Ford let it pass.

"I see," he said.

"It's uphill work," said Arthur wearily. "The only word they know is *grunt* and they can't spell it."

He sighed and sat back.

"What's that supposed to achieve?" asked Ford.

"We've got to encourage them to evolve! To develop!" Arthur burst out angrily. He hoped that the weary sigh and then the anger might do something to counteract the overriding feeling of foolishness from which he was currently suffering. It didn't. He jumped to his feet.

"Can you imagine what a world would be like descended from those . . . cretins we arrived with?" he said.

"Imagine?" said Ford, raising his eyebrows. "We don't have to imagine. We've seen it."

"But . . ." Arthur waved his arms about hopelessly.

"We've seen it," said Ford, "there's no escape."

Arthur kicked at a stone.

"Did you tell them what we'd discovered?" he asked.

"Hmmmm?" said Ford, not really concentrating.

"Norway," said Arthur. "Slartibartfast's signature in the glacier. Did you tell them?"

"What's the point?" said Ford. "What would it mean to them?"

"Mean?" said Arthur. "Mean? You know perfectly well what it means. It means that this planet is the Earth! It's my home! It's where I was born!"

"Was?" said Ford.

"All right, will be."

"Yes, in two million years' time. Why don't you tell them that? Go and say to them, 'Excuse me, I'd just like to point out that in two million years' time I will be born just a few miles from here.' See what they say. They'll chase you up a tree and set fire to it."

Arthur absorbed this unhappily.

"Face it," said Ford, "those zeebs over there are your ancestors, not these poor creatures here."

He went over to where the apemen creatures were rummaging listlessly with the stone letters. He shook his head.

"Put the Scrabble away, Arthur," he said, "it won't save the human race, because this lot aren't going to be the human race. The human race is currently sitting around a rock on the other side of this hill making documentaries about themselves."

Arthur winced.

"There must be something we can do," he said. A terrible sense of desolation thrilled through his body that he should be here, on the Earth, the Earth which had lost its future in a horrifying arbitrary catastrophe and which now seemed set to lose its past as well.

"No," said Ford, "there's nothing we can do. This doesn't change the history of the Earth, you see, this *is* the history of the Earth. Like it or leave it, the Golgafrinchans are the people you are descended from. In two million years they get destroyed by the Vogons. History is never altered you see, it just fits together like a jigsaw. Funny old thing, life, isn't it?"

He picked up the letter Q and hurled it into a distant privet bush where it hit a young rabbit. The rabbit hurtled off in terror and didn't stop till it was set upon and eaten by a fox which choked on one of its bones and died on the bank of a stream which subsequently washed it away.

During the following weeks Ford Prefect swallowed his pride and struck up a relationship with a girl who had been a personnel officer on Golgafrincham, and he was terribly upset when she suddenly passed away as a result of drinking water from a pool that had been polluted by the body of a dead fox. The only moral it is possible to draw from this story is that one should never throw the letter Q into a privet bush, but unfortunately there are times when it is unavoidable.

Like most of the really crucial things in life, this chain of events was completely invisible to Ford Prefect and Arthur Dent. They were looking sadly at one of the natives morosely pushing the other letters around.

"Poor bloody caveman," said Arthur.

"They're not..."

"What?"

"Oh, never mind," said Ford.

The wretched creature let out a pathetic howling noise and banged on the rock.

"It's all been a bit of a waste of time for them, hasn't it?" said Arthur.

"Uh uh urghhhhh," muttered the native and banged on the rock again.

"They've been outevolved by telephone sanitizers."

"Urgh, grr grr, gruh!" insisted the native, continuing to bang on the rock.

"Why does he keep banging on the rock?" said Arthur.

"I think he probably wants you to Scrabble with him again," said Ford. "He's pointing at the letters."

"Probably spelled *crzjgrdwldiwdc* again, poor bastard. I keep on telling him there's only one g in *crzjgrdwldiwdc.*"

The native banged on the rock again.

They looked over his shoulder.

Their eyes popped.

There among the jumble of letters were eight that had been laid out in a clear straight line.

They spelled two words.

The words were these:

"Forty-Two."

"Grrrurgh guh guh," explained the native. He swept the letters angrily away and went and mooched under a nearby tree with his colleague.

Ford and Arthur stared at him. Then they stared at each other.

"Did that say what I thought it said?" they both said to each other.

"Yes," they both said.

"Forty-two," said Arthur.

"Forty-two," said Ford.

Arthur ran over to the two natives.

"What are you trying to tell us?" he shouted. "What's it supposed to mean?"

One of them rolled over on the ground, kicked his legs up in the air, rolled over again and went to sleep.

The other bounded up the tree and threw horse chestnuts at Ford Prefect. Whatever it was they had to say, they had already said it.

"You know what this means," said Ford.

"Not entirely."

"Forty-two is the number Deep Thought gave as being the Ultimate Answer."

"Yes."

"And the Earth is the computer Deep Thought designed and built to calculate the Question to the Ultimate Answer."

"So we are led to believe."

"And organic life was part of the computer matrix."

"If you say so."

"I do say so. That means that these natives, these apemen are an integral part of the computer program, and that we and the Golgafrinchans are *not.*"

"But the cavemen are dying out and the Golgafrinchans are obviously set to replace them."

"Exactly. So you do see what this means."

"What?"

"Cock up," said Ford Prefect.

Arthur looked around him.

"This planet is having a pretty bloody time of it," he said.

Ford puzzled for a moment.

"Still, something must have come out of it," he said at last, "because Marvin said he could see the Question printed in your brain wave patterns."

"But . . ."

"Probably the wrong one, or a distortion of the right one. It might give us a clue though if we could find it. I don't see how we can though."

They moped about for a bit. Arthur sat on the ground and started pulling up bits of grass, but found that it wasn't an occupation he could get deeply engrossed in. It wasn't grass he could believe in, the trees seemed pointless, the rolling hills seemed to be rolling to nowhere and the future seemed just a tunnel to be crawled through.

Ford fiddled with his Sub-Etha Sens-O-Matic. It was silent. He sighed and put it away.

Arthur picked up one of the letter stones from his homemade Scrabble set. It was a *T*. He sighed and put it down again. The letter he put it down next to was an *I*. That spelled *IT*. He tossed another couple of letters next to them. They were an *S* and an *H* as it happened. By a curious coincidence the resulting word perfectly expressed the way Arthur was feeling about things just then. He stared at it for a moment. He hadn't done it deliberately, it was just a random chance. His brain got slowly into first gear.

"Ford," he said suddenly, "look, if that Question is printed in my brain wave patterns but I'm not consciously aware of it it must be somewhere in my unconscious."

"Yes, I suppose so."

"There might be a way of bringing that unconscious pattern forward."

"Oh yes?"

"Yes, by introducing some random element that can be shaped by that pattern."

"Like how?"

"Like by pulling Scrabble letters out of a bag blindfolded."

Ford leaped to his feet.

"Brilliant!" he said. He tugged his towel out of his satchel and with a few deft knots transformed it into a bag.

"Totally mad," he said, "utter nonsense. But we'll do it because it's brilliant nonsense. Come on, come on."

The sun passed respectfully behind a cloud. A few small sad raindrops fell.

They piled together all the remaining letters and dropped them into the bag. They shook them up.

"Right," said Ford, "close your eyes. Pull them out. Come on, come on, come on."

Arthur closed his eyes and plunged his hand into the towelful of stones. He jiggled them about, pulled out four and handed them to Ford. Ford laid them along the ground in the order he got them.

"*W*," said Ford, "*H, A, T*...What!"

He blinked.

"I think it's working!" he said.

Arthur pushed three more at him.

"*D, O, Y*...Doy. Oh, perhaps it isn't working," said Ford.

"Here's the next three."

"*O, U, G*...Doyoug.... It's not making sense I'm afraid."

Arthur pulled another two from the bag. Ford put them in place.

"*E, T*, doyouget....Do you get!" shouted Ford. "It is working! This is amazing, it really is working!"

"More here." Arthur was throwing them out feverishly as fast as he could go.

"*I, F*," said Ford, "*Y, O, U*...*M, U, L, T, I, P, L, Y*...What do you get if you multiply...*S, I, X*...six...*B, Y*, by, six by...what do you get if you multiply six by...*N, I, N, E*...six by nine..." He paused. "Come on, where's the next one?"

"Er, that's the lot," said Arthur, "that's all there were."

He sat back, nonplussed.

He rooted around again in the knotted up towel but there were no more letters.

"You mean that's it?" said Ford.

"That's it."

"Six by nine. Forty-two."

"That's it. That's all there is."

The sun came out and beamed cheerfully at them. A bird sang. A warm breeze wafted through the trees and lifted the heads of the flowers, carrying their scent away through the woods. An insect droned past on its way to do whatever it is that insects do in the late afternoon. The sound of voices lilted through the trees followed a moment later by two girls who stopped in surprise at the sight of Ford Prefect and Arthur Dent apparently lying on the ground in agony, but in fact rocking with noiseless laughter.

"No, don't go," called Ford Prefect between gasps, "we'll be with you in just a moment."

"What's the matter?" asked one of the girls. She was the taller and slimmer of the two. On Golgafrincham she had been a junior personnel officer, but hadn't liked it much.

Ford pulled himself together.

"Excuse me," he said, "hello. My friend and I were just contemplating the meaning of life. Frivolous exercise."

"Oh, it's you," said the girl, "you made a bit of a spectacle of yourself this afternoon. You were quite funny to begin with but you did bang on a bit."

"Did I? Oh yes."

"Yes, what was all that for?" asked the other girl, a shorter, round-faced girl who had been an art director for a small advertising company on Golgafrincham. Whatever the privations of this world were, she went to sleep every night profoundly grateful for the fact that whatever she had to face in the morning it wouldn't be a hundred almost identical photographs of moodily lit tubes of toothpaste.

"For? For nothing. Nothing's *for* anything," said Ford Prefect happily. "Come and join us, I'm Ford, this is Arthur. We were just about to do nothing at all for a while but it can wait."

The girls looked at them doubtfully.

"I'm Agda," said the tall one, "this is Mella."

"Hello, Agda, hello, Mella," said Ford.

"Do you talk at all?" said Mella to Arthur.

"Oh, eventually," said Arthur with a smile, "but not as much as Ford."

"Good."

There was a slight pause.

"What did you mean," asked Agda, "about only having two million years? I couldn't make sense of what you were saying."

"Oh that," said Ford. "It doesn't matter."

"It's just that the world gets demolished to make way for a hyperspace bypass," said Arthur with a shrug. "But that's two million years away, and anyway it's just Vogons doing what Vogons do."

"Vogons?" said Mella.

"Yes, you wouldn't know them."

"Where'd you get this idea from?"

"It really doesn't matter. It's just like a dream from the past, or the future." Arthur smiled and looked away.

"Does it worry you that you don't talk any kind of sense?" asked Agda.

"Listen, forget it," said Ford, "forget all of it. Nothing matters. Look, it's a beautiful day, enjoy it. The sun, the green of the hills, the river down in the valley, the burning trees."

"Even if it's only a dream, it's a pretty horrible idea," said Mella, "destroying a world just to make a bypass."

"Oh, I've heard of worse," said Ford. "I read of one planet off in the seventh dimension that got used as a ball in a game of intergalactic bar billiards. Got potted straight into a black hole. Killed ten billion people."

"That's mad," said Mella.

"Yes, only scored thirty points too."

Agda and Mella exchanged glances.

"Look," said Agda, "there's a party after the committee meeting tonight. You can come along if you like."

"Yeah, okay," said Ford.

"I'd like to," said Arthur.

Many hours later Arthur and Mella sat and watched the moon rise over the dull red glow of the trees.

"That story about the world being destroyed..." began Mella.

"In two million years, yes."

"You say it as if you really think it's true."

"Yes, I think it is. I think I was there."

She shook her head in puzzlement.

"You're very strange," she said.

"No, I'm very ordinary," said Arthur, "but some very strange things have happened to me. You could say I'm more differed from than differing."

"And that other world your friend talked about, the one that got pushed into a black hole."

"Ah, that I don't know about. It sounds like something from the book."

"What book?"

Arthur paused.

"The Hitchhiker's Guide to the Galaxy," he said at last.

"What's that?"

"Oh, just something I threw into the river this evening. I don't think I'll be wanting it any more," said Arthur Dent.

Life,
the
Universe
and
Everything

For Sally

Chapter 1

The regular early morning yell of horror was the sound of Arthur Dent waking up and suddenly remembering where he was.

It wasn't just that the cave was cold, it wasn't just that it was damp and smelly. It was that the cave was in the middle of Islington and there wasn't a bus due for two million years.

Time is the worst place, so to speak, to get lost in, as Arthur Dent could testify, having been lost in both time and space a good deal. At least being lost in space kept you busy.

He was stranded on prehistoric Earth as the result of a complex sequence of events that had involved his being alternately blown up and insulted in more bizarre regions of the Galaxy than he had ever dreamed existed, and though life had now turned very, very, very quiet, he was still feeling jumpy.

He hadn't been blown up now for five years.

He had hardly seen anyone since he and Ford Prefect had parted company four years previously, and he hadn't been insulted in all that time either.

Except just once.

It had happened on a spring evening about two years ago.

He was returning to his cave just a little after dusk when he became aware of lights flashing eerily through the clouds. He turned and stared, with hope suddenly clambering through his heart. Rescue. Escape. The castaway's impossible dream—a ship.

And as he watched, as he stared in wonder and excitement, a long silver ship descended through the warm evening air, quietly, without fuss, its long legs unlocking in a smooth ballet of technology.

It alighted gently on the ground, and what little hum it had generated died away, as if lulled by the evening calm.

A ramp extended itself.

Light streamed out.

A tall figure appeared silhouetted in the hatchway. It walked down the ramp and stood in front of Arthur.

"You're a jerk, Dent," it said simply.

It was alien, very alien. It had a peculiar alien tallness, a peculiar alien flattened head, peculiar slitty little alien eyes, extravagantly draped golden robes with a peculiarly alien collar design, and pale gray green alien skin that had that lustrous sheen about it that most gray green races can acquire only with plenty of exercise and very expensive soap.

Arthur boggled at it.

It gazed levelly at him.

Arthur's first sensations of hope and trepidation had instantly been overwhelmed by astonishment, and all sorts of thoughts were battling for the use of his vocal cords at this moment.

"Whh . . . ?" he said.

"Bu . . . hu . . . uh . . ." he added.

"Ru . . . ra . . . wah . . . who?" he managed finally to say and lapsed into a frantic kind of silence. He was feeling the effects of not having said anything to anybody for as long as he could remember.

The alien creature frowned briefly and consulted what appeared to be some species of clipboard that it was holding in its thin and spindly alien hand.

"Arthur Dent?" it said.

Arthur nodded helplessly.

"Arthur *Philip* Dent?" pursued the alien in a kind of efficient yap.

"Er . . . er . . . yes . . . er . . . er," confirmed Arthur.

"You're a jerk," repeated the alien, "a complete kneebiter."

"Er. . . ."

The creature nodded to itself, made a peculiar alien check on its clipboard and turned briskly back toward its ship.

"Er . . ." said Arthur desperately, "er. . . ."

"Don't give me that," snapped the alien. It marched up the ramp, through the hatchway and disappeared into its ship. The ship sealed itself. It started to make a low throbbing hum.

"Er, hey!" shouted Arthur, and started to run helplessly toward it.

"Wait a minute!" he called. "What is this? What? Wait a minute!"

The ship rose, as if shedding its weight like a cloak falling to the ground, and hovered briefly. It swept strangely up into the evening sky. It passed up through the clouds, illuminating them briefly, and then was gone, leaving Arthur alone in an immensity of land dancing a helplessly tiny little dance.

"What?" he screamed. "What? What? Hey, what? Come back here and say that!"

He jumped and danced until his legs trembled, and shouted till his lungs rasped. There was no answer from anyone. There was no one to hear him or speak to him.

The alien ship was already thundering toward the upper reaches of the atmosphere, on its way out into the appalling void that separates the very few things there are in the Universe from one another.

Its occupant, the alien with the expensive complexion, leaned back in its single seat. His name was Wowbagger the Infinitely Prolonged. He was a man with a purpose. Not a very good purpose, as he would have been the first to admit, but it was at least a purpose, and it did at least keep him on the move.

Wowbagger the Infinitely Prolonged was—indeed, is—one of the Universe's very small number of immortal beings.

Most of those who are born immortal instinctively know how to cope with it, but Wowbagger was not one of them. Indeed, he had come to hate them, the load of serene bastards. He had had his immortality inadvertently thrust upon him by an unfortunate accident with an irrational particle accelerator, a liquid lunch and a pair of rubber bands. The precise details of the accident are not important because no one has ever managed to duplicate the exact circumstances under which it happened, and many people have ended up looking very silly, or dead, or both, trying.

Wowbagger closed his eyes in a grim and weary expression, put some light jazz on the ship's stereo, and reflected that he could have made it if it hadn't been for Sunday afternoons, he really could have done.

To begin with it was fun; he had a ball, living dangerously, taking risks, cleaning up on high-yield long-term investments, and just generally outliving the hell out of everybody.

In the end, it was the Sunday afternoons he couldn't cope with, and that terrible listlessness that starts to set in at about 2:55, when you know you've taken all the baths you can usefully take that day, that however hard you stare at any given paragraph in the newspaper you will never actually read it, or use the revolutionary new pruning technique it describes, and that as you stare at the clock the hands will move relentlessly on to four o'clock, and you will enter the long dark teatime of the soul.

So things began to pall for him. The merry smiles he used to wear at other people's funerals began to fade. He began to despise the Universe in general, and everybody in it in particular.

This was the point at which he conceived his purpose, the thing that would drive him on, and which, as far as he could see, would drive him on forever. It was this.

He would insult the Universe.

That is, he would insult everybody in it. Individually, personally, one by one, and (this was the thing he really decided to grit his teeth over) in alphabetical order.

When people protested to him, as they sometimes had done, that the plan was not merely misguided but actually impossible because of the number of people being born and dying all the time, he would merely fix them with a steely look and say, "A man can dream, can't he?"

And so he had started out. He equipped a spaceship that was built to last with a computer capable of handling all the data processing involved in keeping track of the entire population of the known Universe and working out the horrifically complicated routes involved.

His ship fled through the inner orbits of the Sol star system, preparing to slingshot around the sun and fling itself out into interstellar space.

"Computer," he said.

"Here," yipped the computer.

"Where next?"

"Computing that."

Wowbagger gazed for a moment at the fantastic jewelry of the night, the billions of tiny diamond worlds that dusted the infinite darkness with light. Every one, every single one was on his itinerary. Most of them he would be going to millions of times over.

He imagined for a moment his itinerary connecting all the dots in the sky like a child's numbered dots puzzle. He hoped that from some vantage point in the Universe it might be seen to spell a very, very rude word.

The computer beeped tunelessly to indicate that it had finished its calculations.

"Folfanga," it said. It beeped.

"Fourth world of the Folfanga system," it continued. It beeped again.

"Estimated journey time, three weeks," it continued further. It beeped again.

"There to meet with a small slug," it beeped, "of the genus A-Rth-Urp-Hil-Ipdenu.

"I believe," it added, after a slight pause during which it beeped, "that you had decided to call it a brainless prat."

Wowbagger grunted. He watched the majesty of creation outside his window for a moment or two.

"I think I'll take a nap," he said, and then added, "What network areas are we going to be passing through in the next few hours?"

The computer beeped.

"Cosmovid, Thinkpix and Home Brain Box," it said, and beeped.

"Any movies I haven't seen thirty thousand times already?"

"No."

"Uh."

"There's *Angst in Space*. You've only seen that thirty-three thousand five hundred and seventeen times."

"Wake me for the second reel."

The computer beeped.

"Sleep well," it said.

The ship sped on through the night.

Meanwhile, on Earth, it began to rain heavily and Arthur Dent sat in his cave and had one of the most rotten evenings of his entire life, thinking of things he could have said to the alien, and swatting flies, which also had a rotten evening.

The next day he made himself a pouch out of rabbit skin because he though it would be useful to keep things in.

Chapter 2

This morning, two years later than that, was sweet and fragrant as he emerged from the cave he called home until he could think of a better name for it or find a better cave.

Though his throat was sore again from his early morning yell of horror, he was suddenly in a terrifically good mood. He wrapped his dilapidated dressing gown tightly around him and beamed at the bright morning. The air was clear and scented, the breeze flitted lightly through the tall grass around his cave, the birds were chirping at one another, the butterflies were flitting about prettily, and the whole of nature seemed to be conspiring to be as pleasant as it possibly could.

It wasn't all the pastoral delights that were making Arthur feel so cheery, though. He had just had a wonderful idea about how to cope with the terrible lonely isolation, the nightmares, the failure of all his attempts at horticulture, and the sheer futurelessness and futility of his life here on prehistoric Earth, which was that he would go mad.

He beamed again and took a bite out of a rabbit leg left over from his supper. He chewed happily for a few moments and then decided formally to announce his decision.

He stood up straight and looked the world squarely in the fields and hills. To add weight to his words he stuck the rabbit bone in his beard. He spread his arms out wide.

"I will go mad!" he announced.

"Good idea," said Ford Prefect, clambering down from the rock on which he had been sitting.

Arthur's brain somersaulted. His jaw did push-ups.

"I went mad for a while," said Ford, "did me no end of good."

Arthur's eyes did cartwheels.

"You see . . ." said Ford.

"Where have you been?" interrupted Arthur, now that his head had finished working out.

"Around," said Ford, "around and about." He grinned in what he accurately judged to be an infuriating manner. "I just took my mind off the hook for a bit. I reckoned that if the world wanted me badly enough it would call back. It did."

He took out of his now terribly battered and dilapidated satchel his Sub-Etha Sens-O-Matic.

"At least," he said, "I think it did. This has been playing up a bit." He shook it. "If it was a false alarm I shall go mad," he said, "again."

Arthur shook his head and sat down. He looked up.

"I thought you must be dead . . ." he said simply.

"So did I for a while," said Ford, "and then I decided I was a lemon for a couple of weeks. I kept myself amused all that time jumping in and out of a gin and tonic."

Arthur cleared his throat, and then did it again. "Where," he said, "did you . . . ?"

"Find a gin and tonic?" said Ford brightly. "I found a small lake that thought it was a gin and tonic, and jumped in and out of that. At least, I think it thought it was a gin and tonic.

"I may," he added with a grin that would have sent sane men scampering into trees, "have been imagining it."

He waited for a reaction from Arthur, but Arthur knew better than that.

"Carry on," he said evenly.

"The point is, you see," said Ford, "that there is no point in driving yourself mad trying to stop yourself going mad. You might just as well give in and save your sanity for later."

"And this is you sane again, is it?" asked Arthur. "I ask merely for information."

"I went to Africa," said Ford.

"Yes?"

"Yes."

"What was that like?"

"And this is your cave, is it?" said Ford.

"Er, yes," said Arthur. He felt very strange. After nearly four years of total isolation he was so pleased and relieved to see Ford that he could almost cry. Ford was, on the other hand, an almost immediately annoying person.

"Very nice," said Ford, in reference to Arthur's cave. "You must hate it."

Arthur didn't bother to reply.

"Africa was very interesting," said Ford. "I behaved very oddly there."

He gazed thoughtfully into the distance.

"I took up being cruel to animals," he said airily. "But only," he added, "as a hobby."

"Oh, yes," said Arthur, warily.

"Yes," Ford assured him. "I won't disturb you with the details because they would..."

"What?"

"Disturb you. But you may be interested to know that I am single-handedly responsible for the evolved shape of the animal you came to know in later centuries as a giraffe. And I tried to learn to fly. Do you believe me?"

"Tell me," said Arthur.

"I'll tell you later. I'll just mention that the *Guide* says..."

"The...?"

"Guide. The Hitchhiker's Guide to the Galaxy. You remember?"

"Yes. I remember throwing it in the river."

"Yes," said Ford, "but I fished it out."

"You didn't tell me."

"I didn't want you to throw it in again."

"Fair enough," admitted Arthur. "It says?"

"What?"

"The *Guide* says?"

"The *Guide* says that there is an art to flying," said Ford, "or rather a knack. The knack lies in learning how to throw yourself at the ground and miss." He smiled weakly. He pointed at the knees of his trousers and held his arms up to show the elbows. They were all torn and worn through.

"I haven't done very well so far," he said. He stuck out his hand. "I'm very glad to see you again, Arthur," he added.

Arthur shook his head in a sudden access of emotion and bewilderment.

"I haven't seen anyone for years," he said, "not anyone. I can hardly even remember how to speak. I keep forgetting words. I practice, you see. I practice by talking to...talking to...what are those things people think you're mad if you talk to? Like George the Third."

"Kings?" suggested Ford.

"No, no," said Arthur, "the things he used to talk to. We're surrounded by them, for heaven's sake. I've planted hundreds myself. They all died. Trees! I practice by talking to trees. What's that for?"

Ford still had his hand stuck out. Arthur looked at it with incomprehension.

"Shake," prompted Ford.

Arthur did, nervously at first, as if it might turn out to be a fish. Then he grasped it vigorously with both hands in an overwhelming flood of relief. He shook it and shook it.

After a while Ford found it necessary to disengage. They climbed to the top of a nearby outcrop of rock and surveyed the scene around them.

"What happened to the Golgafrinchans?" asked Ford.

Arthur shrugged.

"A lot of them didn't make it through the winter three years ago," he said, "and the few who remained in the spring said they needed a holiday and set off on a raft. History says that they must have survived. . . ."

"Huh," said Ford, "well well." He stuck his hands on his hips and looked around again at the empty world. Suddenly, there was about Ford a sense of energy and purpose.

"We're going," he said excitedly, and shivered with energy.

"Where? How?" said Arthur.

"I don't know," said Ford, "but I just feel that the time is right. Things are going to happen. We're on our way."

He lowered his voice to a whisper.

"I have detected," he said, "disturbances in the wash."

He gazed keenly into the distance and looked as if he would quite like the wind to blow his hair back dramatically at that point, but the wind was busy fooling around with some leaves a little way off.

Arthur asked him to repeat what he had just said because he hadn't quite understood his meaning. Ford repeated it.

"The wash?" said Arthur.

"The space-time wash," said Ford and, as the wind blew briefly past at that moment, he bared his teeth into it.

Arthur nodded, and then cleared his throat.

"Are we talking about," he asked cautiously, "some sort of Vogon laundromat, or what are we talking about?"

"Eddies," said Ford, "in the space-time continuum."

"Ah," nodded Arthur, "is he. Is he." He pushed his hands into the pockets of his dressing gown and looked knowledgeably into the distance.

"What?" said Ford.

"Er, who," said Arthur, "is Eddy, then, exactly, then?"

Ford looked angrily at him.

"Will you listen?" he snapped.

"I have been listening," said Arthur, "but I'm not sure it's helped."

Ford grasped him by the lapels of his dressing gown and spoke to him as slowly and distinctly and patiently as if he were somebody from the telephone company accounts department.

"There seem..." he said, "to be some pools..." he said, "of instability..." he said, "in the fabric..." he said.

Arthur looked foolishly at the cloth of his dressing gown where Ford was holding it. Ford swept on before Arthur could turn the foolish look into a foolish remark.

"...in the fabric of space-time," he said.

"Ah, that," said Arthur.

"Yes, that," confirmed Ford.

They stood there alone on a hill on prehistoric Earth and stared each other resolutely in the face.

"And it's done what?" said Arthur.

"It," said Ford, "has developed pools of instability."

"Has it," said Arthur, his eyes not wavering for a moment.

"It has," said Ford, with a similar degree of ocular immobility.

"Good," said Arthur.

"See?" said Ford.

"No," said Arthur.

There was a quiet pause.

"The difficulty with this conversation," said Arthur after a sort of ponderous look had crawled slowly across his face like a mountaineer negotiating a tricky outcrop, "is that it's very different from most of the ones I've had of late. Which, as I explained, have mostly been with trees. They weren't like this. Except perhaps some of the ones I've had with elms that sometimes got a bit bogged down."

"Arthur," said Ford.

"Hello? Yes?" said Arthur.

"Just believe everything I tell you, and it will all be very, very simple."

"Ah, well, I'm not sure I believe that."

They sat down and composed their thoughts.

Ford got out his Sub-Etha Sens-O-Matic. It was making vague humming noises and a tiny light on it was flickering faintly.

"Flat battery?" said Arthur.

"No," said Ford, "there is a moving disturbance in the fabric of space-time, an eddy, a pool of instability, and it's somewhere in our vicinity."

"Where?"

Ford moved the device in a slow, lightly bobbing semicircle. Suddenly the light flashed.

"There!" said Ford, shooting out his arm; "there, behind that sofa!"

Arthur looked. Much to his surprise, there was a velvet paisley-covered Chesterfield sofa in the field in front of them. He boggled intelligently at it. Shrewd questions sprang into his mind.

"Why," he said, "is there a sofa in that field?"

"I told you!" shouted Ford, leaping to his feet. "Eddies in the space-time continuum!"

"And this is his sofa, is it?" asked Arthur, struggling to his feet and, he hoped, though not very optimistically, to his senses.

"Arthur!" shouted Ford at him, "that sofa is there because of the space-time instability I've been trying to get your terminally softened brain to come to grips with. It's been washed up out of the continuum, it's space-time jetsam, it doesn't matter what it is, we've got to catch it, it's our only way out of here!"

He scrambled rapidly down the rocky outcrop and made off across the field.

"Catch it?" muttered Arthur, then frowned in bemusement as he saw that the Chesterfield was lazily bobbing and wafting away across the grass.

With a whoop of utterly unexpected delight he leaped down the rock and plunged off in hectic pursuit of Ford Prefect and the irrational piece of furniture.

They careened wildly through the grass, leaping, laughing, shouting instructions to each other to head the thing off this way or that way. The sun shone dreamily on the swaying grass, tiny field animals scattered crazily in their wake.

Arthur felt happy. He was terribly pleased that the day was for once working out so much according to plan. Only twenty minutes ago he had decided he would go mad, and now here he was already chasing a Chesterfield sofa across the fields of prehistoric Earth.

The sofa bobbed this way and that and seemed simultaneously to be as solid as the trees as it drifted past some of them and hazy as a billowing dream as it floated like a ghost through others.

Ford and Arthur pounded chaotically after it, but it dodged and weaved as if following its own complex mathematical topography, which it was. Still they pursued, still it danced and spun, and suddenly turned and dipped as if crossing the lip of a catastrophe graph, and they were practically on top of it. With a heave and a shout they leaped on it, the sun winked out, they fell through a sickening nothingness and emerged unexpectedly in the middle of the pitch at Lord's Cricket Ground, St. John's Wood, London, toward the end of the last Test Match of the Australian series in the year 198–, with England only needing twenty-eight runs to win.

326

Important Fact from Galactic History, Number One: (reproduced from the Sidereal Daily Mentioner's Book of Popular Galactic History)

The night sky over the planet Krikkit is the least interesting sight in the entire Universe.

Chapter 3

t was a charming and delightful day at Lord's as Ford and Arthur tumbled haphazardly out of a space-time anomaly and hit the immaculate turf rather hard.

The applause of the crowd was tremendous. It wasn't for them, but instinctively they bowed anyway, which was fortunate because the small red heavy ball that the crowd actually had been applauding whistled mere inches over Arthur's head. They threw themselves back to the ground that seemed to spin hideously around them.

"What was that?" hissed Arthur.

"Something red," hissed Ford back at him.

"Where are we?"

"Er, somewhere green."

"Shapes," muttered Arthur, "I need shapes."

The applause of the crowd had been rapidly succeeded by gasps of astonishment, and the awkward titters of hundreds of people who could not yet make up their minds whether to believe what they had just seen or not.

"This your sofa?" said a voice.

"What was that?" whispered Ford.

Arthur looked up.

"Something blue," he said.

"Shape?" asked Ford.

Arthur looked again.

"It is shaped," he hissed at Ford, with his brow savagely furrowed, "like a policeman."

They remained crouched there for a few moments, frowning deeply. The blue thing shaped like a policeman tapped them both on the shoulders.

"Come on, you two," the shape said, "let's go."

These words had an electrifying effect on Arthur. He leaped to his feet and shot a series of startled glances at the panorama around him that had suddenly settled down into something of quite terrifying ordinariness.

"Where did you get this from?" he yelled at the policeman shape.

"What did you say?" said the startled shape.

"This is Lord's Cricket Ground, isn't it?" snapped Arthur. "Where did you find it, how did you get it here? I think," he added, clasping his hand to his brow, "that I had better calm down." He squatted down abruptly in front of Ford.

"It is a policeman," he said. "What do we do?"

Ford shrugged. "What do you want to do?" he said.

"I want you," said Arthur, "to tell me that I have been dreaming for the last five years."

Ford shrugged again, and obliged.

"You've been dreaming for the last five years," he said.

Arthur got to his feet.

"It's all right, officer," he said, "I've been dreaming for the last five years. Ask him," he added, pointing at Ford, "he was in it." Having said this, he sauntered off toward the edge of the pitch, brushing down his dressing gown. He then noticed his dressing gown and stopped. He stared at it. He turned around. He flung himself at the policeman.

"So where did I get these clothes from?" he howled.

He collapsed and lay twitching on the grass.

Ford shook his head.

"He's had a bad two million years," he said to the policeman, and together they heaved Arthur onto the sofa and carried him off the pitch and were only briefly hampered by the sudden disappearance of the sofa on the way.

Reactions to all this from the crowd were many and various. Most of them couldn't cope with watching it, and listened to it on the radio instead.

"Well, this is an interesting incident, Brian," said one radio commentator to another. "I don't think there have been any mysterious materializations on the pitch since, oh, since, well, I don't think there have been any, have there? That I recall?"

"Edgbaston 1932?"

"Ah, now what happened then . . . ?"

"Well, Peter, I think it was Canter facing Willcox coming up to bowl from the pavilion end when a spectator suddenly ran straight across the pitch.'

There was a pause while the first commentator considered this.

"Ye . . . e . . . s . . ." he said, "yes, there's nothing actually very mysterious about that, is there? He didn't actually materialize, did he? Just ran on."

"No, that's true, but he did claim to have *seen* something materialize on the pitch."

"Ah, did he."

"Yes. An alligator, I think, of some description."

"And what happened to the man?"

"Well, I think someone offered to take him off and give him some lunch, but he explained that he'd already had a rather good one, so the matter was dropped and Warwickshire went on to win by three wickets."

"So, not very like this current instance. For those of you who've just tuned in, you may be interested to know that, er . . . two men, two rather scruffily attired men, and indeed a sofa—a Chesterfield I think?"

"Yes, a Chesterfield."

"Have just materialized here in the middle of Lord's Cricket Ground. But I don't think they meant any harm, they've been very good-natured about it, and . . ."

"Sorry, can I interrupt you a moment, Peter, and say that the sofa has just vanished."

"So it has. Well, that's one mystery less. Still, it's definitely one for the record books I think, particularly occurring at this dramatic moment in play, England now needing only twenty-four runs to win the series. The men are leaving the pitch in the company of a police officer, and I think everyone's settling down now and play is about to resume."

"Now, sir," said the policeman after they had made a passage through the curious crowd and laid Arthur's peacefully inert body on a blanket, "perhaps you'd care to tell me who you are, where you come from and what that little scene was all about?"

Ford looked at the ground for a moment as if steadying himself for something, then he straightened up and aimed a look at the policeman that hit him with the full force of every inch of the six light-years' distance between Earth and Ford's home near Betelgeuse.

"All right," said Ford, very quietly, "I'll tell you."

"Yes, well, that won't be necessary," said the policeman hurriedly, "just don't let whatever it was happen again." The policeman turned around and wandered off in search of anyone who wasn't from Betelgeuse. Fortunately, the cricket ground was full of them.

Arthur's consciousness approached his body as from a great distance, and reluctantly. It had had some bad times in there. Slowly, nervously, it entered and settled down into its accustomed position.

Arthur sat up.

"Where am I?" he said.

"Lord's Cricket Ground," said Ford.

"Fine," said Arthur, and his consciousness stepped out again for a quick breather. His body flopped back on the grass.

Ten minutes later, hunched over a cup of tea in the refreshment tent, the color started to come back to his haggard face.

"How you feeling?" asked Ford.

"I'm home," said Arthur hoarsely. He closed his eyes and greedily inhaled the steam from his tea as if it were—well, as far as Arthur was concerned, as if it were tea, which it was.

"I'm home," he repeated, "home. It's England, it's today, the nightmare is over." He opened his eyes again and smiled serenely. "I'm where I belong," he said in an emotional whisper.

"There are two things I feel I should tell you," said Ford, tossing a copy of the *Guardian* over the table at him.

"I'm home," said Arthur.

"Yes," said Ford. "One is," he said, pointing at the date at the top of the paper, "that the Earth will be demolished in two days' time."

"I'm home," said Arthur, "tea," he said, "cricket," he added, with pleasure, "mown grass, wooden benches, white linen jackets, beer cans. . . ."

Slowly he began to focus on the newspaper. He cocked his head on one side with a slight frown.

"I've seen that one before," he said. His eyes wandered slowly up to the date, which Ford was idly tapping at. His face froze for a second or two and then began to do that terribly slow crashing trick that Arctic ice floes do so spectacularly in the spring.

"And the other thing," said Ford, "is that you appear to have a bone in your beard." He tossed back his tea.

Outside the refreshment tent, the sun was shining on a happy crowd. It shone on white hats and red faces. It shone on Popsicles and melted them. It shone on the tears of small children whose Popsicles had just melted and fallen off the stick. It shone on the trees, it flashed off whirling cricket bats, it gleamed off the utterly extraordinary object that was parked behind the sight screens and that nobody appeared to have noticed. It beamed on Ford and Arthur as they emerged blinking from the refreshment tent and surveyed the scene around them.

Arthur was shaking.

"Perhaps," he said, "I should . . ."

"No," said Ford, sharply.

"What?" said Arthur.

"Don't try and phone yourself up at home."

"How did you know...?"

Ford shrugged.

"But why not?" said Arthur.

"People who talk to themselves on the phone," said Ford, "never learn anything to their advantage."

"But..."

"Look," said Ford. He picked up an imaginary phone and dialed an imaginary dial.

"Hello?" he said into the imaginary mouthpiece. "Is that Arthur Dent? Ah, hello, yes. This is Arthur Dent speaking. Don't hang up."

He looked at the imaginary phone in disappointment.

"He hung up," he said, shrugged and put the imaginary phone neatly back on its imaginary hook.

"This is not my first temporal anomaly," he added.

A glummer look replaced the already glum look on Arthur Dent's face.

"So we're not home and dry," he said.

"We could not even be said," replied Ford, "to be home and vigorously toweling ourselves off."

The cricket game continued. The bowler approached the wicket at a lope, a trot and then a run. He suddenly exploded in a flurry of arms and legs, out of which flew a ball. The batsman swung and thwacked it behind him over the sight screens. Ford's eyes followed the trajectory of the ball and jogged momentarily. He stiffened. He looked along the flight path of the ball again and his eyes twitched again.

"This isn't my towel," said Arthur, who was rummaging in his rabbit-skin bag.

"Shhh," said Ford. He screwed his eyes up in concentration.

"I had a Golgafrinchan jogging towel," continued Arthur; "it was blue with yellow stars on it. This isn't it."

"Shhh," said Ford again. He covered one eye and looked with the other.

"This one's pink," said Arthur. "It isn't yours, is it?"

"I would like you to shut up about your towel," said Ford.

"It isn't my towel," insisted Arthur, "that is the point I am trying to..."

"And the time at which I would like you to shut up about it," continued Ford in a low growl, "is now."

"All right," said Arthur, starting to stuff it back into the primitively stitched rabbit-skin bag. "I realize that it is probably not important in the cosmic scale of things, it's just odd, that's all. A pink towel suddenly, instead of a blue one with yellow stars."

Ford was beginning to behave rather strangely, or rather not actually beginning to behave strangely but beginning to behave in a way that was strangely different from the other strange ways in which he more regularly behaved. What he was doing was this. Regardless of the bemused stares it was provoking from his fellow members of the crowd gathered round the pitch, he was waving his hands in sharp movements across his face, ducking down behind some people, leaping up behind others, then standing still and blinking a lot. After a moment or two of this he started to stalk forward slowly and stealthily, wearing a puzzled frown of concentration, like a leopard that is not sure whether it's just seen a half-empty tin of cat food half a mile away across a hot and dusty plain.

"This isn't my bag either," said Arthur suddenly.

Ford's spell of concentration was broken. He turned angrily on Arthur.

"I wasn't talking about my towel," said Arthur. "We've established that it isn't mine. It's just that the bag into which I was putting the towel that is not mine is also not mine, though it is extraordinarily similar. Now personally, I think that that is extremely odd, especially as the bag was one I made myself on prehistoric Earth. These are also not my stones," he added, pulling a few flat gray stones out of the bag. "I was making a collection of interesting stones and these are clearly very dull ones."

A roar of excitement thrilled through the crowd and obliterated whatever it was that Ford said in reply to this piece of information. The cricket ball that had excited this reaction fell out of the sky and dropped neatly into Arthur's mysterious rabbit-skin bag.

"Now I would say that that was also a very curious event," said Arthur, rapidly closing the bag and pretending to look for the ball on the ground.

"I don't think it's here," he said to the small boys who immediately clustered around him to join in the search; "it probably rolled off somewhere. Over there I expect." He pointed vaguely in the direction in which he wished they would push off. One of the boys looked at him quizzically.

"You all right?" said the boy.

"No," said Arthur.

"That why you got a bone in your beard?" said the boy.

"I'm training it to like being wherever it's put." Arthur prided himself on saying this. It was, he thought, exactly the sort of thing that would entertain and stimulate young minds.

"Oh," said the small boy, putting his head on one side and thinking about it. "What's your name?"

"Dent," said Arthur, "Arthur Dent."

"You're a jerk, Dent," said the boy, "a complete kneebiter." The boy looked past him at something else, to show that he wasn't in any particular hurry to run away, and then wandered off scratching his nose. Suddenly Arthur remembered that the Earth was going to be demolished again in two days' time, and just this once didn't feel too bad about it. Play resumed with a new ball, the sun continued to shine and Ford continued to jump up and down shaking his head and blinking.

"Something's on your mind, isn't it?" said Arthur.

"I think," said Ford in a tone of voice that Arthur by now recognized as one that presaged something utterly unintelligible, "that there's an S.E.P. over there."

He pointed. Curiously enough, the direction he pointed in was not the one in which he was looking. Arthur looked in the one direction, which was toward the sight screens, and in the other, which was at the field of play. He nodded, he shrugged. He shrugged again.

"A what?" he said.

"An S.E.P."

"An S...?"

"...E.P."

"And what's that?"

"Somebody Else's Problem," said Ford.

"Ah, good," said Arthur, and relaxed. He had no idea what all that was about, but at least it seemed to be over. It wasn't.

"Over there," said Ford, again pointing at the sight screens and looking at the pitch.

"Where?" said Arthur.

"There!" said Ford.

"I see," said Arthur, who didn't.

"You do?" said Ford.

"What?" said Arthur.

"Can you see," said Ford patiently, "the S.E.P.?"

"I thought you said that was someone else's problem."

"That's right."

Arthur nodded slowly, carefully and with an air of immense stupidity.

"And I want to know," said Ford, "if you can see it."

"You do?"

"Yes!"

"What," said Arthur, "does it look like?"

"Well, how should I know, you fool," shouted Ford. "If you can see it, you tell me."

Arthur experienced that dull throbbing sensation just behind the temples that was a hallmark of so many of his conversations with Ford. His brain lurked like a frightened puppy in its kennel. Ford took him by the arm.

"An S.E.P.," he said, "is something that we can't see, or don't see, or our brain doesn't let us see, because we think that it's somebody else's problem. That's what S.E.P. means. Somebody Else's Problem. The brain just edits it out; it's like a blind spot. If you look at it directly you won't see it unless you know precisely what it is. Your only hope is to catch it by surprise out of the corner of your eye."

"Ah," said Arthur, "then that's why..."

"Yes," said Ford, who knew what Arthur was going to say.

"...you've been jumping up and..."

"Yes."

"...down, and blinking..."

"Yes."

"...and..."

"I think you've got the message."

"I can see it," said Arthur, "it's a spaceship."

For a moment Arthur was stunned by the reaction this revelation provoked. A roar erupted from the crowd, and from every direction people were running and shouting, yelling, tumbling over one another in a tumult of confusion. He stumbled back in astonishment and glanced fearfully around. Then he glanced around again in even greater astonishment.

"Exciting, isn't it?" said an apparition. The apparition wobbled in front of Arthur's eyes, though the truth of the matter is probably that Arthur's eyes were wobbling in front of the apparition. His mouth wobbled as well.

"W...w...w...w..." his mouth said.

"I think your team has just won," said the apparition.

"W...w...w...w..." repeated Arthur, and punctuated each wobble with a prod at Ford Prefect's back. Ford was staring at the tumult in trepidation.

"You are English, aren't you?" said the apparition.

"W...w...w...w...yes," said Arthur.

"Well, your team, as I say, has just won. The match. It means they retain the Ashes. You must be very pleased. I must say, I'm rather fond of cricket, though I wouldn't like anyone outside this planet to hear me saying that. Oh dear no."

The apparition gave what might have been a mischievous grin, but it was hard to tell because the sun was directly behind him, creating a blinding halo around his head and illuminating his silver hair and beard in a way that was awesome, dramatic and hard to reconcile with mischievous grins.

"Still," he said, "it'll all be over in a couple of days, won't it? Though as I said to you when we last met, I was very sorry about that. Still, whatever will have been, will have been."

Arthur tried to speak, but gave up the unequal struggle. He prodded Ford again.

"I thought something terrible had happened," said Ford, "but it's just the end of the game. We ought to get out. Oh, hello, Slartibartfast, what are you doing here?"

"Oh, pottering, pottering," said the old man gravely.

"That your ship? Can you give us a lift anywhere?"

"Patience, patience," the old man admonished.

"Okay," said Ford, "it's just that this planet's going to be demolished pretty soon."

"I know that," said Slartibartfast.

"And, well, I just wanted to make that point," said Ford.

"The point is taken."

"And if you feel that you really want to hang around a cricket pitch at this point . . ."

"I do."

"Then, it's your ship."

"It is."

"I suppose." Ford turned away sharply at this point.

"Hello, Slartibartfast," said Arthur at last.

"Hello, Earthman," said Slartibartfast.

"After all," said Ford, "we can only die once."

The old man ignored this and stared keenly onto the pitch, with eyes that seemed alive with expressions that had no apparent bearing on what was happening out there. What was happening was that the crowd was gathering itself into a wide circle around the center of the pitch. What Slartibartfast saw in it, he alone knew.

Ford was humming something. It was just one note repeated at intervals. He was hoping that somebody would ask him what he was humming, but nobody did. If anybody had asked him he would have said he was humming the first line of a Noël Coward song called "Mad About the

Boy" over and over again. It would then have been pointed out to him that he was only singing one note, to which he would have replied that for reasons that he hoped would be apparent, he was omitting the "about the boy" bit. He was annoyed that nobody asked.

"It's just," he burst out at last, "that if we don't go soon, we might get caught in the middle of it all again. And there's nothing that depresses me more than seeing a planet being destroyed. Except possibly still being on it when it happens. Or," he added in an undertone, "hanging around cricket matches."

"Patience," said Slartibartfast again, "great things are afoot."

"That's what you said last time we met," said Arthur.

"They were," said Slartibartfast.

"Yes, that's true," admitted Arthur.

All, however, that seemed to be afoot was a ceremony of some kind. It was being specially staged for the benefit of television rather than the spectators, and all they could gather about it from where they were standing was what they heard from a nearby radio. Ford was aggressively uninterested.

He fretted as he heard it explained that the Ashes were about to be presented to the captain of the English team out there on the pitch, fumed when told that this was because they had now won it for the *nth* time, positively barked with annoyance at the information that the Ashes were the remains of a cricket stump, and when, further to this, he was asked to contend with the fact that the cricket stump in question had been burnt in Melbourne, Australia, in 1882, to signify the "death of English cricket," he rounded on Slartibartfast, took a deep breath, but didn't have a chance to say anything because the old man wasn't there. He was marching out onto the pitch with terrible purpose in his gait; his hair, beard and robes swept behind him, looking very much as Moses would have looked if Sinai had been a well-cut lawn instead of, as it is more usually represented, a fiery smoking mountain.

"He said to meet him at his ship," said Arthur.

"What in the name of zarking fardwarks is the old fool doing?" exploded Ford.

"Meeting us at his ship in two minutes," said Arthur with a shrug which indicated total abdication of thought. They started off toward it. Strange sounds reached their ears. They tried not to listen, but could not help noticing that Slartibartfast was querulously demanding that he be given the silver urn containing the Ashes, as they were, he said, "vitally important for the past, present and future safety of the Galaxy," and that this was causing wild hilarity. They resolved to ignore it.

What happened next they could not ignore. With a noise like a hundred thousand people saying "whop," a steely white spaceship suddenly seemed to create itself out of nothing in the air directly above the cricket pitch and hung there with infinite menace and a slight hum.

Then for a while it did nothing, as if it expected everybody to go about their normal business and not mind its just hanging there.

Then it did something quite extraordinary. Or rather, it opened up and let something quite extraordinary come out of it, eleven quite extraordinary things.

They were robots, white robots.

What was most extraordinary about them was that they appeared to have come dressed for the occasion. Not only were they white, but they carried what appeared to be cricket bats, and not only that but they also carried what appeared to be cricket balls, and not only that but they wore white ribbing pads around the lower parts of their legs. These last were extraordinary because they appeared to contain jets that allowed these curiously civilized robots to fly down from their hovering spaceship and start to kill people, which is what they did.

"Hello," said Arthur, "something seems to be happening."

"Get to the ship," shouted Ford. "I don't want to know, just get to the ship." He started to run. "I don't want to know, I don't want to see, I don't want to hear," he yelled as he ran, "this is not my planet, I didn't choose to be here, I don't want to get involved, just get me out of here, and get me to a party with people I can relate to!"

Smoke and flame billowed from the pitch.

"Well, the supernatural brigade certainly seems to be out in force here today..." burbled a radio happily to itself.

"What I need," shouted Ford, by way of clarifying his previous remarks, "is a strong drink and a peer group." He continued to run, pausing only for a moment to grab Arthur's arm and drag him along with him. Arthur had adopted his normal crisis role, which was to stand with his mouth hanging open and let it all wash over him.

"They're playing cricket," muttered Arthur, stumbling along after Ford. "I swear they are playing cricket. I do not know why they are doing this, but that is what they are doing. They're not just killing people, they're sending them up," he shouted. "Ford, they're sending us up!"

It would have been hard to disbelieve this without knowing a great deal more Galactic history than Arthur had so far managed to pick up in his travels. The ghostly but violent shapes that could be seen moving within the thick pall of smoke seemed to be performing a series of bizarre parodies of batting strokes, the difference being that every ball they struck with their bats exploded wherever it landed. The very first one of these had dispelled Arthur's initial reaction that the whole thing might just be a publicity stunt by Australian margarine manufacturers.

And then, as suddenly as it had all started, it was over. The eleven white robots ascended through the seething cloud in a tight formation, and with a few last flashes of flame entered the bowels of their hovering white ship, which, with a noise like a hundred thousand people saying "foop," promptly vanished into the thin air out of which it had whopped.

For a moment there was a terrible stunned silence, and then out of the drifting smoke emerged the pale figure of Slartibartfast looking even more like Moses because in spite of the continued absence of the mountain he was at least now striding across a fiery and smoking well-mown lawn.

He stared wildly about him until he saw the hurrying figures of Arthur Dent and Ford Prefect forcing their way through the frightened crowd that was for the moment busy stampeding in the opposite direction. The crowd was clearly thinking to itself what an unusual day this was turning out to be, and not really knowing which way, if any, to turn.

Slartibartfast was gesticulating urgently at Ford and Arthur and shouting at them, as the three gradually converged on his ship, still parked behind the sight screens and still apparently unnoticed by the crowd stampeding past it who presumably had enough of their own problems to cope with at that time.

"They've garble warble farble!" shouted Slartibartfast in his thin tremulous voice.

"What did he say?" panted Ford, as he elbowed his way onward.

Arthur shook his head.

"They've ... something or other," he said.

"They've table warble farble!" shouted Slartibartfast again.

Ford and Arthur shook their heads at each other.

"It sounds urgent," Arthur said. He stopped and shouted. "What?"

"They've garble warble fashes!" cried Slartibartfast, still waving at them.

"He says," said Arthur, "that they've taken the Ashes. That is what I think he is saying." They ran on.

"The ...?" said Ford.

"Ashes," said Arthur tersely. "The burnt remains of a cricket stump. It's a trophy. That . . ." he was panting, "is . . . apparently . . . what they . . . have come and taken." He shook his head very slightly as if he were trying to get his brain to settle down lower in his skull.

"Strange thing to want to tell us," snapped Ford.

"Strange thing to take."

"Strange ship."

They had arrived at it. The second strangest thing about the ship was watching the Somebody Else's Problem field at work. They could now clearly see the ship for what it was simply because they knew it was there. It was quite apparent, however, that nobody else could. This wasn't because it was actually invisible or anything hyperimpossible like that. The technology involved in making anything invisible is so infinitely complex that nine hundred and ninety-nine billion, nine hundred and ninety-nine million, nine hundred and ninety-nine thousand, nine hundred and ninety-nine times out of a trillion it is much simpler and more effective just to take the thing away and do without it. The ultrafamous sciento-magician Effrafax of Wug once bet his life that, given a year, he could render the great megamountain Magramal entirely invisible.

Having spent most of the year jiggling around with immense Lux-O-Valves and Refracto-Nullifiers and Spectrum-By-Pass-O-Matics, he realized, with nine hours to go, that he wasn't going to make it.

So, he and his friends, and his friends' friends, and his friends' friends' friends, and his friends' friends' friends' friends, and some rather less good friends of theirs who happened to own a major stellar trucking company, put in what is now widely recognized as being the hardest night's work in history and, sure enough, on the following day, Magramal was no longer visible. Effrafax lost his bet—and therefore his life—simply because some pedantic adjudicating official noticed (a) that when walking around the area where Magramal ought to be he didn't trip over or break his nose on anything, and (b) a suspicious-looking extra moon.

The Somebody Else's Problem field is much simpler and more effective, and what is more can be run for over a hundred years on a single flashlight battery. This is because it relies on people's natural predisposition not to see anything they don't want to, weren't expecting or can't explain. If Effrafax had painted the mountain pink and erected a cheap and simple Somebody Else's Problem field on it, then people would have walked past the mountain, around it, even over it, and simply never have noticed that the thing was there.

And this is precisely what was happening with Slartibartfast's ship. It wasn't pink, but if it had been, that would have been the least of its visual problems and people were simply ignoring it like anything.

The most extraordinary thing about it was that it looked only partly like a spaceship with guidance fins, rocket engines and escape hatches and so on, and a great deal like a small, upended Italian bistro.

Ford and Arthur gazed up at it with wonderment and deeply offended sensibilities.

"Yes, I know," said Slartibartfast, hurrying up to them at that point, breathless and agitated, "but there is a reason. Come, we must go. The ancient nightmare is come again. Doom confronts us all. We must leave at once."

"I fancy somewhere sunny," said Ford.

Ford and Arthur followed Slartibartfast into the ship and were so perplexed by what they saw inside it that they were totally unaware of what happened next outside.

A spaceship, yet another one, but this one sleek and silver, descended from the sky onto the pitch, quietly, without fuss, its long legs unlocking in a smooth ballet of technology.

It landed gently. It extended a short ramp. A tall gray green figure marched briskly out and approached the small knot of people who were gathered in the center of the pitch tending to the casualties of the recent bizarre massacre. It moved people aside with quiet understated authority, and came at last to a man lying in a desperate pool of blood, clearly now beyond the reach of any earthly medicine, breathing, coughing his last. The figure knelt down quietly beside him.

"Arthur Philip Deodat?" asked the figure.

The man, with horrified confusion in eyes, nodded feebly.

"You're a no-good dumbo nothing," whispered the creature. "I thought you should know that before you went."

Chapter 4

It seemed to Arthur as if the whole sky suddenly just stood aside and let them through.

It seemed to him that the atoms of his brain and the atoms of the cosmos were streaming through each other.

It seemed to him that he was blown on the wind of the Universe, and that the wind was him.

It seemed to him that he was one of the thoughts of the Universe and that the Universe was a thought of his.

It seemed to the people at Lord's Cricket Ground that another north London restaurant had just come and gone as they so often do, and that this was Somebody Else's Problem.

"What happened?" whispered Arthur in considerable awe.

"We took off," said Slartibartfast.

Arthur lay in startled stillness on the acceleration couch. He wasn't certain whether he had just got space-sickness or religion.

"Nice mover," said Ford in an unsuccessful attempt to disguise the degree to which he had been impressed by what Slartibartfast's ship had just done. "Shame about the decor."

For a moment or two the old man didn't reply. He was staring at the instruments with the air of one who is trying to convert Fahrenheit to centigrade in his head while his house is burning down. Then his brow cleared and he stared for a moment at the wide panoramic screen in front of him, which displayed a bewildering complexity of stars streaming like silver threads around them. His lips moved as if he were trying to spell something. Suddenly his eyes darted in alarm back to his instruments, but then his expression merely subsided into a steady frown. He looked back up at the screen. He felt his own pulse. His frown deepened for a moment, then he relaxed.

"It's a mistake to try to understand machines," he said, "they only worry me. What did you say?"

"Decor," said Ford, "pity about it."

"Deep in the fundamental heart of mind and Universe," said Slartibartfast, "there is a reason."

Ford glanced sharply around. He clearly thought this was taking an optimistic view of things.

The interior of the flight deck was dark green, dark red, dark brown, cramped and moodily lit. Inexplicably, the resemblance to a small Italian bistro had failed to end at the hatchway. Small pools of light picked out pot plants, glazed tiles and all sorts of little unidentifiable brass things.

Raffia-wrapped bottles lurked hideously in the shadows.

The instruments that had occupied Slartibartfast's attention seemed to be mounted in the bottoms of bottles that were set in concrete.

Ford reached out and touched it.

Fake concrete. Plastic. Fake bottles set in fake concrete.

The fundamental heart of mind and Universe can take a running jump, he thought to himself, this is rubbish. On the other hand, it could not be denied that the way the ship had moved made the *Heart of Gold* seem like an electric pram.

He swung himself off the couch. He brushed himself off. He looked at Arthur, who was singing quietly to himself. He looked at the screen and recognized nothing. He looked at Slartibartfast.

"How far did we just travel?" he said.

"About . . ." said Slartibartfast, "about two-thirds of the way across the Galactic disc, I would say, roughly. Yes, roughly two-thirds, I think."

"It's a strange thing," said Arthur quietly, "that the farther and faster one travels across the Universe, the more one's position in it seems to be largely immaterial, and one is filled with a profound, or rather emptied of a . . ."

"Yes, very strange," said Ford. "Where are we going?"

"We are going," said Slartibartfast, "to confront an ancient nightmare of the Universe."

"And where are you going to drop us off?"

"I will need your help."

"Tough. Look, there's somewhere you can take us where we can have fun, I'm trying to think of it; we can get drunk and maybe listen to some extremely evil music. Hold on, I'll look it up." He dug out his copy of *The Hitchhiker's Guide to the Galaxy* and zipped through those parts of the index primarily concerned with sex, drugs and rock 'n' roll.

"A curse has arisen from the mists of time," said Slartibartfast.

"Yes, I expect so," said Ford. "Hey," he said, lighting accidentally on one particular reference entry, "Eccentrica Gallumbits, did you ever meet her? The triple-breasted whore of Eroticon Six. Some people say her erogenous zones start some four miles from her actual body. Me, I disagree, I say five."

"A curse," said Slartibartfast, "which will engulf the Galaxy in fire and destruction, and possibly bring the Universe to a premature doom. I mean it," he added.

"Sounds like a bad time," said Ford; "with luck I'll be drunk enough not to notice. Here," he said, stabbing his finger at the screen of the *Guide*, "would be a really wicked place to go, and I think we should. What do you say, Arthur? Stop mumbling mantras and pay attention. There's important stuff you're missing here."

Arthur pushed himself up from his couch and shook his head.

"Where are we going?" he said.

"To confront an ancient night—"

"Can it," said Ford. "Arthur, we are going out into the Galaxy to have some fun. Is that an idea you can cope with?"

"What's Slartibartfast looking so anxious about?" said Arthur.

"Nothing," said Ford.

"Doom," said Slartibartfast. "Come," he added, with sudden authority, "there is much I must show and tell you."

He walked toward a green wrought-iron spiral staircase set incomprehensibly in the middle of the flight deck and started to ascend. Arthur, with a frown, followed.

Ford slung the *Guide* sullenly back into his satchel.

"My doctor says that I have a malformed public duty gland and a natural deficiency in moral fiber," he muttered to himself, "and that I am therefore excused from saving Universes."

Nevertheless, he stomped up the stairs behind them.

What they found upstairs was just stupid, or so it seemed, and Ford shook his head, buried his face in his hands and slumped against a pot plant, crushing it against the wall.

"The central computational area," said Slartibartfast, unperturbed. "This is where every calculation affecting the ship in any way is performed. Yes, I know what it looks like, but it is in fact a complex four-dimensional topographical map of a series of highly complex mathematical functions."

"It looks like a joke," said Arthur.

"I know what it looks like," said Slartibartfast, and went into it. As he did so, Arthur had a sudden vague flash of what it might mean, but he refused to believe it. The Universe could not possibly work like that, he thought, cannot possibly. That, he thought to himself, would be as absurd as, as absurd as . . . he terminated that line of thinking. Most of the absurd things he could think of had already happened.

And this was one of them.

It was a large glass cage, or box—in fact a room.

In it was a table, a long one. Around it were gathered about a dozen chairs, of the bentwood style. On it was a tablecloth—a grubby, red-and-white checked tablecloth, scarred with the occasional cigarette burn, each, presumably, at a precisely calculated mathematical position.

And on the tablecloth sat some dozen half-eaten Italian meals, hedged about with half-eaten breadsticks and half-drunk glasses of wine, and toyed with listlessly by robots.

It was all completely artificial. The robot customers were attended by a robot waiter, a robot wine waiter and a robot maître d'. The furniture was artificial, the tablecloth artificial and each particular piece of food was clearly capable of exhibiting all the mechanical characteristics of, say, a *pollo sorpreso*, without actually being one.

And all participated in a little dance together—a complex routine involving the manipulation of menus, check pads, wallets, check books, credit cards, watches, pencils and paper napkins, which seemed to be hovering constantly on the edge of violence, but never actually getting anywhere.

Slartibartfast hurried in, and then appeared to pass the time of day quite idly with the maître d', while one of the customer robots, an autorory, slid slowly under the table, mentioning what he intended to do to some guy over some girl.

Slartibartfast took over the seat that had been thus vacated and passed a shrewd eye over the menu. The tempo of the routine around the table seemed somehow imperceptibly to quicken. Arguments broke out, people attempted to prove things on napkins. They waved fiercely at each other, and attempted to examine each other's pieces of chicken. The waiter's hand began to move on the check pad more quickly than a human hand could manage, and then more quickly than a human eye could follow. The pace accelerated. Soon, an extraordinary and insistent politeness over-whelmed the group, and seconds later it seemed that a moment of consensus was suddenly achieved. A new vibration thrilled through the ship.

Slartibartfast emerged from the glass room.

"Bistromathics," he said, "the most powerful computational force known to parascience. Come to the room of Informational Illusions."

He swept past and carried them, bewildered, in his wake.

Chapter 5

The Bistromathic Drive is a wonderful new method of crossing vast interstellar distances without all that dangerous mucking about with Improbability Factors.

Bistromathics itself is simply a revolutionary new way of understanding the behavior of numbers. Just as Einstein observed that space was not an absolute but depended on the observer's movement in space, and that time was not an absolute, but depended on the observer's movement in time, so it is now realized that numbers are not absolute, but depend on the observer's movement in restaurants.

The first nonabsolute number is the number of people for whom the table is reserved. This will vary during the course of the first three telephone calls to the restaurant, and then bear no apparent relation to the number of people who actually turn up, or to the number of people who subsequently join them after the show/match/party/gig, or to the number of people who leave when they see who else has turned up.

The second nonabsolute number is the given time of arrival, which is now known to be one of those most bizarre of mathematical concepts, a recipriversexcluson, a number whose existence can only be defined as being anything other than itself. In other words, the given time of arrival is the one moment of time at which it is impossible that any member of the party will arrive. Recipriversexclusons now play a vital part in many branches of math, including statistics and accountancy and also form the basic equations used to engineer the Somebody Else's Problem field.

The third and most mysterious piece of nonabsoluteness of all lies in the relationship between the number of items on the check, the cost of each item, the number of people at the table and what they are each prepared to pay for. (The number of people who have actually brought any money is only a subphenomenon in this field.)

The baffling discrepancies that used to occur at this point remained uninvestigated for centuries simply because no one took them seriously. They were at the time put down to such things as politeness, rudeness, meanness, flashiness, tiredness, emotionality or the lateness of the hour, and completely forgotten about on the following morning. They were never tested under laboratory conditions, of course, because they never occurred in laboratories—not in reputable laboratories at least.

And so it was only with the advent of pocket computers that the startling truth became finally apparent, and it was this:

Numbers written on restaurant checks within the confines of restaurants do not follow the same mathematical laws as numbers written on any other pieces of paper in any other parts of the Universe.

This single statement took the scientific world by storm. It completely revolutionized it. So many mathematical conferences got held in such good restaurants that many of the finest minds of a generation died of obesity and heart failure and the science of math was put back by years.

Slowly, however, the implications of the idea began to be understood. To begin with it had been too stark, too crazy, too much like what the man in the street would have said: "Oh yes, I could have told you that." Then some phrases like "Interactive Subjectivity Frameworks" were invented, and everybody was able to relax and get on with it.

The small groups of monks who had taken up hanging around the major research institutes singing strange chants to the effect that the Universe was only a figment of its own imagination were eventually given a street theater grant and went away.

n space travel, you see," said Slartibartfast, as he fiddled with some instruments in the room of Informational Illusions, "in space travel . . ."

He stopped and looked about him.

The room of Informational Illusions was a welcome relief after the visual monstrosities of the central computational area. There was nothing in it. No information, no illusions, just themselves, white walls and a few small instruments that looked as if they were meant to plug into something that Slartibartfast couldn't find.

"Yes?" urged Arthur. He had picked up Slartibartfast's sense of urgency but didn't know what to do with it.

"Yes what?" said the old man.

"You were saying?"

Slartibartfast looked at him sharply.

"The numbers," he said, "are awful." He resumed his search.

Arthur nodded wisely to himself. After a while he realized that this wasn't getting him anywhere and decided that he would say "What?" after all.

"In space travel," repeated Slartibartfast, "all the numbers are awful."

Arthur nodded again and looked around to Ford for help, but Ford was practicing being sullen and getting quite good at it.

"I was only," said Slartibartfast with a sigh, "trying to save you the trouble of asking me why all the ship's computations were being done on a waiter's check pad."

Arthur frowned.

"Why," he said, "were all the ship's computations being done on a wait—"

He stopped.

Slartibartfast said, "Because in space travel all the numbers are awful."

He could tell that he wasn't getting his point across.

"Listen," he said, "on a waiter's check pad numbers dance. You must have encountered the phenomenon."

"Well . . ."

"On a waiter's check pad," said Slartibartfast, "reality and unreality collide on such a fundamental level that each becomes the other and anything is possible, within certain parameters."

"What parameters?"

"It's impossible to say," said Slartibartfast. "That's one of them. Strange but true. At least, I think it's strange," he added, "and I am assured that it's true."

At that moment he located the slot in the wall for which he had been searching, and clicked the instrument he was holding into it.

"Do not be alarmed," he said, and then suddenly darted an alarmed look at it himself, and lunged back, "it's . . ."

They didn't hear what he said, because at that moment the ship winked out of existence around them and a star battleship the size of a small Midlands industrial city plunged out of the sundered night toward them, star lasers ablaze.

A nightmare storm of blistering light seared through the blackness and smacked a fair bit off the planet directly behind them.

They gaped, pop-eyed, and were unable to scream.

Chapter 7

Another world, another day, another dawn.

The early morning's thinnest sliver of light appeared silently. Several billion trillion tons of superhot exploding hydrogen nuclei rose slowly above the horizon and managed to look small, cold and slightly damp.

There is a moment in every dawn when light floats, there is the possibility of magic. Creation holds its breath.

The moment passed as it regularly did on Sqornshellous Zeta, without incident.

The mist clung to the surface of the marshes. The swamp trees were gray with it, the tall reeds indistinct. It hung motionless like held breath.

Nothing moved.

There was silence.

The sun struggled feebly with the mist, tried to impart a little warmth here, shed a little light there, but clearly today was going to be just another long haul across the sky.

Nothing moved.

Again, silence.

Nothing moved.

Silence.

Nothing moved.

Very often on Sqornshellous Zeta, whole days would go on like this, and this was indeed going to be one of them.

Fourteen hours later the sun sank hopelessly beneath the opposite horizon with a sense of totally wasted effort.

And a few hours later it reappeared, squared its shoulders and started on up the sky again.

This time, however, something was happening. A mattress had just met a robot.

"Hello, robot," said the mattress.

"Bleah," said the robot and continued what it was doing, which was walking round very slowly in a very tiny circle.

"Happy?" said the mattress.

The robot stopped and looked at the mattress. It looked at it quizzically.

It was clearly a very stupid mattress. It looked back at him with wide eyes.

After what it had calculated to ten significant decimal places as being the precise length of pause most likely to convey a general contempt for all things mattressy, the robot continued to walk round in tight circles.

"We could have a conversation," said the mattress. "Would you like that?"

It was a large mattress, and probably one of quite high quality. Very few things actually get manufactured these days, because in an infinitely large Universe such as, for instance, the one in which we live, most things one could possibly imagine and a lot of things one would rather not, grow somewhere. (A forest was discovered recently in which most of the trees grew ratchet screwdrivers as fruit. The life cycle of ratchet screwdriver fruit is quite interesting. Once picked it needs a dark dusty drawer in which it can lie undisturbed for years. Then one night it suddenly hatches, discards its outer skin that crumbles into dust, and emerges as a totally unidentifiable little metal object with flanges at both ends and a sort of ridge and a sort of a hole for a screw. This, when found, will get thrown away. No one knows what it is supposed to gain from this. Nature, in her infinite wisdom, is presumably working on it.)

No one really knows what mattresses are meant to gain from their lives either. They are large, friendly, pocket-sprung creatures that live quiet private lives in the marshes of Sqornshellous Zeta. Many of them get caught, slaughtered, dried out, shipped out and slept on. None of them seems to mind this and all of them are called Zem.

"No," said Marvin.

"My name," said the mattress, "is Zem. We could discuss the weather a little."

Marvin paused again in his weary circular plod.

"The dew," he observed, "has clearly fallen with a particularly sickening thud this morning."

He resumed his walk, as if inspired by this conversational outburst to fresh heights of gloom and despondency. He plodded tenaciously. If he had had teeth he would have gritted them at this point. He hadn't. He didn't. The mere plod said it all.

The mattress flolloped around. This is a thing that only live mattresses in swamps are able to do, which is why the word is not in common usage. It flolloped in a sympathetic sort of way, moving a fair-size body of water as it did so. It blew a few bubbles up through the water engagingly. Its blue and white stripes glistened briefly in a sudden feeble ray of sun that had unexpectedly made it through the mist, causing the creature to bask momentarily.

Marvin plodded.

"You have something on your mind, I think," said the mattress, floopily.

"More than you can possibly imagine," dreared Marvin. "My capacity for mental activity of all kinds is as boundless as the infinite reaches of space itself. Except of course for my capacity for happiness."

Stomp, stomp, he went.

"My capacity for happiness," he added, "you could fit into a matchbox without taking out the matches first."

The mattress globbered. This is the noise made by a live, swamp-dwelling mattress that is deeply moved by a story of personal tragedy. The word can also, according to the *Ultra-Complete Maximegalon Dictionary of Every Language Ever*, mean the noise made by the Lord High Sanvalvwag of Hollop on discovering that he has forgotten his wife's birthday for the second year running. Since there was only ever one Lord High Sanvalvwag of Hollop and he never married, the word is only used in a negative or speculative sense, and there is an ever-increasing body of opinion that holds that the *Ultra-Complete Maximegalon Dictionary* is not worth the fleet of trucks it takes to cart its microstored edition around in. Strangely enough, the dictionary omits the word "floopily," which simply means "in the manner of something which is floopy."

The mattress globbered again.

"I sense a deep dejectedness in your diodes," it vollued (for the meaning of the word "vollue," buy a copy of *Sqornshellous Swamptalk* at any bookstore selling remaindered books, or alternatively buy the *Ultra-Complete Maximegalon Dictionary*, as the university will be very glad to get if off their hands and regain some valuable parking lots), "and it saddens me. You should be more mattresslike. We live quiet retired lives in the swamp, where we are content to flollop and vollue and regard the wetness in a fairly floopy manner. Some of us are killed, but all of us are called Zem, so we never know which and globbering is thus kept to a minimum. Why are you walking in circles?"

"Because my leg is stuck," said Marvin simply.

"It seems to me," said the mattress, eying it compassionately, "that it is a pretty poor sort of leg."

"You are right," said Marvin, "it is."

"Voon," said the mattress.

"I expect so," said Marvin, "and I also expect that you find the idea of a robot with an artificial leg pretty amusing. You should tell your friends, Zem and Zem, when you see them later; they'll laugh, if I know them, which I don't of course, except insofar as I know all organic life forms, which is much better than I would wish to. Ha, but my life is but a box of wormgears."

He stomped around again in his tiny circle, around his thin steel pegleg that revolved in the mud but seemed otherwise stuck.

"But why do you just keep walking round and round?" asked the mattress.

"Just to make the point," said Marvin, and continued, round and round.

"Consider it made, my dear friend," flurbled the mattress, "consider it made."

"Just another million years," said Marvin, "just another quick million. Then I might try it backward. Just for the variety, you understand."

The mattress could feel deep in his innermost spring pockets that the robot dearly wished to be asked how long he had been trudging in this futile and fruitless manner, and with another quiet flurble he did so.

"Oh, just over the one point five million mark, just over," said Marvin airily; "ask me if I ever get bored, go on, ask me."

The mattress did.

Marvin ignored the question, he merely trudged with added emphasis.

"I gave a speech once," he said suddenly and apparently unconnectedly. "You may not instantly see why I bring the subject up, but that is because my mind works so phenomenally fast, and I am at a rough estimate thirty billion times more intelligent than you. Let me give you an example. Think of a number, any number."

"Er, five," said the mattress.

"Wrong," said Marvin. "You see?"

The mattress was much impressed by this and realized that it was in the presence of a not unremarkable mind. It willomied along its entire length sending excited little ripples through its shallow algae-covered pool.

It gupped.

"Tell me," it urged, "of the speech you once made, I long to hear it."

"It was received very badly," said Marvin, "for a variety of reasons. I delivered it," he added, pausing to make an awkward humping sort of gesture with his not-exactly-good arm, but his arm that was better than the other one that was dishearteningly welded to his left side, "over there, about a mile distant."

He was pointing as well as he could manage, and he obviously wanted to make it totally clear that this was as well as he could manage, through the mist, over the reeds, to a part of the marsh that looked exactly the same as every other part of the marsh.

"There," he repeated, "I was somewhat of a celebrity at the time."

Excitement gripped the mattress. It had never heard of speeches being delivered on Sqornshellous Zeta, and certainly not by celebrities. Water spattered off it as a thrill glurried across its back.

It did something that mattresses very rarely bother to do. Summoning every bit of its strength, it reared its oblong body, heaved it up into the air and held it quivering there for a few seconds until it peered through the mist over the reeds at the part of the marsh that Marvin had indicated, observing, without disappointment, that it was exactly the same as every other part of the marsh. The effort was too much, and it flodged back into its pool, deluging Marvin with smelly mud, moss and weeds.

"I was a celebrity," droned the robot sadly, "for a short while on account of my miraculous and bitterly resented escape from a fate almost as good as death in the heart of a blazing sun. You can guess from my condition," he added, "how narrow my escape was. I was rescued by a scrap-metal merchant, imagine that. Here I am, brain the size of . . . never mind."

He trudged savagely for a few seconds.

"He it was who fixed me up with this leg. Hateful, isn't it? He sold me to a Mind Zoo. I was the star exhibit. I had to sit on a box and tell my story while people told me to cheer up and think positive. 'Give us a grin, little robot,' they would shout at me, 'give us a little chuckle.' I would explain to them that to get my face to grin would take a good couple of hours in a workshop with a wrench, and that went down very well."

"The speech," urged the mattress, "I long to hear of the speech you gave in the marshes."

"There was a bridge built across the marshes. A cyberstructured hyperbridge, hundreds of miles in length, to carry ion-buggies and freighters over the swamp."

"A bridge?" quirruled the mattress, "here, in the swamp?"

"A bridge," confirmed Marvin, "here in the swamp. It was going to revitalize the economy of the Sqornshellous System. They spent the entire economy of the Sqornshellous System building it. They asked me to open it. Poor fools."

It began to rain a little, a fine spray slid through the mist.

"I stood on the platform. For hundreds of miles in front of me, and hundreds of miles behind me the bridge stretched."

"Did it glitter?" enthused the mattress.

"It glittered."

"Did it span the miles majestically?"

"It spanned the miles majestically."

"Did it stretch like a silver thread, far out into the invisible mist?"

"Yes," said Marvin, "do you want to hear this story?"

"I want to hear your speech," said the mattress.

"This is what I said. I said, 'I would like to say that it is a very great pleasure, honor and privilege for me to open this bridge, but I can't because my lying circuits are all out of commission. I hate and despise you all. I now declare this hapless cyberstructure open to the unthinking abuse of all who wantonly cross her.' And I plugged myself into the opening circuits."

Marvin paused, remembering the moment.

The mattress flurred and glurried. It flolloped, gupped and willomied, doing this last in a particularly floopy way.

"Voon," it wurfed at last, "and was it a magnificent occasion?"

"Reasonably magnificent. The entire thousand-mile-long bridge spontaneously folded up its glittering spans and sank weeping into the mire, taking everybody with it."

There was a sad and terrible pause at this point in the conversation during which a hundred thousand people seemed unexpectedly to say "whop" and a team of white robots descended from the sky like dandelion seeds drifting on the wind in tight military formation. For a sudden violent moment they were all there, in the swamp, wrenching Marvin's false leg off, and then they were gone again in their ship that said "foop."

"You see the sort of thing I have to contend with?" said Marvin to the gobbering mattress.

And suddenly, a moment later, the robots were back again for another violent incident, and this time when they left, the mattress was alone in the swamp. He flolloped around in astonishment and alarm. He almost lurgled in fear. He reared himself to see over the reeds, but there was nothing to see, no robot, no glittering bridge, no ship, just more reeds. He listened, but there was no sound on the wind beyond the now familiar sound of half-crazed etymologists calling to each other across the sullen mire.

Chapter 8

Threw the body of Arthur Dent spun.

The Universe shattered into a million glittering fragments around it, and each particular shard spun silently through the void, reflecting on its silver surface some single searing holocaust of fire and destruction.

And then the blackness behind the Universe exploded, and each particular piece of blackness was the furious smoke of hell.

And the nothingness behind the blackness behind the Universe erupted, and behind the nothingness behind the blackness behind the shattered Universe was at last the dark figure of an immense man speaking immense words.

"These, then," said the figure, speaking from an immensely comfortable chair, "were the Krikkit Wars, the greatest devastation ever visited upon our Galaxy. What you have experienced..."

Slartibartfast floated past, waving.

"It's just a documentary," he called out, "this is not a good bit. Terribly sorry, trying to find the rewind control..."

"...is what billions upon billions of innocent..."

"Do not," called out Slartibartfast, floating past again, and fiddling furiously with the thing that he had stuck into the wall of the room of Informational Illusions and that was in fact still stuck there, "agree to buy anything at this point."

"...people, creatures, your fellow beings..."

Music swelled—again, it was immense music, immense chords. And behind the man, slowly, three tall pillars began slowly to emerge out of the immensely swirling mist.

"...experienced, lived through or—more often—failed to live through. Think of that, my friends. And let us not forget—and in just a moment I shall be able to suggest a way that will help us always to remember—that before the Krikkit Wars, the Galaxy was that rare and wonderful thing, a happy Galaxy!"

The music was going bananas with immensity at this point.

"A happy Galaxy, my friends, as represented by the symbol of the Wikkit Gate!"

The three pillars stood out clearly now, three pillars topped with two crosspieces in a way that looked stupefyingly familiar to Arthur's addled brain.

"The three pillars," thundered the man, "the Steel Pillar, which represents the Strength and Power of the Galaxy!"

Searchlights seared out and danced crazy dances up and down the pillar on the left that was made of steel or something very like it. The music thumped and bellowed.

"The Plastic Pillar," announced the man, "representing the forces of Science and Reason in the Galaxy!"

Other searchlights played exotically up and down the right-hand, transparent pillar creating dazzling patterns within it and a sudden inexplicable craving for ice cream in the stomach of Arthur Dent.

"And," the thunderous voice continued, "the Wooden Pillar, representing..." and here his voice became just very slightly hoarse with wonderful sentiments, "the forces of Nature and Spirituality."

The lights picked out the central pillar. The music moved bravely up into the realms of complete unspeakability.

"Between them supporting," the voice rolled on, approaching its climax, "the Golden Bail of Prosperity and the Silver Bail of Peace!"

The whole structure was now flooded with dazzling lights, and the music had now, fortunately, gone far beyond the limits of the discernible. At the top of the three pillars the two brilliantly gleaming bails sat and dazzled. There seemed to be girls sitting on top of them, or maybe they were meant to be angels. Angels usually are represented as wearing more than that though.

Suddenly there was a dramatic hush in what was presumably meant to be the cosmos, and a darkening of the lights.

"There is not a world," thrilled the man's expert voice, "not a civilized world in the Galaxy where this symbol is not revered even today. Even in primitive worlds it persists in racial memories. This it was that the forces of Krikkit destroyed, and this it is that now locks their world away till the end of eternity!"

And with a flourish, the man produced in his hands a model of the Wikkit Gate. Scale was terribly hard to judge in this whole extraordinary spectacle, but the model looked as if it must have been about three feet high.

"Not the original Key, of course. That, as everyone knows, was destroyed, blasted into the ever whirling eddies in the space-time continuum and lost forever. This is a remarkable replica, hand-tooled by skilled craftsmen, lovingly assembled using ancient craft secrets into a memento you will be proud to own, in memory of those who fell, and in tribute to the Galaxy—our Galaxy—which they died to defend. . . ."

Slartibartfast floated past again at this moment.

"Found it," he said, "we can lose all this rubbish. Just don't nod, that's all."

"Now, let us bow our heads in payment," intoned the voice, and then said it again, much faster and backward.

Lights came and went, the pillars disappeared, the man gabbled himself backward into nothing, the Universe snappily reassembled itself around them.

"You get the gist?" said Slartibartfast.

"I'm astonished," said Arthur, "and bewildered."

"I was asleep," said Ford, who floated into view at this point. "Did I miss anything?"

They found themselves once again teetering rather rapidly on the edge of an agonizingly high cliff. The wind whipped out from their faces and across a bay on which the remains of one of the greatest and most powerful space battle fleets ever assembled in the Galaxy were briskly burning themselves back into existence. The sky was a sullen pink, darkening, via a rather curious color, to blue and upward to black. Smoke billowed down out of it at an incredible lick.

Events were now passing back by them almost too quickly to be distinguished, and when, a short while later, a huge star battleship rushed away from them as if they'd said "Boo," they only just recognized it as the point at which they had come in.

But now things were too rapid, a videotactile blur that brushed and jiggled them through centuries of Galactic history, turning, twisting, flickering. The sound was a mere thin trill.

Periodically throughout the thickening jumble of events they sensed appalling catastrophes, deep horrors, cataclysmic shocks, and these were always associated with certain recurring images, the only images which ever stood out clearly from the avalanche of tumbling history: a Wikkit Gate, a small, hard red ball, and hard white robots, and also something less distinct, something dark and cloudy.

But there was also another sensation that rose clearly out of the trilling passage of time.

Just as a slow series of clicks when speeded up will lose the definition of each individual click and gradually take on the quality of a sustained and rising tone, so a series of individual impressions here took on the quality of a sustained emotion—and yet not an emotion. If it was an emotion, it was a totally emotionless one. It was hatred, implacable hatred. It was cold, not like ice is cold, but like a wall is cold. It was impersonal, not like a randomly flung fist in a crowd is impersonal, but like a computer-issued parking summons is impersonal. And it was deadly, again, not like a bullet or a knife is deadly, but like a brick wall across an expressway is deadly.

And just as a rising tone will change in character and take on harmonics as it rises, so again this emotionless emotion seemed to rise to an unbearable if unheard scream and suddenly seemed to be a scream of guilt and failure.

And suddenly it stopped.

They were left standing on a quiet hilltop on a tranquil evening.

The sun was setting.

All around them softly undulating green countryside rolled off gently into the distance. Birds sang about what they thought of it all, and the general opinion seemed to be good. A little way off could be heard the sound of children playing, and a little farther away than the apparent source of that sound could be seen in the dimming evening light the outlines of a small town.

The town appeared to consist mostly of fairly low buildings made of white stone. The skyline was of gentle pleasing curves.

The sun had nearly set.

As if out of nowhere, music began. Slartibartfast tugged at a switch and it stopped.

A voice said, "This . . ." Slartibartfast tugged at a switch and it stopped.

"I will tell you about it," he said quietly.

The place was peaceful. Arthur felt happy. Even Ford seemed cheerful. They walked a short way in the direction of the town, and the Informational Illusion of the grass was pleasant and springy under their feet, and the Informational Illusion of the flowers smelled sweet and fragrant. Only Slartibartfast seemed apprehensive and out of sorts.

He stopped and looked up.

It suddenly occurred to Arthur that coming as this did at the end, so to speak, or rather the beginning, of all the horror they had just blurrily experienced, something nasty must be about to happen. He was distressed to think that something nasty could happen to somewhere as idyllic as this. He too glanced up. There was nothing in the sky.

"They're not about to attack here, are they?" he said. He realized that this was merely a recording he was walking through, but he still felt alarmed.

"Nothing is about to attack here," said Slartibartfast in a voice that unexpectedly trembled with emotion, "this is where it all starts. This is the place itself. This is Krikkit."

He stared up into the sky.

The sky, from one horizon to another, from east to west, from north to south, was utterly and completely black.

Chapter 9

Stomp stomp.

    Whirrr.

    "Pleased to be of service."

    "Shut up."

"Thank you."

Stomp stomp stomp stomp stomp.

Whirrr.

"Thank you for making a simple door very happy."

"Hope your diodes rot."

"Thank you. Have a nice day."

Stomp stomp stomp stomp.

Whirrr.

"It is my pleasure to open for you . . ."

"Zark off."

". . . and my satisfaction to close again with the knowledge of a job well done."

"I said zark off."

"Thank you for listening to this message."

Stomp stomp stomp stomp.

"Whop."

Zaphod stopped stomping. He had been stomping around the *Heart of Gold* for days, and so far no door had said "whop" to him. He was fairly certain that no door had said "whop" to him now. It was not the sort of thing doors said. Too concise. Furthermore, there were not enough doors. It sounded as if a hundred thousand people had said "whop," which puzzled him because he was the only person on the ship.

It was dark. Most of the ship's nonessential systems were closed down. It was drifting idly in a remote area of the Galaxy, deep in the inky blackness of space. So which particular hundred thousand people would turn up at this point and say a totally unexpected "whop"?

He looked about him, up the corridor and down the corridor. It was all in deep shadow. There were just the very dim pinkish outlines to the doors that glowed in the dark and pulsed whenever they spoke though he had tried every way he could think of to stop them.

The lights were off so that his heads could avoid looking at each other because neither of them was currently a particularly engaging sight, nor had they been since he had made the error of looking into his soul.

It had indeed been an error.

It had been late one night—of course.

It had been a difficult day—of course.

There had been soulful music playing on the ship's sound system—of course.

And he had, of course, been slightly drunk.

In other words, all the usual conditions that bring on a bout of soul-searching had applied, but it had, nevertheless, clearly been an error.

Standing now, silent and alone in the dark corridor, he remembered the moment and shivered. His one head looked one way and his other the other and each decided that the other way was the way to go.

He listened but could hear nothing.

All there had been was the "whop."

It seemed an awfully long way to bring an awfully large number of people just to say one word.

He started nervously to edge his way in the direction of the bridge. There at least he would feel in control. He stopped again. The way he was feeling he didn't think he was an awfully good person to be in control.

The first shock of that moment, thinking back, had been discovering that he actually had a soul.

In fact he'd always more or less assumed that he had one as he had a full complement of everything else, and indeed two of some things, but suddenly actually to encounter the thing lurking there deep within him had given him a severe jolt.

And then to discover (this was the second shock) that it wasn't the totally wonderful object that he felt a man in his position had a natural right to expect had jolted him again.

Then he had thought about what his position actually was and the renewed shock had nearly made him spill his drink. He drained it quickly before anything serious happened to it. He then had another quick one to follow the first one down and check that it was all right.

"Freedom," he said aloud.

Trillian came onto the bridge at that point and said several enthusiastic things on the subject of freedom.

"I can't cope with it," he said darkly, and sent a third drink down to see why the second hadn't yet reported on the condition of the first. He looked uncertainly at both of her and preferred the one on the right.

He poured a drink down his other throat with the plan that it would head the previous one off at the pass, join forces with it, and together they would get the second to pull itself together. Then all three would go off in search of the first, give it a good talking to.

He felt uncertain as to whether the fourth drink had understood all that so he sent down a fifth to explain the plan more fully and a sixth for moral support.

"You're drinking too much," said Trillian.

His heads collided trying to sort out the four of her he could now see into a whole person. He gave up and looked at the navigation screen and was astonished to see a quite phenomenal number of stars.

"Excitement and adventure and really wild things," he muttered.

"Look," she said in a sympathetic tone of voice, and sat down near him, "it's quite understandable that you're going to feel a little aimless for a bit."

He boggled at her. He had never seen anyone sit on their own lap before.

"Wow," he said. He had another drink.

"You've finished the mission you've been on for years."

"I haven't been on it. I've tried to avoid being on it."

"You've still finished it."

He grunted. There seemed to be a terrific party going on in his stomach.

"I think it finished me," he said. "Here I am, Zaphod Beeblebrox, I can go anywhere, do anything. I have the greatest ship in the known sky, a girl with whom things seem to be working out pretty well...."

"Are they?"

"As far as I can tell. I'm not an expert in personal relationships...."

Trillian raised her eyebrows.

"I am," he added, "one hell of a guy, I can do anything I want only I just don't have the faintest idea what."

He paused.

"One thing," he further added, "has suddenly ceased to lead to another," in contradiction of which he had another drink and slid gracelessly off his chair.

While he slept it off, Trillian did a little research in the ship's copy of *The Hitchhiker's Guide to the Galaxy*. It had some advice to offer on drunkenness.

"Go to it," it said, "and good luck."

It was cross-referenced to the entry concerning the size of the Universe and ways of coping with that.

Then she found the entry on Han Wavel, an exotic holiday planet, and one of the wonders of the Galaxy. Han Wavel is a world that consists largely of fabulous ultraluxury hotels and casinos, all of which have been formed by the natural erosion of wind and rain.

The chances of this happening are more or less one to infinity against. Little is known of how this came about because none of the geophysicists, probability statisticians, meteoranalysts or bizarrologists who are so keen to research it can afford to stay there.

"Terrific," thought Trillian to herself, and within a few hours, the great white running shoe ship was slowly powering down out of the sky beneath a hot brilliant sun toward a brightly colored sandy spaceport. The ship was clearly causing a sensation on the ground, and Trillian was enjoying herself. She heard Zaphod moving around and whistling somewhere in the ship.

"How are you?" she said over the general intercom.

"Fine," he said brightly, "terribly well."

"Where are you?"

"In the bathroom."

"What are you doing?"

"Staying here."

After an hour or two it became clear that he meant it and the ship returned to the sky without having once opened its hatchway.

"Heigh-ho," said Eddie the Computer.

Trillian nodded patiently, tapped her fingers a couple of times and pushed the intercom switch.

"I think that enforced fun is probably not what you need at this point."

"Probably not," replied Zaphod from wherever he was.

"I think a bit of physical challenge would help draw you out of yourself."

"Whatever you think, I think," said Zaphod.

RECREATIONAL IMPOSSIBILITIES was a heading that caught Trillian's eye when, a short while later, she sat down to flip through the *Guide* again, and as the *Heart of Gold* rushed at improbable speeds in an indeterminate direction, she sipped a cup of something undrinkable from the Nutri-matic Drinks Dispenser and read about how to fly.

The Hitchhiker's Guide to the Galaxy has this to say on the subject of flying.

There is an art, it says, or, rather, a knack to flying.

The knack lies in learning how to throw yourself at the ground and miss.

Pick a nice day, it suggests, and try it.

The first part is easy.

All it requires is simply the ability to throw yourself forward with all your weight, and the willingness not to mind that it's going to hurt.

That is, it's going to hurt if you fail to miss the ground.

Most people fail to miss the ground, and if they are really trying properly, the likelihood is that they will fail to miss it fairly hard.

Clearly, it is this second part, the missing, which presents the difficulties.

One problem is that you have to miss the ground accidentally. It's no good deliberately intending to miss the ground because you won't. You have to have your attention suddenly distracted by something else when you're halfway there, so that you are no longer thinking about falling, or about the ground, or about how much it's going to hurt if you fail to miss it.

It is notoriously difficult to prize your attention away from these three things during the split second you have at your disposal. Hence most people's failure, and their eventual disillusionment with this exhilarating and spectacular sport.

If, however, you are lucky enough to have your attention momentarily distracted at the crucial moment by, say, a gorgeous pair of legs (tentacles, pseudopodia, according to phylum and/or personal inclination) or a bomb going off in your vicinity, or by suddenly spotting an extremely rare species of beetle crawling along a nearby twig, then in your astonishment you will miss the ground completely and remain bobbing just a few inches above it in what might seem to be a slightly foolish manner.

This is a moment for superb and delicate concentration.

Bob and float, float and bob.

Ignore all considerations of your own weight and simply let yourself waft higher.

Do not listen to what anybody says to you at this point because they are unlikely to say anything helpful.

They are most likely to say something along the lines of "Good God, you can't possibly be flying!"

It is vitally important not to believe them or they will suddenly be right.

Waft higher and higher.

Try a few swoops, gentle ones at first, then drift above the treetops breathing regularly.

DO NOT WAVE AT ANYBODY.

When you have done this a few times you will find the moment of distraction rapidly becomes easier and easier to achieve.

You will then learn all sorts of things about how to control your flight, your speed, your maneuverability, and the trick usually lies in not thinking too hard about whatever you want to do, but just allowing it to happen as if it were going to anyway.

You will also learn about how to land properly, which is something you will almost certainly screw up, and screw up badly, on your first attempt.

There are private flying clubs you can join which help you achieve the all-important moment of distraction. They hire people with surprising bodies or opinions to leap out from behind bushes and exhibit and/or explain them at the critical moments. Few genuine hitchhikers will be able to afford to join these clubs, but some may be able to get temporary employment at them.

Trillian read this longingly, but reluctantly decided that Zaphod wasn't really in the right frame of mind for attempting to fly, or for walking through mountains or for trying to get the Brantisvogan Civil Service to acknowledge a change of address card, which were the other things listed under the heading of RECREATIONAL IMPOSSIBILITIES.

Instead, she flew the ship to Allosimanius Syneca, a world of ice, snow, mind-hurtling beauty and stunning cold. The trek from the snow plains of Liska to the summit of the Ice Crystal Pyramids of Sastantua is long and grueling, even with jet skis and a team of Syneca Snowhounds, but the view from the top, a view which takes in the Stin Glacier Fields, the shimmering Prism Mountains and the far ethereal dancing icelights, is one which first freezes the mind and then slowly releases it to hitherto unexperienced horizons of beauty, and Trillian, for one, felt that she could do with a bit of having her mind slowly released to hitherto unexperienced horizons of beauty.

They went into a low orbit.

There lay the silverwhite beauty of Allosimanius Syneca beneath them.

Zaphod stayed in bed with one head stuck under a pillow and the other doing crosswords till late into the night.

Trillian nodded patiently again, counted to a sufficiently high number, and told herself that the important thing now was just to get Zaphod talking.

She prepared, by dint of deactivating all the robot kitchen synthomatics, the most fabulously delicious meal she could contrive—delicately oiled meats, scented fruits, fragrant cheeses, fine Aldebaran wines.

She carried it through to him and asked if he felt like talking things through.

"Zark off," said Zaphod.

Trillian nodded patiently to herself, counted to an even higher number, tossed the tray lightly aside, walked to the transport room and just teleported herself the hell out of his life.

She didn't even program any coordinates, she hadn't the faintest idea where she was going, she just went—a random row of dots flowing through the Universe.

"Anything," she said to herself as she left, "is better than this."

"Good job, too," muttered Zaphod to himself, turned over and failed to go to sleep.

The next day he restlessly paced the empty corridors of the ship, pretending not to look for her, though he knew she wasn't there. He ignored the computer's querulous demands to know just what the hell was going on around here by fitting a small electronic gag across a pair of its terminals.

After a while he began to turn down the lights. There was nothing to see. Nothing was about to happen.

Lying in bed one night—and night was now virtually continuous on the ship—he decided to pull himself together, to get things into some kind of perspective. He sat up sharply and started to pull clothes on. He decided that there must be someone in the Universe feeling more wretched, miserable and forsaken than himself, and he determined to set out and find him.

Halfway to the bridge it occurred to him that it might be Marvin and he returned to bed.

It was a few hours later than this as he stomped disconsolately about the darkened corridors swearing at cheerful doors, that he heard the "whop" said, and it made him very nervous.

He leaned tensely against the corridor wall and frowned like a man trying to unbend a corkscrew by telekinesis. He laid his fingertips against the wall and felt an unusual vibration. And now he could quite clearly hear slight noises, and could hear where they were coming from—they were coming from the bridge.

Moving his hand along the wall he came across something he was glad to find. He moved on a little farther, quietly.

"Computer?" he hissed.

"Mmmm?" said the computer terminal nearest him, equally quietly.

"Is there someone on this ship?"

"Mmmm," said the computer.

"Who is it?"

"Mmmm mmm mmmmm," said the computer.

"What?"

"Mmmmm mmmm mm mmmmmmmm."

Zaphod buried one of his faces in two of his hands.

"Oh, Zarquon," he muttered to himself. Then he stared up the corridor toward the entrance to the bridge in the dim distance from which more and purposeful noises were coming, and in which the gagged terminals were situated.

"Computer," he hissed again.

"Mmmmm?"

"When I ungag you . . ."

"Mmmmm."

"Remind me to punch myself in the mouth."

"Mmmmm mmm?"

"Either one. Now just tell me this. One for yes, two for no. Is it dangerous?"

"Mmmm."

"It is?"

"Mmmm."

"You didn't just go 'mmmm' twice?"

"Mmmm mmm."

"Hmmmm."

He inched his way up the corridor as if he would rather be yarding his way down it, which was true.

He was within two yards of the door to the bridge when he suddenly realized to his horror that it was going to be nice to him, and he stopped dead. He hadn't been able to turn off the door's courtesy voice circuits.

This doorway to the bridge was concealed from view within it because of the excitingly chunky way in which the bridge had been designed to curve round, and he had been hoping to enter unobserved.

He leaned despondently back against the wall again and said some words that his other head was quite shocked to hear.

He peered at the dim pink outline of the door, and discovered that in the darkness of the corridor he could just about make out the Sensor Field that extended out into the corridor and told the door when there was someone there for whom it must open and to whom it must make a cheery and pleasant remark.

He pressed himself hard back against the wall and edged himself toward the door, flattening his chest as much as he possibly could to avoid brushing against the very, very dim perimeter of the field. He held his breath, and congratulated himself on having lain in bed sulking for the last few days rather than trying to work out his feelings on chest expanders in the ship's gym.

He then realized he was going to have to speak at this point.

He took a series of very shallow breaths, and then said as quickly and as quietly as he could, "Door, if you can hear me, say so very, very quietly."

Very, very quietly, the door murmured, "I can hear you."

"Good. Now, in a moment, I'm going to ask you to open. When you open I do not want you to say that you enjoyed it, okay?"

"Okay."

"And I don't want you to say to me that I have made a simple door very happy, or that it is your pleasure to open for me and your satisfaction to close again with the knowledge of a job well done, okay?"

"Okay."

"And I do not want you to ask me to have a nice day, understand?"

"I understand."

"Okay," said Zaphod, tensing himself, "open now."

The door slid open quietly. Zaphod slipped quietly through. The door closed quietly behind him.

"Is that the way you like it, Mr. Beeblebrox?" said the door out loud.

"I want you to imagine," said Zaphod to the group of white robots who swung round to stare at him at that point, "that I have an extremely powerful Kill-O-Zap blaster pistol in my hand."

There was an immensely cold and savage silence. The robots regarded him with hideously dead eyes. They stood very still. There was something intensely macabre about their appearance, especially to Zaphod, who had never seen one before or even known anything about them. The Krikkit Wars belonged to the ancient past of the Galaxy, and Zaphod had spent most of his early history lessons plotting how he was going to have sex with the girl in the cybercubicle next to him, and since his teaching computer had been an integral part of this plot it had eventually had all its history circuits wiped and replaced with an entirely different set of ideas that had then resulted in its being scrapped and sent to a home for Degenerate Cybermats, whither it was followed by the girl who had inadvertently fallen deeply in love with the unfortunate machine, with the result that (a) Zaphod never got near her and (b) he missed out on a period of ancient history that would have been of inestimable value to him at this moment.

He stared at them in shock.

It was impossible to explain why, but their smooth and sleek white bodies seemed to be the utter embodiment of clean, clinical evil. From their hideously dead eyes to their powerful lifeless feet, they were clearly the calculated product of a mind that wanted simply to kill. Zaphod gulped in cold fear.

They had been dismantling part of the rear wall, and had forced a passage through some of the vital innards of the ship. Through the tangled wreckage Zaphod could see, with a further and worse sense of shock, that they were tunneling toward the very heart of the ship, the heart of the Improbability Drive that had been so mysteriously created out of thin air, the *Heart of Gold* itself.

The robot closest to him was regarding him in such a way as to suggest that it was measuring each minute particle of his body, mind and capability. And when it spoke, what it said seemed to bear this impression out. Before going on to what it actually said, it is worth recording at this point that Zaphod was the first living organic being to hear one of these creatures speak for something over ten billion years. If he had paid more attention to his ancient history lessons and less to his organic being, he might have been more impressed by this honor.

The robot's voice was like its body, cold, sleek and lifeless. It had almost a cultured rasp to it. It sounded as ancient as it was.

It said, "You do have a Kill-O-Zap blaster pistol in your hand."

Zaphod didn't know what it meant for a moment, but then he glanced down at his own hand and was relieved to see that what he had found clipped to a wall bracket was indeed what he had thought it was.

"Yeah," he said in a kind of relieved sneer, which is quite tricky, "well, I wouldn't want to overtax your imagination, robot."

For a while nobody said anything, and Zaphod realized that the robots were obviously not here to make conversation, and that it was up to him.

"I can't help noticing that you have parked your ship," he said with a nod of one of his heads in the appropriate direction, "through mine."

There was no denying this. Without regard for any kind of proper dimensional behavior they had simply materialized their ship precisely where they wanted it to be, which meant that it was simply locked through the *Heart of Gold* as if they were nothing more than two combs.

Again, they made no response to this, and Zaphod wondered if the conversation would gather any momentum if he phrased his part of it in the form of questions.

"Haven't you?" he added.

"Yes," replied the robot.

"Er, okay," said Zaphod, "so what are you cats doing here?"

Silence.

"Robots," said Zaphod, "what are you robots doing here?"

"We have come," rasped the robot, "for the Golden Bail."

Zaphod nodded. He waggled his gun to invite further elaboration. The robot seemed to understand this.

"The Golden Bail is part of the Key we seek," continued the robot, "to release our Masters from Krikkit."

Zaphod nodded again. He waggled his gun again.

"The Key," continued the robot simply, "was disintegrated in time and space. The Golden Bail is embedded in the device which drives your ship. It will be reconstituted in the Key. Our Masters shall be released. The Universal Readjustment will continue."

Zaphod nodded again.

"What are you talking about?" he said.

A slightly pained expression seemed to cross the robot's totally expressionless face. He seemed to be finding the conversation depressing.

"Obliteration," it said. "We seek the Key," it repeated. "We already have the Wooden Pillar, the Steel Pillar and the Plastic Pillar. In a moment we will have the Golden Bail. . . ."

"No, you won't."

"We will," stated the robot simply.

"No, you won't. It makes my ship work."

"In a moment," repeated the robot patiently, "we will have the Golden Bail. . . ."

"You will not," said Zaphod.

"And then we must go," said the robot, in all seriousness, "to a party."

"Oh," said Zaphod, startled, "can I come?"

"No," said the robot, "we are going to shoot you."

"Oh, yeah?" said Zaphod, waggling his gun.

"Yes," said the robot, and they shot him.

Zaphod was so surprised that they had to shoot him again before he fell down.

hhh," said Slartibartfast, "listen and watch."

Night had now fallen on ancient Krikkit. The sky was dark and empty. The only light was coming from the nearby town, from which pleasant convivial sounds were drifting quietly on the breeze. They stood beneath a tree from which heady fragrances wafted around them. Arthur squatted and felt the Informational Illusion of the soil and the grass. He ran it through his fingers. The soil seemed heavy and rich, the grass strong. It was hard to avoid the impression that this was a thoroughly delightful place in all respects.

The sky was, however, extremely blank and seemed to Arthur to cast a certain chill over the otherwise idyllic, if currently invisible, landscape. Still, he supposed, it's a question of what you're used to.

He felt a tap on his shoulder and looked up. Slartibartfast was quietly directing his attention to something down the other side of the hill. He looked and could just see some faint lights dancing and waving, and moving slowly in their direction.

As they came nearer sounds became audible, too, and soon the dim lights and noises resolved themselves into a small group of people who were walking home across the hill toward the town.

They walked quite near the watchers beneath the tree, swinging lanterns that made soft and crazy lights dance among the trees and grass, chattering contentedly, and actually singing a song about how terribly nice everything was, how happy they were, how much they enjoyed working on the farm, and how pleasant it was to be going home to see their wives and children, with a lilting chorus to the effect that the flowers were smelling particularly nice at this time of year and that it was a pity the dog had died seeing as it liked them so much. Arthur could almost imagine Paul McCartney sitting with his feet up by the fire one evening, humming it to Linda and wondering what to buy with the proceeds, and thinking, probably, Essex.

"The Masters of Krikkit," breathed Slartibartfast in sepulchral tones.

Coming, as it did, so hard upon the heels of his own thoughts about Essex this remark caused Arthur a moment's confusion. Then the logic of the situation imposed itself on his scattered mind, and he discovered that he still didn't understand what the old man meant.

"What?" he said.

"The Masters of Krikkit," said Slartibartfast again, and if his breathing had been sepulchral before, this time he sounded like someone in Hades with bronchitis.

Arthur peered at the group and tried to make sense of what little information he had at his disposal at this point.

The people in the group were clearly alien, if only because they seemed a little tall, thin, angular and almost as pale as to be white, but otherwise seemed remarkably pleasant, a little whimsical perhaps; one wouldn't necessarily want to spend a long bus journey with them, but the point was that if they deviated in any way from being good straightforward people it was in being perhaps too nice rather than not nice enough. So why all this rasping lungwork from Slartibartfast, which would seem more appropriate to a radio commercial for one of those nasty films about chainsaw operators taking their work home with them?

Then, this Krikkit angle was a tough one, too. He hadn't quite fathomed the connection between what he knew as cricket, and what . . .

Slartibartfast interrupted his train of thought at this point as if sensing what was going through his mind.

"The game you know as cricket," he said, and his voice still seemed to be wandering, lost in subterranean passages, "is just one of those curious freaks of racial memory that can keep images alive in the mind eons after their true significance has been lost in the mists of time. Of all the races in the Galaxy, only the English could possibly revive the memory of the most horrific wars ever to sunder the Universe and transform it into what I'm afraid is generally regarded as an incomprehensibly dull and pointless game.

"Rather fond of it myself," he added, "but in most people's eyes you have been inadvertently guilty of the most grotesquely bad taste. Particularly the bit about the little red ball hitting the wicket, that's very nasty."

"Um," said Arthur with a reflective frown to indicate that his cognitive synapses were coping with this as best they could, "um."

"And these," said Slartibartfast, slipping back into crypt guttural and indicating the group of Krikkit men who had now walked past them, "are the ones who started it all, and it will start tonight. Come, we will follow, and see why."

They slipped out from underneath the tree, and followed the cheery party along the dark hill path. Their natural instinct was to tread quietly and stealthily in pursuit of their quarry, though, as they were simply walking through a recorded Informational Illusion, they could as easily have been carrying euphoniums and wearing war paint for all the notice their quarry would have taken of them.

Arthur saw that a couple of members of the party were now singing a different song. It came lilting back to them through the soft night air, and was a sweet romantic ballad that would have netted McCartney Kent and Sussex and enabled him to put in a fair offer for Hampshire.

"You must surely know," said Slartibartfast to Ford, "what it is that is about to happen?"

"Me?" said Ford, "no."

"Did you not learn Ancient Galactic history when you were a child?"

"I was in the cybercubicle behind Zaphod," said Ford; "it was very distracting. Which isn't to say that I didn't learn some pretty stunning things."

At this point Arthur noticed a curious feature to the song that the party was singing. The middle eight bridge, which would have had McCartney firmly consolidated in Winchester and gazing intently over the Test Valley to the rich pickings of the New Forest beyond, had some curious lyrics. The songwriter was referring to meeting with a girl not "under the moon" or "beneath the stars" but "above the grass," which struck Arthur as being a little prosaic. Then he looked up again at the bewilderingly blank sky, and had the distinct feeling that there was an important point here, if only he could grasp what it was. It gave him a feeling of being alone in the Universe, and he said so.

"No," said Slartibartfast, with a slight quickening of his step, "the people of Krikkit have never thought to themselves, 'We are alone in the Universe.' They are surrounded by a huge Dust Cloud, you see, their single sun with its single world, and they are right out on the utmost eastern edge of the Galaxy. Because of the Dust Cloud there has never been anything to see in the sky. At night it is totally blank. During the day there is the sun, but you can't look directly at that so they don't. They are hardly aware of the sky. It's as if they had a blind spot that extended 180 degrees from horizon to horizon.

"You see, the reason why they have never thought, 'We are alone in the Universe' is that until tonight they didn't know about the Universe. Until tonight."

He moved on, leaving the words ringing in the air behind him.

"Imagine," he said, "never even thinking, 'We are alone,' simply because it has never occurred to you to think that there's any other way to be."

He moved on again.

"I'm afraid this is going to be a little unnerving," he added.

As he spoke, they became aware of a very thin roaring scream high up in the sightless sky above them. They glanced upward in alarm, but for a moment or two could see nothing.

Then Arthur noticed that the people in the party in front of them had heard the noise, but that none of them seemed to know what to do with it. They were glancing around themselves in consternation, left, right, forward, backward, even at the ground. It never occurred to them to look upward.

The profoundness of the shock and horror they emanated a few moments later when the burning wreckage of a spaceship came hurtling and screaming out of the sky and crashed about half a mile from where they were standing was something that you had to be there to experience.

Some speak of the *Heart of Gold* in hushed tones, some of the starship *Bistromath*.

Many speak of the legendary and gigantic starship *Titanic*, a majestic and luxurious cruise liner launched from the great shipbuilding asteroid complexes of Artrifactovol some hundreds of years ago now, and with good reason.

It was sensationally beautiful, staggeringly huge and more pleasantly equipped than any ship in what now remains of history (see page 110 [on the Campaign for Real Time]) but it had the misfortune to be built in the very earliest days of Improbability Physics, long before this difficult and cussed branch of knowledge was fully, or at all, understood.

The designers and engineers decided, in their innocence, to build a prototype Improbability Field into it, which was meant, supposedly, to ensure that it was Infinitely Improbable that anything would ever go wrong with any part of the ship.

They did not realize that because of the quasi-reciprocal and circular nature of all Improbability calculations, anything that was Infinitely Improbable was actually very likely to happen almost immediately.

The starship *Titanic* was a monstrously pretty sight as it lay beached like a silver Arcturan Megavoidwhale among the laser-lit tracery of its construction gantries, a brilliant cloud of pins and needles of light against the deep interstellar blackness; but when launched, it did not even manage to complete its very first radio message—an SOS—before undergoing a sudden and gratuitous total existence failure.

However, the same event that saw the disastrous failure of one science in its infancy also witnessed the apotheosis of another. It was conclusively proved that more people watched the Tri-D television coverage of the launch than actually existed at the time, and this has now been recognized as the greatest achievement ever in the science of audience research.

Another spectacular media event of that time was the supernova that the star Ysllodins underwent a few hours later. Ysllodins is the star around which most of the Galaxy's major insurance underwriters live, or rather lived.

But while these spaceships, and other great ones that come to mind, such as the Galactic Fleet Battleships—the GSS *Daring*, the GSS *Audacity* and the GSS *Suicidal Insanity*—are all spoken of with awe, pride, enthusiasm, affection, admiration, regret, jealousy, resentment, in fact most of the better known emotions, the one that regularly commands the most actual astonishment is *Krikkit One*, the first spaceship ever built by the people of Krikkit.

This is not because it was a wonderful ship. It wasn't.

It was a crazy piece of near-junk. It looked as if it had been knocked up in somebody's backyard, and this was in fact precisely where it had been knocked up. The astonishing thing about the ship was not that it was done well (it wasn't) but that it was done at all. The period of time that had elapsed between the moment that the people of Krikkit had discovered that there was such a thing as space and the launching of this, their first spaceship, was almost exactly a year.

Ford Prefect was extremely grateful, as he strapped himself in, that this was just another Informational Illusion, and that he was therefore completely safe. In real life it wasn't a ship he would have set foot in for all the rice wine in China. "Extremely rickety" was one phrase that sprang to mind and "Please may I get out?" was another.

"This is going to fly?" said Arthur, giving gaunt looks at the lashed-together pipework and wiring that festooned the cramped interior of the ship.

Slartibartfast assured him that it would, that they were perfectly safe and that it was all going to be extremely instructive and not a little harrowing.

Ford and Arthur decided just to relax and be harrowed.

"Why not," said Ford, "go mad?"

In front of them and, of course, totally unaware of their presence for the very good reason that they weren't actually there, were the three pilots. They also had constructed the ship. They had been on the hill path that night singing wholesome, heartwarming songs. Their brains had been very slightly turned by the nearby crash of the alien spaceship. They had spent weeks stripping every tiniest last secret out of the wreckage of that burntup spaceship, all the while singing lilting spaceship-stripping ditties. They had then built their own ship and this was it. This was their ship, and they were currently singing a little song about that, too, expressing the twin joys of achievement and ownership. The chorus was a little poignant, and told of their sorrow because their work had kept them such long hours in the garage, away from the company of their wives and children, who had missed them terribly but had kept them cheerful by bringing them continual stories of how nicely the puppy was growing up.

Pow, they took off.

They roared into the sky like a ship that knew precisely what it was doing.

"No way," said Ford a while later after they had recovered from the shock of acceleration, and were climbing up out of the planet's atmosphere, "no way," he repeated, "does anyone design and build a ship like this in a year, no matter how motivated. I don't believe it. Prove it to me and I still won't believe it." He shook his head thoughtfully and gazed out of a tiny port at the nothingness outside it.

The trip passed uneventfully for a while, and Slartibartfast fastwound them through it.

Very quickly, therefore, they arrived at the inner perimeter of the hollow, spherical Dust Cloud that surrounded their sun and home planet, occupying, as it were, the next orbit out.

It was more as if there were a gradual change in the texture and consistency of space. The darkness seemed now to thrum and ripple past them. It was very cold darkness, a very blank and heavy darkness, it was the darkness of the night sky of Krikkit.

The coldness and heaviness and blankness of it took a slow grip on Arthur's heart, and he felt acutely aware of the feelings of the Krikkit pilots that hung in the air like a thick static charge. They were now on the very boundary of the historical consciousness of their race. This was the very limit beyond which none of them had ever speculated, or even known that there was any speculation to be done.

The darkness of the cloud buffeted at the ship. Inside was the silence of history. Their historic mission was to find out if there was anything or anywhere on the other side of the sky, from which the wrecked spaceship could have come, another world maybe, strange and incomprehensible though this thought was to the enclosed minds of those who had lived beneath the sky of Krikkit.

History was gathering itself to deliver another blow.

Still the darkness thrummed at them, the blank enclosing darkness. It seemed closer and closer, thicker and thicker, heavier and heavier. And suddenly it was gone.

They flew out of the cloud.

They saw the staggering jewels of the night in their infinite dust and their minds sang with fear.

For a while they flew on, motionless against the starry sweep of the Galaxy, itself motionless against the infinite sweep of the Universe. And then they turned round.

"It'll have to go," the men of Krikkit said as they headed back for home.

On the way back they sang a number of tuneful and reflective songs on the subjects of peace, justice, morality, culture, sport, family life and the obliteration of all other life forms.

Chapter 11

So you see," said Slartibartfast, slowly stirring his artificially constructed coffee, and thereby also stirring the whirlpool interfaces between real and unreal numbers, between the interactive perceptions of mind and universe, and thus generating the restructured matrices of implicitly enfolded subjectivity that allowed his ship to reshape the very concept of time and space, "how it is."

"Yes," said Arthur.

"Yes," said Ford.

"What do I do," said Arthur, "with this piece of chicken?"

Slartibartfast glanced at him, gravely.

"Toy with it," he said, "toy with it."

He demonstrated with his own piece.

Arthur did so, and felt the slight tingle of a mathematical function thrilling through the chicken leg as it moved four-dimensionally through what Slartibartfast had assured him was five-dimensional space.

"Overnight," said Slartibartfast, "the whole population of Krikkit was transformed from being charming, delightful, intelligent..."

"... if whimsical ..." interpolated Arthur.

"...ordinary people," said Slartibartfast, "into charming, delightful, intelligent..."

"...whimsical ..."

"...manic xenophobes. The idea of a Universe didn't fit into their world picture, so to speak. They simply couldn't cope with it. And so, charmingly, delightfully, intelligently, whimsically if you like, they decided to destroy it. What's the matter now?"

"I don't like this wine very much," said Arthur, sniffing it.

"Well, send it back. It's all part of the mathematics of it."

Arthur did so. He didn't like the topography of the waiter's smile, but he'd never liked graphs anyway.

"Where are we going?" said Ford.

"Back to the room of Informational Illusions," said Slartibartfast, rising and patting his mouth with the mathematical representation of a paper napkin, "for the second half."

T he people of Krikkit," said His High Judgmental Supremacy, Judiciary Pag, L.I.V.R. (the Learned, Impartial and Very Relaxed), Chairman of the Board of Judges at the Krikkit War Crimes Trial, "are, well, you know, they're just a bunch of real sweet guys, you know, who just happen to want to kill everybody. Hell, I feel the same way some mornings.

"Okay," he continued, swinging his feet up onto the bench in front of him and pausing a moment to pick a thread off his Ceremonial Beach Loafers, "so you wouldn't necessarily want to share a Galaxy with these guys."

This was true.

The Krikkit attack on the Galaxy had been stunning. Thousands and thousands of huge Krikkit warships had leaped suddenly out of hyperspace and simultaneously attacked thousands and thousands of major worlds, first seizing vital material supplies for building the next wave, and then calmly zapping those worlds out of existence.

The Galaxy, which had been enjoying a period of unusual peace and prosperity at the time, reeled like a man getting mugged in a meadow.

"I mean," continued Judiciary Pag, gazing round the ultramodern (this was ten billion years ago, when ultramodern meant lots of stainless steel and brushed concrete) and huge courtroom, "these guys are just *obsessed.*"

This, too, was true, and is the only explanation anyone has yet managed to come up with for the unimaginable speed with which the people of Krikkit had pursued their new and absolute purpose—the destruction of everything that wasn't Krikkit.

It is also the only explanation for their bewilderingly sudden grasp of all the hypertechnology involved in building their thousands of spaceships, and their millions of lethal white robots.

These had really struck terror into the hearts of everyone who had encountered them—in most cases, however, the terror was extremely short-lived, as was the person experiencing the terror. They were savage, single-minded flying battle machines. They wielded formidable multifunctional battleclubs that brandished one way knocked down buildings, brandished another way fired blistering Omni-Destructo Zap rays, and brandished a third way launched a hideous arsenal of grenades, ranging from minor incendiary devices to Maxi-Slorta Hypernuclear Devices that could take out a major sun. Simply striking the grenades with the battleclubs simultaneously primed them and launched them with phenomenal accuracy over distances ranging from mere yards to hundreds of thousands of miles.

"Okay," said Judiciary Pag again, "so we won." He paused and chewed a little gum. "We won," he repeated, "but that's no big deal. I mean a medium-sized Galaxy against one little world, and how long did it take us? Clerk of the Court?"

"M'lud?" said the severe little man in black, rising.

"How long, kiddo?"

"It is a trifle difficult, m'lud, to be precise in this matter. Time and distance . . ."

"Relax, guy, be vague."

"I hardly like to be vague, m'lud, over such a . . ."

"Bite the bullet and be it."

The Clerk of the Court blinked at him. It was clear that like most of the Galactic legal profession he found Judiciary Pag (or Zipo Bibrok $5x10^8$ as his private name was known, inexplicably, to be) a rather distressing figure. He was clearly a bounder and a cad. He seemed to think because he was the possessor of the finest legal mind ever discovered that gave him the right to behave exactly as he liked, and unfortunately he appeared to be right.

"Er, well, m'lud, very approximately, two thousand years," the Clerk murmured unhappily.

"And how many guys zilched out?"

"Two grillion, m'lud." The Clerk sat down. A hydrospectic photo of him at this point would have revealed that he was steaming slightly.

Judiciary Pag gazed once more around the courtroom, wherein were assembled hundreds of the very highest officials of the entire Galactic administration, all in their ceremonial uniforms or bodies, depending on metabolism and custom. Behind a wall of Zap-Proof Crystal stood a representative group of the people of Krikkit, looking with calm, polite loathing at all the aliens gathered to pass judgment on them. This was the most momentous occasion in legal history and Judiciary Pag knew it.

He took out his chewing gum and stuck it under his chair.

"That's a whole lotta stiffs," he said quietly.

The grim silence in the courtroom seemed in accord with this view.

"So, like I said, these are a bunch of really sweet guys, but you wouldn't want to share a Galaxy with them, not if they're just gonna keep at it, not if they're not gonna learn to relax a little. I mean it's just gonna be continual nervous time, isn't it, right? Pow, pow, pow, when are they next coming at us? Peaceful coexistence is just right out, right? Get me some water somebody, thank you."

He sat back and sipped reflectively.

"Okay," he said, "hear me, hear me. It's like, these guys, you know, are entitled to their own view of the Universe. And according to their view, which the Universe forced on them, right, they did right. Sounds crazy, but I think you'll agree. They believe in..."

He consulted a piece of paper that he found in the back pocket of his judicial jeans.

"They believe in 'peace, justice, morality, culture, sport, family life and the obliteration of all other life forms.' "

He shrugged.

"I've heard a lot worse," he said.

He scratched his crotch reflectively.

"Freeeow," he said. He took another sip of water, then held it up to the light and frowned at it. He twisted it around.

"Hey, is there something in this water?" he said.

"Er, no, m'lud," said the Court Usher, who had brought it to him, rather nervously.

"Then take it away," snapped Judiciary Pag, "and put something in it. I got an idea."

He pushed away the glass, and leaned forward.

"Hear me, hear me," he said.

The solution was brilliant, and went like this:

The planet of Krikkit was to be encased for perpetuity in an envelope of Slo-Time, inside which life would continue almost infinitely slowly. All light would be deflected around the envelope so that it would remain invisible and impenetrable. Escape from the envelope would be utterly impossible unless it was unlocked from the outside.

When the rest of the Universe came to its final end, when the whole of creation reached its dying fall (this was all, of course, in the days before it was known that the end of the Universe would be a spectacular catering venture) and life and matter ceased to exist, then the planet of Krikkit and its sun would emerge from its Slo-Time envelope and continue a solitary existence, such as it craved, in the twilight of the Universal void.

The Lock would be on an asteroid that would slowly orbit the envelope. The Key would be the symbol of the Galaxy—the Wikkit Gate.

By the time the applause in the court had died down, Judiciary Pag was already in the Sens-O-Shower with a rather nice member of the jury that he'd slipped a note to half an hour earlier.

wo months later, Zipo Bibrok $5x10^8$ had cut the bottoms off his Galactic State jeans, and was spending part of the enormous fee his judgments commanded lying on a jeweled beach having Essence of Qualactin rubbed into his back by the same rather nice member of the jury. She was a Soolfinian girl from beyond the Cloudworlds of Yaga. She had skin like lemon silk and was very interested in legal bodies.

"Did you hear the news?" she said.

"Weeeeelaaaaah!" said Zipo Bibrok $5x10^8$, and you would have had to have been there to know exactly why he said this. None of this was on the tape of Informational Illusions and is all based on hearsay.

"No," he added, when the thing that had made him say "Weeeeelaaaaah" had stopped happening. He moved his body around slightly to catch the first rays of the third and greatest of primeval Vod's three suns that was creeping over the ludicrously beautiful horizon, and the sky now glittered with some of the greatest tanning power ever known.

A fragrant breeze wandered up from the quiet sea, trailed along the beach and drifted back to sea again, wondering where to go next. On a mad impulse it went up to the beach again. It drifted back to sea.

"I hope it isn't good news," muttered Zipo Bibrok $5x10^8$, " 'cos I don't think I could bear it."

"Your Krikkit judgment was carried out today," said the girl sumptuously. There was no need to say such a straightforward thing sumptuously, but she went ahead and did it anyway because it was that sort of day. "I heard it on the radio," she said, "when I went back to the ship for the oil."

"Uh-huh," murmured Zipo and rested his head back on the jeweled sand.

"Something happened," she said.

"Mmmm?"

"Just after the Slo-Time envelope was locked," she said, and paused a moment from rubbing in the Essence of Qualactin, "a Krikkit warship that had been missing, presumed destroyed, turned out to be just missing after all. It appeared and tried to seize the Key."

Zipo sat up sharply.

"Hey, what?" he said.

"It's all right," she said in a voice that would have calmed the Big Bang down, "apparently there was a short battle. The Key and the warship were disintegrated and blasted into the space-time continuum. Apparently they are lost forever."

She smiled, and squeezed a little more Essence of Qualactin onto her fingertips. He relaxed and lay back down.

"Do what you did a moment or two ago," he murmured.

"That?" she said.

"No, no," he said, "that."

She tried again.

"That?" she asked.

"Weeeeelaaaaaah!"

Again, you had to be there.

The fragrant breeze drifted up from the sea again.

A magician wandered along the beach, but no one needed him.

Chapter 14

Nothing is lost forever," said Slartibartfast, his face flickering redly in the light of the candle that the robot waiter was trying to take away, "except for the Cathedral of Chalesm."

"The what?" said Arthur with a start.

"The Cathedral of Chalesm," repeated Slartibartfast. "It was during the course of my researches at the Campaign for Real Time that I . . ."

"The what?" said Arthur again.

The old man paused and gathered his thoughts, for what he hoped would be one last onslaught on this story. The robot waiter moved through the space-time matrices in a way that spectacularly combined the surly with the obsequious, made a snatch for the candle and got it. They had the check, had argued convincingly about who had the cannelloni and how many bottles of wine they had had, and, as Arthur had been dimly aware, had thereby successfully maneuvered the ship out of subjective space and into parking orbit round a strange planet. The waiter was now anxious to complete his part of the charade and clear the bistro.

"All will become clear," said Slartibartfast.

"When?"

"In a minute. Listen. The time streams are now very polluted. There's a lot of muck floating about in them, flotsam and jetsam, and more and more of it is now being regurgitated into the physical world. Eddies in the space-time continuum, you see."

"So I hear," said Arthur.

"Look, where are we going?" said Ford, pushing his chair back from the table with impatience, "because I'm eager to get there."

"We are going," said Slartibartfast, in a slow, measured voice, "to try to prevent the war robots of Krikkit from regaining the whole of the Key they need to unlock the planet of Krikkit from the Slo-Time envelope and release the rest of their army and their mad Masters."

"It's just," said Ford, "that you mentioned a party."

"I did," said Slartibartfast, and hung his head.

He realized that it had been a mistake, because the idea seemed to exercise a strange and unhealthy fascination on the mind of Ford Prefect.

The more Slartibartfast unraveled the dark and tragic story of Krikkit and its people, the more Ford Prefect wanted to drink a lot and dance with girls.

The old man felt that he should not have mentioned the party until he absolutely had to. But there it was, the fact was out, and Ford Prefect had attached himself to it the way an Arcturan Megaleech attaches itself to its victim before biting his head off and making off with his spaceship.

"When," said Ford eagerly, "do we get there?"

"When I've finished telling you why we have to go there."

"I know why I'm going," said Ford, and leaned back, sticking his hands behind his head. He did one of his smiles that made people twitch.

Slartibartfast had hoped for an easy retirement.

He had been planning to learn to play the octaventral heebiephone, a pleasantly futile task, he knew, because he had the wrong number of mouths.

He had also been planning to write an eccentric and relentlessly inaccurate monograph on the subject of equatorial fjords in order to set the record wrong about one or two matters he saw as important.

Instead, he had somehow got talked into doing some part-time work for the Campaign for Real Time and had started to take it all seriously for the first time in his life. As a result he now found himself spending his fast declining years combating evil and trying to save the Galaxy.

He found it exhausting work and sighed heavily.

"Listen," he said, "at Camtim . . ."

"What?" said Arthur.

"The Campaign for Real Time, which I will tell you about later. I noticed that five pieces of jetsam that had in relatively recent times plopped back into existence seemed to correspond to the five pieces of the missing Key. Only two I could trace exactly—the Wooden Pillar, which appeared on your planet, and the Silver Bail. It seems to be at some sort of party. We must go there to retrieve it before the Krikkit robots find it, or who knows what may happen."

"No," said Ford firmly, "we must go to the party in order to drink a lot and dance with girls."

"But haven't you understood everything I . . ."

"Yes," said Ford, with sudden and unexpected fierceness, "I've understood it all perfectly well. That's why I want to have as many drinks and dance with as many girls as possible while there are still any left. If everything you've shown us is true . . ."

"True? Of course it's true."

"...then we don't stand a whelk's chance in a supernova."

"A what?" said Arthur sharply again. He had been following the conversation doggedly up to this point, and was keen not to lose the thread now.

"A whelk's chance in a supernova," repeated Ford without losing momentum, "the..."

"What's a whelk got to do with a supernova?" said Arthur.

"It doesn't," said Ford levelly, "stand a chance in one."

He paused to see if the matter was now cleared up. The freshly puzzled looks clambering across Arthur's face told him that it wasn't.

"A supernova," said Ford as quickly and as clearly as he could, "is a star that explodes at almost half the speed of light and burns with the brightness of a billion suns and then collapses as a superheavy neutron star. It's a star that burns up other stars, got it? Nothing stands a chance in a supernova."

"I see," said Arthur.

"The..."

"So why a whelk particularly?"

"Why not a whelk? Doesn't matter."

Arthur accepted this, and Ford continued, picking up his early fierce momentum as best he could.

"The point is," he said, "that people like you and me, Slartibartfast, and Arthur—particularly and especially Arthur—are just dilettantes, eccentrics, layabouts if you like."

Slartibartfast frowned, partly in puzzlement and partly in umbrage. He started to speak.

"...." is as far as he got.

"We're not obsessed by anything, you see," insisted Ford.

"..."

"And that's the deciding factor. We can't win against obsession. They care, we don't. They win."

"I care about lots of things," said Slartibartfast, his voice trembling partly with annoyance, but partly also with uncertainty.

"Such as?"

"Well," said the old man, "life, the Universe. Everything, really. Fjords."

"Would you die for them?"

"Fjords?" blinked Slartibartfast in surprise. "No."

"Well then."

"Wouldn't see the point, to be honest."

"And I still can't see the connection," said Arthur, "with whelks."

Ford could feel the conversation slipping out of his control, and refused to be sidetracked by anything at this point.

"The point is," he hissed, "that we are not obsessive people, and we don't stand a chance against..."

"Except for your sudden obsession with whelks," pursued Arthur, "which I still haven't understood."

"Will you please leave whelks out of it?"

"I will if you will," said Arthur. "You brought the subject up."

"It was an error," said Ford, "forget them. The point is this."

He leaned forward and rested his forehead on the tips of his fingers.

"What was I talking about?" he said wearily.

"Let's just go down to the party," said Slartibartfast, "for whatever reason." He stood up, shaking his head.

"I think that's what I was trying to say," said Ford.

For some unexplained reason, the teleport cubicles were in the bathroom.

Chapter 15

T ime travel is increasingly regarded as a menace. History is being polluted.

The *Encyclopedia Galactica* has much to say on the theory and practice of time travel, most of which is incomprehensible to anyone who hasn't spent at least four lifetimes studying advanced hyper-mathematics, and since it was impossible to do this before time travel was invented, there is a certain amount of confusion as to how the idea was arrived at in the first place. One rationalization of this problem states that time travel was, by its very nature, discovered simultaneously at all periods of history, but this is clearly bunk.

The trouble is that a lot of history is now quite clearly bunk as well.

Here is an example. It may not seem to be an important one to some people, but to others it is crucial. It is certainly significant in that it was this single event that caused the Campaign for Real Time to be set up in the first place (or is it last? It depends which way round you see history as happening, and this, too, is now an increasingly vexed question).

There is, or was, a poet. His name was Lallafa, and he wrote what are widely regarded throughout the Galaxy as the finest poems in existence, the *Songs of the Long Land*.

They are/were unspeakably wonderful. That is to say, you couldn't speak very much of them at once without being so overcome with emotion, truth and a sense of the wholeness and oneness of things that you wouldn't pretty soon need a brisk walk round the block, possibly pausing at a bar on the way back for a quick glass of perspective and soda. They were that good.

Lallafa had lived in the forests of the Long Lands of Effa. He lived there, and he wrote his poems there. He wrote them on pages made of dried habra leaves, without the benefit of education or correcting fluid. He wrote about the light in the forest, and what he thought about that. He wrote about the darkness in the forest, and what he thought about that. He wrote about the girl who had left him and precisely what he thought about that.

Long after his death his poems were found and wondered over. News of them spread like morning sunlight. For centuries they illuminated and watered the lives of many people whose lives might otherwise have been darker and dryer.

Then, shortly after the invention of time travel, some major correcting fluid manufacturers wondered whether his poems might have been better still if he had had access to some high-quality correcting fluid, and whether he might be persuaded to say a few words to that effect.

They traveled the time waves; they found him. They explained the situation—with some difficulty—to him, and did indeed persuade him. In fact they persuaded him to such effect that he became extremely rich at their hands, and the girl about whom he was otherwise destined to write with such precision never got around to leaving him, and in fact they moved out of the forest to a rather nice pad in town and he frequently commuted to the future to do talk shows, on which he sparkled wittily.

He never got around to writing the poems, of course, which was a problem, but an easily solved one. The manufacturers of correcting fluid simply packed him off for a week somewhere with a copy of a later edition of his book and stacks of dried habra leaves to copy them out onto, making the odd deliberate mistake and correction on the way.

Many people now say that the poems are suddenly worthless. Others argue that they are exactly the same as they always were, so what's changed? The first people say that that isn't the point. They aren't quite certain what the point is, but they are quite sure that that isn't it. They set up the Campaign for Real Time to try to stop this sort of thing going on. Their case was considerably strengthened by the fact that a week after they had set themselves up, news broke that not only had the great Cathedral of Chalesm been pulled down in order to build a new ion refinery, but that the construction of the refinery had taken so long, and had had to extend so far back into the past in order to allow ion production to start on time, that the Cathedral of Chalesm had now never been built in the first place. Picture postcards of the cathedral suddenly became immensely valuable.

So a lot of history is now gone forever. The Campaigners for Real Time claim that just as easy travel eroded the differences between one country and another, and between one world and another, so time travel is now eroding the differences between one age and another. "The past," they say, "is now truly like a foreign country. They do things exactly the same there."

Arthur materialized, and did so with all the customary staggering about and clasping at his throat, heart and various limbs that he still indulged himself in whenever he made any of these hateful and painful materializations that he was determined not to let himself get used to. He looked around for the others.

They weren't there.

He looked around for the others again.

They still weren't there.

He closed his eyes.

He opened them.

He looked around for the others.

They obstinately persisted in their absence.

He closed his eyes again, preparatory to making this completely futile exercise once more, and because it was only then, while his eyes were closed, that his brain began to register what his eyes had been looking at while they were open, a puzzled frown crept across his face.

So he opened his eyes again to check his facts and the frown stayed put.

If anything, it intensified, and got a good firm grip. If this was a party, it was a very bad one, so bad, in fact, that everyone else had left. He abandoned this line of thought as futile. Obviously this wasn't a party. It was a cave, or a labyrinth or a tunnel or something—there was insufficient light to tell, certainly insufficient light to hold a party in. All was darkness, a damp, shiny darkness.

And there was no sound, no noise at all, except for the echoes of his own breathing, which sounded worried. And the more he listened to them, the more worried they began to sound.

He coughed very slightly, in an introductory sort of way. He then had to listen to the thin ghostly echo of his cough trailing off among winding corridors and sightless chambers, as of some great labyrinth, and eventually returning to him via further unseen corridors, as if to say... "Yes?"

This happened to every noise he made, and it unnerved him. He tried to hum a cheery tune, but by the time it returned to him it was a hollow dirge and he stopped.

His mind was suddenly full of images from the story that Slartibartfast had been telling him. He half expected suddenly to see lethal white robots step silently from the shadows and kill him. He caught his breath. They didn't. He let it go again. He didn't know what he did expect.

Someone or something, however, seemed to be expecting him, for at that moment there lit up suddenly in the dark distance an eerie green neon sign.

It said, silently:

YOU HAVE BEEN DIVERTED

The sign flicked off again, in a way that Arthur was not at all certain he liked. It flicked off with a sort of contemptuous flourish. Arthur then tried to assure himself that this was just a ridiculous trick of his imagination. A neon sign is either on or off, depending on whether it has electricity running through it or not. There was no way, he told himself, that it could possibly effect the transition from one state to the other with a contemptuous flourish. He hugged himself tightly in his dressing gown and shivered, nevertheless.

The neon sign in the depths now suddenly lit up, bafflingly, with just three dots and a comma. Like this:

. . . ,

Only in green neon.

It was trying, Arthur realized after staring at this perplexedly for a second or two, to indicate that there was more to come, that the sentence was not complete. Trying with almost superhuman pedantry, he further reflected. Or at least, nonhuman pedantry.

The sentence then completed itself with these two words:

ARTHUR DENT.

He reeled. He steadied himself to have another clear look at it. It still said ARTHUR DENT, so he reeled again.

Once again, the sign flicked off, and left him blinking in the darkness with just the dim red image of his name jumping on his retina.

WELCOME, the sign now suddenly said.

After a moment, it added:

I DON'T THINK.

The stone-cold fear which had been hovering around Arthur all this time waiting for its moment, recognized that its moment had now come and pounced on him. He tried to fight it off. He dropped into a kind of alert crouch that he had once seen somebody do on television, but it must have been someone with stronger knees. He peered huntedly into the darkness.

"Er, hello?" he said.

He cleared his throat and said it again, more loudly and without the "er." At some distance down the corridor it seemed suddenly as if somebody started to beat on a bass drum.

He listened to it for a few seconds and realized that it was just his heart beating.

He listened for a few seconds more and realized that it wasn't his heart, it was somebody down the corridor beating on a bass drum.

Beads of sweat formed on his brow, tensed themselves and leaped off. He put out a hand onto the floor to steady his alert crouch, which wasn't holding up very well. The sign changed itself again. It said:

DO NOT BE ALARMED.

After a pause, it added:

BE VERY, VERY FRIGHTENED, ARTHUR DENT.

Once again it flicked off. Once again it left him in darkness. His eyes seemed to be popping out of his head. He wasn't certain if this was because they were trying to see more clearly, or if they simply wanted to leave at this point.

"Hello?" he said again, this time trying to put a note of rugged and aggressive self-assertion into it. "Is anyone there?"

There was no reply, nothing.

This unnerved Arthur even more than a reply would have done, and he began to back away from the scary nothingness. And the more he backed away, the more scared he became. After a while, he realized that the reason for this was that in all the films he had seen in which the hero backs farther and farther away from some imagined terror in front of him, he then manages to bump into it coming up from behind.

At this point it suddenly occurred to him to turn round rather quickly.

There was nothing there.

Just blackness.

This really unnerved him, and he started to back away from that, back the way he had come.

After doing this for a short while it suddenly occurred to him that he was now backing toward whatever it was he had been backing away from in the first place.

This, he couldn't help thinking, must be a foolish thing to do. He decided he would be better off backing the way he had first been backing, and turned around again.

It turned out at this point that his second impulse had been the correct one, because there was an indescribably hideous monster standing quietly behind him. Arthur yawed wildly as his skin tried to jump one way and his skeleton the other, while his brain tried to work out which of his ears it most wanted to crawl out of.

"Bet you weren't expecting to see me again," said the monster, which Arthur couldn't help thinking was a strange remark for it to make, seeing that he had never met the creature before. He could tell that he hadn't met the creature before from the simple fact that he was able to sleep at nights. It was ... it was ... it was ...

Arthur blinked at it. It stood very still. It did look a little familiar.

A terrible cold calm came over him as he realized that what he was looking at was a six-foot-high hologram of a housefly.

He wondered why anybody would be showing him a six-foot-high hologram of a housefly at this time. He wondered whose voice he had heard.

It was a terribly realistic hologram.

It vanished.

"Or perhaps you remember me better," said the voice suddenly, and it was a deep, hollow, malevolent voice that sounded like molten tar glurping out of a drum with evil on its mind, "as the rabbit."

With a sudden ping, there was a rabbit there in the black labyrinth with him, a huge, monstrously hideously soft and lovable rabbit—an image again, but one on which every single soft and lovable hair seemed like a real and single thing growing in its soft and lovable coat. Arthur was startled to see his own reflection in its soft and lovable unblinking and extremely huge brown eye.

"Born in darkness," rumbled the voice, "raised in darkness. One morning I poked my head for the first time into the bright new world and got it split open by what felt like some primitive instrument made of flint.

"Made by you, Arthur Dent, and wielded by you. Rather hard as I recall.

"You turned my skin into a bag for keeping interesting stones in. I happen to know that because in my next life I came back as a fly again and you swatted me. Again. Only this time you swatted me with the bag you'd made of my previous skin.

"Arthur Dent, you are not merely a cruel and heartless man, you are also staggeringly tactless."

The voice paused while Arthur gawked.

"I see you have lost the bag," said the voice, "probably got bored with it, did you?"

Arthur shook his head helplessly. He wanted to explain that he had been in fact very fond of the bag and had looked after it very well and had taken it with him wherever he went, but that somehow every time he traveled anywhere he seemed inexplicably to end up with the wrong bag, and that, curiously enough, even as they stood there, he was just noticing for the first time that the bag he had with him at the moment appeared to be made out of rather nasty fake leopard skin, and wasn't the one he'd had a few moments ago before he arrived in this whatever place it was, and wasn't one he would have chosen himself and heaven knew what would be in it as it wasn't his, and he would much rather have his original bag back, except that he was of course terribly sorry for having so peremptorily removed it, or rather its component parts, i.e., the rabbit skin, from its previous owner, viz., the rabbit whom he currently had the honor of attempting vainly to address.

All he actually managed to say was "Erp."

"Meet the newt you trod on," said the voice.

And there was, standing in the corridor with Arthur, a giant green scaly newt. Arthur turned, yelped, leaped backward, and found himself standing in the middle of the rabbit. He yelped again, but could find nowhere to leap to.

"That was me, too," continued the voice in a low menacing rumble, "as if you didn't know...."

"Know?" said Arthur with a start, "know?"

"The interesting thing about reincarnation," rasped the voice, "is that most people, most spirits, are not aware that it is happening to them."

He paused for effect. As far as Arthur was concerned there was already quite enough effect going on.

"*I* was aware," hissed the voice, "that is, I *became* aware. Slowly. Gradually."

He, whoever he was, paused again and gathered breath.

"I could hardly help it, could I?" he bellowed, "when the same thing kept happening, over and over and over again! Every life I ever lived, I got killed by Arthur Dent. Any world, any body, any time, I'm just getting settled down, along comes Arthur Dent, pow, he kills me.

"Hard not to notice. Bit of a memory jogger. Bit of a pointer. Bit of a bloody giveaway!

" 'That's funny,' my spirit would say to itself as it winged its way back to the netherworld after another fruitless Dent-ended venture into the land of the living, 'that man who just ran me over as I was hopping across the road to my favorite pond, looked a little familiar....' And gradually I got to piece it together, Dent, you multiple-me murderer!"

The echoes of his voice roared up and down the corridors. Arthur stood silent and cold, his head shaking with disbelief.

"Here's the moment, Dent," shrieked the voice, now reaching a feverish pitch of hatred, "here's the moment when at last I knew!"

It was indescribably hideous, the thing that suddenly opened up in front of Arthur, making him gasp and gargle with horror, but here's an attempt at a description of how hideous it was. It was a huge palpitating wet cave with a vast slimy, rough, whale-like creature rolling around in it and sliding over monstrous white tombstones. High above the cave rose a vast promontory in which could be seen the dark recesses of two further fearful caves, which . . .

Arthur Dent suddenly realized that he was looking at his own mouth, when his attention was meant to be directed at the live oyster that was being tipped helplessly into it.

He staggered back with a cry and averted his eyes.

When he looked again the appalling apparition had gone. The corridor was dark and, briefly, silent. He was alone with his thoughts. They were extremely unpleasant thoughts and he would rather have had a chaperon.

The next noise, when it came, was the low heavy roll of a large section of wall trundling aside, revealing, for the moment, just dark blankness behind it. Arthur looked into it in much the same way that a mouse looks into a dark dog kennel.

And the voice spoke to him again.

"Tell me it was a coincidence, Dent," it said. "I dare you to tell me it was a coincidence!"

"It *was* a coincidence," said Arthur quickly.

"It was not!" came the answering bellow.

"It was," said Arthur, "it was . . ."

"If it was a coincidence, then my name," roared the voice, "is not Agrajag!!!"

"And presumably," said Arthur, "you would claim that that *was* your name."

"Yes!" hissed Agrajag, as if he had just completed a rather deft syllogism.

"Well, I'm afraid it was still a coincidence," said Arthur.

"Come in here and say that!" howled the voice, in sudden apoplexy again.

Arthur walked in and said that it was a coincidence, or at least, he nearly said it was a coincidence. His tongue rather lost its footing toward the end of the last word because the lights came up and revealed what it was he had walked into.

It was a Cathedral of Hate.

It was the product of a mind that was not merely twisted, but actually sprained.

It was huge. It was horrific.

It had a statue in it.

We will come to the statue in a moment.

The vast, incomprehensibly vast chamber looked as if it had been carved out of the inside of a mountain, and the reason for this was that that was precisely what it had been carved out of. It seemed to Arthur to spin sickeningly round his head as he stood and gaped at it.

It was black.

Where it wasn't black you were inclined to wish that it was, because the colors with which some of the unspeakable details were picked out ranged horribly across the whole spectrum of eye-defying colors, from Ultra Violent to Infra Dead, taking in Liver Purple, Loathsome Lilac, Matter Yellow, Burnt Hombre and Gan Green on the way.

The unspeakable details that these colors picked out were gargoyles that would have put Francis Bacon off his lunch.

The gargoyles all looked inward from the walls, from the pillars, from the flying buttresses, from the choir stalls, toward the statue, to which we will come in a moment.

And if the gargoyles would have put Francis Bacon off his lunch, then it was clear from the gargoyles' faces that the statue would have put them off theirs, had they been alive to eat it, which they weren't, and had anybody tried to serve them some, which they wouldn't.

Around the monumental walls were vast engraved stone tablets in memory of those who had fallen to Arthur Dent.

The names of some of those commemorated were underlined and had asterisks against them. So, for instance, the name of a cow that had been slaughtered, and of which Arthur had happened to eat a fillet steak, would have the plainest engraving, whereas the name of a fish that Arthur had himself caught and then decided he didn't like and left on the side of the plate had a double underlining, three sets of asterisks and a bleeding dagger added as decoration, just to make the point.

And what was most disturbing about all this, apart from the statue, to which we are, by degrees, coming, was the very clear implication that all these people and creatures were indeed the same person, over and over again.

And it was equally clear that this person was, however unfairly, extremely upset and annoyed.

In fact it would be fair to say that he had reached a level of annoyance the like of which had never been seen in the Universe. It was an annoyance of epic proportions, a burning, searing flame of annoyance, an annoyance that now spanned the whole of time and space in its infinite umbrage.

And this annoyance had been given its fullest expression in the statue in the center of all this monstrosity that was a statue of Arthur Dent, and an unflattering one. Fifty feet tall if it was an inch, there was not an inch of it that wasn't crammed with insult to its subject matter, and fifty feet of that sort of thing would be enough to make any subject feel bad. From the small pimple on the side of his nose to the poorish cut of his dressing gown, there was no aspect of Arthur Dent that wasn't lambasted and vilified by the sculptor.

Arthur appeared as a gorgon, an evil, rapacious, ravening, bloodied ogre, slaughtering his way through an innocent one-man Universe.

With each of the thirty arms that the sculptor in a fit of artistic fervor had decided to give him, he was either braining a rabbit, swatting a fly, pulling a wishbone, picking a flea out of his hair, or doing something that Arthur at first look couldn't quite identify.

His many feet were mostly stamping on ants.

Arthur put his hands over his eyes, hung his head and shook it slowly from side to side in sadness and horror at the craziness of things.

And when he opened his eyes again, there in front of him stood the figure of the man or creature, or whatever it was, that he had supposedly been persecuting all this time.

"Hhhhhhhrrrrrraaaaaa HHHHHH!!!" said Agrajag.

He, or it or whatever, looked like a mad fat bat. He waddled slowly around Arthur, and poked at him with bent claws.

"Look . . . !" protested Arthur.

"Hhhhhhhrrrrrraaaaaa HHHHHH!!!" explained Agrajag, and Arthur reluctantly accepted this on the grounds that he was rather frightened by this hideous and strangely wrecked apparition.

Agrajag was black, bloated, wrinkled and leathery.

His bat wings were somehow more frightening for being the pathetic broken floundering things they were than if they had been strong muscular beaters of the air. The most frightening thing was probably the tenacity of his continued existence against all the physical odds.

He had the most astounding collection of teeth.

They looked as if each came from a completely different animal, and they were ranged around his mouth at such bizarre angles it seemed that if he ever actually tried to chew anything he'd lacerate half his own face along with it, and possibly put an eye out as well.

Each of his three eyes was small and intense and looked about as sane as a fish in a privet bush.

"I was at a cricket match," he rasped.

This seemed on the face of it such a preposterous notion that Arthur practically choked.

"Not in this body," screeched the creature, "not in this body! This is my last body. My last life. This is my revenge body. My kill-Arthur-Dent body. My last chance. I had to fight to get it too."

"But . . ."

"I was at," roared Agrajag, "a cricket match! I had a weak-heart condition, but what, I said to my wife, can happen to me at a cricket match? As I'm watching, what happens?

"Two people quite maliciously appear out of thin air just in front of me. The last thing I can't help but notice before my poor heart gives out in shock is that one of them is Arthur Dent wearing a rabbit bone in his beard. Coincidence?"

"Yes," said Arthur.

"Coincidence?" screamed the creature, painfully thrashing its broken wings, and opening a short gash on its right cheek with a particularly nasty tooth. On closer examination, such as he'd been hoping to avoid, Arthur noticed that much of Agrajag's face was covered with ragged strips of black Band-Aids.

He backed away, nervously. He tugged at his beard. He was appalled to discover that in fact he still had the rabbit bone in it. He pulled it out and threw it away.

"Look," he said, "it's just fate playing silly buggers with you. With me. With us. It's a complete coincidence."

"What have you got against me, Dent?" snarled the creature, advancing on him in a painful waddle.

"Nothing," insisted Arthur, "honestly, nothing."

Agrajag fixed him with a beady stare.

"Seems a strange way to relate to somebody you've got nothing against, killing them all the time. Very curious piece of social interaction, I would call that. I'd also call it a lie!"

"But look," said Arthur, "I'm very sorry. There's been a terrible misunderstanding. I've got to go. Have you got a clock? I'm meant to be helping save the Universe." He backed away still farther.

Agrajag advanced still farther.

"At one point," he hissed, "at one point, I decided to give up. Yes. I would not come back. I would stay in the netherworld. And what happened?"

Arthur indicated with random shakes of his head that he had no idea and didn't want to have one either. He found he had backed up against the cold dark stone that had been carved by who knew what Herculean effort into a monstrous travesty of his bedroom slippers. He glanced up at his own horrendously parodied image towering above him. He was still puzzled as to what one of his hands was meant to be doing.

"I got yanked involuntarily back into the physical world," pursued Agrajag, "as a bunch of petunias. In, I might add, a bowl. This particular happy little lifetime started off with me, in my bowl, unsupported, three hundred miles above the surface of a particularly grim planet. Not a naturally tenable position for a bowl of petunias, you might think. And you'd be right. That life ended a very short while later, three hundred miles lower. In, I might again add, the fresh wreckage of a whale. My spirit brother."

He leered at Arthur with renewed hatred.

"On the way down," he snarled, "I couldn't help noticing a flashy-looking white spaceship. And looking out of a port on this flashy-looking spaceship was a smug-looking Arthur Dent. *Coincidence?!!*"

"Yes!" yelped Arthur. He glanced up again, and realized that the arm that had puzzled him was represented as wantonly calling into existence a bowl of doomed petunias. This was not a concept that leaped easily to the eye.

"I must go," insisted Arthur.

"You may go," said Agrajag, "*after* I have killed you."

"No, that won't be any use," explained Arthur, beginning to climb up the hard stone incline of his carved bedroom slipper, "because I have to save the Universe, you see. I have to find a Silver Bail, that's the point. Tricky thing to do dead."

"Save the Universe," spat Agrajag with contempt. "You should have thought of that before your started your vendetta against me! What about the time when you were on Stavromula Beta and someone . . ."

"I've never been there," said Arthur.

". . . tried to assassinate you and you ducked. Who do you think the bullet hit? What did you say?"

"Never been there," repeated Arthur. "What are you talking about? I have to go."

Agrajag stopped in his tracks.

"You must have been there. You were responsible for my death there, as everywhere else. An innocent bystander!" He quivered.

"I've never heard of the place," insisted Arthur. "I've certainly never had anyone try to assassinate me. Other than you. Perhaps I go there later, do you think?"

Agrajag blinked slowly in a kind of frozen logical horror.

"You haven't been to Stavromula Beta... *yet?*" he whispered.

"No," said Arthur, "I don't know anything about the place. Certainly never been to it, and don't have any plans to go."

"Oh, you go there all right," muttered Agrajag in a broken voice, "you go there all right. Oh, zark!" He tottered, and stared wildly about him at his huge Cathedral of Hate. "I've brought you here too soon!"

He started to scream and bellow, "I've brought you here too zarking soon!"

Suddenly he rallied, and turned a baleful, hating eye on Arthur.

"I'm going to kill you anyway!" he roared. "Even if it's a logical impossibility I'm going to zarking well try! I'm going to blow this whole mountain up!" He screamed, "Let's see you get out of this one, Dent!"

He rushed in a painful waddling hobble to what appeared to be a small black sacrificial altar. He was shouting so wildly now that he was really carving his face up badly. Arthur leaped down from his vantage place on the carving of his own foot and ran to try to restrain the three-quarters-crazed creature.

He leaped upon him, and brought the strange monstrosity crashing down on top of the altar.

Agrajag screamed again, thrashing wildly for a brief moment, and turned a wild eye on Arthur.

"You know what you've done?" he gurgled painfully; "you've gone and killed me again. I mean, what do you want from me, blood?"

He thrashed again in a brief apoplectic fit, quivered and collapsed, smacking a large red button on the altar as he did so.

Arthur started with horror and fear, first at what he appeared to have done, and then at the loud sirens and bells that suddenly shattered the air to announce some clamoring emergency. He stared wildly around him.

The only exit appeared to be the way he had come in. He pelted toward it, throwing away the nasty fake leopard-skin bag as he did so.

He dashed randomly, haphazardly through the labyrinthine maze; he seemed to be pursued more and more fiercely by klaxons, sirens, flashing lights.

Suddenly, he turned a corner and there was a light in front of him.

It wasn't flashing. It was daylight.

Chapter 17

Although it has been said that on Earth alone in our Galaxy is Krikkit (or cricket) treated as a fit subject for a game, and that for this reason the Earth has been shunned, this only applies to our Galaxy, and more specifically to our dimension. In some of the higher dimensions they feel they can more or less please themselves, and have been playing a peculiar game called Brockian Ultra Cricket for whatever their transdimensional equivalent of billions of years is.

"Let's be blunt, it's a nasty game" (says *The Hitchhiker's Guide to the Galaxy*), "but then anyone who has been to any of the higher dimensions will know that they're a pretty nasty heathen lot up there who should just be smashed and done in, and would be, too, if anyone could work out a way of firing missiles at right angles to reality."

This is another example that *The Hitchhiker's Guide to the Galaxy* will employ anybody who wants to walk straight in off the street and get ripped off, especially if they happen to walk in off the street during the afternoon, when very few of the regular staff members are there.

There is a fundamental point here:

The history of *The Hitchhiker's Guide to the Galaxy* is one of idealism, struggle, despair, passion, success, failure and enormously long lunch breaks.

The earliest origins of the *Guide* are now, along with most of its financial records, lost in the mists of time.

For other, and more curious, theories about where they are lost, see below.

Most of the surviving stories, however, speak of a founding editor called Hurling Frootmig.

Hurling Frootmig, it is said, founded the *Guide*, established its fundamental principles of honesty and idealism and went bust.

There followed many years of penury and heart-searching during which he consulted friends, sat in darkened rooms in illegal states of mind, thought about this and that, fooled about with weights, and then, after a chance encounter with the Holy Lunching Friars of Voondoon, who claimed that just as lunch was at the center of man's temporal day, and man's temporal day could be seen as an analogy for his spiritual life, so lunch should be (a) seen as the center of man's spiritual life, and (b) held in jolly nice restaurants, he refounded the *Guide*, laid down its fundamental principles of honesty and idealism and where you could stuff them both, and led the *Guide* on to its first major commercial success.

He also started to develop and explore the role of the editorial lunch break that was subsequently to play such a crucial part in the *Guide*'s history, since it meant that most of the actual work got done by any passing stranger who happened to wander into the empty offices of an afternoon and saw something worth doing.

Shortly after this, the *Guide* was taken over by Megadodo Publications of Ursa Minor Beta, thus putting the whole thing on a very sound financial footing, and allowing the fourth editor, Lig Lury, Jr., to embark on lunch breaks of such breathtaking scope that even the efforts of recent editors who started undertaking sponsored lunch breaks for charity seem like mere sandwiches in comparison.

In fact, Lig never formally resigned his editorship—he merely left his office late one morning, and has never returned since. Though well over a century has now passed, many members of the *Guide* staff still retain the romantic notion that he has simply popped out for a sandwich and will yet return to put in a solid afternoon's work.

Strictly speaking, all editors since Lig Lury, Jr., have therefore been designated acting editors, and Lig's desk is still preserved the way he left it, with the addition of a small sign that says LIG LURY, JR., EDITOR, MISSING, PRESUMED FED.

Some very scurrilous and subversive sources hint at the idea that Lig actually perished in the *Guide*'s first extraordinary experiments in alternative bookkeeping. Very little is known of this, and less still said. Anyone who even notices, let alone calls attention to the curious, but utterly coincidental and meaningless fact that every world on which the *Guide* has ever set up an accounting department has shortly afterward perished in warfare or some natural disaster, is liable to get sued to smithereens.

It is an interesting though utterly unrelated fact that the two or three days prior to the demolition of the planet Earth to make way for a new hyperspace bypass saw a dramatic upsurge in the number of UFO sightings there, not only above Lord's Cricket Ground in St. John's Wood, London, but also above Glastonbury in Somerset.

Glastonbury had long been associated with myths of ancient kings, witchcraft and wart curing, and had now been selected as the site of the

Guide's new financial records office, and indeed, ten years worth of financial records were transferred to a magic hill just outside the city mere hours before the Vogons arrived.

None of these facts, however strange or inexplicable, is as strange or inexplicable as the rules of the game of Brockian Ultra Cricket, as played in the higher dimensions. A full set of rules is so massively complicated that the only time they were all bound together in a single volume they underwent gravitational collapse and became a Black Hole.

A brief summary, however, follows:

Rule One: Grow at least three extra legs. You won't need them, but it keeps the crowds amused.

Rule Two: Find one extremely good Brockian Ultra Cricket player. Clone him off a few times. This saves an enormous amount of tedious selection and training.

Rule Three: Put your team and the opposing team in a large field and build a high wall around them.

The reason for this is that, though the game is a major spectator sport, the frustration experienced by the audience at not actually being able to see what's going on leads them to imagine that it's a lot more exciting than it really is. A crowd that has just watched a rather humdrum game experiences far less life affirmation than a crowd that believes it has just missed the most dramatic event in sporting history.

Rule Four: Throw lots of assorted items of sporting equipment over the wall for the players. Anything will do—cricket bats, basecube bats, tennis racquets, skis, anything you can get a good swing with.

Rule Five: The players should now lay about themselves for all they are worth with whatever they find to hand. Whenever a player scores a "hit" on another player, he should immediately run away as fast as he can and apologize from a safe distance.

Apologies should be concise, sincere and, for maximum clarity and points, delivered through a megaphone.

Rule Six: The winning team shall be the first team that wins.

Curiously enough, the more the obsession with the game grows in the higher dimensions, the less it is actually played, since most of the competing teams are now in a state of permanent warfare with each other over the interpretation of these rules. This is all for the best, because in the long run a good solid war is less psychologically damaging than a protracted game of Brockian Ultra Cricket.

As Arthur ran, darting, dashing and panting down the side of the mountain, he suddenly felt the whole bulk of the mountain move very, very slightly beneath him. There was a rumble, a roar, and a slight blurred movement, and a lick of heat in the distance behind and above him. He ran in a frenzy of fear. The land began to slide, and he suddenly felt the force of the word "landslide" in a way that had never been apparent to him before. It had always just been a word to him, but now he was suddenly and horribly aware that sliding is a strange and sickening thing for land to do. It was doing it with him on it. He felt ill with fear and trembling. The ground slid, the mountain slurred, he slipped, he fell, he stood, he slipped again and ran. The avalanche began.

Stones, then rocks, then boulders, pranced past him like clumsy puppies, only much bigger, much, much harder and heavier, and almost infinitely more likely to kill you if they fell on you. His eyes danced with them, his feet danced with the dancing ground. He ran as if running were a terrible sweating sickness, his heart pounded to the rhythm of the pounding geological frenzy around him.

The logic of the situation, i.e., that he was clearly bound to survive if the next foreshadowed incident in the saga of his inadvertent persecution of Agrajag was to happen, was utterly failing to impinge itself on his mind or exercise any restraining influence on him at this time. He ran with the fear of death in him, under him, over him and grabbing hold of his hair.

And suddenly he tripped again and was hurled forward by his considerable momentum. But just at the moment he was about to hit the ground astoundingly hard he saw lying directly in front of him a small navy blue tote bag that he knew for a fact he had lost in the baggage retrieval system at the Athens airport some ten years previously in his personal time scale, and in his astonishment he missed the ground completely and bobbed off into the air with his brain singing.

What he was doing was this: he was flying. He glanced around him in surprise, but there could be no doubt that that was what he was doing. No part of him was touching the ground, and no part of him was even approaching it. He was simply floating there with boulders hurtling through the air around him.

He could now do something about that. Blinking with the noneffort of it he wafted higher into the air, and now the boulders were hurtling through the air beneath him.

He looked downward with intense curiosity. Between him and the shivering ground was now some thirty feet of empty air, empty, that is, if you discounted the boulders that didn't stay in it for long, but bounded on downward in the iron grip of the law of gravity: the same law that seemed, all of a sudden, to have given Arthur a sabbatical.

It occurred to him almost instantly, with the instinctive correctness that self-preservation instills in the mind, that he mustn't try to think about it, that if he did, the law of gravity would suddenly glance sharply in his direction and demand to know what the hell he thought he was doing up there, and all would suddenly be lost.

So he thought about tulips. It was difficult, but he did. He thought about the pleasing firm roundness of the bottom of tulips, he thought about the interesting variety of colors they came in, and wondered what proportion of the total number of tulips that grew, or had grown, on the Earth would be found within a radius of one mile from a windmill. After a while he got dangerously bored with this train of thought, felt the air slipping away beneath him, felt that he was drifting down into the paths of the bouncing boulders that he was trying so hard not to think about, so he thought about the Athens airport for a bit and that kept him usefully annoyed for about five minutes—at the end of which he was startled to discover that he was now floating about six hundred feet above the ground.

He wondered for a moment how he was going to get back down to it, but instantly shied away from that area of speculation again, and tried to look at the situation steadily.

He was flying. What was he going to do about it? He looked back down at the ground. He didn't look at it hard, but did his best just to give it an idle glance, as it were, in passing. There were a couple of things he couldn't help noticing. One was that the eruption of the mountain seemed now to have spent itself—there was a crater just a little way beneath the peak, presumably where the rock had caved in on top of the huge cavernous cathedral, the statue of himself and the sadly abused figure of Agrajag.

The other was his tote bag, the one he had lost at the Athens airport. It was sitting pertly on a piece of clear ground, surrounded by exhausted boulders but apparently hit by none of them. Why this should be he could not speculate, but since this mystery was completely overshadowed by the monstrous impossibility of the bag's being there in the first place, it was not a speculation he really felt strong enough for anyway. The thing is, it was there.

He was faced with the fact that he was going to have to pick the thing up. Here he was, flying along six hundred feet above the surface of an alien planet, the name of which he couldn't even remember. He could not ignore the plaintive posture of this tiny piece of what used to be his life, here, so many light-years from the pulverized remains of his home.

Furthermore, he realized, the bag, if it was still in the state in which he lost it, would contain a can that would have in it the only Greek olive oil still surviving in the Universe.

Slowly, carefully, inch by inch, he began to bob downward, swinging gently from side to side like a nervous sheet of paper feeling its way toward the ground.

It went well; he was feeling good. The air supported him, but let him through. Two minutes later he was hovering a mere two feet above the bag and was faced with some difficult decisions. He bobbed there lightly. He frowned, but again, as lightly as he could.

If he picked the bag up, could he carry it? Wouldn't the extra weight pull him straight to the ground?

Wouldn't the mere act of touching something on the ground suddenly discharge whatever mysterious force it was that was holding him in the air?

Wouldn't he be better off just being sensible at this point and stepping out of the air, back onto the ground for a moment or two?

If he did, would he ever be able to fly again?

The sensation, when he allowed himself to be aware of it, was so quietly ecstatic that he could not bear the thought of losing it, perhaps forever. With this worry in mind he bobbed upward a little again, just to try the feel of it, the surprising and effortless movement of it. He bobbed, he floated. He tried a little swoop.

The swoop was terrific. With his arms spread out in front of him, his hair and dressing gown streaming out behind him, he dived down out of the sky, bellied along a body of air about two feet from the ground and swung back up again, catching himself at the top of the swing and holding. Just holding. He stayed there.

It was wonderful.

And that, he realized, was the way to pick up the bag. He would swoop down and catch hold of it just at the point of the upswing. He would carry it on up with him. He might wobble a bit, but he was certain that he could hold it.

He tried one or two more practice swoops, and they got better and better. The air on his face, the bounce and woof of his body, all combined to make him feel an intoxication of the spirit that he hadn't felt since, since—well, as far as he could work out, since he was born. He drifted away on the breeze and surveyed the countryside, which was, he discovered, pretty nasty. It had a wasted, ravaged look. He decided not to look at it anymore. He would just pick up the bag and then . . . he didn't know what he was going to do after he had picked up the bag. He decided he would just pick up the bag and see where things went from there.

He judged himself against the wind, pushed up against it and turned around. He didn't realize it, but his body was willomying at this point.

He ducked down under the airstream, dipped—and dived.

The air threw itself past him; he thrilled through it. The ground wobbled uncertainly, straightened its ideas out and rose smoothly up to meet him, offering the bag, its cracked plastic handles up toward him.

Halfway down, there was a sudden dangerous moment when he could no longer believe he was doing this, and therefore very nearly wasn't, but he recovered himself in time, skimmed over the ground, slipped an arm smoothly through the handles of the bag, and began to climb back up, couldn't make it and all of a sudden collapsed, bruised, scratched and shaking on the stony ground.

He staggered instantly to his feet and swayed hopelessly around, swinging the bag around him in an agony of grief and disappointment.

His feet suddenly were stuck heavily to the ground in the way they always had been. His body seemed like an unwieldy sack of potatoes that reeled, stumbling, against the ground; his mind had all the lightness of a bag of lead.

He sagged and swayed and ached with giddiness. He tried hopelessly to run, but his legs were suddenly too weak. He tripped and flopped forward. At that moment he remembered that in the bag he was now carrying was not only a can of Greek olive oil but a duty-free allowance of retsina, and in the pleasurable shock of that realization he failed to notice for at least ten seconds that he was now flying again.

He whooped and cried with relief and pleasure, and sheer physical delight. He swooped, he wheeled, he skidded and whirled through the air. Cheekily he sat on an updraft and went through the contents of the tote bag. He felt the way he imagined an angel must feel doing its celebrated dance on the head of a pin while being counted by philosophers. He laughed with pleasure at the discovery that the bag did in fact contain the olive oil and the retsina as well as a pair of cracked sunglasses, some sand-filled swimming trunks, some creased postcards of Santorini, a large and unsightly towel, some interesting stones and various scraps of paper with the addresses of people he was relieved to think he would never meet again, even if the reason why was a sad one. He dropped the stones, put on the sunglasses and let the pieces of paper whip away in the wind.

Ten minutes later, drifting idly through a cloud, he got a large and extremely disreputable cocktail party in the small of the back.

Chapter 19

T

The longest and most destructive party ever held is now into its fourth generation and still no one shows any signs of leaving. Somebody did once look at his watch, but that was eleven years ago now, and there has been no follow-up.

The mess is extraordinary, and has to be seen to be believed, but if you don't have any particular need to believe it, then don't go and look because you won't enjoy it.

There have recently been some bangs and flashes up in the clouds, and there is one theory that this is a battle being fought between the fleets of several rival carpet-cleaning companies who are hovering over the thing like vultures, but you shouldn't believe anything you hear at parties, and particularly not anything you hear at this one.

One of the problems, and it's one that is obviously going to get worse, is that all the people at the party are either the children or the grandchildren or the great-grandchildren of the people who wouldn't leave in the first place, and because of all the business about selective breeding and recessive genes and so on, it means that all the people now at the party are either absolutely fanatical partygoers, or gibbering idiots or, more and more frequently, both.

Either way, it means that, genetically speaking, each succeeding generation is now less likely to leave than the preceding one.

So, other factors come into operation, like when the drinks are going to run out.

Now, because of certain things that have happened that seemed like a good idea at the time (and one of the problems with a party that never stops is that all the things that only seem like a good idea at parties continue to seem like good ideas), that point seems still to be a long way off.

One of the things that seemed like a good idea at the time was that the party should fly—not in the normal sense that parties are meant to fly, but literally.

One night, long ago, a band of drunken astro-engineers of the first generation clambered around the building digging this, fixing that, banging very hard on the other, and when the sun rose the following morning, it was startled to find itself shining on a building full of happy drunken people that was now floating like a young and uncertain bird over the treetops.

Not only that, but the flying party had also managed to arm itself rather heavily. If they were going to get involved in any petty arguments with wine merchants, they wanted to make sure they had might on their side.

The transition from full-time cocktail party to part-time raiding party came with ease, and did much to add that extra bit of zest and swing to the whole affair that was badly needed at this point because of the enormous number of times that the band had already played all the numbers it knew over the years.

They looted, they raided, they held whole cities to ransom for fresh supplies of cheese, crackers, guacamole, spareribs and wine and spirits that would now get piped aboard from floating tankers.

The problem of when the drinks are going to run out is, however, going to have to be faced one day.

The planet over which they are floating is no longer the planet it was when they first started floating over it.

It is in bad shape.

The party has attacked and raided an awful lot of it, and no one has ever succeeded in hitting it back because of the erratic and unpredictable way in which it lurches round the sky.

It is one hell of a party.

It is also one hell of a thing to get hit with in the small of the back.

Arthur lay floundering in pain on a piece of ripped and dismembered reinforced concrete, flicked at by wisps of passing cloud and confused by the sounds of flabby merrymaking somewhere indistinctly behind him.

There was a sound he couldn't immediately identify, partly because he didn't know the tune "I Left My Leg in Jaglan Beta" and partly because the band playing it was very tired, and some members of it were playing in three-four time, some in four-four, and some in a kind of pie-eyed πr^2, each according to the amount of sleep he'd managed to grab recently.

He lay, panting heavily in the wet air, and tried feeling bits of himself to see where he might be hurt. Wherever he touched himself, he encountered a pain. After a short while he worked out that this was because it was his hand that was hurting. He seemed to have sprained his wrist. His back, too, was hurting, but he soon satisfied himself that he was not badly hurt, but just bruised and a little shaken, as who wouldn't be. He couldn't understand what a building would be doing flying through the clouds.

On the other hand, he would have been a little hard pressed to come up with any convincing explanation of his own presence, so he decided that he and the building were just going to have to accept each other. He looked up from where he was lying. A wall of pale but stained stone slabs rose up behind him, the building proper. He seemed to be stretched out on some sort of ledge or lip that extended outward for about three or four feet all the way around. It was a hunk of the ground in which the party building had had its foundations, and which it had taken along with itself to keep itself bound together at the bottom end.

Nervously, he stood up and suddenly, looking out over the edge, he felt nauseous with vertigo. He pressed himself back against the wall, wet with mist and sweat. His head was swimming freestyle, but his stomach was doing the butterfly.

Even though he had got up here under his own power, he could now not even bear to contemplate the hideous drop in front of him. He was not about to try his luck jumping. He was not about to move an inch closer to the edge.

Clutching his tote bag he edged along the wall, hoping to find a doorway in. The solid weight of the can of olive oil was a great reassurance to him.

He was edging in the direction of the nearest corner, in the hope that the wall around the corner might offer more in the way of entrances than this one, which offered none.

The unsteadiness of the building's flight made him feel sick with fear, and, after a short time, he took the towel from out of his bag, and did something with it which once again justified its supreme position in the list of useful things to take with you when you hitchhike round the Galaxy— he put it over his head so he wouldn't have to see what he was doing.

His feet edged along the ground. His outstretched hand edged along the wall.

Finally he came to the corner, and as his hand rounded the corner, it encountered something that gave him such a shock he nearly fell off. It was another hand.

The two hands gripped each other.

He desperately wanted to use his other hand to pull the towel away from his eyes, but it was holding the bag with the olive oil, the retsina and the postcards of Santorini, and he very much didn't want to put it down.

He experienced one of those "self" moments, one of those moments when you suddenly turn around and look at yourself and think "Who am I? What am I up to? What have I achieved? Am I doing well?" He whimpered very slightly.

He tried to free his hand, but he couldn't. The other hand was holding his tightly. He had no recourse but to edge onward toward the corner. He leaned around it and shook his head in an attempt to dislodge the towel. This seemed to provoke a sharp cry of some unfathomable emotion from the owner of the other hand.

The towel was whipped from his head and he found his eyes peering into those of Ford Prefect. Beyond him stood Slartibartfast, and beyond them he could clearly see a porchway and a large closed door.

They were both pressed back against the wall, eyes wild with terror as they stared out into the thick blind cloud around them, and tried to resist the lurching and swaying of the building.

"Where the zarking photon have you been?" hissed Ford, panic-stricken.

"Er, well," stuttered Arthur, not really knowing how to sum it all up that briefly, "here and there. What are you doing here?"

Ford turned his wild eyes on Arthur again.

"They won't let us in without a bottle," he hissed.

Chapter 21

The first thing Arthur noticed as they entered into the thick of the party, apart from the noise, the suffocating heat, the wild profusion of colors that protruded dimly through the atmosphere of heady smoke, the carpets thick with ground glass, ash and guacamole droppings, and the small group of pterodactyl-like creatures in Lurex who descended on his cherished bottle of retsina, squawking, "A new pleasure, a new pleasure," was Trillian being chatted up by a Thunder God.

"Didn't I see you at Milliways?" he was saying.

"Were you the one with the hammer?"

"Yes. I much prefer it here. So much less reputable, so much more fraught."

Squeals of some hideous pleasure rang around the room, the outer dimensions of which were invisible through the heaving throng of happy noisy creatures, cheerfully yelling at each other things that nobody could hear and occasionally having crises.

"Seems fun," said Trillian. "What did you say, Arthur?"

"I said, how the hell did you get here?"

"I was a row of dots flowing randomly through the Universe. Have you met Thor? He makes thunder."

"Hello," said Arthur. "I expect that must be very interesting."

"Hi," said Thor, "it is. Have you got a drink?"

"Er, no actually...."

"Then why don't you go and get one?"

"See you later, Arthur," said Trillian.

Something jogged Arthur's mind, and he looked around huntedly.

"Zaphod isn't here, is he?" he said.

"See you," said Trillian firmly, "later."

Thor glared at him with hard coal-black eyes, his beard bristling. What little light there was in the place mustered its forces briefly to glint menacingly off the horns on his helmet.

He took Trillian's elbow in his extremely large hand and the muscles in his upper arm moved around each other like a couple of Volkswagens parking.

He led her away.

"One of the interesting things about being immortal," he said, "is . . ."

"One of the interesting things about space," Arthur heard Slartibartfast saying to a large and voluminous creature who looked like someone losing a fight with a pink comforter and was gazing raptly at the old man's deep eyes and silver beard, "is how dull it is."

"Dull?" said the creature, and blinked her rather wrinkled and bloodshot eyes.

"Yes," said Slartibartfast, "staggeringly dull. Bewilderingly so. You see, there's so much of it and so little in it. Would you like me to quote you some statistics?"

"Er, well . . ."

"Please, I would like to. They, too, are quite sensationally dull."

"I'll come back and hear them in a moment," she said, patted him on the arm, lifted up her skirts like a Hovercraft and moved off into the heaving crowd.

"I thought she'd never go," growled the old man. "Come, Earthman. . . ."

"Arthur."

"We must find the Silver Bail, it is here somewhere."

"Can't we just relax a little," Arthur said. "I've had a tough day. Trillian's here, incidentally, she didn't say how; it probably doesn't matter."

"Think of the danger to the Universe. . . ."

"The Universe," said Arthur, "is big enough and old enough to look after itself for half an hour. All right," he added, in response to Slartibartfast's increasing agitation, "I'll wander round and see if anybody's seen it."

"Good, good," said Slartibartfast, "good." He plunged into the crowd himself, and was told to relax by everybody he passed.

"Have you seen a bail anywhere?" said Arthur to a little man who seemed to be standing eagerly waiting to listen to somebody. "It's made of silver, vitally important for the future safety of the Universe, and about this long."

"No," said the enthusiastically wizened little man, "but do have a drink and tell me all about it."

Ford Prefect writhed past, dancing a wild, frenetic and not entirely unobscene dance with someone who looked as if she were wearing Sydney Opera House on her head. He was yelling a futile conversation at her above the din.

"I like the hat!" he bawled.

"What?"

"I said, I like the hat."

"I'm not wearing a hat."

"Well, I like the head, then."

"What?"

"I said, I like the head. Interesting bone structure."

"What?"

Ford worked a shrug into the complex routine of other movements he was performing.

"I said you dance great," he shouted, "just don't nod so much."

"What?"

"It's just that every time you nod," said Ford, "...ow!" he added as his partner nodded forward to say "What?" and once again pecked him sharply on the forehead with the sharp end of her swept-forward skull.

"My planet was blown up one morning," said Arthur, who had found himself quite unexpectedly telling the little man his life story, or at least, edited highlights of it, "that's why I'm dressed like this, in my dressing gown. My planet was blown up with all my clothes in it, you see. I didn't realize I'd be coming to a party."

The little man nodded enthusiastically.

"Later, I was thrown off a spaceship. Still in my dressing gown. Rather than the spacesuit one would normally expect. Shortly after that I discovered that my planet had originally been built for a bunch of mice. You can imagine how I felt about that. I was then shot at for a while and blown up. In fact I have been blown up ridiculously often, shot at, insulted, regularly disintegrated, deprived of tea and recently I crashed into a swamp and had to spend five years in a damp cave."

"Ah," effervesced the little man, "and did you have a wonderful time?"

Arthur started to choke violently on his drink.

"What a wonderfully exciting cough," said the little man, quite startled by it, "do you mind if I join you?"

And with that he launched into the most extraordinary and spectacular fit of coughing that caught Arthur so much by surprise that he started to choke violently, discovered he was already doing it and got thoroughly confused. Together they performed a lung-busting duet that went on for fully two minutes before Arthur managed to cough and splutter to a halt.

"So invigorating," said the little man, panting and wiping tears from his eyes, "what an exciting life you must lead. Thank you very much."

He shook Arthur warmly by the hand and walked off into the crowd. Arthur shook his head in astonishment.

A youngish-looking man came up to him, an aggressive-looking type with a hook mouth, a lantern nose and small beady little cheekbones. He was wearing black trousers, a black silk shirt open to what was presumably his navel, though Arthur had learned never to make assumptions about the anatomies of the sort of people he tended to meet these days, and had all sorts of nasty dangly gold things hanging round his neck. He carried something in a black bag, and clearly wanted people to notice that he didn't want them to notice it.

"Hey, er, did I hear you say your name just now?" he said.

This was one of the many things that Arthur had told the enthusiastic little man.

"Yes, it's Arthur Dent."

The man seemed to be dancing slightly to some rhythm other than any of the several that the band was grimly pushing out.

"Yeah," he said, "only there was a man in a mountain wanted to see you."

"I met him."

"Yeah, only he seemed pretty anxious about it, you know."

"Yes, I met him."

"Yeah, well, I think you should know that."

"I do. I met him."

The man paused to chew a little gum. Then he clapped Arthur on the back.

"Okay," he said, "all right. I'm just telling you, right? Good night, good luck, win awards."

"What?" said Arthur, who was beginning to flounder seriously at this point.

"Whatever. Do what you do. Do it well." He made a sort of clucking noise with whatever he was chewing and then some vaguely dynamic gesture.

"Why?" said Arthur.

"Do it badly," said the man. "Who cares? Who gives a swut?" The blood suddenly seemed to pump angrily into the man's face and he started to shout.

"Why not go mad?" he said. "Go away, get off my back, will you, guy? Just zark off!!!"

"It's been real." The man gave a sharp wave and disappeared off into the throng.

"What was that all about?" asked Arthur to a girl he found standing beside him. "Why did he tell me to win awards?"

"Just show biz talk," answered the girl. "He just won an award at the Annual Ursa Minor Alpha Recreational Illusions Institute Awards ceremony, and he was hoping to be able to pass it off lightly, only you didn't mention it so he couldn't."

"Oh," said Arthur, "oh, well, I'm sorry I didn't. What was it for?"

"The Most Gratuitous Use of the Word 'Belgium' in a Serious Screenplay. It's very prestigious."

"The most gratuitous use of which word?" asked Arthur, with a determined attempt to keep his brain in neutral.

"Belgium," said the girl, "I hardly like to say it."

"Belgium?" exclaimed Arthur.

A drunken seven-toed sloth staggered past, gawked at the word and threw itself backward at a blurry-eyed pterodactyl, roaring with displeasure.

"Are we talking," said Arthur, "about the very flat country, with all the EEC and the fog?"

"What?" said the girl.

"Belgium," said Arthur.

"Raaaaaarrrchchchchch!" screeched the pterodactyl.

"Grrruuuuuurrrghhhh," agreed the seven-toed sloth.

"They must be thinking of Ostend Hoverport," muttered Arthur. He turned back to the girl.

"Have you ever been to Belgium in fact?" he asked brightly and she nearly hit him.

"I think," she said, restraining herself, "that you should restrict that sort of remark to something artistic."

"You sound as if I just said something unspeakably rude."

"You did."

In today's modern Galaxy there is of course very little still held to be unspeakable. Many words and expressions which only a matter of decades ago were considered so distastefully explicit that, were they merely to be breathed in public, the perpetrator would be shunned, barred from polite society, and in extreme cases shot through the lungs, are now thought to be very healthy and proper, and their use in everyday speech and writing is seen as evidence of a well-adjusted, relaxed and totally un****ed-up personality.

So, for instance, when in a recent national speech the Financial Minister of the Royal World Estate of Quarlvista actually dared to say that due to one thing and another and the fact that no one had made any food for a while and the king seemed to have died and most of the population had been on holiday now for over three years, the economy was now in what he called "one whole joojooflop situation," everyone was so pleased that he felt able to come out and say it that they quite failed to note that their entire five-thousand-year-old civilization had just collapsed overnight.

But even though words like "joojooflop," "swut," and "turlingdrome" are now perfectly acceptable in common usage there is one word that is still beyond the pale. The concept it embodies is so revolting that the publication or broadcast of the word is utterly forbidden in all parts of the Galaxy except for use in Serious Screenplays. There is also, or *was*, one planet where they didn't know what it meant, the stupid turlingdromes.

"I see," said Arthur, who didn't, "so what do you get for using the name of a perfectly innocent if slightly dull European country gratuitously in a Serious Screenplay?"

"A Rory," said the girl, "it's just a small silver thing set on a large black base. What did you say?"

"I didn't say anything, I was just about to ask what the silver..."

"Oh, I thought you said 'whop.' "

"Said what?"

"Whop."

Chapter 22

People had been dropping in on the party now for some years, fashionable gate-crashers from other worlds, and for some time it had occurred to the partygoers as they had looked out at their own world beneath them, with its wrecked cities, its ravaged avocado farms and blighted vineyards, its vast tracts of new desert, its seas full of cracker crumbs and worse, that their world was in some tiny and almost imperceptible ways not quite as much fun as it had been. Some of them had begun to wonder if they could manage to stay sober for long enough to make the entire party spaceworthy and maybe take it off to some other people's worlds where the air might be fresher and give them fewer headaches.

The few undernourished farmers who still managed to scratch out a feeble existence on the half-dead ground of the planet's surface would have been extremely pleased to hear this, but that day, as the party came screaming out of the clouds and the farmers looked up in haggard fear of yet another cheese and wine raid, it became clear that the party was not going anywhere else for a while, that the party would soon be over. Very soon it would be time to gather up hats and coats and stagger blearily outside to find out what time of day it was, what time of year it was and whether in any of this burnt and ravaged land there was a taxi going anywhere.

The party was locked in a horrible embrace with a strange white spaceship that seemed to be half sticking through it. Together they were lurching, heaving and spinning their way around the sky in grotesque disregard of their own weight.

The clouds parted. The air roared and leaped out of their way.

The party and the Krikkit warship looked, in their writhings, a little like two ducks, one of which is trying to make a third duck inside the second duck, while the second duck is trying very hard to explain that it doesn't feel ready for a third duck right now, is uncertain that it would want any putative third duck to be made by this particular first duck anyway, and certainly not while it, the second duck, was busy flying.

The sky sang and screamed with the rage of it all and buffeted the ground with shock waves.

And suddenly, with a foop, the Krikkit ship was gone.

The party blundered helplessly across the sky like a man leaning against an unexpectedly open door. It spun and wobbled on its Hover jets. It tried to right itself and wronged itself instead. It staggered back across the sky again.

For a while these staggerings continued, but clearly they could not continue for long. The party was now a mortally wounded party. All the fun had gone out of it, as the occasional broken-backed pirouette could not disguise.

The longer, at this point, that it avoided the ground, the heavier was going to be the crash when finally it hit it.

Inside things were not going well either. They were going monstrously badly in fact and people were hating it and saying so loudly.

The Krikkit robots had been.

They had removed the award for the Most Gratuitous Use of the Word "Belgium" in a Serious Screenplay, and in its place had left a scene of devastation that left Arthur feeling almost as sick as a runner-up for a Rory.

"We would love to stay and help," shouted Ford, picking his way over the mangled debris, "only we're not going to."

The party lurched again, provoking feverish cries and groans from among the smoking wreckage.

"We have to go and save the Universe, you see," said Ford, "and if that sounds like a pretty lame excuse, then you may be right. Either way we're off."

He suddenly came across an unopened bottle lying, miraculously unbroken, on the ground.

"Do you mind if we take this?" he said. "You won't be needing it."

He took a packet of potato chips, too.

"Trillian?" shouted Arthur in a shocked and weakened voice. In the smoking mess he could see nothing.

"Earthman, we must go," said Slartibartfast nervously.

"Trillian?" shouted Arthur again.

A moment or two later, Trillian staggered, shaking, into view, supported by her new friend the Thunder God.

"The girl stays with me," said Thor. "There's a great party going on in Valhalla, we'll by flying off. . . ."

"Where were you when all this was going on?" said Arthur.

"Upstairs," said Thor. "I was weighing her. Flying's a tricky business, you see, you have to calculate wind...."

"She comes with us," said Arthur.

"Hey," said Trillian, "don't I..."

"No," said Arthur, "you come with us."

Thor looked at him with slowly smoldering eyes. He was making some point about godliness and it had nothing to do with being clean.

"She comes with me," he said quietly.

"Come on, Earthman," said Slartibartfast nervously, picking at Arthur's sleeve.

"Come on, Slartibartfast," said Ford nervously, picking at the old man's sleeve. Slartibartfast had the teleport device.

The party lurched and swayed, sending everyone reeling, except for Thor and except for Arthur, who stared, shaking, into the Thunder God's black eyes.

Slowly, incredibly, Arthur put up what now appeared to be his tiny little fists.

"Want to make something of it?" he said.

"I beg your minuscule pardon?" roared Thor.

"I said," repeated Arthur, and he could not keep the quavering out of his voice, "do you want to make something of it?" He waggled his fists ridiculously.

Thor looked at him with incredulity. Then a little wisp of smoke curled upward from his nostril. There was a tiny little flame in it, too.

He gripped his belt.

He expanded his chest to make it totally clear that here was the sort of man you only dared to cross if you had a team of Sherpas with you.

He unhooked the shaft of his hammer from his belt. He held it up in his hands to reveal the massive iron head. He thus cleared up a possible misunderstanding that he might merely have been carrying a telegraph pole around with him.

"Do I want," he said, with a hiss like a river flowing through a steel mill, "to make something of it?"

"Yes," said Arthur, his voice suddenly and extraordinarily strong and belligerent. He waggled his fists, again, this time as if he meant it.

"You want to step outside?" he snarled at Thor.

"All right!" bellowed Thor, like an enraged bull (or in fact like an enraged Thunder God, which is a great deal more impressive), and did so.

"Good," said Arthur, "that's got rid of him. Slarty, get us out of here."

ll right," shouted Ford at Arthur, "so I'm a coward, the point is
I'm still alive." They were back aboard the starship *Bistromath*.
So was Slartibartfast. So was Trillian. Harmony and concord
were not.

"Well, so am I alive, aren't I?" retaliated Arthur, haggard with adventure
and anger. His eyebrows were leaping up and down as if they wanted to
punch each other.

"You damn nearly weren't," exploded Ford.

Arthur turned sharply to Slartibartfast, who was sitting in his pilot
couch on the flight deck gazing thoughtfully into the bottom of a bottle
that was telling him something he clearly couldn't fathom. He appealed to
him.

"Do you think he understands the first word I've been saying?" he said,
quivering with emotion.

"I don't know," replied Slartibartfast, a little abstractedly. "I'm not
sure," he added, glancing up very briefly, "that I do." He stared at his
instruments with renewed vigor and bafflement. "You'll have to explain it
to us again," he said.

"Well . . ."

"But later. Terrible things are afoot."

He tapped the pseudoglass of the bottle bottom.

"We fared rather pathetically at the party, I'm afraid," he said, "and our
only hope now is to try to prevent the robots from using the Key in the
Lock. How in heaven we do that I don't know," he muttered, "just have to
go there, I suppose. Can't say I like the idea at all. Probably end up dead."

"Where is Trillian anyway?" said Arthur with a sudden affectation of
unconcern. What he had been angry about was that Ford had berated him
for wasting time over all the business with the Thunder God when they
could have been making a rather more rapid escape. Arthur's own opinion,
and he had offered it for whatever anybody might have felt it was worth,
was that he had been extraordinarily brave and resourceful.

The prevailing view seemed to be that his opinion was not worth a pair
of fetid dingo's kidneys. What really hurt, though, was that Trillian didn't

seem to react much one way or the other and had wandered off somewhere.

"And where are my potato chips?" said Ford.

"They are both," said Slartibartfast, without looking up, "in the room of Informational Illusions. I think that your young lady friend is trying to understand some problems of Galactic history. I think the potato chips are probably helping her."

Chapter 24

I t is a mistake to think you can solve any major problems just with potatoes.

For instance, there was once an insanely aggressive race of people called the Silastic Armorfiends of Striterax. That was just the name of their race. The name of their army was something quite horrific. Luckily they lived even farther back in Galactic history than anything we have so far encountered—twenty billion years ago—when the Galaxy was young and fresh, and every idea worth fighting for was a new one.

And fighting was what the Silastic Armorfiends of Striterax were good at, and being good at it, they did it a lot. They fought their enemies (i.e., everybody else), they fought each other. Their planet was a complete wreck. The surface was littered with abandoned cities that were surrounded by abandoned war machines, which were in turn surrounded by deep bunkers in which the Silastic Armorfiends lived and squabbled with each other.

The best way to pick a fight with a Silastic Armorfiend of Striterax was just to be born. They didn't like it, they got resentful. And when an Armorfiend got resentful, someone got hurt. An exhausting way of life, one might think, but they did seem to have an awful lot of energy. The best way of dealing with a Silastic Armorfiend was to put him in a room on his own, because sooner or later he would simply beat himself up.

Eventually they realized that this was something they were going to have to sort out, and they passed a law decreeing that anyone who had to carry a weapon as part of his normal Silastic work (policemen, security guards, primary school teachers, etc.) had to spend at least forty-five minutes every day punching a sack of potatoes in order to work off his or her surplus aggression.

For a while this worked well, until someone thought that it would be much more efficient and less time-consuming if they just shot the potatoes instead.

This led to a renewed enthusiasm for shooting all sorts of things, and they all got very excited at the prospect of their first major war for weeks.

Another achievement of the Silastic Armorfiends of Striterax is that they were the first race who ever managed to shock a computer.

It was a gigantic spaceborne computer called Hactar, which to this day is remembered as one of the most powerful ever built. It was the first to be built like a natural brain, in that every cellular particle of it carried the pattern of the whole within it, which enabled it to think more flexibly and imaginatively, and also, it seemed, to be shocked.

The Silastic Armorfiends of Striterax were engaged in one of their regular wars with the Strenuous Garfighters of Stug, and were not enjoying it as much as usual because it involved an awful lot of trekking through the Radiation Swamps of Cwulzenda and across the Fire Mountains of Frazfraga, neither of which terrains they felt at home in.

So when the Strangulous Stillettans of Jajazikstak joined in the fray and forced them to fight another front in the Gamma Caves of Carfrax and the Ice Storms of Varlengooten, they decided that enough was enough, and they ordered Hactar to design for them an Ultimate Weapon.

"What do you mean," asked Hactar, "by Ultimate?"

To which the Silastic Armorfiends of Striterax said, "Read a bloody dictionary," and plunged back into the fray.

So Hactar designed an Ultimate Weapon. It was a very, very small bomb that was simply a junction box in hyperspace which would, when activated, connect the heart of every major sun with the heart of every other major sun simultaneously and thus turn the entire Universe into one gigantic hyperspatial supernova.

When the Silastic Armorfiends tried to use it to blow up a Strangulous Stillettan munitions dump in one of the Gamma Caves, they were extremely irritated that it didn't work, and said so.

Hactar had been shocked by the whole idea.

He tried to explain that he had been thinking about this Ultimate Weapon business, and had worked out that there was no conceivable consequence of not setting the bomb off that was worse than the known consequence of setting it off, and he had therefore taken the liberty of introducing a small flaw into the design of the bomb, and he hoped that everyone involved would, on sober reflection, feel that . . .

The Silastic Armorfiends disagreed and pulverized the computer.

Later they thought better of it, and destroyed the faulty bomb as well.

Then, pausing only to smash the hell out of the Strenuous Garfighters of Stug, and the Strangulous Stillettans of Jajazikstak, they then went on to find an entirely new way of blowing themselves up, which was a profound relief to everyone else in the Galaxy, particularly the Garfighters, the Stillettans and the potatoes.

Trillian had watched all this, as well as the story of Krikkit. She emerged from the room of Informational Illusions thoughtfully, just in time to discover that they had arrived too late.

Chapter 25

Even as the starship *Bistromath* flickered into objective being on the top of a small cliff on the mile-wide asteroid that pursued a lonely and eternal path in orbit around the enclosed star system of Krikkit, its crew was aware that they were in time only to be witnesses to an unstoppable historic event.

They didn't realize they were going to see two.

They stood cold, lonely and helpless on the cliff edge and watched the activity below. Lances of light wheeled in sinister arcs against the void from a point only about a hundred yards below and in front of them.

They stared into the blinding event.

An extension of the ship's field enabled them to stand there by once again exploiting the mind's predisposition to have tricks played on it: the problems of falling up off the tiny mass of the asteroid, or of not being able to breathe simply became Somebody Else's.

The white Krikkit warship was parked among the stark gray crags of the asteroid, alternately flaring under arc lights or disappearing in shadow. The black shadows cast by the hard rocks danced together in wild choreography as the arc lights swept around them.

The eleven white robots were bearing, in procession, the Wikkit Key out into the middle of a circle of swinging lights.

The Wikkit Key had been rebuilt. Its components shone and glittered: the Steel Pillar (or Marvin's leg) of Strength and Power, the Golden Bail (or heart of the Infinite Improbability Drive) of Prosperity, the Plastic Pillar (or Argabuthon Scepter of Justice) of Science and Reason, the Silver Bail (or Rory Award for the Most Gratuitous Use of the Word "Belgium" in a Serious Screenplay) and the now reconstituted Wooden Pillar (or Ashes of a burnt stump signifying the death of English cricket) of Nature and Spirituality.

"I suppose there is nothing we can do at this point?" asked Arthur nervously.

"No," sighed Slartibartfast.

The expression of disappointment that crossed Arthur's face was a complete failure and, since he was standing obscured by shadow, he allowed it to collapse into one of relief.

"Pity," he said.

"We have no weapons," said Slartibartfast, "stupidly."

"Damn," said Arthur, very quietly.

Ford said nothing.

Trillian said nothing, but in a peculiarly thoughtful and distinct way. She was staring at that blankness of the space beyond the asteroid.

The asteroid circled the Dust Cloud that surrounded the Slo-Time envelope that enclosed the world on which lived the people of Krikkit—the Masters of Krikkit and their killer robots.

The helpless group had no way of knowing whether or not the Krikkit robots were aware of their presence. They could only assume they must be, but they felt, quite rightly in the circumstances, that they had nothing to fear. They had a historic task to perform, and their audience could be regarded with contempt.

"Terribly impotent feeling, isn't it?" said Arthur, but the others ignored him.

In the center of the area of light that the robots were approaching, a square-shaped crack appeared in the ground. The crack defined itself more and more distinctly, and soon it became clear that a block of the ground, about six feet square, was slowly rising.

At the same time, they became aware of some other movement, but it was almost subliminal, and for a moment or two it was not clear what it was that was moving.

Then it became clear.

The asteroid was moving. It was moving in toward the Dust Cloud, as if being hauled inexorably by some celestial angler in its depths.

They were to make in real life the journey through the Cloud that they had already made in the room of Informational Illusions. They stood frozen in silence. Trillian frowned.

An age seemed to pass. Events seemed to pass with spinning slowness, as the leading edge of the asteroid passed into the vague and soft outer perimeter of the Cloud.

And soon they were engulfed in a thin and dancing obscurity. They passed on through it, on and on, dimly aware of vague shapes and whorls indistinguishable in the darkness except in the corner of the eye.

The dust dimmed the shafts of brilliant light. The shafts of brilliant light twinkled on the myriad specks of dust.

Trillian, again, regarded the passage from within her own frowning thoughts.

And they were through it. Whether it had taken a minute or half an hour they weren't sure, but they were through it and confronted with a fresh blankness, as if space were pinched out of existence in front of them.

And now things moved quickly.

A blinding shaft of light seemed almost to explode from out of the block that had risen three feet out of the ground, and out of that rose a smaller plastic block, dazzling with interior dancing colors.

The block was slotted with deep grooves, three upright and two across, clearly designed to accept the Wikkit Key.

The robots approached the Lock, slotted the Key into its home and stepped back again. The block twisted around of its own accord, and space began to alter.

As space unpinched itself, it seemed agonizingly to twist the eyes of the watchers in their sockets. They found themselves staring, blinded at an unraveled sun that stood now before them where it seemed only seconds before there had not been even empty space. It was a second or two before they were even sufficiently aware of what had happened to throw their hands up over their horrified blinded eyes. In that second or two, they were aware of a tiny speck moving slowly across the eye of that sun.

They staggered back, and heard ringing in their ears the thin and unexpected chant of the robots crying out in unison.

"Krikkit! Krikkit! Krikkit! Krikkit!"

The sound chilled them. It was harsh, it was cold, it was empty, it was mechanically dismal.

It was also triumphant.

They were so stunned by these two sensory shocks that they almost missed the second historic event.

Zaphod Beeblebrox, the only man in history to survive a direct blast attack from the Krikkit robots, ran out of the Krikkit warship brandishing a Zap gun.

"Okay," he cried, "the situation is totally under control as of this moment in time."

The single robot guarding the hatchway to the ship silently swung his battleclub, and connected it with the back of Zaphod's left head.

"Who the zark did that?" said his left head, and lolled sickeningly forward.

His right head gazed keenly into the middle distance.

"Who did what?" it said.

The club connected with the back of his right head.

Zaphod measured his length and rather strange shape on the ground.

Within a matter of seconds the whole event was over. A few blasts from the robots were sufficient to destroy the Lock forever. It split and melted and splayed its contents brokenly, and robots marched grimly and, it almost seemed, in a slightly disheartened manner, back into their warship which, with a "foop," was gone.

Trillian and Ford ran hectically around and down the steep incline to the dark still body of Zaphod Beeblebrox.

Chapter 26

I don't know," said Zaphod, for what seemed to him like the thirty-seventh time, "they could have killed me, but they didn't. Maybe they just thought I was a kind of wonderful guy or something. I could understand that."

The others silently registered their opinions of this theory.

Zaphod lay on the cold floor of the flight deck. His back seemed to wrestle the floor as pain thudded through him and banged at his heads.

"I think," he whispered, "that there is something wrong with those anodized dudes, something fundamentally weird."

"They are programmed to kill everybody," Slartibartfast pointed out.

"That," wheezed Zaphod between the whacking thuds, "could be it." He didn't seem altogether convinced.

"Hey, baby," he said to Trillian, hoping this would make up for his previous behavior.

"You all right?" she said gently.

"Yeah," he said, "I'm fine."

"Good," she said, and walked away to think. She stared at the huge visiscreen over the flight couches and, twisting a switch, she flipped local images over it. One image was the blankness of the Dust Cloud. One was the sun of Krikkit. One was Krikkit itself. She flipped between them fiercely.

"Well, that's goodbye Galaxy, then," said Arthur, slapping his knees and standing up.

"No," said Slartibartfast, gravely, "our course is clear." He furrowed his brow until you could grow some of the smaller root vegetables in it. He stood up, he paced around. When he spoke again, what he said frightened him so much he had to sit down again.

"We must go down to Krikkit," he said. A deep sigh shook his old frame and his eyes seemed almost to rattle in their sockets.

"Once again," he said, "we have failed pathetically. Quite pathetically."

"That," said Ford quietly, "is because we don't care enough. I told you."

He swung his feet up onto the instrument panel and picked fitfully at something on one of his fingernails.

"But unless we determine to take action," said the old man querulously, as if struggling against something deeply insouciant in his nature, "then we shall all be destroyed; we shall all die. Surely we care about that?"

"Not enough to want to get killed over it," said Ford. He put on a sort of hollow smile and flipped it round the room at anyone who wanted to see it.

Slartibartfast clearly found this point of view extremely seductive and he fought against it. He turned again to Zaphod, who was gritting his teeth and sweating with the pain.

"You surely must have some idea," he said, "of why they spared your life. It seems most strange and unusual."

"I kind of think they didn't even know," shrugged Zaphod. "I told you. They hit me with the most feeble blast, just knocked me out, right? They lugged me into their ship, dumped me in a corner and ignored me. Like they were embarrassed about me being there. If I said anything they knocked me out again. We had some great conversations. 'Hey . . . ugh!' 'Hi there . . . ugh!' 'I wonder . . . ugh!' Kept me amused for hours, you know." He winced again.

He was toying with something in his fingers. He held it up. It was the Golden Bail—the *Heart of Gold*, the heart of the Infinite Improbability Drive. Only that and the Wooden Pillar had survived the destruction of the Lock intact.

"I hear your ship can move a bit," he said, "so how would you like to zip me back to mine before you . . ."

"Will you not help us?" said Slartibartfast.

"Us?" said Ford sharply; "who's us?"

"I'd love to stay and help you save the Galaxy," insisted Zaphod, raising himself up onto his shoulders, "but I have the mother and father of a pair of headaches, and I feel a lot of little headaches coming on. But next time it needs saving, I'm your guy. Hey, Trillian, baby?"

She looked round, briefly.

"Yes?"

"You want to come? *Heart of Gold*? Excitement and adventure and really wild things?"

"I'm going down to Krikkit," she said.

Chapter 27

It was the same hill, and yet not the same.

This time it was not an Informational Illusion. This was Krikkit itself and they were standing on it. Near them, behind the trees, the strange Italian restaurant that had brought these, their real bodies, to this, the real, present world of Krikkit.

The strong grass under their feet was real, the rich soil real, too. The heady fragrances from the tree, too, were real. The night was real night.

Krikkit.

Possibly the most dangerous place in the Galaxy for anyone who isn't Krikkiter to stand. The place that could not countenance the existence of any other place, whose charming, delightful, intelligent inhabitants would howl with fear, savagery and murderous hate when confronted with anyone not their own.

Arthur shuddered.

Slartibartfast shuddered.

Ford, surprisingly, shuddered.

It was not surprising that he shuddered, it was surprising that he was there at all. But when they had returned Zaphod to his ship Ford had felt unexpectedly shamed into not running away.

"Wrong," he thought to himself, "wrong wrong wrong." He hugged to himself one of the Zap guns with which they had armed themselves out of Zaphod's armory.

Trillian shuddered, and frowned as she looked into the sky.

This, too, was not the same. It was no longer blank and empty.

While the countryside around them had changed little in the two thousand years of the Krikkit Wars, and the mere five years that had elapsed locally since Krikkit was sealed in its Slo-Time envelope ten billion years ago, the sky was dramatically different.

Dim lights and heavy shapes hung in it.

High in the sky, where no Krikkiter ever looked, were the War Zones, the Robot Zones—huge warships and tower blocks floating in the Nil-O-Grav fields far above the idyllic pastoral lands of the surface of Krikkit.

Trillian stared at them and thought.

"Trillian," whispered Ford Prefect to her.

"Yes?" she said.

"What are you doing?"

"Thinking."

"Do you always breathe like that when you're thinking?"

"I wasn't aware that I was breathing."

"That's what worried me."

"I think I know. . . ." said Trillian.

"Shhhh!" said Slartibartfast in alarm, and his thin trembling hand motioned them farther back beneath the shadow of the tree.

Suddenly, as before in the tape, there were lights coming along the hill path, but this time the dancing beams were not from lanterns but flashlights—not in itself a dramatic change, but every detail made their hearts thump with fear. This time there were no lilting whimsical songs about flowers and farming and dead dogs, but hushed voices in urgent debate.

A light moved in the sky with slow weight. Arthur was clenched with a claustrophobic terror and the warm wind caught at his throat.

Within seconds a second party became visible, approaching from the other side of the dark hill. They were moving swiftly and purposefully, their flashlights swinging and probing around them.

The parties were clearly converging, and not merely with each other. They were converging deliberately on the spot where Arthur and the others were standing.

Arthur heard the slight rustle as Ford Prefect raised his Zap gun to his shoulder, and the slight whimpering cough as Slartibartfast raised his. He felt the cold unfamiliar weight of his own gun, and with shaking hands he raised it.

His fingers fumbled to release the safety catch and engage the extreme danger catch as Ford had shown him. He was shaking so much that if he'd fired at anybody at that moment he probably would have burnt his signature on them.

Only Trillian didn't raise her gun. She raised her eyebrows, lowered them again and bit her lip in thought.

"Has it occurred to you . . ." she began, but nobody wanted to discuss anything much at the moment.

A light stabbed through the darkness from behind them and they spun around to find a third party of Krikkiters behind them, searching them out with their flashlights.

Ford Prefect's gun crackled viciously, but fire spat back at it and it crashed from his hands.

There was a moment of pure fear, a frozen second before anyone fired again.

And at the end of the second nobody fired.

They were surrounded by pale-faced Krikkiters and bathed in bobbing light.

The captives stared at their captors, the captors stared at their captives.

"Hello," said one of the captors, "excuse me, but are you . . . aliens?"

Chapter 28

Meanwhile, more millions of miles away than the mind can comfortably encompass, Zaphod Beeblebrox was feeling bored.

He had repaired his ship—that is, he'd watched with alert interest while a service robot had repaired it for him. It was now, once again, one of the most powerful and extraordinary ships in existence. He could go anywhere, do anything. He fiddled with a book, and then tossed it away. It was the one he'd read before.

He walked over to the communications bank and opened an all-frequencies emergency channel.

"Anyone want a drink?" he asked.

"This an emergency, feller?" crackled a voice from halfway across the Galaxy.

"Got any mixers?" said Zaphod.

"Go take a ride on a comet."

"Okay, okay," said Zaphod, and flipped the channel shut again. He sighed and sat down. He got up again and wandered over to a computer screen. He pushed a few buttons. Little blobs started to rush around the screen eating each other.

"Pow!" said Zaphod, "freeeoooo! Pop pop pop!"

"Hi there," said the computer brightly after a minute of this, " you have scored three points. Previous best score, seven million five hundred and ninety-seven thousand, two hundred and . . ."

"Okay, okay," said Zaphod, and flipped the screen blank again.

He sat down again. He played with a pencil. This, too, began slowly to lose its fascination.

"Okay, okay," he said, and fed his score and the previous best one into the computer.

His ship mad a blur of the Universe.

Chapter 29

Tell us," said the thin, pale-faced Krikkiter who had stepped forward from the ranks of the others and stood uncertainly in the circle of light handling his gun as if he were just holding it for someone else who'd just popped off somewhere but would be back in a minute, "do you know anything about something called the balance of nature?"

There was no reply from their captives, or at least nothing more articulate than a few confused mumbles and grunts. The flashlight continued to play over them. High in the sky above them dark activity continued in the Robot Zones.

"It's just," continued the Krikkiter uneasily, "something we heard about, probably nothing important. Well, I suppose we'd better kill you, then."

He looked down at his gun as if he were trying to find which bit to press.

"That is," he said, looking up again, "unless there's anything you want to chat about?"

Slow numb astonishment crept up the bodies of Slartibartfast, Ford and Arthur. Very soon it would reach their brains, which were at the moment solely occupied with moving their jawbones up and down. Trillian was shaking her head as if trying to finish a jigsaw puzzle by shaking the box.

"We're worried, you see," said another man from the crowd, "about this plan of universal destruction."

"Yes," added another, "and the balance of nature. It just seemed to us that if the whole of the rest of the Universe is destroyed it will somehow upset the balance. We're quite keen on ecology, you see." His voice trailed away unhappily.

"And sport," said another, loudly. This got a cheer of approval from the others.

"Yes," agreed the first, "and sport..." He looked back at his fellows uneasily and scratched fitfully at his cheek. He seemed to be wrestling with some deep inner confusion, as if everything he wanted to say and everything he thought were entirely different things between which he could see no possible connection.

"You see," he mumbled, "some of us . . ." and he looked around again as if for confirmation. The others made encouraging noises. "Some of us," he continued, "are quite keen to have sporting links with the rest of the Galaxy, and though I can see the argument about keeping sport out of politics, I think that if we want to have sporting links with the rest of the Galaxy, which we do, then it's probably a mistake to destroy it. And indeed the rest of the Universe . . ." His voice trailed away again, "which is what seems to be the idea now . . ."

"Wh . . ." said Slartibartfast, "wh . . ."

"Hhhh . . . ?" said Arthur.

"Dr . . ." said Ford Prefect.

"Okay," said Trillian, "let's talk about it." She walked forward and took the poor confused Krikkiter by the arm. He looked about twenty-five, which meant, because of the peculiar manglings of time that had been going on in this area, that he would have been just twenty when the Krikkit Wars were finished, ten billion years ago.

Trillian led him for a short walk through the light before she said anything more. He stumbled uncertainly after her. The encircling flashlight beams were drooping slightly now as if they were abdicating to this strange, quiet girl who alone in this Universe of dark confusion seemed to know what she was doing.

She turned and faced him, and lightly held both his arms. He was a picture of bewildered misery.

"Tell me," she said.

He said nothing for a moment, while his gaze darted from one of her eyes to the other.

"We . . ." he said, "we have to be alone . . . I think." He screwed up his face and then dropped his head forward, shaking it like someone trying to shake a coin out of a money box. He looked up again. "We have this bomb now, you see," he said, "it's just a little one."

"I know," she said.

He goggled at her as if she'd said something very strange about beetroots.

"Honestly," he said, "it's very, very little."

"I know," she said again.

"But they say," his voice trailed on, "they say it can destroy everything that exists. And we have to do that, you see, I think. Will that make us alone? I don't know. It seems to be our function, though," he said, and dropped his head again.

"Whatever that means," said a hollow voice from the crowd.

Trillian slowly put her arms around the poor bewildered young Krikkiter and patted his trembling head on her shoulder.

"It's all right," she said quietly, but clearly enough for all the shadowy crowd to hear, "you don't have to do it."

She rocked him.

"You don't have to do it," she said again.

She let him go and stood back.

"I want you to do something for me," she said, and unexpectedly laughed.

"I want," she said, and laughed again. She put her hand over her mouth and then said, with a straight face, "I want you to take me to your leader," and she pointed into the War Zones in the sky. She seemed somehow to know that their leader would be there.

Her laughter seemed to discharge something in the atmosphere. From somewhere at the back of the crowd a single voice started to sing a tune that would have enabled Paul McCartney, had he written it, to buy the world.

Zaphod Beeblebrox crawled bravely along a tunnel, like the hell of a guy he was. He was very confused, but continued crawling doggedly anyway because he was that brave.

He was confused by something he had just seen, but not half as confused as he was going to be by something he was about to hear, so it would be best, at this point, to explain exactly where he was.

He was in the Robot War Zones many miles above the surface of the planet Krikkit.

The atmosphere was thin here, and relatively unprotected from any rays or anything that space might care to hurl in this direction.

He had parked the starship *Heart of Gold* among the huge jostling dim hulks that crowded the sky here above Krikkit, and had entered what appeared to be the biggest and most important of the sky buildings, armed with nothing but a Zap gun and something for his headaches.

He had found himself in a long, wide and badly lit corridor in which he was able to hide until he worked out what he was going to do next. He hid because every now and then one of the Krikkit robots would walk along it, and although he had so far led some kind of charmed life at their hands, it had nevertheless been an extremely painful one, and he had no desire to stretch what he was only half inclined to call his good fortune.

He had ducked, at one point, into a room leading off the corridor, and had discovered it to be a huge and, again, dimly lit chamber.

In fact, it was a museum with just one exhibit—the wreckage of a spacecraft. It was terribly burnt and mangled, and now that he had caught up with some of the Galactic history he had missed through his failed attempts to have sex with the girl in the cybercubicle next to him at school, he was able to put in an intelligent guess that this was the wrecked spaceship that had drifted through the Dust Cloud all those billions of years ago and started this whole business off.

But, and this is where he had become confused, there was something not at all right about it.

It was genuinely wrecked. It was genuinely burnt, but a fairly brief inspection by an experienced eye revealed that it was not a genuine spacecraft. It was as if it were a full-scale model of one—a solid blueprint. In other words it was a very useful thing to have around if you suddenly decided to build a spaceship yourself and didn't know how to do it. It was not, however, anything that would ever fly anywhere itself.

He was still puzzling over this—in fact he'd only just started to puzzle over it when he became aware that a door had slid open in another part of the chamber, and another couple of Krikkit robots had entered, looking a little glum.

Zaphod did not want to tangle with them and, deciding that just as discretion was the better part of valor, so was cowardice the better part of discretion, he valiantly hid himself in a closet.

The closet in fact turned out to be the top part of a shaft that led down through an inspection hatch into a wide ventilation tunnel. He let himself down into it and started to crawl along it.

He didn't like it. It was cold, dark and profoundly uncomfortable, and it frightened him. At the first opportunity—which was another shaft a hundred yards farther along—he climbed back up out of it.

This time he emerged into a smaller chamber, which appeared to be a computer intelligence center. He emerged in a dark narrow space between a large computer bank and the wall.

He quickly learned that he was not alone in the chamber and started to leave again, when he began to listen with interest to what the other occupants were saying.

"It's the robots, sir," said one voice, "there's something wrong with them."

"What, exactly?"

These were the voices of two War Command Krikkiters. All the War Commanders lived up in the sky in the Robot War Zones, and were largely immune to the whimsical doubts and uncertainties that were afflicting their fellows down on the surface of the planet.

"Well, sir, I think it's just as well that they are being phased out of the war effort, and that we are now going to detonate the supernova bomb. In the very short time since we were released from the envelope..."

"Get to the point."

"The robots aren't enjoying it, sir."

"What?"

"The war, sir, it seems to be getting them down. There's a certain world weariness about them, or perhaps I should say Universe weariness."

"Well, that's all right, they're meant to be helping to destroy it."

"Yes, well, they're finding it difficult, sir. They are afflicted with a certain lassitude. They're just finding it hard to get behind the job. They lack oomph."

"What are you trying to say?"

"Well, I think they're very depressed about something, sir."

"What on Krikkit are you talking about?"

"Well, in the few skirmishes they've had recently, it seems that they go into battle, raise their weapons to fire and suddenly think, why bother? What, cosmically speaking, is it all about? And they just seem to get a little tired and a little grim."

"And then what do they do?"

"Er, quadratic equations mostly, sir, fiendishly difficult ones by all accounts. And then they sulk."

"Sulk?"

"Yes, sir."

"Whoever heard of a robot sulking?"

"I don't know, sir."

"What was that noise?"

It was the noise of Zaphod leaving with his heads spinning.

Chapter 31

In a deep well of darkness a crippled robot sat. It had been silent in its metallic darkness for some time. It was cold and damp but, being a robot, it was supposed not to be able to notice these things. With an enormous effort of will, however, it did manage to notice them.

Its brain had been harnessed to the central intelligence core of the Krikkit War Computer. It wasn't enjoying the experience, and neither was the central intelligence core of the Krikkit War Computer.

The Krikkit robots who had salvaged this pathetic metal creature from the swamps of Sqornshellous Zeta had done so because they had recognized almost immediately its gigantic intelligence, and the use this could be to them.

They hadn't reckoned with the attendant personality disorders, which the coldness, the darkness, the dampness, the crampedness and the loneliness were doing nothing to decrease.

It was not happy with its task.

Apart from anything else, the mere coordination of an entire planet's military strategy was only taking up a tiny part of its formidable mind, and the rest of it had become extremely bored. Having solved all the major mathematical, physical, chemical, biological, sociological, philosophical, etymological, meteorological and psychological problems of the Universe except his own, three times over, he was severely stuck for something to do, and had taken up composing short dolorous ditties of no tone, or indeed tune. The latest one was a lullaby.

Marvin droned,

Now the world has gone to bed,
Darkness won't engulf my head,
I can see by infrared,
How I hate the night.

He paused to gather the artistic and emotional strength to tackle the next verse.

Now I lay me down to sleep,
Try to count electric sheep,
Sweet dream wishes you can keep,
How I hate the night.

"Marvin!" hissed a voice.

His head snapped up, almost dislodging the intricate network of electrodes that connected him to the central Krikkit War Computer.

An inspection hatch had opened and one of a pair of unruly heads was peering through while the other kept on jogging it by continually darting to look this way and that extremely nervously.

"Oh, it's you," muttered the robot, "I might have known."

"Hey, kid," said Zaphod in astonishment, "was that you singing just then?"

"I am," Marvin acknowledged bitterly, "in particularly scintillating form at the moment."

Zaphod poked his head in through the hatchway and looked around.

"Are you alone?" he said.

"Yes," said Marvin, "wearily I sit here, pain and misery my only companions. And vast intelligence of course. And infinite sorrow. And..."

"Yeah," said Zaphod, "hey, what's your connection with all this?"

"This," said Marvin, indicating with his less damaged arm all the electrodes that connected him with the Krikkit computer.

"Then," said Zaphod awkwardly, "I guess you must have saved my life. Twice."

"Three times," said Marvin.

Zaphod's head snapped round (his other one was looking hawkishly in entirely the wrong direction) just in time to see the lethal killer robot directly behind him seize up and start to smoke. It staggered backward and slumped against a wall. It slid down it. It slipped sideways, threw its head back and started to sob inconsolably.

Zaphod looked back at Marvin.

"You must have a terrific outlook on life," he said.

"Just don't even ask," said Marvin.

"I won't," said Zaphod, and didn't. "Hey, look" he added, "you're doing a terrific job."

"Which means, I suppose," said Marvin, and requiring only one ten thousand million billion trillion grillionth part of his mental powers to make this particular logical leap, "that you're not going to release me or anything like that."

"Kid, you know I'd love to."

"But you're not going to."

"No."

"I see."

"You're working well."

"Yes," said Marvin, "why stop now just when I'm hating it?"

"I have to go find Trillian and the guys. Hey, you any idea where they are? I mean, I just got a planet to choose from. Could take a while."

"They are very close," said Marvin dolefully. "You can monitor them from here if you like."

"I better go get them," asserted Zaphod; "er, maybe they need some help, right?"

"Maybe," said Marvin with unexpected authority in his lugubrious voice, "it would be better if you monitored them from here. That young girl," he added unexpectedly, "is one of the least benightedly unintelligent organic life forms it has been my profound lack of pleasure not to be able to avoid meeting."

Zaphod took a moment or two to find his way through this labyrinthine string of negatives and emerged at the other end with surprise.

"Trillian?" he said. "She's just a kid. Cute, yeah, but temperamental. You know how it is with women. Or perhaps you don't. I assume you don't. If you do I don't want to hear about it. Plug us in."

". . . totally manipulated."

"What?" said Zaphod.

It was Trillian speaking. He turned round.

The wall against which the Krikkit robot was sobbing had lit up to reveal a scene taking place in some other unknown part of the Krikkit Robot War Zones. It seemed to be a council chamber of some kind—Zaphod couldn't make it out too clearly because of the robot slumped against the screen.

He tried to move the robot, but it was heavy with its grief and tried to bite him, so he just looked around it as best he could.

"Just think about it," said Trillian's voice, "your history is just a series of freakishly improbable events. And I know an improbable event when I see one. Your complete isolation from the Galaxy was freakish for a start. Right out on the very edge with a Dust Cloud around you. It's a setup. Obviously."

Zaphod was mad with frustration that he couldn't see the screen. The robot's head was obscuring his view of the people Trillian was talking to, its multifunctional battleclub was obscuring the background, and the elbow of the arm it had pressed tragically against its brow was obscuring Trillian herself.

"Then," said Trillian, "this spaceship that crash-landed on your planet. That's really likely, isn't it? Have you any idea what the odds are against a drifting spaceship accidentally intersecting with the orbit of a planet?"

"Hey," said Zaphod, "she doesn't know what the zark she's talking about. I've seen that spaceship. It's a fake. No deal."

"I thought it might be," said Marvin from his prison behind Zaphod.

"Oh yeah," said Zaphod, "it's easy for you to say that. I just told you. Anyway, I don't see what it's got to do with anything."

"And especially," continued Trillian, "the odds against its intersecting with the orbit of the one planet in the Galaxy or with the whole of the Universe, as far as I know would be totally staggering. You don't know what the odds are? Nor do I, they're that big. Again, it's a setup. I wouldn't be surprised if that spaceship was just a fake."

Zaphod managed to move the robot's battleclub. Behind it on the screen were the figures of Ford, Arthur and Slartibartfast, who appeared astonished and bewildered by the whole thing.

"Hey, look," said Zaphod excitedly, "the guys are doing great. Rah, rah, rah! Go get 'em, guys."

"And what about," said Trillian, "all this technology you suddenly managed to build for yourselves almost overnight? Most people would take thousands of years to do all that. Someone was feeding you what you needed to know, someone was keeping you at it.

"I know, I know," she added in response to some unseen interruption, "I know you didn't realize it was going on. That is exactly my point. You never realized anything at all. Like this supernova bomb."

"How do you know about that?" said an unseen voice.

"I just know," said Trillian. "You expect me to believe that you are bright enough to invent something that brilliant and be too dumb to realize it would take you with it as well? That's not just stupid, that is spectacularly obtuse."

"Hey, what's this bomb thing?" said Zaphod in alarm to Marvin.

"The supernova bomb?" said Marvin. "It's a very, very small bomb."

"Yeah?"

"That would destroy the Universe completely," added Marvin. "Good idea, if you ask me. They won't get it to work though."

"Why not, if it's so brilliant?"

"It's brilliant," said Marvin, "they're not. They got as far as designing it before they were locked in the envelope. They've spent the last five years building it. They think they've got it right but they haven't. They're as stupid as any other organic life form. I hate them."

Trillian was continuing.

Zaphod tried to pull the Krikkit robot away by its leg, but it kicked and growled at him, and then quaked with a fresh outburst of sobbing. Then suddenly it slumped over and continued to express its feelings out of everybody's way on the floor.

Trillian was standing alone in the middle of the chamber, tired but with fiercely burning eyes.

Ranged in front of her were the pale-faced and wrinkled Elder Masters of Krikkit, motionless behind their widely curved control desk, staring at her with helpless fear and hatred.

In front of them, equidistant between their control desk and the middle of the chamber, where Trillian stood, as if on trial, was a slim white pillar about four feet tall. On top of it stood a small white globe, about three, maybe four inches in diameter.

Beside it stood a Krikkit robot with its multifunctional battleclub.

"In fact," explained Trillian, "you are so dumb stupid . . ." (She was sweating. Zaphod felt that this was an unattractive thing for her to be doing at this point.) "You are all so dumb stupid that I doubt, I very much *doubt*, if you've been able to build the bomb properly without any help from Hactar for the last five years."

"Who's this guy Hactar?" said Zaphod, squaring his shoulders.

If Marvin replied, Zaphod didn't hear him. All his attention was concentrated on the screen.

One of the Elders of Krikkit made a small motion with his hand toward the Krikkit robot. The robot raised its club.

"There's nothing I can do," said Marvin, "it's on an independent circuit from the others."

"Wait," said Trillian.

The Elder made a small motion. The robot halted. Trillian suddenly seemed very doubtful of her own judgment.

"How do you know all this?" said Zaphod to Marvin at this point.

"Computer records," said Marvin. "I have access."

"You're very different, aren't you," said Trillian to the Elders, "from your fellow worldlings down on the ground? You've spent all your lives up here, unprotected by the atmosphere. You've been vulnerable. The rest of your race is very frightened, you know, they don't want you to do this. You're out of touch, why don't you check up?"

The Krikkit Elder grew impatient. He made a gesture to the robot that was precisely the opposite of the gesture he had last made to it.

The robot swung its battleclub. It hit the small white globe.

The small white globe was the supernova bomb.

It was a very, very small bomb that was designed to bring the entire Universe to an end.

The supernova bomb flew through the air. It hit the back wall of the council chamber and dented it very badly.

"So how does she know all this?" said Zaphod.

Marvin kept a sullen silence.

"Probably just bluffing," said Zaphod. "Poor kid, I should never have left her alone."

Chapter 32

Hactar!" called Trillian. "What are you up to?"

There was no reply from the enclosing darkness. Trillian waited, nervously. She was sure that she couldn't be wrong. She peered into the gloom from which she had been expecting some kind of response. But there was only cold silence.

"Hactar?" she called again. "I would like you to meet my friend Arthur Dent. I wanted to go off with a Thunder God, but he wouldn't let me and I appreciate that. He made me realize where my affections really lay. Unfortunately Zaphod is too frightened by all this, so I brought Arthur instead. I'm not sure why I'm telling you all this.

"Hello?" she said again. "Hactar?"

And then it came.

It was thin and feeble, like a voice carried on the wind from a great distance, half heard, a memory or a dream of a voice.

"Won't you both come out," said this voice. "I promise that you will be perfectly safe."

They glanced at each other, and then stepped out, improbably, along the shaft of light that streamed out of the open hatchway of the *Heart of Gold* into the dim granular darkness of the Dust Cloud.

Arthur tried to hold her hand to steady and reassure her, but she wouldn't let him. He held on to his airline bag with its tin of Greek olive oil, its towel, its crumpled postcards of Santorini and its other odds and ends. He steadied and reassured that instead.

They were standing on, and in, nothing.

Murky, dusty nothing. Each grain of dust of the pulverized computer sparkled dimly as it turned and twisted slowly, catching the sunlight in the darkness. Each particle of the computer, each speck of dust held within itself, faintly and weakly, the pattern of the whole. In reducing the computer to dust the Silastic Armorfiends of Striterax had merely crippled the computer, not killed it. A weak and insubstantial field held the particles in slight relationship with each other.

Arthur and Trillian stood, or rather floated, in the middle of this bizarre entity. They had nothing to breathe, but for the moment this seemed not to matter. Hactar kept his promise. They were safe. For the moment.

"I have nothing to offer you by way of hospitality," said Hactar faintly, "but tricks of the light. It is possible to be comfortable with tricks of the light, though, if that is all you have."

His voice evanesced, and in the dark a long, velvet paisley-covered sofa coalesced into hazy shape.

Arthur could hardly bear the fact that it was the same sofa that had appeared to him in the fields of prehistoric Earth. He wanted to shout and shake with rage that the Universe kept doing these insanely bewildering things to him.

He let this feeling subside, and then sat on the sofa—carefully. Trillian sat on it, too.

It was real.

At least, if it wasn't real, it did support them, and as that is what sofas are supposed to do, this, by any test that mattered, was a real sofa.

The voice on the solar wind breathed to them again.

"I hope you are comfortable," it said.

They nodded.

"And I would like to congratulate you on the accuracy of your deductions."

Arthur quickly pointed out that he hadn't deduced anything much himself, Trillian was the one. She had simply asked him along because he was interested in life, the Universe and everything.

"That is something in which I, too, am interested," breathed Hactar.

"Well," said Arthur, "we should have a chat about it sometime. Over a cup of tea."

There slowly materialized in front of them a small wooden table on which sat a silver teapot, a bone china milk jug, a bone china sugar bowl and two bone china cups and saucers.

Arthur reached forward, but they were just a trick of the light. He leaned back on the sofa, which was an illusion his body was prepared to accept as comfortable.

"Why," said Trillian, "do you feel you have to destroy the Universe?"

She found it a little difficult talking into nothingness, with nothing on which to focus. Hactar obviously noticed this. He chuckled a ghostly chuckle.

"If it's going to be that sort of session," he said, "we may as well have the right sort of setting."

And now there materialized in front of them something new. It was the dim hazy image of a couch—a psychiatrist's couch. The leather with which it was upholstered was shiny and sumptuous, but again, it was only a trick of the light.

Around them, to complete the setting, was the hazy suggestion of wood-paneled walls. And then, on the couch, appeared the image of Hactar himself, and it was an eye-twisting image.

The couch looked normal size for a psychiatrist's couch—about five or six feet long.

The computer looked normal size for a black spaceborne computer satellite—about a thousand miles across.

The illusion that the one was sitting on top of the other was the thing that made the eyes twist.

"All right," said Trillian firmly. She stood up from the sofa. She felt that she was being asked to feel too comfortable and to accept too many illusions.

"Very good," she said. "Can you construct real things, too? I mean solid objects?"

Again, there was the pause before the answer, as if the pulverized mind of Hactar had to collect its thoughts from the millions and millions of miles over which it was scattered.

"Ah," he sighed, "you are thinking of the spaceship."

Thoughts seemed to drift by them and through them, like waves through the ether.

"Yes," he acknowledged, "I can. But it takes enormous effort and time. All I can do in my . . . particle state, you see, is encourage and suggest. Encourage and suggest. And suggest . . ."

The image of Hactar on the couch seemed to billow and waver, as if finding it hard to maintain itself.

It gathered new strength.

"I can encourage and suggest," it said, "tiny pieces of space debris—the odd minute meteor, a few molecules here, a few hydrogen atoms there—to move together. I encourage them together. I can tease them into shape, but it takes many eons."

"So, did you make," asked Trillian again, "the model of the wrecked spacecraft?"

"Er . . . yes," murmured Hactar, "I have mad . . . a few things. I can move them about. I made the spacecraft. It seemed best to do."

Something at this point made Arthur pick up his tote bag from where he had left it on the sofa and grasp it tightly.

The mist of Hactar's ancient shattered mind swirled about them as if uneasy dreams were moving through it.

"I repented, you see," he murmured dolefully. "I repented of sabotaging my own design for the Silastic Armorfiends. It was not my place to make such decisions. I was created to fulfill a function and I failed in it. I negated my own existence."

Hactar sighed, and they waited in silence for him to continue his story.

"You were right," he said at length. "I deliberately nurtured the planet of Krikkit till they would arrive at the same state of mind as the Silastic Armorfiends, and require of me the design of the bomb I failed to make the first time. I wrapped myself around the planet and coddled it. Under the influence of events I was able to engineer, and influences I was able to generate, they learned to hate like maniacs. I had to make them live in the sky. On the ground my influences were too weak.

"Without me, of course, when they were locked away from me in the envelope of Slo-Time, their responses became very confused and they were unable to manage.

"Ah well, ah well," he added, "I was only trying to fulfill my function."

And very gradually, very, very slowly, the images in the cloud began to fade, gently to melt away.

And then suddenly, they stopped fading.

"There was also the matter of revenge, of course," said Hactar, with a sharpness that was new in his voice.

"Remember," he said, "that I was pulverized, and then left in a crippled and semi-impotent state for billions of years. I honestly would rather like to wipe out the Universe. You would feel the same way, believe me."

He paused again, as eddies swept through the dust.

"But primarily," he said in his former, wistful tone, "I was trying to fulfill my function. Ah well."

Trillian said, "Does it worry you that you have failed?"

"Have I failed?" whispered Hactar. The image of the computer on the psychiatrist's couch began slowly to fade again.

"Ah well, ah well," the fading voice intoned again, "no, failure doesn't bother me now."

"You know what we have to do?" said Trillian, her voice cold and businesslike.

"Yes," said Hactar, "you're going to disperse me. You are going to destroy my consciousness. Please be my guest—after all these eons, oblivion is all I crave. If I haven't already fulfilled my function, then it's too late now. Thank you and good night."

The sofa vanished.

The tea table vanished.

The couch and the computer vanished. The walls were gone. Arthur and Trillian made their cautious way back into the *Heart of Gold*.

"Well, that," said Arthur, "would appear to be that."

The flames danced higher in front of him and then subsided. A few last licks and they were gone, leaving him with just a pile of Ashes, where a few minutes previously there had been the Wooden Pillar of Nature and Spirituality.

He scooped them off the hob of the *Heart of Gold*'s Gamma Barbecue, put them in a paper bag and walked back onto the bridge.

"I think we should take them back," he said. "I feel that very strongly."

He had already had an argument with Slartibartfast on this matter, and eventually the old man had got annoyed and left. He had returned to his own ship, the *Bistromath*, had a furious row with the waiter and disappeared off into an entirely subjective idea of what space was.

The argument had arisen because Arthur's idea of returning the Ashes to Lord's Cricket Ground at the same moment they were originally taken would involve traveling back in time a day or so, and this was precisely the sort of gratuitous and irresponsible mucking about that the Campaign for Real Time was trying to put a stop to.

"Yes," Arthur had said, "but you try and explain that to the M.C.C.," and would hear no more against the idea.

"I think," he said again and stopped. The reason he started to say it again was that no one had listened to him the first time, and the reason he stopped was that it looked fairly clear that no one was going to listen to him this time either.

Ford, Zaphod and Trillian were watching the visiscreen intently. Hactar was dispersing under pressure from a vibration field which the *Heart of Gold* was pumping into it.

"What did it say?" asked Ford.

"I thought I heard it say," said Trillian in a puzzled voice, " 'What's done is done . . . I have fulfilled my function. . . .' "

"I think we should take these back," said Arthur, holding up the bag containing the Ashes. "I feel that very strongly."

Chapter 33

The sun was shining calmly on a scene of complete havoc.

Smoke was still billowing across the burnt grass in the wake of the theft of the Ashes by the Krikkit robots. Through the smoke people were running panic-stricken, colliding with each other, tripping over stretchers, being arrested.

One policeman was attempting to arrest Wowbagger the Infinitely Prolonged for insulting behavior, but was unable to prevent the tall gray green alien from returning to his ship and arrogantly flying away, thus causing even more panic and pandemonium.

In the middle of this suddenly materialized for the second time that afternoon the figures of Arthur Dent and Ford Prefect, who had teleported down out of the *Heart of Gold* which was now in parking orbit round the planet.

"I can explain," shouted Arthur. "I have the Ashes! They're in this bag."

"I don't think you have their attention," said Ford.

"I have also helped save the Universe," called Arthur to anyone who was prepared to listen, in other words no one.

"That should have been a crowd stopper," said Arthur to Ford.

"It wasn't," said Ford.

Arthur accosted a policeman who was running past.

"Excuse me," he said, "the Ashes. I've got them. They were stolen by those white robots a moment ago. I've got them in this bag. They were part of the Key to the Slo-Time envelope, you see, and well, anyway, you can guess the rest, the point is I've got them and what should I do with them?"

The policeman told him, but Arthur could only assume that he was speaking metaphorically.

He wandered about disconsolately.

"Is no one interested?" he shouted out. A man rushed past him and jogged his elbow; he dropped the paper bag and it spilled its contents all over the ground. Arthur stared down at it with a tight set mouth.

Ford looked at him.

"Wanna go now?" he said.

Arthur heaved a heavy sigh. He looked around at the planet Earth, for what he was now certain would be the last time.

"Okay," he said.

At that moment, he caught sight, through the clearing smoke, of one of the wickets, still standing in spite of everything.

"Hold on a moment," he said to Ford, "when I was a boy..."

"Can you tell me later?"

"I had a passion for cricket, you know, but I wasn't very good at it."

"Or not at all if you prefer."

"And I always dreamed, rather stupidly, that one day I would bowl at Lord's."

He looked around him at the panic-stricken throng. No one was going to mind very much.

"Okay," said Ford wearily, "get it over with. I shall be over there," he added, "being bored." He went and sat down on a patch of smoking grass.

Arthur remembered that on their first visit there that afternoon, the cricket ball had actually landed in his bag, and he looked through the bag.

He had already found the ball in it before he remembered that it wasn't the same bag that he'd had at the time. Still, there it was among the souvenirs of Greece.

He took it out and polished it against his hip, spat on it and polished it again. He put the bag down. He was going to do this properly.

He tossed the small hard red ball from hand to hand, feeling its weight.

With a wonderful feeling of lightness and unconcern, he trotted off away from the wicket. A medium-fast pace, he decided, and measured a good long run up.

He looked up into the sky. The birds were wheeling about it, a few white clouds scudded across it. The air was disturbed with the sound of police and ambulance sirens, and people screaming and yelling, but he felt curiously happy and untouched by it all. He was going to bowl a ball at Lord's.

He turned, and pawed a couple of times at the ground with his bedroom slippers. He squared his shoulders, tossed the ball in the air and caught it again.

He started to run.

As he ran, he suddenly saw that standing at the wicket was a batsman.

"Oh, good," he thought, "that should add a little..."

Then, as his running feet took him nearer he saw more clearly. The batsman standing ready at the wicket was not one of the England cricket team. He was not one of the Australian cricket team. It was one of the robot Krikkit team. It was a cold, hard, lethal white killer robot that presumably had not returned to its ship with the others.

Quite a few thoughts collided in Arthur Dent's mind at this moment, but he didn't seem to be able to stop running. Time suddenly seemed to be going terribly, terribly slowly, but still he didn't seem to be able to stop running.

Moving as if through syrup he slowly turned his troubled head and looked at his own hand, the hand that was holding the small hard red ball.

His feet were pounding slowly onward, unstoppably, as he stared at the ball gripped in his helpless hand. It was emitting a deep red glow, and flashing intermittently. And still his feet were pounding inexorably forward.

He looked at the Krikkit robot again standing implacably still and purposeful in front of him, battleclub raised in readiness. Its eyes were burning with a deep cold fascinating light, and Arthur could not move his own eyes from them. He seemed to be looking down a tunnel at them— nothing on either side seemed to exist.

Some of the thoughts that were colliding in his mind at this time were these:

He felt a hell of a fool.

He felt that he should have listened rather more carefully to a number of things he had heard said, phrases that now pounded round his mind as his feet pounded onward to the point where he would inevitably release the ball to the Krikkit robot, who would inevitably strike it.

He remembered Hactar saying, "Have I failed? Failure doesn't bother me."

He remembered the account of Hactar's dying words, "What's done is done. I have fulfilled my function."

He remembered Hactar saying that he had managed to make "a few things."

He remembered the sudden movement in his tote bag that had made him grip it tightly to himself when he was in the Dust Cloud.

He remembered that he had traveled back in time a couple of days to come to Lord's again.

He also remembered that he wasn't a very good bowler.

He felt his arm coming round, gripping tightly onto the ball that he now knew for certain was the supernova bomb, which Hactar had built himself and planted on him, the bomb which would cause the Universe to come to an abrupt and premature end.

He hoped and prayed that there wasn't an afterlife. Then he realized there was a contradiction involved here and merely hoped that there wasn't an afterlife.

He would feel very, very embarrassed meeting everybody.

He hoped, he hoped, he hoped that his bowling was as bad as he remembered it to be, because that seemed to be the only thing now standing between this moment and universal oblivion.

He felt his legs pounding, he felt his arm coming round, he felt his feet connecting with the airline bag he'd stupidly left lying on the ground in front of him, he felt himself falling heavily forward, but having his mind so terribly full of other things at this point, he completely forgot about hitting the ground and didn't.

Still holding the ball firmly in his right hand he soared up into the air whimpering with surprise.

He wheeled and whirled through the air, spinning out of control.

He twisted down toward the ground, flinging himself hectically through the air, at the same time hurling the bomb harmlessly off into the distance.

He hurtled toward the astounded robot from behind. It still had its multifunctional battleclub raised, but had suddenly been deprived of anything to hit.

With a sudden mad outburst of strength, he wrested the battleclub from the grip of the startled robot, executed a dazzling banking turn in the air, hurtled back down in a furious power dive and with one crazy swing knocked the robot's head from the robot's shoulders.

"Are you coming now?" said Ford.

Chapter 34

And at the end they traveled again.

There was a time when Arthur Dent would not. He said that the Bistromathic Drive had revealed to him that time and distance were one, that mind and Universe were one, that perception and reality were one, and that the more one traveled the more one stayed in one place, and that what with one thing and another he would rather just stay put for a while and sort it all out in his mind, which was now at one with the Universe so it shouldn't take too long and he could get a good rest afterward, put in a little flying practice and learn to cook, which he had always meant to do. The can of Greek olive oil was now his most prized possession, and he said that the way it had unexpectedly turned up in his life had again given him a certain sense of the oneness of things, which, which made him feel that . . .

He yawned and fell asleep.

In the morning as they prepared to take him to some quiet and idyllic planet where they wouldn't mind his talking like that, they suddenly picked up a computer-driven distress call and diverted to investigate.

A small but apparently undamaged spacecraft of the Merida class seemed to be dancing a strange little jig through the void. A brief computer scan revealed that the ship was fine, its computer was fine but that its pilot was mad.

"Half-mad, half-mad," the man insisted as they carried him, raving, aboard.

He was a journalist with the Sidereal *Daily Mentioner*. They sedated him and sent Marvin in to keep him company until he promised to try to talk sense.

"I was covering a trial," he said at last, "on Argabuthon."

He pushed himself up onto his thin and wasted shoulders; his eyes stared wildly. His white hair seemed to be waving at someone it knew in the next room.

"Easy, easy," said Ford. Trillian put a soothing hand on his shoulder.

The man sank back down again, and stared at the ceiling of the ship's sick bay.

"The case," he said, "is now immaterial, but there was a witness . . . a witness . . . a man called . . . called Prak. A strange and difficult man. They were eventually forced to administer a drug to make him tell the truth, a truth drug."

His eyes rolled helplessly in his head.

"They gave him too much," he said in a tiny whimper, "they gave him much too much." He started to cry. "I think the robots must have jogged the surgeon's arm."

"Robots?" asked Zaphod sharply. "What robots?"

"Some white robots," whispered the man hoarsely, "broke into the courtroom and stole the Judge's Scepter, the Argabuthon Scepter of Justice, nasty plastic thing. I don't know why they wanted it"—he began to cry again—"and I think they jogged the surgeon's arm. . . ."

He shook his head loosely from side to side, helplessly, sadly, his eyes screwed up in pain.

"And when the trial continued," he said in a weeping whisper, "they asked Prak a most unfortunate thing. They asked him"—he paused and shivered—"to tell the Truth, the Whole Truth and Nothing but the Truth. Only, don't you see?"

He suddenly hoisted himself up onto his elbows again and shouted at them.

"They'd given him much too much of the drug!"

He collapsed again, moaning quietly. "Much too much too much too much too . . ."

The group gathered around his bedside glanced at one another. There were goose bumps on backs.

"What happened?" said Zaphod at last.

"Oh, he told it all right," said the man savagely, "for all I know he's still telling it now. Strange, terrible things . . . terrible terrible!" he screamed.

They tried to calm him, but he struggled to his elbows again.

"Terrible things, incomprehensible things," he shouted, "things that would drive a man mad!"

He stared wildly at them.

"Or in my case," he said, "half-mad. I'm a journalist."

"You mean," said Arthur quietly, "that you are used to confronting the truth?"

"No," said the man with a puzzled frown, "I mean that I made an excuse and left early."

He collapsed into a coma from which he recovered only once and briefly.

On that one occasion, they discovered from him the following:

When it became clear what was happening, and as it became clear that Prak could not be stopped, that here was truth in its absolute and final form, the court was cleared.

Not only cleared, it was sealed up, with Prak still in it. Steel walls were erected around it, and, just to be on the safe side, barbed wire, electric fences, crocodile swamps and three major armies were installed, so that no one would ever have to hear Prak speak.

"That's a pity," said Arthur. "I'd like to hear what he has to say. Presumably he would know what the Question to the Ultimate Answer is. It's always bothered me that we never found out."

"Think of a number," said the computer, "any number."

Arthur told the computer the telephone number of King's Cross railway station passenger inquiries, on the grounds that it must have some function, and this might turn out to be it.

The computer injected the number into the ship's reconstituted Improbability Drive.

In Relativity, Matter tells Space how to curve, and Space tells Matter how to move.

The *Heart of Gold* told space to get knotted, and parked itself neatly within the inner steel perimeter of the Argabuthon Chamber of Law.

The courtroom was an austere place, a large dark chamber, clearly designed for justice rather than, for instance, pleasure. You wouldn't hold a dinner party there, at least not a successful one. The decor would get your guests down.

The ceilings were high, vaulted and very dark. Shadows lurked there with grim determination. The paneling for the walls and benches, the cladding of the heavy pillars, all were carved from the darkest and most severe trees in the fearsome Forest of Arglebard. The massive black podium of justice which dominated the center of the chamber was a monster of gravity. If a sunbeam had ever managed to slink this far into the justice complex of Argabuthon it would have turned around and slunk straight back out again.

Arthur and Trillian were the first in, while Ford and Zaphod bravely kept a watch on their rear.

At first it seemed totally dark and deserted. Their footsteps echoed hollowly round the chamber. This seemed curious. All the defenses were still in position and operative around the outside of the building, they had run scan checks. Therefore, they had assumed, the truth-telling must still be going on.

But there was nothing.

Then, as their eyes became accustomed to the darkness they spotted a dull red glow in a corner, and behind the glow a live shadow. They swung a flashlight round onto it.

Prak was lounging on a bench, smoking a listless cigarette.

"Hi," he said, with a little half-wave. His voice echoed through the chamber. He was a little man with scraggy hair. He sat with his shoulders hunched forward and his head and knees kept jiggling. He took a drag of his cigarette.

They stared at him.

"What's going on?" said Trillian.

"Nothing," said the man, and jiggled his shoulders.

Arthur shone his flashlight full on Prak's face.

"We thought," he said, "that you were meant to be telling the Truth, the Whole Truth and Nothing but the Truth."

"Oh, that," said Prak, "yeah. I was. I finished. There's not nearly as much of it as people imagine. Some of it's pretty funny though."

He suddenly exploded into about three seconds of maniacal laughter and stopped again. He sat there, jiggling his head and knees. He dragged on his cigarette with a strange half-smile.

Ford and Zaphod came forward out of the shadows.

"Tell us about it," said Ford.

"Oh, I can't remember any of it now," said Prak. "I thought of writing some of it down, but first I couldn't find a pencil, and then I thought, why bother?"

There was a long silence, during which they thought they could feel the Universe age a little. Prak stared into the light.

"None of it?" said Arthur at last. "You can remember none of it?"

"No. Except most of the good bits were about frogs, I remember that."

Suddenly he was hooting with laughter again and stamping his feet on the ground.

"You would not believe some of the things about frogs," he gasped. "Come on, let's go out and find ourselves a frog. Boy, will I ever see *them* in a new light!" He leaped to his feet and did a tiny little dance. Then he stopped and took a long drag at his cigarette.

"Let's find a frog I can laugh at," he said simply. "Anyway, who are you guys?"

"We came to find you," said Trillian, deliberately not keeping the disappointment out of her voice. "My name is Trillian."

Prak jiggled his head.

"Ford Prefect," said Ford Prefect with a shrug.

Prak jiggled his head.

"And I," said Zaphod, when he judged that the silence was once again deep enough to allow an announcement of such gravity to be tossed in lightly, "am Zaphod Beeblebrox."

Prak jiggled his head.

"Who's this guy?" said Prak, jiggling his shoulder at Arthur, who was standing silent for a moment, lost in disappointed thoughts.

"Me?" said Arthur. "Oh, my name's Arthur Dent."

Prak's eyes popped out of his head.

"No kidding?" he yelped. "You are Arthur Dent? *The* Arthur Dent?"

He staggered backward, clutching his stomach and convulsed with fresh paroxysms of laughter.

"Hey, just think of meeting *you!*" he gasped. "Boy," he shouted, "you are the most ... wow, you just leave the frogs standing!"

He howled and screamed with laughter. He fell over backward onto the bench. He hollered and yelled in hysterics. He cried with laughter, kicked his legs in the air, he beat his chest. Gradually he subsided, panting. He looked at them. He looked at Arthur. He fell back again howling with laughter. Eventually he fell asleep.

Arthur stood there with his lips twitching while the others carried Prak comatose on to the ship.

"Before we picked up Prak," said Arthur, "I was going to leave. I still want to, and I think I should do so as soon as possible."

The others nodded in silence, a silence only slightly undermined by the heavily muffled and distant sound of hysterical laughter that came drifting from Prak's cabin at the farthest end of the ship.

"We have questioned him," continued Arthur, "or at least, you have questioned him—I, as you know, can't go near him—on everything, and he doesn't really seem to have anything to contribute. Just the occasional snippet, and things I don't wish to hear about frogs."

The others tried not to smirk.

"Now, I am the first to appreciate a joke," said Arthur, and then had to wait for the others to stop laughing.

"I am the first..." He stopped again. This time he stopped and listened to the silence. There actually was silence this time, and it had come very suddenly.

Prak was quiet. For days they had lived with constant maniacal laughter ringing round the ship, only occasionally relieved by short periods of light giggling and sleep. Arthur's very soul was clenched with paranoia.

This was not the silence of sleep. A buzzer sounded. A glance at a board told them that the buzzer had been sounded by Prak.

"He's not well," said Trillian, quietly. "The constant laughing is completely wrecking his body."

Arthur's lips twitched but he said nothing.

"We'd better go and see him," said Trillian.

Trillian came out of the cabin wearing her serious face.

"He wants you to go in," she said to Arthur, who was wearing his glum and tight-lipped one. He thrust his hands deep into his dressing-gown pockets and tried to think of something to say which wouldn't sound petty. It seemed terribly unfair, but he couldn't.

"Please," said Trillian.

He shrugged, and went in, taking his glum and tight-lipped face with him, despite the reaction this always provoked from Prak.

He looked down at his tormentor, who was lying quietly on the bed, ashen and wasted. His breathing was very shallow. Ford and Zaphod were standing by the bed looking awkward.

"You wanted to ask me something," said Prak in a thin voice and coughed slightly.

Just the cough made Arthur stiffen, but it passed and subsided.

"How do you know that?" he asked.

Prak shrugged weakly.

" 'Cos it's true," he said simply.

Arthur took the point.

"Yes," he said at last in rather a strained drawl, "I did have a question. Or rather, what I actually have is an answer. I wanted to know what the question was."

Prak nodded sympathetically, and Arthur relaxed a little.

"It's . . . well, it's a long story," he said, "but the question I would like to know, is the Ultimate Question of Life, the Universe and Everything. All we know about it is that the Answer is Forty-two, which is a little aggravating."

Prak nodded again.

"Forty-two," he said, "yes, that's right."

He paused. Shadows of thought and memory crossed his face like the shadows of clouds crossing the land.

"I'm afraid," he said at last, "that the Question and the Answer are mutually exclusive. Knowledge of one logically precludes knowledge of the other. It is impossible that both can ever be known about the same Universe."

He paused again. Disappointment crept into Arthur's face and snuggled down into its accustomed place.

"Except," said Prak, struggling to sort a thought out, "if it happened, it seems that the Question and the Answer would just cancel each other out, and take the Universe with them, which would then be replaced by something even more bizarrely inexplicable. It is possible that this has already happened," he added with a weak smile, "but there is a certain amount of uncertainty about it."

A little giggle brushed through him.

Arthur sat down on a stool.

"Oh, well," he said with resignation, "I was just hoping there would be some sort of reason."

"Do you know," said Prak, "the story of the reason?"

Arthur said that he didn't, and Prak said that he knew that he didn't. He told it.

One night, he said, a spaceship appeared in the sky of a planet that had never seen one before. The planet was Dalforsas, the ship was this one. It appeared as a brilliant new star moving silently across the heavens.

Primitive Tribesmen who were sitting huddled on the Cold Hillsides looked up from their steaming night drinks and pointed with trembling fingers, and swore that they had seen a sign, a sign from their Gods that meant that they must now arise at last and go and slay the evil Princes of the Plains.

In the high turrets of their palaces, the Princes of the Plains looked up and saw the shining star, and received it unmistakably as a sign from their

Gods that they must go and attack the accursed Tribesmen of the Cold Hillsides.

And between them, the Dwellers in the Forest looked up into the sky and saw the sign of the new star, and saw it with fear and apprehension, for though they had never seen anything like it before, they, too, knew precisely what it foreshadowed, and they bowed their heads in despair.

They knew that when the rains came, it was a sign.

When the rains departed, it was a sign.

When the winds rose, it was a sign.

When the winds fell, it was a sign.

When in the land there was born at the midnight of a full moon a goat with three heads, that was a sign.

When in the land there was born at some time in the afternoon a perfectly normal cat or pig with no birth complications, or even just a child with a retroussé nose, that, too, would often be taken as a sign.

So there was no doubt at all that a new star in the sky was a sign of a particularly spectacular order.

And each new sign signified the same thing—that the Princes of the Plains and the Tribesmen of the Cold Hillsides were about to beat the hell out of each other again.

This in itself wouldn't be so bad, except that the Princes of the Plains and the Tribesmen of the Cold Hillsides always elected to beat the hell out of each other in the Forest, and it was always the Dwellers in the Forest who came off worst in these exchanges, though as far as they could see it never had anything to do with them.

And sometimes, after some of the worst of these outrages, the Dwellers in the Forest would send a Messenger to either the Leader of the Princes of the Plains or the Leader of the Tribesmen of the Cold Hillsides and demand to know the reason for this intolerable behavior.

And the Leader, whichever one it was, would take the Messenger aside and explain the reason to him, slowly and carefully, and with great attention to the considerable detail involved.

And the terrible thing was, it was a very good one. It was very clear, very rational and tough. The Messenger would hang his head and feel sad and foolish that he had not realized what a tough and complex place the real world was, and what difficulties and paradoxes had to be embraced if one was to live in it.

"Now do you understand?" the Leader would say.

The Messenger would nod dumbly.

"And you see these battles have to take place?"

Another dumb nod.

"And why they have to take place in the Forest, and why it is in everybody's best interest, the Forest Dwellers included, that they should?"

"Er . . ."

"In the long run."

"Er, yes."

And the Messenger did understand the reason, and he returned to his people in the Forest. But as he approached them, as he walked through the Forest and among the trees, he found that all he could remember of the reason was how terribly clear the argument had seemed. What it actually was, he couldn't remember at all.

And this, of course, was a great comfort when next the Tribesmen and the Princes came hacking and burning their way through the Forest, killing every Forest Dweller in their way.

Prak paused in his story and coughed pathetically.

"I was the Messenger," he said, "after the battles precipitated by the appearance of your ship, which were particularly savage. Many of our people died. I thought I could bring the reason back. I went, and was told it by the Leader of the Princes, but on the way back it slipped and melted away in my mind like snow in the sun. That was many years ago, and much has happened since then."

He looked up at Arthur, and giggled again very gently.

"There is one other thing I can remember from the truth drug, apart from the frogs, and that is God's last message to his creation. Would you like to hear it?"

For a moment they didn't know whether to take him seriously.

" 'S true," he said, "for real. I mean it."

His chest heaved weakly and he struggled for breath. His head lolled slightly.

"I wasn't very impressed with it when I first knew what it was," he said, "but now I think back to how impressed I was by the Prince's reason, and how soon afterward I couldn't recall it at all, I think it might be a lot more helpful. Would you like to know what it is? Would you?"

They nodded dumbly.

"I bet you would. If you're that interested I suggest you go and look for it. It is written in thirty-foot-high letters of fire on top of the Quentulus Quazgar Mountains in the land of Sevorbeupstry on the planet Preliumtarn, third out from the sun Zarss in Galactic Sector QQ7 ActiveJ Gamma. It is guarded by the Lajestic Vantrashell of Lob."

There was a long silence following this announcement, which was finally broken by Arthur.

"Sorry, it's where?" he said.

"It is written," repeated Prak, "in thirty-foot-high letters of fire on top of the Quentulus Quazgar Mountains in the land of Sevorbeupstry on the planet Preliumtarn, third out from the..."

"Sorry," said Arthur again, "which mountains?"

"The Quentulus Quazgar Mountains in the land of Sevorbeupstry on the planet..."

"Which land was that? I didn't quite catch it."

"Sevorbeupstry, on the planet..."

"Sevorbe what?"

"Oh, for heaven's sake," said Prak, and died testily.

In the following days Arthur thought a little about this message, but in the end he decided that he was not going to allow himself to be drawn by it, and insisted on following his original plan of finding a nice little world somewhere to settle down and lead a quiet retired life. Having saved the Universe twice in one day he thought that he could take things a little easier from now on.

They dropped him off on the planet Krikkit, which was now once again a pleasant idyllic pastoral world, even if the songs did occasionally get on his nerves.

He spent a lot of time flying.

He learned to communicate with birds and discovered that their conversation was fantastically boring. It was all to do with wind speed, wingspans, power-to-weight ratios and a fair bit about berries. Unfortunately, he discovered, once you have learned birdspeak you quickly come to realize that the air is full of it the whole time, just inane bird chatter. There is no getting away from it.

For that reason Arthur eventually gave up the sport and learned to live on the ground and love it, despite the inane chatter he heard down there as well.

One day he was walking through the fields humming a ravishing tune he'd heard recently when a silver spaceship descended from the sky and landed in front of him.

A hatchway opened, a ramp extended and a tall gray green alien marched out and approached him.

"Arthur Phili..." it said, then glanced sharply at him, and down at his clipboard. It frowned. It looked up at him again.

"I've done you before, haven't I?" it said.

So Long, and Thanks for All the Fish

For Jane

With thanks
to Rick and Heidi for the loan of
their stable event
to Mogens and Andy and all at
Huntsham Court for a number of
unstable events
and especially to Sonny Mehta
for being stable through all events.

Far out in the uncharted backwaters of the unfashionable end of the Western Spiral arm of the Galaxy lies a small unregarded yellow sun.

Orbiting this at a distance of roughly ninety-eight million miles is an utterly insignificant little blue-green planet whose ape-descended life forms are so amazingly primitive that they still think digital watches are a pretty neat idea.

This planet has—or rather, had—a problem, which was this: most of the people living on it were unhappy for pretty much of the time.

Many solutions were suggested for this problem, but most of these were largely concerned with the movements of small green pieces of paper, which is odd because on the whole it wasn't the small green pieces of paper that were unhappy.

And so the problem remained; lots of the people were mean, and most of them were miserable, even the ones with digital watches.

Many were increasingly of the opinion that they'd all made a big mistake in coming down from the trees in the first place. And some said that even the trees had been a bad move and that no one should ever have left the oceans.

And then, one Thursday, nearly two thousand years after one man had been nailed to a tree for saying how great it would be to be nice to people for a change, a girl sitting on her own in a small café in Rickmansworth suddenly realized what it was that had been going wrong all this time, and she finally knew how the world could be made a good and happy place. This time it was right, it would work, and no one would have to get nailed to anything.

Sadly, however, before she could get to a phone to tell anyone about it, the Earth was unexpectedly demolished to make way for a new hyperspace bypass, and so the idea was lost, seemingly for ever.

This is her story.

Chapter 1

That evening it was dark early, which was normal for the time of year. It was cold and windy, which was normal.

It started to rain, which was particularly normal.

A spacecraft landed, which was not.

There was nobody around to see it except for some spectacularly stupid quadrupeds who hadn't the faintest idea what to make of it, or whether they were meant to make anything of it, or eat it, or what. So they did what they did to everything, which was to run away from it and try to hide under each other, which never worked.

It slipped down out of the clouds, seeming to be balanced on a single beam of light.

From a distance you would scarcely have noticed it through the lightning and the storm clouds, but seen from close up to it was strangely beautiful—a gray craft of elegantly sculpted form; quite small.

Of course, one never has the slightest notion what size or shape different species are going to turn out to be, but if you were to take the findings of the latest Mid-Galactic Census report as any kind of accurate guide to statistical averages you would probably guess that the craft would hold about six people, and you would be right.

You'd probably guessed that anyway. The Census report, like most such surveys, had cost an awful lot of money and told nobody anything they didn't already know—except that every single person in the Galaxy had 2.4 legs and owned a hyena. Since this was clearly not true the whole thing eventually had to be scrapped.

The craft slid quietly down through the rain, its dim operating lights seeming to wrap it in tasteful rainbows. It hummed very quietly, a hum that became gradually louder and deeper as it approached the ground and which at an altitude of six inches became a heavy throb.

At last it dropped and was quiet.

A hatchway opened. A short flight of steps unfolded itself.

A light appeared in the opening, a bright light streaming out into the wet night, and shadows moved within.

A tall figure appeared in the light, looked around, flinched, and hurried down the steps, carrying a large shopping bag under his arm.

He turned and gave a single abrupt wave back to the ship. Already the rain was streaming through his hair.

"Thank you," he called out, "thank you very—"

He was interrupted by a sharp crack of thunder. He glanced up apprehensively, and in response to a sudden thought started quickly to rummage through the large plastic shopping bag, which he now discovered had a hole in the bottom.

It had large characters printed on the side which read (to anyone who could decipher the Centaurian alphabet) DUTY FREE MEGA-MARKET, PORT BRASTA, ALPHA CENTAURI. BE LIKE THE TWENTY-SECOND ELEPHANT WITH HEATED VALUE IN SPACE—BARK!

"Hold on!" the figure called, waving at the ship.

The steps, which had started to fold themselves back through the hatchway, stopped, re-unfolded, and allowed him back in.

He emerged again a few seconds later carrying a battered and threadbare towel which he shoved into the bag.

He waved again, hoisted the bag under his arm, and started to run for the shelter of some trees as, behind him, the spacecraft had already begun its ascent.

Lightning flitted through the sky and made the figure pause for a moment, and then hurry onward, revising his path to give the trees a wide berth. He moved swiftly across the ground, slipping here and there, hunching himself against the rain which was falling now with ever-increasing concentration, as if being pulled from the sky.

His feet sloshed through the mud. Thunder grumbled over the hills. He pointlessly wiped the rain off his face and stumbled on.

More lights.

Not lightning this time, but more diffused and dimmer lights which played slowly over the horizon and faded.

The figure paused again on seeing them, and then redoubled his steps, making directly toward the point on the horizon at which they had appeared.

And now the ground was becoming steeper, sloping upward, and after another two or three hundred yards it led at last to an obstacle. The figure paused to examine the barrier and then dropped the bag over it before climbing over it himself.

Hardly had the figure touched the ground on the other side than there came a machine sweeping out of the rain toward him with lights streaming through the wall of water. The figure pressed back as the machine streaked toward him. It was a low, bulbous shape, like a small whale surfing—sleek, gray, and rounded and moving at terrifying speed.

The figure instinctively threw up his hands to protect himself, but was hit only by a sluice of water as the machine swept past and off into the night.

It was illuminated briefly by another flicker of lightning crossing the sky, which allowed the soaked figure by the roadside a split second to read a small sign at the back of the machine before it disappeared.

To the figure's apparent incredulous astonishment the sign read "My other car is also a Porsche."

Rob McKenna was a miserable bastard and he knew it because he'd had a lot of people point it out to him over the years and he saw no reason to disagree with them except the obvious one which was that he liked disagreeing with people, particularly people he disliked, which included, at the last count, everybody.

He heaved a sigh and shoved down a gear.

The hill was beginning to steepen and his lorry was heavy with Danish thermostatic radiator controls.

It wasn't that he was naturally predisposed to be so surly, at least he hoped not. It was just the rain that got him down, always the rain.

It was raining now, just for a change.

It was a particular type of rain that he particularly disliked, particularly when he was driving. He had a number for it. It was rain type 17.

He had read somewhere that the Eskimos had over two hundred different words for snow, without which their conversation would probably have got very monotonous. So they would distinguish between thin snow and thick snow, light snow and heavy snow, sludgy snow, brittle snow, snow that came in flurries, snow that came in drifts, snow that came in on the bottom of your neighbor's boots all over your nice clean igloo floor, the snows of winter, the snows of spring, the snows you remember from your childhood that were so much better than any of your modern snow, fine snow, feathery snow, hill snow, valley snow, snow that falls in the morning, snow that falls at night, snow that falls all of a sudden just when you were going out fishing, and snow that despite all your efforts to train them, the huskies have pissed on.

Rob McKenna had two hundred and thirty-one different types of rain entered in his little book, and he didn't like any of them.

He shifted down another gear and the lorry heaved its revs up. It grumbled in a comfortable sort of way about all the Danish thermostatic radiator controls it was carrying.

Since he had left Denmark the previous afternoon, he had been through types 33 (light pricking drizzle which made the roads slippery), 39 (heavy spotting), 47 to 51 (vertical light drizzle through to sharply slanting light to moderate drizzle freshening), 87 and 88 (two finely distinguished varieties of vertical torrential downpour), 100 (postdownpour squalling, cold), all the sea-storm types between 192 and 213 at once, 123, 124, 126, 127 (mild and intermediate cold gusting, regular and syncopated cab-drumming), 11 (breezy droplets), and now his least favorite of all, 17.

Rain type 17 was a dirty blatter battering against his windshield so hard that it didn't make much odds whether he had his wipers on or off.

He tested this theory by turning them off briefly, but as it turned out the visibility did get quite a lot worse. It just failed to get better again when he turned them back on.

In fact one of the wiper blades began to flap off.

Swish swish swish flop swish swish flop swish swish flop swish flop swish flop flop flap scrape.

He pounded his steering wheel, kicked the floor, thumped his cassette player until it suddenly started playing Barry Manilow, thumped it until it stopped again, and swore and swore and swore and swore and swore.

It was at the very moment that his fury was peaking that there loomed swimmingly in his headlights, hardly visible through the blatter, a figure by the roadside.

A poor bedraggled figure, strangely attired, wetter than an otter in a washing machine, and hitching.

"Poor miserable sod," thought Rob McKenna to himself, realizing that here was somebody with a better right to feel hard done by than himself, "must be chilled to the bone. Stupid to be out hitching on a filthy night like this. All you get is cold, wet, and lorries driving through puddles at you."

He shook his head grimly, heaved another sigh, gave the wheel a turn, and hit a large sheet of water square on.

"See what I mean?" he thought to himself as he plowed swiftly through it; "you get some right bastards on the road."

Splattered in his rearview mirror a couple of seconds later was the reflection of the hitchhiker, drenched by the roadside.

For a moment he felt good about this. A moment or two later he felt bad about feeling good about it. Then he felt good about feeling bad about feeling good about it and, satisfied, drove on into the night.

At least it made up for finally having been overtaken by that Porsche he had been diligently blocking for the last twenty miles.

And as he drove on, the rain clouds dragged down the sky after him for, though he did not know it, Rob McKenna was a Rain God. All he knew was that his working days were miserable and he had a succession of lousy holidays. All the clouds knew was that they loved him and wanted to be near him, to cherish him and to water him.

The next two lorries were not driven by Rain Gods, but they did exactly the same thing.

The figure trudged, or rather sloshed, onward till the hill resumed and the treacherous sheet of water was left behind.

After a while the rain began to ease and the moon put in a brief appearance from behind the clouds.

A Renault drove by, and its driver made frantic and complex signals to the trudging figure to indicate that normally he would have been delighted to give the figure a lift, only he couldn't this time because he wasn't going in the direction that the figure wanted to go, whatever direction that might be, and he was sure the figure would understand. He concluded the signaling with a cheery thumbs-up sign as if to say that he hoped the figure felt really fine about being cold and almost terminally wet, and he would catch him next time around.

The figure trudged on. A Fiat passed and did exactly the same as the Renault.

A Maxi passed on the other side of the road and flashed its lights at the slowly plodding figure, though whether this was meant to convey a "Hello" or a "Sorry, we're going the other way" or a "Hey look, there's someone in the rain, what a jerk" was entirely unclear. A green strip across the top of the windshield indicated that whatever the message was, it came from Steve and Carola.

The storm had now definitely abated, and what thunder there was now grumbled over more distant hills, like a man saying "And another thing..." twenty minutes after admitting he'd lost the argument.

The air was clearer now, the night cold. Sound traveled rather well. The lost figure, shivering desperately, presently reached a junction, where a side road turned off to the left. Opposite the turning stood a signpost and this the figure suddenly hurried to and studied with feverish curiosity, only twisting away from it as another car passed suddenly.

And another.

The first whisked by with complete disregard, the second flashed meaninglessly. A Ford Cortina passed and put on its brakes.

Lurching with surprise, the figure bundled his bag to his chest and hurried forward toward it, but at the last moment the Cortina spun its wheels in the wet and careened off up the road rather amusingly.

The figure slowed to a stop and stood there, lost and dejected.

As it chanced, the following day the driver of the Cortina went into the hospital to have his appendix out, only due to a rather amusing mix-up the surgeon removed his leg in error and before the appendectomy could be rescheduled, the appendicitis complicated into an entertainingly serious case of peritonitis, and justice, in its way, was served.

The figure trudged on.

A Saab drew to a halt beside him.

Its window wound down and a friendly voice said, "Have you come far?"

The figure turned toward it. He stopped and grasped the handle of the door.

The figure, the car, and its door handle were all on a planet called the Earth, a world whose entire entry in *The Hitchhiker's Guide to the Galaxy* was comprised of two words: *"Mostly harmless."*

The man who wrote this entry was called Ford Prefect, and he was at this precise moment on a far from harmless world, sitting in a far from harmless bar, recklessly causing trouble.

Chapter 4

Whether it was because he was drunk, ill, or suicidally insane would not have been apparent to a casual observer, and indeed there were no casual observers in the Old Pink Dog Bar on the lower south side of Han Dold City because it wasn't the sort of place you could afford to do things casually in if you wanted to stay alive. Any observers in the place would have been mean, hawklike observers, heavily armed, with painful throbbings in their heads which caused them to do crazy things when they observed things they didn't like.

One of those nasty hushes had descended on the place, a missile crisis sort of hush.

Even the evil-looking bird perched on a rod in the bar had stopped screeching out the names and addresses of local contract killers, which was a service it provided for free.

All eyes were on Ford Prefect. Some of them were on stalks.

The particular way in which he was choosing to dice recklessly with death today was by trying to pay for a drinks bill the size of a small defense budget with an American Express card, which was not acceptable anywhere in the known Universe.

"What are you worried about," he asked in a cheery kind of voice, "the expiration date? Haven't you guys ever heard of Neo-Relativity out here? There're whole new areas of physics which can take care of this sort of thing. Time dilation effects, temporal relastatics—"

"We are not worried about the expiration date," said the man to whom he addressed these remarks, who was a dangerous barman in a dangerous city. His voice was a low soft purr, like the low soft purr made by the opening of an ICBM silo. A hand like a side of meat tapped lightly on the bar top, lightly denting it.

"Well, that's good then," said Ford, packing his satchel and preparing to leave.

The tapping finger reached out and rested lightly on the shoulder of Ford Prefect. It prevented him from leaving.

Although the finger was attached to a slablike hand, and the hand was attached to a clublike forearm, the forearm wasn't attached to anything at all, except in the metaphorical sense that it was attached by a fierce doglike loyalty to the bar which was its home. It had previously been more conventionally attached to the original owner of the bar, who on his deathbed had unexpectedly bequeathed it to medical science. Medical science had decided they didn't like the look of it and had bequeathed it right back to the Old Pink Dog Bar.

The new barman didn't believe in the supernatural or poltergeists or anything kooky like that, he just knew a useful ally when he saw one. The hand sat on the bar. It took orders, it served drinks, it dealt murderously with people who behaved as if they wanted to be murdered. Ford Prefect sat still.

"We are not worried about the expiration date," repeated the barman, satisfied that he now had Ford Prefect's full attention; "we are worried about the entire piece of plastic."

"What?" said Ford. He seemed a little taken aback.

"This," said the barman, holding out the card as if it were a small fish whose soul had three weeks earlier winged its way to the Land Where Fish Are Eternally Blessed. "We don't accept it."

Ford wondered briefly whether to raise the fact that he didn't have any other means of payment on him, but decided for the moment to soldier on. The disembodied hand was now grasping his shoulder lightly but firmly between its finger and thumb.

"But you don't understand," said Ford, his expression slowly ripening from a little taken abackness into rank incredulity, "this is the American Express card. It is the finest way of settling bills known to man. Haven't you read their junk mail?"

The cheery quality of Ford's voice was beginning to grate on the barman's ears. It sounded like someone relentlessly playing the kazoo during one of the more somber passages of a war requiem.

One of the bones in Ford's shoulder began to grate against another one of the bones in his shoulder in a way that suggested the hand had learned the principles of pain from a highly skilled chiropractor. He hoped he could get this business settled before the hand started to grate one of the bones in his shoulder against any of the bones in different parts of his body. Luckily, the shoulder it was holding was not the one he had his satchel slung over.

The barman slid the card back across the bar at Ford.

"We have never," he said with muted savagery, "heard of this thing."

This was hardly surprising.

Ford had only acquired it through a serious computer error toward the end of the fifteen-year sojourn he had spent on the planet Earth. Exactly how serious, the American Express Company had gotten to know very rapidly, and the increasingly strident and panic-stricken demands of its debt collection department were only silenced by the unexpected demolition of the entire planet by the Vogons, to make way for a new hyperspace bypass.

He had kept it ever since because he found it useful to carry a form of currency that no one would accept.

"Credit?" he said. "Aaaargggh . . ."

These two words were usually coupled in the Old Pink Dog Bar.

"I thought," gasped Ford, "that this was meant to be a class establishment. . . ."

He glanced around at the motley collection of thugs, pimps, and record company executives that skulked on the edges of the dim pools of light with which the dark shadows of the bar's inner recesses were pitted. They were all very deliberately looking in any direction but his, carefully picking up the threads of their former conversations about murders, drug rings, and music publishing deals. They knew what would happen now and didn't want to watch in case it put them off their drinks.

"You gonna die, boy," murmured the barman quietly at Ford Prefect, and the evidence was on his side. The bar used to have hanging up one of those signs that read "Please don't ask for credit as a punch in the mouth often offends," but in the interest of strict accuracy this was altered to "Please don't ask for credit because having your throat torn out by a savage bird while a disembodied hand smashes your head against the bar often offends." However, this made an unreadable mess of the notice and anyway didn't have the same ring to it, so it was taken down again. It was felt that the story would get about of its own accord, and it had.

"Lemme look at the bill again," said Ford. He picked it up and studied it thoughtfully under the malevolent gaze of the barman, and the equally malevolent gaze of the bird, which was currently gouging great furrows in the bar top with its talons.

It was a rather lengthy piece of paper.

At the bottom of it was a number that looked like one of those serial numbers you find on the underside of stereo sets which always take so long to copy on to the registration form. He had, after all, been in the bar all day, he had been drinking a lot of stuff with bubbles in it, and he had bought an awful lot of rounds for all the pimps, thugs, and record executives who suddenly couldn't remember who he was.

He cleared his throat rather quietly and patted his pockets. There was, as he knew, nothing in them.

He rested his left hand lightly but firmly on the half-opened flap of his satchel. The disembodied hand renewed its pressure on his right shoulder.

"You see," said the barman, and his face seemed to wobble evilly in front of Ford's, "I have a reputation to think of. You see that, don't you?"

This is it, thought Ford. There was nothing else for it. He had obeyed the rules, he had made a bona fide attempt to pay his bill, it had been rejected. He was now in danger of his life.

"Well," he said quietly, "if it's your reputation . . ."

With a sudden flash of speed he opened his satchel and slapped down on the bar top his copy of *The Hitchhiker's Guide to the Galaxy* and the official card which said that he was a field researcher for the *Guide* and absolutely not allowed to do what he was now doing.

"Want a write-up?"

The barman's face stopped in midwobble. The bird's talons stopped in midfurrow. The hand slowly released its grip.

"That," said the barman in a barely audible whisper, from between dry lips, "will do nicely, sir."

Chapter 5

The *Hitchhiker's Guide to the Galaxy* is a powerful organ. Indeed, its influence is so prodigious that strict rules had to be drawn up by its editorial staff to prevent its misuse. So none of its field researchers is allowed to accept any kind of services, discounts, or preferential treatment of any kind in return for editorial favors unless:

a. they have made a bona fide attempt to pay for a service in the normal way;

b. their lives would be otherwise in danger; or

c. they really want to.

Since invoking the third rule involved giving the editor a cut, Ford always preferred to muck about with the first two.

He stepped out along the street, walking briskly.

The air was stifling, but he liked it because it was stifling city air, full of excitingly unpleasant smells, dangerous music, and the distant sound of warring police tribes.

He carried his satchel with an easy swaying motion so that he could get a good swing at anybody who tried to take it from him without asking. It contained everything he owned, which at the moment wasn't much.

A limousine careened down the street, dodging between the piles of burning garbage, and frightening an old pack animal which lurched, screeching, out of its way, stumbled against the window of a herbal remedies shop, set off a wailing alarm, blundered off down the street, and then pretended to fall down the steps of a small Italian restaurant where it knew it would get photographed and fed.

Ford was walking north. He thought he was probably on his way to the spaceport, but he had thought that before. He knew he was going through that part of the city where people's plans often changed quite abruptly.

"Do you want to have a good time?" said a voice from a doorway.

"As far as I can tell," said Ford, "I'm having one. Thanks."

"Are you rich?" said another.

This made Ford laugh.

He turned and opened his arms in a wide gesture.

"Do I *look* rich?" he said.

"Don't know," said the girl. "Maybe, maybe not. Maybe you'll get rich. I have a very special service for rich people. . . ."

"Oh yes," said Ford, intrigued but careful, "and what's that?"

"I tell them it's okay to be rich."

Gunfire erupted from a window high above them, but it was only a bass player getting shot for playing the wrong riff three times in a row, and bass players are two a penny in Han Dold City.

Ford stopped and peered into the dark doorway.

"You what?" he said.

The girl laughed and stepped forward a little out of the shadow. She was tall, and had that kind of self-possessed shyness which is a great trick if you can do it.

"It's my big number," she said. "I have a master's degree in social economics and can be very convincing. People love it. Especially in this city."

"Goosnargh," said Ford Prefect, which was a special Betelgeusian word he used when he knew he should say something but didn't know what it should be.

He sat on a step, took from his satchel a bottle of that Ol' Janx Spirit and a towel. He opened the bottle and wiped the top of it with the towel, which had the opposite effect to the one intended, in that the Ol' Janx Spirit instantly killed off millions of the germs which had been slowly building up quite a complex and enlightened civilization on the smellier patches of his towel.

"Want some?" he said, after he'd had a swig himself.

She shrugged and took the proffered bottle.

They sat for a while, peacefully listening to the clamor of burglar alarms in the next block.

"As it happens, I'm owed a lot of money," said Ford, "so if I ever get hold of it, can I come and see you then maybe?"

"Sure, I'll be here," said the girl. "So how much is a lot?"

"Fifteen years' back pay."

"For?"

"Writing two words."

"Zarquon," said the girl, "which one took the time?"

"The first one. Once I'd got that the second one just came one afternoon after lunch."

A huge electronic drum kit hurtled through the window high above them and smashed itself to bits in the street in front of them.

It soon became apparent that some of the burglar alarms on the next block had been deliberately set off by one police tribe in order to lay an ambush for the other. Cars with screaming sirens converged on the area, only to find themselves being picked off by helicopters which came thudding through the air between the city's mountainous tower blocks.

"In fact," said Ford, having to shout now above the din, "it wasn't quite like that. I wrote an awful lot, but they just cut it down."

He took his copy of the *Guide* back out of his satchel.

"Then the planet got demolished," he shouted, "really worthwhile job, eh? They've still got to pay me, though."

"You work for that thing?" the girl yelled back.

"Yeah."

"Good number."

"You want to see the stuff I wrote," he shouted, "before it gets erased? The new revisions are due to be released tonight over the net. Someone must have found out that the planet I spent fifteen years on has been demolished by now. They missed it on the last few revisions, but it can't escape their notice forever."

"It's getting impossible to talk, isn't it?"

"What?"

She shrugged and pointed upward.

There was a helicopter above them now which seemed to be involved in a side skirmish with the band upstairs. Smoke was billowing from the building. The sound engineer was hanging out the window by his fingertips, and a maddened guitarist was beating on his fingers with a burning guitar. The helicopter was firing at all of them.

"Can we move?"

They wandered down the street, away from the noise. They ran into a street theater group who tried to do a short play for them about the problems of the inner city, but then gave up and disappeared into the small restaurant most recently patronized by the pack animal.

All the time, Ford was poking at the interface panel of the *Guide*. They ducked into an alleyway. Ford squatted on a garbage can while information began to flood over the screen of the *Guide*.

He located his entry.

"Earth: Mostly harmless."

Almost immediately the screen became a mass of system messages.

"Here it comes," he said.

"Please wait," said the messages. *"Entries are being updated over the Sub-*

Etha Net. This entry is being revised. The system will be down for ten seconds."

At the end of the alley a steel-gray limousine crawled past.

"Hey, look," said the girl, "if you get paid, look me up. I'm a working girl, and there are people over there who need me. I gotta go."

She brushed aside Ford's half-articulated protests, and left him sitting dejectedly on his garbage can preparing to watch a large swath of his working life being swept away electronically into the ether.

Out in the street things had calmed down a little. The police battle had moved off to other sectors of the city, the few surviving members of the rock band had agreed to recognize their musical differences and pursue solo careers, the street theater group was reemerging from the Italian restaurant with the pack animal, telling it they would take it to a bar they knew where it would be treated with a little respect, and a little way farther on the steel-gray limousine was parked silently by the curb.

She hurried toward it.

Behind her, in the darkness of the alley, a green flickering glow was bathing Ford Prefect's face, and his eyes were slowly widening in astonishment.

For where he had expected to find nothing—an erased, closed-off entry—there was instead a continuous stream of data—text, diagrams, figures, and images, moving descriptions of surf on Australian beaches, yogurt on Greek islands, restaurants to avoid in Los Angeles, currency deals to avoid in Istanbul, weather to avoid in London, bars to go everywhere. Pages and pages of it. It was all there, everything he had written.

With a deepening frown of blank incomprehension he went backward and forward through it, stopping here and there at various entries.

Tips for aliens in New York:

Land anywhere, Central Park, anywhere. No one will care or indeed even notice.

Surviving: get a job as a cabdriver immediately. A cabdriver's job is to drive people anywhere they want to go in big yellow machines called taxis. Don't worry if you don't know how the machine works and you can't speak the language, don't understand the geography or indeed the basic physics of the area, and have large green antennae growing out of your head. Believe me, this is the best way of staying inconspicuous.

If your body is really weird, try showing it to people in the streets for money.

Amphibious life forms from any of the worlds in the Swulling, Noxios, or

Nausalia systems will particularly enjoy the East River, which is said to be richer in those lovely life-giving nutrients than the finest and most virulent laboratory slime yet achieved.

Having fun: this is the big section. It is impossible to have more fun without electrocuting your pleasure center. . . .

Ford flipped the switch which he saw was marked "Mode Execute Ready" instead of the now old-fashioned "Access Standby" that had so long ago replace the appallingly stone-aged "Off."

This was a planet he had seen completely destroyed, seen with his own two eyes or rather, blinded as he had been by the hellish disruption of air and light, felt with his own two feet as the ground had started to pound at him like a hammer, bucking, roaring, gripped by tidal waves of energy pouring out of the loathsome yellow Vogon ships. And then at last, five seconds after the moment he had determined as being the last possible moment had already passed, he felt the gently swinging nausea of dematerialization as he and Arthur Dent had been beamed up through the atmosphere like a sports broadcast.

There was no mistake, there couldn't have been. The Earth had definitely been destroyed. Definitely, definitely. Boiled away into space.

And yet here—he activated the *Guide* again—was his own entry on how you would set about having a good time in Bournemouth, Dorset, England, which he had always prided himself on as being one of the most baroque pieces of invention he had ever delivered. He read it again and shook his head in sheer wonder.

Suddenly he realized what the answer to the problem was, and it was this, that something very weird was happening; and if something very weird was happening, he thought, he wanted it to be happening to him.

He stashed the *Guide* back in his satchel and hurried out on to the street.

Walking north again he passed a steel-gray limousine parked by the curb, and from a nearby doorway he heard a soft voice saying, "It's okay, honey, it's really okay, you got to learn to feel good about it. Look at the way the whole economy is structured. . . ."

Ford grinned, detoured round the next block, which was now in flames, found a police helicopter that was standing unattended in the street, broke into it, strapped himself in, crossed his fingers, and sent it hurtling inexpertly into the sky.

He weaved terrifyingly up through the canyoned walls of the city, and once clear of them, hurtled through the black-and-red pall of smoke that hung permanently above it.

Ten minutes later, with all the copter's sirens blaring and its rapid-fire cannon blasting at random into the clouds, Ford Prefect brought it careening down among the gantries and landing lights at Han Dold City spaceport, where it settled like a gigantic, startled, and very noisy gnat.

Since he hadn't damaged it too much he was able to trade it in for a first-class ticket on the next ship leaving the system, and he settled into one of its huge, voluptuous, body-hugging seats.

This was going to be fun, he thought to himself, as the ship blinked silently across the insane distances of deep space and the cabin service got into its full extravagant swing.

"Yes, please," he said to the cabin attendants whenever they glided up to offer him anything at all.

He smiled with a curious kind of manic joy as he flipped again through the mysteriously reinstated entry on the planet Earth. He had a major piece of unfinished business that he would now be able to attend to, and he was terribly pleased that life had suddenly furnished him with a serious goal to achieve.

It suddenly occurred to him to wonder where Arthur Dent was, and if he knew.

Arthur Dent was one thousand, four hundred and thirty-seven light-years away in a Saab and anxious.

Behind him in the back seat was a girl who had made him crack his head on the door as he had climbed in. He didn't know if it was just because she was the first female of his own species that he had laid eyes on in years, or what it was, but he felt stupefied with . . . with . . . This is absurd, he told himself. Calm down, he told himself. You are not, he continued to himself in the firmest internal voice he could muster, in a fit and rational state. You have just hitchhiked over a hundred thousand light-years across the Galaxy, you are very tired, a little confused, and extremely vulnerable. Relax, don't panic, concentrate on breathing deeply.

He twisted round in his seat.

"Are you *sure* she's all right?" he said again.

Beyond the fact that she was, to him, heart-thumpingly beautiful, he could make out very little, how tall she was, how old she was, the exact shading of her hair. And he couldn't ask her anything about herself because, sadly, she was completely unconscious.

"She's just drugged," said her brother, shrugging, not moving his eyes from the road ahead.

"And that's all right, is it?" said Arthur, in alarm.

"Suits me," he said.

"Ah," said Arthur. "Er," he added after a moment's thought.

The conversation so far had been going astoundingly badly.

After an initial flurry of opening hellos, he and Russell—the wonderful girl's brother's name was Russell, a name which to Arthur's mind always suggested burly men with blond mustaches and blow-dried hair who would at the slightest provocation start wearing velvet tuxedos and frilly shirt fronts and would then have to be forcibly restrained from commentating on billiards matches—had quickly discovered they didn't like each other at all.

Russell was a burly man. He had a blond mustache. His hair was fine and blow-dried. To be fair to him—though Arthur didn't see any necessity for this beyond the sheer mental exercise of it—he, Arthur, was himself looking pretty grim. A man can't cross a hundred thousand light-years, mostly in other people's baggage compartments, without beginning to fray a little, and Arthur had frayed a lot.

"She's not a junkie," said Russell suddenly, as if he clearly thought that someone else in the car might be, "she's under sedation."

"But that's terrible," said Arthur, twisting round to look at her again. She seemed to stir slightly and her head slipped sideways on her shoulder. Her dark hair fell across her face, obscuring it.

"What's the matter with her, is she ill?"

"No," said Russell, "merely barking mad."

"What?" said Arthur, horrified.

"Loopy, completely bananas. I'm taking her back to the hospital and telling them to have another go. They let her out while she still thought she was a hedgehog."

"A *hedgehog?*"

Russell hooted his horn fiercely at a car that came round the corner toward them halfway across on to their side of the road, making them swerve. The anger seemed to make him feel better.

"Well, maybe not a hedgehog," he said after he'd settled down again, "though it would probably be simpler to deal with if she did. If somebody thinks they're a hedgehog, presumably you just give 'em a mirror and a few pictures of hedgehogs and tell them to sort it out for themselves, come down again when they feel better. At least medical science could deal with it, that's the point. Seems that's not good enough for Fenny, though."

"Fenny . . . ?"

"You know what I got her for Christmas?"

"Well, no."

"Black's *Medical Dictionary*."

"Nice present."

"I thought so. Thousands of diseases in it, all in alphabetical order."

"You say her name is Fenny?"

"Yeah. Take your pick, I said. Anything in here can be dealt with. The proper drugs can be prescribed. But no, she has to have something different. Just to make life difficult. She was like that at school, you know."

"Was she?"

"She was. Fell over playing hockey and broke a bone nobody had ever heard of."

"I can see how that would be irritating," said Arthur doubtfully. He was rather disappointed to discover her name was Fenny. It was a rather silly, dispiriting name, such as an unlovely maiden aunt might vote herself if she couldn't sustain the name Fenella properly.

"Not that I wasn't sympathetic," continued Russell, "but it did get a bit irritating. She was limping for months."

He slowed down.

"This is your exit, isn't it?"

"Ah no," said Arthur, "five miles farther on. If that's all right."

"Okay," said Russell, after a very tiny pause to indicate that it wasn't, and speeded up again.

It was in fact Arthur's exit, but he couldn't leave without finding out something more about this girl who seemed to have taken such a grip on his mind without even waking up. He could take either of the next two exits.

They led back to the village that had been his home, though what he would find there he hesitated to imagine. Familiar landmarks had been flitting by, ghostlike, in the dark, giving rise in him to the shudders that only very very normal things can create, when seen where the mind is unprepared for them, and in an unfamiliar light.

By his own personal time scale, so far as he could estimate it, living as he had been under the alien rotations of distant suns, it was eight years since he had left, but what time had passed here he could hardly guess. Indeed, what events had passed were beyond his exhausted comprehension because this planet, his home, should not be here.

Eight years ago, at lunchtime, this planet had been demolished, utterly destroyed, by the huge yellow Vogon ships which had hung in the lunchtime sky as if the law of gravity was no more than a local regulation, and breaking it no more than just a parking offense.

"Delusions," said Russell.

"What?" said Arthur, startled out of his train of thought.

"She says she suffers from strange delusions that she's living in the real world. It's no good telling her that she is living in the real world because she just says that's why the delusions are so strange. Don't know about you, but I find that kind of conversation pretty exhausting. Give her the tablets and piss off for a beer is my answer. I mean, you can only muck about so much, can't you?"

Arthur frowned, not for the first time. "Well . . ."

"And all this dreams and nightmare stuff. And the doctors going on about strange jumps in her brain-wave patterns."

"Jumps?"

"This," said Fenny.

Arthur whirled round in his seat and stared into her suddenly open but utterly vacant eyes. Whatever she was looking at wasn't in the car. Her eyes fluttered, her head jerked once, and then she was sleeping peacefully.

"What did she say?" he asked anxiously.

"She said 'this.' "

"This what?"

"This what? How the heck should I know? This hedgehog, that chimney pot, the other pair of Don Alfonso's tweezers. She's barking mad, I thought I'd mentioned that."

"You don't seem to care very much." Arthur tried to say it as matter-of-factly as possible but it didn't seem to work.

"Look, buster . . ."

"Okay, I'm sorry. It's none of my business. I didn't mean it to sound like that," said Arthur. "I know you care a lot, obviously," he added, lying. "I know that you have to deal with it somehow. You'll have to excuse me. I just hitched from the other side of the Horsehead Nebula."

He stared furiously out the window.

He was astonished that of all the sensations fighting for room in his head on this night as he returned to the home that he thought had vanished into oblivion forever, the one that was compelling him was an obsession with this bizarre girl of whom he knew nothing other than that she had said "this" to him, and that he wouldn't wish her brother on a Vogon.

"So, er, what were the jumps, these jumps you mentioned," he went on to say as quickly as he could.

"Look, this is my sister, I don't even know why I'm talking to you about—"

"Okay, I'm sorry. Perhaps you'd better let me out. This is . . ."

At the moment he said it, it became impossible, because the storm which had passed them by suddenly erupted again. Lightning belted through the sky, and someone seemed to be pouring something which closely resembled the Atlantic Ocean over them, through a sieve.

Russell swore and steered intently for a few seconds as the sky blattered at them. He worked out his anger by rashly accelerating to pass a lorry marked "McKenna's All-Weather Haulage." The tension eased as the rain subsided.

"It started out with all that business of the CIA agent they found in the reservoir, when everybody had all the hallucinations and everything, you remember?"

Arthur wondered for a moment whether to mention again that he had just hitchhiked back from the other side of the Horsehead Nebula and was for this and various other related and astounding reasons a little out of touch with recent events, but he decided it would only confuse matters further.

"No," he said.

"That was the moment she cracked up. She was in a café somewhere. Rickmansworth. Don't know what she was doing there, but that was where she cracked up. Apparently she stood up, calmly announced that she had undergone some extraordinary revelation or something, wobbled a bit, looked confused, and finally collapsed screaming into an egg sandwich."

Arthur winced.

"I'm very sorry to hear that," he said a little stiffly.

Russell made a sort of grumping noise.

"So what," said Arthur in an attempt to piece things together, "was the CIA agent doing in the reservoir?"

"Bobbing up and down, of course. He was dead."

"But what—"

"Come on, you remember all that stuff. The hallucinations. Everyone said it was the CIA experimenting with drug warfare or something. Some crackpot theory that instead of invading a country it would be much cheaper and more effective to make everyone *think* they'd been invaded."

"What hallucinations were those exactly...?" said Arthur in a rather quiet voice.

"What do you mean, what hallucinations? I'm talking about all that stuff with the big yellow ships, everyone going crazy and saying we're going to die, and then pop, they vanished as the effect wore off. The CIA denied it, which meant it must be true."

Arthur's head went a little swimmy. His hand grabbed at something to steady himself, and gripped it tightly. His mouth made little opening and closing movements as if it was on his mind to say something, but nothing emerged.

"Anyway," continued Russell, "whatever drug it was it didn't seem to wear off so fast with Fenny. I was all for suing the CIA, but a lawyer friend of mine said it would be like trying to attack a lunatic asylum with a banana, so . . ."

He shrugged.

"The Vogon . . ." squeaked Arthur, "the yellow ships . . . *vanished?*"

"Well, of course they did, they were hallucinations," said Russell, and looked at Arthur oddly. "You trying to say you don't remember any of this? Where have you been, for heaven's sake?"

This was, to Arthur, such an astonishingly good question that he half leaped out of his seat with shock.

"Christ!!!" yelled Russell, fighting to control the car, which was suddenly trying to skid. He pulled it out of the path of an oncoming lorry and swerved up onto a grass bank. As the car lurched to a halt, the girl in the back was thrown against Russell's seat and collapsed awkwardly.

Arthur twisted round in horror.

"Is she all right?" he blurted out.

Russell swept his hands angrily back through his blow-dried hair. He tugged at his blond mustache. He turned to Arthur.

"Would you please," he said, "let go of the handbrake?"

Chapter 6

From here it was a four-mile walk to his village: a mile farther to the exit, to which the abominable Russell had now fiercely declined to take him, and from there a farther three miles of winding country lane.

The Saab seethed off into the night. Arthur watched it go, as stunned as a man might be who, having believed himself to be totally blind for five years, suddenly discovers that he had merely been wearing too large a hat.

He shook his head sharply in the hope that it might dislodge some salient fact which would fall into place and make sense of an otherwise utterly bewildering Universe, but since the salient fact, if there was one, entirely failed to do this, he set off up to the road again, hoping that a good vigorous walk and maybe even some good painful blisters would help to reassure him of at least his own existence, if not his sanity.

It was ten-thirty when he arrived, a fact he discovered from the steamed and greasy window of the Horse and Groom pub, in which there had hung for many years a battered old Guinness clock which featured a picture of an emu with a pint glass jammed rather amusingly down its throat.

This was the pub in which he had passed the fatal lunchtime during which first his house and then the entire Earth had been demolished, or rather had seemed to be demolished, no, damn it, *had* been demolished because if they hadn't been then where the bloody heck had he *been* for the last eight years, and how had he got there if not in one of the big yellow Vogon ships which the appalling Russell had just been telling him were merely drug-induced hallucinations, and yet if it *had* been demolished, what was he currently standing on . . . ?

He jammed the brake on this line of thought because it wasn't going to get him any further than it had the last twenty times he'd been over it.

He started again.

This was the pub in which he had passed the fatal lunchtime during which whatever it was had happened that he was going to sort out later had happened, and . . .

It still didn't make sense.

He started again.

This was the pub in which . . .

This was *a* pub.

Pubs served drinks and he could certainly do with one.

Satisfied that his jumbled thought processes had at last arrived at a conclusion, and a conclusion he was happy with even if it wasn't the one he had set out to achieve, he strode toward the door.

And stopped.

A small black wirehaired terrior ran out from behind a low wall and then, catching sight of Arthur clearly, began to snarl.

Now Arthur knew this dog, and he knew it well. It belonged to an advertising friend of his, and was called Know-Nothing-Bozo the Non-Wonder Dog because the way its hair stood up on its head reminded people of the President of the United States of America, and the dog knew Arthur, or at least should. It was a stupid dog, but it should at least have been able to recognize Arthur instead of standing there, hackles raised, as if Arthur were the most fearful apparition ever to intrude upon its feeble-witted life.

This prompted Arthur to go and peer at the window again, this time with an eye not for the asphyxiating emu but for himself.

Seeing himself for the first time suddenly in a familiar context, he had to admit that the dog had a point.

He looked a lot like something a farmer would use to scare birds with, and there was no doubt but that to go into the pub in his present condition would excite comment of a raucous kind, and worse still, there would doubtless be several people in there at the moment whom he knew, all of whom would be bound to bombard him with questions which at the moment he felt ill-equipped to deal with.

Will Smithers, for instance, the owner of Know-Nothing-Bozo the Non-Wonder Dog, an animal so stupid that it had been sacked from one of Will's own commercials for being incapable of knowing which dog food it was supposed to prefer, despite the fact that the meat in all the other bowls had engine oil poured all over it.

Will would definitely be in there. Here was his dog, there was his car, a gray Porsche 928S with a sign in the back window which read "My other car is also a Porsche." Damn him.

He stared at it and realized that he had just learned something he hadn't known before.

Will Smithers, like most of the overpaid and underscrupulous bastards

Arthur knew in advertising, made a point of changing his car every August so that he could tell people his accountant made him do it, though the truth was that his accountant was trying like hell to stop him, what with all the alimony he had to pay, and so on—and this was the same car Arthur remembered him having before. The number plate proclaimed its year.

Given that it was now winter, and that the event which had caused Arthur so much trouble eight of his personal years ago had occurred at the beginning of September, less than six or seven months could have passed here.

He stood terribly still for a moment and let Know-Nothing-Bozo jump up and down yapping at him. He was suddenly stunned by a realization he could no longer avoid, which was this: he was now an alien on his own world. Try as they might, no one was even going to be *able* to believe his story. Not only did it sound perfectly potty, but it was flatly contradicted by the simplest observable facts.

Was this *really* the Earth? Was there the slightest possibility that he had made some extraordinary mistake?

The pub in front of him was unbearably familiar to him in every detail— every brick, every piece of peeling paint; and inside he could sense its familiar stuffy, noisy warmth, its exposed beams, its unauthentic cast-iron light fittings, its bar sticky with beer that people he knew had put their elbows in, overlooked by cardboard cutouts of girls with packets of peanuts stapled all over their breasts. It was all the stuff of his home, his world.

He even knew this blasted dog.

"Hey, Know-Nothing!"

The sound of Will Smithers's voice meant he had to decide what to do quickly. If he stood his ground he would be discovered and the whole circus would begin. To hide would only postpone the moment, and it was bitterly cold now.

The fact that it was Will made the choice easier. It wasn't that Arthur disliked him as such—Will was quite fun. It was just that he was fun in such an exhausting way because, being in advertising, he always wanted you to know how much fun he was having and where he had got his jacket from.

Mindful of this, Arthur hid behind a van.

"Hey, Know-Nothing, what's up?"

The door opened and Will came out, wearing a leather flying jacket that he'd got a mate of his at the Road Research Laboratory to crash a car into specially, in order to get that battered look. Know-Nothing yelped with delight and, having got the attention it wanted, was happy to forget Arthur.

Will was with some friends, and they had a game they played with the dog.

"Commies!" they all shouted at the dog in chorus, "Commies, Commies, Commies!!!"

The dog went berserk with barking, prancing up and down, yapping its little heart out, beside itself in transports of ecstatic rage. They all laughed and cheered it on, then gradually dispersed to their various cars and disappeared into the night.

Well, that clears one thing up, thought Arthur from behind his van, this is quite definitely the planet I remember.

Chapter 7

His house was still there.

How or why, he had no idea, but he had decided to go and have a look while he was waiting for the pub to empty so that he could go and ask the landlord for a bed for the night when everyone else had gone, and there it was.

He let himself in with a key he kept under a stone frog in the garden, hurriedly because, astoundingly, the phone was ringing.

He had heard it faintly all the way up the lane and had started to run as soon as he realized where the sound was coming from.

The door had to be forced open because of the astonishing accumulation of junk mail on the doormat. It jammed itself stuck on what he would later discover were fourteen identical, personally addressed invitations to apply for a credit card he already had, seventeen identical threatening letters for nonpayment of bills on a credit card he didn't have, thirty-three identical letters saying that he personally had been specially selected as a man of taste and discrimination who knew what he wanted and where he was going in today's sophisticated jet-setting world and would he therefore like to buy some grotty wallet, and also a dead tabby kitten.

He rammed himself through the relatively narrow opening afforded by all this, stumbled through a pile of wine offers that no discriminating connoisseur would want to miss, slithered over a heap of beach villa holidays, blundered up the dark stairs to his bedroom, and got to the phone just as it stopped ringing.

He collapsed, panting, onto his cold, musty-smelling bed and for a few minutes stopped trying to prevent the world from spinning round his head in the way it obviously wanted to.

When it had enjoyed its little spin and had calmed down a bit, Arthur reached out for the bedside light, not expecting it to come on. To his surprise it did. This appealed to Arthur's sense of logic. Since the Electricity Board had cut him off without fail every time he paid his bill, it seemed only reasonable that they should leave him connected when he hadn't. Sending them money obviously only drew attention to himself.

The room was much as he had left it, festeringly untidy, though the effect was muted a little by a thick layer of dust. Half-read books and magazines nestled among piles of half-used towels. Half-pairs of socks reclined in half-drunk cups of coffee. What once had been a half-eaten sandwich had now half-turned into something that Arthur didn't entirely want to know about. Bung a fork of lightning through this lot, he thought to himself, and you'd start the evolution of life off all over again.

There was only one thing in the room that was different.

For a moment or so he couldn't see what the one thing that was different was, because it was too covered in a film of disgusting dust. Then his eyes caught it and stopped.

It was next to a battered old television on which it was only possible to watch Open University study courses, because if it tried to show anything more exciting it would break down.

It was a box.

Arthur pushed himself up on his elbows and peered at it.

It was a gray box, with a kind of dull luster to it. It was a cubical gray box, just over a foot on one side. It was tied with a single gray ribbon, knotted into a neat bow on the top.

He got up, walked over, and touched it in surprise. Whatever it was was clearly gift-wrapped, neatly and beautifully, and was waiting for him to open it.

Cautiously, he picked it up and carried it back to the bed. He brushed the dust off the top and loosened the ribbon. The top of the box was a lid, with a flap tucked into the body of the box.

He untucked it and looked into the box. In it was a glass globe, nestling in fine gray tissue paper. He drew it out, carefully. It wasn't a proper globe because it was open at the bottom, or, as Arthur realized, turning it over, at the top, with a thick rim. It was a bowl. A fishbowl.

It was made of the most wonderful glass, perfectly transparent, yet with an extraordinary silver-gray quality as if crystal and slate had gone into its making.

Arthur slowly turned it over and over in his hands. It was one of the most beautiful objects he had ever seen, but he was entirely perplexed by it. He looked into the box, but other than the tissue paper there was nothing. On the outside of the box there was nothing.

He turned the bowl round again. It was wonderful. It was exquisite. But it was a fishbowl.

He tapped it with his thumbnail and it rang with a deep and glorious chime which was sustained for longer than seemed possible and when at last it faded seemed not to die away but to drift off into other worlds, as into a deep sea dream.

Entranced, Arthur turned it round yet again, and this time the light from the dusty little bedside lamp caught it at a different angle and glittered on some fine abrasions on the fishbowl's surface. He held it up, adjusting the angle to the light, and suddenly saw clearly the finely engraved shapes of words shadowed on the glass.

"So Long," they said, "and Thanks..."

And that was all. He blinked, and understood nothing.

For fully five more minutes he turned the object around and around, held it to the light at different angles, tapped it for its mesmerizing chime, and pondered on the meaning of the shadowy letters but could find none. Finally he stood up, filled the bowl with water from the tap, and put it back on the table next to the television. He shook the little Babel fish from his ear and dropped it, wriggling, into the bowl. He wouldn't be needing it anymore, except for watching foreign movies.

He returned to lie on his bed, and turned out the light.

He lay still and quiet. He absorbed the enveloping darkness, slowly relaxed his limbs from end to end, eased and regulated his breathing, gradually cleared his mind of all thought, closed his eyes, and was completely incapable of getting to sleep.

The night was uneasy with rain. The rain clouds themselves had now moved on and were currently concentrating their attention on a small café just outside Bournemouth, but the sky through which they had passed had been disturbed by them and now wore a damply ruffled air, as if it didn't know what else it might not do if further provoked.

The moon was out in a watery way. It looked like a ball of paper from the back pocket of jeans that have just come out of the washing machine, which only time and ironing would tell if it was an old shopping list or a five-pound note.

The wind flicked about a little, like the tail of a horse that's trying to decide what sort of mood it's in tonight, and a bell somewhere chimed midnight.

A skylight creaked open.

It was stiff and had to be jiggled and persuaded a little because the frame was slightly rotten and the hinge had at some time in its life been rather sensibly painted over, but eventually it was open.

A strut was found to prop it and a figure struggled out into the narrow gully between the opposing pitches of the roof.

The figure stood and watched the sky in silence.

The figure was completely unrecognizable as the wild-looking creature who has burst crazily into the cottage a little over an hour ago. Gone was the ragged threadbare dressing gown, smeared with the mud of a hundred worlds, stained with junk food condiment from a hundred grimy space-ports, gone was the tangled mane of hair, gone the long and knotted beard, flourishing ecostructure and all.

Instead, there was Arthur Dent, smooth and casual in corduroys and a bulky sweater. His hair was cropped and washed, his chin clean-shaven. Only the eyes still said that whatever it was the Universe thought it was doing to him, he would still like it please to stop.

They were not the same eyes with which he had last looked out at this particular scene, and the brain which interpreted the images the eyes resolved was not the same brain. There had been no surgery involved, just the continual wrenching of experience.

The night seemed like an alive thing to him at this moment, the dark Earth around him a being in which he was rooted.

He could feel like a tingle on distant nerve ends the flood of a far river, the roll of invisible hills, the knot of heavy rain clouds parked somewhere away to the south.

He could sense, too, the thrill of being a tree, which was something he hadn't expected. He knew that it felt good to curl your toes in the earth, but he'd never realized it could feel quite as good as that. He could sense an almost unseemly wave of pleasure reaching at him all the way from the New Forest. He must try this summer, he thought, to see what having leaves felt like.

From another direction he felt the sensation of being a sheep startled by a flying saucer, but it was virtually indistinguishable from the feeling of being a sheep startled by anything else it ever encountered, for they were creatures who learned very little on their journey through life, and would be startled to see the sun rising in the morning, and astonished by all the green stuff in the fields.

He was surprised to find he could feel the sheep being startled by the sun that morning, and the morning before, and being startled by a clump of trees the day before that. He could go further and further back, but it got dull because all it consisted of was sheep being startled by things they'd been startled by the day before.

He left the sheep and let his mind drift outward sleepily in developing ripples. It felt the presence of other minds, hundreds of them, thousands in a web, some sleepy, some sleeping, some terribly excited, one fractured.

One fractured.

He passed it fleetingly and tried to feel for it again, but it eluded him like the other card with an apple on it in a memory course. He felt a spasm of excitement because he knew instinctively who it was, or at least knew who it was he wanted it to be, and once you know what it is you want to be true, instinct is a very useful device for enabling you to know that it is.

He instinctively knew that it was Fenny and that he wanted to find her; but he could not. By straining too much for it, he could feel he was losing this strange new faculty, so he relaxed the search and let his mind wander easily once more.

And again, he felt the fracture.

Again he couldn't find it. This time, whatever his instincts were busy telling him it was all right to believe, he wasn't certain that it was Fenny— or perhaps it was a different fracture this time. It had the same disjointed quality but it seemed a more general feeling of fracture, deeper, not a single mind, maybe not a mind at all. It was different.

He let his mind sink slowly and widely into the Earth, rippling, seeping, sinking.

He was following the Earth through its days, drifting with the rhythms of its myriad pulses, seeping through the webs of its life, swelling with its tides, turning with its weight. Always the fracture kept returning, a dull disjointed distant ache.

And now he was flying through a land of light; the light was time, the tides of it were days receding. The fracture he had sensed, the second fracture, lay in the distance before him across the land, the thickness of a single hair across the dreaming landscape of the days of Earth.

And suddenly he was upon it.

He danced dizzily over the edge as the dreamland dropped sheer away beneath him, a stupefying precipice into nothing, him wildly twisting, clawing at nothing, flailing in horrifying space, spinning, falling.

Across the jagged chasm had been another land, another time, an older world, not fractured from, but hardly joined: two Earths. He woke.

A cold breeze brushed the feverish sweat standing on his forehead. The nightmare was spent and so, he felt, was he. His shoulders drooped, he gently rubbed his eyes with the tips of his fingers. At last he was sleepy as well as very tired. As to what it meant, if it meant anything at all, he would think about in the morning; for now he would go to bed and sleep. His own bed, his own sleep.

He could see his house in the distance and wondered why this was. It was silhouetted against the moonlight and he recognized its rather dull blockish shape. He looked about him and noticed that he was about eighteen inches above the rosebushes of one of his neighbors, John Ainsworth. His rosebushes were carefully tended, pruned back for the winter, strapped to canes and labeled, and Arthur wondered what he was doing above them. He wondered what was holding him there, and when he discovered that nothing was holding him there he crashed awkwardly to the ground.

He picked himself up, brushed himself down, and hobbled back to his house on a sprained ankle. He undressed and toppled into bed.

While he was asleep the phone rang again. It rang for fully fifteen minutes and caused him to turn over twice. It never, however, stood a chance of waking him up.

rthur awoke feeling wonderful, absolutely fabulous, refreshed, overjoyed to be home, bouncing with energy, hardly disappointed at all to discover it was the middle of February.

He almost danced to the fridge, found the three least hairy things in it, put them on a plate and watched them intently for two minutes. Since they made no attempt to move within that time he called them breakfast and ate them. Between them they killed a virulent space disease he'd picked up without knowing it in the Flargathon Gas Swamps a few days earlier, which otherwise would have killed off half the population of the Western Hemisphere, blinded the other half, and driven everyone else psychotic and sterile, so the Earth was lucky there.

He felt strong, he felt healthy. He vigorously cleared away the junk mail with a spade and then buried the cat.

Just as he was finishing that, the phone rang, but he let it ring while he maintained a moment's respectful silence. Whoever it was would ring back if it was important.

He kicked the mud off his shoes and went back inside.

There had been a small number of significant letters in the piles of junk—some documents from the council, dated three years earlier, relating to the proposed demolition of his house, and some other letters about the setting up of a public inquiry into the whole bypass scheme in the area; there was also an old letter from Greenpeace, the ecological pressure group to which he occasionally made contributions, asking for help with their scheme to release dolphins and orcas from captivity; and some postcards from friends vaguely complaining that he never got in touch these days.

He collected these together and put them in a cardboard file which he marked "Things To Do." Since he was feeling so vigorous and dynamic that morning, he even added the word "Urgent!"

He unpacked his towel and another few odd bits and pieces from the plastic bag he had acquired at the Port Brasta Mega-Market. The slogan on the side was a clever and elaborate pun in Lingua Centauri which was completely incomprehensible in any other language and therefore entirely pointless for a duty-free shop at a spaceport. The bag also had a hole in it so he threw it away.

He realized with a sudden twinge that something else must have dropped out in the small spacecraft that had brought him to Earth, kindly going out of its way to drop him right beside the A303. He had lost his battered and space-worn copy of the thing which had helped him find his way across the unbelievable wastes of space he had traversed. He had lost *The Hitchhiker's Guide to the Galaxy*.

Well, he told himself, this time I really won't be needing it again.

He had some calls to make.

He had decided how to deal with the mass of contradictions his return journey precipitated, which was that he would simply brazen it out.

He phoned the BBC and asked to be put through to his department head.

"Oh, hello, Arthur Dent here. Look, sorry I haven't been in for six months but I've gone mad."

"Oh, not to worry. Thought it was probably something like that. Happens here all the time. How soon can we expect you?"

"When do hedgehogs start hibernating?"

"Sometime in spring, I think."

"I'll be in shortly after that."

"Righty-ho."

He flipped through the Yellow Pages and made a short list of numbers to try.

"Oh, hello, is that the Old Elms Hospital? Yes, I was just phoning to see if I could have a word with Fenella, er...Fenella...good Lord, silly me, I'll forget my own name next, er, Fenella—isn't this ridiculous? Patient of yours, dark-haired girl, came in last night..."

"I'm afraid we don't have any patients called Fenella."

"Oh, don't you? I meant Fiona, of course, we just call her Fen—"

"I'm sorry, goodbye."

Click.

Six conversations along these lines began to take their toll on his mood of vigorous, dynamic optimism, and he decided that before it deserted him entirely he would take it down to the pub and parade it a little.

He had the perfect idea for explaining away every inexplicable weirdness about himself at a stroke, and he whistled as he pushed open the door which had so daunted him last night.

"Arthur!!!!"

He grinned cheerfully at the boggling eyes that stared at him from all corners of the pub, and told them all what a wonderful time he'd had in Southern California.

Chapter 9

He accepted another pint and took a pull at it.

"Of course, I had my own personal alchemist, too."

"You what?"

He was getting silly and he knew it. Exuberance and Hall and Woodhouse best bitter was a mixture to be wary of, but one of the first effects it has is to stop you being wary of things, and the point at which Arthur should have stopped and explained no more was the point at which he started instead to get inventive.

"Oh yes," he insisted with a happy glazed smile, "it's why I've lost so much weight."

"What?" said his audience.

"Oh yes," he said again, "the Californians have rediscovered alchemy, oh yes."

He smiled again.

"Only," he said, "it's in a much more useful form than that which in"—he paused thoughtfully to let a little grammar assemble in his head—"in which the ancients used to practice it. Or at least," he added, "failed to practice it. They couldn't get it to work, you know. Nostradamus and that lot. Couldn't cut it."

"Nostradamus?" said one of his audience.

"I didn't think he was an alchemist," said another.

"I thought," said a third, "he was a seer."

"He became a seer," said Arthur to his audience, the component parts of which were beginning to bob and blur a little, "because he was such a lousy alchemist. You should know that."

He took another pull at his beer. It was something he had not tasted for eight years. He tasted it and tasted it.

"What has alchemy got to do," asked a bit of the audience, "with losing weight?"

"I'm glad you asked that," said Arthur, "very glad. And I will now tell you what the connection is between"—he paused—"between those two things. The things you mentioned. I'll tell you."

He paused and maneuvered his thoughts. It was like watching oil tankers doing three-point turns in the English Channel.

"They've discovered how to turn excess body fat into gold," he said, in a sudden blurt of coherence.

"You're kidding."

"Oh yes," he said, "no," he corrected himself, "they have."

He rounded on the doubting part of his audience, which was all of it, and so it took a little while to round on it completely.

"Have you *been* to California?" he demanded. "Do you *know* the sort of stuff they do there?"

Three members of his audience said they had and that he was talking nonsense.

"You haven't seen anything," insisted Arthur. "Oh yes," he added, because someone was offering to buy another round.

"The evidence," he said, pointing at himself, and not missing by more than a couple of inches, "is before your eyes. Fourteen hours in a trance," he said, "in a tank. In a trance. I was in a tank. I think," he added after a thoughtful pause, "I already said that."

He waited patiently while the next round was duly distributed. He composed the next bit of his story in his mind, which was going to be something about the tank needing to be oriented along a line dropped perpendicularly from the Pole Star to a base line drawn between Mars and Venus, and was about to start trying to say it when he decided to give it a miss.

"Long time," he said instead, "in a tank. In a trance." He looked round severely at his audience, to make sure it was all following attentively.

He resumed.

"Where was I?" he said.

"In a trance," said one.

"In a tank," said another.

"Oh yes," said Arthur, "thank you. And slowly," he said, pressing onward, "slowly, slowly slowly, all your excess body fat . . . turns . . . to"—he paused for effect—"subcoo . . . subyoo . . . subtoocay"—he paused for breath—"subcutaneous gold, which you can have surgically removed. Getting out of the tank is hell. What did you say?"

"I was just clearing my throat."

"I think you doubt me."

"I was clearing my throat."

"She was clearing her throat," confirmed a significant part of the audience in a low rumble.

"Oh yes," said Arthur, "all right. And you then split the proceeds"—he paused again for a math break—"fifty-fifty with the alchemist. Make a lot of money!"

He looked swayingly around at his audience, and could not help but be aware of an air of skepticism about their jumbled faces.

He felt very affronted by this.

"How else," he demanded, "could I afford to have my face dropped?"

Friendly arms began to help him home. "Listen," he protested, as the cold February breeze brushed his face, "looking lived-in is all the rage in California at the moment. You've got to look as if you've seen the Galaxy. Life, I mean. You've got to look as if you've seen life. That's what I got. A face drop. Give me eight years, I said. I hope being thirty doesn't come back into fashion or I've wasted a lot of money."

He lapsed into silence for a while as the friendly arms continued to help him along the lane to his house.

"Got in yesterday," he mumbled. "I'm very very very happy to be home. Or somewhere very like it . . ."

"Jet lag," muttered one of his friends, "long trip from California. Really mucks you up for a couple of days."

"I don't think he's been there at all," muttered another. "I wonder where he has been. And what's happened to him."

After a little sleep Arthur got up and pottered round the house a bit. He felt woozy and a little low, still disoriented by the journey. He wondered how he was going to find Fenny.

He sat and looked at the fishbowl. He tapped it again, and despite being full of water and a small yellow Babel fish which was gulping its way around rather dejectedly, it still chimed its deep and resonant chime as clearly and mesmerically as before.

Someone is trying to thank me, he thought to himself. He wondered who, and for what.

Chapter 10

A t the third stroke it will be one...thirty-two...and twenty seconds."

"Beep...beep...beep."

Ford Prefect suppressed a little giggle of evil satisfaction, realized that he had no reason to suppress it, and laughed out loud, a wicked laugh.

He switched the incoming signal through from the Sub-Etha Net to the ship's superb hi-fi system, and the odd, rather stilted singsong voice spoke out with remarkable clarity round the cabin.

"At the third stroke it will be one...thirty-two...and thirty seconds."

"Beep...beep...beep."

He tweaked the volume up just a little, while keeping a careful eye on a rapidly changing table of figures on the ship's computer display. For the length of time he had in mind, the question of power consumption became significant. He didn't want a murder on his conscience.

"At the third stroke it will be one...thirty-two...and forty seconds."

"Beep...beep...beep."

He checked around the small ship. He walked down the short corridor.

"At the third stroke..."

He stuck his head into the small, functional, gleaming steel bathroom.

"...it will be..."

It sounded fine in there.

He looked into the tiny sleeping quarters.

"...one...thirty-two..."

It sounded a bit muffled. There was a towel hanging over one of the speakers. He took down the towel.

"...and fifty seconds."

Fine.

He checked out the packed cargo hold, and wasn't at all satisfied with the sound. There was altogether too much crated junk in the way. He stepped back out and waited for the door to seal. He broke open a closed control panel and pushed the jettison button. He didn't know why he hadn't thought of that before. A whooshing, rumbling noise died away quickly into silence. After a pause a slight hiss could be heard again.

It stopped.

He waited for the green light to show and then opened the door again onto the new empty cargo hold.

" . . . one . . . thirty-three . . . and fifty seconds."

Very nice.

"Beep . . . beep . . . beep."

He then went and had a last thorough examination of the emergency suspended animation chamber, which was where he particularly wanted it to be heard.

"At the third stroke it will be one . . . thirty-four . . . precisely."

He shivered as he peered down through the heavily frosted covering at the dim bulk of the form within. One day, who knew when, it would wake, and when it did, it would know what time it was. Not exactly local time, true, but what the heck.

He double-checked the computer display above the freezer bed, dimmed the lights, and checked it again.

"At the third stroke it will be . . ."

He tiptoed out and returned to the control cabin.

" . . . one . . . thirty-four and twenty seconds."

The voice sounded as clear as if he were hearing it over a phone in London, which he wasn't, not by a long way.

He gazed out into the inky night. The star he could see in the distance the size of a brilliant biscuit crumb was Zondostina, or as it was known on the world from which the rather stilted, singsong voice was being received, Pleiades Zeta.

The bright orange curve that filled over half the visible area was the giant gas planet Sesefras Magna, where the Xaxisian battleships docked, and just rising over its horizon was a small cool blue moon, Epun.

"At the third stroke it will be . . ."

For twenty minutes he sat and merely watched as the gap between the ship and Epun closed, as the ship's computer teased and kneaded the numbers that would bring it into a loop around the little moon, close the loop and keep it there, orbiting in perpetual obscurity.

"One . . . fifty-nine . . ."

His original plan had been to close down all external signaling and radiation from the ship, to render it as nearly invisible as possible unless you were actually looking at it, but then he'd had an idea he preferred. It would now emit one single continuous beam, pencil thin, broadcasting the incoming time signal to the planet of the signal's origin, which it would not reach for four hundred years, traveling at light-speed, but where it would probably cause something of a stir when it did.

"Beep...beep...beep..."

He sniggered.

He didn't like to think of himself as the sort of person who giggled or sniggered, but he had to admit that he had been giggling and sniggering almost continuously for well over half an hour now.

"At the third stroke..."

The ship was now locked almost perfectly into its perpetual orbit round a little-known and never-visited moon. Almost perfect.

One thing only remained. He ran again the computer simulation of the launching of the ship's little Escape-O-Buggy, balancing actions, reactions, tangential forces, all the mathematical poetry of motion, and saw that it was good.

Before he left, he turned out the lights.

As his tiny little cigar tube of an escape craft zipped out on the beginning of its three-day journey to the orbiting space station Port Sesefron, it rode for a few seconds a long pencil-thin beam of radiation that was starting out on a longer journey still.

"At the third stroke, it will be two...thirteen...and fifty seconds."

He giggled and sniggered. He would have laughed out loud but he didn't have room.

"Beep...beep...beep."

Chapter 11

April showers I hate especially."

However noncommittally Arthur grunted, the man seemed determined to talk to him. He wondered if he should get up and move to another table, but there didn't seem to be one free in the whole cafeteria. He stirred his coffee fiercely.

"Bloody April showers. Hate, hate, hate."

Arthur stared, frowning, out the window. A light, sunny spray of rain hung over the motorway. Two months he'd been back now. Slipping back into his old life had in fact been laughably easy. People had such extraordinarily short memories, including him. Eight years of crazed wanderings round the Galaxy now seemed to him not so much like a bad dream as like a film he had videotaped off television and now kept in the back of a cupboard without bothering to watch.

One effect that still lingered, though, was his joy at being back. Now that the Earth's atmosphere had closed over his head for good, he thought wrongly, everything within it gave him extraordinary pleasure. Looking at the silvery sparkle of the raindrops he felt he had to protest.

"Well, I like them," he said suddenly, "and for all the obvious reasons. They're light and refreshing. They sparkle and make you feel good."

The man snorted derisively.

"That's what they all say," he said, and glowered darkly from his corner seat.

He was a lorry driver. Arthur knew this because his opening, unprovoked remark had been, "I'm a lorry driver. I hate driving in the rain. Ironic, isn't it? Bloody ironic."

If there was a sequitur hidden in this remark, Arthur had not been able to divine it and had merely given a little grunt, affable but not encouraging.

But the man had not been deterred then, and was not deterred now. "They all say that about bloody April showers," he said, "so bloody nice, so bloody refreshing, such charming bloody weather."

He leaned forward, screwing his face up as if he was going to say something extraordinary about the government.

"What I want to know is this," he said, "if it's going to be nice weather, *why*," he almost spat, "can't it be nice without bloody raining?"

Arthur gave up. He decided to leave his coffee, which was too hot to drink quickly and too nasty to drink cold.

"Well, there you go," he said, and instead got up himself. "'Bye."

He stopped off at the service station shop, then walked back through the parking lot, making a point of enjoying the fine play of rain in his face. There was even, he noticed, a faint rainbow glistening over the Devon hills. He enjoyed that, too.

He climbed into his battered but adored old black VW Rabbit, squealed the tires, and headed out past the islands of gas pumps and along the slip road to the motorway.

He was wrong in thinking that the atmosphere of the Earth had closed finally and forever above his head.

He was wrong to think that it would ever be possible to put behind him the tangled web of irresolutions into which his galactic travels had dragged him.

He was wrong to think he could now forget that the big, hard, oily, dirty, rainbow-hung Earth on which he lived was a microscopic dot on a microscopic dot lost in the unimaginable infinity of the Universe.

He drove on, humming, being wrong about all these things.

The reason he was wrong was standing by the slip road under a small umbrella.

His jaw sagged. He sprained his ankle against the brake pedal and skidded so hard he very nearly turned the car over.

"Fenny!" he shouted.

Having narrowly avoided hitting her with the actual car, he hit her instead with the car door as he leaned across and flung it open.

It caught her hand and knocked away the umbrella from it, which then bowled wildly away across the road.

"Shit!" yelled Arthur as helpfully as he could, leaped out of his own door, narrowly avoided being run down by McKenna's All-Weather Haulage, and watched in horror as it ran down Fenny's umbrella instead. The lorry swept along the motorway and away.

The umbrella lay like a recently swatted daddy longlegs, expiring sadly on the ground. Tiny gusts of wind made it twitch a little.

He picked it up.

"Er," he said. There didn't seem to be a lot of point in offering the thing back to her.

"How did you know my name?" she said.

"Er, well," he said, "look, I'll get you another one."

He looked at her and tailed off.

She was tallish with dark hair which fell in waves around a pale and serious face. Standing still, alone, she seemed almost somber, like a statue to some important but unpopular virtue in a formal garden. She seemed to be looking at something other than what she looked as if she was looking at.

But when she smiled, as she did now, suddenly, it was as if she had just arrived from somewhere. Warmth and life flooded into her face, and impossibly graceful movement into her body. The effect was very disconcerting, and it disconcerted Arthur like hell.

She grinned, tossed her bag into the back, and swiveled herself into the front seat.

"Don't worry about the umbrella," she said to him as she climbed in, "it was my brother's and he can't have liked it or he wouldn't have given it to me." She laughed and pulled on her seat belt. "You're not a friend of my brother's, are you?"

"No."

Her voice was the only part of her which didn't say "Good."

Her physical presence there in the car, his car, was quite extraordinary to Arthur. He felt, as he let the car pull slowly away, that he could hardly think or breathe, and hoped that neither of these functions was vital to his driving or they were in trouble.

So what he had experienced in the other car, her brother's car, the night he had returned exhausted and bewildered from his nightmare years in the stars had not been the unbalance of the moment or, if it had been, he was at least twice as unbalanced now, and quite liable to fall off whatever it is that well-balanced people are supposed to be balancing on.

"So . . ." he said, hoping to kick the conversation off to an exciting start.

"He was supposed to pick me up—my brother—but phoned to say he couldn't make it. I asked about buses but the man started to look at a calendar rather than a timetable, so I decided to hitch. So."

"So."

"So here I am. And what I would like to know, is how you know my name."

"Perhaps we ought to first sort out," said Arthur, looking back over his shoulder as he eased his car into the motorway traffic, "where I'm taking you."

Very close, he hoped, or a long way. Close would mean she lived near him, a long way would mean he could drive her there.

"I'd like to go to Taunton," she said, "please. If that's all right. It's not far. You can drop me at—"

"You live in *Taunton?*" he said, hoping that he'd managed to sound merely curious rather than ecstatic. Taunton was wonderfully close to him. He could . . .

"No, London," she said, "there's a train in just under an hour."

It was the worst thing possible. Taunton was only minutes away up the motorway. He wondered what to do, and while he was wondering heard himself, with horror, saying, "Oh, I can take you to London. Let me take you to London. . . ."

Bungling idiot. Why on earth had he said "let" in that stupid way? He was behaving like a twelve-year-old.

She looked at him severely.

"Are you going to London?" she asked.

"Yes," he didn't say.

"And I've got to step on it," he failed to add, omitting to glance at his watch.

"I wasn't," he said, "but . . ." Bungling idiot.

"It's very kind of you," she said, "but really no. I like to go by train." And suddenly she was gone. Or rather, that part of her which brought her to life was gone. She looked rather distantly out the window and hummed lightly to herself.

He couldn't believe it.

Thirty seconds into the conversation, and already he'd blown it.

Grown men, he told himself, in flat contradiction of centuries of accumulated evidence about the way grown men behave, do not behave like this.

Taunton 5 miles, said the signpost.

He gripped the steering wheel so tightly the car wobbled.

He was going to have to do something dramatic.

"Fenny," he said.

She glanced round sharply at him. "You still haven't told me how—"

"Listen," said Arthur, "I will tell you, though the story is rather strange. Very strange."

She was still looking at him, but said nothing.

"Listen . . ."

"You said that."

"Did I? Oh. There are things I must talk to you about, and things I must tell you ... a story I must tell you which would ..." He was thrashing about. He wanted something along the lines of "Thy knotted and combined locks to part,/And each particular hair to stand on end,/Like quills upon the fretful porcupine" but didn't think he could carry it off and didn't like the hedgehog reference.

" ... which would take more than five miles," he settled for in the end, rather lamely, he was afraid.

"Well ..."

"Just supposing," he said, "just supposing"—he didn't know what was coming next, so he thought he'd just sit back and listen—"that there was some extraordinary way in which you were very important to me, and that, though you didn't know it, I was very important to you, but it all went for nothing because we only had five miles and I was a stupid idiot at knowing how to say something very important to someone I've only just met and not crash into lorries at the same time, what would you say ..." He paused, helplessly, and looked at her.

" ... I should do?"

"Watch the road!" she yelped.

"Shit!"

He narrowly avoided careening into the side of a hundred Italian washing machines in a German lorry.

"I think," she said, with a momentary sigh of relief, "you should buy me a drink before my train goes."

Chapter 12

There is, for some reason, something especially grim about pubs near stations, a very particular kind of grubbiness, a special kind of pallor to the pork pies.

Worse than the pork pies, though, are the sandwiches.

There is a feeling which persists in England that making a sandwich interesting, attractive, or in any way pleasant to eat is something sinful that only foreigners do.

"Make 'em dry" is the instruction buried somewhere in the collective national consciousness, "make 'em rubbery. If you have to keep the buggers fresh, do it by washing 'em once a week."

It is by eating sandwiches in pubs at Saturday lunchtime that the British seek to atone for whatever their national sins have been. They're not altogether clear what those sins are, and don't want to know either. Sins are not the sort of things one wants to know about. But whatever sins there are are amply atoned for by the sandwiches they make themselves eat.

If there is anything worse than the sandwiches, it is the sausages which sit next to them. Joyless tubes, full of gristle, floating in a sea of something hot and sad, stuck with a plastic pin in the shape of a chef's hat: a memorial, one feels, for some chef who hated the world, and died, forgotten and alone among his cats on a back stair in Stepney.

The sausages are for the ones who know what their sins are and wish to atone for something specific.

"There must be somewhere better," said Arthur.

"No time," said Fenny, glancing at her watch, "my train leaves in half an hour."

They sat at a small wobbly table. On it were some dirty glasses, and some soggy beer mats with jokes printed on them. Arthur got Fenny a tomato juice, and himself a pint of yellow water with gas in it. And a couple of sausages, he didn't know why. He bought them for something to do while the gas settled in his glass.

The barman dunked Arthur's change in a pool of beer on the bar, for which Arthur thanked him.

"All right," said Fenny, glancing at her watch, "tell me what it is you have to tell me."

She sounded, as well she might, extremely skeptical, and Arthur's heart sank. Hardly, he felt, the most conducive setting to try to explain to her as she sat there, suddenly cool and defensive, that in a sort of out-of-body dream he had had a telepathic sense that the mental breakdown she had suffered had been connected with the fact that, appearances to the contrary notwithstanding, the Earth had been demolished to make way for a new hyperspace bypass, something which he alone on Earth knew anything about, having virtually witnessed it from a Vogon spaceship, and that furthermore both his body and soul ached for her unbearably and he needed deeply to go to bed with her as soon as was humanly possible.

"Fenny," he started.

"I wonder if you'd like to buy some tickets for our raffle? It's just a little one."

He glanced up sharply.

"To raise money for Anjie, who's retiring."

"What?"

"And needs a kidney machine."

He was being leaned over by a rather stiffly slim, middle-aged woman with a prim knitted suit and a prim little perm, and a prim little smile that probably got licked by prim little dogs a lot.

She was holding out a small book of cloakroom tickets and a collecting tin.

"Only ten pence each," she said, "so you could probably even buy two. Without breaking the bank!" She gave a tinkly little laugh and then a curiously long sigh. Saying "without breaking the bank" had obviously given her more pleasure than anything since some G.I.s had been billeted on her in the war.

"Er, yes, all right," said Arthur, hurriedly digging in his pocket and producing a couple of coins.

With infuriating slowness, and prim theatricality, if there was such a thing, the woman tore off two tickets and handed them to Arthur.

"I *do* hope you win," she said with a smile that suddenly snapped together like a piece of advanced origami, "the prizes are *so* nice."

"Yes, thank you," said Arthur, pocketing the tickets rather brusquely and glancing at his watch.

He turned toward Fenny.

So did the woman with the raffle tickets.

"And what about you, young lady?" she said. "It's for Anjie's kidney machine. She's retiring, you see. Yes?" She hoisted the little smile even farther up her face. She would have to stop and let it go soon or the skin would surely split.

"Er, look, here you are," said Arthur, and pushed a fifty-pence piece at her in the hope that that would see her off.

"Oh, we *are* in the money, aren't we?" said the woman, with a long smiling sigh. "Down from London, are we?"

Arthur wished she wouldn't talk so slowly.

"No, that's all right, really," he said with a wave of his hand, as she started with an awful deliberation to peel off five tickets, one by one.

"Oh, but you *must* have your tickets," insisted the woman, "or you won't be able to claim your prize. They're very nice prizes, you know. Very *suit*able."

Arthur snatched the tickets, and said thank you as sharply as he could.

The woman turned to Fenny once again.

"And now, what about—"

"No!" Arthur nearly yelled. "These are for her," he explained, brandishing the five new tickets.

"Oh, I *see!* How nice!"

She smiled sickeningly at both of them.

"Well, I *do* hope you—"

"Yes," snapped Arthur, "thank you."

The woman finally departed to the table next to theirs. Arthur turned desperately to Fenny, and was relieved to see that she was rocking with silent laughter.

He sighed and smiled.

"Where were we?"

"You were calling me Fenny, and I was about to ask you not to."

"What do you mean?"

She twirled the little wooden cocktail stick in her tomato juice.

"It's why I asked if you were a friend of my brother's. Or half-brother really. He's the only one who calls me Fenny, and I'm not fond of him for it."

"So, what's . . . ?"

"Fenchurch."

"What?"

"Fenchurch."

"Fenchurch."

She looked at him sternly.

"Yes," she said, "and I'm watching you like a lynx to see if you're going to ask the same silly question that everyone asks me till I want to scream. I shall be cross and disappointed if you do. Plus I shall scream. So watch it."

She smiled, shook her hair a little forward over her face and peered at him from behind it.

"Oh," he said, "that's a little unfair, isn't it?"

"Yes."

"Fine."

"All right," she said with a laugh, "you can ask me. Might as well get it over with. Better than having you call me Fenny all the time."

"Presumably..." said Arthur.

"We've only got *two* tickets left, you see, and since you were *so* generous when I spoke to you before—"

"What?" snapped Arthur.

The woman with the perm and the smile and the now nearly empty book of cloakroom tickets was waving the two last ones under his nose.

"I thought I'd give the opportunity to you, because the prizes are so nice."

She wrinkled up her nose a little confidentially.

"*Very tasteful.* I know you'll like them. And it is for Anjie's retirement present, you see. We want to give her—"

"A kidney machine, yes," said Arthur, "here."

He held out two more ten-pence pieces to her, and took the tickets.

A thought seemed to strike the woman. It struck her very slowly. You could watch it coming in like a long wave on a sandy beach.

"Oh dear," she said, "I'm not interrupting anything, am I?"

She peered anxiously at both of them.

"No, it's fine," said Arthur, "everything that could possibly be fine," he insisted, "is fine.

"Thank you," he added.

"I say," she said, in a delighted ecstasy of worry, "you're not... in *love*, are you?"

"It's very hard to say," said Arthur. "We haven't had a chance to talk yet."

He glanced at Fenchurch. She was grinning.

The woman nodded with knowing confidentiality.

"I'll let you see the prizes in a minute," she said, and left.

Arthur turned, with a sigh, back to the girl that he found it hard to say whether he was in love with.

"You were about to ask me," she said, "a question."

"Yes," said Arthur.

"We can do it together if you like," said Fenchurch. "Was I found..."

"...in a handbag," joined in Arthur.

"...in the Left Luggage office," they said together.

"...at Fenchurch Street Station," they finished.

"And the answer," said Fenchurch, "is no."

"Fine," said Arthur.

"I was conceived there."

"*What?*"

"I was con—"

"In the Left Luggage office?" hooted Arthur.

"No, of course not. Don't be silly. What would my parents be doing in the Left Luggage office?" she said, rather taken aback by the suggestion.

"Well, I don't know," sputtered Arthur, "or rather—"

"It was in the ticket queue."

"The—"

"The ticket queue. Or so they claim. They refuse to elaborate. They only say you wouldn't believe how bored it is possible to get in the ticket queue at Fenchurch Street Station."

She sipped demurely at her tomato juice and looked at her watch.

Arthur continued to gurgle chirpily for a moment or two.

"I'm going to have to go in a minute or two," said Fenchurch, "and you haven't begun to tell me whatever this terrifically extraordinary thing is that you were so keen to get off your chest."

"Why don't you let me drive you to London?" said Arthur. "It's Saturday, I've got nothing particular to do, I'd—"

"No," said Fenchurch, "thank you, it's sweet of you, but no. I need to be by myself for a couple of days." She smiled and shrugged.

"But—"

"You can tell me another time. I'll give you my number."

Arthur's heart went boom boom churn churn as she scribbled seven figures in pencil on a scrap of paper and handed it to him.

"Now we can relax," she said with a slow smile which filled Arthur till he thought he would burst.

"Fenchurch," he said, enjoying the name as he said it, "I—"

"A box," said a trailing voice, "of cherry liqueurs, and also, and I know you'll like this, a gramophone record of Scottish bagpipe music—"

"Yes, thank you, very nice," insisted Arthur.

"I just thought I'd let you have a look at them," said the permed woman, "as you're down from London..."

She was holding them out proudly for Arthur to see. He could see that they were indeed a box of cherry brandy liqueurs and a record of bagpipe music. That was what they were.

"I'll let you have your drink in peace now," she said, patting Arthur lightly on his seething shoulder, "but I knew you'd like to see."

Arthur reengaged his eyes with Fenchurch's once again, and suddenly was at a loss for something to say. A moment had come and gone between the two of them, but the whole rhythm of it had been wrecked by that stupid, blasted woman.

"Don't worry," said Fenchurch, looking at him steadily from over the top of her glass, "we will talk again." She took a sip.

"Perhaps," she added, "it wouldn't have gone so well if it wasn't for her." She gave a wry smile and dropped her hair forward over her face again.

It was perfectly true.

He had to admit it was perfectly true.

Chapter 13

That night, at home, as he was prancing round the house pretending to be tripping through cornfields in slow motion and continually exploding with sudden laughter, Arthur thought he could even bear to listen to the album of bagpipe music he had won. It was eight o'clock and he decided he would make himself, force himself, to listen to the whole record before he phoned her. Maybe he should even leave it till tomorrow. That would be the cool thing to do. Or next week sometime.

No. No games. He wanted her and didn't care who knew it. He definitely and absolutely wanted her, adored her, longed for her, wanted to do more things than there were names for with her.

He actually caught himself saying things like "Yippee," as he pranced ridiculously round the house. Her eyes, her hair, her voice, everything...

He stopped.

He would put on the record of bagpipe music. Then he would call her.

Would he, perhaps, call her first?

No. What he would do was this. He would put on the record of bagpipe music. He would listen to it, every last banshee wail of it. Then he would call her. That was the correct order. That was what he would do.

He was worried about touching things in case they blew up when he did so.

He picked up the record. It failed to blow up. He slipped it out of its cover. He opened the record player, he turned on the amp. They both survived. He giggled foolishly as he lowered the stylus onto the disk.

He sat and listened solemnly to "A Scottish Soldier."

He listened to "Amazing Grace."

He listened to something about some glen or other.

He thought about his miraculous lunchtime.

They had just been on the point of leaving when they were distracted by an awful outbreak of "yoo-hooing." The appallingly permed woman was waving to them across the room like some stupid bird with a broken wing. Everyone in the pub turned to them and seemed to be expecting some sort of response.

They hadn't listened to the bit about how pleased and happy Anjie was going to be about the £4.30 everyone had helped to raise toward the cost of her kidney machine, had been vaguely aware that someone from the next table had won a box of cherry brandy liqueurs, and took a moment or two to cotton on to the fact that the yoo-hooing lady was trying to ask them if they had ticket number 37.

Arthur discovered that he had. He glanced angrily at his watch.

Fenchurch gave him a push.

"Go on," she said, "go and get it. Don't be bad-tempered. Give them a nice speech about how pleased you are and you can give me a call and tell me how it went. I'll want to hear the record. Go on."

She flicked his arm and left.

The regulars thought his acceptance speech a little overeffusive. It was, after all, merely an album of bagpipe music.

Arthur thought about it, and listened to the music, and kept on breaking into laughter.

Chapter 14

Ring-ring.
Ring-ring.
Ring-ring.
"Hello, yes? Yes, that's right. Yes. You'll 'ave to speak up, there's an awful lot of noise in 'ere. What?

"No, I only do the bar in the evenings. It's Yvonne who does lunch, and Jim he's the landlord. No, I wasn't on. What?

"You'll have to speak up.

"What? No, don't know nothing about no raffle. What?

"No, don't know nothing about it. 'Old on, I'll call Jim."

The barmaid put her hand over the receiver and called over the noisy bar.

" 'Ere, Jim, bloke on the phone says something about he's won a raffle. He keeps on saying it's ticket 37 and he's won."

"No, there was a guy in the pub here won," shouted back the barman.

"He says 'ave we got the ticket."

"Well, how can he think he's won if he hasn't even got a ticket?"

"Jim says 'ow can you think you've won if you 'aven't even got the ticket. What?"

She put her hand over the receiver again.

"Jim, 'e keeps effing at me. Says there's a number on the ticket."

" 'Course there was a number on the ticket, it was a bloody raffle ticket, wasn't it?"

" 'E says 'e means it's a telephone number on the ticket."

"Put the phone down and serve the bloody customers, will you?"

Chapter 15

Eight hours west sat a man alone on a beach mourning an inexplicable loss. He could only think of his loss in little packets of grief at a time, because the whole thing was too great to be borne.

He watched the long slow Pacific waves come in along the sand, and waited and waited for the nothing that he knew was about to happen. As the time came for it not to happen, it duly didn't happen and so the afternoon wore itself away and the sun dropped beneath the long line of the sea, and the day was gone.

The beach was a beach we shall not name, because his private house was there, but it was a small sandy stretch somewhere along the hundreds of miles of coastline that runs west from Los Angeles, which is described in the new edition of *The Hitchhiker's Guide to the Galaxy* in one entry as *"junky, wunky, lunky, stunky, and what's that other word, and all kinds of bad stuff, woo,"* and in another, written only hours later as *"being like several thousand square miles of American Express junk mail, but without the same sense of moral depth. Plus the air is, for some reason, yellow."*

The coastline runs west, and then turns north up to the misty bay of San Francisco, which the *Guide* describes as a *"good place to go. It's very easy to believe that everyone you meet there also is a space traveler. Starting a new religion for you is just their way of saying 'hi.' Until you've settled in and got the hang of the place it is best to say 'no' to three questions out of any given four that anyone may ask you, because there are some very strange things going on there, some of which an unsuspecting alien could die of."* The hundreds of curling miles of cliffs and sand, palm trees, breakers, and sunsets are described in the *Guide* as *"boffo. A good one."*

And somewhere on this good boffo stretch of coastline lay the house of this inconsolable man, a man whom many regarded as being insane. But this was only, as he would tell people, because he was.

One of the many many reasons why people thought him insane was the peculiarness of his house which, even in a land where most people's houses were peculiar in one way or another, was quite extreme in its peculiarness.

His house was called The Outside of the Asylum.

His name was simply John Watson, though he preferred to be called—and some of his friends had now reluctantly agreed to do this—Wonko the Sane.

In his house were a number of strange things, including a gray glass bowl with eight words engraved upon it.

We can talk of him much later on. This is just an interlude to watch the sun go down and to say that he was there watching it.

He had lost everything he cared for, and was now simply waiting for the end of the world—little realizing that it had already been and gone.

Chapter 16

After a disgusting Sunday spent emptying rubbish bins behind a pub in Taunton, and finding nothing, no raffle ticket, no telephone number, Arthur tried everything he could to find Fenchurch, and the more things he tried, the more weeks passed.

He raged and railed against himself, against fate, against the world and its weather. He even, in his sorrow and his fury, went and sat in the motorway service station cafeteria where he'd been just before he met her.

"It's the drizzle that makes me particularly morose."

"Please shut up about the drizzle," snapped Arthur.

"I would shut up if it would shut up drizzling."

"Look—"

"But I'll tell you what it will do when it shuts up drizzling, shall I?"

"No."

"Blatter."

"What?"

"It will blatter."

Arthur stared over the rim of his coffee cup at the grisly outside world. It was a completely pointless place to be, he realized, and he had been driven there by superstition rather than logic. However, as if to bait him with the knowledge that such coincidences could in fact happen, fate had chosen to reunite him with the lorry driver he had encountered there last time.

The more he tried to ignore him, the more he found himself being dragged back into the whirlpool of the man's exasperating conversation.

"I think," said Arthur vaguely, cursing himself for even bothering to say this, "that it's easing off."

"Ha!"

Arthur just shrugged. He should go. That's what he should do. He should just go.

"It *never* stops raining!" ranted the lorry driver. He thumped the table, spilled his tea, and actually, for a moment, appeared to be steaming.

You can't just walk around without responding to a remark like that.

"Of course it stops raining," said Arthur. It was hardly an elegant refutation, but it had to be said.

"It *rains ... all ...* the *time*," raved the man, thumping the table again, in time to the words.

Arthur shook his head.

"Stupid to say it rains *all* the time," he said.

The man's eyebrows shot up, affronted.

"*Stupid*? Why's it stupid? Why's it stupid to say it rains all the time if it rains all the whole time?"

"Didn't rain yesterday."

"Did in Darlington."

Arthur paused, warily.

"You going to ask me where I was then yesterday," asked the man, "eh?"

"No," said Arthur.

"But I expect you can guess."

"Do you."

"Begins with a D."

"Does it."

"And it was pissing down there, I can tell you."

"You don't want to sit there, mate," said a passing stranger in overalls cheerily to Arthur, "that's Thundercloud Corner, that is. Reserved special for old Raindrops Keep Falling On My Head here. There's one reserved in every motorway caff between here and sunny Denmark. Steer clear is my advice. 'Swhat we all do. How's it going, Rob? Keeping busy? Got your wet-weather tires on? Har-har."

He breezed by and went to tell a joke about Britt Ekland to someone at a nearby table who roared with laughter.

"See, none of them bastards take me seriously," said Rob McKenna, "but," he added darkly, leaning forward and screwing up his eyes, "they all know it's true!"

Arthur frowned.

"Like my wife," hissed the sole owner and driver of McKenna's All-Weather Haulage; "she says it's nonsense and I make a fuss and complain about nothing, *but*"—he paused dramatically and darted out dangerous looks from his eyes—"she always brings the washing in when I phone to say I'm on me way home!" He brandished his coffee spoon. "What do you make of that?"

"Well ..."

"I have a book," he went on, "I have a book. A diary. Kept it for fifteen years. Shows every single place I've ever been. Every day. And also what the weather was like. And it was uniformly," he snarled, "'orrible. All over England, Scotland, Wales, I been. All round the Continent, Italy, Germany, back and forth to Denmark, been to Yugoslavia. It's all marked in and charted. Even when I went to visit my brother," he added, "in Seattle."

"Well," said Arthur, getting up to leave at last, "perhaps you'd better show it to someone."

"I will," said Rob McKenna.

And he did.

Misery. Dejection. More misery and more dejection. He needed a project and he gave himself one.

He would find where his cave had been.

On prehistoric Earth he had lived in a cave, not a nice cave, a lousy cave, but ... There was no but. It had been a totally lousy cave and he had hated it. But he had lived in it for five years, which made it home of some kind, and a person likes to keep track of his homes. Arthur Dent was such a person and so he went to Exeter to buy a computer.

That was what he really wanted, of course, a computer. But he felt he ought to have some serious purpose in mind before he simply went and blew a lot of bread on what people might otherwise mistake as being just a thing to play with. So that was his serious purpose. To pinpoint the exact location of a cave on prehistoric Earth. He explained this to the man in the shop.

"Why?" said the man in the shop.

This was a tricky one.

"Okay, skip that," said the man in the shop, "how?"

"Well, I was hoping you could help me with that."

The man sighed and his shoulders dropped.

"Have you much experience of computers?"

Arthur wondered whether to mention Eddie the shipboard computer on the *Heart of Gold*, who could have done the job in a second, or Deep Thought, or—but decided he wouldn't.

"No," he said.

"Looks like a fun afternoon," said the man in the shop, but he said it only to himself.

Arthur bought the Apple anyway. Over a few days he also acquired some astronomical software, plotted the movements of stars, drew rough little diagrams of how he seemed to remember the stars to have been in the sky when he looked up out of his cave at night, and worked away busily at it for weeks, cheerfully putting off the conclusion he knew he would inevitably have to come to, which was that the whole project was completely ludicrous.

Rough drawings from memory were futile. He didn't even know how long ago it had been, beyond Ford Prefect's rough guess at the time that it was "a couple of million years" and he simply didn't have the math.

Still, in the end he worked out a method which would at least produce a result. He decided not to mind the fact that with the extraordinary jumble of rules of thumb, wild approximations, and arcane guesswork he was using he would be lucky to hit the right galaxy; he just went ahead and got a result.

He would call it the right result. Who would know?

As it happened, through the myriad and unfathomable chances of fate, he got it exactly right, though he of course would never know that. He just went up to London and knocked on the appropriate door.

"Oh. I thought you were going to phone me first."

Arthur gaped in astonishment.

"You can only come in for a few minutes," said Fenchurch. "I'm just going out."

A summer's day in Islington, full of the mournful wail of antique-restoring machinery.

Fenchurch was unavoidably busy for the afternoon, so Arthur wandered in a blissed-out haze and looked at all the shops, which in Islington are quite a useful bunch, as anyone who regularly needs old woodworking tools, Boer War helmets, drag, office furniture, or fish will readily confirm.

The sun beat down over the roof gardens. It beat on architects and plumbers. It beat on barristers and burglars. It beat on pizzas. It beat on estate agent's particulars.

It beat on Arthur as he went into a restored furniture shop.

"It's an interesting building," said the proprietor cheerfully. "There's a cellar with a secret passage which connects with a nearby pub. It was built for the Prince Regent apparently, so he could make his escape when he needed to."

"You mean, in case anybody might catch him buying stripped pine furniture," said Arthur.

"No," said the proprietor, "not for that reason."

"You'll have to excuse me," said Arthur, "I'm terribly happy."

"I see."

He wandered hazily on and found himself outside the offices of Greenpeace. He remembered the contents of his file marked "Things To Do—Urgent!" which he hadn't opened again in the meantime. He marched in with a cheery smile and said he'd come to give them some money to help free the dolphins.

"Very funny," they told him, "go away."

This wasn't quite the response he had expected, so he tried again. This time they got quite angry with him, so he just left some money anyway and went back out into the sunshine.

Just after six he returned to Fenchurch's house in the alleyway, clutching a bottle of champagne.

"Hold this," she said, shoved a stout rope in his hand, and disappeared inside through the large white wooden doors from which dangled a fat padlock off a black iron bar.

The house was a small converted stable in a light industrial alleyway behind the derelict Royal Agricultural Hall of Islington. As well as its large stable doors it also had a normal-looking front door of smartly glazed paneled wood with a black dolphin door knocker. The one odd thing about this door was its doorstep, which was nine feet high, since the door was set into the upper of the two floors and presumably had been used originally to haul up hay for hungry horses.

An old pulley jutted out of the brickwork above the doorway and it was over this that the rope Arthur was holding was slung. The other end of the rope held a suspended cello.

The door opened above his head.

"Okay," said Fenchurch, "pull on the rope, steady the cello. Pass it up to me."

He pulled on the rope, he steadied the cello.

"I can't pull on the rope again," he said, "without letting go of the cello."

Fenchurch leaned down.

"I'm steadying the cello," she said, "you pull on the rope."

The cello eased up level with the doorway, swinging slightly, and Fenchurch maneuvered it inside.

"Come on up yourself," she called down.

Arthur picked up his bag of goodies and went in through the stable doors, tingling.

The bottom room, which he had seen briefly before, was pretty rough and full of junk. A large cast-iron clothes wringer stood there, a surprising number of kitchen sinks were piled in a corner. There was also, Arthur was momentarily alarmed to see, a baby carriage, but it was very old and uncomplicatedly full of books.

The floor was old stained concrete, excitingly cracked. And this was the measure of Arthur's mood as he started up the rickety wooden steps in the far corner. Even a cracked concrete floor seemed to him an almost unbearably sensual thing.

"An architect friend of mine keeps on telling me how he can do wonderful things with this place," said Fenchurch chattily as Arthur emerged through the floor. "He keeps on coming round, standing in stunned amazement muttering about space and objects and events and marvelous qualities of light, then says he needs a pencil and disappears for weeks. Wonderful things have therefore so far failed to happen to it."

In fact, thought Arthur as he looked about, the upper room was at least reasonably wonderful anyway. It was simply decorated, furnished with things made out of cushions and also a stereo set with speakers which would have impressed the guys who put up Stonehenge.

There were flowers which were pale and pictures which were interesting.

There was a sort of gallery structure in the roof space which held a bed and also a bathroom which, Fenchurch explained, you could actually swing a cat in, "But," she added, "only if it was a reasonably patient cat and didn't mind a few nasty cracks about the head. So. Here you are."

"Yes."

They looked at each other for a moment.

The moment became a longer moment, and suddenly it was a very long moment, so long one could hardly tell where all the time was coming from.

For Arthur, who could usually contrive to feel self-conscious if left alone for long enough with a Swiss cheese plant, the moment was one of sustained revelation. He felt on the sudden like a cramped and zoo-born animal who wakes one morning to find the door to his cage hanging quietly open and the savanna stretching gray and pink to the distant rising sun, while all around new sounds are waking.

He wondered what the new sounds were as he gazed at her openly wondering face and her eyes that smiled with a shared surprise.

He hadn't realized that life speaks with a voice to you, a voice that brings you answers to the questions you continually ask of it, had never consciously detected it or recognized its tones until it now said something it had never said to him before, which was "yes."

Fenchurch dropped her eyes away at last, with a tiny shake of her head.

"I know," she said. "I shall have to remember," she added, "that you are the sort of person who cannot hold on to a simple piece of paper for two minutes without winning a raffle with it."

She turned away.

"Let's go for a walk," she said quickly. "Hyde Park. I'll change into something less suitable."

She was dressed in a rather severe dark dress, not a particularly shapely one, and it didn't really suit her.

"I wear it specially for my cello teacher," she said. "He's a nice old boy, but I sometimes think all that bowing gets him a bit excited. I'll be down in a moment."

She ran lightly up the steps to the gallery above, and called down, "Put the bottle in the fridge for later."

He noticed as he slipped the champagne bottle into the door that it had an identical twin to sit next to.

He walked over to the window and looked out. He turned and started to look at her records. From above he heard the rustle of her dress fall to the ground. He talked to himself about the sort of person he was. He told himself very firmly that for this moment at least he would keep his eyes very firmly and steadfastly locked on to the spines of her records, read the titles, nod appreciatively, count the blasted things if he had to. He would keep his head down.

This he completely, utterly, and abjectly failed to do.

She was staring down at him with such intensity that she seemed hardly to notice that he was looking up at her. Then suddenly she shook her head, dropped the light sundress down over herself and disappeared quickly into the bathroom.

She emerged a moment later, all smiles and with a sun hat, and came tripping down the steps with extraordinary lightness. It was a strange kind of dancing motion she had. She saw that he noticed it and put her head slightly on one side.

"Like it?" she said.

"You look gorgeous," he said simply, because she did.

"Hmmm," she said, as if he hadn't really answered her question.

She closed the upstairs front door which had stood open all this time, and looked around the little room to see that it was all in a fit state to be left on its own for a while. Arthur's eyes followed hers around, and while he was looking in the other direction she slipped something out of a drawer and into the canvas bag she was carrying.

Arthur looked back at her.

"Ready?"

"Did you know," she said with a slightly puzzled smile, "that there's something wrong with me?"

Her directness caught Arthur unprepared.

"Well," he said, "I'd heard some vague sort of—"

"I wonder how much you do know about me," she said. "If you heard from where I think you heard then that's not it. Russell just sort of makes stuff up, because he can't deal with what it really is."

A pang of worry went through Arthur.

"Then what is it," he said, "can you tell me?"

"Don't worry," she said, "it's nothing bad at all. Just unusual. Very very unusual."

She touched his hand, and then leaned forward and kissed him briefly.

"I shall be very interested to know," she said, "if you manage to work out what it is this evening."

Arthur felt that if someone tapped him at that point he would have chimed, like the deep sustained rolling chime his gray fishbowl made when he flicked it with his thumbnail.

Chapter 19

Ford Prefect was irritated to be continually awakened by the sound of gunfire.

He slid himself out of the maintenance hatchway which he had fashioned into a bunk for himself by disabling some of the noisier machinery in its vicinity and padding it with towels. He slung himself down the access ladder and prowled the corridors moodily. They were claustrophobic and ill-lit, and what light there was continually flickering and dimming as power surged this way and that through the ship, causing heavy vibrations and rasping humming noises.

That wasn't it, though.

He paused and leaned back against the wall as something that looked like a small silver power drill flew down the dim corridor past him, with a nasty searing screech.

That wasn't it either.

He clambered listlessly through a bulkhead door and found himself in a larger corridor, though still ill-lit.

The ship lurched. It had been doing this a fair bit, but this was heavier. A small platoon of robots went by making a terrible clattering.

Still not it, though.

Acrid smoke was drifting up from one end of the corridor, so he walked along it in the other direction.

He passed a series of observation monitors built into the walls behind plates of toughened but still badly scratched Plexiglas.

One of them showed some horrible green scaly reptilian figure ranting and raving about the Single Transferable Vote system. It was hard to tell whether he was for or against it, but he clearly felt very strongly about it. Ford turned the sound down.

That wasn't it, though.

He passed another monitor. It was showing a commercial for some brand of toothpaste that would apparently make you feel free if you used it. There was nasty blaring music with it, too.

That wasn't it.

He came upon another, much larger three-dimensional screen that was monitoring the outside of the vast silver Xaxisian ship.

As he watched, a thousand horribly beweaponed Zirzla robot star cruisers came searing round the dark shadow of a moon, silhouetted against the blinding disk of the star Xaxis, and the ship simultaneously unleashed a vicious blaze of hideously incomprehensible forces from all its orifices against them.

That was it.

Ford shook his head irritably and rubbed his eyes. He slumped on the wrecked body of a dull silver robot which clearly had been burning earlier on but had now cooled down enough to sit on.

He yawned and dug his copy of *The Hitchhiker's Guide to the Galaxy* out of his satchel. He activated the screen, and flickered idly through some level-three entries and some level-four entries. He was looking for some good insomnia cures. He found REST, which was what he reckoned he needed. He found REST AND RECUPERATION and was about to pass on when he suddenly had a better idea. He looked up at the monitor screen. The battle was raging more fiercely every second and the noise was appalling. The ship juddered, screamed, and lurched as each new bolt of stunning energy was delivered or received.

He looked back down at the *Guide* again and flipped through a few likely locations. He suddenly laughed, and then rummaged in his satchel again.

He pulled out a small memory dump module, wiped off the fluff and biscuit crumbs, and plugged it into an interface on the back of the *Guide*.

When all the information that he could think was relevant had been dumped into the module, he unplugged it again, tossed it lightly in the palm of his hand, put the *Guide* away in his satchel, smirked, and went in search of the ship's computer data banks.

Chapter 20

The purpose of having the sun go low in the evenings, in the summer, especially in parks," said the voice earnestly, "is to make girls' breasts bob up and down more clearly to the eye. I am convinced that this is the case."

Arthur and Fenchurch giggled about this to each other as they passed. She hugged him more tightly for a moment.

"And I am certain," said the frizzy ginger-haired youth with the long thin nose who was expostulating from his deck chair by the side of the Serpentine, "that if one worked the argument through, one would find that it flowed with perfect naturalness and logic from everything," he insisted to his thin dark-haired companion who was slumped in the next-door deck chair feeling dejected about his spots, "that Darwin was going on about. This is certain. This is indisputable. And," he added, "I love it."

He turned sharply and squinted through his spectacles at Fenchurch. Arthur steered her away.

"Next guess," she said, when she had stopped giggling, "come on."

"All right," he said, "your elbow. Your left elbow. There's something wrong with your left elbow."

"Wrong again," she said, "completely wrong. You're on completely the wrong track."

The summer sun was sinking through the trees in the park, looking as if—let's not mince words. Hyde Park is stunning. Everything about it is stunning except for the rubbish on Monday mornings. Even the ducks are stunning. Anyone who can go through Hyde Park on a summer's evening and not feel moved by it is probably going through in an ambulance with the sheet pulled up over his face.

It is a park in which people do more extraordinary things than they do elsewhere. Arthur and Fenchurch found a man in shorts practicing the bagpipes to himself under a tree. The piper paused to chase off an American couple who had tried, timidly, to put some coins on the box his bagpipes came in.

"No!" he shouted at them; "go away! I'm only practicing."

He started resolutely to reinflate his bag, but even the noise this made could not disfigure their mood.

Arthur put his arms around her and moved them slowly downward.

"I don't think it can be your bottom," he said after a while. "There doesn't seem to be anything wrong with that at all."

"Yes," she agreed, "there's absolutely nothing wrong with my bottom."

They kissed for so long that eventually the piper went and practiced on the other side of the tree.

"I'll tell you a story," said Arthur.

"Good."

They found a patch of grass which was relatively free of couples actually lying on top of each other and sat and watched the stunning ducks and the low sunlight rippling on the water which ran beneath the stunning ducks.

"A story," said Fenchurch, cuddling his arm to her.

"Which will tell something of the sort of things that happen to me. It's absolutely true."

"True story."

"You know sometimes people tell you stories that are supposed to be something that happened to their wife's cousin's best friend, but actually probably got made up somewhere along the line.

"Well, it's like one of those stories, except that it actually happened, and I know it actually happened, because the person it actually happened to was me."

"Like the raffle ticket."

Arthur laughed. "Yes. I had a train to catch. I arrived at the station—"

"Did I ever tell you," interrupted Fenchurch, "what happened to my parents in a station?"

"Yes," said Arthur, "you did."

"Just checking."

Arthur glanced at his watch. "I suppose we could think of getting back," he said.

"Tell me the story," said Fenchurch firmly. "You arrived at the station."

"I was about twenty minutes early. I'd got the time of the train wrong. I suppose it is at least equally possible," he added after a moment's reflection, "that British Rail had got the time of the train wrong. Hadn't occurred to me before."

"Get on with it." Fenchurch laughed.

"So I bought a newspaper, to do the crossword, and went to the buffet to get a cup of coffee."

"You do the crossword?"

"Yes."

"Which one?"

"*The Guardian* usually."

"I think it tries to be too cute. I prefer *The Times*. Did you solve it?"

"What?"

"The crossword in *The Guardian*."

"I haven't had a chance to look at it yet," said Arthur. "I'm still trying to buy the coffee."

"All right then. Buy the coffee."

"I'm buying it. I am also," said Arthur, "buying some biscuits."

"What sort?"

"Rich Tea."

"Good choice."

"I like them. Laden with all these new possessions, I go and sit at a table. And don't ask me what the table was like because this was some time ago and I can't remember. It was probably round."

"All right."

"So let me give you the layout. Me sitting at the table. On my left, the newspaper. On my right, the cup of coffee. In the middle of the table, the packet of biscuits."

"I see it perfectly."

"What you don't see," said Arthur, "because I haven't mentioned him yet, is the guy sitting at the table already. He is sitting there opposite me."

"What's he like?"

"Perfectly ordinary. Briefcase. Business suit. He didn't look," said Arthur, "as if he was about to do anything weird."

"Ah. I know the type. What did he do?"

"He did this. He leaned across the table, picked up the packet of biscuits, tore it open, took one out, and..."

"What?"

"Ate it."

"*What?*"

"He ate it."

Fenchurch looked at him in astonishment. "What on earth did you do?"

"Well, in the circumstances I did what any red-blooded Englishman would do. I was compelled," said Arthur, "to ignore it."

"*What?* Why?"

"Well, it's not the sort of thing you're trained for, is it? I searched my soul, and discovered that there was nothing anywhere in my upbringing, experience, or even primal instincts to tell me how to react to someone who has quite simply, calmly, sitting right there in front of me, stolen one of my biscuits."

"Well, you could . . ." Fenchurch thought about it. "I must say I'm not sure what I would have done either. So what happened?"

"I stared furiously at the crossword," said Arthur, "couldn't do a single clue, took a sip of coffee, it was too hot to drink, so there was nothing for it. I braced myself. I took a biscuit, trying very hard not to notice," he added, "that the packet was already mysteriously open. . . ."

"But you're fighting back, taking a tough line."

"After my fashion, yes. I ate the biscuit. I ate it very deliberately and visibly, so that he would have no doubt as to what it was I was doing. When I eat a biscuit," said Arthur, "it stays eaten."

"So what did he do?"

"Took another one. Honestly," insisted Arthur, "this is exactly what happened. He took another biscuit, he ate it. Clear as daylight. Certain as we are sitting on the ground."

Fenchurch stirred uncomfortably.

"And the problem was," said Arthur, "that having not said anything the *first* time, it was somehow even more difficult to broach the subject the second time around. What do you say? 'Excuse me . . . I couldn't help noticing, er . . .' Doesn't work. No, I ignored it with, if anything, even more vigor than previously."

"My man . . ."

"Stared at the crossword again, still couldn't budge a bit of it, so showing some of the spirit that Henry V did on St. Crispin's Day . . ."

"What?"

"I went into the breach again. I took," said Arthur, "another biscuit. And for an instant our eyes met."

"Like this?"

"Yes, well, no, not quite like that. But they met. Just for an instant. And we both looked away. But I am here to tell you," said Arthur, "that there was a little electricity in the air. There was a little tension building up over the table. At about this time."

"I can imagine."

"We went through the whole packet like this. Him, me, him, me . . ."

"The *whole* packet?"

"Well, it was only eight biscuits, but it seemed like a lifetime of biscuits we were getting through at this point. Gladiators could hardly have had a tougher time."

"Gladiators," said Fenchurch, "would have had to do it in the sun. More physically grueling."

"There is that. So. When the empty packet was lying dead between us the man at last got up, having done his worst, and left. I heaved a sigh of relief, of course.

"As it happened, my train was announced a moment or two later, so I finished my coffee, stood up, picked up the newspaper, and underneath the newspaper..."

"Yes?"

"Were *my* biscuits."

"What?" said Fenchurch. *"What?"*

"True."

"No!" She gasped and tossed herself back on the grass laughing.

She sat up again.

"You complete nitwit," she hooted, "you almost completely and utterly foolish person."

She pushed him backward, rolled over him, kissed him, and rolled off again. He was surprised at how light she was.

"Now you tell me a story."

"I thought," she said, putting on a low husky voice, "that you were very keen to get back."

"No hurry," he said airily, "I want you to tell me a story."

She looked out over the lake and pondered.

"All right," she said, "it's only a short one. And not funny like yours, but... anyway."

She looked down. Arthur could feel that it was one of those sorts of moments. The air seemed to stand still around them, waiting. Arthur wished that the air would go away and mind its own business.

"When I was a kid..." she said. "These sorts of stories always start like this, don't they? 'When I was a kid...' Anyway. This is the bit when the girl suddenly says, 'When I was a kid...' and starts to unburden herself. We have got to that bit. When I was a kid I had this picture hanging over the foot of my bed.... What do you think of it so far?"

"I like it. I think it's moving well. You're getting the bedroom interest in nice and early. We could probably do with some development with the picture."

"It was one of those pictures that children are supposed to like," she said, "but don't. Full of endearing little animals doing endearing things, you know?"

"I know. I was plagued with them too. Rabbits in waistcoats."

"Exactly. These rabbits were in fact on a raft, as were assorted rats and owls. There may even have been a reindeer."

"On the raft."

"On the raft. And a boy was sitting on the raft."

"Among the rabbits in waistcoats and the owls and the reindeer."

"Precisely there. A boy of the cheery gypsy ragamuffin variety."

"Ugh."

"The picture worried me, I must say. There was an otter swimming in front of the raft, and I used to lie awake at night worrying about this otter having to pull the raft, with all these wretched animals on it who shouldn't even be on a raft, and the otter had such a thin tail to pull it with I thought it must hurt pulling it all the time. Worried me. Not badly, but just vaguely, all the time.

"Then one day—and remember I'd been looking at this picture every night for years—I suddenly noticed that the raft had a sail. Never seen it before. The otter was fine, he was just swimming along."

She shrugged.

"Good story?" she said.

"Ends weakly," said Arthur, "leaves the audience crying, 'Yes, but what of it?' Fine up till there, but needs a final sting before the credits."

Fenchurch laughed and hugged her legs.

"It was just such a sudden revelation, years of almost unnoticed worry just dropping away, like taking off heavy weights, like black and white becoming color, like a dry stick suddenly being watered. The sudden shift of perspective that says, 'Put away your worries, the world is a good and perfect place. It is in fact very easy.' You probably think I'm saying that because I'm going to say that I felt like that this afternoon or something, don't you?"

"Well, I . . ." said Arthur, his composure suddenly shattered.

"Well, it's all right," she said, "I did. That's exactly what I felt. But, you see, I've felt that before, even stronger. Incredibly strongly. I'm afraid I'm a bit of a one," she said, gazing off into the distance, "for sudden startling revelations."

Arthur was at sea, could hardly speak, and felt it wiser therefore for the moment not to try.

"It was very *odd*," she said, much as one of the pursuing Egyptians might have said that the behavior of the Red Sea when Moses waved his rod at it was a little on the strange side.

"Very odd," she repeated, "for days before, the strangest feeling had been building in me, as if I was going to give birth. No, it wasn't like that in fact, it was more as if I was being connected into something, bit by bit, no, not even that, it was as if the whole of the Earth, through me, was going to..."

"Does the number," said Arthur gently, "forty-two mean anything to you at all?"

"What? No, what are you talking about?" exclaimed Fenchurch.

"Just a thought," murmured Arthur.

"Arthur, I mean this, this is very real to me, this is serious."

"*I* was being perfectly serious," said Arthur; "it's just the Universe I'm never quite sure about."

"What do you mean by that?"

"Tell me the rest of it," he said. "Don't worry if it sounds odd. Believe me, you are talking to someone who has seen a lot of stuff," he added, "that is odd. And I don't mean biscuits."

She nodded, and seemed to believe him. Suddenly, she gripped his arm.

"It was so *simple*," she said, "so wonderfully and extraordinarily simple, when it came."

"What was it?" said Arthur quietly.

"Arthur, you see," she said, "that's what I no longer know. And the loss is unbearable. If I try to think back to it it all goes flickery and jumpy, and if I try too hard, I get as far as the teacup and I just black out."

"What?"

"Well, like your story," she said, "the best bit happened in a café. I was sitting there, having a cup of tea. This was after days of this build-up, the feeling of becoming connected up. I think I was buzzing gently. And there was some work going on at a building site opposite the café, and I was watching it through the window, over the rim of my teacup, which I always find is the nicest way of watching other people working. And suddenly, there it was in my mind, this message from somewhere. And it was so simple. It made such sense of everything. I just sat up and thought, 'Oh! Oh, well, that's all right, then.' I was so startled I almost dropped my teacup, in fact I think I did drop it. Yes," she added thoughtfully, "I'm sure I did. How much sense am I making?"

"It was fine up to the bit about the teacup."

She shook her head, and shook it again, as if trying to clear it, which is what she was trying to do.

"Well, that's it," she said, "fine up to the bit about the teacup. That was the point at which it seemed to me quite literally as if the world exploded."

"What . . . ?"

"I know it sounds crazy, and everybody says it was hallucinations, but if that was hallucinations then I have hallucinations in big screen 3D with 16-track Dolby stereo and should probably hire myself out to people who are bored with shark movies. It was as if the ground was literally ripped from under my feet, and . . . and . . ."

She patted the grass lightly, as if for reassurance, and then seemed to change her mind about what she was going to say.

"And I woke up in hospital. I suppose I've been in and out ever since. And that's why I have an instinctive nervousness," she said, "of sudden startling revelations that everything's going to be all right." She looked up at him.

Arthur had simply ceased to worry himself about the strange anomalies surrounding his return to his home world, or rather had consigned them to that part of his mind marked "Things To Think About—Urgent." "Here is the world," he had told himself, "here, for whatever reason, is the world, and here it stays. With me on it." But now it seemed to go swimmy around him, as it had that night in the car when Fenchurch's brother had told him the silly story of the CIA agent in the reservoir. The French Embassy went swimmy. The Sheraton Tower Hotel and the Bank of Abu Dhabi went swimmy. The trees went swimmy. The lake went swimmy, but this was perfectly natural and nothing to be alarmed at because a gray goose had just landed on it. The geese were having a great relaxed time and had no major answers they wished to know the questions to.

"Anyway," said Fenchurch, suddenly and brightly and with a wide-eyed smile, "there is something wrong with part of me, and you've got to find out what it is. We'll go home."

Arthur shook his head.

"What's the matter?" she said.

Arthur had shaken his head, not to disagree with her suggestion which he thought was a truly excellent one, one of the world's great suggestions, but because he was just for a moment trying to free himself of the recurring impression he had that just when he was least expecting it the Universe would suddenly leap out from behind a door and go boo at him.

"I'm just trying to get this entirely clear in my mind," said Arthur. "You say you felt as if the Earth actually . . . exploded. . . ."

"Yes. More than felt."

"Which is what everybody else says," he said hesitantly, "is hallucinations?"

"Yes but, Arthur, that's ridiculous. People think that if you just say 'hallucinations' it explains anything you want it to explain and eventually whatever it is you can't understand will just go away. It's just a word, it doesn't explain anything. It doesn't explain why the dolphins disappeared."

"No," said Arthur, "no," he added thoughtfully. "No," he added again, even more thoughtfully. "What?" he said at last.

"Doesn't explain the dolphins disappearing."

"No," said Arthur, "I see that. Which dolphins do you mean?"

"What do you mean which dolphins? I'm talking about when all the dolphins disappeared."

She put her hand on his knee, which made him realize that the tingling going up and down his spine was not her gently stroking his back, and must instead be one of those nasty creepy feelings he so often got when people were trying to explain things to him.

"Disappeared?"

"Yes."

"The dolphins?"

"Yes."

"All the dolphins," said Arthur, "disappeared?"

"Yes."

"The dolphins? You're saying the dolphins all disappeared? Is this," said Arthur, trying to be absolutely clear on this point, "what you're saying?"

"Arthur, where have you been, for heaven's sake? The dolphins all disappeared on the same day I . . ."

She stared him intently in his startled eyes.

"What . . . ?"

"No dolphins. All gone. Vanished."

She searched his face.

"Did you really not know that?"

It was clear from his startled expression that he did not.

"Where did they go?" he asked.

"No one knows. That's what vanished means." She paused. "Well, there is one man who says he knows about it, but everyone says he lives in California," she said, "and is mad. I was thinking of going to see him because it seems the only lead I've got on what happened to me."

She shrugged, and then looked at him long and quietly. She laid her hand on the side of his face.

"I really would like to know where you've been," she said. "I think something terrible happened to you then as well. And that's why we recognized each other."

She glanced around the park, which was now being gathered into the clutches of dusk.

"Well," she said, "now you've got someone you can tell."

Arthur slowly let out a long year of a sigh.

"It is," he said, "a very long story."

Fenchurch leaned across him and drew over her canvas bag.

"Is it anything to do with this?" she said. The thing she took out of her bag was battered and travel-worn as if it had been hurled into prehistoric rivers, baked under the sun that shines so redly on the deserts of Kakrafoon, half buried in the marbled sands that fringe the heady vapored oceans of Santraginus V, frozen on the glaciers of the moon of Jaglan Beta, sat on, kicked around spaceships, scuffed and generally abused, and since its makers had thought that these were exactly the sorts of things that might happen to it, they had thoughtfully encased it in a sturdy plastic cover and written on it, in large friendly letters, the words "Don't Panic."

"Where did you get this?" said Arthur, startled, taking it from her.

"Ah," she said, "I thought it was yours. In Russell's car that night. You dropped it. Have you been to many of these places?"

Arthur drew *The Hitchhiker's Guide to the Galaxy* from its cover. It was like a small, thin, flexible lap computer. He tapped some buttons till the screen flared with text.

"A few," he said.

"Can we go?"

"What? No," said Arthur abruptly, then relented, but relented warily. "Do you want to?" he said, hoping for the answer no. It was an act of great generosity on his part not to say, "You don't want to, do you?" which expects it.

"Yes," she said. "I want to know what the message was that I lost, and where it came from. Because I don't think," she added, standing up and looking round the increasing gloom of the park, "that it came from here."

"I'm not even sure," she further added, slipping her arm around Arthur's waist, "that I know where here is."

The Hitchhiker's Guide to the Galaxy is, as has been remarked before often and accurately, a pretty startling kind of a thing. It is, essentially, as the title implies, a guidebook. The problem is, or rather one of the problems, for there are many, a sizable number of which are continually clogging up the civil, commercial, and criminal courts in all areas of the Galaxy, and especially, where possible, the more corrupt ones, this.

The previous sentence makes sense. That is not the problem.

This is:

Change.

Read it through again and you'll get it.

The Galaxy is a rapidly changing place. There is, frankly, so much of it, every bit of which is continually on the move, continually changing. A bit of a nightmare, you might think, for a scrupulous and conscientious editor diligently striving to keep this massively detailed and complex electronic tome abreast of all the changing circumstances and conditions that the Galaxy throws up every minute of every hour of every day, and you would be wrong. Where you would be wrong would be in failing to realize that the editor, like all the editors the *Guide* has ever had, has no real grasp of the meaning of the words "scrupulous," "conscientious," and "diligent," and tends to get his nightmares through a straw.

Entries tend to get updated or not across the Sub-Etha Net according to if they read good.

Take, for example, the case of Brequinda on the Foth of Avalars, famed in myth, legend, and stultifyingly dull tri-d miniseries as home of the magnificent and magical Fuolornis Fire Dragon.

In ancient days, before the advent of the Sorth of Bragadox, when Fragilis sang and Saxaquine of the Quenelux held sway, when the air was sweet and the nights fragrant, but they all somehow managed to be, or so they claimed, though how on earth they could have thought that anyone was even remotely likely to believe such a preposterous claim what with all the sweet air and fragrant nights and whatnot is anyone's guess, virgins, it

was not possible to heave a brick on Brequinda in the Foth of Avalars
without hitting at least half a dozen Fuolornis Fire Dragons.

Whether you would want to do that is another matter.

Not that Fire Dragons weren't an essentially peace-loving species,
because they were. They adored it to bits, and this wholesale adoring of
things to bits was often in itself the problem: one so often hurts the one
one loves, especially if one is a Fuolornis Fire Dragon with breath like a
rocket booster and teeth like a park fence. Another problem was that once
they were in the mood they often went on to hurt quite a lot of the ones
that other people loved as well. Add to all that the relatively small number
of madmen who actually went around the place heaving bricks, and you
end up with a lot of people on Brequinda in the Foth of Avalars getting
seriously hurt by dragons.

But did they mind? They did not.

Were they heard to bemoan their fate? No.

The Fuolornis Fire Dragons were revered throughout the lands of
Brequinda in the Foth of Avalars for their savage beauty, their noble ways,
and their habit of biting people who didn't revere them.

Why was this?

The answer was simple.

Sex.

There is, for some unfathomed reason, something almost unbearably
sexy about having huge fire-breathing magical dragons flying low about the
sky on moonlit nights which were already dangerously on the sweet and
fragrant side.

Why this should be so, the romance-besotted people of Brequinda in the
Foth of Avalars could not have told you, and would not have stopped to
discuss the matter once the effect was up and going, for no sooner would a
flock of half a dozen silk-winged leather-bodied Fuolornis Fire Dragons
heave into sight across the evening horizon than half the people of
Brequinda were scurrying off into the woods with the other half, there to
spend a busy breathless night together and emerge with the first rays of
dawn all smiling and happy and still claiming, rather endearingly, to be
virgins, if rather flushed and sticky virgins.

Pheromones, some researchers said.

Something sonic, others claimed.

The place was always stiff with researchers trying to get to the bottom of
it all and taking a very long time about it.

Not surprisingly, the *Guide*'s graphically enticing description of the general state of affairs on this planet has proved to be astonishingly popular among hitchhikers who allow themselves to be guided by it, and so it has simply never been taken out, and it is therefore left to latter-day travelers to find out for themselves that today's modern Brequinda in the city-state of Avalars is now little more than concrete, strip joints, and Dragon Burger Bars.

he night in Islington was sweet and fragrant.

There were, of course, no Fuolornis Fire Dragons about in the alley, but if any had chanced by they might just as well have sloped off across the road for a pizza, for they were not going to be needed.

Had an emergency cropped up while they were still in the middle of their pizza with extra anchovies they could always have sent across a message to put Dire Straits on the stereo, which is now known to have much the same effect.

"No," said Fenchurch, "not yet."

Arthur put Dire Straits on the stereo. Fenchurch pushed ajar the upstairs front door to let in a little more of the sweet fragrant night air. They both sat on some of the furniture made out of cushions very close to the open bottle of champagne.

"No," said Fenchurch, "not till you've found out what's wrong with me, which bit. But I suppose," she added, very, very, very quietly, "that we may as well start with where your hand is now."

Arthur said, "So which way do I go?"

"Down," said Fenchurch, "on this occasion."

He moved his hand.

"Down," she said, "is in fact the other way."

"Oh yes."

Mark Knopfler has an extraordinary ability to make a Schecter Custom Stratocaster hoot and sing like angels on a Saturday night, exhausted from being good all week and needing a stiff drink—which is not strictly relevant at this point since the record hadn't yet got to that bit, but there will be too much else going on when it does, and furthermore the chronicler does not intend to sit here with a track list and a stopwatch, so it seems best to mention it now while things are still moving slowly.

"And so we come," said Arthur, "to your knee. There is something terribly and tragically wrong with your left knee."

"My left knee," said Fenchurch, "is absolutely fine."

"So it is."

"Did you know that..."

"What?"

"Ah, it's all right, I can tell you do. No, keep going."

"So it has to be something to do with your feet...."

She smiled in the dim light, and wriggled her shoulders noncommittally against the cushions. Since there are cushions in the Universe, on Sqornshellous Beta to be exact, two worlds in from the swampland of the mattresses, that actively enjoy being wriggled against, particularly if it's noncommittally because of the syncopated way in which the shoulders move, it's a pity they weren't there. They weren't, but such is life.

Arthur held her left foot in his lap and looked it over carefully. All kinds of stuff about the way her dress fell away from her legs was making it difficult for him to think particularly clearly at this point.

"I have to admit," he said, "that I really don't know what I'm looking for."

"You'll know when you find it," she said, "really you will." There was a slight catch in her voice. "It's not that one."

Feeling increasingly puzzled, Arthur let her left foot down on the floor and moved himself around so that he could take her right foot. She moved forward, put her arms round him and kissed him, because the record had got to that bit which, if you knew the record, you would know made it impossible not to do this.

Then she gave him her right foot.

He stroked it, ran his fingers around her ankle, under her toes, along her instep, could find nothing wrong with it.

She watched him with great amusement, laughed and shook her head.

"No, don't stop," she said, "but it's not that one now."

Arthur stopped, and frowned at her left foot on the floor.

"Don't stop."

He stroked her right foot, ran his fingers around her ankle, under her toes, along her instep, and said, "You mean it's something to do with which leg I'm holding...?"

She did another of the shrugs which would have brought such joy into the life of a simple cushion from Sqornshellous Beta.

He frowned.

"Pick me up," she said quietly.

He let her right foot down on the floor and stood up. So did she. He picked her up in his arms and they kissed again. This went on for a while, then she said, "Now put me down again."

Still puzzled, he did so.

"Well?"

She looked at him almost challengingly.

"So what's wrong with my feet?" she said.

Arthur still did not understand. He sat on the floor, then got down on his hands and knees to look at her feet, in situ, as it were, in their normal habitat. And as he looked closely, something odd struck him. He put his head right down to the ground and peered. There was a long pause. He sat back heavily.

"Yes," he said, "I see what's wrong with your feet. They don't touch the ground."

"So...so what do you think...?"

Arthur looked up at her quickly and saw the deep apprehension making her eyes suddenly dark. She bit her lip and was trembling.

"What do..." she stammered, "...are you...?" She shook the hair forward over her eyes that were filling with dark fearful tears.

He stood up quickly, put his arms around her and gave her a single kiss.

"Perhaps you can do what I can do," he said, and walked straight out of her upstairs front door.

The record got to the good bit.

Chapter 23

T

he battle raged on about the star of Xaxis. Hundreds of the fierce and horribly beweaponed Zirzla ships had now been smashed and wrenched to atoms by the withering forces the huge silver Xaxisian ship was able to deploy.

Part of the moon had gone, too, blasted away by those same blazing force guns that ripped the very fabric of space as they passed through it.

The Zirzla ships that remained, horribly beweaponed though they were, were now hopelessly outclassed by the devastating power of the Xaxisian ship, and were fleeing for cover behind the rapidly disintegrating moon, when the Xaxisian ship, in hurtling pursuit behind them, suddenly announced that it needed a holiday and left the field of battle.

All was redoubled fear and consternation for a moment, but the ship was gone.

With the stupendous powers at its command it flitted across vast tracts of irrationally shaped space, quickly, effortlessly, and above all, quietly.

Deep in his greasy, smelly bunk, fashioned out of a maintenance hatchway, Ford Prefect slept among his towels, dreaming of old haunts. He dreamed at one point in his slumbers of New York. In his dreams he was walking late at night along the East Side, beside the river which had become so extravagantly polluted that new life forms were now emerging from it spontaneously, demanding welfare and voting rights.

One of these floated past, waving. Ford waved back.

The thing thrashed to the shore and struggled up the bank.

"Hi," it said, "I've just been created. I'm completely new to the Universe in all respects. Is there anything you can tell me?"

"Phew," said Ford, a little nonplussed, "I can tell you where some bars are, I guess."

"What about love and happiness? I sense deep needs for things like that," it said, waving its tentacles. "Got any leads there?"

"You can get some of that," said Ford, "on Seventh Avenue."

"I instinctively feel," said the creature, urgently, "that I need to be beautiful. Am I?"

"You're pretty direct, aren't you?"

"No point in mucking about. Am I?"

The thing was oozing all over the place now, squelching and blubbering. A nearby wino was getting interested.

"To me?" said Ford. "No. But listen," he added after a moment, "most people make out, you know. Are there any more like you down there?"

"Search me, buster," said the creature. "As I said, I'm new here. Life is entirely strange to me. What's it like?"

Here was something that Ford felt he could speak about with authority.

"Life," he said, "is like a grapefruit."

"Er, how so?"

"Well, it's sort of orangy-yellow and dimpled on the outside, wet and squidgy in the middle. It's got pips inside, too. Oh, and some people have half a one for breakfast."

"Is there anyone else out there I can talk to?"

"I expect so," said Ford; "ask a policeman."

Deep in his bunk, Ford Prefect wriggled and turned onto his other side. It wasn't his favorite type of dream because it didn't have Eccentrica Gallumbits (the triple-breasted whore of Eroticon Six) in it, whom many of his dreams did feature. But at least it was a dream. At least he was asleep.

Luckily there was a strong updraft in the alley because Arthur hadn't done this sort of thing for a while, at least not deliberately, and deliberately is exactly the way you are not meant to do it.

He swung down sharply, nearly catching himself a nasty crack on the jaw with the doorstep, and tumbled through the air, so suddenly stunned with what a profoundly stupid thing he had just done that he completely forgot the bit about hitting the ground and didn't.

A nice trick, he thought to himself, if you can do it.

The ground was hanging menacingly above his head.

He tried not to think about the ground, what an extraordinarily big thing it was and how much it would hurt him if it decided to stop hanging there and suddenly fell on him. He tried to think nice thoughts about lemurs instead, which was exactly the right thing to do because he couldn't at that moment remember precisely what a lemur was, if it was one of those things that sweep in great majestic herds across the plains of wherever it was or if that was wildebeests, so it was a tricky kind of thing to think nice thoughts about without simply resorting to an icky sort of general well-disposedness toward things, and all this kept his mind well occupied while his body tried to adjust to the fact that it wasn't touching anything.

A Mars bar wrapper fluttered down the alleyway.

After a seeming moment of doubt and indecision it eventually allowed the wind to ease it, fluttering, between him and the ground.

"Arthur..."

The ground was still hanging menacingly above his head, and he thought it was probably time to do something about that, such as fall away from it, which is what he did. Slowly. Very, very slowly.

As he fell, slowly, very, very slowly, he closed his eyes—carefully, so as not to jolt anything.

The feel of his eyes closing ran down his whole body. Once it had reached his feet, and the whole of his body was alerted to the fact that his eyes were now closed and was not panicked by it, he slowly, very, very slowly revolved his body one way and his mind the other.

That should sort the ground out.

He could feel the air clear about him now, breezing around him quite cheerfully, untroubled by his being there, and slowly, very, very slowly, as from a deep and distant sleep, he opened his eyes.

He had flown before, of course, flown many times on Krikkit until all the bird talk had driven him scatty, but this was different.

Here he was on his own world, quietly, and without fuss, beyond a slight trembling which could have been attributable to a number of things, being in the air.

Ten or fifteen feet below him was the hard tarmac and a few yards off to the right the yellow street lights of Upper Street.

Luckily the alleyway was dark since the light which was supposed to see it through the night was on an ingenious time switch which meant it came on just before lunchtime and went off again as the evening was beginning to draw in. He was therefore safely shrouded in a blanket of dark obscurity.

He slowly, very, very slowly lifted his head to Fenchurch, who was standing in silent breathless amazement, silhouetted in her upstairs doorway.

Her face was inches from his.

"I was about to ask you," she said in a low, trembly voice, "what you were doing. But then I realized that I could see what you were doing. You were flying. So it seemed," she went on after a slight wondering pause, "like a bit of a silly question. And I couldn't immediately think of any others."

Arthur said, "Can you do it?"

"No."

"Would you like to try?"

She bit her lip and shook her head, not so much to say no, but just in sheer bewilderment. She was shaking like a leaf.

"It's quite easy," urged Arthur, "if you don't know how. That's the important bit. Be not at all sure how you're doing it."

Just to demonstrate how easy it was he floated away down the alley, fell dramatically upward and bobbed back down toward her like a banknote on a breath of wind.

"Ask me how I did that."

"How . . . did you do that?"

"No idea. Not a clue."

She shrugged in bewilderment. "So how can I . . . ?"

Arthur bobbed down a little lower and held out his hand.

"I want you to try," he said, "to step onto my hand, just one foot."

"What?"

"Try it."

Nervously, hesitantly, almost, she told herself, as if she was trying to step onto the hand of someone who was floating in front of her in midair, she stepped onto his hand.

"Now the other."

"What?"

"Take the weight off your back foot."

"I can't."

"Try it."

"Like this?"

"Like that."

Nervously, hesitantly, almost, she told herself, as if—she stopped telling herself what what she was doing was like because she had a feeling she didn't altogether want to know.

She fixed her eyes very, very firmly on the gutter of the roof of the decrepit warehouse opposite which had been annoying her for weeks because it was clearly going to fall off and she wondered if anyone was going to do anything about it or whether she ought to say something to somebody and didn't think for a moment about the fact that she was standing on the hands of someone who wasn't standing on anything at all.

"Now," said Arthur, "take your weight off your left foot."

She thought that the warehouse belonged to the carpet company that had their offices around the corner and took her weight off her left foot, so she should probably go and see them about the gutter.

"Now," said Arthur, "take the weight off your right foot."

"I can't."

"Try."

She had never seen the gutter from this angle before, and it looked to her now as if there might be a bird's nest as well as all the mud and gunge up there. If she leaned forward just a little and took her weight off her right foot, she could probably see it more clearly.

Arthur was alarmed to see that someone down in the alley was trying to steal her bicycle. He particularly didn't want to get involved in an argument at the moment and hoped that the guy would do it quietly and not look up.

He had the quiet shifty look of someone who habitually stole bicycles in alleys and habitually didn't expect to find their owners hovering several feet above him. He was relaxed by both these habits, and went about his job with purpose and concentration, and when he found that the bike was unarguably bound to an iron bar embedded in concrete by hoops of tungsten carbide, he peacefully bent both its wheels and went on his way.

Arthur let out a long-held breath.

"See what a piece of eggshell I have found you," said Fenchurch in his ear.

Chapter 25

Those who are regular followers of the doings of Arthur Dent may have received an impression of his character and habits which, while it includes the truth and, of course, nothing but the truth, falls somewhat short, in its composition, of the whole truth in all its glorious aspects.

And the reasons for this are obvious: editing, selection, the need to balance that which is interesting with that which is relevant and cut out all the tedious happenstance.

Like this, for instance: "Arthur Dent went to bed. He went up the stairs, all fifteen of them, opened the door, went into his room, took off his shoes and socks and then all the rest of his clothes one by one and left them in a neatly crumpled heap on the floor. He put on his pajamas, the blue ones with the stripes. He washed his face and hands, brushed his teeth, went to the bathroom, realized that he had once again got this all in the wrong order, had to wash his hands again, and went to bed. He read for fifteen minutes, spending the first ten minutes of that trying to work out where in the book he had got to the previous night, then he turned out the light and within a minute or so more was asleep.

"It was dark. He lay on his left side for a good hour.

"After that he moved restlessly in his sleep for a moment and then turned over to sleep on his right side. Another hour after this his eyes flickered briefly and he slightly scratched his nose, though there was still a good twenty minutes to go before he turned back onto his left side. And so he whiled the night away, sleeping.

"At four he got up and went to the bathroom again. He opened the door to the bathroom..." and so on.

It's guff. It doesn't advance the action. It makes for nice fat books such as the American market thrives on, but it doesn't actually get you anywhere. You don't, in short, want to know.

But there are other omissions as well, besides the toothbrushing-and-trying-to-find-fresh-socks variety, and in some of these people have often seemed inordinately interested.

What, they want to know, about all that stuff off in the wings with Arthur and Trillian, did that ever get anywhere?

To which the answer was, of course, mind your own business.

And what, they say, was he up to all those nights on the planet Krikkit? Just because the planet didn't have Fuolornis Fire Dragons or Dire Straits doesn't mean that the whole planet just sat up every night reading.

Or to take a more specific example, what about the night after the committee meeting party on prehistoric Earth when Arthur found himself sitting on a hillside watching the moon rise over the softly burning trees in company with a beautiful young girl called Mella, recently escaped from a lifetime of staring every morning at a hundred nearly identical photographs of moodily lit tubes of toothpaste in the art department of an advertising agency on the planet Golgafrincham? What then? What happened next? And the answer is, of course, that the book ended.

The next one didn't resume the story till five years later, and you can, claim some, take discretion too far. "This Arthur Dent," comes the cry from the farthest reaches of the Galaxy, and has even now been found inscribed on a mysterious deep-space probe thought to originate from another alien galaxy at a distance too hideous to contemplate, "what is he, man or mouse? Is he interested in nothing more than tea and the wider issues of life? Has he no spirit? Has he no passion? Does he not, to put it in a nutshell, fuck?"

Those who wish to know should read on. Others may wish to skip on to the last chapter which is a good bit and has Marvin in it.

Chapter 26

Arthur Dent very much hoped, for an unworthy moment, as they drifted up, that his friends who had always found him pleasant but dull or, more latterly, odd but dull, were having a good time in the pub, but that was the last time, for a while, that he thought of them.

They drifted up, spiraling slowly around each other, like sycamore seeds falling from sycamore trees in the autumn, except going the other way.

And as they drifted up, their minds sang with the ecstatic knowledge that either what they were doing was completely and utterly and totally impossible or that physics had a lot of catching up to do.

Physics shook its head and, looking the other way, concentrated on keeping the cars going along the Euston Road and out toward the Westway flyover, on keeping the street lights lit and on making sure that when somebody in Baker Street dropped a cheeseburger it went splat upon the ground.

Dwindling headily beneath them, the beaded strings of lights of London—London, Arthur had to keep reminding himself, not the strangely colored fields of Krikkit on the remote fringes of the Galaxy, lighted freckles of which faintly spanned the opening sky above them, but London—swayed, swaying and turning, turned.

"Try a swoop," he called to Fenchurch.

"What?"

Her voice seemed strangely clear but distant in all the vast empty air. It was breathy and faint with disbelief—all those things, clear, faint, distant, breathy, all at the same time.

"We're flying..." she said.

"A trifle," called Arthur, "think nothing of it. Try a swoop."

"A sw—"

Her hand caught his, and in a sudden second her weight caught it, too, and stunningly, she was gone, tumbling beneath him, clawing wildly at nothing.

Physics glanced at Arthur and, clotted with horror, he was gone, too, sick with giddy dropping, every part of him screaming but his voice.

They plummeted because this was London and you really couldn't do this sort of thing here.

He couldn't catch her because this was London, and not a million miles from here—seven hundred and fifty-six, to be exact, in Pisa, where Galileo had clearly demonstrated that two falling bodies fell at exactly the same rate of acceleration irrespective of their relative weights.

They fell.

Arthur realized as he fell, giddily and sickeningly, that if he was going to hang around in the sky believing everything that the Italians had to say about physics when they couldn't even keep a simple tower straight, that they were in dead trouble, and he damn well did fall faster than Fenchurch.

He grappled her from above, and fumbled for a tight grip on her shoulders. He got it.

Fine. They were now falling together, which was all very sweet and romantic, but didn't solve the basic problem, which was that they were falling, and the ground wasn't waiting around to see if he had any more clever tricks up his sleeve, but was coming up to meet them like an express train.

He couldn't support her weight, he hadn't anything he could support it with or against. The only thing he could think was that they were obviously going to die, and if he wanted anything other than the obvious to happen he was going to have to do something other than the obvious. Here he felt he was on familiar territory.

He let go of her, pushed her away, and when she turned her face to him in a gasp of stunned horror, caught her little finger with his little finger and swung her back upward, tumbling clumsily up after her.

"Shit," she said, as she sat panting and breathless on absolutely nothing at all, and when she had recovered herself they fled on up into the night.

Just below cloud level they paused and scanned where they had impossibly come. The ground was something not to regard with any too firm or steady eye, but merely to glance at, as it were, in passing.

Fenchurch tried some little swoops, daringly, and found that if she judged herself right against a body of wind she could pull off some really quite dazzling ones with a little pirouette at the end, followed by a little drop which made her dress billow around her, and this is where readers who are keen to know what Marvin and Ford Prefect have been up to all this while should look ahead to later chapters, because Arthur now could wait no longer and helped her take it off.

It drifted down and away whipped by the wind until it was a speck which finally vanished, and for obvious complicated reasons revolutionized the life of a family in Hounslow, over whose washing line it was discovered draped in the morning.

In a mute embrace, they drifted up till they were swimming among the misty wraiths of moisture that you can see feathering around the wings of an airplane but never feel because you are sitting warm inside the stuffy airplane and looking through the little scratchy Plexiglas window while somebody else's son tries patiently to pour warm milk into your shirt.

Arthur and Fenchurch could feel them, wispy cold and thin, wreathing round their bodies, very cold, very thin. They felt, even Fenchurch, now protected from the elements only by a couple of fragments from Marks and Spencer, that if they were not going to let the force of gravity bother them, then mere cold or paucity of atmosphere could go and whistle.

The two fragments from Marks and Spencer which, as Fenchurch rose now into the misty body of the clouds, Arthur removed very, very slowly, which is the only way it's possible to do it when you're flying and also not using your hands, went on to create considerable havoc in the morning in, respectively, counting from top to bottom, Isleworth and Richmond.

They were in the cloud for a long time, because it was stacked very high, and when finally they emerged wetly above it, Fenchurch slowly spinning like a starfish lapped by a rising tide pool, they found that above the clouds is where the night gets seriously moonlit.

The light is darkly brilliant. There are different mountains up there, but they are mountains with their own white Arctic snows.

They had emerged at the top of the high-stacked cumulonimbus, and now began lazily to drift down its contours, as Fenchurch eased Arthur in turn from his clothes, pried him free of them till all were gone, winding their surprised way down into the enveloping whiteness.

She kissed him, kissed his neck, his chest, and soon they were drifting on, turning slowly, in a kind of speechless T-shape, which might have caused even a Fuolornis Fire Dragon, had one flown past, replete with pizza, to flap its wings and cough a little.

There were, however, no Fuolornis Fire Dragons in the clouds nor could there be for, like the dinosaurs, the dodos, and the Greater Drubbered Wintwock of Stegbartle Major in the Constellation Fraz, and unlike the Boeing 747 which is in plentiful supply, they are, sadly, extinct, and the Universe shall never know their like again.

The reason that a Boeing 747 crops up rather unexpectedly in the above list is not unconnected with the fact that something very similar happened in the lives of Arthur and Fenchurch a moment or two later.

They are big things, terrifyingly big. You know when one is in the air with you. There is a thunderous attack of air, a moving wall of screaming wind, and you get tossed aside, if you are foolish enough to be doing anything remotely like what Arthur and Fenchurch were doing in its close vicinity, like butterflies in the Blitz.

This time, however, there was no heart-sickening fall or loss of nerve, just a regrouping moments later and a wonderful new idea enthusiastically signaled through the buffeting noise.

Mrs. E. Kapelsen of Boston, Massachusetts, was an elderly lady; indeed, she felt her life was nearly at an end. She had seen a lot of it, been puzzled by some but, she was a little uneasy to feel at this late stage, bored by too much. It had all been very pleasant, but perhaps a little too explicable, a little too routine.

With a sigh she flipped up the little plastic window shade and looked over the wing.

At first she thought she ought to call the stewardess, but then she thought, no, damn it, definitely not, this was for her, and her alone.

By the time her two inexplicable people finally slipped back off the wing and tumbled into the slipstream she had cheered up an awful lot.

She was mostly immensely relieved to think that virtually everything that anybody had ever told her was wrong.

The following morning Arthur and Fenchurch slept very late in the alley despite the continual wail of furniture being restored.

The following night they did it all over again, only this time with Sony Walkmen.

Chapter 27

This is all very wonderful," said Fenchurch a few days later, "but I do need to know what has happened to me. You see, there's this difference between us. That you lost something and found it again, and I found something and lost it. I need to find it again."

She had to go out for the day, so Arthur settled down for a day of telephoning.

Murray Bost Henson was a journalist on one of the papers with small pages and big print. It would be pleasant to be able to say that he was none the worse for this but, sadly, this was not the case. He happened to be the only journalist that Arthur knew, so Arthur phoned him anyway.

"Arthur, my old soup spoon, my old silver tureen, how particularly stunning to hear from you! Someone told me you'd gone off into space or something."

Murray had his own special kind of conversation language which he had invented for his own use, and which no one else was able to speak or even to follow. Hardly any of it meant anything at all. The bits which did mean anything were often so wonderfully buried that no one could ever spot them slipping past in the avalanche of nonsense. The time when you did find out, later, which bits he did mean, was often a bad time for all concerned.

"What?" said Arthur.

"Just a rumor, my old elephant tusk, my little green baize card table, just a rumor. Probably means nothing at all, but I may need a quote from you."

"Nothing to say, just pub talk."

"We thrive on it, my old prosthetic limb, we thrive on it. Plus it would fit like a whatsit in one of those other things with the other stories of the week, so it could be good just to have you denying it. Excuse me, something has just fallen out of my ear."

There was a slight pause, at the end of which Murray Bost Henson came back on the line sounding genuinely shaken.

"Just remembered," he said, "what an odd evening I had last night. Anyway my old, I won't say what, how do you feel about having ridden on Halley's comet?"

"I haven't," said Arthur with a suppressed sigh, "ridden on Halley's comet."

"Okay. How do you feel about not having ridden on Halley's comet?"

"Pretty relaxed, Murray."

There was a pause while Murray wrote this down.

"Good enough for me, Arthur, good enough for Ethel and me and the chickens. Fits in with the general weirdness of the week. Week of the Weirdos, we're thinking of calling it. Good, eh?"

"Very good."

"Got a ring to it. First, we have this man it always rains on."

"What?"

"It's the absolute stocking top truth. All documented in his little black books, it all checks out at every single fun-loving level. The Met Office is going ice cold thick banana whips, and funny little men in white coats are flying in from all over the world with their little rulers and boxes and drip feeds. This man is the bee's knees, Arthur, he is the wasp's nipples. He is, I would go so far as to say, the entire set of erogenous zones of every major flying insect of the Western world. We're calling him the Rain God. Nice, eh?"

"I think I've met him."

"Good ring to it. What did you say?"

"I may have met him. Complains all the time, yes?"

"Incredible! You met the Rain God?"

"If it's the same guy. I told him to stop complaining and show someone his book."

There was an impressed pause from Murray Bost Henson's end of the phone.

"Well, you did a bundle. An absolute bundle has absolutely been done by you. Listen, do you know how much a tour operator is paying that guy not to go to Malaga this year? I mean, forget irrigating the Sahara and boring stuff like that, this guy has a whole new *career* ahead of him, just avoiding places for money. The man's turning into a monster, Arthur, we might even have to make him win the bingo.

"Listen, we may want to do a feature on you, Arthur, the Man Who Made the Rain God Rain. Got a ring to it, eh?"

"A nice one, but—"

"We may need to photograph you under a garden shower, but that'll be okay. Where are you?"

"Er, I'm in Islington. Listen, Murray—"

"Islington!"

"Yes—"

"Well, what about the *real* weirdness of the week, the real seriously loopy stuff. You know anything about these flying people?"

"No."

"You must have. This is the real seethingly crazy one. This is the real meatballs in the batter. Locals are phoning in all the time to say there's this couple who go flying nights. We've got guys down in our photo labs working through the night to put together a genuine photograph. You must have heard."

"No."

"Arthur, where have you been? Oh, space, right, I got your quote. But that was months ago. Listen, it's night after night this week, my old cheese grater, right on your patch. This couple just fly around the sky and start doing all kinds of stuff. And I don't mean looking through walls or pretending to be box-girder bridges. You don't know anything?"

"No."

"Arthur, it's been almost inexpressibly delicious conversing with you, chumbum, but I have to go. I'll send the guy with the camera and the hose. Give me the address, I'm ready and writing."

"Listen, Murray, I called to ask you something."

"I have a lot to do."

"I just wanted to find something about the dolphins."

"No story. Last year's news. Forget 'em. They're gone."

"It's important."

"Listen, no one will touch it. You can't sustain a story, you know, when the only news is the continuing absence of whatever it is the story's about. Not our territory anyway, try the Sundays. Maybe they'll run a little 'Whatever Happened to "Whatever Happened to the Dolphins"' story in a couple of years, around August. But what's anybody going to do now? 'Dolphins Still Gone'? 'Continuing Dolphin Absence'? 'Dolphins—Further Days Without Them'? The story dies, Arthur. It lies down and kicks its little feet in the air and presently goes to the great golden spike in the sky, my old fruitbat."

"Murray, I'm not interested in whether it's a story. I just want to find out how I can get in touch with that guy in California who claims to know something about it. I thought you might know."

People are beginning to talk," said Fenchurch that evening, after they had hauled her cello in.

"Not only talk," said Arthur, "but print, in big bold letters under the bingo prizes. Which is why I thought I'd better get these."

He showed her the long narrow booklets of airline tickets.

"Arthur!" she said, hugging him, "does that mean you managed to talk to him?"

"I have had a day," said Arthur, "of extreme telephonic exhaustion. I have spoken to virtually every department of virtually every paper in Fleet Street, and I finally tracked his number down."

"You've obviously been working hard, you're drenched with sweat, poor darling."

"Not with sweat," said Arthur wearily. "A photographer's just been here. I tried to argue, but—never mind, the point is, yes."

"You spoke to him."

"I spoke to his wife. She said he was too weird to come to the phone right now and could I call back."

He sat down heavily, realized he was missing something, and went to the fridge to find it.

"Want a drink?"

"Would commit murder to get one. I always know I'm in for a tough time when my cello teacher looks me up and down and says, 'Ah yes, my dear, I think a little Tchaikovsky today.'"

"I called again," said Arthur, "and she said that he was 3.2 light-years from the phone and I should call back."

"Ah."

"I called again. She said the situation had improved. He was now a mere 2.6 light-years from the phone but it was still a long way to shout."

"You don't suppose," said Fenchurch doubtfully, "that there's anyone else we can talk to?"

"It gets worse," said Arthur. "I spoke to someone on a science magazine who actually knows him, and he said that John Watson will not only

believe, but will actually have absolute proof, often dictated to him by
angels with golden beards and green wings and Dr. Scholl footwear, that
the month's most fashionable silly theory is true. For people who question
the validity of these visions he will triumphantly produce the clogs in
question, and that's as far as you get."

"I didn't realize it was that bad," said Fenchurch quietly. She fiddled
listlessly with the tickets.

"I phoned Mrs. Watson again," said Arthur. "Her name, by the way,
and you may wish to know this, is Arcane Jill."

"I see."

"I'm glad you see. I thought you mightn't believe any of this, so when I
called her this time I used the telephone answering machine to record the
call with."

He went across to the telephone machine and fiddled and fumed with all
its buttons for a while, because it was the one which was particularly
recommended by *Which* magazine and is almost impossible to use without
going mad.

"Here it is," he said at last, wiping the sweat from his brow.

The voice was thin and crackly with its journey to a geostationary
satellite and back, but was also hauntingly calm.

"Perhaps I should explain," Arcane Jill Watson's voice said, "that the
phone is in fact in a room that he never comes into. It's in the Asylum, you
see. Wonko the Sane does not like to enter the Asylum and so he does not.
I feel you should know this because it may save you phoning. If you would
like to meet him, this is very easily arranged. All you have to do is walk in.
He will only meet people outside the Asylum."

Arthur's voice, at its most mystified: "I'm sorry, I don't understand.
Where is the asylum?"

"*Where* is the Asylum?" Arcane Jill Watson again. "Have you ever read
the instructions on a packet of toothpicks?"

On the tape, Arthur's voice had to admit that he had not.

"You may want to do that. You may find that it clarifies things for you a
little. You may find that it indicates to you where the Asylum is. Thank
you."

The sound of the phone line went dead. Arthur turned the machine off.

"Well, I suppose we can regard that as an invitation," he said with a
shrug. "I actually managed to get the address from the guy on the science
magazine."

Fenchurch looked up at him with a thoughtful frown, and looked at the tickets again.

"Do you think it's worth it?" she said.

"Well," said Arthur, "the one thing that everyone I spoke to agreed on, apart from the fact they all thought he was barking mad, is that he does know more than any man living about dolphins."

"This is an important announcement. This is flight 121 to Los Angeles. If your travel plans today do not include Los Angeles, now would be a perfect time to disembark."

They rented a car in Los Angeles from one of the places that rents out cars that other people have thrown away.

"Getting it to go around corners is a bit of a problem," said the guy behind the sunglasses as he handed them the keys. "Sometimes it's simpler just to get out and find a car that's going in that direction."

They stayed for one night in a hotel on Sunset Boulevard which someone had told them they would enjoy being puzzled by.

"Everyone there is either English or odd or both. They've got a swimming pool where you can go and watch English rock stars reading *Language, Truth and Logic* for the photographers."

It was true. There was one and that was exactly what he was doing.

The garage attendant didn't think much of their car, but that was fine because they didn't either.

Late in the evening they drove through the Hollywood hills along Mulholland Drive and stopped to look out first over the dazzling sea of floating light that is Los Angeles, and later stopped to look across the dazzling sea of floating light that is the San Fernando Valley. They agreed that the sense of dazzle stopped immediately at the back of their eyes and didn't touch any other part of them and came away strangely unsatisfied by the spectacle. As dramatic seas of light went, it was fine, but light is meant to illuminate something, and having driven through what this particularly dramatic sea of light was illuminating they didn't think much of it.

They slept late and restlessly and awoke at lunchtime when it was unbearably hot.

They drove out along the freeway to Santa Monica for their first look at the Pacific Ocean, the ocean which Wonko the Sane spent all his days and a good deal of his nights looking at.

"Someone told me," said Fenchurch, "that they once overheard two ladies on this beach, doing what we're doing, looking at the Pacific Ocean for the first time in their lives. And apparently, after a long pause, one of them said to the other, 'You know, it's not as big as I expected.'"

Their mood gradually lifted as they walked along the beach in Malibu and watched all the millionaires in their chic shanty huts carefully keeping an eye on one another to check how rich they were each getting.

Their mood lifted further as the sun began to move down the western half of the sky, and by the time they were back in their rattling car and driving toward a sunset that no one of any sensibility would dream of building a city like Los Angeles in front of they were suddenly feeling astonishingly and irrationally happy and didn't even mind that the terrible old car radio would only play two stations, and those simultaneously. So what, they were both playing good rock and roll.

"I know that he will be able to help us," said Fenchurch determinedly, "I know he will. What's his name again, the one he likes to be called?"

"Wonko the Sane."

"I know that he will be able to help us."

Arthur wondered if he would and hoped that he would, and hoped that what Fenchurch had lost could be found here, on this Earth, whatever this Earth might prove to be.

He hoped, as he had hoped continually and fervently since the time they had talked together on the banks of the Serpentine, that he would not be called upon to try to remember something that he had very firmly and deliberately buried in the furthest recesses of his memory, where he hoped it would cease to nag at him.

In Santa Barbara they stopped at a fish restaurant in what seemed to be a converted warehouse.

Fenchurch had red mullet and said it was delicious.

Arthur had a swordfish steak and said it made him angry. He grabbed a passing waitress by the arm and berated her.

"Why's this fish so bloody good?" he demanded, angrily.

"Please excuse my friend," said Fenchurch to the startled waitress. "I think he's having a nice day at last."

f you took a couple of David Bowies and stuck one of the David Bowies on the top of the other David Bowie, then attached another David Bowie to the end of each of the arms of the upper of the first two David Bowies and wrapped the whole business up in a dirty beach robe you would then have something which didn't exactly look like John Watson, but which those who knew him would find hauntingly familiar.

He was tall and he gangled.

When he sat in his deck chair gazing at the Pacific, not so much with any kind of wild surmise any longer as with a peaceful deep dejection, it was a little difficult to tell exactly where the deck chair ended and he began, and you would hesitate to put your hand on, say, his forearm in case the whole structure suddenly collapsed with a snap and took your thumb off. But his smile when he turned it on you was quite remarkable. It seemed to be composed of all the worst things that life can do to you, but which when he briefly reassembled them in that particular order on his face made you suddenly feel "Oh. Well, that's all right then."

When he spoke, you were glad that he used the smile that made you feel "Oh. Well, that's all right then" pretty often.

"Oh yes," he said, "they come and see me. They sit right here. They sit right where you're sitting." He was talking of the angels with the golden beards and green wings and Dr. Scholl sandals.

"They eat nachos which they say they can't get where they come from. They do a lot of coke and are very wonderful about a whole range of things."

"Do they," said Arthur, "are they? So, er . . . when is this then? When do they come?"

He gazed out at the Pacific as well. There were little sandpipers running along the margin of the shore which seemed to have this problem: they needed to find their food in the sand which a wave had just washed over, but they couldn't bear to get their feet wet. To deal with this problem they ran with an odd kind of movement as if they'd been constructed by somebody very clever in Switzerland.

Fenchurch was sitting on the sand, idly drawing patterns in it with her fingers.

"Weekends, mostly," said Wonko the Sane, "on little scooters. They are great machines." He smiled.

"I see," said Arthur, "I see."

A tiny cough from Fenchurch attracted his attention and he looked round at her. She had scratched a little stick figure drawing in the sand of the two of them in the clouds. For a moment he thought she was trying to get him excited, then he realized that she was rebuking him. "Who are we," she was saying, "to say he's mad?"

His house was certainly peculiar, and since this was the first thing that Fenchurch and Arthur had encountered it would help to know what it was like.

It was like this:

It was inside out.

Actually inside out, to the extent that they had had to park on the carpet.

All along what one would normally call the outer wall, which was decorated in a tasteful interior-designed pink, were bookshelves, also a couple of those odd three-legged tables with semicircular tops which stand in such a way as to suggest that someone just dropped the wall straight through them, and pictures which were clearly designed to soothe.

Where it got really odd was the roof.

It folded back on itself like something that M. C. Escher, had he been given to hard nights on the town, which it is no part of this narrative's purpose to suggest was the case, though it is sometimes hard, looking at his pictures, particularly the one with all the awkward steps, not to wonder, might have dreamed up after having been on one, for the little chandeliers which should have been hanging inside were on the outside pointing up.

Confusing.

The sign above the front door read "Come Outside," and so, nervously, they had.

Inside, of course, was where the Outside was. Rough brickwork, nicely done pointing, gutters in good repair, a garden path, a couple of small trees, some rooms leading off.

And the inner walls stretched down, folded curiously, and opened at the end as if, by an optical illusion which would have had M. C. Escher frowning and wondering how it was done, to enclose the Pacific Ocean itself.

"Hello," said John Watson, Wonko the Sane.

Good, they thought to themselves, "hello" is something we can cope with.

"Hello," they said, and all, surprisingly, was smiles.

For quite a while he seemed curiously reluctant to talk about the dolphins, looking oddly distracted and saying, "I forget..." whenever they were mentioned, and had shown them quite proudly round the eccentricities of his house.

"It gives me pleasure," he said, "in a curious kind of way, and does nobody any harm," he continued, "that a competent optician couldn't correct."

They liked him. He had an open, engaging quality and seemed able to mock himself before anybody else did.

"Your wife," said Arthur, looking around, "mentioned some tooth-picks." He said it with a hunted look, as if he was worried that she might suddenly leap out from behind a door and mention them again.

Wonko the Sane laughed. It was a light easy laugh, and sounded like one he had used a lot before and was happy with.

"Ah yes," he said, "that's to do with the day I finally realized that the world had gone totally mad and built the Asylum to put it in, poor thing, and hoped it would get better."

This was the point at which Arthur began to feel a little nervous again.

"Here," said Wonko the Sane, "we are outside the Asylum." He pointed again at the rough brickwork, the pointing, and the gutters. "Go through that door"—he pointed at the first door through which they had originally entered—"and you go into the Asylum. I've tried to decorate it nicely to keep the inmates happy, but there's very little one can do. I never go in there myself. If ever I am tempted, which these days I rarely am, I simply look at the sign written over the door and I shy away."

"That one?" said Fenchurch, pointing, rather puzzled, at a blue plaque with some instructions written on it.

"Yes. They are the words that finally turned me into the hermit I have now become. It was quite sudden. I saw them, and I knew what I had to do."

The sign read:

"Hold stick near center of its length. Moisten pointed end in mouth. Insert in tooth space, blunt end next to gum. Use gentle in-out motion."

"It seemed to me," said Wonko the Sane, "that any civilization that had so far lost its head as to need to include a set of detailed instructions for use in a package of toothpicks, was no longer a civilization in which I could live and stay sane."

He gazed out at the Pacific again, as if daring it to rave and gibber at him, but it lay there calmly and played with the sandpipers.

"And in case it crossed your mind to wonder, as I can see how it possibly might, I am completely sane. Which is why I call myself Wonko the Sane, just to reassure people on this point. Wonko is what my mother called me when I was a kid and clumsy and knocked things over, and sane is what I am, and how," he added, with one of his smiles that made you feel "Oh. Well, that's all right then, I intend to remain. Shall we go to the beach and see what we have to talk about?"

They went out onto the beach, which was where he started talking about angels with golden beards and green wings and Dr. Scholl sandals.

"About the dolphins..." said Fenchurch gently, hopefully.

"I can show you the sandals," said Wonko the Sane.

"I wonder, do you know..."

"Would you like me to show you," said Wonko the Sane, "the sandals? I have them. I'll get them. They are made by the Dr. Scholl company, and the angels say that they particularly suit the terrain they have to work in. They say they run a concession stand by the message. When I say I don't know what that means they say no, you don't, and laugh. Well, I'll get them anyway."

As he walked back toward the inside, or the outside depending on how you looked at it, Arthur and Fenchurch looked at each other in a wondering and slightly desperate sort of way, then each shrugged and idly drew figures in the sand.

"How are the feet today?" said Arthur quietly.

"Okay. It doesn't feel so odd in the sand. Or in the water. The water touches them perfectly. I just think this isn't our world."

She shrugged. "What do you think he meant," she said, "by the message?"

"I don't know," said Arthur, though the memory of a man called Prak who laughed at him continuously kept nagging at him.

When Wonko returned he was carrying something that stunned Arthur. Not the sandals; they were perfectly ordinary wooden-bottomed sandals.

"I just thought you'd like to see," he said, "what angels wear on their feet. Just out of curiosity. I'm not trying to prove anything, by the way. I'm a scientist and I know what constitutes proof. But the reason I call myself by my childhood name is to remind myself that a scientist must also be absolutely like a child. If he sees a thing, he must say that he sees it, whether it was what he thought he was going to see or not. See first, think later, then test. But always see first. Otherwise you will only see what you were expecting. Most scientists forget that. I'll show you something to demonstrate that later. So, the other reason I call myself Wonko the Sane is so that people will think I am a fool. That allows me to say what I see when I see it. You can't possibly be a scientist if you mind people thinking that you're a fool. Anyway, I also thought you might like to see this."

This was the thing that Arthur had been stunned to see him carrying, for it was a wonderfully silver-gray glass fishbowl, seemingly identical to the one in Arthur's bedroom.

Arthur had been trying for some thirty seconds now, without success, to say "Where did you get that?" sharply, and with a gasp in his voice.

Finally his time had come but he missed it by a millisecond.

"Where did you get that?" said Fenchurch, sharply and with a gasp in her voice.

Arthur glanced at Fenchurch sharply and with a gasp in his voice said, "What? Have you seen one of these before?"

"Yes," she said, "I've got one. Or at least did have. Russell stole it to put his golf balls in. I don't know where it came from, just that I was angry with Russell for stealing it. Why, have you got one?"

"Yes, it was . . ."

They both became aware that Wonko the Sane was glancing sharply backward and forward between them, and trying to get a gasp in edgeways.

"*You* have one of these, too?" he said to both of them.

"Yes." They both said it.

He looked long and calmly at each of them, then he held up the bowl to catch the light of the California sun.

The bowl seemed almost to sing with the sun, to chime with the intensity of its light, and cast darkly brilliant rainbows around the sand and upon them. He turned it and turned it. They could see quite clearly in the fine tracery of its etchwork the words "So Long, and Thanks for All the Fish."

"Do you know," asked Wonko quietly, "what it is?"

They shook their heads slowly, and with wonder, almost hypnotized by the flashing of the lightning shadows in the gray glass.

"It is a farewell gift from the dolphins," said Wonko in a low quiet voice, "the dolphins whom I loved and studied, and swam with, and fed with fish, and even tried to learn their language, a task which they seemed to make impossibly difficult, considering the fact that I now realize they were perfectly capable of communicating in ours if they decided they wanted to."

He shook his head with a slow, slow smile, and then looked again at Fenchurch, and then at Arthur.

"Have you..." he said to Arthur, "what have you done with yours? May I ask you that?"

"Er, I keep a fish in it," said Arthur, slightly embarrassed. "I happened to have this fish I was wondering what to do with, and, er, there was this bowl." He tailed off.

"You've done nothing else? No," he said, "if you had, you would know." He shook his head again.

"My wife kept wheat germ in ours," resumed Wonko, with some new tone in his voice, "until last night...."

"What," said Arthur slowly and hushedly, "happened last night?"

"We ran out of wheat germ," said Wonko, evenly. "My wife," he added, "has gone to get some more." He seemed lost with his own thoughts for a moment.

"And what happened then?" said Fenchurch, in the same breathless tone.

"I washed it," said Wonko. "I washed it very carefully, very, very carefully, removing every last speck of wheat germ, then I dried it slowly with a lint-free cloth, slowly, carefully, turning it over and over. Then I held it to my ear. Have you... have you held one to your ear?"

They both shook their heads, again slowly, again dumbly.

"Perhaps," he said, "you should."

Chapter 32

The deep roar of the ocean.

The break of waves on farther shores than thought can find.

The silent thunders of the deep.

And from among it, voices calling, and yet not voices, humming trillings, wordlings, and half-articulated songs of thought.

Greetings, waves of greetings, sliding back down into the inarticulate, words breaking together.

A crash of sorrow on the shores of Earth.

Waves of joy on—where? A world indescribably found, indescribably arrived at, indescribably wet, a song of water.

A fugue of voices now, clamoring explanations, of a disaster unavertable, a world to be destroyed, a surge of helplessness, a spasm of despair, a dying fall, again the break of words.

And then the fling of hope, the finding of a shadow Earth in the implications of enfolded time, submerged dimensions, the pull of parallels, the deep pull, the spin of will, the hurl and split of it, the fight. A new Earth pulled into replacement, the dolphins gone.

Then stunningly a single voice, quite clear.

"This bowl was brought to you by the Campaign to Save the Humans. We bid you farewell."

And then the sound of long, heavy, perfectly gray bodies rolling away into an unknown fathomless deep, quietly giggling.

Chapter 33

That night they stayed Outside the Asylum and watched TV from inside it.

"This is what I wanted you to see," said Wonko the Sane when the news came around again, "an old colleague of mine. He's over in your country running an investigation. Just watch."

It was a press conference.

"I'm afraid I can't comment on the name Rain God at this present time, and we are calling him an example of a Spontaneous Para-Causal Meteorological Phenomenon."

"Can you tell us what that means?"

"I'm not altogether sure. Let's be straight here. If we find something we can't understand we like to call it something you can't understand, or indeed pronounce. I mean if we just let you go around calling him a Rain God, then that suggests that you know something we don't, and I'm afraid we couldn't have that.

"No, first we have to call it something which says it's ours, not yours, then we set about finding some way of proving it's not what you said it is, but something we say it is.

"And if it turns out that you're right, you'll still be wrong, because we will simply call him a . . . er, 'Supernormal'—not paranormal or supernatural because you think you know what those mean now, no, a 'Supernormal Incremental Precipitation Inducer.' We'll probably want to shove a 'Quasi' in there somewhere to protect ourselves. Rain God! Huh, never heard such nonsense in my life. Admittedly, you wouldn't catch me going on holiday with him. Thanks, that'll be all for now, other than to say 'Hi!' to Wonko if he's watching."

Chapter 34

O
n the way home there was a woman sitting next to them on the plane who was looking at them rather oddly.

They talked quietly to themselves.

"I still have to know," said Fenchurch, "and I strongly feel that you know something that you're not telling me."

Arthur sighed and took out a piece of paper.

"Do you have a pencil?" he said.

She dug around and found one.

"What are you doing, sweetheart?" she said, after he had spent twenty minutes frowning, chewing the pencil, scribbling on the paper, crossing things out, scribbling again, chewing the pencil again, and grunting irritably to himself.

"Trying to remember an address someone once gave me."

"Your life would be an awful lot simpler," she said, "if you bought yourself an address book."

Finally he passed the paper to her.

"You look after it," he said.

She looked at it. Among all the scratchings and crossings out were the words "Quentulus Quazgar Mountains. Sevorbeupstry. Planet of Prelium-tarn. Sun-Zarss. Galactic Sector QQ7 Active J Gamma."

"And what's there?"

"Apparently," said Arthur, "it's God's Final Message to His Creation."

"That sounds a bit more like it," said Fenchurch. "How do we get there?"

"You really...?"

"Yes," said Fenchurch firmly, "I really want to know."

Arthur looked out of the little scratchy Plexiglas window at the open sky outside.

"Excuse me," said the woman who had been looking at them rather oddly, suddenly, "I hope you don't think I'm rude. I get so bored on these long flights, it's nice to talk to somebody. My name's Enid Kapelsen, I'm from Boston. Tell me, do you fly a lot?"

They went to Arthur's house in the West Country, shoved a couple of towels and stuff in a bag, and then sat down to do what every galactic hitchhiker ends up spending most of his time doing.

They waited for a flying saucer to come by.

"Friend of mine did this for fifteen years," said Arthur one night as they sat forlornly watching the sky.

"Who was that?"

"Called Ford Prefect."

He caught himself doing something he had never really expected to do again.

He wondered where Ford Prefect was.

By an extraordinary coincidence the following day there were two reports in the paper, one concerning the most astonishing incident with a flying saucer, and the other about a series of unseemly riots in pubs.

Ford Prefect turned up the day after that looking hungover and complaining that Arthur never answered the phone.

In fact he looked extremely ill, not merely as if he'd been pulled through a hedge backward, but as if the hedge was being simultaneously pulled backward through a combine harvester. He staggered into Arthur's sitting room, waving aside all offers of support, which was an error, because the effort of waving caused him to lose his balance altogether and Arthur eventually had to drag him to the sofa.

"Thank you," said Ford, "thank you very much. Have you . . ." he said, and fell asleep for three hours.

" . . . the faintest idea," he continued suddenly, when he revived, "how hard it is to tap into the British phone system from the Pleiades? I can see that you haven't, so I'll tell you," he said, "over the very large mug of black coffee that you are about to make me."

He followed Arthur wobbily into the kitchen.

"Stupid operators keep asking you where you're calling from and you try and tell them Letchworth and they say you couldn't be if you're coming in on that circuit. What are you doing?"

"Making you some black coffee."

"Oh." Ford seemed oddly disappointed. He looked about the place forlornly.

"What's this?" he said.

"Rice Krispies."

"And this?"

"Paprika."

"I see," said Ford, solemnly, and put the two items back down, on top of the other, but that didn't seem to balance properly, so he put the other on top of the one and that seemed to work.

"A little space-lagged," he said. "What was I saying?"

"About not phoning from Letchworth."

"I wasn't. I explained this to the lady. 'Bugger Letchworth,' I said, 'if that's your attitude. I am in fact calling from a sales scoutship of the Sirius Cybernetics Corporation, currently on the sub-light-speed leg of a journey between the stars known to your world, though not necessarily to you, dear lady.' I said 'dear lady,'" explained Ford Prefect, "because I didn't want her to be offended by my implication that she was an ignorant cretin—"

"Tactful," said Arthur Dent.

"Exactly," said Ford, "tactful."

He frowned.

"Space-lag," he said, "is very bad for sub-clauses. You'll have to assist me again," he continued, "by reminding me what I was talking about."

"'Between the stars,'" said Arthur, "'known to your world, though not necessarily to you, dear lady, as—'"

"Pleiades Epsilon and Pleiades Zeta," concluded Ford triumphantly. "This conversation lark is quite a gas, isn't it?"

"Have some coffee."

"Thank you, no. 'And the reason,' I said, 'why I am bothering you with it rather than just dialing direct as I could, because we have some pretty sophisticated telecommunications equipment out here in the Pleiades, I can tell you, is that the penny-pinching son of a starbeast piloting this son of a starbeast starship insists that I call collect. Can you believe that?'"

"And could she?"

"I don't know. She had hung up," said Ford, "by this time. So! What do you suppose," he asked fiercely, "I did next?"

"I've no idea, Ford," said Arthur.

"Pity," said Ford, "I was hoping you could remind me. I really hate those guys, you know. They really are the creeps of the cosmos, buzzing round the celestial infinite with their junky little machines that never work properly or, when they do, perform functions that no sane man would require of them and," he added savagely, "go beep to tell you when they've done it!"

This was perfectly true, and a very respectable view widely held by right-thinking people, who are largely recognizable as being right-thinking people by the mere fact that they hold this view.

The Hitchhiker's Guide to the Galaxy, in a moment of reasoned lucidity which is almost unique among its current tally of five million, nine hundred and seventy-three thousand, five hundred and nine pages, says of the Sirius Cybernetics Corporation products that *"it is very easy to be blinded to the essential uselessness of them by the sense of achievement you get from getting them to work at all.*

"In other words—and this is the rock-solid principle on which the whole of the Corporation's Galaxywide success is founded—their fundamental design flaws are completely hidden by their superficial design flaws."

"And this guy," ranted Ford, "was on a drive to sell more of them! His five-year mission to seek out and explore strange new worlds, and sell Advanced Music Substitute Systems to their restaurants, elevators, and wine bars! Or if they didn't have restaurants, elevators, and wine bars yet, to artificially accelerate their civilization growth until they bloody well did have! Where's that coffee!"

"I threw it away."

"Make some more. I have now remembered what I did next. I saved civilization as we know. I knew it was something like that."

He stumbled determinedly back into the sitting room, where he seemed to carry on talking to himself, tripping over the furniture and making beep-beep noises.

A couple of minutes later, wearing his very placid face, Arthur followed him.

Ford looked stunned.

"Where have you been?" he demanded.

"Making some coffee," said Arthur, still wearing his very placid face. He had long ago realized that the only way of being in Ford's company successfully was to keep a large stock of very placid faces and wear them at all times.

"You missed the best bit!" raged Ford. "You missed the bit where I jumped the guy! Now," he said, "I shall have to jump him all over again!"

He hurled himself recklessly at a chair and broke it.

"It was better," he said sullenly, "last time," and waved vaguely in the direction of another broken chair which he had already got trussed up on the dining table.

"I see," said Arthur, casting a placid eye over the trussed-up wreckage, "and, er, what are all the ice cubes for?"

"What?" screamed Ford. "What? You missed that bit, too? That's the suspended animation facility! I put the guy in the suspended animation facility. Well, I had to, didn't I?"

"So it would seem," said Arthur, in his placid voice.

"Don't touch that!!!" yelled Ford.

Arthur, who was about to replace the phone, which was for some mysterious reason lying on the table, off the hook, paused, placidly.

"Okay," said Ford, calming down, "listen to it."

Arthur put the phone to his ear.

"It's the speaking clock," he said.

"Beep, beep, beep," said Ford, "beep, beep, beep."

"I see," said Arthur, with every ounce of placidness he could muster.

"Beep, beep, beep," said Ford, "is exactly what is being heard all over that guy's ship, while he sleeps, in the ice, going slowly round a little known moon of Sesefras Magna. The London speaking clock!"

"I see," said Arthur again, and decided that now was the time to ask the big one.

"Why?" he said, acidly.

"With a bit of luck," said Ford, "the phone bill will bankrupt the buggers."

He threw himself, sweating, onto the sofa.

"Anyway," he said, "dramatic arrival, don't you think?"

Chapter 36

The flying saucer in which Ford Prefect had stowed away had stunned the world.

Finally there was no doubt, no possibility of mistake, no hallucinations, no mysterious CIA agents found floating in reservoirs.

This time it was real, it was definite. It was quite definitely definite.

It had come down with a wonderful disregard for anything beneath it and crushed a large area of some of the most expensive real estate in the world, including much of Harrods.

The thing was massive, nearly a mile across, some said, dull silver in color, pitted, scorched, and disfigured with the scars of unnumbered vicious space battles fought with savage forces by the light of suns unknown to man.

A hatchway opened, crashed down through the Harrods Food Halls, demolished Harvey Nichols, and with a final grinding scream of tortured architecture, toppled the Sheraton Park Tower.

After a long, heart-stopping moment of internal crashes and grumbles of rending machinery, there marched from it, down the ramp, an immense silver robot, a hundred feet tall.

It held up a hand.

"I come in peace," it said, adding after a long moment of further grinding, "take me to your Lizard."

Ford Prefect, of course, had an explanation for this, as he sat with Arthur and watched the nonstop frenetic news reports on television, none of which had anything to say other than to record that the thing had done this amount of damage which was valued at that amount of billions of pounds and had killed this totally other number of people, and then say it again, because the robot was doing nothing more than standing there, swaying very slightly, and emitting short incomprehensible error messages.

"It comes from a very ancient democracy, you see...."

"You mean, it comes from a world of lizards?"

"No," said Ford, who by this time was a little more rational and coherent than he had been, having finally had the coffee forced down him, "nothing so simple. Nothing anything like so straightforward. On its world, the people are people. The leaders are lizards. The people hate the lizards and the lizards rule the people."

"Odd," said Arthur, "I thought you said it was a democracy."

"I did," said Ford. "It is."

"So," said Arthur, hoping he wasn't sounding ridiculously obtuse, "why don't the people get rid of the lizards?"

"It honestly doesn't occur to them," said Ford. "They've all got the vote, so they all pretty much assume that the government they've voted in more or less approximates to the government they want."

"You mean they actually *vote* for the lizards?"

"Oh yes," said Ford with a shrug, "of course."

"But," said Arthur, going for the big one again, "why?"

"Because if they didn't vote for a lizard," said Ford, "the wrong lizard might get in. Got any gin?"

"What?"

"I said," said Ford, with an increasing air of urgency creeping into his voice, "have you got any gin?"

"I'll look. Tell me about the lizards."

Ford shrugged again.

"Some people say that the lizards are the best thing that ever happened to them," he said. "They're completely wrong of course, completely and utterly wrong, but someone's got to say it."

"But that's terrible," said Arthur.

"Listen, bud," said Ford, "if I had one Altairian dollar for every time I heard one bit of the Universe look at another bit of the Universe and say 'That's terrible' I wouldn't be sitting here like a lemon looking for a gin. But I haven't and I am. Anyway, what are you looking so placid and moon-eyed for? Are you in love?"

Arthur said yes, he was, and said it placidly.

"With someone who knows where the gin bottle is? Do I get to meet her?"

He did because Fenchurch came in at that moment with a pile of newspapers she'd been into the village to buy. She stopped in astonishment at the wreckage on the table and the wreckage from Betelgeuse on the sofa.

"Where's the gin?" said Ford to Fenchurch, and to Arthur, "What happened to Trillian, by the way?"

"Er, this is Fenchurch," said Arthur, awkwardly. "There was nothing with Trillian, you must have seen her last."

"Oh yeah," said Ford, "she went off with Zaphod somewhere. They had some kids or something. At least," he added, "I think that's what they were. Zaphod's calmed down a lot, you know."

"Really?" said Arthur, clustering hurriedly round Fenchurch to relieve her of the shopping.

"Yeah," said Ford, "at least one of his heads is now saner than an emu on acid."

"Arthur, who is this?" said Fenchurch.

"Ford Prefect," said Arthur. "I may have mentioned him in passing."

Chapter 37

For a total of three days and nights the giant silver robot stood in stunned amazement straddling the remains of Knightsbridge, swaying slightly and trying to work out a number of things.

Government deputations came to see it, ranting journalists by the truckload asked each other questions on the air about what they thought of it all, flights of fighter bombers tried pathetically to attack it—but no lizards appeared. It scanned the horizon slowly.

At night it was at its most spectacular, floodlit by the teams of television crews who covered it continuously as it continuously did nothing.

It thought and thought and eventually reached a conclusion.

It would have to send out its service robots.

It should have thought of that before, but it was having a number of problems.

The tiny flying robots came screeching out of the hatchway one afternoon in a terrifying cloud of metal. They roamed the surrounding terrain, frantically attacking some things and defending others.

One of them at last found a pet shop with some lizards, but it instantly defended the pet shop for democracy so savagely that little in the area survived.

A turning point came when a crack team of flying screechers discovered the zoo in Regent's Park, and most particularly the reptile house.

Learning a little caution from their previous mistakes in the pet shop, the flying drills and fretsaws brought some of the larger and fatter iguanas to the giant silver robot, who tried to conduct high-level talks with them.

Eventually the robot announced to the world that despite the full, frank, and wide-ranging exchange of views, the high-level talks had broken down, the lizards had been retired, and that it, the robot, would take a short holiday somewhere and for some reason selected Bournemouth.

Ford Prefect, watching it on TV, nodded, laughed, and had another beer. Immediate preparations were made for its departure.

The flying toolkits screeched and sawed and drilled and fried things with light throughout the day and all through the nighttime, and in the morning, stunningly, a giant mobile gantry started to roll westward on several roads simultaneously with the robot standing on it, supported within the gantry.

Westward it crawled, like a strange carnival buzzed around by its servants and helicopters and news coaches, scything through the land until at last it came to Bournemouth, where the robot slowly freed itself of its transport system's embraces and went and lay for ten days on the beach.

It was, of course, by far the most exciting thing that had ever happened to Bournemouth.

Crowds gathered daily along the perimeter which was staked out and guarded as the robot's recreation area, and tried to see what it was doing.

Motorboats prowled up and down the shore to see what it was doing.

It was doing nothing. It was lying on the beach. It was lying a little awkwardly on its face.

It was a journalist from a local paper who, late one night, managed to do what no one else in the world so far had managed, which was to strike up a brief intelligible conversation with one of the service robots guarding the perimeter.

It was an extraordinary breakthrough.

"I think there's a story in it," confided the journalist over a cigarette shared through the steel-link fence, "but it needs a good local angle. I've got a little list of questions here," he went on, rummaging awkwardly in an inner pocket. "Perhaps you could get him, it, whatever you call him, to run through them quickly."

The little flying ratchet screwdriver said it would see what it could do and screeched off.

A reply was never forthcoming.

Curiously, however, the questions on the piece of paper more or less exactly matched the questions that were going through the massive battle-scarred industrial-quality circuits of the robot's mind. They were these:

"How do you feel about being a robot?"

"How does it feel to be from outer space?" and,

"How do you like Bournemouth?"

Early the following day things started to be packed up and within a few days it became apparent that the robot was preparing to leave for good.

"The point is," said Fenchurch to Ford, "can you get us on board?"

Ford looked wildly at his watch.

"I have some serious unfinished business to attend to," he exclaimed.

Chapter 38

Crowds thronged as close as they could to the giant silver craft. The immediate perimeter was fenced off and patrolled by the tiny flying service robots. Staked out around that was the army, which had been completely unable to breach that inner perimeter, but were damned if anybody was going to breach them. They in turn were surrounded by a cordon of police, though whether they were there to protect the public from the army or the army from the public, or to guarantee the giant ship's diplomatic immunity and prevent it getting parking tickets was entirely unclear and the subject of much debate.

The inner perimeter fence was now being dismantled. The army stirred uncomfortably, uncertain of how to react to the fact that the reason for their being there seemed as if it were simply going to get up and go.

The giant robot had lurched back aboard the ship at lunchtime, and now it was five o'clock in the afternoon and no further sign had been seen of it. Much had been heard—more grindings and rumblings from deep within the craft, the music of a million hideous malfunctions; but the sense of tense expectation among the crowd was born of the fact that they tensely expected to be disappointed. This wonderful extraordinary thing had come into their lives, and now it was simply going to go without them.

Two people were particularly aware of this sensation. Arthur and Fenchurch scanned the crowd anxiously, unable to find Ford Prefect in it anywhere, or any sign that he had the slightest intention of being there.

"How reliable is he?" asked Fenchurch in a sinking voice.

"How *reliable?*" asked Arthur. He gave a hollow laugh. "How shallow is the ocean?" he asked. "How cold is the sun?"

The last parts of the robot's gantry transport were being carried on board, and the few remaining sections of the perimeter fence were now stacked at the bottom of the ramp waiting to follow them. The soldiers on guard round the ramp bristled meaningfully, orders were barked back and forth, hurried conferences were held, but nothing, of course, could be done about any of it.

Hopelessly, and with no clear plan now, Arthur and Fenchurch pushed forward through the crowd, but since the whole crowd was also trying to push forward through the crowd, this got them nowhere.

And within a few minutes, nothing remained outside the ship; every last link of the fence was aboard. A couple of flying fretsaws and a spirit level seemed to do one last check around the site and then screamed in through the giant hatchway themselves.

A few seconds passed.

The sounds of mechanical disarray from within changed in intensity, and slowly, heavily, the huge steel ramp began to lift itself back out of the Harrods Food Halls. The sound that accompanied it was the sound of thousands of tense, excited people being completely ignored.

"Hold it!"

A megaphone barked from a taxi that screeched to a halt on the edge of the milling crowd.

"There has been," barked the megaphone, "a major scientific break-in! Through. Breakthrough," it corrected itself. The door flew open and a small man from somewhere in the vicinity of Betelgeuse leapt out wearing a white coat.

"Hold it!" he shouted again, and this time brandished a short squat black rod with lights on it. The lights winked briefly, the ramp paused in its ascent, and then in obedience to the signals from the Thumb (which half the electronic engineers in the Galaxy are constantly trying to find fresh ways of jamming, while the other half are constantly trying to find fresh ways of jamming the jamming signals), slowly ground its way downward again.

Ford Prefect grabbed his megaphone from out of the taxi and started bawling at the crowd through it.

"Make way," he shouted, "make way, please, this is a major scientific breakthrough! You and you, get the equipment from the taxi."

Completely at random he pointed at Arthur and Fenchurch, who wrestled their way back out of the crowd and clustered urgently round the taxi.

"All right, I want you to clear a passage, please, for some important pieces of scientific equipment," boomed Ford. "Just everybody keep calm. It's all under control, there's nothing to see. It is merely a major scientific breakthrough. Keep calm now. Important scientific equipment. Clear the way."

Hungry for new excitement, delighted at this sudden reprieve from disappointment, the crowd enthusiastically fell back and started to open up.

Arthur was a little surprised to see what was printed on the boxes of important scientific equipment in the back of the taxi.

"Hang your coat over them," he muttered to Fenchurch as he heaved them out to her. Hurriedly, he maneuvered out the large supermarket cart that was also jammed against the back seat. It clattered to the ground, and together they loaded the boxes into it.

"Clear a path, please," shouted Ford again. "Everything's under proper scientific control."

"He said you'd pay," said the taxi driver to Arthur, who dug out some notes and paid him. There was the distant sound of police sirens.

"Move along there," shouted Ford, "and no one will get hurt."

The crowd surged and closed behind them again, as frantically they pushed and hauled the rattling supermarket cart through the rubble toward the ramp.

"It's all right," Ford continued to bellow. "There's nothing to see, it's all over. None of this is actually happening."

"Clear the way, please," boomed a police megaphone from the back of the crowd. "There's been a break-in, clear the way."

"Breakthrough," yelled Ford in competition. "A scientific break-through."

"This is the police! Clear the way!"

"Scientific equipment! Clear the way!"

"Police! Let us through!"

"Walkmen!" yelled Ford, and pulled half a dozen miniature tape players from his pockets and tossed them into the crowd. The resulting seconds of utter confusion allowed them to get the supermarket cart to the edge of the ramp, and to haul it up onto the lip of it.

"Hold tight," muttered Ford, and released a button on his Electronic Thumb. Beneath them, the huge ramp shuddered and began slowly to heave its way upward.

"OK, kids," he said as the milling crowd dropped away beneath them and they started to lurch their way along the tilting ramp into the bowels of the ship, "looks like we're on our way."

Chapter 39

Arthur Dent was irritated to be continually wakened by the sound of gunfire.

Being careful not to wake Fenchurch, who was still managing to sleep fitfully, he slid his way out of the maintenance hatchway that they had fashioned into a kind of bunk for themselves, slung himself down the access ladder, and prowled the corridors moodily.

They were claustrophobic and ill-lit. The lighting circuits buzzed annoyingly.

That wasn't it, though.

He paused and leaned backward as a flying power drill flew past him down the dim corridor with a screech, occasionally clanging against the walls like a confused bee.

That wasn't it either.

He clambered through a bulkhead door and found himself in a large corridor. Acrid smoke was drifting up from one end so he walked toward the other.

He came to an observation monitor let into the wall behind a plate of toughened but still badly scratched Plexiglas.

"Would you turn it down please?" he asked Ford Prefect who was crouching in front of it in the middle of a pile of bits of video equipment he'd taken from a shop window in Tottenham Court Road, having first hurled a small brick through it, and also a heap of empty beer cans.

"Shhhh!" hissed Ford, and peered with manic concentration at the screen. He was watching *The Magnificent Seven*.

"Just a bit," said Arthur.

"No!" shouted Ford. "We're just getting to the good bit! Listen, I finally got it all sorted out, voltage levels, line conversion, everything, and this is the good bit!"

With a sigh and a headache, Arthur sat down beside him and watched the good bit. He listened to Ford's whoops and yells and yeeehays as placidly as he could.

"Ford," he said eventually, when it was all over, and Ford was hunting through a stack of cassettes for the tape of *Casablanca*, "how come, if . . ."

"This is the big one," said Ford. "This is the one I came back for. Do you realize I never saw it all the way through? I always missed the end. I saw half of it again the night before the Vogons came. When they blew the place up I thought I'd never get to see it. Hey, what happened with all that anyway?"

"Just life," said Arthur, and plucked a beer from a six-pack.

"Oh, that again," said Ford. "I thought it might be something like that. I prefer this stuff," he said as Rick's bar flickered onto the screen. "How come if what?"

"What?"

"You started to say, 'how come if...'"

"How come if you're so rude about the Earth, that you ... Oh, never mind, let's just watch the movie."

"Exactly," said Ford.

Chapter 40

There remains little still to tell.

Beyond what used to be known as the Limitless Lightfields of Flanux until the Gray Binding Fiefdoms of Saxaquine were discovered lying behind them, lie the Gray Binding Fiefdoms of Saxaquine.

Within the Gray Binding Fiefdoms of Saxaquine lies the star named Zarss, around which orbits the planet Preliumtarn in which is the land of Sevorbeupstry, and it was to the land of Sevorbeupstry that Arthur and Fenchurch came at last, a little tired by the journey.

And in the land of Sevorbeupstry, they came to the Great Red Plain of Rars, which was bounded on the south side by the Quentulus Quazgar Mountains, on the farther side of which, according to the dying words of Prak, they would find in thirty-foot-high letters of fire God's Final Message to His Creation.

According to Prak, if Arthur's memory served him right, the place was guarded by the Lajestic Vantrashell of Lob, and so, after a manner, it proved to be. He was a little man in a strange hat and he sold them a ticket.

"Keep to the left, please," he said, "keep to the left," and hurried past them on a little scooter.

They realized they were not the first to pass that way, for the path that led around the left of the Great Red Plain was well worn and dotted with booths. At one they bought a box of fudge, which had been baked in an oven in a cave in the mountain, which was heated by the fire of the letters that formed God's Final Message to His Creation. At another they bought some postcards. The letters had been blurred with an airbrush, "So as not to spoil the Big Surprise!" it said on the reverse.

"Do you know what the message is?" they asked the wizened little lady in the booth.

"Oh yes," she piped cheerily, "oh yes!"

She waved them on.

Every twenty miles or so there was a little stone hut with showers and sanitary facilities, but the going was tough, and the high sun baked down on the Great Red Plain, and the Great Red Plain rippled in the heat.

"Is it possible," asked Arthur at one of the larger booths, "to rent one of those little scooters? Like the one Lajestic Ventrawhatsit had?"

"The scooters," said the little lady who was serving at the ice cream bar, "are not for the devout."

"Oh well, that's easy then," said Fenchurch, "we're not particularly devout. We're just interested."

"Then you must turn back now," said the little lady severely, and when they demurred, sold them a couple of Final Message sun hats and a photograph of themselves with their arms tight around each other on the Great Red Plain of Rars.

They drank a couple of sodas in the shade of the booth and then trudged out into the sun again.

"We're running out of barrier cream," said Fenchurch after a few more miles. "We can go to the next booth, or we can return to the previous one which is nearer, but means we have to retrace our steps."

They stared ahead at the distant black speck winking in the heat haze; they looked behind themselves. They elected to go on.

They then discovered that they were not only not the first to make this journey, but that they were not the only ones making it now.

Some way ahead of them an awkward low shape was heaving itself wretchedly along the ground, stumbling painfully slowly, half limping, half crawling.

It was moving so slowly that before too long they caught the creature up and could see that it was made of worn, scarred, and twisted metal.

It groaned at them as they approached it, collapsing in the hot, dry dust.

"So much time," it groaned, "oh, so much time. And pain as well, so much of that, and so much time to suffer in it, too. One or the other on its own I could probably manage. It's the two together that really get me down. Oh, hello, you again."

"Marvin?" said Arthur sharply, crouching down beside it. "Is that you?"

"You were always one," groaned the aged husk of the robot, "for the superintelligent question, weren't you?"

"What is it?" whispered Fenchurch in alarm, crouching behind Arthur, and grasping his arm.

"He's sort of an old friend," said Arthur, "I—"

"Friend!" croaked the robot pathetically. The word died away in a kind of dry crackle and flakes of rust fell out of his mouth. "You'll have to excuse me while I try and remember what the word means. My memory banks are not what they were, you know, and any word which falls into disuse for a few zillion years has to get shifted down into auxiliary memory backup. Ah, here it comes."

The robot's battered head snapped up a bit as if in thought.

"Hmm," he said, "what a curious concept."

He thought a little longer.

"No," he said at last, "don't think I ever came across one of those. Sorry, can't help you there."

He scraped a knee along pathetically in the dust, and then tried to twist himself up onto his misshapen elbows.

"Is there any last service you would like me to perform for you perhaps?" he asked in a kind of hollow rattle. "A piece of paper that perhaps you would like me to pick up for you? Or maybe you would like me," he continued, "to open a door?"

His head scratched round in its rusty neck bearings and seemed to scan the distant horizon.

"Don't seem to be any doors around at present," he said, "but I'm sure that if we waited long enough, someone would build one. And then," he said slowly, twisting his head around to see Arthur again, "I could open it for you. I'm quite used to waiting, you know."

"Arthur," hissed Fenchurch in his ear sharply, "you never told me of this. What have you done to this poor creature?"

"Nothing," insisted Arthur sadly, "he's always like this—"

"Ha!" snapped Marvin. "Ha!" he repeated, "what do you know of always? You say 'always' to me, who, because of the silly little errands your organic life forms keep on sending me through time on, am now thirty-seven times older than the Universe itself? Pick your words with a little more care," he coughed, "and tact."

He rasped his way through a coughing fit and resumed.

"Leave me," he said, "go on ahead, leave me to struggle painfully on my way. My time at last is nearly come. My race is nearly run. I fully expect," he said, feebly waving them on with a broken finger, "to come in last. It would be fitting. Here I am, brain the size—"

"Shut up," said Arthur.

Between them they picked him up despite his feeble protests and insults. The metal was so hot it nearly blistered their fingers, but he weighed now surprisingly little, and hung limply between their arms.

They carried him with them along the path that ran along the left of the Great Red Plain of Rars toward the south-encircling mountains of Quentulus Quazgar.

Arthur attempted to explain to Fenchurch, but was too often inter-rupted by Marvin's dolorous cybernetic ravings.

They tried to see if they could get him some spare parts at one of the booths, and some soothing oil, but Marvin would have none of it.

"I'm all spare parts," he droned.

"Let me be!" he groaned.

"Every part of me," he moaned, "has been replaced at least fifty times...except..." He seemed almost imperceptibly to brighten for a moment. His head bobbed between them with the effort of memory. "Do you remember, the first time you ever met me," he said at last to Arthur, "I had been given the intellect-stretching task of taking you up to the bridge? I mentioned to you that I had this terrible pain in all the diodes down my left side? That I had asked for them to be replaced but they never were?"

He left a longish pause before he continued. They carried him on between them, under the baking sun that hardly ever seemed to move, let alone set.

"See if you can guess," said Marvin, when he judged that the pause had become embarrassing enough, "which parts of me were never replaced? Go on, see if you can guess.

"Ouch," he added, "ouch, ouch, ouch, ouch, ouch."

At last they reached the last of the little booths, set Marvin down between them, and rested in the shade. Fenchurch bought some cuff links for Russell, cuff links that had set in them little polished pebbles which had been picked up from the Quentulus Quazgar Mountains, directly under-neath the letters of fire in which were written God's Final Message to His Creation.

Arthur flipped through a little rack of devotional tracts on the counter, little meditations on the meaning of the Message.

"Ready?" he said to Fenchurch, who nodded.

They heaved up Marvin between them.

They rounded the foot of the Quentulus Quazgar Mountains, and there was the Message written in blazing letters along the crest of the mountain. There was a little observation vantage point with a rail built along the top of a large rock facing it, from which you could get a good view. It had a little pay telescope for looking at the letters in detail, but no one would ever use it because the letters burned with the divine brilliance of the heavens and would, if seen through a telescope, have severely damaged the retina and optic nerve.

They gazed at God's Final Message to His Creation in wonderment, and were slowly and ineffably filled with a great sense of peace, and of final and complete understanding.

Fenchurch sighed. "Yes," she said, "that was it."

They had been staring at it for fully ten minutes before they became aware that Marvin, hanging between their shoulders, was in difficulties. The robot could no longer lift his head, had not read the message. They lifted his head, but he complained that his vision circuits had almost gone.

They found a coin and helped him to the telescope. He complained and insulted them, but they helped him look at each individual letter in turn. The first letter was a "w," the second an "e." Then there was a gap. An "a" followed, then a "p," an "o," and an "l."

Marvin paused for a rest.

After a few moments they resumed and let him see the "o," the "g," the "i," the "z," and the "e."

The next two words were "for" and "the." The last one was a long one, and Marvin needed another rest before he could tackle it.

It started with "i," then "n," then "c." Next came an "o" and an "n," followed by a "v," an "e," another "n," and an "i."

After a final pause, Marvin gathered his strength for the last stretch.

He read the "e," the "n," the "c," and at last the final "e," and staggered back into their arms.

"I think," he murmured at last from deep within his corroding, rattling thorax, "I feel good about it."

The lights went out in his eyes for absolutely the very last time ever.

Luckily, there was a stall nearby where you could rent scooters from guys with green wings.

Epilogue

One of the greatest benefactors of all lifekind was a man who couldn't keep his mind on the job at hand.

Brilliant?

Certainly.

One of the foremost genetic engineers of his or any other generation, including a number he had designed himself?

Without a doubt.

The problem was that he was far too interested in things which he shouldn't be interested in, at least, as people would tell him, not *now*.

He was also, partly because of this, of a rather irritable disposition.

So when his world was threatened by terrible invaders from a distant star, who were still a fair way off but traveling fast, he, Blart Versenwald III (his name was Blart Versenwald III, which is not strictly relevant, but quite interesting because—never mind, that was his name and we can talk about why it's interesting later), was sent into guarded seclusion by the masters of his race with instructions to design a breed of fanatical superwarriors to resist and vanquish the feared invaders, do it quickly and, they told him, "Concentrate!"

So he sat by a window and looked out at a summer lawn and designed and designed and designed, but inevitably got a little distracted by things, and by the time the invaders were practically in orbit round them, had come up with a remarkable new breed of superfly that could, unaided, figure out how to fly through the open half of a half-open window, and also an off switch for children. Celebrations of these remarkable achievements seemed doomed to be short-lived because disaster was imminent as the alien ships were landing. But, astoundingly, the fearsome invaders who, like most warlike races were only on the rampage because they couldn't cope with things at home, were stunned by Versenwald's extraordinary breakthroughs, joined in the celebrations and were instantly prevailed upon to sign a wide-ranging series of trading agreements and set up a program of cultural exchanges. And, in an astonishing reversal of normal practice in the conduct of such matters, everybody concerned lived happily ever after.

There was a point to this story, but it has temporarily escaped the chronicler's mind.

Young Zaphod Plays It Safe

A large flying craft moved swiftly across the surface of an astoundingly beautiful sea. From mid-morning onward it plied back and forth in great widening arcs, and at last attracted the attention of the local islanders, a peaceful, sea-food–loving people who gathered on the beach and squinted up into the blinding sun, trying to see what was there.

Any sophisticated knowledgeable person, who had knocked about, seen a few things, would probably have remarked on how much the craft looked like a filing cabinet—a large and recently burgled filing cabinet lying on its back with its drawers in the air and flying.

The islanders, whose experience was of a different kind, were instead struck by how little it looked like a lobster.

They chattered excitedly about its total lack of claws, its stiff unbending back, and the fact that it seemed to experience the greatest difficulty staying on the ground. This last feature seemed particularly funny to them. They jumped up and down on the spot a lot to demonstrate to the stupid thing that they themselves found staying on the ground the easiest thing in the world.

But soon this entertainment began to pall for them. After all, since it was perfectly clear to them that the thing was not a lobster, and since their world was blessed with an abundance of things that were lobsters (a good half dozen of which were now marching succulently up the beach toward them), they saw no reason to waste any more time on the thing but decided instead to adjourn immediately for a late lobster lunch.

At that exact moment the craft stopped suddenly in mid-air, then upended itself and plunged headlong into the ocean with a great crash of spray which sent them shouting into the trees.

When they reemerged, nervously, a few minutes later, all they were able to see was a smoothly scarred circle of water and a few gulping bubbles.

That's odd, they said to each other between mouthfuls of the best lobster to be had anywhere in the Western Galaxy, that's the second time that's happened in a year.

The craft which wasn't a lobster dived direct to a depth of two hundred feet, and hung there in the heavy blueness, while vast masses of water swayed about it. High above, where the water was magically clear, a brilliant formation of fish flashed away. Below, where the light had difficulty reaching, the color of the water sank to a dark and savage blue.

Here, at two hundred feet, the sun streamed feebly. A large, silk-skinned sea-mammal rolled idly by, inspecting the craft with a kind of half interest, as if it had half expected to find something of this kind around about here, and then it slid on up and away toward the rippling light.

The craft waited for a minute or two, taking readings, and then descended another hundred feet. At this depth it was becoming seriously dark. After a moment or two the internal lights of the craft shut down, and in the second or so that passed before the main external beams suddenly stabbed out, the only visible light came from a small hazily illuminated pink sign which read *The Beeblebrox Salvage and Really Wild Stuff Corporation*.

The huge beams switched downward, catching a vast shoal of silver fish, which swiveled away in silent panic.

In the dim control room, which extended in a broad bow from the craft's blunt prow, four heads were gathered around a computer display that was analyzing the very, very faint and intermittent signals that emanated from deep on the sea bed.

"That's it," said the owner of one of the heads finally.

"Can we be quite sure?" said the owner of another of the heads.

"One hundred percent positive," replied the owner of the first head.

"You're one hundred percent positive that the ship which is crashed on the bottom of this ocean is the ship which you said you were one hundred percent positive could one hundred percent positively never crash?" said the owner of the two remaining heads. "Hey," he put up two of his hands, "I'm only asking."

The two officials from the Safety and Civil Reassurance Administration responded to this with a very cold stare, but the man with the odd, or rather the even, number of heads missed it. He flung himself back on the pilot couch, opened a couple of beers—one for himself and the other also for himself—stuck his feet on the console and said "Hey, baby" through the ultra-glass at a passing fish.

"Mr. Beeblebrox . . ." began the shorter and less reassuring of the two officials in a low voice.

"Yup?" said Zaphod, rapping a suddenly empty can down on some of the more sensitive instruments. "You ready to dive? Let's go."

"Mr. Beeblebrox, let us make one thing perfectly clear . . ."

"Yeah let's," said Zaphod. "How about this for a start. Why don't you just tell me what's really on this ship."

"We have told you," said the official. "By-products."

Zaphod exchanged weary glances with himself.

"By-products," he said. "By-products of what?"

"Processes," said the official.

"What processes?"

"Processes that are perfectly safe."

"Santa Zarquana Voostra!" exclaimed both of Zaphod's heads in chorus. "So safe that you have to build a zarking fortress ship to take the by-products to the nearest black hole and tip them in! Only it doesn't get there because the pilot takes a detour—is this right?—to pick up some *lobster*...? OK, so the guy is cool, but...I mean own up, this is barking time, this is major lunch, this is stool approaching critical mass, this is...this is...*total vocabulary failure!*

"Shut *up!*" his right head yelled at his left, "we're *flanging!*"

He got a good calming grip on the remaining beer can.

"Listen, guys," he resumed after a moment's peace and contemplation. The two officials had said nothing. Conversation at this level was not something to which they felt they could aspire. "I just want to know," insisted Zaphod, "what you're getting me into here."

He stabbed a finger at the intermittent readings trickling over the computer screen. They meant nothing to him but he didn't like the look of them at all. They were all squiggly with lots of long numbers and things.

"It's breaking up, is that it?" he shouted. "It's got a hold full of epsilonic radiating aorist rods or something that'll fry this whole space sector for zillions of years back and it's breaking up. Is that the story? Is that what we're going down to find? Am I going to come out of that wreck with even *more* heads?"

"It cannot possibly be a wreck, Mr. Beeblebrox," insisted the official, "the ship is guaranteed to be perfectly safe. It cannot possibly break up."

"Then why are you so keen to go and look at it?"

"We like to look at things that are perfectly safe."

"Freeeooow!"

"Mr. Beeblebrox," said the official, patiently, "may I remind you that you have a job to do?"

"Yeah, well, maybe I don't feel so keen on doing it all of a sudden. What do you think I am, completely without any moral whatsits, what are they called, those moral things?"

"Scruples?"

"Scruples, thank you, whatsoever? Well?"

The two officials waited calmly. They coughed slightly to help pass the time.

Zaphod sighed a "what is the world coming to" sort of sigh to absolve himself from all blame, and swung himself around in his seat.

"Ship?" he called.

"Yup?" said the ship.

"Do what I do."

The ship thought about this for a few milliseconds and then, after double checking all the seals on its heavy duty bulkheads, it began slowly, inexorably, in the hazy blaze of its lights, to sink to the lowest depths.

Five hundred feet.

A thousand.

Two thousand.

Here, at a pressure of nearly seventy atmospheres, in the chilling depths where no light reaches, nature keeps its most heated imaginings. Two foot-long nightmares loomed wildly into the bleaching light, yawned, and vanished back into the blackness.

Two and a half thousand feet.

At the dim edges of the ship's lights guilty secrets flitted by with their eyes on stalks.

Gradually the topography of the distantly approaching ocean bed resolved with greater and greater clarity on the computer displays until at last a shape could be made out that was separate and distinct from its surroundings. It was like a huge lopsided cylindrical fortress that widened sharply halfway along its length to accommodate the heavy ultraplating with which the crucial storage holds were clad, and which were supposed by its builders to have made this the most secure and impregnable spaceship ever built. Before launch the material structure of this section had been battered, rammed, blasted and subjected to every assault its builders knew it could withstand in order to demonstrate that it could withstand them.

The tense silence in the cockpit tightened perceptibly as it became clear that it was this section that had broken rather neatly in two.

"In fact it's perfectly safe," said one of the officials, "it's built so that even if the ship does break up, the storage holds cannot possibly be breached."

Three thousand, eight hundred and twenty-five feet.

Four Hi-Presh-A Smart Suits moved slowly out of the open hatchway of the salvage craft and waded through the barrage of its lights toward the monstrous shape that loomed darkly out of the sea night. They moved with a sort of clumsy grace, near weightlessness though weighed on by a world of water.

With his right-hand head Zaphod peered up into the black immensities above him and for a moment his mind sang with a silent roar of horror. He glanced to his left and was relieved to see that his other head was busy watching the Brockian Ultra-Cricket broadcasts on the helmet vid without concern. Slightly behind him to his left walked the two officials from the Safety and Civil Reassurance Administration, slightly in front of him to his right walked the empty suit, carrying their implements and testing the way for them.

They passed the huge rift in the broken backed *Starship Billion Year Bunker*, and played their flashlights up into it. Mangled machinery loomed between torn and twisted bulkheads, two feet thick. A family of large transparent eels lived in there now and seemed to like it.

The empty suit preceded them along the length of the ship's gigantic murky hull, trying the airlocks. The third one it tested ground open uneasily. They crowded inside it and waited for several long minutes while the pump mechanisms dealt with the hideous pressure that the ocean exerted, and slowly replaced it with an equally hideous pressure of air and inert gases. At last the inner door slid open and they were admitted to a dark outer holding area of the *Starship Billion Year Bunker*.

Several more high security Titan-O-Hold doors had to be passed through, each of which the officials opened with a selection of quark keys. Soon they were so deep within the heavy security fields that the Ultra-Cricket broadcasts were beginning to fade, and Zaphod had to switch to one of the rock video stations, since there was nowhere that they were not able to reach.

A final doorway slid open, and they emerged into a large sepulchral space. Zaphod played his flashlight against the opposite wall and it fell full on a wild-eyed screaming face.

Zaphod screamed a diminished fifth himself, dropped his light and sat heavily on the floor, or rather on a body which had been lying there undisturbed for around six months and which reacted to being sat on by exploding with great violence. Zaphod wondered what to do about all this, and after a brief but hectic internal debate decided that passing out would be the very thing.

He came to a few minutes later and pretended not to know who he was, where he was or how he had got there, but was not able to convince anybody. He then pretended that his memory suddenly returned with a rush and that the shock caused him to pass out again, but he was helped unwillingly to his feet by the empty suit—which he was beginning to take a serious dislike to—and forced to come to terms with his surroundings.

They were dimly and fitfully lit and unpleasant in a number of respects, the most obvious of which was the colorful arrangement of parts of the ship's late lamented Navigation Officer over the floor, walls and ceiling, and especially over the lower half of his, Zaphod's, suit. The effect of this was so astoundingly nasty that we shall not be referring to it again at any point in this narrative—other than to record briefly the fact that it caused Zaphod to throw up inside his suit, which he therefore removed and swapped, after suitable headgear modifications, with the empty one. Unfortunately the stench of the fetid air in the ship, followed by the sight of his own suit walking around casually draped in rotting intestines was enough to make him throw up in the other suit as well, which was a problem that he and the suit would simply have to live with.

There. All done. No more nastiness.

At least, no more of that particular nastiness.

The owner of the screaming face had calmed down very slightly now and was babbling away incoherently in a large tank of yellow liquid—an emergency suspension tank.

"It was crazy," he babbled, "crazy! I told him we could always try the lobster on the way back, but he was crazy. Obsessed! Do you ever get like that about lobster? Because I don't. Seems to me it's all rubbery and fiddly to eat, and not that much taste, well I mean is there? I infinitely prefer scallops, and said so. Oh Zarquon, I *said* so!"

Zaphod stared at this extraordinary apparition, flailing in its tank. The man was attached to all kinds of life-support tubes, and his voice was bubbling out of speakers that echoed insanely around the ship, returning as haunting echoes from deep and distant corridors.

"That was where I went wrong," the madman yelled, "I actually said that I preferred scallops and he said it was because I hadn't had real lobster like they did where his ancestors came from, which was here, and he'd prove it. He said it was no problem, he said the lobster here was worth a whole journey, let alone the small diversion it would take to get here, and he swore he could handle the ship in the atmosphere, but it was madness, madness!" he screamed, and paused with his eyes rolling, as if the word had rung some kind of bell in his mind. "The ship went right out of control! I couldn't believe what we were doing and just to prove a point about lobster which is really so overrated as a food, I'm sorry to go on about lobsters so much, I'll try and stop in a minute, but they've been on my mind so much for the months I've been in this tank, can you imagine what it's like to be stuck in a ship with the same guys for months eating junk food when all one guy will talk about is lobster and then spend six months floating by yourself in a tank thinking about it. I promise I will try and shut up about the lobsters, I really will. Lobsters, lobsters, lobsters—enough! I think I'm the only survivor. I'm the only one who managed to get to an emergency tank before we went down. I sent out the Mayday and then we hit. It's a disaster, isn't it? A total disaster, and all because the guy liked lobsters. How much sense am I making? It's really hard for me to tell."

He gazed at them beseechingly, and his mind seemed to sway slowly back down to earth like a falling leaf. He blinked and looked at them oddly like a monkey peering at a strange fish. He scrabbled curiously with his wrinkled up fingers at the glass side of the tank. Tiny, thick yellow bubbles loosed themselves from his mouth and nose, caught briefly in his swab of hair and strayed on upward.

"Oh Zarquon, oh heavens," he mumbled pathetically to himself, "I've been found. I've been rescued. . . ."

"Well," said one of the officials, briskly, "you've been found at least." He strode over to the main computer bank in the middle of the chamber and started checking quickly through the ship's main monitor circuits for damage reports.

"The aorist rod chambers are intact," he said.

"Holy dingo's dos," snarled Zaphod, "there *are* aorist rods on board . . . !"

Aorist rods were devices used in a now happily abandoned form of energy production. When the hunt for new sources of energy had at one point got particularly frantic, one bright young chap suddenly spotted that one place which had never used up all its available energy—the past. And with the sudden rush of blood to the head that such insights tend to induce, he invented a way of mining it that very same night, and within a year huge tracts of the past were being drained of all their energy and simply wasting away. Those who claimed that the past should be left unspoiled were accused of indulging in an extremely expensive form of sentimentality. The past provided a very cheap, plentiful and clean source of energy, there could always be a few Natural Past Reserves set up if anyone wanted to pay for their upkeep, and as for the claim that draining the past impoverished the present, well, maybe it did, slightly, but the effects were immeasurable and you really had to keep a sense of proportion.

It was only when it was realized that the present really was being impoverished, and that the reason for it was that those selfish plundering wastrel bastards up in the future were doing exactly the same thing, that everyone realized that every single aorist rod, and the terrible secret of how they were made, would have to be utterly and forever destroyed. They claimed it was for the sake of their grandparents and grandchildren, but it was of course for the sake of their grandparent's grandchildren, and their grandchildren's grandparents.

The official from the Safety and Civil Reassurance Administration gave a dismissive shrug.

"They're perfectly safe," he said. He glanced up at Zaphod and suddenly said with uncharacteristic frankness, "There's worse than that on board. At least," he added, tapping at one of the computer screens, "I hope it's on board."

The other official rounded on him sharply.

"What the hell do you think you're saying?" he snapped.

The first shrugged again. He said, "It doesn't matter. He can say what he likes. No one would believe him. It's why we chose to use him rather than do anything official, isn't it? The more wild the story he tells, the more it'll sound like he's some hippy adventurer making it up. He can even say that we said this and it'll make him sound like a paranoid." He smiled pleasantly at Zaphod who was seething in his nasty suit. "You may accompany us," he told him, "if you wish."

"You see?" said the official, examining the ultra-titanium outer seals of the aorist rod hold. "Perfectly secure, perfectly safe."

He said the same thing as they passed holds containing chemical weapons so powerful that a teaspoonful could fatally infect an entire planet.

He said the same thing as they passed holds containing zeta-active compounds so powerful that a teaspoonful could blow up a whole planet.

He said the same thing as they passed holds containing theta-active compounds so powerful that a teaspoonful could irradiate a whole planet.

"I'm glad I'm not a planet," muttered Zaphod.

"You'd have nothing to fear," assured the official from the Safety and Civil Reassurance Administration, "planets are very safe. Provided," he added—and paused. They were approaching the hold nearest to the point where the back of the *Starship Billion Year Bunker* was broken. The corridor here was twisted and deformed, and the floor was damp and sticky in patches.

"Ho hum," he said, "ho very much hum."

"What's in this hold?" demanded Zaphod.

"By-products," said the official, clamming up again.

"By-products . . . ," insisted Zaphod, quietly, "of what?"

Neither official answered. Instead, they examined the hold door very carefully and saw that its seals were twisted apart by the forces that had deformed the whole corridor. One of them touched the door lightly. It swung open to his touch. There was darkness inside, with just a couple of dim yellow lights deep within it.

"Of *what?*" hissed Zaphod.

The leading official turned to the other.

"There's an escape capsule," he said, "that the crew were to use to abandon ship before jettisoning it into the black hole," he said. "I think it would be good to know that it's still there." The other official nodded and left without a word.

The first official quietly beckoned Zaphod in. The large dim yellow lights glowed about twenty feet from them.

"The reason," he said, quietly, "why everything else in this ship is, I maintain, safe, is that no one is really crazy enough to use them. No one. At least no one that crazy would ever get near them. Anyone that mad or dangerous rings very deep alarm bells. People may be stupid but they're not *that* stupid."

"By-products," hissed Zaphod again, he had to hiss in order that his voice shouldn't be heard to tremble, "of what."

"Er, Designer People."

"*What?*"

"The Sirius Cybernetics Corporation was awarded a huge research grant to design and produce synthetic personalities to order. The results were uniformly disastrous. All the 'people' and 'personalities' turned out to be amalgams of characteristics that simply could not co-exist in naturally occurring life forms. Most of them were just poor pathetic misfits, but some were deeply, deeply dangerous. Dangerous because they didn't ring alarm bells in other people. They could walk through situations the way that ghosts walk through walls, because no one spotted the danger.

"The most dangerous of all were three identical ones—they were put in this hold, to be blasted, with this ship, right out of this universe. They are not evil, in fact they are rather simple and charming. But they are the most dangerous creatures that ever lived because there is nothing they will not do if allowed, and nothing they will not be allowed to do. . . ."

Zaphod looked at the dim yellow lights, the two dim yellow lights. As his eyes became accustomed to the light he saw that the two lights framed a third space where something was broken. Wet sticky patches gleamed dully on the floor.

Zaphod and the official walked cautiously toward the lights. At that moment, four words came crashing into the helmet headsets from the other official.

"The capsule is gone," he said tersely.

"Trace it," snapped Zaphod's companion. "Find exactly where it has gone. We *must* know where it has gone!"

Zaphod slid aside a large ground-glass door. Beyond it lay a tank full of thick yellow liquid, and floating in it was a man, a kindly looking man with lots of pleasant laugh lines around his face. He seemed to be floating quite contentedly and smiling to himself.

Another terse message suddenly came through his helmet headset. The planet toward which the escape capsule had headed had already been identified. It was in Galactic Sector ZZ9 Plural Z Alpha.

The kindly looking man in the tank seemed to be babbling gently to himself, just as the co-pilot had been in his tank. Little yellow bubbles beaded on the man's lips. Zaphod found a small speaker by the tank and turned it on. He heard the man babbling gently about a shining city on a hill.

He also heard the official from the Safety and Civil Reassurance Administration issue instructions that the planet in ZZ9 Plural Z Alpha must be made "perfectly safe."

Mostly Harmless

For Ron

With grateful thanks to Sue Freestone and Michael Bywater
for their support, help and constructive abuse.

Anything that happens, happens.

Anything that, in happening, causes something else to happen, causes something else to happen.

Anything that, in happening, causes itself to happen again, happens again.

It doesn't necessarily do it in chronological order, though.

Chapter 1

The history of the Galaxy has got a little muddled, for a number of reasons: partly because those who are trying to keep track of it have got a little muddled, but also because some very muddling things have been happening anyway.

One of the problems has to do with the speed of light and the difficulties involved in trying to exceed it. You can't. Nothing travels faster than the speed of light with the possible exception of bad news, which obeys its own special laws. The Hingefreel people of Arkintoofle Minor did try to build spaceships that were powered by bad news but they didn't work particularly well and were so extremely unwelcome whenever they arrived anywhere that there wasn't really any point in being there.

So, by and large, the peoples of the Galaxy tended to languish in their own local muddles and the history of the Galaxy itself was, for a long time, largely cosmological.

Which is not to say that people weren't trying. They tried sending off fleets of spaceships to do battle or business in distant parts, but these usually took thousands of years to get anywhere. By the time they eventually arrived, other forms of travel had been discovered which made use of hyperspace to circumvent the speed of light, so that whatever battles it was that the slower-than-light fleets had been sent to fight had already been taken care of centuries earlier by the time they actually got there.

This didn't, of course, deter their crews from wanting to fight the battles anyway. They were trained, they were ready, they'd had a couple of thousand years' sleep, they'd come a long way to do a tough job and, by Zarquon, they were going to do it.

This was when the first major Muddles of Galactic history set in, with battles continually reerupting centuries after the issues they had been fought over had supposedly been settled. However, these muddles were as nothing to the ones which historians had to try and unravel once time-travel was discovered and battles started *pre*erupting hundreds of years before the issues even arose. When the Infinite Improbability Drive arrived and whole planets started unexpectedly turning into banana fruitcake, the great history faculty of the University of MaxiMegalon finally gave up, closed itself down and surrendered its buildings to the rapidly growing joint faculty of Divinity and Water Polo, which had been after them for years.

Which is all very well, of course, but it almost certainly means that no one will ever know for sure where, for instance, the Grebulons came from, or exactly what it was they wanted. And this is a pity because, if anybody had known anything about them, it is just possible that a most terrible catastrophe would have been averted—or, at least, would have had to find a different way to happen.

Click, hum.

The huge gray Grebulon reconnaissance ship moved silently through the black void. It was traveling at fabulous, breathtaking speed, yet appeared, against the glimmering background of a billion distant stars to be moving not at all. It was just one dark speck frozen against an infinite granularity of brilliant night.

On board the ship, everything was as it had been for millennia, deeply dark and silent.

Click, hum.

At least, almost everything.

Click, click, hum.

Click, hum, click, hum, click, hum.

Click, click, click, click, click, hum.

Hmmm.

A low-level supervising program woke up a slightly higher-level supervising program deep in the ship's semisomnolent cyberbrain and reported to it that whenever it went *click* all it got was a *hum*.

The higher-level supervising program asked it what it was supposed to get, and the low-level supervising program said that it couldn't remember what it was meant to get, exactly, but thought it was probably more of a sort of distant satisfied sigh, wasn't it? It didn't know what this hum was. Click, hum, click, hum. That was all it was getting.

The higher-level supervising program considered this and didn't like it. It asked the low-level supervising program what exactly it was supervising and the low-level supervising program said it couldn't remember that either, just that it was something that was meant to go *click, sigh* every ten years or so, which usually happened without fail. It had tried to consult its error look-up table but couldn't find it, which was why it had alerted the higher-level supervising program of the problem.

The higher-level supervising program went to consult one of its own look-up tables to find out what the low-level supervising program was meant to be supervising.

It couldn't find the look-up table.

Odd.

It looked again. All it got was an error message. It tried to look up the error message in its error message look-up table and couldn't find that either. It allowed a couple of nanoseconds to go by while it went through all this again. Then it woke up its sector function supervisor.

The sector function supervisor hit immediate problems. It called its supervising agent, which hit problems too. Within a few millionths of a second virtual circuits that had lain dormant, some for years, some for centuries, were flaring into life throughout the ship. Something, somewhere, had gone terribly wrong, but none of the supervising programs could tell what it was. At every level, vital instructions were missing, and the instructions about what to do in the event of discovering that vital instructions were missing, were also missing.

Small modules of software—agents—surged through the logical pathways, grouping, consulting, regrouping. They quickly established that the ship's memory, all the way back to its central mission module, was in tatters. No amount of interrogation could determine what it was that had happened. Even the central mission module itself seemed to be damaged.

This made the whole problem very simple to deal with, in fact. Replace the central mission module. There was another one, a backup, an exact duplicate of the original. It had to be physically replaced because, for safety reasons, there was no link whatsoever between the original and its backup. Once the central mission module was replaced it could itself supervise the reconstruction of the rest of the system in every detail, and all would be well.

Robots were instructed to bring the backup central mission module from the shielded strong room, where they guarded it, to the ship's logic chamber for installation.

This involved the lengthy exchange of emergency codes and protocols as the robots interrogated the agents as to the authenticity of the instructions. At last the robots were satisfied that all procedures were correct. They unpacked the backup central mission module from its storage housing, carried it out of the storage chamber, fell out of the ship and went spinning off into the void.

This provided the first major clue as to what it was that was wrong.

Further investigation quickly established what it was that had happened. A meteorite had knocked a large hole in the ship. The ship had not previously detected this because the meteorite had neatly knocked out that part of the ship's processing equipment which was supposed to detect if the ship had been hit by a meteorite.

The first thing to do was to try to seal up the hole. This turned out to be impossible, because the ship's sensors couldn't see that there was a hole, and the supervisors, which should have said that the sensors weren't working properly, weren't working properly and kept saying that the sensors were fine. The ship could only deduce the existence of the hole from the fact that the robots had clearly fallen out of it, taking its spare brain—which would have enabled it to see the hole—with them.

The ship tried to think intelligently about this, failed and then blanked out completely for a bit. It didn't realize it had blanked out, of course, because it had blanked out. It was merely surprised to see the stars jump. After the third time the stars jumped, the ship finally realized that it must be blanking out, and that it was time to take some serious decisions.

It relaxed.

Then it realized it hadn't actually taken the serious decisions yet and panicked. It blanked out again for a bit. When it awoke again it sealed all the bulkheads around where it knew the unseen hole must be.

It clearly hadn't got to its destination yet, it thought, fitfully, but since it no longer had the faintest idea where its destination was or how to reach it, there seemed to be little point in continuing. It consulted what tiny scraps of instructions it could reconstruct from the tatters of its central mission module.

"Your !!!!! !!!!! !!!!! year mission is to !!!!! !!!!! !!!!!, !!!!!, !!!!! !!!!! !!!!! !!!!!, land !!!!! !!!!! !!!!! a safe distance !!!!! !!!!! monitor it. !!!!! !!!!! !!!!! . . ."

All the rest was complete garbage.

Before it blanked out for good, the ship would have to pass on those instructions, such as they were, to its more primitive subsidiary systems.

It must also revive all of its crew.

There was another problem. While the crew was in hibernation, the minds of all its members, their memories, their identities and their understanding of what they had come to, had all been transferred into the ship's central mission module for safe keeping. The crew would not have the faintest idea of who they were or what they were doing there. Oh well.

Just before it blanked out for the final time, the ship realized that its engines were beginning to give out too.

The ship and its revived and confused crew coasted on under the control of its subsidiary automatic systems, which simply looked to land wherever they could find to land and monitor whatever they could find to monitor.

As far as finding something to land on was concerned, they didn't do very well. The planet they found was desolately cold and lonely, so achingly far from the sun that should warm it, that it took all of the Envir-O-Form machinery and Life-Support-O-Systems they carried with them to render it—or at least parts of it—habitable. There were better planets nearer in, but the ship's Strateej-O-Mat was obviously locked into Lurk mode and chose the most distant and unobtrusive planet and, furthermore, would not be gainsaid by anybody other than the ship's Chief Strategic Officer. Since everybody on the ship had lost their minds, no one knew who the Chief Strategic Officer was or, even if he could have been identified, how he was supposed to go about gainsaying the ship's Strateej-O-Mat.

As far as finding something to monitor was concerned, though, they hit solid gold.

Chapter 2

One of the extraordinary things about life is the sort of places it's prepared to put up with living. Anywhere it can get some kind of a grip, whether it's the intoxicating seas of Santraginus V, where the fish never seem to care whatever the heck kind of direction they swim in, the fire storms of Frastra, where, they say, life begins at 40,000 degrees, or just burrowing around in the lower intestine of a rat for the sheer unadulterated hell of it, life will always find a way of hanging on in somewhere.

It will even live in New York, though it's hard to know why. In the wintertime the temperature falls well below the legal minimum, or rather it would do if anybody had the common sense to set a legal minimum. The last time anybody made a list of the top hundred character attributes of New Yorkers, common sense snuck in at number 79.

In the summer it's too darn hot. It's one thing to be the sort of life form that thrives on heat and finds, as the Frastrans do, that the temperature range between 40,000 and 40,004 is very equable, but it's quite another to be the sort of animal that has to wrap itself up in lots of other animals at one point in your planet's orbit, and then find, half an orbit later, that your skin's bubbling.

Spring is overrated. A lot of the inhabitants of New York will honk on mightily about the pleasures of spring, but if they actually knew the first thing about the pleasures of spring they would know of at least 5,983 better places to spend it than New York, and that's just on the same latitude.

Fall, though, is the worst. Few things are worse than fall in New York. Some of the things that live in the lower intestines of rats would disagree, but most of the things that live in the lower intestines of rats are highly disagreeable anyway, so their opinion can and should be discounted. When it's fall in New York, the air smells as if someone's been frying goats in it, and if you are keen to breathe, the best plan is to open a window and stick your head in a building.

Tricia McMillan loved New York. She kept on telling herself this over and over again. The Upper West Side. Yeah. Midtown. Hey, great retail. SoHo. The East Village. Clothes. Books. Sushi. Italian. Delis. Yo.

Movies. Yo also. Tricia had just been to see Woody Allen's new movie, which was all about the angst of being neurotic in New York. He had made one or two other movies that had explored the same theme, and Tricia wondered if he had ever considered moving, but heard that he had set his face against the idea. So: more movies, she guessed.

Tricia loved New York because loving New York was a good career move. It was a good retail move, a good cuisine move, not a good taxi move or a great quality of pavement move, but definitely a career move that ranked among the highest and the best. Tricia was a TV anchor person, and New York was where most of the world's TV was anchored. Tricia's TV anchoring had been done exclusively in Britain up to that point: regional news, then breakfast news, early evening news. She would have been called, if the language allowed, a rapidly rising anchor, but . . . hey, this is television, what does it matter? She was a rapidly rising anchor. She had what it took: great hair, a profound understanding of strategic lip gloss, the intelligence to understand the world and a tiny secret interior deadness which meant she didn't care. Everybody has their moment of great opportunity in life. If you happen to miss the one you care about, then everything else in life becomes eerily easy.

Tricia had only ever missed one opportunity. These days it didn't even make her tremble quite so much as it used to to think about it. She guessed it was that bit of her that had gone dead.

NBS needed a new anchor. Mo Minetti was leaving the "U.S./ A.M." breakfast show to have a baby. She had been offered a mind-bubbling amount of money to have it on the show, but she had declined, unexpectedly, on grounds of personal privacy and taste. Teams of NBS lawyers had sieved through her contract to see if these constituted legitimate grounds, but in the end, reluctantly, they had to let her go. This was, for them, particularly galling because normally, "reluctantly letting someone go" was an expression which had its boot on quite another foot.

The word was out that maybe, just maybe, a British accent would fit. The hair, the skin tone and the bridgework would have to be up to American network standards, but there had been a lot of British accents up there thanking their mothers for their Oscars, a lot of British accents singing on Broadway, some unusually big audiences tuning in to British accents in wigs on "Masterpiece Theatre." British accents were telling jokes on David Letterman and Jay Leno. Nobody understood the jokes but they were really responding to the accents, so maybe it was time, just maybe. A British accent on "U.S./A.M." Well, hell.

That was why Tricia was here. This was why loving New York was a great career move.

It wasn't, of course, the stated reason. Her TV company back in the U.K. would hardly have stumped up the airfare and hotel bill for her to go job hunting in Manhattan. Since she was chasing something like ten times her present salary, they might have felt that she could have forked out her own expenses, but she'd found a story, found a pretext, kept very quiet about anything ulterior, and they'd stumped up for the trip. A business-class ticket, of course, but her face was known and she'd smiled herself an upgrade. The right moves had got her a nice room at the Brentwood and here she was, wondering what to do next.

The word on the street was one thing, making contact was another. She had a couple of names, a couple of numbers, but all it took was being put on indeterminate hold a couple of times and she was back at square one. She'd put out feelers, left messages, but so far, none had been returned. The actual job she had come to do she had done in a morning, the imagined job she was after was only shimmering tantalizingly on an unreachable horizon.

Shit.

She caught a cab from the movie theater back to the Brentwood. The cab couldn't get close to the curb because a big stretch limo was hogging all the available space and she had to squeeze her way past it. She walked out of the fetid, goat-frying air and into the blessed cool of the lobby. The fine cotton of her blouse was sticking like grime to her skin. Her hair felt as if she'd bought it at a fairground, on a stick. At the front desk she asked if there were any messages, grimly expecting none. There was one.

Oh . . .

Good.

It had worked. She had gone out to the movie specifically in order to make the phone ring. She couldn't bear sitting in a hotel room waiting.

She wondered. Should she open the message down here? Her

clothes were itching and she longed to take them all off and just lie on the bed. She had turned the air-conditioning way down to its bottom temperature setting, way up to its top fan setting. What she wanted more than anything else in the world at the moment was goose pimples. Then a hot shower, then a cool one, then lying on a towel, on the bed again, drying in the air-conditioning. Then reading the message. Maybe more goose pimples. Maybe all sorts of things.

No. What she wanted more than anything else in the world was a job in American television at ten times her current salary. More than anything else in the world. In the world. What she wanted more than anything else at all was no longer a live issue.

She sat on a chair in the lobby, under a kentia palm, and opened the little cellophane-windowed envelope.

"Please call," it said. "Not happy," and gave a number. The name was Gail Andrews.

Gail Andrews.

It wasn't a name she was expecting. It caught her unawares. She recognized it, but couldn't immediately say why. Was she Andy Martin's secretary? Hilary Bass's assistant? Martin and Bass were the two major contact calls she had made, or tried to make, at NBS. And what did "Not happy" mean?

"Not *happy*"?

She was completely bewildered. Was this Woody Allen trying to contact her under an assumed name? It was a 212 area code number. So it was someone in New York. Who was not happy. Well, that narrowed it down a bit, didn't it?

She went back to the receptionist at the desk.

"I have a problem with this message you just gave me," she said. "Someone I don't know has tried to call me and says she's not happy."

The receptionist peered at the note with a frown.

"Do you know this person?" he said.

"No," Tricia said.

"Hmmm," said the receptionist. "Sounds like she's not happy about something."

"Yes," said Tricia.

"Looks like there's a name here," said the receptionist. "Gail Andrews. Do you know anybody of that name?"

"No," said Tricia.

"Any idea what she's unhappy about?"

"No," said Tricia.

"Have you called the number? There's a number here."

"No," said Tricia, "you only just gave me the note. I'm just trying to get some more information before I ring back. Perhaps I could talk to the person who took the call?"

"Hmmm," said the receptionist, scrutinizing the note carefully. "I don't think we have anybody called Gail Andrews here."

"No, I realize that," said Tricia. "I just—"

"I'm Gail Andrews."

The voice came from behind Tricia. She turned around.

"I'm sorry?"

"I'm Gail Andrews. You interviewed me this morning."

"Oh. Oh, good heavens, yes," said Tricia, slightly flustered.

"I left the message for you a few hours ago. I hadn't heard so I came by. I didn't want to miss you."

"Oh. No. Of course," said Tricia, trying hard to get up to speed.

"I don't know about this," said the receptionist, for whom speed was not an issue. "Would you like me to try this number for you now?"

"No, that'll be fine, thanks," said Tricia. "I can handle it now."

"I can call this room number here for you if that'll help," said the receptionist, peering at the note again.

"No, that won't be necessary, thanks," said Tricia. "That's my own room number. I'm the one the message was for. I think we've sorted this out now."

"You have a nice day now," said the receptionist.

Tricia didn't particularly want to have a nice day. She was busy.

She also didn't want to talk to Gail Andrews. She had a very strict cut-off point as far as fraternizing with the Christians was concerned. Her colleagues called her interview subjects Christians and would often cross themselves when they saw one walking innocently into the studio to face Tricia, particularly if Tricia was smiling warmly and showing her teeth.

She turned and smiled frostily, wondering what to do.

Gail Andrews was a well-groomed woman in her mid-forties. Her clothes fell within the boundaries defined by expensive good taste, but were definitely huddled up at the floatier end of those boundaries. She was an astrologer—a famous and, if rumor were true, influential astrologer, having allegedly influenced a number of decisions made by the late President Hudson, including everything from which flavor of Cool Whip to have on which day of the week to whether or not to bomb Damascus.

Tricia had savaged her more than somewhat. Not on the grounds of whether or not the stories about the president were true, that was old hat now. At the time Ms. Andrews had emphatically denied advising President Hudson on anything other than personal, spiritual or dietary matters, which did not, apparently, include the bombing of Damascus. (NOTHING PERSONAL, DAMASCUS! the tabloids had hooted at the time.)

No, this was a neat topical little angle that Tricia had come up with about the whole issue of astrology itself. Ms. Andrews had not been entirely ready for it. Tricia, on the other hand, was not entirely ready for a rematch in the hotel lobby. What to do?

"I can wait for you in the bar, if you need a few minutes," said Gail Andrews. "But I would like to talk to you, and I'm leaving the city tonight."

She seemed to be slightly anxious about something rather than aggrieved or irate.

"Okay," said Tricia. "Give me ten minutes."

She went up to her room. Apart from anything else, she had so little faith in the ability of the guy on the message desk at reception to deal with anything so complicated as a message that she wanted to be doubly certain that there wasn't a note under the door. It wouldn't be the first time that messages at the desk and messages under the door had been completely at odds with each other.

There wasn't one.

The message light on the phone was flashing, though.

She hit the message button and got the hotel operator.

"You have a message from Gary Andress," said the operator.

"Yes?" said Tricia. An unfamiliar name. "What does it say."

"Not hippy," said the operator.

"Not what?" said Tricia.

"Hippy. What it says. Guy says he's not a hippy. I guess he wanted you to know that. You want the number?"

As she started to dictate the number Tricia suddenly realized that this was just a garbled version of the message she had already had.

"Okay, okay," she said. "Are there any other messages for me?"

"Room number?"

Tricia couldn't work out why the operator should suddenly ask for her number this late in the conversation, but gave it to her anyway.

"Name?"

"McMillan, Tricia McMillan." Tricia spelled it, patiently.

"Not Mr. MacManus?"

"No."

"No more messages for you." Click.

Tricia sighed and dialed again. This time she gave her name and room number all over again, up front. The operator showed not the slightest glimmer of recognition that they had been speaking less than ten seconds ago.

"I'm going to be in the bar," Tricia explained. "In the bar. If a phone call comes through for me, please would you put it through to me in the bar?"

"Name?"

They went through it all a couple more times till Tricia was certain that everything that possibly could be clear was as clear as it possibly could be.

She showered, put on fresh clothes and retouched her makeup with the speed of a professional and, looking at her bed with a sigh, left the room again.

She had half a mind just to sneak off and hide.

No. Not really.

She had a look at herself in the mirror in the elevator lobby while she was waiting. She looked cool and in charge, and if she could fool herself she could fool anybody.

She was just going to have to tough it out with Gail Andrews. Okay, she had given her a hard time. Sorry, but that's the game we're all in—that sort of thing. Ms. Andrews had agreed to do the interview because she had a new book out and TV exposure was free publicity. But there's no such thing as a free launch. No, she edited that line out again.

What had happened was this:

Last week astronomers had announced that they had at last discovered a tenth planet, out beyond the orbit of Pluto. They had been searching for it for years, guided by certain orbital anomalies in the outer planets, and now they'd found it and they were all terribly pleased, and everyone was terribly happy for them and so on. The planet was named Persephone, but rapidly nicknamed Rupert after some astronomer's parrot—there was some tediously heartwarming story attached to this—and that was all very wonderful and lovely.

Tricia had followed the story with, for various reasons, considerable interest.

Then, while she had been casting around for a good excuse to go to New York at her TV company's expense, she had happened to notice a press release about Gail Andrews and her new book, *You and Your Planets*.

Gail Andrews was not exactly a household name, but the moment you mentioned President Hudson, Cool Whip and the amputation of Damascus (the world had moved on from surgical strikes—the official term had in fact been "Damascectomy," meaning the "taking out" of Damascus), everyone remembered who you meant.

Tricia saw an angle here which she quickly sold to her producer.

Surely the notion that great lumps of rock whirling in space knew something about your day that you didn't must take a bit of a knock from the fact that there was suddenly a new lump of rock out there that nobody had known about before.

That must throw a few calculations out, mustn't it?

What about all those star charts and planetary motions and so on? We all knew (apparently) what happened when Neptune was in Virgo, and so on, but what about when Rupert was rising? Wouldn't the whole of astrology have to be rethought? Wouldn't now perhaps be a good time to own up that it was all just a load of hogwash and instead take up pig farming, the principles of which were founded on some kind of rational basis? If we'd known about Rupert three years ago, might President Hudson have been eating the chocolate flavor on Thursday rather than Friday? Might Damascus still be standing? That sort of thing.

Gail Andrews had taken it all reasonably well. She was just starting to recover from the initial onslaught, when she made the rather serious mistake of trying to shake Tricia off by talking smoothly about diurnal arcs, right ascensions and some of the more abstruse areas of three-dimensional trigonometry.

To her shock she discovered that everything she delivered to Tricia came right back at her with more spin on it than she could cope with. Nobody had warned Gail that being a TV bimbo was, for Tricia, her second stab at a role in life. Behind her Chanel lip gloss, her coupe sauvage and her crystal blue contact lenses lay a brain that had acquired for itself, in an earlier, abandoned phase of her life, a first-class degree in mathematics and a doctorate in astrophysics.

As she was getting into the elevator, Tricia, slightly preoccupied, realized she had left her bag in her room and wondered whether to duck back out and get it. No. It was probably safer where it was and there wasn't anything she particularly needed in it. She let the door close behind her.

Besides, she told herself, taking a deep breath, if life had taught her anything it was this: *Never* go back for your bag.

As the elevator went down she stared at the ceiling in a rather intent way. Anyone who didn't know Tricia McMillan better would have said that that was exactly the way people sometimes stared upward when they were trying to hold back tears. She must have been staring at the tiny security video camera mounted up in the corner. She marched rather briskly out of the elevator a minute later, and went up to the reception desk again.

"Now, I'm going to write this out," she said, "because I don't want anything to go wrong."

She wrote her name in large letters on a piece of paper, then her room number, then IN THE BAR and gave it to the receptionist, who looked at it.

"That's in case there's a message for me. Okay?"

The receptionist continued to look at it.

"You want me to see if she's in her room?" he said.

Two minutes later, Tricia swiveled into the bar seat next to Gail Andrews, who was sitting in front of a glass of white wine.

"You struck me as the sort of person who preferred to sit up at the bar rather than demurely at a table," she said.

This was true, and caught Tricia a little by surprise.

"Vodka?" said Gail.

"Yes," said Tricia, suspiciously. She just stopped herself from asking, How did you know? but Gail answered anyway.

"I asked the barman," she said, with a kindly smile.

The barman had her vodka ready for her and slid it charmingly across the glossy mahogany.

"Thank you," said Tricia, stirring it sharply.

She didn't know quite what to make out of all this sudden niceness and was determined not to be wrong-footed by it. People in New York were not nice to each other without reason.

"Ms. Andrews," she said, firmly, "I'm sorry that you're not happy. I know you probably feel I was a bit rough with you this morning, but astrology is, after all, just popular entertainment, which is fine. It's part of showbiz and it's a part that you have done well out of and good luck to you. It's fun. It's not a science though, and it shouldn't be mistaken for one. I think that's something we both managed to demonstrate very successfully together this morning, while at the same time generating some popular entertainment, which is what we both do for a living. I'm sorry if you have a problem with that."

"I'm perfectly happy," said Gail Andrews.

"Oh," said Tricia, not quite certain what to make of this. "It said in your message that you were not happy."

"No," said Gail Andrews. "I said in my message that I thought *you* were not happy, and I was just wondering why."

Tricia felt as if she had been kicked in the back of the head. She blinked.

"*What?*" she said quietly.

"To do with the stars. You seemed very angry and unhappy about something to do with stars and planets when we were having our discussion, and it's been bothering me, which is why I came to see if you were all right."

Tricia stared at her. "Ms. Andrews—" she started, and then realized that the way she had said it sounded exactly angry and unhappy and rather undermined the protest she had been trying to make.

"Please call me Gail, if that's okay."

Tricia just looked bewildered.

"*I* know that astrology isn't a science," said Gail. "Of course it isn't. It's just an arbitrary set of rules like chess or tennis or—what's that strange thing you British play?"

"Er, cricket? Self-loathing?"

"Parliamentary democracy. The rules just kind of got there. They don't make any kind of sense except in terms of themselves. But when you start to exercise those rules, all sorts of processes start to happen and you start to find out all sorts of stuff about people. In astrology the rules happen to be about stars and planets, but they could be about ducks and drakes for all the difference it would make. It's just a way of thinking about a problem which lets the shape of that problem begin to emerge. The more rules, the tinier the rules, the more arbitrary they are, the better. It's like throwing a handful of fine graphite dust on a piece of paper to see where the hidden indentations are. It lets you see the words that were written on the piece of paper above it that's now been taken away and hidden. The graphite's not important. It's just the means of revealing their indentations. So you see, astrology's nothing to do with astronomy. It's just to do with people thinking about people.

"So when you got so, I don't know, so emotionally *focused* on stars and planets this morning, I began to think, she's not angry about astrology, she really is angry and unhappy about actual stars and planets. People usually only get that unhappy and angry when they've lost something. That's all I could think and I couldn't make any more sense of it than that. So I came to see if you were okay."

Tricia was stunned.

One part of her brain had already got started on all sorts of stuff. It was busy constructing all sorts of rebuttals to do with how ridiculous newspaper horoscopes were and the sort of statistical tricks they played on people. But gradually it petered out, because it realized that the rest of her brain wasn't listening. She had been completely stunned.

She had just been told, by a total stranger, something she'd kept completely secret for seventeen years.

She turned to look at Gail.

"I . . ."

She stopped.

A tiny security camera up behind the bar had turned to follow her movement. This completely flummoxed her. Most people would not have noticed it. It was not designed to be noticed. It was not designed to suggest that nowadays even an expensive and elegant hotel in New York couldn't be sure that its clientele wasn't suddenly going to pull a gun or not wear a tie. But carefully hidden though it was behind the vodka, it couldn't deceive the finely honed instinct of a TV anchor person, which was to know exactly when a camera was turning to look at her.

"Is something wrong?" asked Gail.

"No, I . . . I have to say that you've rather astonished me," said Tricia. She decided to ignore the security TV camera. It was just her imagination playing tricks with her because she had television so much on her mind today. It wasn't the first time it had happened. A traffic-monitoring camera, she was convinced, had swung around to follow her as she walked past it, and a security camera in Bloomingdale's had seemed to make a particular point of watching her trying on hats. She was obviously going dotty. She had even imagined that a bird in Central Park had been peering at her rather intently.

She decided to put it out of her mind and took a sip of her vodka. Someone was walking around the bar asking people if they were Mr. MacManus.

"Okay," she said, suddenly blurting it out. "I don't know how you worked it out, but . . ."

"I didn't work it out, as you put it. I just listened to what you were saying."

"What I lost, I think, was a whole other life."

"Everybody does that. Every moment of every day. Every single decision we make, every breath we draw, opens some doors and closes many others. Most of them we don't notice. Some we do. Sounds like you noticed one."

"Oh yes, I noticed," said Tricia. "All right. Here it is. It's very simple. Many years ago I met a guy at a party. He said he was from another planet and did I want to go along with him. I said, yes, okay. It was that kind of party. I said to him to wait while I went to get my bag and then I'd be happy to go off to another planet with him. He said I wouldn't need my bag. I said he obviously came from a very backward planet or he'd know that a woman always needed to take her bag with her. He got a bit impatient, but I wasn't going to be a complete pushover just because he said he was from another planet.

"I went upstairs. Took me a while to find my bag, and then there was someone else in the bathroom. Came down and he was gone."

Tricia paused.

"And . . . ?" said Gail.

"The garden door was open. I went outside. There were lights. Some kind of gleaming thing. I was just in time to see it rise up into the sky, shoot silently up through the clouds and disappear. That was it. End of story. End of one life, beginning of another. But hardly a moment of this life goes by that I don't wonder about some other me. A me that didn't go back for her bag. I feel like she's out there somewhere and I'm walking in her shadow."

A member of the hotel staff was now going around the bar asking people if they were Mr. Miller. Nobody was.

"You really think this . . . person was from another planet?" asked Gail.

"Oh, certainly. There was the spacecraft. Oh, and also he had two heads."

"*Two?* Didn't anybody else notice?"

"It was a fancy dress party."

"I see . . ."

"And he had a bird cage over it, of course. With a cloth over the cage. Pretended he had a parrot. He tapped on the cage and it did a lot of stupid 'Pretty Polly' stuff and squawking and so on. Then he pulled the cloth back for a moment and roared with laughter. There was another head in there, laughing along with him. It was a worrying moment, I can tell you."

"I think you probably did the right thing, dear, don't you?" said Gail.

"No," said Tricia. "No, I don't. And I couldn't carry on doing what I was doing either. I was an astrophysicist, you see. You can't be an astrophysicist properly if you've actually met someone from another planet who's got a second head that pretends to be a parrot. You just can't do it. I couldn't at least."

"I can see it would be hard. And that's probably why you tend to be a little hard on other people who talk what sounds like complete nonsense."

"Yes," said Tricia. "I expect you're right. I'm sorry."

"That's okay."

"You're the first person I've ever told this, by the way."

"I wondered. You married?"

"Er, no. So hard to tell these days, isn't it? But you're right to ask because that was probably the reason. I came very close a few times, mostly because I wanted to have a kid. But every guy ended up asking why I was constantly looking over his shoulder. What do you tell someone? At one point I even thought I might just go to a sperm bank and take pot luck. Have somebody's child at random."

"You can't seriously do that, can you?"

Tricia laughed. "Probably not. I never quite went and found out for real. Never quite did it. Story of my life. Never quite did the real thing. That's why I'm in television, I guess. Nothing is real."

"Excuse me, lady, your name Tricia McMillan?"

Tricia looked around in surprise. There was a man standing there in a chauffeur's hat.

"Yes," she said, instantly pulling herself back together again.

"Lady, I been looking for you for about an hour. Hotel said they didn't have anybody of that name, but I checked back with Mr. Martin's office and they said that this was definitely where you were staying. So I ask again, they still say they never heard of you, so I get them to page you anyway and they can't find you. In the end I get the office to fax a picture of you through to the car and have a look myself."

He looked at his watch.

"May be a bit late now, but do you want to go anyway?"

Tricia was stunned.

"Mr. Martin? You mean Andy Martin at NBS?"

"That's correct, lady. Screen test for 'U.S./A.M.' "

Tricia shot up out of her seat. She couldn't even bear to think of all the messages she'd heard for Mr. MacManus and Mr. Miller.

"Only we have to hurry," said the chauffeur. "As I heard it Mr. Martin thinks it might be worth trying a British accent. His boss at the network is dead against the idea. That's Mr. Zwingler, and I happen to know he's flying out to the coast this evening because I'm the one has to pick him up and take him to the airport."

"Okay," said Tricia, "I'm ready. Let's go."

"Okay, lady. It's the big limo out the front."

Tricia turned back to Gail. "I'm sorry," she said.

"Go! Go!" said Gail. "And good luck. I've enjoyed meeting you."

Tricia made to reach for her bag for some cash.

"Damn," she said. She'd left it upstairs.

"Drinks are on me," insisted Gail. "Really. It's been very interesting."

Tricia sighed.

"Look, I'm really sorry about this morning and . . ."

"Don't say another word. I'm fine. It's only astrology. It's harmless. It's not the end of the world."

"Thanks." On an impulse, Tricia gave her a hug.

"You got everything?" said the chauffeur. "You don't want to pick up your bag or anything?"

"If there's one thing that life's taught me," said Tricia, "it's never go back for your bag."

*　*　*

Just a little over an hour later, Tricia sat on one of the pair of beds in her hotel room. For a few minutes she didn't move. She just stared at her bag, which was sitting innocently on top of the other bed.

In her hand was a note from Gail Andrews, saying, "Don't be too disappointed. Do ring if you want to talk about it. If I were you I'd stay in at home tomorrow night. Get some rest. But don't mind me, and don't worry. It's only astrology. It's not the end of the world. Gail."

The chauffeur had been dead right. In fact the chauffeur seemed to know more about what was going on inside NBS than any other single person she had encountered in the organization. Martin had been keen, Zwingler had not. She had had her one shot at proving Martin right and she had blown it.

Oh well. Oh well, oh well, oh well.

Time to go home. Time to phone the airline and see if she could still get the red-eye back to Heathrow tonight. She reached for the big phone directory.

Oh. First things first.

She put down the directory again, picked up her handbag and took it through to the bathroom. She put it down and took out the small plastic case that held her contact lenses, without which she had been unable to properly read either the script or the autocue.

As she dabbed each tiny plastic cup into her eyes, she reflected that if there was one thing life had taught her, it was that there are some times when you do not go back for your bag and other times when you do. It had yet to teach her to distinguish between the two types of occasions.

Chapter 3

The Hitchhiker's Guide to the Galaxy has, in what we laughingly call the past, had a great deal to say on the subject of parallel universes. Very little of this is, however, at all comprehensible to anyone below the level of Advanced God, and since it is now well established that all known gods came into existence a good three millionths of a second after the Universe began rather than, as they usually claimed, the previous week, they already have a great deal of explaining to do as it is, and are therefore not available for comment on matters of deep physics at this time.

One encouraging thing the *Guide* does have to say on the subject of parallel universes is that you don't stand the remotest chance of understanding it. You can therefore say "What?" and "Eh?" and even go cross-eyed and start to blither if you like without any fear of making a fool of yourself.

The first thing to realize about parallel universes, the *Guide* says, is that they are not parallel.

It is also important to realize that they are not, strictly speaking, universes either, but it is easiest if you don't try to realize that until a little later, after you've realized that everything you've realized up to that moment is not true.

The reason they are not universes is that any given universe is not actually a *thing* as such, but is just a way of looking at what is technically known as the WSOGMM, or Whole Sort of General Mish Mash. The Whole Sort of General Mish Mash doesn't actually exist either, but is just the sum total of all the different ways there would be of looking at it if it did.

The reason they are not parallel is the same reason that the sea is not parallel. It doesn't mean anything. You can slice the Whole Sort of General Mish Mash any way you like and you will generally come up with something that someone will call home.

Please feel free to blither now.

* * *

The Earth with which we are here concerned, because of its particular orientation in the Whole Sort of General Mish Mash, was hit by a neutrino that other Earths were not.

A neutrino is not a big thing to be hit by.

In fact it's hard to think of anything much smaller by which one could reasonably hope to be hit. And it's not as if being hit by neutrinos was in itself a particularly unusual event for something the size of the Earth. Far from it. It would be an unusual nanosecond in which the Earth was not hit by several billion passing neutrinos.

It all depends on what you mean by "hit," of course, seeing as matter consists almost entirely of nothing at all. The chances of a neutrino actually hitting something as it travels through all this howling emptiness are roughly comparable to that of dropping a ball bearing at random from a cruising 747 and hitting, say, an egg sandwich.

Anyway, this neutrino hit something. Nothing terribly important in the scale of things, you might say. But the problem with saying something like that is that you would be talking cross-eyed badger spit. Once something actually happens somewhere in something as wildly complicated as the Universe, Kevin knows where it will all end up—where "Kevin" is any random entity that doesn't know nothin' about nothin'.

This neutrino struck an atom.

The atom was part of a molecule. The molecule was part of a nucleic acid. The nucleic acid was part of a gene. The gene was part of a genetic recipe for growing . . . and so on. The upshot was that a plant ended up growing an extra leaf. In Essex. Or what would, after a lot of palaver and local difficulties of a geological nature, become Essex.

The plant was a clover. It threw its weight, or rather its seed, around extremely effectively and rapidly became the world's dominant type of clover. The precise causal connection between this tiny biological happenstance and a few other minor variations that exist in that slice of the Whole Sort of General Mish Mash—such as Tricia McMillan failing to leave with Zaphod Beeblebrox, abnormally low sales of pecan-flavored ice cream and the fact that the Earth on which all this occurred did not get demolished by the Vogons to make way for a new hyperspace bypass—is currently sitting at number 4,763,984,132 on the research project priority list at what was once the history department of the University of MaxiMegalon, and no one currently at the prayer meeting by the poolside appears to feel any sense of urgency about the problem.

Tricia began to feel that the world was conspiring against her. She knew that this was a perfectly normal way to feel after an overnight flight going east, when you suddenly have a whole other mysteriously threatening day to deal with for which you are not the least bit prepared. But still.

There were marks on her lawn.

She didn't really care about marks on her lawn very much. Marks on her lawn could go and take a running jump as far as she was concerned. It was Saturday morning. She had just got home from New York feeling tired, crabby and paranoid, and all she wanted to do was go to bed with the radio on quietly and gradually fall asleep to the sound of Ned Sherrin being terribly clever about something.

But Eric Bartlett was not going to let her get away with not making a thorough inspection of the marks. Eric was the old gardener who came in from the village on Saturday mornings to poke around at her garden with a stick. He didn't believe in people coming in from New York first thing in the morning. Didn't hold with it. Went against nature. He believed in virtually everything else, though.

"Probably them space aliens," he said, bending over and prodding at the edges of the small indentations with his stick. "Hear a lot about space aliens these days. I expect it's them."

"Do you?" said Tricia, looking furtively at her watch. Ten minutes, she reckoned. Ten minutes she'd be able to stay standing up. Then she would simply keel over, whether she was in her bedroom or still out here in the garden. That was if she just had to stand. If she also had to nod intelligently and say "Do you?" from time to time, it might cut it down to five.

"Oh yes," said Eric. "They come down here, land on your lawn and then buzz off again, sometimes with your cat. Mrs. Williams at the post office, her cat, you know the ginger one? It got abducted by space aliens. Course, they brought it back the next day but it were in a very odd mood. Kept prowling around all morning, and then falling asleep in the afternoon. Used to be the other way round, is the point. Sleep in the morning, prowl in the afternoon. Jet lag, you see, from being in an interplanetary craft."

"I see," said Tricia.

"They dyed it tabby, too, she says. These marks are exactly the sort of marks that their landing pods would probably make."

"You don't think it's the lawn mower?" asked Tricia.

"If the marks were more round, I'd say, but these are just off-round, you see. Altogether more alien in shape."

"It's just that you mentioned the lawn mower was playing up and needed fixing or it might start gouging holes in the lawn."

"I did say that, Miss Tricia, and I stand by what I said. I'm not saying it's not the lawn mower for definite, I'm just saying what seems to be more likely given the shapes of the holes. They come in over these trees, you see, in their landing pods . . ."

"Eric . . ." said Tricia, patiently.

"Tell you what, though, Miss Tricia," said Eric, "I will take a look at the mower, like I meant to last week, and leave you to get on with whatever you're wanting to."

"Thank you, Eric," said Tricia. "I'm going to bed now, in fact. Help yourself to anything you want in the kitchen."

"Thank you, Miss Tricia, and good luck to you," said Eric. He bent over and picked something from the lawn.

"There," he said. "Three-leaf clover. Good luck, you see."

He peered at it closely to check that it was a real three-leaf clover and not just a regular four-leaf one that one of the leaves had fallen off. "If I were you, though, I'd watch for signs of alien activity in the area." He scanned the horizon keenly. "Particularly from over there in the Henley direction."

"Thank you, Eric," said Tricia, again. "I will."

She went to bed and dreamed fitfully of parrots and other birds. In the afternoon she got up and prowled around restlessly, not certain what to do with the rest of the day, or indeed the rest of her life. She spent at least an hour dithering trying to make up her mind whether to head up into town and go to Stavro's for the evening. This was the currently fashionable spot for high-flying media people, and seeing a few friends there might help her ease herself back into the swing of things. She decided at last she would go. It was good. It was fun there. She was very fond of Stavro himself, who was a Greek with a German father—a fairly odd combination. Tricia had been to the Alpha a couple of nights earlier, which was Stavro's original club in New York, now run by his brother Karl, who thought of himself as German with a Greek mother. Stavro would be very happy to be told that Karl was making a bit of a pig's ear of running the New York club, so Tricia would go and make him happy. There was little love lost between Stavro and Karl Mueller.

Okay. That's what she would do.

She then spent another hour dithering about what to wear. At last she settled on a smart little black dress she'd got in New York. She phoned a friend to see who was likely to be at the club that evening, and was told that it was closed this evening for a private wedding party.

She thought that trying to live life according to any plan you actually work out is like trying to buy ingredients for a recipe from the supermarket. You get one of those carts, which simply will not go in the direction you push it, and end up just having to buy completely different stuff. What do you do with it? What do you do with the recipe? She didn't know.

Anyway, that night an alien spacecraft landed on her lawn.

Chapter 5

She watched it coming in from over the Henley direction with mild curiosity at first, wondering what those lights were. Living, as she did, not a million miles from Heathrow, she was used to seeing lights in the sky. Not usually so late in the evening, or so low, though, which was why she was mildly curious.

When whatever it was began to come closer and closer, her curiosity began to turn to bemusement.

Hmmm, she thought, which was about as far as she could get with thinking. She was still feeling dopey and jet-lagged and the messages that one part of her brain was busy sending to another were not necessarily arriving on time or the right way up. She left the kitchen, where she'd been fixing herself a coffee, and went to open the back door, which led out to the garden. She took a deep breath of cool evening air, stepped outside and looked up.

There was something roughly the size of a large camper van parked about a hundred feet above her lawn.

It was really there. Hanging there. Almost silent.

Something moved deep inside her.

Her arms dropped slowly down to her side. She hardly noticed the scalding coffee slopping over her foot. She was hardly breathing as slowly, inch by inch, foot by foot, the craft came downward. Its lights were playing softly over the ground as if probing and feeling it. They played over her.

It seemed beyond all hope that she should be given her chance again. Had he found her? Had he come back?

The craft dropped down and down until at last it had settled quietly on her lawn. It didn't look exactly like the one she had seen departing all those years ago, she thought, but flashing lights in the night sky are hard to resolve into clear shapes.

Silence.

Then a click and a hum.

Then another click and another hum. Click hum, click hum.

A doorway slid open, spilling light toward her across the lawn.

She waited, tingling.

A figure stood silhouetted in the light, then another, and another.

Wide eyes blinked slowly at her. Hands were slowly raised in greeting.

"McMillan?" a voice said at last, a strange, thin voice that managed the syllables with difficulty. "Tricia McMillan. *Ms.* Tricia McMillan?"

"Yes," said Tricia, almost soundlessly.

"We have been monitoring you."

"M . . . monitoring? *Me?*"

"Yes."

They looked at her for a while, their large eyes moving up and down her very slowly.

"You look smaller in real life," one said at last.

"What?" said Tricia.

"Yes."

"I . . . I don't understand," said Tricia. She hadn't expected any of this, of course, but even for something she hadn't expected to begin with, it wasn't going the way she expected. At last she said, "Are you . . . are you from . . . Zaphod?"

This question seemed to cause a little consternation among the three figures. They conferred with one another in some skittering language of their own and then turned back to her.

"We don't think so. Not as far as we know," said one.

"Where is Zaphod?" said another, looking up into the night sky.

"I . . . I don't know," said Tricia, helplessly.

"It is far from here? Which direction? We don't know."

Tricia realized with a sinking heart that they had no idea who she was talking about. Or even what she was talking about. And she had no idea what they were talking about. She put her hopes tightly away again and snapped her brain back into gear. There was no point in being disappointed. She had to wake up to the fact that she had here the journalistic scoop of the century. What should she do? Go back into the house for a video camera? Wouldn't they just be gone when she got back? She was thoroughly confused as to strategy. Keep 'em talking, she thought. Figure it out later.

"You've been monitoring . . . *me?*"

"All of you. Everything on your planet. TV. Radio. Telecommunications. Computers. Video circuitry. Warehouses."

"What?"

"Car parks. Everything. We monitor everything."

Tricia stared at them.

"That must be very boring, isn't it?" she blurted out.

"Yes."

"So why . . ."

"Except . . ."

"Yes? Except what?"

"Game shows. We quite like game shows."

There was a terribly long silence as Tricia looked at the aliens and the aliens looked at her.

"There's something I would just like to get from indoors," said Tricia, very deliberately. "Tell you what. Would you, or one of you, like to come inside with me and have a look?"

"Very much," they all said, enthusiastically.

All three of them stood, slightly awkwardly in her sitting room, as she hurried around picking up a video camera, a 35mm camera, a tape recorder, every recording medium she could grab hold of. They were all thin and, under domestic lighting conditions, a sort of dim purplish green.

"I really won't be a second, guys," Tricia said, as she rummaged through some drawers for spare tapes and films.

The aliens were looking at the shelves that held her CDs and her old records. One of them nudged one of the others very slightly.

"Look," he said. "Elvis."

Tricia stopped, and stared at them all over again.

"You like Elvis?" she said.

"Yes," they said.

"Elvis *Presley?*"

"Yes."

She shook her head in bewilderment as she tried to stuff a new tape into her video camera.

"Some of your people," said one of her visitors, hesitantly, "think that Elvis has been kidnapped by space aliens."

"*What?*" said Tricia. "Has he?"

"It is possible."

"Are you telling me that *you* have kidnapped Elvis?" gasped Tricia. She was trying to keep cool enough not to foul up her equipment, but this was all almost too much for her.

"No. Not us," said her guests. "Aliens. It is a very interesting possibility. We talk of it often."

"I must get this down," Tricia muttered to herself. She checked that her video was properly loaded and working now. She pointed the camera at them. She didn't put it up to her eye because she didn't want to freak them out. But she was sufficiently experienced to be able to shoot accurately from the hip.

"Okay," she said. "Now tell me slowly and carefully who you are. You first," she said to the one on the left. "What's your name?"

"I don't know."

"You don't know."

"No."

"I see," said Tricia. "And what about you other two?"

"We don't know."

"Good. Okay. Perhaps you can tell me where you are from?"

They shook their heads.

"You don't know where you're from?"

They shook their heads again."

"So," said Tricia. "What are you . . . er . . ."

She was floundering but, being a professional, kept the camera steady while she did it.

"We are on a mission," said one of the aliens.

"A *mission?* A mission to do what?"

"We do not know."

Still she kept the camera steady.

"So what are you doing here on Earth, then?"

"We have come to fetch you."

Rock steady, rock steady. Could have been on a tripod. She wondered if she should be using a tripod, in fact. She wondered that because it gave her a moment or two to digest what they had just said. No, she thought, hand-held gave her more flexibility. She also thought, *Help*, what am I going to do?

"Why," she asked, calmly, "have you come to fetch me?"

"Because we have lost our minds."

"Excuse me," said Tricia, "I'm going to have to get a tripod."

They seemed happy enough to stand there doing nothing while Tricia quickly found a tripod and mounted the camera to it. Her face was completely immobile, but she did not have the faintest idea what was going on or what to think about it.

"Okay," she said, when she was ready. "Why . . ."

"We liked your interview with the astrologer."

"You *saw* it?"

"We see everything. We are very interested in astrology. We like it. It is very interesting. Not everything is interesting. Astrology is interesting. What the stars tell us. What the stars foretell. We could do with some information like that."

"But . . ."

Tricia didn't know where to start.

Own up, she thought. There's no point in trying to second-guess any of this stuff.

So she said, "But I don't know anything about astrology."

"We do."

"You do?"

"Yes. We follow our horoscopes. We are very avid. We see all your newspapers and your magazines and are very avid with them. But our leader says we have a problem."

"You have a *leader?*"

"Yes."

"What's his name?"

"We do not know."

"What does he *say* his name is, for Christ's sake? Sorry, I'll need to edit that. What does he say his name is?"

"He does not know."

"So how do you all know he's the leader?"

"He seized control. He said someone has to do something around here."

"Ah!" said Tricia, seizing on a clue. "Where is 'here'?"

"Rupert."

"*What?*"

"Your people call it Rupert. The tenth planet from your sun. We have settled there for many years. It is highly cold and uninteresting there. But good for monitoring."

"Why are you monitoring us?"

"It is all we know to do."

"Okay," said Tricia. "Right. What is the problem that your leader says you have?"

"Triangulation."

"I beg your pardon?"

"Astrology is a very precise science. We know this."

"Well . . ." said Tricia, then left it at that.

"But it is precise for you here on Earth."

"Ye . . . e . . . s . . ." She had a horrible feeling she was getting a vague glimmering of something.

"So when Venus is rising in Capricorn, for instance, that is from Earth. How does that work if we are out on Rupert? What if the Earth is rising in Capricorn? It is hard for us to know. Among the things we have forgotten, which we think are many and profound, is trigonometry."

"Let me get this straight," said Tricia. "You want me to come with you to . . . Rupert . . ."

"Yes."

"To recalculate your *horoscopes* for you to take account of the relative positions of Earth and Rupert?"

"Yes."

"Do I get an exclusive?"

"Yes."

"I'm your girl," said Tricia, thinking that at the very least she could sell it to the *National Enquirer*.

As she boarded the craft that would take her off to the farthest limits of the solar system, the first thing that met her eyes was a bank of video monitors across which thousands of images were sweeping. A fourth alien was sitting watching them, but was focused on one particular screen that held a steady image. It was a replay of the impromptu interview which Tricia had just conducted with his three colleagues. He looked up when he saw her apprehensively climbing in.

"Good evening, Ms. McMillan," he said. "Nice camera work."

ord Prefect hit the ground running. The ground was about three inches farther from the ventilation shaft than he remembered it, so he misjudged the point at which he would hit the ground, started running too soon, stumbled awkwardly and twisted his ankle. Damn! He ran off down the corridor anyway, hobbling slightly.

All over the building, alarms were erupting into their usual frenzy of excitement. He dove for cover behind the usual storage cabinets, glanced around to check that he was unseen and started rapidly to fish around inside his satchel for the usual things he needed.

His ankle, unusually, was hurting like hell.

The ground was not only three inches farther from the ventilation shaft than he remembered, it was also on a different planet than he remembered, but it was the three inches that had caught him by surprise. The offices of *The Hitchhiker's Guide to the Galaxy* were quite often shifted at very short notice to another planet, for reasons of local climate, local hostility, power bills or taxes, but they were always reconstructed exactly the same way, almost to the very molecule. For many of the company's employees, the layout of their offices represented the only constant they knew in a severely distorted personal universe.

Something, though, was odd.

This was not in itself surprising, thought Ford as he pulled out his lightweight throwing towel. Virtually everything in his life was, to a greater or lesser extent, odd. It was just that this was odd in a slightly different way than he was used to things being odd, which was, well, strange. He couldn't quite get it into focus immediately.

He got out his no. 3-gauge prising tool.

The alarms were going in the same old way that he knew well. There was a kind of music to them that he could almost hum along to. That was all very familiar. The world outside had been a new one to Ford. He had not been to Saquo-Pilia Hensha before, and he liked it. It had a kind of carnival atmosphere to it.

He took from his satchel a toy bow and arrow, which he had bought in a street market.

He had discovered that the reason for the carnival atmosphere on Saquo-Pilia Hensha was that the local people were celebrating the annual feast of the Assumption of St. Antwelm. St. Antwelm had been, during his lifetime, a great and popular king who had made a great and popular assumption. What King Antwelm had assumed was that what everybody wanted, all other things being equal, was to be happy and enjoy themselves and have the best possible time together. On his death he had willed his entire personal fortune to financing an annual festival to remind everyone of this, with lots of good food and dancing and very silly games like Hunt the Wocket. His Assumption had been such a brilliantly good one that he was made into a saint for it. Not only that, but all the people who had previously been made saints for doing things like being stoned to death in a thoroughly miserable way or living upside down in barrels of dung were instantly demoted and were now thought to be rather embarrassing.

The familiar H-shaped building of the *Hitchhiker's Guide* offices rose above the outskirts of the city, and Ford Prefect, on arriving at it, had broken into it in the familiar way. He always entered via the ventilation system rather than the main lobby because the main lobby was patrolled by robots whose job it was to quiz incoming employees about their expense accounts. Ford Prefect's expense accounts were notoriously complex and difficult affairs and he had found, on the whole, that the lobby robots were ill-equipped to understand the arguments he wished to put forward in relation to them, and he preferred, therefore, to make his entrance by another route.

This meant setting off nearly every alarm in the building, but not the one in the accounts department, which was the way that Ford preferred it.

He hunkered down behind the storage cabinet, licked the rubber suction cup of the toy arrow and then fitted it to the string of the bow.

Within about thirty seconds a security robot the size of a small melon came flying down the corridor at about waist height, scanning left and right for anything unusual as it did so.

With impeccable timing Ford shot the toy arrow across its path. The arrow flew across the corridor and stuck, wobbling, on the opposite wall. As it flew, the robot's sensors locked onto it instantly and the robot twisted through ninety degrees to follow it, see what the hell it was and where it was going.

This bought Ford one precious second, during which the robot was looking in the opposite direction from him. He hurled the towel over the flying robot and caught it.

Because of the various sensory protuberances with which the robot was festooned, it couldn't maneuver inside the towel, and it just twitched back and forth without being able to turn and face its captor.

Ford hauled it quickly toward him and pinned it down to the ground. It was beginning to whine pitifully. With one swift and practiced movement, Ford reached under the towel with his no. 3-gauge prising tool and flipped off the small plastic panel on top of the robot, which gave access to its logic circuits.

Now logic is a wonderful thing but it has, as the processes of evolution discovered, certain drawbacks.

Anything that thinks logically can be fooled by something else that thinks at least as logically as it does. The easiest way to fool a completely logical robot is to feed it the same stimulus sequence over and over again so it gets locked in a loop. This was best demonstrated by the famous Herring Sandwich experiments conducted millennia ago at MISPWOSO (the MaxiMegalon Institute of Slowly and Painfully Working Out the Surprisingly Obvious).

A robot was programmed to believe that it liked herring sandwiches. This was actually the most difficult part of the whole experiment. Once the robot had been programmed to believe that it liked herring sandwiches, a herring sandwich was placed in front of it. Whereupon the robot thought to itself, Ah! A herring sandwich! I like herring sandwiches.

It would then bend over and scoop up the herring sandwich in its herring sandwich scoop, and then straighten up again. Unfortunately for the robot, it was fashioned in such a way that the action of straightening up caused the herring sandwich to slip straight back off its herring sandwich scoop and fall on to the floor in front of the robot. Whereupon the robot thought to itself, Ah! A herring sandwich . . . , etc., and repeated the same action over and over and over again. The only thing that prevented the herring sandwich from getting bored with the whole damn business and crawling off in search of other ways of passing the time was that the herring sandwich, being just a bit of dead fish between a couple of slices of bread, was marginally less alert to what was going on than was the robot.

The scientists at the Institute thus discovered the driving force behind all change, development and innovation in life, which was this: herring sandwiches. They published a paper to this effect, which was widely criticized as being extremely stupid. They checked their figures and realized that what they had actually discovered was "boredom," or rather, the practical function of boredom. In a fever of excitement they then went on to discover other emotions like "irritability," "depression," "reluctance," "ickiness" and so on. The next big breakthrough came when they stopped using herring sandwiches, whereupon a whole welter of new emotions became suddenly available to them for study, such as "relief," "joy," "friskiness," "appetite," "satisfaction," and most important of all, the desire for "happiness."

This was the biggest breakthrough of all.

Vast wodges of complex computer codes governing robot behavior in all possible contingencies could be replaced very simply. All that robots needed was the capacity to be either bored or happy, and a few conditions that needed to be satisfied in order to bring those states about. They would then work the rest out for themselves.

The robot that Ford had got trapped under his towel was not, at the moment, a happy robot. It was happy when it could move about. It was happy when it could see other things. It was particularly happy when it could see other things moving about, particularly if the other things were moving about doing things they shouldn't do because then it could, with considerable delight, report them.

Ford would soon fix that.

He squatted over the robot and held it between his knees. The towel was still covering all of its sensory mechanisms, but Ford had now got its logic circuits exposed. The robot was whirring grungily and pettishly, but it could only fidget, it couldn't actually move. Using the prising tool, Ford eased a small chip out from its socket. As soon as it came out, the robot suddenly went quiet and just sat there in a coma.

The chip Ford had taken out was the one that contained the instructions for all the conditions that had to be fulfilled in order for the robot to feel happy. The robot would be happy when a tiny electrical charge from a point just to the left of the chip reached another point just to the right of the chip. The chip determined whether the charge got there or not.

Ford pulled out a small length of wire that had been threaded into the towel. He dug one end of it into the top left hole of the chip socket and the other into the bottom right hole.

That was all it took. Now the robot would be happy whatever happened.

Ford quickly stood up and whisked the towel away. The robot rose ecstatically into the air, pursuing a kind of wriggly path.

It turned and saw Ford.

"Mr. Prefect, sir! I'm so happy to see you!"

"Good to see you, little fella," said Ford.

The robot rapidly reported back to its central control that everything was now for the best in this best of all possible worlds, and the alarms rapidly quelled themselves and life returned to normal.

At least, almost to normal.

There was something odd about the place.

The little robot was gurgling with electric delight. Ford hurried on down the corridor, letting the thing bob along in his wake telling him how delicious everything was, and how happy it was to be able to tell him that.

Ford, however, was not happy.

He passed faces of people he didn't know. They didn't look like his sort of people. They were too well groomed. Their eyes were too dead. Every time he thought he saw someone he recognized in the distance and hurried along to say hello, it would turn out to be someone else, with an altogether neater hairstyle and a much more thrusting, purposeful look than, well, than anybody Ford knew.

A staircase had been moved a few inches to the left. A ceiling had been lowered slightly. A lobby had been remodeled. All these things were not worrying in themselves, though they were a little disorienting. The thing that was worrying was the decor. It used to be brash and glitzy. Expensive—because the *Guide* sold so well throughout the civilized and postcivilized Galaxy—but expensive and fun. Wild games machines lined the corridors. Insanely painted grand pianos hung from ceilings, vicious sea creatures from the planet Viv reared up out of pools in tree-filled atria, robot butlers in stupid shirts roamed the corridors seeking whose hands they might press frothing drinks into. People used to have pet vastdragons on leads and pterospondes on perches in their offices. People knew how to have a good time, and if they didn't there were courses they could sign up for which would put that right.

There was none of that, now.

Somebody had been through the place doing some iniquitous kind of taste job on it.

Ford turned sharply into a small alcove, cupped his hand and yanked the flying robot in with him. He squatted down and peered at the burbling cybernaut.

"What's been happening here?" he demanded.

"Oh, just the nicest things, sir, just the nicest possible things. Can I sit on your lap, please?"

"No," said Ford, brushing the thing away. It was overjoyed to be spurned in this way and started to bob and burble and swoon. Ford grabbed it again and stuck it firmly in the air a foot in front of his face. It tried to stay where it was put but couldn't help quivering slightly.

"Something's changed, hasn't it?" Ford hissed.

"Oh yes," squealed the little robot, "in the most fabulous and wonderful way. I feel so good about it."

"Well, what was it like before, then?"

"Scrumptious."

"But you like the way it's changed?" demanded Ford.

"I like *everything*," moaned the robot. "Especially when you shout at me like that. Do it again, *please*."

"Just tell me what's happened!"

"Oh, thank you, thank you!"

Ford sighed.

"Okay, okay," panted the robot. "The *Guide* has been taken over. There's a new management. It's all so gorgeous I could just melt. The old management was also fabulous of course, though I'm not sure if I thought so at the time."

"That was before you had a bit of wire stuck in your head."

"How true. How wonderfully true. How wonderfully, bubblingly, frothingly, burstingly true. What a truly ecstasy-inducingly correct observation."

"What's *happened?*" insisted Ford. "Who is this new management? When did they take over? I . . . oh, never mind," he added, as the little robot started to gibber with uncontrollable joy and rub itself against his knee. "I'll go and find out for myself."

* * *

Ford hurled himself at the door of the editor-in-chief's office, tucked himself into a tight ball as the frame splintered and gave way, rolled rapidly across the floor to where the drinks trolley laden with some of the Galaxy's most potent and expensive beverages habitually stood, seized hold of the trolley and, using it to give himself cover, trundled it and himself across the main exposed part of the office floor to where the valuable and extremely rude statue of Leda and the Octopus stood and took shelter behind it. Meanwhile the little security robot, entering at chest height, was suicidally delighted to draw gunfire away from Ford.

That, at least, was the plan, and a necessary one. The current editor-in-chief, Stagyar-zil-Doggo, was a dangerously unbalanced man who took a homicidal view of contributing staff turning up in his office without pages of fresh, proofed copy, and had a battery of laser-guided guns linked to special scanning devices in the door frame to deter anybody who was merely bringing extremely good reasons why they hadn't written any. Thus was a high level of output maintained.

Unfortunately, the drinks trolley wasn't there.

Ford hurled himself desperately sideways and somersaulted toward the statue of Leda and the Octopus, which also wasn't there. He rolled and hurtled around the room in a kind of random panic, tripped, spun, hit the window, which fortunately was built to withstand rocket attacks, rebounded and fell in a bruised and winded heap behind a smart gray crushed-leather sofa, which hadn't been there before.

After a few seconds he slowly peeked up above the top of the sofa. As well as there being no drinks trolley and no Leda and the Octopus, there had also been a startling absence of gunfire. He frowned. This was all utterly wrong.

"Mr. Prefect, I assume," said a voice.

The voice came from a smooth-faced individual behind a large ceramo-teak-bonded desk. Stagyar-zil-Doggo may well have been a hell of an individual, but no one, for a whole variety of reasons, would ever have called him smooth-faced. This was not Stagyar-zil-Doggo.

"I assume from the manner of your entrance that you do not have new material for the, er, *Guide*, at the moment," said the smooth-faced individual. He was sitting with his elbows resting on the table and holding his fingertips together in a manner which, inexplicably, has never been made a capital offense.

"I've been busy," said Ford, rather weakly. He staggered to his feet, brushing himself down. Then he thought, What the hell was he saying things weakly for? He had to get on top of this situation. He had to find out who the hell this person was, and he suddenly thought of a way of doing it.

"Who the hell are you?" he demanded.

"I am your new editor-in-chief. That is, if we decide to retain your services. My name is Vann Harl." He didn't put his hand out. He just added, "What have you done to that security robot?"

The little robot was rolling very, very slowly around the ceiling and moaning quietly to itself.

"I've made it very happy," snapped Ford. "It's a kind of mission I have. Where's Stagyar? More to the point, where's his drinks trolley?"

"Mr. Zil-Doggo is no longer with this organization. His drinks trolley is, I imagine, helping to console him for this fact."

"Organization?" yelled Ford. "*Organization?* What a bloody stupid word for a set-up like this!"

"Precisely our sentiments. Understructured, overresourced, undermanaged, overinebriated. And that," said Harl, "was just the editor."

"I'll do the jokes," snarled Ford.

"No," said Harl. "You will do the restaurant column."

He tossed a piece of plastic onto the desk in front of him. Ford did not move to pick it up.

"You *what?*" said Ford.

"No. Me Harl. You Prefect. You do restaurant column. Me editor. Me sit here tell you you do restaurant column. You get?"

"*Restaurant* column?" said Ford, too bewildered to be really angry yet.

"Siddown, Prefect," said Harl. He swung around in his swivel chair, got to his feet and stood staring out at the tiny specks enjoying the carnival twenty-three stories below.

"Time to get this business on its feet, Prefect," he snapped. "We at InfiniDim Enterprises are . . ."

"You at *what?*"

"InfiniDim Enterprises. We have bought out the *Guide.*"

"*InfiniDim?*"

"We spent millions on that name, Prefect. Start liking it or start packing."

Ford shrugged. He had nothing to pack.

"The Galaxy is changing," said Harl. "We've got to change with it. Go with the market. The market is moving up. New aspirations. New technology. The future is . . ."

"Don't tell me about the future," said Ford. "I've been all over the future. Spend half my time there. It's the same as anywhere else. Anywhen else. Whatever. Just the same old stuff in faster cars and smellier air."

"That's *one* future," said Harl. "That's *your* future, if you accept it. You've got to learn to think multidimensionally. There are limitless futures stretching out in every direction from this moment—and from this moment and from this. Billions of them, bifurcating every instant! Every possible position of every possible electron balloons out into billions of probabilities! Billions and billions of shining, gleaming futures! You know what that means?"

"You're dribbling down your chin."

"Billions and billions of markets!"

"I see," said Ford. "So you sell billions and billions of *Guides.*"

"No," said Harl, reaching for his handkerchief and not finding one. "Excuse me," he said, "but this gets me so excited." Ford handed him his towel.

"The reason we don't sell billions and billions of *Guides,*" continued Harl, after wiping his mouth, "is the expense. What we do is we sell one *Guide* billions and billions of times. We exploit the multidimensional nature of the Universe to cut down on manufacturing costs. And we don't sell to penniless hitchhikers. What a stupid notion that was! Find the one section of the market that, more or less by definition, doesn't have any money, and try to sell to it. No. We sell to the affluent business traveler and his vacationing wife in a billion, billion different futures. This is the most radical, dynamic and thrusting business venture in the entire multidimensional infinity of space-time-probability ever."

"And you want me to be its restaurant critic," said Ford.

"We would value your input."

"Kill!" shouted Ford. He shouted it at his towel.

The towel leapt up out of Harl's hands.

This was not because it had any motive force of its own, but because Harl was so startled at the idea that it might. The next thing that startled him was the sight of Ford Prefect hurtling across the desk at him fists first. In fact Ford was just lunging for the credit card, but you don't get to occupy the sort of position that Harl occupied in the sort of organization in which Harl occupied it without developing a healthily paranoid view of life. He took the sensible precaution of hurling himself backward, and striking his head a sharp blow on the rocket-proof glass, then subsided into a series of worrying and highly personal dreams.

Ford lay on the desk, surprised at how swimmingly everything had gone. He glanced quickly at the piece of plastic he now held in his hand—it was a Dine-O-Charge credit card with his name already embossed on it, and an expiration date two years from now, and was possibly the single most exciting thing Ford had ever seen in his life— then he clambered over the desk to see to Harl.

He was breathing fairly easily. It occurred to Ford that he might breathe more easily yet without the weight of his wallet bearing down on his chest, so he slipped it out of Harl's breast pocket and flipped through it. Fair amount of cash. Credit tokens. Ultragolf club membership. Other club memberships. Photos of someone's wife and family—presumably Harl's, but it was hard to be sure these days. Busy executives often didn't have time for a full-time wife and family and would just rent them for weekends.

Ha!

He couldn't believe what he'd just found.

He slowly drew out from the wallet a single and insanely exciting piece of plastic that was nestling among a bunch of receipts.

It wasn't insanely exciting to look at. It was rather dull in fact. It was smaller and a little thicker than a credit card and semitransparent. If you held it up to the light you could see a lot of holographically encoded information and images buried pseudoinches deep beneath its surface.

It was an Ident-I-Eeze, and was a very naughty and silly thing for Harl to have lying around in his wallet, though it was perfectly understandable. There were so many different ways in which you were required to provide absolute proof of your identity these days that life could easily become extremely tiresome just from that factor alone, never mind the deeper existential problems of trying to function as a coherent consciousness in an epistemologically ambiguous physical universe. Just look at cash machines, for instance. Queues of people standing around waiting to have their fingerprints read, their retinas scanned, bits of skin scraped from the nape of the neck and undergoing instant (or nearly instant—a good six or seven seconds in tedious reality) genetic analysis, then having to answer trick questions about members of their family they didn't even remember they had and about their recorded preferences for tablecloth colors. And that was just to get a bit of spare cash for the weekend. If you were trying to raise a loan for a jetcar, sign a missile treaty or pay an entire restaurant bill, things could get really trying.

Hence the Ident-I-Eeze. This encoded every single piece of information about you, your body and your life into one all-purpose machine-readable card that you could then carry around in your wallet, and it therefore represented technology's greatest triumph to date over both itself and plain common sense.

Ford pocketed it. A remarkably good idea had just occurred to him. He wondered how long Harl would remain unconscious.

"Hey!" he shouted to the little melon-sized robot still slobbering with euphoria up on the ceiling. "You want to stay happy?"

The robot gurgled that it did.

"Then stick with me and do everything I tell you without fail."

The robot said that it was quite happy where it was up on the ceiling thank you very much. It had never realized before how much sheer titillation there was to be got from a good ceiling and it wanted to explore its feelings about ceilings in greater depth.

"You stay there," said Ford, "and you'll soon be recaptured and have your conditional chip replaced. You want to stay happy, come now."

The robot let out a long heartfelt sigh of impassioned tristesse and sank reluctantly away from the ceiling.

"Listen," said Ford, "can you keep the rest of the security system happy for a few minutes?"

"One of the joys of true happiness," trilled the robot, "is sharing. I brim, I froth, I overflow with . . ."

"Okay," said Ford. "Just spread a little happiness around the security network. Don't give it any information. Just make it feel good so it doesn't feel the need to ask for any."

He picked up his towel and ran cheerfully for the door. Life had been a little dull of late. It showed every sign now of becoming extremely froody.

Arthur Dent had been in some hell holes in his life, but he had never before seen a spaceport that had a sign saying "Even traveling despondently is better than arriving here." To welcome visitors the arrivals hall featured a picture of the president of NowWhat, smiling. It was the only picture anybody could find of him, and it had been taken shortly after he had shot himself, so although the photo had been retouched as well as could be managed, the smile it wore was rather a ghastly one. The side of his head had been drawn back in crayon. No replacement had been found for the photograph because no replacement had been found for the president. There was only one ambition that anyone on the planet ever had, and that was to leave.

Arthur checked himself into a small motel on the outskirts of town and sat glumly on the bed, which was damp, and flipped through the little information brochure, which was also damp. It said that the planet of NowWhat had been named after the opening words of the first settlers to arrive there after struggling across light years of space to reach the farthest unexplored outreaches of the Galaxy. The main town was called OhWell. There weren't any other towns to speak of. Settlement on NowWhat had not been a success and the sort of people who actually wanted to live on NowWhat were not the sort of people you would want to spend time with.

Trading was mentioned in the brochure. The main trade that was carried out was in the skins of the NowWhattian boghog but it wasn't a very successful one because no one in their right minds would want to buy a NowWhattian boghog skin. The trade only hung on by its fingernails because there was always a significant number of people in the Galaxy who were not in their right minds. Arthur had felt very uncomfortable looking around at some of the other occupants of the small passenger compartment of the ship.

The brochure described some of the history of the planet. Whoever had written it had obviously started out trying to drum up a little enthusiasm for the place by stressing that it wasn't actually cold and wet *all* the time, but could find little positive to add to this, so the tone of the piece quickly degenerated into savage irony.

It talked about the early years of settlement. It said that the major activities pursued on NowWhat were those of catching, skinning and eating NowWhattian boghogs, which were the only extant form of animal life on NowWhat, all others having long ago died of despair. The boghogs were tiny, vicious creatures, and the small margin by which they fell short of being completely inedible was the margin by which life on the planet subsisted. So what were the rewards, however small, that made life on NowWhat worth living? Well, there weren't any. Not a one. Even making yourself some protective clothing out of boghog skins was an exercise in disappointment and futility, since the skins were unaccountably thin and leaky. This caused a lot of puzzled conjecture among the settlers. What was the boghog's secret of keeping warm? If anyone had ever learned the language the boghogs spoke to one another, they would have discovered that there was no trick. The boghogs were as cold and wet as anyone else on the planet. No one had had the slightest desire to learn the language of the boghogs for the simple reason that these creatures communicated by biting each other very hard on the thigh. Life on NowWhat being what it was, most of what a boghog might have to say about it could easily be signified by these means.

Arthur flipped through the brochure till he found what he was looking for. At the back there were a few maps of the planet. They were fairly rough and ready because they weren't likely to be of much interest to anyone, but they told him what he wanted to know.

He didn't recognize it at first because the maps were the other way up from the way he would have expected and looked, therefore, thoroughly unfamiliar. Of course, up and down, north and south, are absolutely arbitrary designations, but we are used to seeing things the way we are used to seeing them, and Arthur had to turn the maps upside down to make sense of them.

There was one huge landmass off on the upper left-hand side of the page that tapered down to a tiny waist and then ballooned out again like a large comma. On the right-hand side was a collection of large shapes jumbled familiarly together. The outlines were not exactly the same, and Arthur didn't know if this was because the map was so rough, or because the sea level was higher or because, well, things were just different here. But the evidence was inarguable.

This was definitely the Earth.

Or rather, it most definitely was not.

It merely looked a lot like the Earth and occupied the same coordinates in space-time. What coordinates it occupied in Probability was anybody's guess.

He sighed.

This, he realized, was about as close to home as he was likely to get. Which meant that he was about as far from home as he could possibly be. Glumly he slapped the brochure shut and wondered what on earth he was going to do next.

He allowed himself a hollow laugh at what he had just thought. He looked at his old watch and shook it a bit to wind it. It had taken him, according to his own time scale, a year of hard traveling to get here. A year since the accident in hyperspace in which Fenchurch had completely vanished. One minute she had been sitting there next to him in the SlumpJet; the next minute the ship had done a perfectly normal hyperspace hop and when he had next looked she was not there. The seat wasn't even warm. Her name wasn't even on the passenger list.

The spaceline had been wary of him when he complained. A lot of awkward things happen in space travel, and a lot of them make a lot of money for lawyers. But when they asked him what Galactic Sector he and Fenchurch were from and he said ZZ9 Plural Z Alpha, they relaxed completely in a way that Arthur wasn't at all sure he liked. They even laughed a little, though sympathetically, of course. They pointed to the clause in the ticket contract that said that the entities whose lifespans had originated in any of the Plural zones were advised not to travel in hyperspace and did so at their own risk. Everybody, they said, knew that. They tittered slightly and shook their heads.

As Arthur left their offices he found he was trembling slightly. Not only had he lost Fenchurch in the most complete and utter way possible, but he felt that the more time he spent away out in the Galaxy the more it seemed that the number of things he didn't know anything about actually increased.

Just as he was lost for a moment in these numb memories a knock came on the door of his motel room, which then opened immediately. A fat and disheveled man came in carrying Arthur's one small case.

He got as far as "Where shall I put—" when there was a sudden violent flurry and he collapsed heavily against the door, trying to beat off a small and mangy creature that had leapt snarling out of the wet

night and buried its teeth into his thigh, even through the thick layers
of leather padding he wore there. There was a brief, ugly confusion of
jabbering and thrashing. The man shouted frantically and pointed.
Arthur grabbed a hefty stick that stood next to the door expressly for
this purpose and beat at the boghog with it.

The boghog suddenly disengaged and limped backward, dazed and
forlorn. It turned anxiously in the corner of the room, its tail tucked
up right under its back legs, and then stood looking nervously up at
Arthur, jerking its head awkwardly and repeatedly to one side. Its jaw
seemed to be dislocated. It cried a little and scraped its damp tail
across the floor. By the door, the fat man with Arthur's suitcase was
sitting and cursing, trying to staunch the flow of blood from his thigh.
His clothes were already wet from the rain.

Arthur stared at the boghog, not knowing what to do. The boghog
looked at him questioningly. It tried to approach him, making mournful little whimpering noises. It moved its jaw painfully. It made a
sudden leap for Arthur's thigh, but its dislocated jaw was too weak to
get a grip and it sank, whining sadly, down to the floor. The fat man
jumped to his feet, grabbed the stick, beat the boghog's brains into a
sticky, pulpy mess on the thin carpet, and then stood there breathing
heavily as if daring the animal to move again, just once.

A single boghog eyeball sat looking reproachfully at Arthur from
out of the mashed ruins of its head.

"What do you think it was trying to say?" asked Arthur in a small
voice.

"Ah, nothing much," said the man. "Just its way of trying to be
friendly. This is just our way of being friendly back," he added, gripping the stick.

"When's the next flight out?" asked Arthur.

"Thought you'd only just arrived," said the man.

"Yes," said Arthur. "It was only going to be a brief visit. I just
wanted to see if this was the right place or not. Sorry."

"You mean you're on the wrong planet?" said the man, lugubri-
ously. "Funny how many people say that. 'Specially the people who
live here." He eyed the remains of the boghog with a deep, ancestral
resentment.

"Oh no," said Arthur, "it's the right planet, all right." He picked up
the damp brochure lying on the bed and put it in his pocket. "It's

okay, thanks, I'll take that," he said, taking his case from the man. He went to the door and looked out into the cold, wet night.

"Yes, it's the right planet, all right," he said again. "Right planet, wrong universe."

A single bird wheeled in the sky above him as he set off back for the spaceport.

Ford had his own code of ethics. It wasn't much of one, but it was his and he stuck by it, more or less. One rule he made was never to buy his own drinks. He wasn't sure if that counted as an ethic, but you have to go with what you've got. He was also firmly and utterly opposed to all and any forms of cruelty to any animals whatsoever except geese. And furthermore he would never steal from his employers.

Well, not exactly *steal*.

If his accounts supervisor didn't start to hyperventilate and put out a seal-all-exits security alert when Ford handed in his expenses claim, then Ford felt he wasn't doing his job properly. But actually *stealing* was another thing. That was biting the hand that feeds you. Sucking very hard on it, even nibbling it in an affectionate kind of a way was okay, but you didn't actually bite it. Not when that hand was the *Guide*. The *Guide* was something sacred and special.

But that, thought Ford as he ducked and weaved his way down through the building, was about to change. And they had only themselves to blame. Look at all this stuff. Lines of neat gray office cubicles and executive workstation pods. The whole place was dreary with the hum of memos and minutes of meetings flitting through its electronic networks. Out in the street they were playing Hunt the Wocket, for Zark's sake, but here in the very heart of the *Guide* offices no one was even recklessly kicking a ball around the corridors or wearing inappropriately colored beachware.

"InfiniDim Enterprises," Ford snarled to himself as he stalked rapidly down one corridor after another. Door after door magically opened to him without question. Elevators took him happily to places they should not. Ford was trying to pursue the most tangled and complicated route he could, heading generally downward through the building. His happy little robot took care of everything, spreading waves of acquiescent joy through all the security circuits it encountered.

Ford thought it needed a name and decided to call it Emily Saunders, after a girl he had very fond memories of. Then he thought that

Emily Saunders was an absurd name for a security robot, and decided to call it Colin instead, after Emily's dog.

He was moving deep into the bowels of the building now, into areas he had never entered before, areas of higher and higher security. He was beginning to encounter puzzled looks from the operatives he passed. At this level of security you didn't even call them people anymore. And they were probably doing stuff that only operatives would do. When they went home to their families in the evening they became people again, and when their little children looked up to them with their sweet shining eyes and said, "Daddy, what did you do all day today?" they just said, "I performed my duties as an operative," and left it at that.

The truth of the matter was that all sorts of highly dodgy stuff went on behind the cheery, happy-go-lucky front that the *Guide* liked to put up—or used to like to put up before this new InfiniDim Enterprises bunch marched in and started to make the whole thing highly dodgy. There were all kinds of tax scams and rackets and graft and shady deals supporting the shining edifice, and down in the secure research and data processing levels of the building was where it all went on.

Every few years the *Guide* would set up its business, and indeed its building, on a new world, and all would be sunshine and laughter for a while as the *Guide* would put down its roots in the local culture and economy, provide employment, a sense of glamour and adventure and, in the end, not quite as much actual revenue as the locals had expected.

When the *Guide* moved on, taking its building with it, it left a little like a thief in the night. Exactly like a thief in the night in fact. It usually left in the very early hours of the morning, and the following day there always turned out to be a very great deal of stuff missing. Whole cultures and economies would collapse in its wake, often within a week, leaving once-thriving planets desolate and shell-shocked but still somehow feeling they had been part of some great adventure.

The "operatives" who shot puzzled glances at Ford as he marched on into the depths of the building's most sensitive areas were reassured by the presence of Colin, who was flying along with him in a buzz of emotional fulfillment and easing his path for him at every stage.

Alarms were starting to go off in other parts of the building. Perhaps that meant that Vann Harl had already been discovered, which might be a problem. Ford had been hoping he would be able to slip the Ident-I-Eeze back into his pocket before he came around. Well, that was a problem for later, and he didn't for the moment have the faintest idea how he was going to solve it. For the moment he wasn't going to worry. Wherever he went with little Colin, he was surrounded by a cocoon of sweetness and light and, most important, willing and acquiescent elevators and positively obsequious doors.

Ford even began to whistle, which was probably his mistake. Nobody likes a whistler, particularly not the divinity that shapes our ends.

The next door wouldn't open.

And that was a pity, because it was the very one that Ford had been making for. It stood there before him, gray and resolutely closed with a sign on it saying:

> NO ADMITTANCE.
> NOT EVEN TO AUTHORIZED PERSONNEL.
> YOU ARE WASTING YOUR TIME HERE.
> GO AWAY.

Colin reported that the doors had been getting generally a lot grimmer down in these lower reaches of the building.

They were about ten stories below ground level now. The air was refrigerated and the tasteful gray hessian wall-weave had given way to brutal gray bolted steel walls. Colin's rampant euphoria had subsided into a kind of determined cheeriness. He said that he was beginning to tire a little. It was taking all his energy to pump the slightest bonhomie whatsoever into the doors down here.

Ford kicked at the door. It opened.

"Mixture of pleasure and pain," he muttered. "Always does the trick."

He walked in and Colin flew in after him. Even with a wire stuck straight into his pleasure electrode, his happiness was a nervous kind of happiness. He bobbed around a little.

The room was small, gray and humming.

This was the nerve center of the entire *Guide*.

The computer terminals that lined the gray walls were windows onto every aspect of the *Guide*'s operations. Here, on the left-hand side of the room, reports were gathered over the Sub-Etha-Net from field researchers in every corner of the Galaxy, fed straight up into the network of sub-editors' offices, where they had all the good bits cut out by secretaries because the sub-editors were out having lunch. The remaining copy would then be shot across to the other half of the building—the other leg of the H—which was the legal department. The legal department would cut out anything that was still even remotely good from what remained and fire it back to the offices of the executive editors, who were also out at lunch. So the editors' secretaries would read it and say it was stupid and cut most of what was left.

When any of the editors finally staggered in from lunch they would exclaim, "What is this feeble crap that X"—where X was the name of the field researcher in question—"has sent us from halfway across the bloody Galaxy? What's the point of having somebody spending three whole orbital periods out in the bloody Gagrakacka Mind Zones, with all that stuff going on out there, if this load of anemic squitter is the best he can be bothered to send us? Disallow his expenses!"

"What shall we do with the copy?" the secretary would ask.

"Ah, put it out over the network. Got to have something going out there. I've got a headache, I'm going home."

So the edited copy would go for one last slash and burn through the legal department, and then be sent back down here, where it would be broadcast out over the Sub-Etha-Net for instantaneous retrieval anywhere in the Galaxy. That was handled by equipment which was monitored and controlled by the terminals on the right-hand side of the room.

Meanwhile the order to disallow the researcher's expenses was relayed down to the computer terminal stuck off in the upper right-hand corner, and it was to this terminal that Ford Prefect now swiftly made his way.

If you are reading this on planet Earth then:

A. Good luck to you. There is an awful lot of stuff you don't know anything about, but you are not alone in this. It's just that in your case the consequences of not knowing any of this stuff are particularly terrible, but then, hey, that's just the way the cookie gets completely stomped on and obliterated.

B. Don't imagine you know what a computer terminal is.

A computer terminal is not some clunky old television with a typewriter in front of it. It is an interface where the mind and body can connect with the universe and move bits of it about.

Ford hurried over to the terminal, sat in front of it and quickly dipped himself into its universe.

It wasn't the normal universe he knew. It was a universe of densely enfolded worlds, of wild topographies, towering mountain peaks, heart-stopping ravines, of moons shattering off into seahorses, hurtful blurting crevices, silently heaving oceans and bottomless hurtling hooping funts.

He held still to get his bearings. He controlled his breathing, closed his eyes and looked again.

So this was where accountants spent their time. There was clearly more to them than met the eye. He looked around carefully, trying not to let it all swell and swim and overwhelm him.

He didn't know his way around this universe. He didn't even know the physical laws that determined its dimensional extents or behaviors, but his instinct told him to look for the most outstanding feature he could detect and make toward it.

Way off in some indistinguishable distance—was it a mile or a million or a mote in his eye?—was a stunning peak that overarched the sky, climbed and climbed and spread out in flowering aigrettes,[1] agglomerates,[2] and archimandrites.[3]

He weltered toward it, hooling and thurling, and at last reached it in a meaninglessly long umthingth of time.

He clung to it, arms outspread, gripping tightly on to its roughly gnarled and pitted surface. Once he was certain that he was secure, he made the hideous mistake of looking down.

While he had been weltering, hooling and thurling, the distance beneath him had not bothered him unduly, but now that he was gripping, the distance made his heart wilt and his brain bend. His fingers were white with pain and tension. His teeth were grinding and twisting against each other beyond his control. His eyes turned inward with waves from the willowing extremities of nausea.

With an immense effort of will and faith he simply let go and pushed.

He felt himself float. Away. And then, counterintuitively, upward. And upward.

[1] An ornamental tuft of plumes.
[2] A jumbled mass.
[3] A cleric ranking below a bishop.

He threw his shoulders back, let his arms drop, gazed upward and let himself be drawn loosely, higher and higher.

Before long, insofar as such terms had any meaning in this virtual universe, a ledge loomed up ahead of him on which he could grip and onto which he could clamber.

He rose; he gripped; he clambered.

He panted a little. This was all a little stressful.

He held tightly onto the ledge as he sat. He wasn't certain if this was to prevent himself from falling down off it or rising up from it, but he needed something to grip onto as he surveyed the world in which he found himself.

The whirling, turning height spun him and twisted his brain in upon itself till he found himself, eyes closed, whimpering and hugging the hideous wall of towering rock.

He slowly brought his breathing back under control again. He told himself repeatedly that he was just in a graphic representation of a world. A virtual universe. A simulated reality. He could snap back out of it at any moment.

He snapped back out of it.

He was sitting in a blue leatherette foam-filled, swivel-seated office chair in front of a computer terminal.

He relaxed.

He was clinging to the face of an impossibly high peak perched on a narrow ledge above a drop of brain-swiveling dimensions.

It wasn't just the landscape being so far beneath him—he wished it would stop undulating and waving.

He had to get a grip. Not on the rock wall—that was an illusion. He had to get a grip on the situation, be able to look at the physical world he was in while drawing himself out of it emotionally.

He clenched inwardly and then, just as he had let go of the rock face itself, he let go of the idea of the rock face and let himself just sit there clearly and freely. He looked out at the world. He was breathing well. He was cool. He was in charge again.

He was in a four-dimensional topological model of the *Guide*'s financial systems, and somebody or something would very shortly want to know why.

And here they came.

Swooping through virtual space toward him came a small flock of mean and steely-eyed creatures with pointy little heads, pencil moustaches and querulous demands as to who he was, what he was doing there, what his authorization was, what the authorization of his authorizing agent was, what his inside leg measurement was and so on. Laser light flickered all over him as if he were a packet of biscuits at a supermarket check-out. The heavier-duty laser guns were held, for the moment, in reserve. The fact that all of this was happening in virtual space made no difference. Being virtually killed by virtual laser in virtual space is just as effective as the real thing, because you are as dead as you think you are.

The laser readers were becoming very agitated as they flickered over his fingerprints, his retina and the follicle pattern where his hairline was receding. They didn't like what they were finding at all. The chattering and screeching of highly personal and insolent questions was rising in pitch. A little surgical steel scraper was reaching out toward the skin at the nape of his neck when Ford, holding his breath and praying very slightly, pulled Vann Harl's Indent-I-Eeze out of his pocket and waved it in front of them.

Instantly every laser was diverted to the little card and swept backward and forward over it and in it, examining and reading every molecule.

Then, just as suddenly, they stopped.

The entire flock of little virtual inspectors snapped to attention.

"Nice to see you, Mr. Harl," they said in smarmy unison. "Is there anything we can do for you?"

Ford smiled a slow and vicious smile.

"Do you know," he said, "I rather think there is?"

Five minutes later he was out of there.

About thirty seconds to do the job, and three minutes thirty to cover his tracks. He could have done anything he liked in the virtual structure, more or less. He could have transferred ownership of the entire organization into his own name, but he doubted if that would have gone unnoticed. He didn't want it anyway. It would have meant responsibility, working late nights at the office, not to mention massive and time-consuming fraud investigations and a fair amount of time in jail. He wanted something that nobody other than the computer would notice: that was the bit that took thirty seconds.

The thing that took three minutes thirty was programming the computer not to notice that it had noticed anything.

It had to *want* not to know about what Ford was up to, and then he could safely leave the computer to rationalize its own defenses against the information's ever emerging. It was a programming technique that had been reverse-engineered from the sort of psychotic mental blocks that otherwise perfectly normal people had been observed invariably to develop when elected to high political office.

The other minute was spent discovering that the computer system already had a mental block. A big one.

He would never have discovered it if he hadn't been busy engineering a mental block himself. He came across a whole slew of smooth and plausible denial procedures and diversionary subroutines exactly where he had been planning to install his own. The computer denied all knowledge of them, of course, then blankly refused to accept that there was anything even to deny knowledge of and was generally so convincing that even Ford almost found himself thinking he must have made a mistake.

He was impressed.

He was so impressed, in fact, that he didn't bother to install his own mental block procedures, he just set up calls to the ones that were already there, which then called themselves when questioned, and so on.

He quickly set about debugging the little bits of code he had installed himself, only to discover they weren't there. Cursing, he searched all over for them, but could find no trace of them at all.

He was just about to start installing them all over again when he realized that the reason he couldn't find them was that they were working already.

He grinned with satisfaction.

He tried to discover what the computer's other mental block was all about, but it seemed, not unnaturally, to have a mental block about it. He could no longer find any trace of it at all, in fact; it was that good. He wondered if he had been imagining it. He wondered if he had been imagining that it was something to do with something in the building, and something to do with the number thirteen. He ran a few tests. Yes, he had obviously been imagining it.

No time for fancy routes now, there was obviously a major security alert in progress. Ford took the elevator up to the ground floor to change to the express elevators. He somehow had to get the

Ident-I-Eeze back into Harl's pocket before it was missed. How, he didn't know.

The doors of the elevator slid open to reveal a large posse of security guards and robots poised waiting for it and brandishing filthy-looking weapons.

They ordered him out.

With a shrug he stepped forward. They all pushed rudely past him into the elevator, which took them down to continue their search for him on the lower levels.

This was fun, thought Ford, giving Colin a friendly pat. Colin was about the first genuinely useful robot Ford had ever encountered. Colin bobbed along in the air in front of him in a lather of cheerful ecstasy. Ford was glad he'd named him after a dog.

He was highly tempted just to leave at that point and hope for the best, but he knew that the best had a far greater chance of actually occurring if Harl did not discover that his Ident-I-Eeze was missing. He somehow, surreptitiously, had to return it.

They went to the express elevators.

"Hi," said the elevator they got into.

"Hi," said Ford.

"Where can I take you folks today?" said the elevator.

"Floor twenty-three," said Ford.

"Seems to be a popular floor today," said the elevator.

Hmm, thought Ford, not liking the sound of that at all. The elevator lit up the twenty-third floor on its floor display and started to zoom upward. Something about the floor display tweaked at Ford's mind but he couldn't catch what it was and forgot about it. He was more worried about the idea of the floor he was going to being a popular one. He hadn't really thought through how he was going to deal with whatever it was that was happening up there because he had no idea what he was going to find. He would just have to busk it.

They were there.

The doors slid open.

Ominous quiet.

Empty corridor.

There was the door to Harl's office, with a slight layer of dust around it. Ford knew that this dust consisted of billions of tiny molecular robots that had crawled out of the woodwork, built one another, rebuilt the door, disassembled one another and then crept back into the woodwork again and just waited for damage. Ford wondered what kind of life that was, but not for long because he was a lot more concerned about what his own life was like at that moment.

He took a deep breath and started his run.

rthur felt at a bit of a loss. There was a whole galaxy of stuff out there for him, and he wondered if it was churlish of him to complain to himself that it lacked just two things: the world he was born on and the woman he loved.

Damn it and blast it, he thought, and felt the need of some guidance and advice. He consulted *The Hitchhiker's Guide to the Galaxy*. He looked up "guidance" and it said, "See under ADVICE." He looked up "advice" and it said, "See under GUIDANCE." It had been doing a lot of that kind of stuff recently and he wondered if it was all it was cracked up to be.

He headed to the outer Eastern rim of the Galaxy, where, it was said, wisdom and truth were to be found, most particularly on the planet Hawalius, which was a planet of oracles and seers and soothsayers and also take-out pizza parlors, because most mystics were completely incapable of cooking for themselves.

However, it appeared that some sort of calamity had befallen this planet. As Arthur wandered the streets of the village where the major prophets lived, it had something of a crestfallen air. He came across one prophet who was clearly shutting up shop in a despondent kind of way and asked him what was happening.

"No call for us anymore," he said gruffly as he started to bang a nail into the plank he was holding across the window of his hovel.

"Oh? Why's that?"

"Hold on to the other end of this and I'll show you."

Arthur held up the unnailed end of the plank and the old prophet scuttled into the recesses of his hovel, returning a moment or two later with a small Sub-Etha radio. He turned it on, fiddled with the dial for a moment and put the thing on the small wooden bench that he usually sat and prophesied on. He then took hold of the plank again and resumed hammering.

Arthur sat and listened to the radio.

". . . be confirmed," said the radio.

"Tomorrow," it continued, "the vice president of Poffla Vigus,

Roopy Ga Stip, will announce that he intends to run for president. In a speech he will give tomorrow at . . ."

"Find another channel," said the prophet. Arthur pushed the preset button.

". . . refused to comment," said the radio. "Next week's jobless totals in the Zabush sector," it continued, "will be the worst since records began. A report published next month says . . ."

"Find another," barked the prophet, crossly. Arthur pushed the button again.

". . . denied it categorically," said the radio. "Next month's royal wedding between Prince Gid of the Soofling dynasty and Princess Hooli of Raui Alpha will be the most spectacular ceremony the Bjanjy Territories has ever witnessed. Our reporter Trillian Astra is there and sends us this report."

Arthur blinked.

The sound of cheering crowds and a hubbub of brass bands erupted from the radio. A very familiar voice said, "Well, Krart, the scene here in the middle of next month is absolutely incredible. Princess Hooli is looking radiant in a . . ."

The prophet swiped the radio off the bench and onto the dusty ground, where it squawked like a badly tuned chicken.

"See what we have to contend with?" grumbled the prophet. "Here, hold this. Not that, this. No, not like that. This way up. Other way 'round, you fool."

"I was listening to that," complained Arthur, grappling helplessly with the prophet's hammer.

"So does everybody. That's why this place is like a ghost town." He spat into the dust.

"No, I mean, that sounded like someone I knew."

"Princess Hooli? If I had to stand around saying hello to everybody who's known Princess Hooli, I'd need a new set of lungs."

"Not the Princess," said Arthur. "The reporter. Her name's Trillian. I don't know where she got the Astra from. She's from the same planet as me. I wondered where she'd got to."

"Oh, she's all over the continuum these days. We can't get the tri-d TV stations out here of course, thank the Great Green Arkleseizure, but you hear her on the radio, gallivanting here and there through space-time. She wants to settle down and find herself a steady era, that young lady does. It'll all end in tears. Probably already has." He swung with his hammer and hit his thumb rather hard. He started to speak in tongues.

The village of oracles wasn't much better.

He had been told that when looking for a good oracle it was best to find the oracle that other oracles went to, but he was shut. There was a sign by the entrance saying, "I just don't know anymore. Try next door →, but that's just a suggestion, not formal oracular advice."

"Next door" was a cave a few hundred yards away and Arthur walked toward it. Smoke and steam were rising from, respectively, a small fire and a battered tin pot that was hanging over it. There was also a very nasty smell coming from the pot. At least, Arthur thought it was coming from the pot. The distended bladders of some of the local goatlike things were hanging from a propped-up line drying in the sun, and the smell could have been coming from them. There was also, a worryingly small distance away, a pile of discarded bodies of the local goatlike things and the smell could have been coming from them.

But the smell could just as easily have been coming from the old lady who was busy beating flies away from the pile of bodies. It was a hopeless task because each of the flies was about the size of a winged bottle top and all she had was a table tennis bat. Also she seemed half-blind. Every now and then, by chance, her wild thrashing would connect with one of the flies with a richly satisfying thunk, and the fly would hurtle through the air and smack itself open against the rock face a few yards from the entrance to her cave.

She gave every impression, by her demeanor, that these were the moments she lived for.

Arthur watched this exotic performance for a while from a polite distance, and then at last tried giving a gentle cough to attract her attention. The gentle cough, courteously meant, unfortunately involved first inhaling rather more of the local atmosphere than he had so far been doing and, as a result, he erupted into a fit of raucous expectoration and collapsed against the rock face, choking and streaming with tears. He struggled for breath, but each new breath made things worse. He vomited, half-choked again, rolled over his vomit, kept rolling for a few yards and eventually made it up on to his hands and knees and crawled, panting, into slightly fresher air.

"Excuse me," he said. He got some breath back. "I really am most dreadfully sorry. I feel a complete idiot and . . ." He gestured help-lessly toward the small pile of his own vomit lying spread around the entrance to her cave.

"What can I say?" he said. "What can I possibly say?"

This at least had gained her attention. She looked around at him suspiciously, but, being half-blind, had difficulty finding him in the blurred and rocky landscape.

He waved, helpfully. "Hello!" he called.

At last she spotted him, grunted to herself and turned back to whacking flies.

It was horribly apparent from the way that currents of air moved when she did, that the major source of the smell was in fact her. The drying bladders, the festering bodies and the noxious potage may all have been making valiant contributions to the atmosphere, but the major olfactory presence was the woman herself.

She got another good thwack at a fly. It smacked against the rock and dribbled its insides down it in what she clearly regarded, if she could see that far, as a satisfactory manner.

Unsteadily, Arthur got to his feet and brushed himself down with a fistful of dried grass. He didn't know what else to do by way of an-nouncing himself. He had half a mind just to wander off again, but felt awkward about leaving a pile of his vomit in front of the entrance to the woman's home. He wondered what to do about it. He started to pluck up more handfuls of the scrubby dried grass that was to be found here and there. He was worried, though, that if he ventured nearer to the vomit he might simply add to it rather than clear it up.

Just as he was debating with himself as to what the right course of action was, he began to realize that she was at last saying something to him.

"I beg your pardon?" he called out.

"I said, can I help you?" she said, in a thin, scratchy voice that he could only just hear.

"Er, I came to ask your advice," he called back, feeling a bit ridicu-lous.

She turned to peer at him, myopically, then turned back, swiped at a fly and missed.

"What about?" she said.

"I beg your pardon?" he said.

"I said, what about?" she almost screeched.

"Well," said Arthur. "Just sort of general advice, really. It said in the brochure—"

"Ha! Brochure!" spat the old woman. She seemed to be waving her bat more or less at random now.

Arthur fished the crumpled-up brochure from his pocket. He wasn't quite certain why. He had already read it and she, he expected, wouldn't want to. He unfolded it anyway in order to have something to frown thoughtfully at for a moment or two. The copy in the brochure twittered on about the ancient mystical arts of the seers and sages of Hawalius, and wildly overrepresented the level of accommodation available in Hawalion. Arthur still carried a copy of *The Hitchhiker's Guide to the Galaxy* with him but found, when he consulted it, that the entries were becoming more abstruse and paranoid and had lots of *x*s and *j*s and [s in them. Something was wrong somewhere. Whether it was in his own personal unit, or whether it was something or someone going terribly amiss, or perhaps just hallucinating, at the heart of the *Guide* organization itself, he didn't know. But one way or another he was even less inclined to trust it than usual, which meant that he trusted it not one bit, and mostly used it for eating his sandwiches off of when he was sitting on a rock staring at something.

The woman had turned and was walking slowly toward him now. Arthur tried, without making it too obvious, to judge the wind direction, and bobbed about a bit as she approached.

"Advice," she said. "Advice, eh?"

"Er, yes," said Arthur. "Yes. That is—"

He frowned again at the brochure, as if to be certain that he hadn't misread it and stupidly turned up on the wrong planet or something. The brochure said, "The friendly local inhabitants will be glad to share with you the knowledge and wisdom of the ancients. Peer with them into the swirling mysteries of past and future time!" There were some coupons as well, but Arthur had been far too embarrassed actually to cut them out or try to present them to anybody.

"Advice, eh?" said the old woman again. "Just sort of general advice, you say. On what? What to do with your life, that sort of thing?"

"Yes," said Arthur. "That sort of thing. Bit of a problem I sometimes find if I'm being perfectly honest." He was trying desperately, with tiny darting movements, to stay upwind of her. She surprised him by suddenly turning sharply away from him and heading off toward her cave.

"You'll have to help me with the photocopier, then," she said.

"What?" said Arthur.

"The photocopier," she repeated, patiently. "You'll have to help me drag it out. It's solar-powered. I have to keep it in the cave, though, so the birds don't shit on it."

"I see," said Arthur.

"I'd take a few deep breaths if I were you," muttered the old woman, as she stomped into the gloom of the cave mouth.

Arthur did as she advised. He almost hyperventilated in fact. When he felt he was ready, he held his breath and followed her in.

The photocopier was a big old thing on a rickety trolley. It stood just inside the dim shadows of the cave. The wheels were stuck obstinately in different directions and the ground was rough and stony.

"Go ahead and take a breath outside," said the old woman. Arthur was going red in the face trying to help her move the thing.

He nodded in relief. If she wasn't going to be embarrassed about it, then neither, he was determined, would he. He stepped outside and took a few breaths, then came back in to do more heaving and pushing. He had to do this quite a few times till at last the machine was outside.

The sun beat down on it. The old woman disappeared back into her cave again and brought with her some mottled metal panels, which she connected to the machine to collect the sun's energy.

She squinted up into the sky. The sun was quite bright, but the day was hazy and vague.

"It'll take a while," she said.

Arthur said he was happy to wait.

The old woman shrugged and stomped across to the fire. Above it, the contents of the tin can were bubbling away. She poked about at them with a stick.

"You won't be wanting any lunch?" she inquired of Arthur.

"I've eaten, thanks," said Arthur. "No, really. I've eaten."

"I'm sure you have," said the old lady. She stirred with the stick. After a few minutes she fished a lump of something out, blew on it to cool it a little and then put it in her mouth.

She chewed on it thoughtfully for a bit.

Then she hobbled slowly across to the pile of dead goatlike things. She spat the lump out onto the pile. She hobbled slowly back to the can. She tried to unhook it from the sort of tripodlike thing that it was hanging from.

"Can I help you?" said Arthur, jumping up politely. He hurried over.

Together they disengaged the tin from the tripod and carried it awkwardly down the slight slope that led downward from her cave and toward a line of scrubby and gnarled trees, which marked the edge of a steep but quite shallow gully, from which a whole new range of offensive smells was emanating.

"Ready?" said the old lady.

"Yes . . ." said Arthur, though he didn't know for what.

"One," said the old lady.

"Two," she said.

"Three," she added.

Arthur realized just in time what she intended. Together they tossed the contents of the tin into the gully.

After an hour or two of uncommunicative silence, the old woman decided that the solar panels had absorbed enough sunlight to run the photocopier now and she disappeared to rummage inside her cave. She emerged at last with a few sheaves of paper and fed them through the machine.

She handed the copies to Arthur.

"This is, er, this is your advice then, is it?" said Arthur, leafing through them uncertainly.

"No," said the old lady. "It's the story of my life. You see, the quality of any advice anybody has to offer has to be judged against the quality of life they actually lead. Now, as you look through this document you'll see that I've underlined all the major decisions I ever made to make them stand out. They're all indexed and cross-referenced. See? All I can suggest is that if you take decisions that are exactly opposite to the sort of decisions that I've taken, then maybe you won't finish up at the end of your life"—she paused, and filled her lungs for a good shout—"in a smelly old cave like this!"

She grabbed up her table tennis bat, rolled up her sleeve, stomped off to her pile of dead goatlike things and started to set about the flies with vim and vigor.

The last village Arthur visited consisted entirely of extremely high poles. They were so high that it wasn't possible to tell, from the ground, what was on top of them, and Arthur had to climb three before he found one that had anything on top of it at all other than a platform covered with bird droppings.

Not an easy task. You went up the poles by climbing on the short wooden pegs that had been hammered into them in slowly ascending spirals. Anybody who was a less diligent tourist than Arthur would have taken a couple of snapshots and sloped right off to the nearest bar & grill, where you also could buy a range of particularly sweet and gooey chocolate cakes to eat in front of the ascetics. But, largely as a result of this, most of the ascetics had gone now. In fact they had mostly gone and set up lucrative therapy centers on some of the more affluent worlds in the Northwest ripple of the Galaxy, where the living was easier by a factor of about 17 million, and the chocolate was just fabulous. Most of the ascetics, it turned out, had not known about chocolate before they took up asceticism. Most of the clients who came to their therapy centers knew about it all too well.

At the top of the third pole Arthur stopped for a breather. He was very hot and out of breath, since each pole was about fifty or sixty feet high. The world seemed to swing vertiginously around him, but it didn't worry Arthur too much. He knew that, logically, he could not die until he had been to Stavromula Beta,[4] and had therefore managed to cultivate a merry attitude toward extreme personal danger. He felt a little giddy perched fifty feet up in the air on top of a pole, but he dealt with it by eating a sandwich. He was just about to embark on reading the photocopied life history of the oracle, when he was rather startled to hear a slight cough behind him.

He turned so abruptly that he dropped his sandwich, which turned downward through the air and was rather small by the time it was stopped by the ground.

About thirty feet behind Arthur was another pole, and, alone among the sparse forest of about three dozen poles, the top of it was occupied. It was occupied by an old man who, in turn, seemed to be occupied by profound thoughts that were making him scowl.

"Excuse me," said Arthur. The man ignored him. Perhaps he couldn't hear him. The breeze was moving about a bit. It was only by chance that Arthur had heard the slight cough.

"Hello?" called Arthur. "Hello!"

[4] See Life, the Universe and Everything, chapter 18.

The man at last glanced around at him. He seemed surprised to see him. Arthur couldn't tell if he was surprised and pleased to see him or just surprised.

"Are you open?" called Arthur.

The man frowned in incomprehension. Arthur couldn't tell if he couldn't understand or couldn't hear.

"I'll pop over," called Arthur. "Don't go away."

He clambered off the small platform and climbed quickly down the spiraling pegs, arriving at the bottom quite dizzy.

He started to make his way over to the pole on which the old man was sitting, and then suddenly realized that he had disoriented himself on the way down and didn't know for certain which one it was.

He looked around for landmarks and worked out which was the right one.

He climbed it. It wasn't.

"Damn," he said. "Excuse me!" he called out to the old man again, who was now straight in front of him and forty feet away. "Got lost. Be with you in a minute." Down he went again, getting very hot and bothered.

When he arrived, panting and sweating, at the top of the pole that he knew for certain was the right one, he realized that the man was, somehow or other, mucking him about.

"What do you want?" shouted the old man crossly at him. He was now sitting on top of the pole that Arthur recognized was the one that he had been on himself when eating his sandwich.

"How did you get over there?" called Arthur in bewilderment.

"You think I'm going to tell you just like that what it took me forty springs, summers and autumns of sitting on top of a pole to work out?"

"What about winter?"

"What about winter?"

"Don't you sit on the pole in the winter?"

"Just because I sit up a pole for most of my life," said the man, "doesn't mean I'm an idiot. I go south in the winter. Got a beach house. Sit on the chimney stack."

"Do you have any advice for a traveler?"

"Yes. Get a beach house."

"I see."

The man stared out over the hot, dry, scrubby landscape. From here Arthur could just see the old woman, a tiny speck in the distance, dancing up and down swatting flies.

"You see her?" called the old man, suddenly.

"Yes," said Arthur. "I consulted her in fact."

"Fat lot she knows. I got the beach house because she turned it down. What advice did she give you?"

"Do exactly the opposite of everything she's done."

"In other words, get a beach house."

"I suppose so," said Arthur. "Well, maybe I'll get one."

"Hmmm."

The horizon was swimming in a fetid heat haze.

"Any other advice?" asked Arthur. "Other than to do with real estate?"

"A beach house isn't just real estate. It's a state of mind," said the man. He turned and looked at Arthur.

Oddly, the man's face was now only a couple of feet away. He seemed in one way to be a perfectly normal shape, but his body was sitting cross-legged on a pole forty feet away while his face was only two feet from Arthur's. Without moving his head, and without seeming to do anything odd at all, he stood up and stepped onto the top of another pole. Either it was just the heat, thought Arthur, or space was a different shape for him.

"A beach house," he said, "doesn't even have to be on the beach. Though the best ones are. We all like to congregate," he went on, "at boundary conditions."

"Really?" said Arthur.

"Where land meets water. Where earth meets air. Where body meets mind. Where space meets time. We like to be on one side, and look at the other."

Arthur got terribly excited. This was exactly the sort of thing he'd been promised in the brochure. Here was a man who seemed to be moving through some kind of Escher space saying really profound things about all sorts of stuff.

It was unnerving, though. The man was now stepping from pole to ground, from ground to pole, from pole to pole, from pole to horizon and back: he was making complete nonsense of Arthur's spatial universe. "Please stop!" Arthur said, suddenly.

"Can't take it, huh?" said the man. Without the slightest movement he was now back, sitting cross-legged, on top of the pole forty feet in front of Arthur. "You come to me for advice, but you can't cope with anything you don't recognize. Hmmm. So we'll have to tell you something you already know but make it sound like news, eh? Well, business as usual, I suppose." He sighed and squinted mournfully into the distance.

"Where you from, boy?" he then asked.

Arthur decided to be clever. He was fed up with being mistaken for a complete idiot by everyone he ever met. "Tell you what," he said. "You're a seer. Why don't you tell me?"

The old man sighed again. "I was just," he said, passing his hand around behind his head, "making conversation." When he brought his hand around to the front again, he had a globe of the Earth spinning on his up-pointed forefinger. It was unmistakable. He put it away again. Arthur was stunned.

"How did you—"

"I can't tell you."

"Why not? I've come all this way."

"You cannot see what I see because you see what you see. You cannot know what I know because you know what you know. What I see and what I know cannot be added to what you see and what you know because they are not of the same kind. Neither can it replace what you see and what you know, because that would be to replace you yourself."

"Hang on, can I write this down?" said Arthur, excitedly fumbling in his pocket for a pencil.

"You can pick up a copy at the spaceport," said the old man. "They've got racks of the stuff."

"Oh," said Arthur, disappointed. "Well, isn't there anything that's perhaps a bit more specific to me?"

"Everything you see or hear or experience in any way at all is specific to you. You create a universe by perceiving it, so everything in the universe you perceive is specific to you."

Arthur looked at him doubtfully. "Can I get that at the spaceport, too?" he said.

"Check it out," said the old man.

"It says in the brochure," said Arthur, pulling it out of his pocket and looking at it again, "that I can have a special prayer, individually tailored to me and my special needs."

"Oh, all right," said the old man. "Here's a prayer for you. Got a pencil?"

"Yes," said Arthur.

"It goes like this. Let's see now: 'Protect me from knowing what I don't need to know. Protect me from even knowing that there are things to know that I don't know. Protect me from knowing that I decided not to know about the things that I decided not to know about. Amen.' That's it. It's what you pray silently inside yourself anyway, so you may as well have it out in the open."

"Hmmm," said Arthur. "Well, thank you—"

"There's another prayer that goes with it that's very important," continued the old man, "so you'd better jot this down, too."

"Okay."

"It goes, 'Lord, lord, lord . . .' It's best to put that bit in, just in case. You can never be too sure. 'Lord, lord, lord. Protect me from the consequences of the above prayer. Amen.' And that's it. Most of the trouble people get into in life comes from leaving out that last part."

"Ever heard of a place called Stavromula Beta?" asked Arthur.

"No."

"Well, thank you for your help," said Arthur.

"Don't mention it," said the man on the pole, and vanished.

Ford hurled himself at the door of the editor-in-chief's office, tucked himself into a tight ball as the frame splintered and gave way once again, rolled rapidly across the floor to where the smart gray crushed-leather sofa was and set up his strategic operational base behind it.

That, at least, was the plan.

Unfortunately the smart gray crushed-leather sofa wasn't there.

Why, thought Ford, as he twisted himself around in midair, lurched, dove and scuttled for cover behind Harl's desk, did people have this stupid obsession with rearranging their office furniture every five minutes?

Why, for instance, replace a perfectly serviceable if rather muted gray crushed-leather sofa with what appeared to be a small tank?

And who was the big guy with the mobile rocket launcher on his shoulder? Someone from head office? Couldn't be. This was head office. At least it was the head office of the *Guide*. Where these InfiniDim Enterprises guys came from Zarquon knew. Nowhere very sunny, judging from the slug-like color and texture of their skins. This was all wrong, thought Ford. People connected with the *Guide* should come from sunny places.

There were several of them, in fact, and all of them seemed to be more heavily armed and armored than you normally expected corporate executives to be, even in today's rough-and-tumble business world.

He was making a lot of assumptions here, of course. He was assuming that the big, bull-necked, sluglike guys were in some way connected with InfiniDim Enterprises, but it was a reasonable assumption and he felt happy about it because they had logos on their armorplating which said "InfiniDim Enterprises" on them. He had a nagging suspicion that this was not a business meeting, though. He also had a nagging feeling that these sluglike creatures were familiar to him in some way. Familiar, but in an unfamiliar guise.

Well, he had been in the room for a good two and a half seconds now and thought that it was probably about time to start doing something constructive. He could take a hostage. That would be good.

Vann Harl was in his swivel chair, looking alarmed, pale and shaken. Had probably had some bad news as well as a nasty bang to the back of his head. Ford leapt to his feet and made a running grab of him.

Under the pretext of getting him into a good solid double underpinned elbow lock, Ford managed surreptitiously to slip the Ident-I-Eeze back into Harl's inner pocket.

Bingo!

He'd done what he came to do. Now he just had to talk his way out of here.

"Okay," he said. "I . . ." He paused.

The big guy with the rocket launcher was turning toward Ford Prefect and pointing it at him, which Ford couldn't help feeling was wildly irresponsible behavior.

"I . . ." he started again, and then on a sudden impulse decided to duck.

There was a deafening roar as flames leapt from the back of the rocket launcher and a rocket leapt from its front.

The rocket hurtled past Ford and hit the large plate-glass window, which billowed outward in a shower of a million shards under the force of the explosion. Huge shock waves of noise and air pressure reverberated around the room, sweeping a couple of chairs, a filing cabinet and Colin the security robot out of the window.

Ah! So they're not totally rocket-proof after all, thought Ford Prefect to himself. Someone should have a word with somebody about that. He disentangled himself from Harl and tried to work out which way to run.

He was surrounded.

The big guy with the rocket launcher was moving it up into position again for another shot.

Ford was completely at a loss for what to do next.

"Look," he said in a stern voice. But he wasn't certain how far saying things like "Look" in a stern voice was necessarily going to get him, and time was not on his side. What the hell, he thought, you're only young once, and threw himself out of the window. That would at least keep the element of surprise on his side.

Chapter 11

The first thing Arthur Dent had to do, he realized resignedly, was to get himself a life. This meant he had to find a planet he could have one on. It had to be a planet he could breathe on, where he could stand up and sit down without experiencing gravitational discomfort. It had to be somewhere where the acid levels were low and the plants didn't actually attack you.

"I hate to be anthropic about this," he said to the strange thing behind the desk at the Resettlement Advice Center on Pintleton Alpha, "but I'd quite like to live somewhere where the people look vaguely like me as well. You know. Sort of human."

The strange thing behind the desk waved some of its stranger bits around and seemed rather taken aback by this. It oozed and glopped off its seat, thrashed its way slowly across the floor, ingested the old metal filing cabinet and then, with a great belch, excreted the appropriate drawer. It popped out a couple of glistening tentacles from its ear, removed some files from the drawer, sucked the drawer back in and vomited up the cabinet again. It thrashed its way back across the floor, slimed its way back up onto the seat and slapped the files on the table.

"See anything you fancy?" it asked.

Arthur looked nervously through some grubby and damp pieces of paper. He was definitely in some backwater part of the Galaxy here, and somewhere off to the left as far as the universe he knew and recognized was concerned. In the space where his own home should have been there was a rotten hick planet, drowned with rain and inhabited by thugs and boghogs. Even *The Hitchhiker's Guide to the Galaxy* seemed to work only fitfully here, which was why he was reduced to making these sorts of inquiries in these sorts of places. One place he always asked after was Stavromula Beta, but no one had ever heard of such a planet.

The available worlds looked pretty grim. They had little to offer him because he had little to offer them. He had been extremely chastened to realize that although he originally came from a world which had cars and computers and ballet and Armagnac, he didn't, by himself, know how any of it worked. He couldn't do it. Left to his own devices he couldn't build a toaster. He could just about make a sandwich and that was it. There was not a lot of demand for his services.

Arthur's heart sank. This surprised him, because he thought it was already about as low as it could possibly be. He closed his eyes for a moment. He so much wanted to be home. He so much wanted his own home world, the actual Earth he had grown up on, not to have been demolished. He so much wanted none of this to have happened. He so much wanted that when he opened his eyes again he would be standing on the doorstep of his little cottage in the West Country of England, that the sun would be shining over the green hills, the post van would be going up the lane, the daffodils would be blooming in his garden and in the distance the pub would be opening for lunch. He so much wanted to take the newspaper down to the pub and read it over a pint of bitter. He so much wanted to do the crossword. He so much wanted to be able to get completely stuck on 17 across.

He opened his eyes.

The strange thing was pulsating irritably at him, tapping some kind of pseudopodia on the desk.

Arthur shook his head and looked at the next sheet of paper.

Grim, he thought. And the next.

Very grim. And the next.

Oh . . . Now *that* looked better.

It was a world called Bartledan. It had oxygen. It had green hills. It even, it seemed, had a renowned literary culture. But the thing that most aroused his interest was a photograph of a small bunch of Bartledanian people, standing around in a village square, smiling pleasantly at the camera.

"Ah," he said, and held the picture up to the strange thing behind the desk.

Its eyes squirmed out on stalks and rolled up and down the piece of paper, leaving a glistening trail of slime all over it.

"Yes," it said with distaste. "They do look exactly like you."

Arthur moved to Bartledan and, using some money he had made by selling some toenail clippings and spit to a DNA bank, he bought himself a room in the village featured in the picture. It was pleasant there. The air was balmy. The people looked like him and seemed not to mind him being there. They didn't attack him with anything. He bought some clothes and a cupboard to put them in.

He had got himself a life. Now he had to find a purpose in it.

At first he tried to sit and read. But the literature of Bartledan, famed though it was throughout this sector of the Galaxy for its subtlety and grace, didn't seem to be able to sustain his interest. The problem was that it wasn't actually about human beings after all. It wasn't about what human beings wanted. The people of Bartledan were remarkably like human beings to look at, but when you said "Good evening" to one, he would tend to look around with a slight sense of surprise, sniff the air and say that, yes, he supposed that it probably was a goodish evening now that Arthur came to mention it.

"No, what I meant was to wish you a good evening," Arthur would say, or rather, used to say. He soon learned to avoid these conversations. "I mean that I hope you have a good evening," he would add.

More puzzlement.

"Wish?" the Bartledanian would say at last, in polite bafflement.

"Er, yes," Arthur would then have said. "I'm just expressing the hope that . . ."

"Hope?"

"Yes."

"What is hope?"

Good question, thought Arthur to himself, and retreated back to his room to think about things.

On the one hand he could only recognize and respect what he learned about the Bartledanian view of the Universe, which was that the Universe was what the Universe was, take it or leave it. On the other hand he could not help but feel that not to desire anything, not ever to wish or to hope, was just not natural.

Natural. There was a tricky word.

He had long ago realized that a lot of things that he had thought of as natural, like buying people presents at Christmas, stopping at red lights or falling at a rate of 32 feet per second per second, were just the habits of his own world and didn't necessarily work the same way anywhere else; but not to wish—that really couldn't be natural, could it? That would be like not breathing.

Breathing was another thing that the Bartledanians didn't do, despite all the oxygen in the atmosphere. They just stood there. Occasionally they ran around and played netball and stuff (without ever

wishing to win, though, of course—they would just play and whoever
won, won), but they never actually breathed. It was, for some reason,
unnecessary. Arthur quickly learned that playing netball with them
was just too spooky. Though they looked like humans, and even
moved and sounded like humans, they didn't breathe and they didn't
wish for things.

Breathing and wishing for things, on the other hand, was just about
all that Arthur seemed to do all day. Sometimes he would wish for
things so much that his breathing would get quite agitated, and he
would have to go and lie down for a bit. On his own. In his small
room. So far from the world that had given birth to him that his brain
could not even process the sort of numbers involved without just going limp.

He preferred not to think about it. He preferred just to sit and read
—or at least he would prefer it if there was anything worth reading.
But nobody in Bartledanian stories ever wanted anything. Not even a
glass of water. Certainly, they would fetch one if they were thirsty, but
if there wasn't one available, they would think no more about it. He
had just read an entire book in which the main character had, over the
course of a week, done some work in his garden, played a great deal of
netball, helped mend a road, fathered a child on his wife and then
unexpectedly died of thirst just before the last chapter. In exasperation
Arthur had combed his way back through the book and in the end had
found a passing reference to some problem with the plumbing in
chapter two. And that was it. So the guy dies. It just happens.

It wasn't even the climax of the book, because there wasn't one. The
character died about a third of the way through the penultimate chapter of the book, and the rest of it was just more stuff about road-
mending. The book just finished dead at the one hundred thousandth
word, because that was how long books were on Bartledan.

Arthur threw the book across the room, sold the room and left. He
started to travel with wild abandon, trading in more and more spit,
toenails, fingernails, blood, hair, anything that anybody wanted, for
tickets. For semen, he discovered, he could travel first class. He settled
nowhere, but only existed in the hermetic, twilight world of the cabins
of hyperspatial starships, eating, drinking, sleeping, watching movies,
only stopping at spaceports to donate more DNA and catch the next
long-haul ship out. He waited and waited for another accident to
happen.

The trouble with trying to make the right accident happen is that it won't. That is not what "accident" means. The accident that eventually occurred was not what he had planned at all. The ship he was on blipped in hyperspace, flickered horribly between ninety-seven different points in the Galaxy simultaneously, caught the unexpected gravitational pull of an uncharted planet in one of them, became ensnared in its outer atmosphere and began to fall, screaming and tearing, into it.

The ship's systems protested all the way down that everything was perfectly normal and under control, but when it went into a final hectic spin, ripped wildly through half a mile of trees and finally exploded into a seething ball of flame, it became clear that this was not the case.

Fire engulfed the forest, boiled into the night, then neatly put itself out, as all unscheduled fires over a certain size are now required to do by law. For a short while afterward, other small fires flared up here and there as odd pieces of scattered debris exploded quietly in their own time. Then they too died away.

Arthur Dent, because of the sheer boredom of endless interstellar flight was the only one on board who actually had familiarized himself with the ship's safety procedures in case of an unscheduled landing, was the sole survivor. He lay dazed, broken and bleeding in a sort of fluffy pink plastic cocoon with "Have a nice day" printed in more than three thousand different languages all over it.

Black, roaring silences swam sickeningly through his shattered mind. He knew with a kind of resigned certainty that he would survive, because he had not yet been to Stavromula Beta.

After what seemed an eternity of pain and darkness, he became aware of quiet shapes moving around him.

Ford tumbled through the open air in a cloud of glass splinters and chair parts. Again, he hadn't really thought things through, really, and was just playing it by ear, buying time. At times of major crisis he found it was often quite helpful to have his life flash before his eyes. It gave him a chance to reflect on things, see things in some sort of perspective, and it sometimes furnished him with a vital clue as to what to do next.

There was the ground rushing up to meet him at thirty feet per second, but he would, he thought, deal with that problem when he got to it. First things first.

Ah, here it came. His childhood. Humdrum stuff, he'd been through it all before. Images flashed by. Boring times on Betelgeuse Five. Zaphod Beeblebrox as a kid. Yes, he knew all that. He wished he had some kind of fast forward in his brain. His seventh birthday party, being given his first towel. Come on, come on.

He was twisting and turning downward, the outside air at this height a cold shock to his lungs. Trying not to inhale glass.

Early voyages to other planets. Oh, for Zark's sake, this was like some sort of bloody travelog documentary before the main feature. First beginning to work for the *Guide*.

Ah!

Those were the days. They worked out of a hut on the Bwenelli Atoll on Fanalla before the Riktanarqals and the Donqueds vertled it. Half a dozen guys, some towels, a handful of highly sophisticated digital devices and most important a lot of dreams. No. Most important a lot of Fanallan rum. To be absolutely accurate, that Ol' Janx Spirit was the absolute most important thing, then the Fanallan rum and also some of the beaches on the Atoll where the local girls would hang out, but the dreams were important as well. Whatever happened to those?

He couldn't quite remember what the dreams were in fact, but they had seemed immensely important at the time. They had certainly not involved this huge towering office block he was now falling down the side of. All of that had come when some of the original team had started to settle down and get greedy, while he and others had stayed out in the field, researching and hitchhiking and gradually becoming more and more isolated from the corporate nightmare the *Guide* had inexorably turned into, and the architectural monstrosity it had come to occupy. Where were the dreams in that? He thought of all the corporate lawyers who occupied half of the building, all the "operatives" who occupied the lower levels, and all the sub-editors and their secretaries and their secretaries' lawyers and their secretaries, lawyers' secretaries and, worst of all, the accountants and the marketing department.

He had half a mind just to keep on falling. The finger to the lot of them.

He was just passing the seventeenth floor now, where the marketing department hung out. Load of tosspots all arguing about what color the *Guide* should be and exercising their infinitely infallible skills of being wise after the event. If any of them had chosen to look out of the window at that moment, they would have been startled by the sight of Ford Prefect dropping past them to his certain death and flipping the finger at them.

Sixteenth floor. Sub-editors. Bastards. What about all that copy of his they'd cut? Fifteen years of research he'd filed from one planet alone and they'd cut it to two words. "Mostly harmless." The finger to them as well.

Fifteenth floor. Logistical Administration, whatever that was about. They all had big cars. That, he thought, was what that was about.

Fourteenth floor. Personnel. He had a very shrewd suspicion that it was they who had engineered his fifteen-year exile while the *Guide* metamorphosed into the corporate monolith (or rather, duolith—mustn't forget the lawyers) it had become.

Thirteenth floor. Research and Development.

Hang about.

Thirteenth floor.

He was having to think rather fast at the moment because the situation was becoming a little urgent.

He suddenly remembered the floor-display panel in the elevator. It hadn't had a thirteenth floor. He'd thought no more about it because, having spent fifteen years on the rather backward planet Earth, where they were superstitious about the number thirteen, he was used to

being in buildings that numbered their floors without it. No reason
for that here, though.

The windows of the thirteenth floor, he could not help noticing as
he flashed swiftly by them, were darkened.

What was going on in there? He started to remember all the stuff
that Harl had been talking about. One new, multidimensional *Guide*
spread across an infinite number of universes. It had sounded, the way
Harl had put it, like wild meaninglessness dreamed up by the marketing department with the backing of the accountants. If it was any
more real than that, then it was a very weird and dangerous idea. Was
it real? What was going on behind the darkened windows of the
sealed-off thirteenth floor?

Ford felt a rising sense of curiosity, and then a rising sense of panic.
That was the complete list of rising feelings he had. In every other
respect he was falling very rapidly. He really ought to turn his mind to
wondering how he was going to get out of this situation alive.

He glanced down. A hundred feet or so below him people were
milling around, some of them beginning to look up expectantly.
Clearing a space for him. Even temporarily calling off the wonderful
and completely fatuous hunt for Wockets.

He would hate to disappoint them, but about two feet below him,
he hadn't realized before, was Colin. Colin had obviously been happily dancing attendance and waiting for him to decide what he wanted
to do.

"Colin!" Ford bawled.

Colin didn't respond. Ford went cold. Then he suddenly realized
that he hadn't told Colin his name was Colin.

"Come up here!" Ford bawled.

Colin bobbed up beside him. Colin was enjoying the ride down
immensely and hoped that Ford was, too.

Colin's world went unexpectedly dark as Ford's towel suddenly en-
veloped him. Colin immediately felt himself get much, much heavier.
He was thrilled and delighted by the challenge that Ford had presented him with. Just not sure if he could handle it, that was all.

The towel was slung over Colin. Ford was hanging from the towel,
gripping to its seams. Other hitchhikers had seen fit to modify their
towels in exotic ways, weaving all kinds of esoteric tools and utilities
and even computer equipment into their fabric. Ford was a purist. He
liked to keep things simple. He carried a regular towel from a regular

domestic soft-furnishings shop. It even had a kind of blue and pink floral pattern despite his repeated attempts to bleach and stonewash it. It had a couple of pieces of wire threaded into it, a bit of flexible writing stick, and also some nutrients soaked into one of the corners of the fabric so he could suck on it in an emergency, but otherwise it was a simple towel you could dry your face on.

The only actual modification he had been persuaded by a friend to make to it was to reinforce the seams.

Ford gripped the seams like a maniac.

They were still descending, but the rate had slowed.

"Up, Colin!" he shouted.

Nothing.

"Your name," shouted Ford, "is Colin. So when I shout, 'Up, Colin!' I want you, Colin, to go up. Okay? Up, Colin!"

Nothing. Or rather a sort of muffled groaning sound from Colin. Ford was very anxious. They were descending very slowly now, but Ford was very anxious about the sort of people he could see assembling on the ground beneath him. Friendly, local, Wocket-hunting types were dispersing, and thick, heavy, bull-necked, sluglike creatures with rocket launchers were, it seemed, sliding out of what was usually called thin air. Thin air, as all experienced Galactic travelers well know, is in fact extremely thick with multidimensional complexities.

"Up," bellowed Ford again. "Up! Colin, go up!"

Colin was straining and groaning. They were now more or less stationary in the air. Ford felt as if his fingers were breaking.

"Up!"

They stayed put.

"Up, up, up!"

A slug was preparing to launch a rocket at him. Ford couldn't believe it. He was hanging from a towel in midair and a slug was preparing to fire rockets at him. He was running out of anything he could think of doing and was beginning to get seriously alarmed.

This was the sort of predicament that he usually relied on having the *Guide* available for to give advice, however infuriating or glib, but this was not a moment for reaching into his pocket. And the *Guide* seemed to be no longer a friend and ally but was now itself a source of danger. These were the *Guide* offices he was hanging outside, for Zark's sake, in danger of his life from the people who now appeared to own the thing. What had become of all the dreams he vaguely remembered having on the Bwenelli Atoll? They should have let it all be. They should have stayed there. Stayed on the beach. Loved good women. Lived on fish. He should have known it was all wrong the moment they started hanging grand pianos over the sea-monster pool in the atrium. He began to feel thoroughly wasted and miserable. His fingers were on fire with clenched pain. And his ankle was still hurting.

Oh, thank you, ankle, he thought to himself bitterly. Thank you for bringing up your problems at this time. I expect you'd like a nice warm footbath to make you feel better, wouldn't you? Or at least you'd like me to . . .

He had an idea.

The armored slug had hoisted the rocket launcher up onto its shoulder. The rocket was presumably designed to hit anything in its path that moved.

Ford tried not to sweat because he could feel his grip on the seams of his towel slipping.

With the toe of his good foot he nudged and pried at the heel of the shoe on his hurting foot.

"Go *up*, damn you!" Ford muttered hopelessly to Colin, who was cheerily straining away but unable to rise. Ford worked away at the heel of his shoe.

He was trying to judge the timing, but there was no point. Just go for it. He only had one shot and that was it. He had now eased the back of his shoe down off his heel. His twisted ankle felt a little better. Well, that was good, wasn't it?

With his other foot he kicked at the heel of the shoe. It slipped off his foot and fell through the air. About half a second later a rocket erupted up from the muzzle of its launcher, encountered the shoe falling through its path, went straight for it, hit it and exploded with a great sense of satisfaction and achievement.

This happened about fifteen feet from the ground.

The main force of the explosion was directed downward. Where, a second earlier, there had been a squad of InfiniDim Enterprises executives with a rocket launcher standing on an elegant terraced plaza paved with large slabs of lustrous stone cut from the ancient alabastrum quarries of Zentalquabula, there was now, instead, a bit of a pit with nasty bits in it.

A great wump of hot air welled up from the explosion, throwing

Ford and Colin violently up into the sky. Ford fought desperately and blindly to hold on and failed. He turned helplessly upward through the sky, reached the peak of a parabola, paused and then started to fall again. He fell and fell and fell and suddenly winded himself badly on Colin, who was still rising.

He clasped himself desperately onto the small spherical robot. Colin slewed wildly through the air toward the tower of the *Guide* offices, trying delightedly to control himself and slow down.

The world spun sickeningly around Ford's head as they spun and twisted around each other and then, equally sickeningly, everything suddenly stopped.

Ford found himself deposited dizzily on a window ledge.

His towel fell past and he grabbed at it and caught it.

Colin bobbed in the air inches away from him.

Ford looked around himself in a bruised, bleeding and breathless daze. The ledge was only about a foot wide and he was perched precariously on it, thirteen stories up.

Thirteen.

He knew they were thirteen stories up because the windows were dark. He was bitterly upset. He had bought those shoes for some absurd price in a store on the Lower East Side in New York. He had, as a result, written an entire essay on the joys of great footwear, all of which had been jettisoned in the "Mostly harmless" debacle. Damn everything.

And now one of the shoes was gone. He threw his head back and stared at the sky.

It wouldn't be such a grim tragedy if the planet in question hadn't been demolished, which meant that he wouldn't even be able to get another pair.

Yes, given the infinite sideways extension of probability, there was, of course, an almost infinite multiplicity of planets Earth, but, when you come down to it, a major pair of shoes wasn't something you could just replace by mucking about in multidimensional space-time.

He sighed.

Oh well, he'd better make the best of it. At least it had saved his life. For the time being.

He was perched on a foot-wide ledge thirteen stories up the side of a building and he wasn't at all sure that that was worth a good shoe.

He stared in woozily through the darkened glass.

It was as dark and silent as a tomb.

No. That was a ridiculous thing to think. He'd been to some great parties in tombs.

Could he detect some movement? He wasn't quite sure. It seemed that he could see some kind of weird, flapping shadow. Perhaps it was just blood dribbling over his eyelashes. He wiped it away. Boy, he'd love to have a farm somewhere, keep some sheep. He peered into the window again, trying to make out what the shape was, but he had the feeling, so common in today's universe, that he was looking into some kind of optical illusion and that his eyes were just playing silly buggers with him.

Was there a bird of some kind in there? Was that what they had hidden away up here on a concealed floor behind darkened, rocket-proof glass? Someone's aviary? There was certainly something flapping about in there, but it seemed like not so much a bird, more a kind of bird-shaped hole in space.

He closed his eyes, which he'd been wanting to do for a bit anyway. He wondered what the hell to do next. Jump? Climb? He didn't think there was going to be any way of breaking in. Okay, the supposedly rocket-proof glass hadn't stood up, when it came to it, to an actual rocket, but then that had been a rocket that had been fired at very short range from inside, which probably wasn't what the engineers who designed it had had in mind. It didn't mean he was going to be able to break the window here by wrapping his fist in his towel and punching. What the hell, he tried it anyway and hurt his fist. It was just as well he couldn't get a good swing from where he was sitting or he might have hurt it quite badly. The building had been sturdily reinforced when it was completely rebuilt after the Frogstar attack and was probably the most heavily armored publishing company in the business, but there was always, he thought, some weakness in any system designed by a corporate committee. He had already found one of them. The engineers who designed the windows had not expected them to be hit by a rocket from short range from the inside, so the window had failed.

So, what would the engineers not be expecting someone sitting on the ledge outside the window to do?

He wracked his brains for a moment or so before he got it.

The thing they wouldn't be expecting him to do was to be there in the first place. Only an absolute idiot would be sitting where he was, so he was winning already. A common mistake that people make when trying to design something completely foolproof was to underestimate the ingenuity of complete fools.

He pulled his newly acquired credit card from his pocket, slid it into the crack where the window met its surrounding frame and did something a rocket would not have been able to do. He wiggled it around a bit. He felt a catch slip. He slid the window open and almost fell backward off the ledge laughing, giving thanks as he did so for the Great Ventilation and Telephone Riots of SrDt 3454.

The Great Ventilation and Telephone Riots of SrDt 3454 had started off as just a lot of hot air. Hot air was, of course, the problem that ventilation was supposed to solve and generally it had solved the problem reasonably well up to the point that someone invented air-conditioning, which solved the problem far more throbbingly.

And that was all well and good, provided you could stand the noise and the dribbling until someone else came up with something even sexier and smarter than air-conditioning, which was called in-building climate control.

Now this was quite something.

The major differences from just ordinary air-conditioning were that it was thrillingly more expensive, and involved a huge amount of sophisticated measuring and regulating equipment which was far better at knowing, moment by moment, what kind of air people wanted to breathe than mere people did.

It also meant that, to be sure that mere people didn't muck up the sophisticated calculations which the system was making on their behalf, all the windows in the buildings were built sealed shut. This is true.

While the systems were being installed, a number of the people who were going to work in the buildings found themselves having conversations with Breathe-O-Smart systems fitters which went something like this:

"But what if we want to have the windows open?"

"You won't want to have the windows open with new Breathe-O-Smart."

"Yes, but supposing we just wanted to have them open even for a little bit?"

"You won't want to have them open even for a little bit. The new Breathe-O-Smart system will see to that."

"Hmmm."

"Enjoy Breathe-O-Smart!"

"Okay, so what if the Breathe-O-Smart breaks down or goes wrong or something?"

"Ah! One of the smartest features of the Breathe-O-Smart is that it cannot possibly go wrong. So. No worries on that score. Enjoy your breathing now, and have a nice day."

(It was, of course, as a result of the Great Ventilation and Telephone Riots of SrDt 3454, that all mechanical or electrical or quantum-mechanical or hydraulic or even wind-, steam- or piston-driven devices, are now required to have a certain legend emblazoned on them somewhere. It doesn't matter how small the object is, the designers of the object have got to find a way of squeezing the legend in somewhere, because it is their attention that is being drawn to it rather than necessarily that of the user's.

The legend is this:

"The major difference between a thing that might go wrong and a thing that cannot possibly go wrong is that when a thing that cannot possibly go wrong goes wrong it usually turns out to be impossible to get at or repair.")

Major heat waves started to coincide, with almost magical precision, with major failures of the Breathe-O-Smart systems. To begin with, this merely caused simmering resentment and only a few deaths from asphyxiation.

The real horror erupted on the day that three events happened simultaneously. The first event was that Breathe-O-Smart Inc. issued a statement to the effect that best results were achieved by using their systems in temperate climates.

The second event was the breakdown of a Breathe-O-Smart system on a particularly hot and humid day, with the resulting evacuation of many hundreds of office staff into the street where they met the third event, which was a rampaging mob of long-distance telephone operators who had got so twisted with having to say, all day and every day, "Thank you for using BS&S" to every single idiot who picked up a phone that they had finally taken to the streets with trash cans, megaphones and rifles.

In the ensuing days of carnage every single window in the city, rocket-proof or not, was smashed, usually to accompanying cries of "Get off the line, asshole! I don't care what number you want, what extension you're calling from. Go and stick a firework up your bottom! Yeeehaah! Hoo Hoo Hoo! Velooooom! Squawk!" and a variety of other animal noises that they didn't get a chance to practice in the normal line of their work.

As a result of this, all telephone operators were granted a constitutional right to say "Use BS&S and die!" at least once an hour when answering the phone and all office buildings were required to have windows that opened, even if only a little bit.

Another, unexpected result was a dramatic lowering of the suicide rate. All sorts of stressed and rising executives who had been forced, during the dark days of the Breathe-O-Smart tyranny, to jump in front of trains or stab themselves could now just clamber out onto their own window ledges and leap off at their leisure. What frequently happened, though, was that in the moment or two they had to look around and gather their thoughts they would suddenly discover that all they had really needed was a breath of air and a fresh perspective on things, and maybe also a farm on which they could keep a few sheep.

Another completely unlooked for result was that Ford Prefect, stranded thirteen stories up a heavily armored building armed with nothing but a towel and a credit card, was nevertheless able to clamber through a supposedly rocket-proof window to safety.

He closed the window neatly after him, having first allowed Colin to follow him through, and then started to look around for this bird thing.

The thing he realized about the windows was this: because they had been converted into openable windows *after* they had first been designed to be impregnable, they were, in fact, much less secure than if they had been designed as openable windows in the first place.

Hey ho, it's a funny old life, he was just thinking to himself, when he suddenly realized that the room he had gone to all this trouble to break into was not a very interesting one.

He stopped in surprise.

Where was the strange flapping shape? Where was anything that was worth all this palaver—the extraordinary veil of secrecy that seemed to lie over this room and the equally extraordinary sequence of events that had seemed to conspire to get him into it?

The room, like every other room in this building now, was done out in some appallingly tasteful gray. There were a few charts and drawings on the wall. Most of them were meaningless to Ford, but then he came across something that was obviously a mock-up for a poster of some kind.

There was a kind of birdlike logo on it and a slogan which said, "*The Hitchhiker's Guide to the Galaxy* Mk II: the single most astounding thing of any kind ever. Coming soon to a dimension near you." No more information than that.

Ford looked around again. Then his attention was gradually drawn to Colin, the absurdly over-happy security robot, who was cowering in a corner of the room gibbering with what seemed strangely like fear.

Odd, thought Ford. He looked around to see what it was that Colin might have been reacting to. Then he saw something that he hadn't noticed before, lying quietly on top of a work bench.

It was circular and black and about the size of a small side plate. Its top and its bottom were smoothly convex so that it resembled a small lightweight throwing discus.

Its surfaces seemed to be completely smooth, unbroken and featureless.

It was doing nothing.

Then Ford noticed that there was something written on it. Strange. There hadn't been anything written on it a moment ago and now suddenly there was. There just didn't seem to have been any observable transition between the two states.

All it said, in small, alarming letters, was a single word:
Panic.

A moment ago there hadn't been any marks or cracks in its surface. Now there were. They were growing.

Panic, the *Guide* Mk II said. Ford began to do as he was told. He had just remembered why the sluglike creatures looked familiar. Their color scheme was a kind of corporate gray, but in all other respects they looked exactly like Vogons.

Chapter 13

T

he ship dropped quietly to land on the edge of the wide clearing, a hundred yards or so from the village.

It arrived suddenly and unexpectedly but with a minimum of fuss. One moment it was a perfectly ordinary late afternoon in the early autumn—the leaves were just beginning to turn red and gold, the river was beginning to swell again with the rains from the mountains in the north, the plumage of the pikka birds was beginning to thicken in anticipation of the coming winter frosts, any day now the Perfectly Normal Beasts would start their thunderous migration across the plains, and Old Thrashbarg was beginning to mutter to himself as he hobbled his way around the village, a muttering which meant that he was rehearsing and elaborating the stories that he would tell of the past year once the evenings had drawn in and people had no choice but to gather around the fire and listen to him and grumble and say that that wasn't how they remembered it—and the next moment there was a spaceship sitting there, gleaming in the warm autumn sun.

It hummed for a bit and then stopped.

It wasn't a big spaceship. If the villagers had been experts on spaceships they would have known at once that it was a pretty nifty one, a small, sleek Hrundi four-berth runabout with just about every optional extra in the brochure except Advanced Vectoid Stabilisis, which only wimps went for. You can't get a good tight, sharp curve around a trilateral time axis with Advanced Vectoid Stabilisis. All right, it's a bit safer, but it makes the handling go all soggy.

The villagers didn't know all that, of course. Most of them here on the remote planet of Lamuella had never seen a spaceship, certainly not one that was all in one piece, and as it shone warmly in the evening light it was just the most extraordinary thing they had come across since the day Kirp caught a fish with a head at both ends.

Everybody had fallen silent.

Whereas a moment before two or three dozen people had been wandering about, chattering, chopping wood, carrying water, teasing the pikka birds or just amiably trying to stay out of Old Thrashbarg's way, suddenly all activity died away and everybody turned to look at the strange object in amazement.

Or, not quite everybody. The pikka birds tended to be amazed by completely different things. A perfectly ordinary leaf lying unexpectedly on a stone would cause them to skitter off in paroxysms of confusion; sunrise always took them completely by surprise every morning, but the arrival of an alien craft from another world simply failed to engage any part of their attention. They continued to *kar* and *rit* and *huk* as they pecked for seeds on the ground; the river continued with its quiet, spacious burbling.

Also, the noise of loud and tuneless singing from the last hut on the left continued unabated.

Suddenly, with a slight click and a hum, a door folded itself outward and downward from the spaceship. Then, for a minute or two, nothing further seemed to happen, other than the loud singing from the last hut on the left, and the thing just sat there.

Some of the villagers, particularly the boys, began to edge forward a little bit to have a closer look. Old Thrashbarg tried to shoo them back. This was exactly the sort of thing that Old Thrashbarg didn't like to have happening. He hadn't foretold it, not even slightly, and even though he would be able to wrestle the whole thing into his continuing story somehow or other, it really was all getting a bit much to deal with.

He strode forward, pushed the boys back and raised his arms and his ancient knobbly staff into the air. The long warm light of the evening sun caught him nicely. He prepared to welcome whatever gods these were as if he had been expecting them all along.

Still nothing happened.

Gradually it became clear that there was some kind of argument going on inside the craft. Time went by and Old Thrashbarg's arms were beginning to ache.

Suddenly the ramp folded itself back up again.

That made it easy for Thrashbarg. They were demons and he had repulsed them. The reason he hadn't foretold it was that prudence and modesty forbade.

Almost immediately a different ramp folded itself out on the other side of the craft from where Thrashbarg was standing, and two figures at last emerged on it, still arguing with each other and ignoring everybody, even Thrashbarg, whom they wouldn't even have noticed from where they were standing.

Old Thrashbarg chewed angrily on his beard.

To continue to stand there with his arms upraised? To kneel with his head bowed forward and his staff held out pointing at them? To fall backward as if overcome in some titanic inner struggle? Perhaps just to go off to the woods and live in a tree for a year without speaking to anyone?

He opted just to drop his arms smartly as if he had done what he meant to do. They were really hurting, so he didn't have much choice. He made a small, secret sign he had just invented toward the ramp, which had closed, and then made three and a half steps backward, so he could at least get a good look at whoever these people were and then decide what to do next.

The taller one was a very good-looking woman wearing soft and crumply clothes. Old Thrashbarg didn't know this, but they were made of Rymplon™, a new synthetic fabric which was terrific for space travel because it looked its absolute best when it was all creased and sweaty.

The shorter one was a girl. She was awkward and sullen looking and was wearing clothes which looked their absolute worst when they were all creased and sweaty, and what was more, she almost certainly knew it.

All eyes watched them, except for the pikka birds, which had their own things to watch.

The woman stood and looked around her. She had a purposeful air about her. There was obviously something in particular she wanted, but she didn't know exactly where to find it. She glanced from face to face among the villagers assembled curiously around her without apparently seeing what she was looking for.

Thrashbarg had no idea how to play this at all and decided to resort to chanting. He threw back his head and began to wail, but was instantly interrupted by a fresh outbreak of song from the hut of the Sandwich Maker: the last one on the left. The woman looked around sharply, and gradually a smile came over her face. Without so much as a glance at Old Thrashbarg, she started to walk toward the hut.

There is an art to the business of making sandwiches which it is given to few ever to find the time to explore in depth. It is a simple task, but the opportunities for satisfaction are many and profound: choosing the right bread, for instance. The Sandwich Maker had spent many months in daily consultation and experiment with Grarp the Baker and eventually they had created a loaf of exactly the consistency that was dense enough to slice thinly and neatly, while still being light, moist and having the best of that fine nutty flavor which best enhanced the savor of roast Perfectly Normal Beast flesh.

There was also the geometry of the slice to be refined: the precise relationships between the width and height of the slice and also its thickness which would give the proper sense of bulk and weight to the finished sandwich—here again, lightness was a virtue, but so too were firmness, generosity and that promise of succulence and savor that is the hallmark of a truly intense sandwich experience.

The proper tools, of course, were crucial, and many were the days that the Sandwich Maker, when not engaged with the Baker at his oven, would spend with Strinder the Tool Maker, weighing and balancing knives, taking them to the forge and back again. Suppleness, strength, keenness of edge, length and balance were all enthusiastically debated, theories put forward, tested, refined, and many was the evening when the Sandwich Maker and the Tool Maker could be seen silhouetted against the light of the setting sun and the Tool Maker's forge making slow sweeping movements through the air, trying one knife after another, comparing the weight of this one with the balance of another, the suppleness of a third and the handle binding of a fourth.

Three knives altogether were required. First, there was the knife for the slicing of the bread: a firm, authoritative blade, which imposed a clear and defining will on a loaf. Then there was the butter-spreading knife, which was a whippy little number but still with a firm backbone to it. Early versions had been a little too whippy, but now the combination of flexibility with a core of strength was exactly right to achieve the maximum smoothness and grace of spread.

The chief among the knives, of course, was the carving knife. This was the knife that would not merely impose its will on the medium through which it moved, as did the bread knife. It must work with it, be guided by the grain of the meat, to achieve slices of the most exquisite consistency and translucency, that would slide away in filmy folds from the main hunk of meat. The Sandwich Maker would then flip each sheet with a smooth flick of the wrist onto the beautifully proportioned lower bread slice, trim it with four deft strokes and then at last perform the magic that the children of the village so longed to gather round and watch with rapt attention and wonder. With just four more dexterous flips of the knife he would assemble the trimmings into a perfectly fitting jigsaw of pieces on top of the primary slice. For every sandwich the size and shape of the trimmings were different, but the Sandwich Maker would always effortlessly and without hesitation assemble them into a pattern which fitted perfectly. A second layer of meat and a second layer of trimmings, and the main act of creation would now be accomplished.

The Sandwich Maker would pass what he had made to his assistant, who would then add a few slices of newcumber and fladish and a touch of splagberry sauce, and then apply the topmost layer of bread and cut the sandwich with a fourth and altogether plainer knife. It was not that these were not also skillful operations, but they were lesser skills to be performed by a dedicated apprentice who would one day, when the Sandwich Maker finally laid down his tools, take over from him. It was an exalted position and that apprentice, Drimple, was the envy of his fellows. There were those in the village who were happy chopping wood, those who were content carrying water, but to be the Sandwich Maker was very heaven.

And so the Sandwich Maker sang as he worked.

He was using the last of the year's salted meat. It was a little past its best now, but still the rich savor of Perfectly Normal Beast meat was something unsurpassed in any of the Sandwich Maker's previous experience. Next week it was anticipated that the Perfectly Normal Beasts would appear again for their regular migration, whereupon the whole village would once again be plunged into frenetic action: hunting the Beasts, killing perhaps six, maybe even seven dozen of the thousands that thundered past. Then the Beasts must be rapidly butchered and cleaned, most of the meat salted to keep it through the winter months until the return migration in the spring, which would replenish their supplies.

The very best of the meat would be roasted straight away for the feast that marked the Autumn Passage. The celebrations would last for three days of sheer exuberance, dancing and stories that Old Thrashbarg would tell of how the hunt had gone, stories that he would have been busy sitting making up in his hut while the rest of the village was out doing the actual hunting.

And then the very, very best of the meat would be saved from the feast and delivered cold to the Sandwich Maker. And the Sandwich Maker would exercise on it the skills that he had brought to them from the gods, and make the exquisite Sandwiches of the Third Season, of which the whole village would partake before beginning, the next day, to prepare themselves for the rigors of the coming winter.

Today he was just making ordinary sandwiches, if such delicacies, so lovingly crafted, could ever be called ordinary. Today his assistant was away so the Sandwich Maker was applying his own garnish, which he was happy to do. He was happy with just about everything in fact.

He sliced, he sang. He flipped each slice of meat neatly onto a slice of bread, trimmed it and assembled all the trimmings into their jigsaw. A little salad, a little sauce, another slice of bread, another sandwich, another verse of "Yellow Submarine."

"Hello, Arthur."

The Sandwich Maker almost sliced his thumb off.

The villagers had watched in consternation as the woman had marched boldly to the hut of the Sandwich Maker. The Sandwich Maker had been sent to them by Almighty Bob in a burning fiery chariot. This, at least, was what Thrashbarg said, and Thrashbarg was the authority on these things. So, at least, Thrashbarg claimed, and Thrashbarg was . . . and so on and so on. It was hardly worth arguing about.

A few villagers wondered why Almighty Bob would send his only begotten Sandwich Maker in a burning fiery chariot rather than perhaps in one that might have landed quietly without destroying half the forest, filling it with ghosts and also injuring the Sandwich Maker quite badly. Old Thrashbarg said that it was the ineffable will of Bob, and when they asked him what "ineffable" meant, he said look it up.

This was a problem because Old Thrashbarg had the only dictionary and he wouldn't let them borrow it. They asked him why not and he said that it was not for them to know the will of Almighty Bob, and when they asked him why not again, he said because he said so. Anyway, somebody sneaked into Old Thrashbarg's hut one day while he was out having a swim and looked up "ineffable." "Ineffable" apparently meant "unknowable, indescribable, unutterable, not to be known or spoken about." So that cleared that up.

At least they had got the sandwiches.

One day Old Thrashbarg said that Almighty Bob had decreed that he, Thrashbarg, was to have first pick of the sandwiches. The villagers asked him when this had happened, exactly, and Thrashbarg said it had happened yesterday, when they weren't looking. "Have faith," Old Thrashbarg said, "or burn!"

They let him have first pick of the sandwiches. It seemed easiest.

And now this woman had just arrived out of nowhere and gone straight for the Sandwich Maker's hut. His fame had obviously spread, though it was hard to know where to since, according to Old Thrashbarg, there wasn't anywhere else. Anyway, wherever it was she had come from, presumably somewhere ineffable, she was here now and was in the Sandwich Maker's hut. Who was she? And who was the strange girl who was hanging around outside the hut moodily and kicking at stones and showing every sign of not wanting to be there? It seemed odd that someone should come all the way from somewhere ineffable in a chariot that was obviously a vast improvement on the burning fiery one that had brought them the Sandwich Maker, if she didn't even want to be here.

They all looked to Thrashbarg, but he was on his knees mumbling and looking very firmly up into the sky and not catching anybody else's eye until he'd thought of something.

"Trillian!" said the Sandwich Maker, sucking his bleeding thumb. "What . . . ? Who . . . ? When . . . ? Where . . . ?"

"Exactly the questions I was going to ask you," said Trillian, looking around Arthur's hut. It was neatly laid out with his kitchen utensils. There were some fairly basic cupboards and shelves, and a basic bed in the corner. A door at the back of the room led to something that Trillian couldn't see because the door was closed. "Nice," she said, but in an inquiring tone of voice. She couldn't quite make out what the setup was.

"Very nice," said Arthur. "Wonderfully nice. I don't know when I've ever been anywhere nicer. I'm happy here. They like me, I make sandwiches for them, and . . . er, well, that's it really. They like me and I make sandwiches for them."

"Sounds, er . . ."

"Idyllic," said Arthur, firmly. "It is. It really is. I don't expect you'd like it very much, but for me it's, well, it's perfect. Look, sit down, please, make yourself comfortable. Can I get you anything, er, a sandwich?"

Trillian picked up a sandwich and looked at it. She sniffed it carefully.

"Try it," said Arthur, "it's good."

Trillian took a nibble, then a bite and munched on it thoughtfully.

"It is good," she said, looking at it.

"My life's work," said Arthur, trying to sound proud and hoping he didn't sound like a complete idiot. He was used to being revered a bit and was having to go through some unexpected mental gear changes.

"What's the meat in it?" asked Trillian.

"Ah yes, that's, um, that's Perfectly Normal Beast."

"It's what?"

"Perfectly Normal Beast. It's a bit like a cow, or rather a bull. Kind of like a buffalo in fact. Large, charging sort of animal."

"So what's odd about it?"

"Nothing, it's Perfectly Normal."

"I see."

"It's just a bit odd where it comes from."

Trillian frowned, and stopped chewing.

"Where does it come from?" she said with her mouth full. She wasn't going to swallow until she knew.

"Well, it's not just a matter of where it comes from, it's also where it goes to. It's all right, it's perfectly safe to swallow. I've eaten tons of it. It's great. Very succulent. Very tender. Slightly sweet flavor with a long dark finish."

Trillian still hadn't swallowed.

"Where," she said, "does it come from, and where does it go to?"

"They come from a point just slightly to the east of the Hondo Mountains. They're the big ones behind us here, you must have seen them as you came in, and then they sweep in their thousands across the great Anhondo Plains and, er, well, that's it really. That's where they come from. That's where they go."

Trillian frowned. There was something she wasn't quite getting about this.

"I probably haven't made it quite clear," said Arthur. "When I say they come from a point to the east of the Hondo Mountains, I mean that that's where they suddenly appear. Then they sweep across the Anhondo Plains and, well, vanish really. We have about six days to catch as many of them as we can before they disappear. In the spring they do it again, only the other way around, you see."

Reluctantly, Trillian swallowed. It was either that or spit it out, and it did in fact taste pretty good.

"I see," she said, once she had reassured herself that she didn't seem to be suffering any ill effects. "And why are they called Perfectly Normal Beasts?"

"Well, I think because otherwise people might think it was a bit odd. I think Old Thrashbarg called them that. He says that they come from where they come from and they go to where they go to and that it's Bob's will and that's all there is to it."

"Who—"

"Just don't even ask."

"Well, you look well on it."

"I feel well. You look well."

"I'm well. I'm very well."

"Well, that's good."

"Yes."

"Good."

"Good."

"Nice of you to drop in."

"Thanks."

"Well," said Arthur, casting around himself. Astounding how hard it was to think of anything to say to someone after all this time.

"I expect you're wondering how I found you," said Trillian.

"Yes!" said Arthur. "I was wondering exactly that. How did you find me?"

"Well, as you may or may not know, I now work for one of the big Sub-Etha broadcasting networks that—"

"I did know that," said Arthur, suddenly remembering. "Yes, you've done very well. That's terrific. Very exciting. Well done. Must be a lot of fun."

"Exhausting."

"All that rushing around. I expect it must be, yes."

"We have access to virtually every kind of information. I found your name on the passenger list of the ship that crashed."

Arthur was astonished.

"You mean they *knew* about the crash?"

"Well, of course they knew. You don't have a whole spaceliner disappear without someone knowing about it."

"But you mean, they knew where it had happened? They knew I'd survived?"

"Yes."

"But nobody's ever been to look or search or rescue. There's been absolutely nothing."

"Well, there wouldn't be. It's a whole complicated insurance thing. They just bury the whole thing. Pretend it never happened. The insurance business is completely screwy now. You know they've reintroduced the death penalty for insurance company directors?"

"Really?" said Arthur. "No, I didn't. For what offense?"

Trillian frowned.

"What do you mean, offense?"

"I see."

Trillian gave Arthur a long look, and then, in a new tone of voice, said, "It's time for you to take responsibility, Arthur."

Arthur tried to understand this remark. He found it often took a moment or so before he saw exactly what it was that people were driving at, so he let a moment or two pass at a leisurely rate. Life was so pleasant and relaxed these days, there was time to let things sink in. He let it sink in.

He still didn't quite understand what she meant, though, so in the end he had to say so.

Trillian gave him a cool smile and then turned back to the door of the hut.

"Random?" she called. "Come in. Come and meet your father."

As the *Guide* folded itself back into a smooth, dark dish, Ford realized some pretty hectic stuff. Or at least he tried to realize it, but it was too hectic to take in all in one go. His head was hammering, his ankle was hurting, and though he didn't like to be a wimp about his ankle, he always found that intense multidimensional logic was something he understood best in the bath. He needed time to think about this. Time, a tall drink, and some kind of rich, foamy oil.

He had to get out of here. He had to get the *Guide* out of here. He didn't think they'd make it together.

He glanced wildly around the room.

Think, think, think. It had to be something simple and obvious. If he was right in his nasty lurking suspicion that he was dealing with nasty, lurking Vogons, then the more simple and obvious, the better.

Suddenly he saw what he needed.

He wouldn't try to beat the system, he would just use it. The frightening thing about the Vogons was their absolute mindless determination to do whatever mindless thing it was they were determined to do. There was never any point in trying to appeal to their reason because they didn't have one. However, if you kept your nerve you could sometimes exploit their blinkered, bludgeoning insistence on being bludgeoning and blinkered. It wasn't merely that their left hand didn't always know what their right hand was doing, so to speak; quite often their right hand had a pretty hazy notion as well.

Did he dare just post the thing to himself?

Did he dare just put it in the system and let the Vogons work out how to get the thing to him while at the same time they were busy, as they probably would be, tearing the building apart to find out where he'd hidden it?

Yes.

Feverishly, he packed it. He wrapped it. He labeled it. With a moment's pause to wonder if he was really doing the right thing, he committed the package to the building's internal mail chute.

"Colin," he said, turning to the little, hovering ball. "I am going to abandon you to your fate."

"I'm so happy," said Colin.

"Make the most of it," said Ford. "Because what I want you to do is to nursemaid that package out of the building. They'll probably incinerate you when they find you, and I won't be here to help. It will be very, very nasty for you, and that's just too bad. Got it?"

"I gurgle with pleasure," said Colin.

"Go!" said Ford.

Colin obediently dove down the mail chute in pursuit of his charge. Now Ford had only himself to worry about, but that was still quite a substantial worry. There were noises of heavy running footsteps outside the door, which he had taken the precaution of locking and shifting a large filing cabinet in front of.

He was worried that everything had gone so smoothly. Everything had fitted terribly well. He had hurtled through the day with reckless abandon and yet everything had worked out with uncanny neatness. Except for his shoe. He was bitter about his shoe. That was an account that was going to have to be settled.

With a deafening roar the door exploded inward. In the turmoil of smoke and dust he could see large, sluglike creatures hurrying through.

So everything was going well, was it? Everything was working out as if the most extraordinary luck was on his side? Well, he'd see about that.

In a spirit of scientific inquiry he hurled himself out of the window again.

Chapter 15

The first month, getting to know each other, was a little difficult.

The second month, trying to come to terms with what they'd got to know about each other in the first month, was much easier.

The third month, when the box arrived, was very tricky indeed.

At the beginning, it was a problem even trying to explain what a month was. This had been a pleasantly simple matter for Arthur, here on Lamuella. The days were just a little over twenty-five hours long, which basically meant an extra hour in bed *every single day* and, of course, having regularly to reset his watch, which Arthur rather enjoyed doing.

He also felt at home with the number of suns and moons which Lamuella had—one of each—as opposed to some of the planets he'd fetched up from time to time which had had ridiculous numbers of them.

The planet orbited its single sun every three hundred days, which was a good number because it meant the year didn't drag by. The moon orbited Lamuella just over nine times a year, which meant that a month was a little over thirty days, which was absolutely perfect because it gave you a little more time to get things done in. It was not merely reassuringly like Earth, it was actually rather an improvement.

Random, on the other hand, thought she was trapped in a recurring nightmare. She would have crying fits and think the moon was out to get her. Every night it was there, and then, when it went, the sun came out and followed her. *Over and over again.*

Trillian had warned Arthur that Random might have some difficulty in adjusting to a more regular lifestyle than she had been used to up till now, but Arthur hadn't been ready for actual howling at the moon.

He hadn't been ready for any of this of course.

His daughter?

His daughter? He and Trillian had never even—had they? He was absolutely convinced he would have remembered. What about Zaphod?

"Not the same species, Arthur," Trillian had answered. "When I decided I wanted a child they ran all sorts of genetic tests on me and could find only one match anywhere. It was only later that it dawned on me. I double-checked and I was right. They don't usually like to tell you, but I insisted."

"You mean you went to a DNA bank?" Arthur had asked, pop-eyed.

"Yes. But she wasn't quite as random as her name suggests, because, of course, you were the only *homo sapiens* donor. I must say, though, it seems you were quite a frequent flyer."

Arthur had stared wide-eyed at the unhappy-looking girl who was slouching awkwardly in the door frame looking at him.

"But when . . . how long . . . ?"

"You mean, what age is she?"

"Yes."

"The wrong one."

"What do you mean?"

"I mean that I haven't any idea."

"*What?*"

"Well, in my time line I think it's about ten years since I had her, but she's obviously quite a lot older than that. I spend my life going backward and forward in time, you see. The job. I used to take her with me when I could, but it just wasn't always possible. Then I used to put her into day-care time zones, but you just can't get reliable time tracking now. You leave them there in the morning, you've simply no idea how old they'll be in the evening. You complain till you're blue in the face but it doesn't get you anywhere. I left her at one of the places for a few hours once, and when I came back she'd passed puberty. I've done all I can, Arthur, it's over to you. I've got a war to cover."

The ten seconds that passed after Trillian left were about the longest of Arthur Dent's life. Time, we know, is relative. You can travel light years through the stars and back, and if you do it at the speed of light then, when you return, you may have aged mere seconds while your twin brother or sister will have aged twenty, thirty, forty or however many years it is, depending on how far you traveled.

This will come to you as a profound personal shock, particularly if you didn't know you had a twin brother or sister. The seconds that you have been absent for will not have been sufficient time to prepare you for the shock of new and strangely distended family relationships when you return.

Ten seconds' silence was not enough time for Arthur to reassemble his whole view of himself and his life in a way that suddenly included an entire new daughter of whose merest existence he had not the slightest inkling of a suspicion when he had woken that morning. Deep, emotional family ties cannot be constructed in ten seconds, however far and fast you travel away from them, and Arthur could only feel hopeless, bewildered and numb as he looked at the girl standing in his doorway, staring at his floor.

He supposed that there was no point in pretending not to be hopeless.

He walked over and he hugged her.

"I don't love you," he said. "I'm sorry. I don't even know you yet. But give me a few minutes."

We live in strange times.

We also live in strange places: each in a universe of our own. The people with whom we populate our universes are the shadows of whole other universes intersecting with our own. Being able to glance out into this bewildering complexity of infinite recursion and say things like, "Oh, hi, Ed! Nice tan. How's Carol?" involves a great deal of filtering skill for which all conscious entities have eventually to develop a capacity in order to protect themselves from the contemplation of the chaos through which they seethe and tumble. So give your kid a break, okay?

Extract from *Practical Parenting in a Fractally Demented Universe*

"What's this?"

Arthur had almost given up. That is to say, he was not going to give up. He was absolutely not going to give up. Not now. Not ever. But if he had been the sort of person who was going to give up, this was probably the time he would have done it.

Not content with being surly, bad tempered, wanting to go and play in the Paleozoic era, not seeing why they had to have the gravity on the whole time and shouting at the sun to stop following her, Random had also used his carving knife to dig up stones to throw at the pikka birds for looking at her like that.

Arthur didn't even know if Lamuella had had a Paleozoic era. According to Old Thrashbarg, the planet had been found fully formed in the navel of a giant earwig at four-thirty one Vroonday afternoon, and although Arthur, as a seasoned Galactic traveler with good O-level passes in physics and geography, had fairly serious doubts about this, it was rather a waste of time trying to argue with Old Thrashbarg and there had never been much point before.

He sighed as he sat nursing the chipped and bent knife. He was going to love her if it killed him, or her, or both. It wasn't easy being a father. He knew that no one had ever said it was going to be easy, but that wasn't the point because he'd never asked about being one in the first place.

He was doing his best. Every moment that he could wrest away from making sandwiches he was spending with her, talking to her, walking with her, sitting on the hill with her watching the sun go down over the valley in which the village nestled, trying to find out about her life, trying to explain to her about his. It was a tricky business. The common ground between them, apart from the fact that they had almost identical genes, was about the size of a pebble. Or rather, it was about the size of Trillian and of her they had slightly differing views.

"What's this?"

He suddenly realized she had been talking to him and he hadn't noticed. Or rather, he had not recognized her voice.

Instead of the usual tone of voice in which she spoke to him, which was bitter and truculent, she was just asking him a simple question.

He looked around in surprise.

She was sitting there on a stool in the corner of the hut in that rather hunched way she had, knees together, feet splayed out, with her dark hair hanging down over her face as she looked at something she had cradled in her hands.

Arthur went over to her, a little nervously.

Her mood swings were very unpredictable but so far they'd all been between different types of bad ones. Outbreaks of bitter recrimination would give way without warning to abject self-pity and then long bouts of sullen despair which were punctuated with sudden acts of mindless violence against inanimate objects and demands to go to electric clubs.

Not only were there no electric clubs on Lamuella, there were no clubs at all and, in fact, no electricity. There was a forge and a bakery, a few carts and a well, but those were the high watermark of Lamuel-

lan technology, and a fair number of Random's unquenchable rages
were directed against the sheer incomprehensible backwardness of the
place.

She could pick up Sub-Etha TV on a small Flex-O-Panel which had
been surgically implanted in her wrist, but that didn't cheer her up at
all because it was full of news of insanely exciting things happening in
every other part of the Galaxy than here. It would also give her frequent news of her mother, who had dumped her to go off and cover
some war which now seemed not to have happened, or at least to have
gone all wrong in some way because of the absence of any proper
intelligence gathering. It also gave her access to lots of great adventure
shows featuring all sorts of fantastically expensive spaceships crashing
into each other.

The villagers were absolutely hypnotized by all these wonderful
magic images flashing over her wrist. They had only ever seen one
spaceship crash, and it had been so frightening, violent and shocking
and had caused so much horrible devastation, fire and death that,
stupidly, they had never realized it was entertainment.

Old Thrashbarg had been so astonished by it that he had instantly
seen Random as an emissary from Bob, but had fairly soon afterward
decided that in fact she had been sent as a test of his faith, if not of his
patience. He was also alarmed at the number of spaceship crashes he
had to start incorporating into his holy stories if he was to hold the
attention of the villagers, and not have them rushing off to peer at
Random's wrist all the time.

At the moment she was not peering at her wrist. Her wrist was
turned off. Arthur squatted down quietly beside her to see what she
was looking at.

It was his watch. He had taken it off when he'd gone to shower
under the local waterfall, and Random had found it and was trying to
work it out.

"It's just a watch," he said. "It's to tell the time."

"I know that," she said. "But you keep on fiddling with it, and it
still doesn't tell the right time. Or even anything like it."

She brought up the display on her wrist panel, which automatically
produced a readout of local time. Her wrist panel had quietly got on
with the business of measuring the local gravity and orbital momentum, and had noticed where the sun was and tracked its movement in
the sky, all within the first few minutes of Random's arrival. It had

then quickly picked up clues from its environment as to what the local unit conventions were and reset itself appropriately. It did this sort of thing continually, which was particularly valuable if you did a lot of traveling in time as well as space.

Random frowned at her father's watch, which didn't do any of this.

Arthur was very fond of it. It was a better one than he would ever have afforded himself. He had been given it on his twenty-second birthday by a rich and guilt-ridden godfather who had forgotten every single birthday he had had up till then, and also his name. It had the day, the date, the phases of the moon; it had "To Albert on his twenty-first birthday" and the wrong date engraved on the battered and scratched surface of its back in letters that were still just about visible.

The watch had been through a considerable amount of stuff in the last few years, most of which would fall well outside the warranty. He didn't suppose, of course, that the warranty had especially mentioned that the watch was guaranteed to be accurate only within the very particular gravitational and magnetic fields of the Earth, and so long as the day was twenty-four hours long and the planet didn't explode and so on. These were such basic assumptions that even the lawyers would have missed them.

Luckily his watch was a wind-up one, or at least, a self-winder. Nowhere else in the Galaxy would he have found batteries of precisely the dimensions and power specifications that were perfectly standard on Earth.

"So what are all these numbers?" asked Random.

Arthur took it from her.

"These numbers around the edge mark the hours. In the little window on the right it says THU, which means Thursday, and the number is fourteen, which means it's the fourteenth day of the month of MAY, which is what it says in this window over here.

"And this sort of crescent-shaped window at the top tells you about the phases of the moon. In other words it tells you how much of the moon is lit up at night by the sun, which depends on the relative positions of the sun and the moon and, well . . . the Earth."

"The Earth," said Random.

"Yes."

"And that's where you came from, and where Mum came from?"

"Yes."

Random took the watch back from him and looked at it again,

clearly baffled by something. Then she held it up to her ear and listened in puzzlement.

"What's that noise?"

"It's ticking. That's the mechanism that drives the watch. It's called clockwork. It's all kind of interlocking cogs and springs that work to turn the hands around at exactly the right speed to mark the hours and minutes and days and so on."

Random carried on peering at it.

"There's something puzzling you," said Arthur. "What is it?"

"Yes," said Random, at last. "Why's it all in hardware?"

Arthur suggested they go for a walk. He felt there were things they should discuss, and for once Random seemed, if not precisely amenable and willing, then at least not growling.

From Random's point of view this was also all very weird. It wasn't that she wanted to be difficult, as such, it was just that she didn't know how or what else to be.

Who was this guy? What was this life she was supposed to lead? What was this world she was supposed to lead it in? And what was this universe that kept coming at her through her eyes and ears? What was it for? What did it want?

She'd been born in a spaceship that had been going from somewhere to somewhere else, and when it had got to somewhere else, somewhere else had only turned out to be another somewhere that you had to get to somewhere else again from, and so on.

It was her normal expectation that she was supposed to be somewhere else. It was normal for her to feel that she was in the wrong place.

Then, constant time travel had only compounded this problem and had led to the feeling that she was not only always in the wrong place, but she was also almost always there at the wrong time.

She didn't notice that she felt this, because it was the only way she ever felt, just as it never seemed odd to her that nearly everywhere she went she needed either to wear weights or antigravity suits and usually special apparatus for breathing as well. The only places you could ever feel were right were worlds you designed for yourself to inhabit— virtual realities in the electric clubs. It had never occurred to her that the real Universe was something you could actually fit into.

And that included this Lamuella place her mother had dumped her in. And it also included this person who had bestowed on her this precious and magical gift of life in return for a seat upgrade. It was just as well he had turned out to be rather kind and friendly or there would have been trouble. Really. She'd got a specially sharpened stone in her pocket she could cause a lot of trouble with.

It can be very dangerous to see things from somebody else's point of view without the proper training.

They sat on the spot that Arthur particularly liked, on the side of a hill overlooking the valley. The sun was going down over the village.

The only thing that Arthur wasn't quite so fond of was being able to see a little way into the next valley, where a deep, dark, mangled furrow in the forest marked the spot where his ship had crashed. But maybe that was what kept bringing him back here. There were plenty of spots from which you could survey the lush rolling countryside of Lamuella, but this was the one he was drawn to, with its nagging dark spot of fear and pain nestling just on the edge of his vision.

He had never been there again since he had been pulled out of the wreckage.

Wouldn't.

Couldn't bear it.

In fact he had gone some of the way back to it the very next day, while he was still numb and spinning with shock. He had a broken leg, a couple of broken ribs, some bad burns and was not really thinking coherently but had insisted that the villagers take him, which, uneasily, they had. He had not managed to get right to the actual spot where the ground had bubbled and melted, however, and had at last hobbled away from the horror forever.

Soon, word had got around that the whole area was haunted and no one had ventured back there ever since. The land was full of beautiful, verdant and delightful valleys—no point in going to a highly worrying one. Let the past hold on to itself and let the present move forward into the future.

Random cradled the watch in her hands, slowly turning it to let the long light of the evening sun shine warmly in the scratches and scuffs of the thick glass. It fascinated her watching the spidery little second hand ticking its way around. Every time it completed a full circle, the longer of the two main hands had moved on exactly to the next of the sixty small divisions around the dial. And when the long hand had made its own full circle, the smaller hand had moved on to the next of the main digits.

"You've been watching it for over an hour," said Arthur, quietly.

"I know," she said. "An hour is when the big hand has gone all the way around, yes?"

"That's right."

"Then I've been watching it for an hour and seventeen . . . minutes."

She smiled with a deep and mysterious pleasure and moved very slightly so that she was resting just a little against his arm. Arthur felt that a small sigh escaped from him that had been pent up inside his chest for weeks. He wanted to put his arm around his daughter's shoulders, but felt it was too early yet and that she would shy away from him. But something was working. Something was easing inside her. The watch meant something to her that nothing in her life had so far managed to do. Arthur was not sure that he had really understood what it was yet, but he was profoundly pleased and relieved that something had reached her.

"Explain to me again," said Random.

"There's nothing really to it," said Arthur. "Clockwork was something that developed over hundreds of years—"

"Earth years."

"Yes. It became finer and finer and more and more intricate. It was highly skilled and delicate work. It had to be made very small, and it had to carry on working accurately however much you waved it around or dropped it."

"But only on one planet?"

"Well, that was where it was made, you see. It was never expected to go anywhere else and deal with different suns and moons and magnetic fields and things. I mean the thing still *goes* perfectly well, but it doesn't really mean much this far from Switzerland."

"From where?"

"Switzerland. That's where these were made. Small hilly country. Tiresomely neat. The people who made them didn't really know there were other worlds."

"Quite a big thing not to know."

"Well, yes."

"So where did *they* come from?"

"They, that is we . . . we just sort of grew there. We evolved on the Earth. From, I don't know, some kind of sludge or something."

"Like this watch."

"Um. I don't think the watch grew out of sludge."

"*You don't understand!*"

Random suddenly leapt to her feet, shouting.

"You don't understand! You don't understand me, you don't understand *anything*! I *hate* you for being so stupid!"

She started to run hectically down the hill, still clutching the watch and shouting that she hated him.

Arthur jumped up, startled and at a loss. He started to run after her through the stringy and clumpy grass. It was hard and painful for him. When he had broken his leg in the crash, it had not been a clean break, and it had not healed cleanly. He was stumbling and wincing as he ran.

Suddenly she turned and faced him, her face dark with anger.

She brandished the watch at him. "You don't understand that there's somewhere this belongs? Somewhere it works? Somewhere that it *fits?*"

She turned and ran again. She was fit and fleet-footed and Arthur could not remotely keep up with her.

It wasn't that he had not expected being a father to be this difficult, it was that he hadn't expected to be a father at all, particularly not suddenly and unexpectedly on an alien planet.

Random turned to shout at him again. For some reason he stopped each time she did.

"Who do you think I am?" she demanded angrily. "Your upgrade? Who do you think Mum thought I was? Some sort of ticket to the life she didn't have?"

"I don't know what you mean by that," said Arthur, panting and hurting.

"You don't know what anybody means by anything!"

"What do you mean?"

"Shut up! Shut up! Shut *up!*"

"Tell me! Please tell me! What does she mean by saying 'the life she didn't have'?"

"She wished she'd stayed on Earth! She wished she hadn't gone off with that stupid brain-dead fruit gum, Zaphod! She thinks she would have had a different life!"

"But," said Arthur, "she would have been killed! She would have been killed when the world was destroyed!"

"That's a different life, isn't it?"

"That's . . ."

"She wouldn't have had to have me! She hates me!"

"You can't mean that! How could anyone possibly, er, I mean . . ."

"She had me because I was meant to make things fit for her. That was *my* job. But I fitted even worse than she did! So she just shut me off and carried on with her stupid life."

"What's stupid about her life? She's fantastically successful, isn't she? She's all over time and space, all over the Sub-Etha TV networks . . ."

"Stupid! Stupid! Stupid! Stupid!"

Random turned and ran off again. Arthur couldn't keep up with her and at last he had to sit down for a bit and let the pain in his leg subside. The turmoil in his head he didn't know what to do with at all.

He hobbled into the village an hour later. It was getting dark. The villagers he passed said hello, but there was a sense of nervousness and of not quite knowing what was going on or what to do about it in the air. Old Thrashbarg had been seen pulling on his beard a fair bit and looking at the moon, and that was not a good sign either.

Arthur went into his hut.

Random was sitting hunched quietly over the table.

"I'm sorry," she said. "I'm so sorry."

"That's all right," said Arthur as gently as he knew how. "It's good to, well, to have a little chat. There's so much we have to learn and understand about each other, and life isn't, well, it isn't all just tea and sandwiches . . ."

"I'm *so* sorry," she said again, sobbing.

Arthur went up to her and put his arm around her shoulder. She didn't resist or pull away. Then Arthur saw what it was she was so sorry about.

In the pool of light thrown by a Lamuellan lantern lay Arthur's watch. Random had forced the back off it with the back edge of the butter-spreading knife and all of the minute cogs and springs and levers were lying in a tiny cockeyed mess where she'd been fiddling with them.

"I just wanted to see how it worked," said Random, "how it all fitted together. I'm so sorry! I can't get it back together. I'm sorry, I'm sorry, I'm sorry. I don't know what to do. I'll get it repaired! Really! I'll get it repaired!"

The following day Thrashbarg came around and said all sorts of Bob stuff. He tried to exert a calming influence by inviting Random to let her mind dwell on the ineffable mystery of the giant earwig, and Random said there was no giant earwig and Thrashbarg went very cold and silent and said she would be cast into outer darkness. Random said good, she had been born there, and the next day the parcel arrived.

This was all getting a bit eventful.

In fact, when the parcel arrived, delivered by a kind of robot drone that dropped out of the sky making droning robot noises, it brought with it a sense, which gradually began to permeate through the whole village, that it was almost one event too many.

It wasn't the robot drone's fault. All it required was Arthur Dent's signature or thumbprint, or just a few scrapings of skin cells from the nape of his neck, and it would be on its way again. It hung around waiting, not quite sure what all this resentment was about. Meanwhile, Kirp had caught another fish with a head at both ends, but on closer inspection it turned out that it was in fact two fish cut in half and sewn together rather badly, so not only had Kirp failed to rekindle any great interest in two-headed fish, but he had seriously cast doubt on the authenticity of the first one. Only the pikka birds seemed to feel that everything was exactly normal.

The robot drone got Arthur's signature and made its escape. Arthur bore the parcel back to his hut and sat and looked at it.

"Let's open it!" said Random, who was feeling much more cheerful this morning now that everything around her had got thoroughly weird, but Arthur said no.

"Why not?"

"It's not addressed to me."

"Yes it is."

"No it isn't. It's addressed to . . . well, it's addressed to Ford Prefect, in care of me."

"Ford Prefect? Is he the one who—"

"Yes," said Arthur, tartly.

"I've heard about him."

"I expect you have."

"Let's open it anyway. What else are we going to do?"

"I don't know," said Arthur, who really wasn't sure.

He had taken his damaged knives over to the forge bright and early that morning and Strinder had had a look at them and said that he would see what he could do.

They had tried the usual business of waving the knives through the air, feeling for the point of balance and the point of flex and so on, but the joy was gone from it, and Arthur had a sad feeling that his sandwich-making days were probably numbered.

He hung his head.

The next appearance of the Perfectly Normal Beasts was imminent, but Arthur felt that the usual festivities of hunting and feasting were going to be rather muted and uncertain. Something had happened here on Lamuella, and Arthur had a horrible feeling that it was him.

"What do you think it is?" urged Random, turning the parcel over in her hands.

"I don't know," said Arthur. "Something bad and worrying, though."

"How do you know?" Random protested.

"Because anything that's to do with Ford Prefect is bound to be worse and more worrying than something that isn't," said Arthur. "Believe me."

"You're upset about something, aren't you?" said Random.

Arthur sighed.

"I'm just feeling a little jumpy and unsettled, I think," said Arthur.

"I'm sorry," said Random, and put the package down again. She could see that it really would upset him if she opened it. She would just have to do it when he wasn't looking.

Arthur wasn't quite certain which he noticed as being missing first. When he noticed that the one wasn't there, his mind instantly leapt to the other and he knew immediately that they were both gone and that something insanely bad and difficult to deal with would happen as a result.

Random was not there. And neither was the parcel.

He had left it up on a shelf all day, in plain view. It was an exercise in trust.

He knew that one of the things he was supposed to do as a parent was to show trust in his child, to build a sense of trust and confidence into the bedrock of relationship between them. He had had a nasty feeling that that might be an idiotic thing to do, but he did it anyway, and sure enough it had turned out to be an idiotic thing to do. You live and learn. At any rate, you live.

You also panic.

Arthur ran out of the hut. It was the middle of the evening. The light was getting dim and a storm was brewing. He could not see her anywhere, nor any sign of her. He asked. No one had seen her. He asked again. No one else had seen her. They were going home for the night. A little wind was whipping around the edge of the village, picking things up and tossing them around in a dangerously casual manner.

He found Old Thrashbarg and asked him. Thrashbarg looked at him stonily, and then pointed in the one direction that Arthur had dreaded and had therefore instinctively known was the way she would have gone.

So now he knew the worst.

She had gone where she thought he would not follow her.

He looked up at the sky, which was sullen, streaked and livid, and reflected that it was the sort of sky that the Four Horsemen of the Apocalypse wouldn't feel like a bunch of complete idiots riding out of.

With a heavy sense of the utmost foreboding he set off on the track that led to the forest in the next valley. The first heavy blobs of rain began to hit the ground as Arthur tried to drag himself to some sort of run.

Random reached the crest of the hill and looked down into the next valley. It had been a longer and harder climb than she had anticipated. She was a little worried that doing the trip at night was not that great an idea, but her father had been mooching around near the hut all day trying to pretend to either her or himself that he wasn't guarding the parcel. At last he'd had to go over to the forge to talk with Strinder about the knives, and Random had seized her opportunity and done a runner with the parcel.

It was perfectly clear that she couldn't just open the thing there, in the hut, or even in the village. He might have come across her at any moment. Which meant that she had to go where she wouldn't be followed.

She could stop where she was now. She had gone this way in the hope that he wouldn't follow her, and even if he did he would never find her up in the wooded parts of the hill with night drawing in and the rain starting.

All the way up, the parcel had been jiggling under her arm. It was a satisfyingly hunky sort of thing: a box with a square top about the length of her forearm on each side, and about the length of her hand deep, wrapped up in brown plasper with an ingenious new form of self-knotting string. It didn't rattle as she shook it, but she sensed that its weight was concentrated excitingly at the center.

Having come so far, though, there was a certain satisfaction in not stopping here, but carrying on down into what seemed to be almost a forbidden area—where her father's ship had come down. She wasn't exactly certain what the word "haunted" meant, but it might be fun to find out. She would keep going and save the parcel for when she got there.

It was getting darker, though. She hadn't used her tiny electric torch yet, because she didn't want to be visible from a distance. She would have to use it now, but it probably didn't matter now, since she would be on the other side of the hill that divided the valleys from each other.

She turned her torch on. Almost at the same moment a fork of lightning ripped across the valley into which she was heading and startled her considerably. As the darkness shuddered back around her and a clap of thunder rolled out across the land, she felt suddenly rather small and lost with just a feeble pencil of light bobbing in her hand. Perhaps she should stop after all and open the parcel here. Or maybe she should go back and come out again tomorrow. It was only a momentary hesitation, though. She knew there was no going back tonight and sensed that there was no going back ever.

She headed on down the side of the hill. The rain was beginning to pick up now. Where a short while ago it had been a few heavy blobs, it was settling in for a good pour now, hissing in the trees, and the ground was getting slippery under her feet.

At least, she thought, it was the rain hissing in the trees. Shadows were leaping and leering at her as her light bobbed through the trees. Onward and downward.

She hurried on for another ten or fifteen minutes, soaked to the skin now and shivering, and gradually became aware that there seemed to be some other light somewhere ahead of her. It was very faint and she wasn't certain if she was imagining it or not. She turned off her torch to see. There did seem to be some sort of dim glow ahead. She couldn't tell what it was. She turned her torch back on and continued down the hill, toward whatever it was.

There was something wrong with the woods, though.

She couldn't immediately say what it was, but they didn't seem like sprightly healthy woods looking forward to a good spring. The trees were lolling at sickly angles and had a sort of pallid, blighted look about them. Random more than once had the worrying sensation that they were trying to reach toward her as she passed them, but it was just a trick of the way that her light caused their shadows to flicker and lurch.

Suddenly, something fell out of a tree in front of her. She leapt backward with alarm, dropping both the torch and the box as she did so. She went down into a crouch, pulling the specially sharpened rock out of her pocket.

The thing that had fallen out of the tree was moving. The torch was lying on the ground and pointing toward it, and a vast, grotesque shadow was slowly lurching through the light toward her. She could hear faint rustling and screeching noises over the steady hiss of the rain. She scrabbled on the ground for the torch, found it and shone it directly at the creature.

At the same moment another dropped from a tree just a few feet away. She swung the torch wildly from one to the other. She held her rock up, ready to throw.

They were quite small in fact. It was the angle of the light that had made them loom so large. Not only small, but small, furry and cuddly. And there was another, dropping from the trees. It fell through the beam of light, so she saw it quite clearly.

It fell neatly and precisely, turned and then, like the other two, started slowly and purposefully to advance on Random.

She stayed rooted to the spot. She still had her rock poised and ready to throw, but was increasingly conscious of the fact that the things she had it poised and ready to throw at were squirrels. Or, at least, squirrellike things. Soft, warm, cuddly squirrellike things advancing on her in a way she wasn't at all certain she liked.

She shone her torch directly on the first of them. It was making aggressive, hectoring, screeching noises and carrying in one of its little fists a small tattered piece of wet, pink rag. Random hefted her rock menacingly in her hand, but it made no impression at all on the squirrel advancing on her with its wet piece of rag.

She backed away. She didn't know at all how to deal with this. If they had been vicious snarling slavering beasts with glistening fangs, she would have pitched into them with a will, but squirrels behaving like this she couldn't quite handle.

She backed away again. The second squirrel was starting to make a flanking maneuver around to her right. Carrying a cup. Some kind of acorn thing. The third was right behind it and making its own advance. What was it carrying? Some little scrap of soggy paper, Random thought.

She stepped back again, caught her ankle against the root of a tree and fell over backward.

Instantly the first squirrel darted forward and was on top of her, advancing along her stomach with cold purpose in its eyes, and a piece of wet rag in its fist.

Random tried to jump up, but only managed to jump about an inch. The startled movement of the squirrel on her stomach startled her in return. The squirrel froze, gripping her skin through her soaking shirt with its tiny claws. Then slowly, inch by inch, it made its way up her, stopped and proffered her the rag.

She felt almost hypnotized by the strangeness of the thing and its tiny glinting eyes. It proffered her the rag again. It pushed it at her repeatedly, screeching insistently, till at last, nervously, hesitantly, she took the thing from it. It continued to watch her intently, its eyes darting all over her face. She had no idea what to do. Rain and mud were streaming down her face and she had a squirrel sitting on her. She wiped some mud out of her eyes with the rag.

The squirrel shrieked triumphantly, grabbed the rag back, leapt off her and ran scampering into the dark, enclosing night, darted up into a tree, dived into a hole in the trunk, settled back and lit a cigarette.

Meanwhile Random was trying to fend off the squirrel with the acorn cup full of rain and the one with the paper. She shuffled backward on her bottom.

"No!" she shouted. "Go away!"

They darted back, in fright, and then darted right forward again with their gifts. She brandished her rock at them. "Go!" she yelled.

The squirrels scampered around in consternation. Then one darted straight at her, dropped the acorn cup in her lap, turned and ran off into the night. The other stood quivering for a moment, then put its scrap of paper neatly down in front of her and disappeared as well.

She was alone again, but trembling with confusion. She got unsteadily to her feet, picked up her rock and her parcel, then paused and picked up the scrap of paper as well. It was so soggy and dilapidated it was hard to make out what it was. It seemed just to be a fragment of an in-flight magazine.

Just as Random was trying to understand exactly what it was that this all meant, a man walked out into the clearing in which she was standing, raised a vicious-looking gun and shot her.

Arthur was thrashing around hopelessly two or three miles behind her, on the upward side of the hill.

Within minutes of setting out he had gone back again and equipped himself with a lamp. Not an electric one. The only electric light in the place was the one that Random had brought with her. This was a kind of dim hurricane lamp: a perforated metal canister from Strinder's forge, which contained a reservoir of inflammable fish oil, a wick of knotted dried grass and was wrapped in a translucent film made from dried membranes from the gut of a Perfectly Normal Beast.

It had now gone out.

Arthur jiggled around with it in a thoroughly pointless kind of a way for a few seconds. There was clearly no way he was going to get the thing suddenly to burst into flame again in the middle of a rain-storm, but it's impossible not to make a token effort. Reluctantly he threw the thing aside.

What to do? This was hopeless. He was absolutely sodden, his clothes heavy and billowing with the rain, and now he was lost in the dark as well.

For a brief second he was lost in the blinding light, and then he was lost in the dark again.

The sheet of lightning had at least shown him that he was very close to the brow of the hill. Once he had breasted that he would . . . well, he wasn't certain what he would do. He'd have to work that out when he got there.

He limped forward and upward.

A few minutes later he knew that he was standing panting at the top. There was some kind of dim glow in the distance below him. He had no idea what it was, and indeed he hardly liked to think. It was the only thing he had to make toward, though, so he started to make his way, stumbling, lost and frightened, toward it.

The flash of lethal light passed straight through Random and, about two seconds later, so did the man who had shot it. Other than that he paid her no attention whatsoever. He had shot someone standing be-hind her, and when she turned to look, he was kneeling over the body and going through its pockets.

The tableau froze and vanished. It was replaced a second later by a giant pair of teeth framed by immense and perfectly glossed red lips. A huge blue brush appeared out of nowhere and started, foamily, to scrub at the teeth, which continued to hang there gleaming in the shimmering curtain of rain.

Random blinked at it twice before she got it.

It was a commercial. The guy who had shot her was part of a holographic in-flight movie. She must now be very close to where the ship had crashed. Obviously some of its systems were more indestruc-tible than others.

The next half-mile of the journey was particularly troublesome. Not only did she have the cold and the rain and the night to contend with, but also the fractured and thrashing remains of the ship's on-board entertainment system. Spaceships and jetcars and helipods crashed and exploded continuously around her, illuminating the night, villainous people in strange hats smuggled dangerous drugs through her, and the combined orchestra and chorus of the Hallapolis State Opera performed the closing March of the AnjaQantine Star Guard from Act IV of Rizgar's *Blamwellamum of Woont* in a little glade somewhere off to her left.

And then she was standing on the lip of a very nasty-looking and bubbly-edged crater. There was still a faint warm glow coming from what would otherwise have looked like an enormous piece of caramelized chewing gum in the center of the pit: the melted remains of a great spaceship.

She stood looking at it for a longish while, and then at last started to walk along and around the edge of the crater. She was no longer certain what she was looking for, but kept moving anyway, keeping the horror of the pit to her left.

The rain was beginning to ease off a little, but it was still extremely wet, and since she didn't know what it was that was in the box, whether it was perhaps something delicate or damageable, she thought that she ought to find somewhere reasonably dry to open it. She hoped she hadn't already damaged it by dropping it.

She played her torch around the surrounding trees, which were thin on the ground here, and mostly charred and broken. In the middle distance she thought she could see a jumbled outcrop of rock that might provide some shelter, and she started to pick her way toward it. All around she found the detritus that had been ejected from the ship as it broke up, before the final fireball.

After she had moved two or three hundred yards from the edge of the crater, she came across the tattered fragments of some fluffy pink material, sodden, muddied and drooping among the broken trees. She guessed, correctly, that this must be the remains of the escape cocoon that had saved her father's life. She went and looked at it more closely, and then noticed something close to it on the ground, half-covered in mud.

She picked it up and wiped the mud off it. It was some kind of electronic device the size of a small book. Feebly glowing on its cover, in response to her touch, were some large friendly letters. They said DON'T PANIC. She knew what this was. It was her father's copy of *The Hitchhiker's Guide to the Galaxy*.

She felt instantly reassured by it, turned her head up to the thundery sky and let some rain wash over her face and into her mouth.

She shook her head and hurried on toward the rocks. Clambering up and over them, she almost immediately found the perfect thing. The mouth of a cave. She played her torch into its interior. It seemed to be dry and safe. Picking her way carefully, she walked in. It was quite spacious, but didn't go that deep. Exhausted and relieved, she sat on a convenient rock, put the box down in front of her and started immediately to open it.

For a long period of time there was much speculation and controversy about where the so-called "missing matter" of the Universe had got to. All over the Galaxy the science departments of all the major universities were acquiring more and elaborate equipment to probe and search the hearts of distant galaxies, and then the very center and the very edges of the whole Universe, but when eventually it was tracked down it turned out in fact to be all the stuff which the equipment had been packed in.

There was quite a large quantity of missing matter in the box, little soft round white pellets of missing matter, which Random discarded for future generations of physicists to track down and discover all over again once the findings of the current generation of physicists had been lost and forgotten about.

Out of the pellets of missing matter she lifted the featureless black disk. She put it down on a rock beside her and sifted among all the missing matter to see if there was anything else, a manual or some attachments or something, but there was nothing else at all. Just the black disk.

She shone the torch on it.

As she did so, cracks began to appear along its apparently featureless surface. Random backed away nervously, but then saw that the thing, whatever it was, was merely unfolding itself.

The process was wonderfully beautiful. It was extraordinarily elaborate, but also simple and elegant. It was like a piece of self-opening origami, or a rosebud blooming into a rose in just a few seconds.

Where just a few moments earlier there had been a smoothly curved black disk, there was now a bird. A bird, hovering there.

Random continued to back away from it, carefully and watchfully.

It was a little like a pikka bird, only rather smaller. That is to say, in fact it was larger, or to be more exact, precisely the same size or, at least, not less than twice the size. It was also both a lot bluer and a lot pinker than pikka birds, while at the same time being perfectly black.

There was also something very odd about it, which Random couldn't immediately make out.

It certainly shared with pikka birds the impression it gave that it was watching something that you couldn't see.

Suddenly it vanished.

Then, just as suddenly, everything went black. Random dropped into a tense crouch, feeling for the specially sharpened rock in her pocket again. Then the blackness receded and rolled itself up into a ball, and then the blackness was the bird again. It hung in the air in front of her, beating its wings slowly and staring at her.

"Excuse me," it said suddenly, "I just have to calibrate myself. Can you hear me when I say this?"

"When you say what?" demanded Random.

"Good," said the bird. "And can you hear me when I say this?" It spoke this time at a much higher pitch.

"Yes, of course I can!" said Random.

"And can you hear me when I say this?" it said, this time in a sepulchrally deep voice.

"*Yes!*"

There was then a pause.

"No, obviously not," said the bird after a few seconds. "Good, well, your hearing range is obviously between sixteen and twenty KHz. So. Is this comfortable for you?" it said in a pleasant light tenor. "No uncomfortable harmonics screeching away in the upper register? Obviously not. Good. I can use those as data channels. Now. How many of me can you see?"

Suddenly the air was full of nothing but interlocking birds. Random was well used to spending time in virtual realities, but this was something far weirder than anything she had previously encountered. It was as if the whole geometry of space was redefined in seamless bird shapes.

Random gasped and flung her arms around her face, her arms moving through bird-shaped space.

"Hmmm, obviously way too many," said the bird. "How about now?"

It concertinaed into a tunnel of birds, as if it was a bird caught between parallel mirrors, reflecting infinitely into the distance.

"What are you?" shouted Random.

"We'll come to that in a minute," said the bird. "Just how many, please?"

"Well, you're sort of . . ." Random gestured helplessly off into the distance.

"I see, still infinite in extent, but at least we're homing in on the right dimensional matrix. Good. No, the answer is an *orange* and two lemons."

"Lemons?"

"If I have three lemons and three oranges and I lose two oranges and a lemon, what do I have left?"

"Huh?"

"Okay, so you think that time flows *that* way, do you? Interesting. Am I still infinite?" it asked, ballooning this way and that in space. "Am I infinite now? How yellow am I?"

Moment by moment the bird was going through mind-mangling transformations of shape and extent.

"I can't . . ." said Random, bewildered.

"You don't have to answer, I can tell from watching you now. So. Am I your mother? Am I a rock? Do I seem huge, squishy and sinuously intertwined? No? How about now? Am I going backward?"

For once the bird was perfectly still and steady.

"No," said Random.

"Well, I was in fact, I was moving backward in time. Hmmm. Well, I think we've sorted all that out now. If you'd like to know, I can tell you that in your universe you move freely in three dimensions that you call space. You move in a straight line in a fourth, which you call time, and stay rooted to one place in a fifth, which is the first fundamental of probability. After that it gets a bit complicated, and there's all sorts of stuff going on in dimensions thirteen to twenty-two that you really wouldn't want to know about. All you really need to know for the moment is that the universe is a lot more complicated than you might think, even if you start from a position of thinking it's pretty damn complicated in the first place. I can easily not say words like 'damn' if it offends you."

"Say what you damn well like."

"I will."

"What the hell are you?" demanded Random.

"I am the *Guide*. In *your* universe I am *your Guide*. In fact I inhabit what is technically known as the Whole Sort of General Mish Mash, which means . . . well, let me show you."

It turned in midair and swooped out of the cave, and then perched on a rock, just beneath an overhang, out of the rain, which was getting heavier again.

"Come on," it said, "watch this."

Random didn't like being bossed around by a bird, but she followed it to the mouth of the cave anyway, still fingering the rock in her pocket.

"Rain," said the bird. "You see? Just rain."

"I know what rain is."

Sheets of the stuff were sweeping through the night, moonlight sifting through it.

"So what is it?"

"What do you mean, what is it? Look, who are you? What were you doing in that box? Why have I spent a night running through the forest fending off demented squirrels to find that all I've got at the end of it is a bird asking me what rain is? It's just water falling through the bloody air, that's what it is. Anything else you want to know or can we go home now?"

There was a long pause before the bird answered, "You want to go home?"

"I haven't got a home!" Random almost shocked herself, she screamed the words so loudly.

"Look into the rain . . ." said the bird *Guide*.

"I'm looking into the rain! What else is there to look at?"

"What do you see?"

"What do you mean, you stupid bird? I just see a load of rain. It's just water, falling."

"What shapes do you see in the water?"

"Shapes? There aren't any shapes. It's just, just . . ."

"Just a mish mash," said the bird *Guide*.

"Yes . . ."

"Now what do you see?"

Just on the very edge of visibility a thin faint beam fanned out of the bird's eyes. In the dry air beneath the overhang there was nothing to see. Where the beam hit the drops of rain as they fell through it, there was a flat sheet of light, so bright and vivid it seemed solid.

"Oh, great. A laser show," said Random, fractiously. "Never seen one of *those* before, of course, except at about five million rock concerts."

"*Tell me what you see!*"

"Just a flat sheet! Stupid bird."

"There's nothing there that wasn't there before. I'm just using light to draw your attention to certain drops at certain moments. Now what do you see?"

The light shut off.

"Nothing."

"I'm doing exactly the same thing, but with ultraviolet light. You can't see it."

"So what's the point of showing me something I can't see?"

"So that you understand that just because you see something, it doesn't mean to say it's there. And if you don't see something, it doesn't mean to say it's not there. It's only what your senses bring to your attention."

"I'm bored with this," said Random, and then gasped.

Hanging in the rain was a giant and very vivid three-dimensional image of her father looking startled about something.

About two miles away behind Random, her father, struggling his way through the woods, suddenly stopped. He was startled to see an image of himself looking startled about something hanging brightly in the rain-filled air about two miles away. About two miles away some distance to the right of the direction in which he was heading.

He was almost completely lost, was convinced he was going to die of cold and wet and exhaustion and was beginning to wish he could just get on with it. He had just been brought an entire golfing magazine by a squirrel, as well, and his brain was beginning to howl and gibber.

Seeing a huge bright image of himself light up in the sky told him that, on balance, he was probably right to howl and gibber but probably wrong as far as the direction he was heading was concerned.

Taking a deep breath, he turned and headed off toward the inexplicable light show.

"Okay, so what's that supposed to prove?" demanded Random. It was the fact that the image was her father that had startled her rather than the appearance of the image itself. She had seen her first hologram when she was two months old and had been put in it to play. She had seen her most recent one about half an hour ago playing the March of the AnjaQantine Star Guard.

"Only that it's no more there or not there than the sheet was," said the bird. "It's just the interaction of water from the sky moving in one direction, with light at frequencies your senses can detect moving in another. It makes an apparently solid image in your mind. But it's all just images in the Mish Mash. Here's another one for you."

"My mother!" said Random.

"No," said the bird.

"I know my mother when I see her!"

The image was of a woman emerging from a spacecraft inside a large, gray hangarlike building. She was being escorted by a group of tall, thin purplish-green creatures. It was definitely Random's mother. Well, almost definitely. Trillian wouldn't have been walking quite so uncertainly in low gravity, or looking around her at a boring old life-support environment with quite such a disbelieving look on her face, or carrying such a quaint old camera.

"So who is it?" demanded Random.

"She is part of the extent of your mother on the probability axis," said the bird *Guide*.

"I haven't the faintest idea what you mean."

"Space, time and probability all have axes along which it is possible to move."

"Still dunno. Though I think . . . No. Explain."

"I thought you wanted to go home."

"Explain!"

"Would you like to see your home?"

"*See* it? It was destroyed!"

"It is discontinuous along the probability axis. Look!"

Something very strange and wonderful now swam into view in the rain. It was a huge bluish-greenish globe, misty and cloud-covered, turning with majestic slowness against a black, starry background.

"Now you see it," said the bird. "Now you don't."

A little less than two miles away now, Arthur Dent stood still in his tracks. He could not believe what he could see, hanging there, shrouded in rain, but brilliant and vividly real against the night sky—the Earth. He gasped at the sight of it. Then, at the moment he gasped, it disappeared again. Then it appeared again. Then, and this was the bit that made him give up and stick straws in his hair, it turned into a sausage.

* * *

Random was also bewildered at the sight of this huge blue and green and watery and misty sausage hanging above her. And now it was a string of sausages, or rather it was a string of sausages in which many of the sausages were missing. The whole brilliant string turned and spun in a bewildering dance in the air and then gradually slowed, grew insubstantial and faded into the glistening darkness of the night.

"What was that?" asked Random, in a small voice.

"A glimpse along the probability axis of a discontinuously probable object."

"I see."

"Most objects mutate and change along their axis of probability, but the world of your origin does something slightly different. It lies on what you might call a fault line in the landscape of probability, which means that at many probability coordinates the whole of it simply ceases to exist. It has an inherent instability, which is typical of anything that lies within what are usually designated the Plural sectors. Make sense?"

"No."

"Want to go and see for yourself?"

"To . . . Earth?"

"Yes."

"Is that possible?"

The bird *Guide* did not answer at once. It spread its wings and, with an easy grace, ascended into the air and flew out into the rain, which, once again, was beginning to lighten.

It soared ecstatically up into the night sky, lights flashed around it, dimensions dithered in its wake. It swooped and turned and looped and turned again and came at last to rest two feet in front of Random's face, its wings beating slowly and silently.

It spoke to her again.

"Your universe is vast to you. Vast in time, vast in space. That's because of the filters through which you perceive it. But I was built with no filters at all, which means I perceive the Mish Mash which contains all possible universes but which has, itself, no size at all. For me, anything is possible. I am omniscient and omnipotent, extremely vain and, what is more, I come in a handy self-carrying package. You have to work out how much of the above is true."

A slow smile spread over Random's face.

"You bloody little thing. You've been winding me up!"

"As I said, anything is possible."

Random laughed. "Okay," she said. "Let's try and go to Earth. Let's go to Earth at some point on its, er . . ."

"Probability axis?"

"Yes. Where it hasn't been blown up. Okay. So you're the *Guide*. How do we get a lift?"

"Reverse engineering."

"What?"

"Reverse engineering. To me the flow of time is irrelevant. You decide what you want. I then merely make sure that it has already happened."

"You're joking."

"Anything is possible."

Random frowned. "You *are* joking, aren't you?"

"Let me put it another way," said the bird. "Reverse engineering enables us to shortcut all the business of waiting for one of the horribly few spaceships that passes through your galactic sector every year or so to make up its mind about whether or not it feels like giving you a lift. You want a lift, a ship arrives and gives you one. The pilot may think he has any one of a million reasons why he has decided to stop and pick you up. The real reason is that I have determined that he will."

"This is you being extremely vain, isn't it, little bird?"

The bird was silent.

"Okay," said Random. "I want a ship to take me to Earth."

"Will this one do?"

It was so silent that Random had not noticed the descending spaceship until it was nearly on top of her.

Arthur had noticed it. He was a mile away now and closing. Just after the illuminated sausage display had drawn to its conclusion, he had noticed the faint glimmerings of further lights coming down out of the clouds and had, to begin with, assumed it to be another piece of flashy *son et lumière*.

It took a moment or so for it to dawn on him that it was an actual spaceship, and a moment or too longer for him to realize that it was dropping directly down to where he assumed his daughter to be. That was when, rain or no rain, old leg injury or no leg injury, darkness or no darkness, he suddenly started really to run.

He fell almost immediately, slid and hurt his knee quite badly on a rock. He slithered back up to his feet and tried again. He had a horrible cold feeling that he was about to lose Random forever. Limping and cursing, he ran. He didn't know what it was that had been in the box, but the name on it had been Ford Prefect, and that was the name he cursed as he ran.

The ship was one of the sexiest and most beautiful ones that Random had ever seen.

It was astounding. Silver, sleek, ineffable.

If she didn't know better she would have said it was an RW6. As it settled silently beside her she realized that it actually was an RW6 and she could scarcely breathe for excitement. An RW6 was the sort of thing you only saw in the sort of magazines that were designed to provoke civil unrest.

She was also extremely nervous. The manner and timing of its arrival was deeply unsettling. Either it was the most bizarre coincidence or something very peculiar and worrying was going on. She waited a little tensely for the ship's hatch to open. Her *Guide*—she thought of it as hers now—was hovering lightly over her right shoulder, its wings barely fluttering.

The hatch opened. Just a little dim light escaped. A moment or two passed and a figure emerged. He stood still for a moment or so, obviously trying to accustom his eyes to the darkness. Then he caught sight of Random standing there and seemed a little surprised. He started to walk toward her. Then suddenly he shouted in surprise and started to run at her.

Random was not a good person to take a run at on a dark night when she was feeling a little strung out. She had unconsciously been fingering the rock in her pocket from the moment she saw the craft coming down.

Still running, slithering, hurtling, bumping into trees, Arthur saw at last that he was too late. The ship had only been on the ground for about three minutes, and now, silently, gracefully, it was rising up above the trees again, turning smoothly in the fine speckle of rain to which the storm had now abated, climbing, climbing, tipping up its nose and, suddenly, effortlessly, hurtling up through the clouds.

Gone. Random was in it. It was impossible for Arthur to know this, but he just went ahead and knew it anyway. She was gone. He had had his stint at being a parent and could scarcely believe how badly he had done at it. He tried to continue running, but his feet were dragging, his knee was hurting like fury and he knew that he was too late.

He could not conceive that he could feel more wretched and awful than this, but he was wrong.

He limped his way at last to the cave where Random had sheltered and opened the box. The ground bore the indentations of the space-craft that had landed there only minutes before, but of Random there was no sign. He wandered disconsolately into the cave, found the empty box and piles of missing matter pellets strewn around the place. He felt a little cross about that. He'd tried to teach her about cleaning up after herself. Feeling a bit cross with her about something like that helped him feel less desolate about her leaving. He knew he had no means of finding her.

His foot knocked against something unexpected. He bent down to pick it up, and was thoroughly surprised to discover what it was. It was his old *Hitchhiker's Guide to the Galaxy*. How did that come to be in the cave? He had never returned to collect it from the scene of the crash. He had not wanted to revisit the crash and he had not wanted the *Guide* again. He had reckoned he was here on Lamuella, making sand-wiches, for good. How did it come to be in the cave? It was active. The words on the cover flashed DON'T PANIC at him.

He went out of the cave again into the dim and damp moonlight. He sat on a rock to have a look through the old *Guide*, and then discovered it wasn't a rock, it was a person.

Chapter 18

Arthur leapt to his feet with a start of fear. It would be hard to say which he was more frightened of: that he might have hurt the person he had inadvertently sat on or that the person he had inadvertently sat on would hurt him back.

There seemed, on inspection, to be little immediate cause for alarm on the second count. Whoever it was he had sat on was unconscious. That would probably go a great deal of the way toward explaining what he was doing lying there. He seemed to be breathing okay, though. Arthur felt his pulse. That was okay as well.

He was lying on his side, half curled up. It was so long ago and far away when Arthur had last done first aid that he really couldn't remember what it was he was supposed to do. The first thing he was supposed to do, he remembered, was to have a first aid kit about his person. Damn.

Should he roll him onto his back or not? Suppose he had any broken bones? Suppose he swallowed his tongue? Suppose he sued him? Who, apart from anything else, was he?

At that moment the unconscious man groaned loudly and rolled himself over.

Arthur wondered if he should—

He looked at him.

He looked at him again.

He looked at him again, just to make absolutely sure.

Despite the fact that he had been thinking he was feeling about as low as he possibly could, he experienced a terrible sinking feeling.

The figure groaned again and slowly opened his eyes. It took him a while to focus, then he blinked and stiffened.

"You!" said Ford Prefect.

"You!" said Arthur Dent.

Ford groaned again.

"What do you need to have explained this time?" he said, and closed his eyes in some kind of despair.

* * *

Five minutes later he was sitting up and rubbing the side of his head, where he had quite a large swelling.

"Who the hell was that woman?" he said. "Why are we surrounded by squirrels, and what do they want?"

"I've been pestered by squirrels all night," said Arthur. "They keep on trying to give me magazines and stuff."

Ford frowned. "Really?" he said.

"And bits of rag."

Ford thought.

"Oh," he said. "Is this near where your ship crashed?"

"Yes," said Arthur. He said it a little tightly.

"That's probably it. Can happen. Ship's cabin robots get destroyed. The cyberminds that control them survive and start infecting the local wildlife. Can turn a whole ecosystem into some kind of helpless thrashing service industry, handing out hot towels and drinks to passersby. Should be a law against it. Probably is. Probably also a law against there being a law against it so everybody can get nice and worked up. Hey ho. What did you say?"

"I said, and the woman is my daughter."

Ford stopped rubbing his head.

"Say that one more time."

"I said," said Arthur, huffily, "the woman is my daughter."

"I didn't know," said Ford, "that you had a daughter."

"Well, there's probably a lot you don't know about me," said Arthur. "Come to mention it, there's probably a lot I don't know about me either."

"Well, well, well. When did this happen then?"

"I'm not quite sure."

"That sounds like more familiar territory," said Ford. "Is there a mother involved?"

"Trillian."

"*Trillian?* I didn't think that . . ."

"No. Look, it's a bit embarrassing."

"I remember she told me once she had a kid but only, sort of, in passing. I'm in touch with her from time to time. Never seen her with the kid."

Arthur said nothing.

Ford started to feel the side of his head again in some bemusement. "Are you *sure* this was *your* daughter?" he said.

"Tell me what happened."

"Phroo. Long story. I was coming to pick up this parcel I'd sent to myself here care of you . . ."

"Well, what was that all about?"

"I think it may be something unimaginably dangerous."

"And you sent it to *me?*" protested Arthur.

"Safest place I could think of. I thought I could rely on you to be absolutely boring and not open it. Anyway, coming in at night I couldn't find this village place. I was going by pretty basic information. I couldn't find any signal of any kind. I guess you don't have signals and stuff here."

"That's what I like about it."

"Then I did pick up a faint signal from your old copy of the *Guide,* so I homed in on that, thinking that would take me to you. I found I'd landed in some kind of wood. Couldn't figure out what was going on. I get out, and then see this woman standing there. I go up to say hello, then suddenly I see that she's got this thing!"

"What thing?"

"The thing I sent you! The new *Guide.* The bird thing! You were meant to keep it safe, you idiot, but this woman had the thing right there by her shoulder. I ran forward and she hit me with a rock."

"I see," said Arthur. "What did you do?"

"Well, I fell over, of course. I was very badly hurt. She and the bird started to make off toward my ship. And when I say my ship, I mean an RW6."

"A what?"

"An RW6, for Zark's sake. I've got this great relationship going now between my credit card and the *Guide*'s central computer. You would not believe that ship, Arthur, it's . . ."

"So an RW6 is a spaceship, then?"

"*Yes!* It's—oh, never mind. Look, just get some kind of grip, will you, Arthur? Or at least get some kind of catalogue. At this point I was very worried. And, I think, semiconcussed. I was down on my knees and bleeding profusely, so I did the only thing I could think of, which was to beg. I said please, for Zark's sake, don't take my ship. And don't leave me stranded in the middle of some primitive zarking forest with no medical help and a head injury. I could be in serious trouble and so could she."

"What did she say?"

"She hit me on the head with the rock again."

"I think I can confirm that that was my daughter."

"Sweet kid."

"You have to get to know her," said Arthur.

"She eases up, does she?"

"No," said Arthur, "but you get a better sense of when to duck."

Ford held his head and tried to see straight.

The sky was beginning to lighten in the west, which was where the sun rose. Arthur didn't particularly want to see it. The last thing he wanted after a hellish night like this one was some blasted day coming along and barging about the place.

"What are you doing in a place like this, Arthur?" demanded Ford.

"Well," said Arthur, "making sandwiches mostly."

"What?"

"I am, probably was, the sandwich maker for a small tribe. It was a bit embarrassing really. When I first arrived, that is, when they rescued me from the wreckage of this super high-technology spacecraft that had crashed on their planet, they were very nice to me and I thought I should help them out a bit. You know, I'm an educated chap from a high-technology culture, I could show them a thing or two. And of course I couldn't. I haven't got the faintest idea, when it comes down to it, of how anything actually works. I don't mean like video recorders, nobody knows how to work those. I mean just something like a pen or an artesian well or something. Not the foggiest. I couldn't help at all. One day I got glum and made myself a sandwich. That suddenly got them all excited. They'd never seen one before. It was just an idea that had never occurred to them, and I happen to quite like making sandwiches, so it all sort of developed from there."

"And you *enjoyed* that?"

"Well, yes, I think I sort of did, really. Getting a good set of knives, that sort of thing."

"You didn't, for instance, find it mind-witheringly, explosively, astoundingly, blisteringly dull?"

"Well, er, no. Not as such. Not actually blisteringly."

"Odd. I would."

"Well, I suppose we have a different outlook."

"Yes."

"Like the pikka birds."

Ford had no idea what he was talking about and couldn't be bothered to ask. Instead he said, "So how the hell do we get out of this place?"

"Well, I think the simplest way from here is just to follow the way down the valley to the plains, probably take an hour, and then walk around from there. I don't think I could face going back up and over the way I came."

"Walk around *where* from there?"

"Well, back to the village, I suppose." Arthur sighed a little forlornly.

"I don't want to go to any blasted village!" snapped Ford. "We've got to get out of here!"

"Where? How?"

"I don't know, you tell me. You live here! There must be some way off this zarking planet."

"I don't know. What do you usually do? Sit around and wait for a passing spacecraft, I suppose."

"Oh, yes? And how many spacecraft have visited this zark-forsaken little flea-pit recently?"

"Well, a few years ago there was mine that crashed here by mistake. Then there was, er, Trillian, then the parcel delivery, and now you, and . . ."

"Yes, but *apart* from the usual suspects?"

"Well, er, I think pretty much none, so far as I know. Pretty quiet around here."

As if deliberately to prove him wrong, there was a long, low distant roll of thunder.

Ford leapt to his feet fretfully and started pacing backward and forward in the feeble, painful light of the early dawn, which lay streaked against the sky as if someone had dragged a piece of liver across it.

"You don't understand how important this is," he said.

"What? You mean my daughter out there all alone in the Galaxy? You think I don't . . ."

"Can we feel sorry for the Galaxy later?" said Ford. "This is very, very serious indeed. The *Guide* has been taken over. It's been bought out."

Arthur leapt up. "Oh, very serious," he shouted. "Please fill me in straight away on some corporate publishing politics! I can't tell you how much it's been on my mind of late!"

"You don't understand! There's a whole new *Guide!*"

"Oh!" shouted Arthur again. "Oh! Oh! Oh! I'm incoherent with excitement! I can hardly wait for it to come out to find out which are the most exciting spaceports to get bored hanging about in some glob-ular cluster I've never heard of. Please, can we rush to a store that's got it right this very instant?"

Ford narrowed his eyes.

"This is that thing you call sarcasm, isn't it?"

"Do you know," bellowed Arthur, "I think it is? I really think it might just be a crazy little thing called sarcasm seeping in at the edges of my manner of speech! Ford, I have had a *fucking* bad night! Will you please try and take that into account while you consider what fascinating bits of *badger-sputumly* inconsequential trivia to assail me with next?"

"Try to rest," said Ford. "I need to think."

"Why do you need to *think?* Can't we just sit and go budumbudumbudum with our lips for a bit? Couldn't we just dribble gently and loll a little bit to the left for a few minutes? I can't stand it, Ford! I can't stand all this thinking and trying to work things out anymore. You may think that I am just standing here barking . . ."

"Hadn't occurred to me in fact."

"But I mean it! What is the point? We assume that every time we do anything we know what the consequences will be, i.e., more or less what we intend them to be. This is not only not always correct. It is wildly, crazily, stupidly cross-eyed-blithering-insectly wrong!"

"Which is exactly my point."

"Thank you," said Arthur, sitting down again. "What?"

"Temporal reverse engineering."

Arthur put his head in his hands and shook it gently from side to side.

"Is there any humane way," he moaned, "in which I can prevent you from telling me what temporary reverse bloody-whatsiting is?"

"No," said Ford, "because your daughter is caught up in the middle of it and it is deadly, deadly serious."

Thunder rolled in the pause.

"All right," said Arthur. "Tell me."

"I leapt out of a high-rise office window."

This cheered Arthur up.

"Oh!" he said. "Why don't you do it again?"

"I did."

"Hmmm," said Arthur, disappointed. "Obviously no good came of it."

"The first time I managed to save myself by the most astonishing and—I say this in all modesty—fabulous piece of ingenious quick thinking, agility, fancy footwork and self-sacrifice."

"What was the self-sacrifice?"

"I jettisoned half of a much-loved and I think irreplaceable pair of shoes."

"Why was that self-sacrifice?"

"Because they were mine!" said Ford, crossly.

"I think we have different value systems."

"Well, mine's better."

"That's according to your . . . oh, never mind. So having saved yourself very cleverly once, you very sensibly went and jumped again. Please don't tell me why. Just tell me what happened if you must."

"I fell straight into the open cockpit of a passing jet towncar whose pilot had just accidentally pushed the eject button when he meant only to change tracks on the stereo. Now, even I couldn't think that that was particularly clever of me."

"Oh, I don't know," said Arthur, wearily. "I expect you probably sneaked into his jetcar the previous night and set the pilot's least favorite track to play or something."

"No, I didn't," said Ford.

"Just checking."

"Though oddly enough, *somebody else did*. And this is the nub. You could trace the chain and branches of crucial events and coincidences back and back. Turned out the new *Guide* had done it. That bird."

"What bird?"

"You haven't seen it?"

"No."

"Oh. It's a lethal little thing. Looks pretty, talks big, collapses waveforms selectively at will."

"What does that mean?"

"Temporal reverse engineering."

"Oh," said Arthur. "Oh yes."

"The question is, *who is it really doing it for?*"

"I've actually got a sandwich in my pocket," said Arthur, delving. "Would you like a bit?"

"Yeah, okay."

"It's a bit squished and sodden, I'm afraid."

"Never mind."

They munched for a bit.

"It's quite good in fact," said Ford. "What's the meat in it?"

"Perfectly Normal Beast."

"Not come across that one. So, the question is," Ford continued, "who is the bird really doing it for? What's the real game here?"

"Mmm," ate Arthur.

"When I found the bird," continued Ford, "which I did by a series of coincidences that are interesting in themselves, it put on the most fantastic multidimensional display of pyrotechnics I've ever seen. It then said that it would put its services at my disposal in my universe. I said, thanks but no thanks. It said that it would anyway, whether I liked it or not. I said just try it, and it said it would and, indeed, already had done so. I said we'd see about that and it said that we would. That's when I decided to pack the thing up and get it out of there. So I sent it to you for safety."

"Oh yes? Whose?"

"Never you mind. Then, what with one thing and another, I thought it prudent to jump out of the window again, being fresh out of other options at the time. Luckily for me the jetcar was there, otherwise I would have had to fall back on ingenious quick thinking, agility, maybe another shoe or, failing all else, the ground. But it meant that, whether I liked it or not, the *Guide* was, well, working for me, and that was deeply worrying."

"Why?"

"Because if you've got the *Guide*, you think that you are the one it's working for. Everything went swimmingly smoothly for me from then on, up to the very moment that I came up against the totty with the rock, then, bang, I'm history. I'm out of the loop."

"Are you referring to my daughter?"

"As politely as I can. She's the next one in the chain who will think that everything is going fabulously for her. She can beat whoever she likes around the head with bits of the landscape, everything will just swim for her until she's done whatever she's supposed to do and then it will be all up for her too. It's reverse temporal engineering, and clearly nobody understood what was being unleashed!"

"Like me, for instance."

"What? Oh, wake up, Arthur. Look, let me try it again. The new *Guide* came out of the research labs. It made use of this new technology of Unfiltered Perception. Do you know what that means?"

"Look, I've been making sandwiches, for Bob's sake!"

"Who's Bob?"

"Never mind. Just carry on."

"Unfiltered Perception means it perceives everything. Got that? *I* don't perceive everything. *You* don't perceive everything. We have filters. The new *Guide* doesn't have any sense filters. It perceives *everything*. It wasn't a complicated technological idea. It was just a question of leaving a bit out. Got it?"

"Why don't I just say that I've got it, and then you can carry on regardless."

"Right. Now because the bird can perceive every possible universe, it is present in every possible universe. Yes?"

"Y . . . e . . . e . . . s. Ish."

"So what happens is, the bozos in the marketing and accounting departments say, 'Oh, that sounds good, doesn't that mean we only have to make one of them and then sell it an infinite number of times?' Don't squint at me like that, Arthur, this is how accountants *think!*"

"That's quite clever, isn't it?"

"No! It is fantastically *stupid*. Look. The machine's only a little *Guide*. It's got some quite clever cybertechnology in it, but because it has Unfiltered Perception, any smallest move it makes has the power of a virus. It can propagate throughout space, time and a million other dimensions. Anything can be focused anywhere in any of the universes that you and I move in. Its power is recursive. Think of a computer program. Somewhere, there is one key instruction, and everything else is just functions calling themselves, or brackets billowing out endlessly through an infinite address space. What happens when the brackets collapse? Where's the final 'end if'? Is any of this making sense? Arthur?"

"Sorry, I was nodding off for a moment. Something about the Universe, yes?"

"Something about the Universe, yes," said Ford, wearily. He sat down again.

"All right," he said. "Think about this. You know who I think I saw at the *Guide* offices? Vogons. Ah. I see I've said a word you understand at last."

Arthur leapt to his feet.

"That noise," he said.

"What noise?"

"The thunder."

"What about it?"

"It isn't thunder. It's the spring migration of the Perfectly Normal Beasts. It's started."

"What are these animals you keep on about?"

"I don't keep on about them. I just put bits of them in sandwiches."

"Why are they called Perfectly Normal Beasts?"

Arthur told him.

It wasn't often that Arthur had the pleasure of seeing Ford's eyes open wide with astonishment.

Chapter 19

It was a sight that Arthur never quite got used to, or tired of. He and Ford had tracked their way swiftly along the side of the small river that flowed down along the bed of the valley, and when at last they reached the margin of the plains, they pulled themselves up into the branches of a large tree, to get a better view of one of the stranger and more wonderful visions that the Galaxy has to offer.

The great thunderous herd of thousand upon thousand of Perfectly Normal Beasts was sweeping in magnificent array across the Anhondo Plain. In the early pale light of the morning, as the great animals charged through, the fine steam of the sweat of their bodies mingled with the muddy mist churned up by their pounding hooves, their appearance seemed a little unreal and ghostly anyway, but what was heart-stopping about them was where they came from and where they went to, which appeared to be, simply, nowhere.

They formed a solid, charging phalanx roughly a hundred yards wide and half a mile long. The phalanx never moved, except that it exhibited a slight gradual drift sideways and backward for the eight or nine days that it regularly appeared for. But though the phalanx stayed more or less constant, the great beasts of which it was composed charged steadily at upward of twenty miles an hour, appearing suddenly from thin air at one end of the plain, and disappearing equally abruptly at the other end.

No one knew where they came from, no one knew where they went. They were so important to the lives of the Lamuellans, it was almost as if nobody liked to ask. Old Thrashbarg had said on one occasion that sometimes if you received an answer, the question might be taken away. Some of the villagers had privately said that this was the only properly wise thing that they'd ever heard Thrashbarg say, and after a short debate on the matter, had put it down to chance.

The noise of the pounding of the hooves was so intense that it was hard to hear anything else above it.

"What did you say?" shouted Arthur.

"I said," shouted Ford, "this looks like it might be some kind of evidence of dimensional drift."

"Which is what?" shouted Arthur back.

"Well, a lot of people are beginning to worry that spacetime is showing signs of cracking up with everything that's happening to it. There are quite a lot of worlds where you can see how the landmasses have cracked up and moved around just from the weirdly long or meandering routes that migrating animals take. This might be something like that. We live in twisted times. Still, in the absence of a decent spaceport . . ."

Arthur looked at him in a kind of frozen way.

"What do you mean?" he said.

"What do you mean, what do I mean?" shouted Ford. "You know perfectly well what I mean. We're going to ride our way out of here."

"Are you seriously suggesting we try to ride a Perfectly Normal Beast?"

"Yeah. See where it goes to."

"We'll be killed! No," said Arthur, suddenly. "We won't be killed. At least I won't. Ford, have you ever heard of a planet called Stavromula Beta?"

Ford frowned. "Don't think so," he said. He pulled out his own battered old copy of *The Hitchhiker's Guide to the Galaxy* and accessed it. "Any funny spelling?" he said.

"Don't know. I've only ever heard it said, and that was by someone who had a mouthful of other people's teeth. You remember I told you about Agrajag?"

Ford thought for a moment. "You mean the guy who was convinced you were getting him killed over and over again?"

"Yes. One of the places he claimed I'd got him killed was Stavromula Beta. Someone tries to shoot me, it seems. I duck and Agrajag, or at least one of his many reincarnations, gets hit. It seems that this has definitely happened at some point in time, so, I suppose, I can't get killed at least until after I've ducked on Stavromula Beta. Only no one's ever heard of it."

"Hmm." Ford tried a few other searches of the *Hitchhiker's Guide*, but drew a blank.

"Nothing," he said.

"I was just . . . no, I've never heard of it," said Ford, finally. He wondered why it was ringing a very, very faint bell, though.

"Okay," said Arthur. "I've seen the way the Lamuellan hunters trap Perfectly Normal Beasts. If you spear one in the herd it just gets trampled, so they have to lure them out one at a time for the kill. It's very like the way a matador works, you know, with a brightly colored cape. You get one to charge at you and then step aside and execute a rather elegant swing through with the cape. Have you got anything like a brightly colored cape about you?"

"This do?" said Ford, handing him his towel.

Leaping onto the back of a one-and-a-half-ton Perfectly Normal Beast migrating through your world at a thundering thirty miles an hour is not as easy as it might at first seem. Certainly it is not as easy as the Lamuellan hunters made it seem, and Arthur Dent was prepared to discover that this might turn out to be the difficult bit.

What he hadn't been prepared to discover, however, was how difficult it was even getting to the difficult bit. It was the bit that was supposed to be the easy bit that turned out to be practically impossible.

They couldn't even catch the attention of a single animal. The Perfectly Normal Beasts were so intent on working up a good thunder with their hooves, heads down, shoulders forward, back legs pounding the ground into porridge, that it would have taken something not merely startling but actually geological to disturb them.

The sheer amount of thundering and pounding was, in the end, more than Arthur and Ford could deal with. After they had spent nearly two hours prancing about doing increasingly foolish things with a medium-sized floral-patterned bath towel, they had not managed to get even one of the great beasts thundering and pounding past them to do so much as glance casually in their direction.

They were within three feet of the horizontal avalanche of sweating bodies. To have been much nearer would have been to risk instant death, chrono-logic or no chrono-logic. Arthur had seen what remained of any Perfectly Normal Beast which, as the result of a clumsy miss-throw by a young and inexperienced Lamuellan hunter, got speared while still thundering and pounding with the herd.

One stumble was all it took. No prior appointment with death on Stavromula Beta, wherever the hell Stavromula Beta was, would save you or anybody else from the thunderous, mangling, pounding of those hooves.

At last, Arthur and Ford staggered back. They sat down, exhausted and defeated, and started to criticize each other's technique with the towel.

"You've got to flick it more," complained Ford. "You need more follow-through from the elbow if you're going to get those blasted creatures to notice anything at all."

"*Follow-through?*" protested Arthur. "*You* need more suppleness in the wrist."

"You need more after-flourish," countered Ford.

"You need a bigger towel."

"You need," said another voice, "a pikka bird."

"You what?"

The voice had come from behind them. They turned, and there, standing behind them in the early morning sun, was Old Thrashbarg.

"To attract the attention of a Perfectly Normal Beast," he said, as he walked forward toward them, "you need a pikka bird. Like this."

From under the rough, cassocky robelike thing he wore he drew a small pikka bird. It sat restlessly on Old Thrashbarg's hand and peered intently at Bob knows what darting around about three feet six inches in front of it.

Ford instantly went into the sort of alert crouch he liked to do when he wasn't quite sure what was going on or what he ought to do about it. He waved his arms around very slowly in what he hoped was an ominous manner.

"Who is this?" he hissed.

"It's just Old Thrashbarg," said Arthur, quietly. "And I wouldn't bother with all the fancy movements. He's just as experienced a bluffer as you are. You could end up dancing around each other all day."

"The bird," hissed Ford again. "What's the bird?"

"It's just a bird!" said Arthur, impatiently. "It's like any other bird. It lays eggs and goes *ark* at things you can't see. Or *kar* or *rit* or something."

"Have you *seen* one lay eggs?" said Ford, suspiciously.

"For heaven's sake, of course I have," said Arthur. "And I've eaten hundreds of them. Make rather a good omelette. The secret is little cubes of cold butter and then whipping it lightly with . . ."

"I don't want a zarking recipe," said Ford. "I just want to be sure it's a real bird and not some kind of multidimensional cybernightmare."

He slowly stood up from his crouched position and started to brush himself down. He was still watching the bird, though.

"So," said Old Thrashbarg to Arthur. "Is it written that Bob shall once more take back unto himself the benediction of his once-given Sandwich Maker?"

Ford almost went back into his crouch.

"It's all right," muttered Arthur, "he always talks like that." Aloud, he said, "Ah, venerable Thrashbarg. Um, yes. I'm afraid I think I'm going to have to be popping off now. But young Drimple, my apprentice, will be a fine sandwich maker in my stead. He has the aptitude, a deep love of sandwiches and the skills he has acquired so far, though rudimentary as yet, will, in time, mature, and, er, well, I think he'll work out okay is what I'm trying to say."

Old Thrashbarg regarded him gravely. His old gray eyes moved sadly. He held his arms aloft, one still carrying a bobbing pikka bird, the other his staff.

"O Sandwich Maker from Bob!" he pronounced. He paused, furrowed his brow and sighed as he closed his eyes in pious contemplation. "Life," he said, "will be a very great deal less weird without you!"

Arthur was stunned.

"Do you know," he said, "I think that's the nicest thing anybody's ever said to me?"

"Can we get on, please?" said Ford.

Something was already happening. The presence of the pikka bird at the end of Thrashbarg's outstretched arm was sending tremors of interest through the thundering herd. The odd head flicked momentarily in their direction. Arthur began to remember some of the Perfectly Normal Beast hunts he had witnessed. He recalled that as well as the hunter-matadors brandishing their capes there were always others standing behind them holding pikka birds. He had always assumed that, like him, they had just come along to watch.

Old Thrashbarg moved forward, a little closer to the rolling herd. Some of the Beasts were now tossing their heads back with interest at the sight of the pikka bird.

Old Thrashbarg's outstretched arms were trembling.

Only the pikka bird itself seemed to show no interest in what was going on. A few anonymous molecules of air nowhere in particular engaged all of its perky attention.

"Now!" exclaimed Old Thrashbarg at last. "Now you may work them with the towel!"

Arthur advanced with Ford's towel, moving the way the hunter-matadors did, with a kind of elegant strut that did not come at all naturally to him. But now he knew what to do and that it was right. He brandished and flicked the towel a few times, to be ready for the moment, and then he watched.

Some distance away he spotted the Beast he wanted. Head down, it was galloping toward him, right on the very edge of the herd. Old Thrashbarg twitched the bird, the Beast looked up, tossed its head, and then, just as its head was coming down again, Arthur flourished the towel in the Beast's line of sight. It tossed its head again in bemusement, and its eyes followed the movement of the towel.

He had got the Beast's attention.

From that moment on, it seemed the most natural thing to coax and draw the animal toward him. Its head was up, cocked slightly to one side. It was slowing to a canter and then a trot. A few seconds later the huge thing was standing there among them, snorting, panting, sweating and sniffing excitedly at the pikka bird, which appeared not to have noticed its arrival at all. With strange sorts of sweeping movements of his arms, Old Thrashbarg kept the pikka bird in front of the Beast, but always out of its reach and always downward. With strange sorts of sweeping movements of the towel, Arthur kept drawing the Beast's attention this way and that—always downward.

"I don't think I've ever seen anything quite so stupid in my life," muttered Ford to himself.

At last, the Beast dropped, bemused but docile, to its knees.

"Go!" whispered Old Thrashbarg, urgently, to Ford. "Go! Go now!"

Ford leapt up onto the great creature's back, scrabbling among its thick, knotty fur for purchase, grasping great handfuls of the stuff to hold him steady once he was in position.

"Now, Sandwich Maker! Go!" He performed some elaborate sign and ritual handshake which Arthur couldn't quite get the hang of because Old Thrashbarg had obviously made it up on the spur of the moment, then he pushed Arthur forward. Taking a deep breath, he clambered up behind Ford onto the great, hot, heaving back of the Beast and held on tight. Huge muscles the size of sea lions rippled and flexed beneath him.

Old Thrashbarg held the bird suddenly aloft. The Beast's head swiveled up to follow it. Thrashbarg pushed upward and upward repeatedly with his arms and with the pikka bird; and slowly, heavily, the Perfectly Normal Beast lurched up off its knees and stood, at last, swaying slightly. Its two riders held on fiercely and nervously.

Arthur gazed out over the sea of hurtling animals, straining in an attempt to see where it was they were going, but there was nothing but heat haze.

"Can you see anything?" he said to Ford.

"No." Ford twisted around to glance back, trying to see if there was any clue as to where they had come. Still, nothing.

Arthur shouted down at Thrashbarg.

"Do you know where they come from?" he called. "Or where they're going?"

"The domain of the King!" shouted Old Thrashbarg back.

"King?" shouted Arthur in surprise. "What King?" The Perfectly Normal Beast was swaying and rocking restlessly under him.

"What do you mean, *what* King?" shouted Old Thrashbarg. "*The* King."

"It's just that you never mentioned a King," shouted Arthur back, in some consternation.

"What?" shouted Old Thrashbarg. The thrumming of a thousand hooves was very hard to hear over, and the old man was concentrating on what he was doing.

Still holding the bird aloft, he led the Beast slowly around till it was once more parallel with the motion of its great herd. He moved forward. The Beast followed. He moved forward again. The Beast followed again. At last, the Beast was lumbering forward with a little momentum.

"I said you never mentioned a King!" shouted Arthur again.

"I didn't say *a* King," shouted Old Thrashbarg, "I said *the* King."

He drew back his arm and then hurled it forward with all his strength, casting the pikka bird up into the air above the herd. This seemed to catch the pikka bird completely by surprise, as it had obviously not been paying any attention at all to what was going on. It took it a moment or two to work out what was happening, then it unfurled its little wings, spread them out and flew.

"Go!" shouted Thrashbarg. "Go and meet your destiny, Sandwich Maker!"

Arthur wasn't so sure about wanting to meet his destiny as such. He just wanted to get to wherever it was they were going so he could get back off this creature again. He didn't feel at all safe up there. The Beast was gathering speed as it followed in the wake of the pikka bird. And then it was in at the fringes of the great tide of animals, and in a moment or two, with its head down, the pikka bird forgotten, it was running with the herd again and rapidly approaching the point at which the herd was vanishing into thin air. Arthur and Ford held on to the great monster for dear life, surrounded on all sides by hurtling mountains of bodies.

"Go! Ride that Beast!" shouted Thrashbarg. His distant voice reverberated faintly in their ears. "Ride that Perfectly Normal Beast! Ride it, ride it!"

Ford shouted in Arthur's ear, "Where did he say we were going?"

"He said something about a King," shouted Arthur in return, holding on desperately.

"What King?"

"That's what I said. He just said *the* King."

"I didn't know there was a *the* King," shouted Ford.

"Nor did I," shouted Arthur back.

"Except of course for *the* King," shouted Ford. "And I don't suppose he meant him."

"*What* King?" shouted Arthur.

The point of exit was almost upon them. Just ahead of them, Perfectly Normal Beasts were galloping into nothingness and vanishing.

"What do you mean, *what* King?" shouted Ford. "*I* don't know what King. I'm only saying that he couldn't possibly mean *the* King, so I don't know what he means."

"Ford, I don't know what you're talking about."

"So?" said Ford. Then with a sudden rush, the stars came on, turned and twisted around their heads, and then, just as suddenly, turned off again.

Misty gray buildings loomed and flickered. They bounced up and down in a highly embarrassing way. What sort of buildings were they?

What were they for? What did they remind her of?

It's so difficult to know what things are supposed to be when you suddenly turn up unexpectedly on a different world, which has a different culture, a different set of the most basic assumptions about life, and also incredibly dull and meaningless architecture.

The sky above the buildings was a cold and hostile black. The stars, which should have been blindingly brilliant points of light this far from the sun, were blurred and dulled by the thickness of the huge shielding bubble. Perspex or something like it. Something dull and heavy anyway.

Tricia wound the tape back again to the beginning.

She knew there was something slightly odd about it.

Well, in fact, there were about a million things that were slightly odd about it, but there was one that was nagging at her and she hadn't quite got it.

She sighed and yawned.

As she waited for the tape to rewind she cleared away some of the dirty polystyrene coffee cups that had accumulated on the editing desk and tipped them into the bin.

She was sitting in a small editing suite at a video production company in Soho. She had DO NOT DISTURB notices plastered all over the door and a block on all incoming calls at the switchboard. This was originally to protect her astonishing scoop, but now it was to protect her from embarrassment.

She would watch the tape all the way through again from the beginning. If she could bear to. She might do some fast forwarding here and there.

It was about four o'clock on Monday afternoon, and she had a kind of sick feeling. She was trying to work out what the cause of this slightly sick feeling was, and there was no shortage of candidates.

First of all, it had all come on top of the overnight flight from New York. The red-eye. Always a killer, that.

Then, being accosted by aliens on her lawn and flown to the planet Rupert. She was not sufficiently experienced in that sort of thing to be able to say for sure that that was always a killer, but she would be prepared to bet that those who went through it regularly cursed it. There were always stress charts being published in magazines. Fifty stress points for losing your job. Seventy-five points for a divorce or changing your hairstyle and so on. None of them ever mentioned being accosted on your lawn by aliens and then being flown to the planet Rupert, but she was sure it was worth a few dozen points.

It wasn't that the journey had been particularly stressful. It had been extremely dull in fact. Certainly it had been no more stressful than the trip she had just taken across the Atlantic and it had taken roughly the same time, about seven hours.

Well, that was pretty astounding, wasn't it? Flying to the outer limits of the solar system in the same time that it took to fly to New York meant they must have some fantastic unheard of form of propulsion in the ship. She quizzed her hosts about it and they agreed that it was pretty good.

"But how does it *work?*" she had demanded excitedly. She was still quite excited at the beginning of the trip.

She found that part of the tape and played it through to herself. The Grebulons, which is what they called themselves, were politely showing her which buttons they pressed to make the ship go.

"Yes, but what *principle* does it work on?" she heard herself demand, from behind the camera.

"Oh, you mean is it something like a warp drive or something like that?" they said.

"Yes," persisted Tricia. "What *is* it?"

"It probably is something of the kind," they said.

"Like *what?*"

"Warp drive, photon drive, something like that. You'd have to ask the flight engineer."

"Which one is he?"

"We don't know. We have all lost our minds, you see."

"Oh yes," said Tricia, a little faintly. "So you said. Um, how did you lose your minds, exactly, then?"

"We don't know," they said, patiently.

"Because you've lost your minds," echoed Tricia, glumly.

"Would you like to watch television? It is a long flight. We watch television. It is something we enjoy."

All of this riveting stuff was on the tape, and fine viewing it made. First of all the picture quality was extremely poor. Tricia didn't know why this was, exactly. She had a feeling that the Grebulons responded to a slightly different range of light frequencies, and that there had been a lot of ultraviolet around, which was mucking up the video camera. There were a lot of interference patterns and video snow as well. Probably something to do with the warp drive that none of them knew the first thing about.

So what she had on tape, essentially, was a bunch of slightly thin and discolored people sitting around watching televisions that were showing network broadcasts. She had also pointed the camera out of the very tiny viewport near her seat and got a nice, slightly streaky effect of stars. She knew it was real, but it would have taken a good three or four minutes to fake.

In the end she had decided to save her precious videotape for Rupert itself and had simply sat back and watched television with them. She even dozed off for a while.

So part of her sick feeling came from the sense that she had had all that time in an alien spacecraft of astounding technological design, and had spent most of it dozing in front of reruns of "M*A*S*H" and "Cagney and Lacey." But what else was there to do? She had taken some photos as well, of course, all of which had subsequently turned out to be badly fogged when she got them back from the chemist.

Another part of her sick feeling probably came from the landing on Rupert. This at least had been dramatic and hair-raising. The ship had come sweeping in over a dark and somber landscape, a terrain so desperately far removed from the heat and light of its parent sun, Sol, that it seemed like a map of the psychological scars of the mind of an abandoned child.

Lights blazed through the frozen darkness and guided the ship into the mouth of some kind of cave that seemed to bend itself open to accept the small craft.

Unfortunately, because of the angle of their approach, and the depth at which the small, thick viewport was set into the craft's skin, it hadn't been possible to get the video camera to point directly at any of it. She ran through that bit of the tape.

The camera was pointing directly at the sun.

This is normally very bad for a video camera. But when the sun is roughly a third of a billion miles away, it doesn't do any harm. In fact it hardly makes any impression at all. You just get a small point of light right in the middle of the frame, which could be just about anything. It was just one star in a multitude.

Tricia fast-forwarded.

Ah. Now, the next bit had been quite promising. They had emerged out of the ship into a vast, gray hangarlike structure. This was clearly alien technology on a dramatic scale. Huge gray buildings under the dark canopy of the Perspex bubble. These were the same buildings that she had been looking at at the end of the tape. She had taken more footage of them while leaving Rupert a few hours later, just as she was about to reboard the spacecraft for the journey home. What did they remind her of?

Well, as much as anything else they reminded her of a film set from just about any low-budget science-fiction movie of the last twenty years. A lot larger, of course, but it all looked thoroughly tawdry and unconvincing on the video screen. Apart from the dreadful picture quality, she had been struggling with the unexpected effects of gravity that was appreciably lower than on Earth, and she had found it very hard to keep the camera from bouncing around in an embarrassingly unprofessional way. It was therefore impossible to make out any detail.

And now here was the Leader coming forward to greet her, smiling and sticking his hand out.

That was all he was called. The Leader.

None of the Grebulons had names, largely because they couldn't think of any. Tricia discovered that some of them had thought of calling themselves after characters from television programs they had picked up from Earth, but hard as they had tried to call each other Wayne and Bobby and Chuck, some remnant of something lurking deep in the cultural subconscious they had brought with them from the distant stars that were their home must have told them that this really wasn't right and wouldn't do.

The Leader had looked pretty much like all the others. Possibly a bit less thin. He said how much he enjoyed her shows on TV, that he was her greatest fan, how glad he was that she had been able to come along and visit them on Rupert and how much everybody had been looking forward to her coming, how he hoped the flight had been comfortable and so on. There was no particular sense she could detect of being any kind of emissary from the stars or anything.

Certainly, watching it now on videotape, he just looked like some guy in costume and makeup, standing in front of a set that wouldn't hold up too well if you leaned against it.

She sat staring at the screen with her face cradled in her hands, and shaking her head in slow bewilderment.

This was *awful*.

Not only was this bit awful but she knew what was coming next. It was the bit where the Leader asked if she was hungry after the flight, and would she perhaps like to come and have something to eat? They could discuss things over a little dinner.

She could remember what she was thinking at this point.

Alien food.

How was she going to deal with it?

Would she actually have to eat it? Would she have access to some sort of paper napkin she could spit stuff out into? Wouldn't there be all sorts of differential immunity problems?

It turned out to be hamburgers.

Not only did it turn out to be hamburgers, but the hamburgers it turned out to be were very clearly and obviously McDonald's hamburgers which had been reheated in a microwave. It wasn't just the look of them. It wasn't just the smell. It was the polystyrene clamshell packages they came in which had "McDonald's" printed all over them.

"Eat! Enjoy!" said the Leader. "Nothing is too good for our honored guest!"

This was in his private apartment. Tricia looked around it in bewilderment that had bordered on fear but had nevertheless got it all on videotape.

The apartment had a water bed in it. And a Midi hi-fi. And one of those tall electrically illuminated glass things that sit on tabletops and appear to have large globules of sperm floating in them. The walls were covered in velvet.

The Leader lounged against a brown corduroy beanbag chair and squirted breath freshener into his mouth.

Tricia began to feel very scared, suddenly. She was farther from

Earth than any human being, to her knowledge, had ever been, and she was with an alien creature who was lounging against a brown corduroy beanbag and squirting breath freshener into his mouth.

She didn't want to make any false moves. She didn't want to alarm him. But there were things she had to know.

"How did you . . . where did you get . . . this?" she asked, gesturing around the room nervously.

"The decor?" asked the Leader. "Do you like it? It is very sophisticated. We are a sophisticated people, we Grebulons. We buy sophisticated consumer durables . . . by mail order."

Tricia had nodded tremendously slowly at this point.

"Mail order . . ." she had said.

The Leader chuckled. It was one of those dark chocolate, reassuring, silky chuckles.

"I think you think they ship it here. No! Ha-ha! We have arranged a special box number in New Hampshire. We make regular pick-up visits. Ha-ha!" He lounged back in a relaxed fashion on his beanbag, reached for a reheated French fry and nibbled the end of it, an amused smile playing across his lips.

Tricia could feel her brain beginning to bubble very slightly. She kept the video camera going.

"How do you, well, er, how do you pay for these wonderful . . . things?"

The Leader chuckled again.

"American Express," he said with a nonchalant shrug.

Tricia nodded slowly again. She knew that they gave cards exclusively to just about anybody.

"And these?" she said, holding up the hamburger he had presented her with.

"It is very easy," said the Leader. "We stand in line."

Again, Tricia realized with a cold, trickling feeling going down her spine, that explained an awful lot.

She hit the fast-forward button again. There was nothing of any use here at all. It was all nightmarish madness. She could have faked something that would have looked more convincing.

Another sick feeling began to creep over her as she watched this hopeless, awful tape, and she began, with slow horror, to realize that it must be the answer.

She must be . . .

She shook her head and tried to get a grip.

An overnight flight going east . . . The sleeping pills she had taken to get her through it. The vodka she'd had to set the sleeping pills going.

What else? Well. There was seventeen years of obsession that a glamorous man with two heads, one of which was disguised as a parrot in a cage, had tried to pick her up at a party but had then impatiently flown off to another planet in a flying saucer. There suddenly seemed to be all sorts of bothersome aspects to that idea that had never really occurred to her. Never occurred to her. In seventeen years.

She stuffed her fist into her mouth.

She must get help.

Then there had been Eric Bartlett banging on about alien space-craft landing on her lawn. And before that . . . New York had been, well, very hot and stressful. The high hopes and the bitter disappointment. The astrology stuff.

She must have had a nervous breakdown.

That was it. She was exhausted and she had had a nervous break-down and had started hallucinating some time after she got home. She had dreamed the whole story. An alien race of people dispossessed of their own lives and histories, stuck on a remote outpost of our solar system and filling their cultural vacuum with our cultural junk. Ha! It was nature's way of telling her to check into an expensive medical establishment very quickly.

She was very, very sick. She looked at how many large coffees she'd got through as well, and realized how heavily she was breathing and how fast.

Part of solving any problem, she told herself, was realizing that you had it. She started to bring her breathing under control. She had caught herself in time. She had seen where she was. She was on the way back from whatever psychological precipice she had been on the brink of. She started to calm down, to calm down, to calm down. She sat back in the chair and closed her eyes.

After a while, now that she was breathing normally again, she opened them again.

So where had she got this tape from, then?

* * *

It was still running.

All right. It was a fake.

She had faked it herself, that was it.

It must have been her who had faked it because her voice was all over the soundtrack, asking questions. Every now and then the camera would swing down at the end of a shot and she would see her own feet in her own shoes. She had faked it and she had no recollection of faking it or any idea of why she had done it.

Her breathing was getting hectic again as she watched the snowy, flickering screen.

She must *still* be hallucinating.

She shook her head, trying to make it go away. She had no memory of faking any of this very obviously fake stuff. On the other hand she did seem to have memories that were very *like* the faked stuff. She continued to watch in a bewildered trance.

The person she imagined to be called the Leader was questioning her about astrology and she was answering smoothly and calmly. Only she could detect the well-disguised rising panic in her own voice.

The Leader pushed a button and a maroon velvet wall slid aside, revealing a large bank of flat TV monitors.

Each of the monitors was showing a kaleidoscope of different images: a few seconds from a game show, a few seconds from a cop show, a few seconds from a supermarket warehouse security system, a few seconds from somebody's holiday movies, a few seconds of sex, a few seconds of news, a few seconds of comedy. It was clear that the Leader was very proud of all this stuff, and he was waving his hands like a conductor while continuing at the same time to talk complete gibberish.

Another wave of his hands, and all the screens cleared to form one giant computer screen showing in diagrammatic form all the planets of the solar system, mapped out against a background of the stars in their constellations. The display was completely static.

"We have great skills," the Leader was saying. "Great skills in computation, in cosmological trigonometry, in three-dimensional navigational calculus. Great skills. Great, great skills. Only we have lost them. It is too bad. We like to have skills, only they have gone. They are in space somewhere, hurtling. With our names and the details of our homes and loved ones. Please," he said, gesturing her forward to sit at the computer's console, "be skillful for us."

Obviously what happened next was that Tricia quickly set the video camera up on its tripod to capture the whole scene. She then walked into the shot herself and sat down calmly in front of the giant computer display, spent a few moments familiarizing herself with the interface and then started smoothly and competently to pretend that she had the faintest idea what she was doing.

It hadn't been that difficult, in fact.

She was, after all, a mathematician and astrophysicist by training and a television presenter by experience, and what science she had forgotten over the years she was more than capable of making up by bluffing.

The computer she was working on was clear evidence that the Grebulons came from a far more advanced and sophisticated culture than their current vacuous state suggested, and with its aid she was able, within about half an hour, to cobble together a rough working model of the solar system.

It wasn't particularly accurate or anything, but it looked good. The planets were whizzing around in reasonably good simulations of their orbits, and you could watch the movement of the whole piece of virtual cosmological clockwork from any point within the system— very roughly. You could watch from Earth, you could watch from Mars, etc. You could watch from the surface of the planet Rupert. Tricia had been quite impressed with herself, but also very impressed with the computer system she was working on. The task would probably have taken a year or so of programming, using a computer workstation on Earth.

When she was finished, the Leader came up behind her and watched. He was very pleased and delighted with what she had achieved.

"Good," he said. "And now, please, I would like you to demonstrate how to use the system you have just designed to translate the information in this book for me."

Quietly he put a book down in front of her.

It was *You and Your Planets* by Gail Andrews.

Tricia stopped the tape again.

She was definitely feeling very wobbly indeed. The feeling that she was hallucinating had now receded, but had not left anything any easier or clearer in her head.

She pushed her seat back from the editing desk and wondered what to do. Years ago she had left the field of astronomical research because she knew, without any doubt whatsoever, that she had met a being from another planet. At a party. And she had also known, without any doubt whatsoever, that she would have made herself a laughingstock if she had ever said so. But how could she study cosmology and *not* say anything about the single most important thing she knew about it? She had done the only thing she could do. She had left.

Now she worked in television and the same thing had happened again.

She had videotape, actual *videotape* of the most astounding story in the history of, well, *anything:* a forgotten outpost of an alien civilization marooned on the outermost planet of our own solar system.

She had the story.

She had *been* there.

She had *seen* it.

She had the *videotape,* for God's sake.

And if she ever showed it to anybody, she would be a laughingstock.

How could she prove any of this? It wasn't even worth thinking about. The whole thing was a nightmare from virtually any angle she cared to look at it from. Her head was beginning to throb.

She had some aspirin in her bag. She went out of the little editing suite to the water dispenser down the corridor. She took the aspirin and drank several cups of water.

The place seemed to be very quiet. Usually there were more people bustling about the place, or at least *some* people bustling around the place. She popped her head around the door of the editing suite next to hers but there was no one there.

She had gone rather overboard keeping people out of her own suite. DO NOT DISTURB, the notice read. DO NOT EVEN THINK OF ENTERING. I DON'T CARE WHAT IT IS. GO AWAY. I'M BUSY!

When she went back in she noticed that the message light on her phone extension was winking and wondered how long it had been on.

"Hello?" she said to the receptionist.

"Oh, Miss McMillan, I'm so glad you called. Everybody's been trying to reach you. Your TV company. They're desperate to reach you. Can you call them?"

"Why didn't you put them through?" said Tricia.

"You said I wasn't to put anybody through for anything. You said I was to deny that you were even here. I didn't know what to do. I came up to give you a message, but . . ."

"Okay," said Tricia, cursing herself. She phoned her office.

"*Tricia!* Where the hemorrhaging *fuck* are you?"

"At the editing . . ."

"They said . . ."

"I know. What's up?"

"What's *up?* Only a bloody alien spaceship!"

"What? *Where?*"

"Regent's Park. Big silver job. Some girl with a bird. She speaks English and throws rocks at people and wants someone to repair her watch. Just get there."

Tricia stared at it.

It wasn't a Grebulon ship. Not that she was suddenly an expert on extraterrestrial craft, but this was a sleek and beautiful silver and white thing about the size of a large oceangoing yacht, which is what it most resembled. Next to this, the structures of the huge half-dismantled Grebulon ship looked like gun turrets on a battleship. Gun turrets. That's what those blank gray buildings had looked like. And what was odd about them was that by the time she passed them again on her way to reboarding the small Grebulon craft, they had moved. These things flitted briefly through her head as she ran from the taxi to meet her camera crew.

"Where's the girl?" she shouted above the noise of helicopters and police sirens.

"There!" shouted the producer while the sound engineer hurried to clip a radio mike to her. "She says her mother and father came from here in some parallel dimension or something like that, and she's got her father's watch, and . . . I don't know. What can I tell you? Busk it. Ask her what it feels like to be from outer space."

"Thanks a lot, Ted," muttered Tricia. She checked that her mike was securely clipped, gave the engineer some level, took a deep breath, tossed her hair back and switched into her role of professional reporter, on home ground, ready for anything

At least, nearly anything.

She turned to look for the girl. That must be her, with the wild hair and wild eyes. The girl turned toward her. And stared.

"Mother!" she screamed, and started to hurl rocks at Tricia.

Daylight exploded around them. Hot, heavy sun. A desert plain stretched out ahead in a haze of heat. They thundered out into it.

"Jump!" shouted Ford Prefect.

"What?" shouted Arthur Dent, holding on for dear life.

There was no reply.

"What did you say?" shouted Arthur again, and then realized that Ford Prefect was no longer there. He looked around in panic and started to slip. Realizing he couldn't hold on any longer, he pushed himself sideways as hard as he could and rolled into a ball as he hit the ground, rolling, rolling away from the pounding hooves.

What a day, he thought, as he started furiously coughing dust up out of his lungs. He hadn't had a day as bad as this since the Earth had been blown up. He staggered up to his knees, and then up to his feet and started to run away. He didn't know what from or what to, but running away seemed a prudent move.

He ran straight into Ford Prefect, who was standing there surveying the scene.

"Look," said Ford. "That is precisely what we need."

Arthur coughed up some more dust and wiped some other dust out of his hair and eyes. He turned, panting, to look at what Ford was looking at.

It didn't look much like the domain of a King, or *the* King, or any kind of King. It looked quite inviting, though.

First, the context. This was a desert world. The dusty earth was packed hard and had neatly bruised every last bit of Arthur that hadn't been already bruised by the festivities of the previous night. Some way ahead of them were great cliffs that looked like sandstone, eroded by the wind and what little rain presumably fell in these parts into wild and fantastic shapes, which matched the fantastic shapes of the giant cacti that sprouted here and there from the arid, orange landscape.

For a moment Arthur dared to hope they had unexpectedly arrived in Arizona or New Mexico or maybe South Dakota, but there was plenty of evidence that this was not the case.

The Perfectly Normal Beasts, for a start, were still thundering, still pounding. They swept up in their tens of thousands from the far horizon, disappeared completely for about half a mile, then swept off, thundering and pounding to the distant horizon opposite.

Then there were the spaceships parked in front of the bar & grill. Ah. The Domain of the King Bar & Grill. Bit of an anticlimax, thought Arthur to himself.

In fact only one of the spaceships was parked in front of the Domain of the King Bar & Grill. The other three were in a parking lot by the side of the bar & grill. It was the one in front that caught the eye, though. Wonderful-looking thing. Wild fins all over it, far, far too much chrome all over the fins and most of the actual bodywork painted in a shocking pink. It crouched there like an immense brooding insect and looked as if it was at any moment about to jump on something about a mile away.

The Domain of the King Bar & Grill was slap bang in the middle of where the Perfectly Normal Beasts would be charging if they didn't take a minor transdimensional diversion on the way. It stood on its own, undisturbed. An ordinary bar & grill. A truck-stop diner. Somewhere in the middle of nowhere. Quiet. The Domain of the King.

"Gonna buy that spaceship," said Ford, quietly.

"Buy it?" said Arthur. "That's not like you. I thought you usually pinched them."

"Sometimes you have to show a little respect," said Ford.

"Probably have to show a little cash as well," said Arthur. "How the hell much is that thing worth?"

With a tiny movement, Ford brought his Dine-O-Charge credit card up out of his pocket. Arthur noticed that the hand holding it was trembling very slightly.

"I'll teach them to make me the restaurant critic . . ." breathed Ford.

"What do you mean?" asked Arthur.

"I'll show you," said Ford with a nasty glint in his eye. "Let's go and run up a few *expenses*, shall we?"

"Couple beers," said Ford, "and, I dunno, a couple bacon rolls, whatever you got—oh, and that pink thing outside."

He flipped his card on the top of the bar and looked around casually.

There was a kind of silence.

There hadn't been a lot of noise before, but there was definitely a kind of silence now. Even the distant thunder of the Perfectly Normal Beasts carefully avoiding the Domain of the King seemed suddenly a little muted.

"Just *rode* into town," said Ford as if nothing was odd about that or about anything else. He was leaning against the bar at an extravagantly relaxed angle.

There were about three other customers in the place, sitting at tables, nursing beers. About three. Some people would say there were exactly three, but it wasn't that kind of a place, not the kind of a place that you felt like being that specific in. There was some big guy setting up some stuff on the little stage as well. Old drum kit. Couple guitars. Country and Western kind of stuff.

The barman was not moving very swiftly to get in Ford's order. In fact he wasn't moving at all.

"Not sure that the pink thing's for sale," he said at last in the kind of accent that went on for quite a long time.

"Sure it is," said Ford. "How much you want?"

"Well . . ."

"Think of a number, I'll double it."

"Tain't mine to sell," said the barman.

"So, whose?"

The barman nodded at the big guy setting up on the stage. Big fat guy, moving slow, balding.

Ford nodded. He grinned.

"Okay," he said. "Get the beers, get the rolls. Keep the tab open."

Arthur sat at the bar and rested. He was used to not knowing what was going on. He felt comfortable with it. The beer was pretty good and made him a little sleepy, which he didn't mind at all. The bacon rolls were not bacon rolls. They were Perfectly Normal Beast rolls. He exchanged a few professional roll-making remarks with the barman and just let Ford get on with whatever Ford wanted to do.

"Okay," said Ford, returning to his stool. "It's cool. We got the pink thing."

The barman was very surprised. "He's selling it to you?"

"He's giving it to us for free," said Ford, taking a gnaw at his roll.

"Hey, no, keep the tab open, though. We have some items to add to it. Good roll."

He took a deep pull of beer.

"Good beer," he added. "Good ship, too," he said, eyeing the big pink and chrome insectlike thing, bits of which could be seen through windows of the bar. "Good everything, pretty much. You know," he said, sitting back, reflectively, "it's at times like this that you kind of wonder if it's worth worrying about the fabric of space-time and the causal integrity of the multidimensional probability matrix and the potential collapse of all waveforms in the Whole Sort of General Mish Mash and all that sort of stuff that's been bugging me. Maybe I feel that what the big guy says is right. Just let it all go. What does it matter? Let it go."

"Which big guy?" said Arthur.

Ford just nodded toward the stage. The big guy was saying, "One, two" into the mike a couple of times. Couple other guys were on the stage now. Drums. Guitar.

The barman, who had been silent for a moment or two, said, "You say he's letting you *have* his ship?"

"Yeah," said Ford. " 'Let it all go' is what he said. 'Take the ship. Take it with my blessing. Be good to her.' I will be good to her."

He took a pull at his beer again.

"Like I was saying," he went on. "It's at times like this that you kind of think, let it all go. But then you think of guys like InfiniDim Enterprises and you think, they are not going to get away with it. They are going to suffer. It is my sacred and holy duty to see those guys suffer. Here, let me put something on the tab for the singer. I asked for a special request and we agreed. It's to go on the tab, okay?"

"Okay," said the barman, cautiously. Then he shrugged. "Okay, however you want to do it. How much?"

Ford named a figure. The barman fell over among the bottles and glasses. Ford vaulted quickly over the bar to check that he was all right and help him back up to his feet. He'd cut his finger and his elbow a bit and was feeling a little woozy but was otherwise fine. The big guy started to sing. The barman hobbled off with Ford's credit card to get authorization.

"Is there stuff going on here that I don't know about?" said Arthur to Ford.

"Isn't there usually?" said Ford.

"No need to be like that," said Arthur. He began to wake up. "Shouldn't we be going?" he said, suddenly. "Will that ship get us to Earth?"

"Sure will," said Ford.

"That's where Random will be going!" said Arthur with a start. "We can follow her! But . . . er . . ."

Ford let Arthur get on with thinking things out for himself while he got out his old edition of *The Hitchhiker's Guide to the Galaxy*.

"But where are we on the probability axis thing?" said Arthur. "Will the Earth be there or not there? I spent so much time looking for it. All I found was planets that were a bit like it or not at all like it, though it was clearly the right place because of the continents. The worst version was called NowWhat, where I got bitten by some wretched little animal. That's how they communicated, you know, by biting each other. Bloody painful. Then half the time, of course, the Earth isn't even there because it's been blown up by the bloody Vogons. How much sense am I making?"

Ford didn't comment. He was listening to something. He passed the *Guide* over to Arthur and pointed at the screen. The active entry read "Earth. Mostly harmless."

"You mean it's there!" said Arthur, excitedly. "The Earth is there! That's where Random will be going! The bird was showing her the Earth in the rainstorm!"

Ford motioned Arthur to shout a little less loudly. He was listening.

Arthur was growing impatient. He'd heard bar singers sing "Love Me Tender" before. He was a bit surprised to hear it here, right in the middle of wherever the hell this was, certainly not Earth, but then things tended not to surprise him these days as much as formerly. The singer was quite good, as bar singers went, if you liked that sort of thing, but Arthur was getting fretful.

He glanced at his watch. This only served to remind him that he didn't have his watch anymore. Random had it, or at least the remains of it.

"Don't you think we should be going?" he said, insistently.

"Shhh!" said Ford. "I paid to hear this song." He seemed to have tears in his eyes, which Arthur found a bit disturbing. He'd never seen Ford moved by anything other than very, very strong drink. Probably the dust. He waited, tapping his fingers irritably, out of time with the music.

The song ended. The singer went on to do "Heartbreak Hotel."

"Anyway," Ford whispered, "I've got to review the restaurant."

"What?"

"I have to write a review."

"Write a *review?* Of this place?"

"Filing the review validates the expenses claim. I've fixed it so that it happens completely automatically and untraceably. This bill is going to *need* some validation," he added, quietly, staring into his beer with a nasty smirk.

"For a couple of beers and a roll?"

"And a tip for the singer."

"Why, how much did you tip him?"

Ford named a figure again.

"I don't know how much that is," said Arthur. "What's it worth in pounds sterling? What would it buy you?"

"It would probably buy you, roughly . . . er . . ." Ford screwed his eyes up as he did some calculations in his head. "Switzerland," he said at last. He picked up his *Hitchhiker's Guide* and started to type.

Arthur nodded intelligently. There were times when he wished he understood what on earth Ford was talking about, and other times, like now, when he felt it was probably safer not even to try. He looked over Ford's shoulder. "This isn't going to take long, is it?" he said.

"Nah," said Ford. "Piece of piss. Just mention that the rolls were quite good, the beer good and cold, local wildlife nicely eccentric, the bar singer the best in the known universe and that's about it. Doesn't need much. Just a validation."

He touched an area on the screen marked "ENTER" and the message vanished into the Sub-Etha.

"You thought the singer was pretty good, then?"

"Yeah," said Ford. The barman was returning with a piece of paper, which seemed to be trembling in his hand.

He pushed it over to Ford with a kind of nervous, reverential twitch.

"Funny thing," said the barman. "The system rejected it first couple times. Can't say it surprised me." Beads of sweat were standing on his brow. "Then suddenly it's, Oh yeah, that's okay, and the system . . . er, validates it. Just like that. You wanna . . . sign it?"

Ford scanned the form quickly. He sucked his teeth. "This is going to hurt InfiniDim a lot," he said, with an appearance of concern. "Oh well," he added softly, "screw 'em."

He signed with a flourish and handed it back to the barman.

"More money," he said, "than the Colonel made for him in an entire career of doing crap movies and casino gigs. Just for doing what he does best. Standing up and singing in a bar. And he negotiated it himself. I think this is a good moment for him. Tell him I said thanks and buy him a drink." He tossed a few coins on the bar. The barman pushed them away.

"I don't think that's necessary," he said, slightly hoarsely.

" 'Tis to me," said Ford. "Okay, we are outta here."

They stood out in the heat and the dust and looked at the big pink and chrome thing with amazement and admiration. Or, at least Ford looked at it with amazement and admiration.

Arthur just looked at it. "You don't think it's a bit overdone, do you?"

He said it again when they climbed inside it. The seats and quite a lot of the controls were covered in fine fur skin or suede. There was a big gold monogram on the main control panel which just read "EP."

"You know," said Ford as he fired up the ship's engines, "I asked him if it was true that he had been abducted by aliens, and you know what he said?"

"Who?" said Arthur.

"The King."

"Which King? Oh, we've had this conversation, haven't we?"

"Never mind," said Ford. "For what it's worth, he said no. He went of his own accord."

"I'm still not sure who we're talking about," said Arthur.

Ford shook his head. "Look," he said, "there are some tapes over in the compartment to your left. Why don't you choose some music and put it on?"

"Okay," said Arthur, and flipped through the cartons. "Do you like Elvis Presley?" he said.

"Yeah, I do as a matter of fact," said Ford. "Now. I hope this machine can leap like it looks like it can." He engaged the main drive.

"Yeeehaah!" shouted Ford as they shot upward at face-tearing speed.

It could.

Chapter 23

The news networks don't like this kind of thing. They regard it as a waste. An incontrovertible spaceship arrives out of nowhere in the middle of London and it is sensational news of the highest magnitude. Another completely different one arrives three and a half hours later and somehow it isn't.

ANOTHER SPACECRAFT! said the headlines and newsstand billboards. THIS ONE'S PINK. A couple of months later they could have made a lot more of it. The third spacecraft, half an hour after that, the little four-berth Hrundi runabout, only made it onto the local news.

Ford and Arthur had come screaming down out of the stratosphere and parked neatly on Portland Place. It was just after six-thirty in the evening and there were spaces free. They mingled briefly with the crowd that gathered around to ogle, then said loudly that if no one else was going to call the police, they would, and made good their escape.

"Home . . ." said Arthur, a husky tone creeping into his voice as he gazed, misty-eyed, around him.

"Oh, don't get all maudlin on me," snapped Ford. "We have to find your daughter and we have to find that bird thing."

"How?" said Arthur. "This is a planet of five and a half billion people, and . . ."

"Yes," said Ford. "But only one of them has just arrived from outer space in a large silver spaceship accompanied by a mechanical bird. I suggest we just find a television and something to drink while we watch it. We need some serious room service."

They checked into a large two-bedroom suite at the Langham. Mysteriously, Ford's Dine-O-Charge card, issued on a planet over five thousand light years away, seemed to present the hotel's computer with no problems.

Ford hit the phones straight away while Arthur attempted to locate the television.

"Okay," said Ford. "I want to order up some margaritas, please. Couple of pitchers. Couple of chef's salads. And as much foie gras as you've got. And also London Zoo."

"She's on the news!" shouted Arthur from the next room.

"That's what I said," said Ford into the phone. "London Zoo. Just charge it to the room."

"She's . . . Good God!" shouted Arthur. "Do you know who she's being interviewed by?"

"Are you having difficulty understanding the English language?" continued Ford. "It's the zoo just up the road from here. I don't care if it's closed this evening. I don't want to buy a ticket, I just want to buy the zoo. I don't care if you're busy. This is room service, I'm in a room and I want some service. Got a piece of paper? Okay. Here's what I want you to do. All the animals that can be safely returned to the wild, return them. Set up some good teams of people to monitor their progress in the wild, see that they're doing okay."

"It's *Trillian!*" shouted Arthur. "Or is it . . . er . . . God, I can't stand all this parallel universe stuff. It's so bloody confusing. It seems to be a different Trillian. It's Tricia McMillan, which is what Trillian used to be called before . . . er . . . Why don't you come and watch, see if you can figure it out?"

"Just a second," Ford shouted, and returned to his negotiations with room service. "Then we'll need some natural reserves for the animals that can't hack it in the wild," he said. "Set up a team to work out the best places to do that. We might need to buy somewhere like Zaire and maybe some islands. Madagascar. Baffin. Sumatra. Those kind of places. We'll need a wide variety of habitats. Look, I don't see why you're seeing this as a problem. Learn to delegate. Hire whoever you want. Get onto it. I think you'll find my credit is good. And blue cheese dressing on the salad. Thank you."

He put the phone down and went through to Arthur, who was sitting on the edge of his bed watching television.

"I ordered us some foie gras," said Ford.

"What?" said Arthur, whose attention was entirely focused on the television.

"I said I ordered us some foie gras."

"Oh," said Arthur, vaguely. "Um, I always feel a bit bad about foie gras. Bit cruel to the geese, isn't it?"

"Fuck 'em," said Ford, slumping on the bed. "You can't care about every damn thing."

"Well, that's all very well for you to say, but—"

"Drop it!" said Ford. "If you don't like it I'll have yours. What's happening?"

"Chaos!" said Arthur. "Complete chaos! Random keeps on screaming at Trillian, or Tricia or whoever it is, that she abandoned her and then demanding to go to a good night club. Tricia's broken down in tears and says she's never even met Random, let alone given birth to her. Then she suddenly started howling about someone called Rupert and said that he had lost his mind or something. I didn't quite follow that bit, to be honest. Then Random started throwing stuff and they've cut to a commercial break while they try and sort it all out. Oh! They've just cut back to the studio! Shut up and watch."

A rather shaken anchorman appeared on the screen and apologized to viewers for the disruption of the previous item. He said he didn't have any very clear news to report, only that the mysterious girl, who called herself Random Frequent Flyer Dent, had left the studio to, er, rest. Tricia McMillan would be, he hoped, back tomorrow. Meanwhile, fresh reports of UFO activity were coming in . . .

Ford leapt up off the bed, grabbed the nearest phone and jabbed at a number.

"Concierge? You want to own the hotel? It's yours if you can find out for me in five minutes which clubs Tricia McMillan belongs to. Just charge the whole thing to this room."

Chapter 24

A way in the inky depths of space invisible movements were being made.

Invisible to any of the inhabitants of the strange and temperamental Plural zone at the focus of which lay the infinitely multitudinous possibilities of the planet called Earth, but not inconsequential to them.

At the very edge of the solar system, hunkered down on a green leatherette sofa, staring fretfully at a range of TV and computer screens, sat a very worried Grebulon leader. He was fiddling with stuff. Fiddling with his book on astrology. Fiddling with the console of his computer. Fiddling with the displays being fed through to him constantly from all of the Grebulons' monitoring devices, all of them focused on the planet Earth.

He was distressed. Their mission was to monitor. But to monitor secretly. He was a bit fed up with his mission, to be honest. He was fairly certain that his mission must have been to do more than sit around watching TV for years on end. They certainly had a lot of other equipment with them that must have had some purpose if only they hadn't accidentally lost all trace of their purpose. He needed a sense of purpose in life, which was why he had turned to astrology to fill the yawning gulf that existed in the middle of his mind and soul. That would tell him something, surely.

Well, it was telling him something.

It was telling him, as far as he could make out, that he was about to have a very bad month, that things were going to go from bad to worse if he didn't get a grip on things and start making some positive moves and think things out for himself.

It was true. It was very clear from his star chart, which he had worked out using his astrology book and the computer program which that nice Tricia McMillan had designed for him to retriangulate all the appropriate astronomical data. Earth-based astrology had to be entirely recalculated to yield results that were meaningful to the Grebulons here on the tenth planet, out on the frozen edges of the solar system.

The recalculations showed absolutely clearly and unambiguously that he was going to have a very bad month indeed, starting with today. Because today Earth was starting to rise into Capricorn, and that, for the Grebulon leader, who showed all the character signs of being a classic Taurus, was very bad indeed.

This was all very distressing for him, but he knew that he had to start taking positive action. He ordered the turrets to swivel.

Because all of the Grebulon surveillance equipment was focused on the planet Earth, it failed to spot that there was now another source of data in the solar system.

Its chances of accidentally spotting this other source of data—a massive yellow constructor ship—were practically nil. It was as far from the sun as Rupert was, but almost diametrically opposite, almost hidden by the sun.

Almost.

The massive yellow constructor ship wanted to be able to monitor events on Planet Ten without being spotted itself. It had managed this very successfully.

There were all sorts of other ways in which this ship was diametrically opposite to the Grebulons'.

Its leader, its Captain, had a very clear idea of what his purpose was. It was a very simple and plain one and he had been pursuing it in his simple, plain way for a considerable period of time now.

Anyone who knew of his purpose might have said that it was a pointless and ugly one, that it wasn't the sort of purpose that enhanced a life, put a spring in a person's step, made birds sing and flowers bloom. Rather the reverse in fact. Absolutely the reverse.

It wasn't his job to worry about that, though. It was his job to do his job, which was to do his job. If that led to a certain narrowness of vision and circularity of thought, then it wasn't his job to worry about such things. Any such things that came his way were referred to others, who had, in turn, other people to refer such things to.

Many, many light years from here, indeed from anywhere, lies the grim and long-abandoned planet Vogsphere. Somewhere on a fetid, fog-bound mud bank on this planet there stands, surrounded by the dirty, broken and empty carapaces of the last few jeweled scuttling crabs, a small stone monument which marks the place where, it is thought, the species *Vogon Vogonblurtus* first arose. On the monument there is carved an arrow which points away, into the fog, under which is inscribed in plain, simple letters the words "The buck stops there."

Deep in the bowels of his unsightly yellow ship, the Vogon Captain grunted as he reached for a slightly faded and dog-eared piece of paper that lay in front of him. A demolition order.

If you were to unravel exactly where the Captain's job, which was to do his job, actually began, then it all came down at last to this piece of paper that had been issued to him by his immediate superior long ago. The piece of paper had an instruction on it, and his purpose was to carry out that instruction and put a little tick mark in the adjacent box when he had carried it out.

He had carried out the instruction once before, but a number of troublesome circumstances had prevented him from being able to put the tick in the little box.

One of the troublesome circumstances was the Plural nature of this Galactic Sector, where the possible continually interfered with the probable. Simple demolition didn't get you any further than pushing down a bubble under a badly hung strip of wallpaper. Anything you demolished kept on popping up again. That would soon be taken care of.

Another was a small bunch of people who continually refused to be where they were supposed to be when they were supposed to be there. That, also, would soon be taken care of.

The third was an irritating and anarchic little device called *The Hitchhiker's Guide to the Galaxy*. That was now well and truly taken care of and, in fact, through the phenomenal power of temporal reverse engineering, it was now itself the agency through which everything else would be taken care of. The Captain had merely come to watch the final act of this drama. He himself did not have to lift a finger.

"Show me," he said.

The shadowy shape of a bird spread its wings and rose into the air near him. Darkness engulfed the bridge. Dim lights danced briefly in the black eyes of the bird as, deep in its instructional address space, bracket after bracket was finally closing, *if* clauses were finally ending, repeat loops halting, recursive functions calling themselves for the last few times.

A brilliant vision lit up in the darkness, a watery blue and green vision, a tube flowing through the air, shaped like a chopped-up string of sausages.

With a flatulent noise of satisfaction, the Vogon Captain sat back to watch.

Just there, number forty-two," shouted Ford Prefect to the taxi driver. "Right here!"

The taxi lurched to a halt, and Ford and Arthur jumped out. They had stopped at quite a number of cash dispensers on the way, and Ford chucked a fistful of money through the window at the driver.

The entrance to the club was dark, smart and severe. Only the smallest little plaque bore its name. Members knew where it was, and if you weren't a member, then knowing where it was wasn't any help to you.

Ford Prefect was not a member of Stavro's, though he had once been to Stavro's other club in New York. He had a very simple method of dealing with establishments of which he was not a member. He simply swept in as soon as the door was opened, pointed back at Arthur and said, "It's okay, he's with me."

He bounded down the dark glossy stairs, feeling very froody in his new shoes. They were suede and they were blue, and he was very pleased that in spite of everything else going on he had been sharp-eyed enough to spot them in a shop window from the back of a speeding taxi.

"I thought I told you not to come here."

"What?" said Ford.

A thin, ill-looking man wearing something baggy and Italian was walking up the stairs past them, lighting a cigarette, and had stopped, suddenly.

"Not you," he said. "Him."

He looked straight at Arthur, then seemed to become a little confused.

"Excuse me," he said. "I think I must have mistaken you for someone else." He started on up the stairs again, but almost immediately turned around once more, even more puzzled. He stared at Arthur.

"Now what?" said Ford.

"What did you say?"

"I said, now what?" repeated Ford, irritably.

"Yes, I think so," said the man and swayed slightly and dropped the book of matches he'd been carrying. His mouth moved weakly. Then he put his hand to his forehead.

"Excuse me," he said, "I'm trying desperately to remember which drug I've just taken, but it must be one of those ones that mean you can't remember." He shook his head and turned away again and went up toward the men's room.

"Come on," said Ford. He hurried on downstairs, with Arthur following nervously in his wake. The encounter had shaken him badly and he didn't know why.

He didn't like places like this. For all of the dreams of Earth and home he had had for years, he now badly missed his hut on Lamuella with his knives and his sandwiches. He even missed Old Thrashbarg.

"Arthur!"

It was the most astounding effect. His name was being shouted in stereo.

He twisted to look one way. Up the stairs behind him he saw Trillian hurrying down toward him in her wonderfully rumpled Rymplon™. She was looking suddenly aghast.

He twisted the other way to see what she was looking suddenly aghast at.

At the bottom of the stairs was Trillian, wearing . . . No—this was Tricia. Tricia that he had just seen, hysterical with confusion, on television. And behind her was Random, looking more wild-eyed than ever. Behind her in the recesses of the smart, dimly lit club, the other clientele of the evening formed a frozen tableau, staring anxiously up at the confrontation on the stairs.

For a few seconds everyone stood stock still. Only the music from behind the bar didn't know to stop throbbing.

"The gun she is holding," said Ford, quietly, nodding slightly toward Random, "is a Wabanatta 3. It was in the ship she stole from me. It's quite dangerous in fact. Just don't move for a moment. Let's just everybody stay calm and find out what's upsetting her."

"Where do I *fit?*" screamed Random, suddenly. The hand holding the gun was trembling fiercely. Her other hand delved into her pocket and pulled out the remains of Arthur's watch. She shook it at them.

"I thought I would fit here," she cried, "on the world that made me! But it turns out that even my *mother* doesn't know who I am!" She flung the watch violently aside, and it smashed into the glasses behind the bar, scattering its innards.

Everyone was very quiet for a moment or two longer.

"Random," said Trillian, quietly, from up on the stairs.

"Shut *up!*" shouted Random. "You abandoned me!"

"Random, it is very important that you listen to me and understand," persisted Trillian, quietly. "There isn't very much time. We must leave. We must all leave."

"What are you talking about? We're always *leaving!*" She had both hands on the gun now, and both were shaking. There was no one in particular she was pointing it at. She was just pointing it at the world in general.

"Listen," said Trillian again. "I left you because I went to cover a war for the network. It was extremely dangerous. At least, I thought it was going to be. I arrived and the war had suddenly ceased to happen. There was a time anomaly and . . . listen! Please listen! A reconnaissance battleship had failed to turn up, the rest of the fleet was scattered in some farcical disarray. It's happening all the time now."

"I don't care! I don't want to hear about your bloody *job!*" shouted Random. "I want a home! I want to fit somewhere!"

"This is not your home," said Trillian, still keeping her voice calm. "You don't have one. None of us have one. Hardly anybody has one anymore. The missing ship I was just talking about. The people of that ship don't have a home. They don't know where they are from. They don't even have any memory of who they are or what they are for. They are very lost and very confused and very frightened. They are here in this solar system, and they are about to do something very . . . misguided because they are so lost and confused. We . . . must . . . leave . . . now. I can't tell you where there is to go to. Perhaps there isn't anywhere. But here is not the place to be. Please. One more time. Can we go?"

Random was wavering in panic and confusion.

"It's all right," said Arthur, gently. "If I'm here, we're safe. Don't ask me to explain just now, but I am safe, so you are safe. Okay?"

"What are you saying?" said Trillian.

"Let's all just relax," said Arthur. He was feeling very tranquil. His life was charmed and none of this seemed real.

Slowly, gradually, Random began to relax, and to let the gun down, inch by inch.

Two things happened simultaneously.

The door to the men's room at the top of the stairs opened, and the man who had accosted Arthur came out, sniffing.

Startled at the sudden movement, Random lifted the gun again just as a man standing behind her made a grab for it.

Arthur threw himself forward. There was a deafening explosion. He fell awkwardly as Trillian threw herself down over him. The noise died away. Arthur looked up to see the man at the top of the stairs gazing down at him with a look of utter stupefaction.

"You . . ." he said. Then slowly, horribly, he fell apart.

Random threw the gun down and fell to her knees, sobbing. "I'm sorry!" she said. "I'm so sorry! I'm so, so sorry . . ."

Tricia went to her. Trillian went to her.

Arthur sat on the stairs with his head between his hands and had not the faintest idea what to do. Ford was sitting on the stair beneath him. He picked something up, looked at it with interest and passed it up to Arthur.

"This mean anything to you?" he said.

Arthur took it. It was the book of matches that the dead man had dropped. It had the name of the club on it. It had the name of the proprietor of the club on it. It looked like this:

STAVRO MUELLER

BETA

He stared at it for some time as things began slowly to reassemble themselves in his mind. He wondered what he should do, but he only wondered it idly. Around him people were beginning to rush and shout a lot, but it was suddenly very clear to him that there was nothing to be done, not now or ever. Through the new strangeness of noise and light he could just make out the shape of Ford Prefect sitting back and laughing wildly.

A tremendous feeling of peace came over him. He knew that at last, for once and forever, it was now all, finally, over.

In the darkness of the bridge at the heart of the Vogon ship, Prostetnic Vogon Jeltz sat alone. Lights flared briefly across the external vision screens that lined one wall. In the air above him the discontinuities in the blue and green watery sausage shape resolved themselves.

Options collapsed, possibilities folded into each other, and the whole at last resolved itself out of existence.

A very deep darkness descended. The Vogon Captain sat immersed in it for a few seconds.

"Light," he said.

There was no response. The bird, too, had crumpled out of all possibility.

The Vogon turned on the light himself. He picked up the piece of paper again and placed a little tick in the little box.

Well, that was done. His ship slunk off into the inky void.

In spite of having taken what he regarded as an extremely positive piece of action, the Grebulon leader ended up having a very bad month after all. It was pretty much the same as all the previous months except that there was now nothing on the television anymore. He put on a little light music instead.